# THE BOOK OF
# DEVAULTUS
## THE DARK DECEIVER CHRONICLES
### BOOK I
#### J.A. ROGGIE

GRINNING BARD PRESS

# CONTENTS

# PRELUDE

The tavern roared with life. A thick haze of pipe smoke hung in the air, mingling with the scent of spilled ale, roasted meats, and a faint tang of sweat. Tonight, the Timberwell Inn buzzed louder than it had in months. Every table was occupied, the hearth crackling and spitting embers that danced in the air. Cara, the barkeep, worked the room like a queen commanding her court, her laughter chiming above the noise.

Cara was the heart and soul of the Timberwell. Her auburn hair, streaked with silver, was tied up in a practical bun, though a few strands rebelliously framed her face. Her figure, while no longer youthful, still turned heads. She had the kind of confidence that made her magnetic, and her sharp tongue kept even the rowdiest drunkards in line. Her trusty cook, Baxter, toiled away in the kitchen, his belly straining against his stained apron. Baxter was gruff, perpetually grumbling about something, but his food was the kind that could warm even the coldest heart.

Then there was Lilly, the new serving girl, a bubbly raven-black-haired woman with an infectious laugh. She was the kind of girl who seemed to float rather than walk, her skirts swishing as she moved. The patrons loved her, their cheers and laughter growing louder with every ale she delivered. She was a star performer in the grand, chaotic play that was the Timberwell Inn.

The tavern was alive with raucous laughter and the clatter of tankards as ale flowed freely. Harvest had just ended, and the air was thick with the scent of spiced mead and roasted meats. The people were merry, their worries drowning in the revelry of hard-earned celebration.

A burly older man, his hands calloused from years of labor, threw his head back with a booming laugh, slamming his mug onto the table. Beside him, a lanky, sun-worn man staggered across the floor, dancing drunkenly, his steps wild and uncoordinated to the amusement of the crowd.

A petite woman perched on a man's lap on the other side of the room, her chest bouncing with every delighted giggle at whatever sweet nonsense he had just whispered in her ear. Everywhere, the warmth of good company and strong drink filled the space, the night promising indulgence, mischief, and many good nights of drinking to come.

The tavern door flew open with a deafening crash, the wood shuddering from the impact. Conversation died instantly as every head turned toward the entrance. A lone figure staggered inside, his silhouette stark against the dim glow of the setting sun. He clutched his arm, fingers slick with fresh blood, crimson droplets pattering onto the dusty floorboards. A sharp gasp rippled between the gathered patrons.

Cara, behind the bar, dropped the mug she'd been wiping down, the ceramic shattering upon impact. "Bloody hell!" she snapped, already moving around the counter with surprising speed. "Get off your arse and help him!"

Several men sprang into action, catching the injured man before he could collapse. His face was pale and strained, sweat clinging to his brow, but even through the pain, a lopsided, almost amused grin tugged at the corner of his lips.

The large man, his face still flushed from drink and laughter, lurched to his feet, the merriment draining from his expression as he unsheathed the worn blade at his belt. The steel gleamed dully in the dim tavern light as he strode toward the door, his heavy boots thudding against the wooden floorboards. Peering into the darkness beyond, he narrowed his eyes, trying to pierce the night's shroud.

A few other men followed suit, emboldened either by curiosity or by their ale. One man, younger but just as rough-handed, leaned in beside him. "Do ye see anything?" the older man muttered, glancing back at the injured lad who had stumbled in, blood staining his clothes.

"It's too dark to tell," the older man replied, shifting uneasily. "But I don't see a damned thing."

Eiko was a quiet town, a place where trouble was more likely to involve a drunken brawl over a farmer's daughter than anything truly threatening. Most nights, the worst thing that happened was some fool having too much ale and throwing a sluggish punch at a friend who had been a little too friendly with his kin.

And yet, something about tonight felt different. The laughter had died down, the weight of unease settling over the room like a thick fog.

Lilly knelt beside the young man, rolling her eyes at the sorry state of him. "That's a nasty one," she muttered, pulling a cloth from her belt and pressing it firmly against the wound. "Not the worst I've seen, but you're not walking this one off." She lifted her gaze and spotted Jim standing off to the side, uncertain. "Jim! Stop gawking and go get the healer, now. It's not life-threatening, but it's deep, and I don't fancy watching him bleed all over the floor."

Jim wasn't the sharpest tool in the shed, but what he lacked in wit, he made up for in heart. He was a man who meant well, even if he rarely had a clear idea of what "well" actually was. A good soul, through and through, he was the kind of fellow who'd leap to help without ever thinking about how, or if, he even could.

Another man, broader and heavier set, pushed himself up from his seat, his arms thick with the hardened muscle of a life spent in relentless labor. "I'll go with you, Jim," he rumbled, his deep voice steady but edged with a quiet seriousness. "Just in case there's actually somethin' out there."

His gaze swept over the gathered patrons, the warmth of drink and merriment now dampened by unease. He squared his shoulders and pointed a thick, calloused finger at the lot of them. "Bar the door. Don't let anyone in unless it's us or the Healer. No exceptions."

Without waiting for a response, he turned on his heel and stepped out after Jim, the two men vanishing into the night's embrace, the heavy wooden door creaking shut behind them.

Two other men hurried forward, their hands gripping the heavy drawbar as they heaved it into place, the thick wood settling with a solid *thunk* against the doorframe. One of them, a wiry man with a weathered face, peered through the small window; his breath could be seen in the chilly night air as he watched Jim and his companion disappear down the dimly lit cobblestone street.

The flickering lanterns lining the road cast long, restless shadows, stretching and twisting with each step the men took toward the Healer's house. The night swallowed them quickly, the sounds of the tavern behind them now muffled and distant. Inside, the remaining patrons held their breath, ears straining for any sound, be it a friendly call or something far worse.

Lilly worked quickly, securing a makeshift bandage around the wound with practiced hands. "Hold still, alright? You'll be fine, but let's not test fate."

The man gave a shaky, breathless chuckle. "I made it," he murmured, his voice strained yet triumphant. "By the gods, I actually made it."

A nearby patron, one of the older regulars, raised an eyebrow. "Made it from where, lad?"

Another man, older but still sturdy from years of labor, stepped forward, his brow furrowed as he eyed the injured young man with growing unease. His calloused fingers tightened around the mug in his hand, knuckles whitening.

"Aye, lad... and what did this to ye?" he asked, his voice steady but laced with concern. His gaze flicked toward the barred door, as if he expected whatever horror lurked outside to come crashing through at any moment. "How many are out there?"

A tense hush settled over the room, the usual warmth of the tavern dampened by an unseen threat. Every ear strained for an answer, every heartbeat pounding just a little harder.

As they eased him into a chair, Cara shoved a tankard of ale into his trembling hands. "Drink," she ordered, watching as he took a long, greedy gulp before slamming the mug onto the table with a satisfying *thunk*.

His grin widened, a flash of startlingly white teeth against the grime and blood smeared across his face.

The young man let out a weary sigh, his shoulders slumping as if the weight of his journey had finally settled on him. He shook his head, glancing toward the barred door before turning his gaze back to the expectant faces around him.

"I don't think you'll find anyone out there," he admitted, his voice low, carrying the exhaustion of someone who had spent too long looking over his shoulder. "I lost them a day's time ago. Just a few bandits, that's all. Took everything I had, my cart, my steed, and every damned thing on it."

His fingers twitched toward his side, brushing against the torn fabric of his tunic where blood had seeped through. He winced slightly, more from the memory than the pain. "Bastards left me with nothing but the clothes on my back... and even those, they damn near took."

The tavern remained silent for a moment, save for the crackling of the fire and the distant howl of the wind outside. Then, a few of the men exchanged looks, expressions shifting from tension to something closer to pity, while others still held on to their suspicion. After all, trouble had a way of following the lost and desperate, and the last thing Eiko needed was a reason for it to come knocking.

The young man let out another sigh, this one heavier, as if it carried the weight of all he'd lost. He raised his cup and took a slow swig, savoring the burn as the ale slid down his throat. For a moment, he simply stared into the amber liquid, swirling it idly before speaking again.

"Forgive my rudeness," he said, his voice rough but steady. His weary eyes flicked up to the men around him, their wary expressions a mix of concern and suspicion. "It's been a long road... longer still when you've got nothing left to your name."

He set the cup down with a dull clunk, fingers lingering on its rim as if anchoring himself. "Name's Marko Dela'Fonta," he finally offered, the words slow, deliberate. "Not that it means much anymore."

The firelight flickered across his face, casting shadows that made him look even more hollowed out than he already was. The men exchanged glances; some softening, others remaining cautious. Trouble rarely came alone, and a man who had been stripped of everything had little to lose.

He brushed a few damp strands of hair away from his eyes, and leaned forward, eyes glinting with mischief and adrenaline.

"And, oh, do I have a tale for you."

The crowd leaned in, curiosity crackling in the air like the embers in the hearth. Marko's voice, though hoarse, carried the kind of energy that demanded attention.

"Now," he began, his gaze sweeping the room, "allow me to set the stage. I used to work at a tavern much like this one. A little place called the Sweetwater Inn, run by Caralana Sweetwater herself, a woman as sharp as her name suggests. Our cook, Fro'dovin, was a mountain of a man with hands like hammers and a temper to match. He made the best damned stew in the land, or so we all thought."

Marko paused for dramatic effect, taking another sip of ale. "Then came Lindgurth."

A murmur ran through the crowd. Cara crossed her arms, one eyebrow raised. "Lindgurth? What kind of name is that?"

"The kind you don't forget," Marko said, a gleam in his eye. "He showed up one day, looking for work. Caralana took him in as Fro'dovin's apprentice. Now, Lindgurth was... different. Quiet, sharp-eyed, and unnervingly skilled with a blade. He wasn't just good, he was extraordinary. The man could dice an onion so fine, it turned to mist. Fro'dovin didn't like him much, probably because Lindgurth was better at cooking than he'd ever be. But he couldn't deny the results."

Marko gestured with his tankard, nearly spilling its contents. "Lindgurth created dishes that brought people from miles away. Like the Chaktaka Steak. You've heard of it, haven't you?"

The room erupted with exclamations. "Chaktaka Steak? That was Fro'dovin's recipe!" someone shouted.

Marko grinned knowingly. "That's what they want you to think. Truth is, Lindgurth invented it. But he let Fro'dovin take the credit. Said he didn't care about fame or recognition. He was just there to earn some coin and perfect his craft."

He leaned forward, his voice dropping to a conspiratorial whisper. "But cooking wasn't his only skill. Lindgurth was a master of knives, and not just in the kitchen. The man could throw a blade and hit a fly mid-flight. He practiced every day, honing his craft like a warrior sharpening his sword."

The tension in the room was palpable. Even Lilly had stopped bouncing around, her tray of mugs forgotten as she hung on Marko's every word.

"One day," Marko continued, "during the busy part of the day, Lindgurth was asked to go to town for some ingredients. He wandered into the wrong part of town, a place where shadows hid more than just darkness. That's when it happened..."

Marko trailed off, his eyes darting around the room as if he was expecting danger to leap from the corners. The crowd leaned in closer, breaths held in suspense.

"What happened?" Cara prompted, her voice unusually soft.

Marko smirked, his fingers tightening around the tankard. "Well, that, my friends, is where the real story begins."

# CHAPTER I
# THE KNIFE BEHIND THE APRON

Lindgurth hadn't spent much time in the city, at least during the day. Tyranus was a particularly nasty place, ruled by a tangled web of power-hungry houses. At first glance, it seemed the countless gangs that prowled the streets held control, but Lindgurth knew better. No gang operated without being deep in the pocket of a noble Lord. The illusion of law and order was just that: an illusion. The Lords let the people believe they were protecting them from the criminals, but in truth, those criminals were just another tool of their rule.

And above even the Lords, there were the gods, the massive dragons that occasionally darkened the sky with their colossal forms. Rumors whispered of their ability to take on humanoid shapes, to walk among the people unnoticed. No one dared speak ill of the gods, for one might be standing beside you at any moment. But when they soared through the heavens, their vast shadows blotting out the twin suns, there was no mistaking their presence. Lindgurth half suspected they did it purely to remind the city who truly ruled.

The world had not always been like this. The old stories spoke of lush forests, flowing rivers, and great cities built in harmony with the land. But that was before the Mage Wars, before the truth about magic had been revealed. Magic had always been powerful, but no one had understood the cost, not until it was too late. Every spell, every incantation, pulled life directly from the world, draining it of its vitality. Fields withered, rivers dried to cracked earth, and entire regions once teeming with life became nothing more than endless wastelands of sand and stone.

It had taken less than a hundred years to reduce the world to what it was now. Deserts stretched as far as the eye could see, swallowing entire civilizations in waves of dust. Food was scarce, and survival was a daily struggle. People ate whatever they could find: vermin, insects, even the bones of the dead if they could grind them fine enough. Many races had abandoned their old ways entirely, turning to cannibalism to survive. Nothing went to waste.

Unless, of course, you were a Lord.

The streets of Tyranus were alive with the clatter of carts and the sharp calls of merchants hawking their wares. Leatherworkers displayed their finely stitched armor, padded and reinforced with layers of bone plates or thick hide. A butcher carved into the remains of some great beast, its ribs long and curved like the frame of a ship. And, in place of the usual blacksmiths one might expect in a city, there were artisans shaping weapons from whatever materials they could scavenge.

A craftsman sat beneath a canopy of stretched animal hide, meticulously sharpening a dagger made from a jagged piece of obsidian. Another tested the balance of a spear tipped with sharpened bone, its shaft reinforced with strips of sinew and tightly wrapped leather. A rare few displayed weapons edged with slivers of metal; thin, precious filaments scavenged from ruins or melted down from ancient relics, hammered into weapons only the wealthiest could afford.

Lindgurth knew better than to linger. Here, everything had a price, and if you weren't careful, that price could be your own hide.

His steps slowed as he came upon a street performer, a young man adorned in peculiar garb with his face painted in bright colors. The performer twirled and danced, juggling wooden balls in an elaborate display of dexterity. A woman accompanied him, playing a lute, her nimble fingers coaxing out a jaunty melody that set the crowd tapping their feet. Children laughed and clapped, utterly entranced. Lindgurth found himself nodding along, his foot instinctively keeping time with the music. It wasn't the finest performance he had ever heard, but entertainment was entertainment. He had certainly endured worse.

Shaking himself from the distraction, he refocused. He was on an errand today, sent to procure supplies for the kitchen. Fro'dovin would not be pleased if he returned empty-handed. However, just as he turned towards the market stalls, something unusual caught his eye.

A beast.

Not just any beast, but a creature unlike any he had encountered before. It stood tall, a formidable lizard-like thing with thick, plated armor running along its back. Its head bore imposing, curved horns, and its beak-like snout jutted forward in a way that suggested it could snap bone with ease. Lindgurth tilted his head, intrigued. A clawed foot stamped against the ground to ward off a few overzealous children who had dared to get too close.

"How peculiar," Lindgurth mused aloud, stepping forward without hesitation. He had seen the common feathered lizard mounts that populated the city, ill-tempered things, always as likely to bite their owners as they were their enemies. Some said their aggression was a byproduct of the harsh desert landscape they hailed from. But this creature... this was something else entirely.

Ignoring the children's wary retreat, Lindgurth strode right up to the beast. It snorted in warning, eyes narrowing at his approach. Yet, rather than heed the silent threat, he reached out a hand, intent on feeling the creature's tough, plated hide.

Before his fingers could make contact, the door to the adjacent shop slammed open with a bang. Out stormed a massive man clad in nothing but a loincloth, and a horned helm perched atop his head. A colossal bone battle-axe resting easily in one meaty hand.

"Away with you, git! Are ye lookin' to lose an arm?!" the man bellowed, his voice a rolling thunder that sent the nearby children scurrying.

Lindgurth froze, his casual curiosity replaced with a flicker of genuine fear. His gaze shifted from indifferent to alarmed in an instant. Scrambling back, he forced a nervous chuckle. "No, of course not, sir," he stammered.

Unfortunately, the beast had already picked up on its master's agitation. It lunged with terrifying speed, its beak snapping mere inches from Lindgurth's face. A spray of spittle hit his cheek, and he let out an undignified yelp, stumbling backward and landing flat on his rear.

The warrior burst into booming laughter, slapping his knee at the spectacle. "Be gone with ye! Consider yourself lucky you've still got all your fingers!"

Lindgurth didn't need to be told twice. The moment the opportunity presented itself, he scrambled to his feet and bolted, his heart pounding like a war drum against his ribs. Behind him, the mocking laughter of the onlookers followed, echoing off the walls like a chorus of cruel specters. He ignored them, pushing forward, his feet pounding against the uneven cobblestones as he ducked into the nearest alley.

This was no ordinary alleyway; it was an infamously dangerous stretch, a place where even the bravest hesitated to tread. Years of arcane warfare had left their mark, scarring the very bones of the city. A jagged wound in reality itself tore through the ground along the left side of the alley, an Abyss so deep that the bottom remained swallowed in darkness. It was said that once something, or someone, fell in, they were never seen again.

To his right, the backs of buildings loomed like silent sentinels, their walls marred with soot, old battle scars, and the desperate claw marks of those who had tried to escape whatever horror lurked within this passage. The rumors were enough to make even the most hardened cutthroats wary. There were stories of men being dragged into the Abyss, their screams cut short as they vanished into nothingness. Of thieves ambushing the unfortunate, their pockets emptied before their bodies were kicked over the edge, their fates left to whatever horrors lay below.

Lindgurth hesitated for only a breath, his pulse a frantic staccato against his throat. The danger here was undeniable, but so was the necessity. This alley was the fastest route to his destination, and time was not a luxury he could afford. Steeling himself, he stepped deeper into the shadows, where the city's light dared not follow.

He took a cautious step forward, then froze.

Ahead, movement.

A scuffle.

And then, as he crept closer, he saw them. Three men, an unnervingly tall, lanky elf, a burly barbarian, and a human with a wicked grin. The elf had his bony fingers wrapped around the wrist of a struggling blonde woman, his sharp teeth glinting as he dragged his tongue up the side of her neck. She let out a desperate cry, thrashing against her captors.

Lindgurth had heard tales of elves before. They were a ruthless people, savage, monstrous. Travelers passing through the Inn spoke in hushed tones of their carnivorous ways, of how many an unfortunate soul had met their end in the jaws of one of these creatures.

The scene before him only confirmed the rumors.

Nearby, a guard was held fast by the barbarian, his arms pinned behind him in an iron grip. The human, giggling like a deranged child, drove a jagged bone dagger repeatedly into the guard's gut. Blood splattered across the sand in sickening bursts as the guard's eyes went dull. The woman's struggles weakened as horror twisted her face.

Lindgurth watched, his instincts urging him to turn away. This was none of his concern. He had business to attend to. But just as he prepared to slip into the shadows, her eyes met his.

A silent plea.

Damn it all.

"That's right, you little bitch, be gone with you," the barbarian sneered, tossing the guard's lifeless body to the side.

The human licked his bloodstained blade and turned his gaze to Lindgurth.

Lindgurth remained still. "I have no quarrel with you," he said evenly. "Let me pass, and I'll be on my way."

The human cackled wildly. The barbarian cracked his knuckles, stepping to Lindgurth's left, cutting off his escape. The woman whimpered, anticipating yet another slaughter.

"Oh, lad," the barbarian rumbled, a grin splitting his scarred face. "It's too late for that."

And with these words, he lunged.

Lindgurth barely had time to react before a massive hand wrapped around his throat, lifting him from the ground as if he were weightless. The barbarian's rancid breath hit his face, and yellowed teeth sneered at him.

A thud could be heard as the woman was tossed against the wall of a nearby building.

The elf giggled, licking his lips. "Ohhh... let me have a taste."

Lindgurth did not look at the barbarian. He did not struggle.

Instead, his body shimmered, rippling like the surface of disturbed water.

Then, in a blur, his hand shot up, clawed fingers wrapping around the barbarian's thick neck. No longer the hand of a man, but something reptilian. Something monstrous. His claws tore deep, blood gushing as he squeezed. The barbarian's grip slackened, and Lindgurth yanked him downward, pulling him into a crouch as the elf's eyes widened in terror.

The elf turned and ran. Lindgurth smirked.

His attention flicked back to the barbarian. The brute's face twisted in horror as Lindgurth's claws dug deeper. With a sharp tug, he pulled the man's tongue from his shredded throat.

"What's the matter?" he murmured, a wicked grin curling his lips. "Not so talkative now, are we?"

Releasing the limp body, he gave the barbarian a final shove, watching as he tumbled over the cliff's edge and into the scar. He turned to face the human, but the coward had already vanished into the night.

Sighing, Lindgurth thought, *What a shame. I'll have to deal with them later.*

A soft groan behind him reminded him of the woman. He quickly willed his hand back to its human form before approaching her.

"Miss, are you alright?" he asked, kneeling at her side.

Her eyes darted to the blood on his hands. "What... what happened to the men?"

He smiled. "They thought guards were coming. They ran."

Of course, he knew this was not a believable lie. But perhaps she was too much of a shock to see through it.

She stared at him for a long moment before nodding. "We should leave."

He agreed. Though he wondered why he had intervened at all.

That wasn't like him.


Lindgurth's ears pricked at the sound of movement behind him. Whipping around, he spotted several guards, their armor identical to the fallen woman's protector lying lifeless on the ground. Their faces were stern, swords drawn, as they closed in on him. The woman stepped between them, her voice cutting through the tension like a blade.

"Do not harm this man," she commanded firmly, her tone brooking no argument. "He came to my aid."

The guards hesitated but didn't lower their weapons. Instead, they positioned themselves protectively in front of her, pushing her gently but firmly behind their shielded forms. Lindgurth raised his hands, a mask of fear painted across his face. His sharp eyes flicked between the guards, gauging their movements, calculating his next step if the situation turned sour. To his relief, the woman's intervention held their aggression at bay.

Lindgurth bowed his head slightly, his voice wavered in fear. "My apologies, milady. I must be on my way. I have pressing matters that need my attention."

The woman studied him for a moment before nodding. "Very well. Thank you, kind sir. But tell me, who might I call my hero?"

The word struck Lindgurth, and he hesitated, caught off guard. *Hero?* The thought was almost laughable, yet oddly appealing. After all, it was a far cry from the reputation of his former life. A grin tugged at the corner of his lips, but he suppressed it. Straightening his posture, he delivered a flourishing bow so grandiose, it seemed more suited to a nobleman than a simple cook.

"I am called Lindgurth, ma'am," he said, his voice smooth and practiced.

The woman inclined her head gracefully. "Very well, Lindgurth. I bid you farewell and thank you again for your help." With that, she turned and left, her guards forming a protective wall as they escorted her away.

Lindgurth let out a quiet sigh of relief once they disappeared. That had been far too close. What in the name of the gods had possessed him to intervene? It wasn't like him to meddle in affairs that didn't concern him, especially when doing so risked complicating his life. Sure, he loved attention, but only when it suited him, and this was not one of those times. Shaking his head, he turned and slipped out of the alley, eager to put the ordeal behind him.

To his immense relief, the rest of his errand passed uneventfully. He bartered skillfully in the market, haggling prices down with the kind of charm and quick wit that would make a merchant's head spin. By the time he was done, his bags were brimming with fresh fruits and vegetables purchased at a steal. Of course, Lindgurth would tell anyone who asked that he was the finest negotiator to ever grace the cobblestone streets of the city.

On his way back to the Sweetwater Inn, the streets buzzed with activity. Wily wenches called out to him with flirtatious grins, some even trying to tug him aside with promises of "alone time." He waved them off with a practiced ease, his mind focused elsewhere. Such distractions were beneath him, at least for now. As he strolled through the bustling main street, his sharp eyes caught sight of a group of cloaked figures cornering a man and woman in a shadowy alley. He itched to investigate, but he forced himself to look away. He'd already played the hero once today, and that was quite enough for one lifetime, or at least for one afternoon.

Rounding the corner, he finally arrived at the Sweetwater Inn. A couple of busty wenches loitered near the entrance, one of them cackling as she spotted him.

"'Ello, Lindgurth! Fancy a bit of fun tonight?" she teased, her grin as wicked as her intentions.

He smirked but waved her off with a flourish of his hand. "Not tonight, ladies. I've got more pressing matters."

Pushing through the inn's doors, he was greeted by the chaotic din of a lively tavern. The patrons were singing, dancing, and clapping along to the tuneless strumming of a particularly uninspired bard. Lindgurth wove through the crowd with practiced ease, making his way to the kitchen where Fro'dovin was hard at work.

"Did ye get the things I needed?" Fro'dovin barked without so much as a glance in Lindgurth's direction.

"Of course," Lindgurth replied, dropping the sack of goods onto the table with a satisfying thud. He tossed the leftover coins beside it.

Fro'dovin paused his chopping to eye the coins suspiciously. "There's a bit left over. You got everything on the list, right?"

"Every last item," Lindgurth assured him with a confident grin. "Managed to strike a good deal."

Fro'dovin opened the sack and inspected its contents with a critical eye. Satisfied, he gave a nod of approval. "Good job, lad," he said, clapping Lindgurth on the back with enough force to make him stumble.

Grabbing a knife, Lindgurth joined Fro'dovin in chopping vegetables. The blade, freshly sharpened by his own hand, sliced through the produce like butter. As he worked, his mind wandered, unbidden, back to the memory of his fingers ripping through the barbarian's throat earlier that day. A dark smile played on his lips, but he quickly masked it, focusing on the task at hand.

"Find yourself any trouble out there?" Fro'dovin asked, his tone casual but laced with curiosity.

"Not a bit," Lindgurth lied smoothly, his grin unwavering. "Pretty dull, actually."

Fro'dovin chuckled. "Good. Now get outta here, lad. I'll finish up. You look like you could use some rest after braving the city."

"Thank you," Lindgurth replied, wiping down his knife before heading toward the stairs.

He climbed to the second floor and paused at his door, his eyes scanning the hallway. Reaching up, he plucked a thin strand of hair from the doorframe. Undisturbed. Good. He slipped inside, bolted the door, and checked the window. The second strand of hair was still in place, confirming that no one had tampered with his room.

Satisfied, he moved to the large chest at the foot of his bed, unlocking it with a small key. Inside lay his lute, a seemingly unassuming instrument that he carefully lifted out. Beneath it, hidden by a false bottom, were bags of coins, a set of vibrant purple and black clothing, and a wooden mask. The mask's one-sided grin, painted stark white, stared up at him like a ghostly reminder of his secret life.

Lindgurth's lips curled into a pleased smirk as he secured the chest again. He sat on the edge of his bed, cradling the lute in his hands. As he plucked at the strings, a melody filled the room, rich and hauntingly beautiful. The notes carried the warmth of spring and the bittersweet promise of fleeting moments.

Setting the lute aside, Lindgurth lay back on the bed. His eyes drifted shut, and for the first time that day, he allowed himself to relax. Whatever tomorrow held, he would face it, but tonight, he would rest.

Lindgurth stretched, rolling his shoulders as a long, deep yawn rumbled from his chest. He blinked the sleep from his eyes, his gaze sweeping across the dimly lit room, searching for the slightest sign of disturbance. Everything was exactly as he had left it. Still, he remained on edge. Paranoia was a survival response he had long since learned to trust. Every morning, he woke with the same lingering thought: *Has someone snuck in while I slept? Has some clever bastard slipped a blade between my ribs while I lay vulnerable?*

Not this time. He was alone. Safe, for now.

But unfinished business nagged at him, coiling in the back of his mind like a viper waiting to strike. The two who had fled the alley... their survival was a problem. If they spoke, if they whispered his name in the wrong ears, word of his involvement would spread like wildfire. That simply would not do.

With a low sigh, he swung his legs over the side of the bed and planted his feet on the cold wooden floor. His fingers absently traced the hilt of the dagger strapped to his thigh. He had work to do.

He made his way to the chest at the foot of his bed, unlocking it with practiced ease. Reaching inside, he carefully pulled free the mask and wide-brimmed hat, placing them on the bed before retrieving the garments of black and deep violet. The fabric felt familiar, like a second skin, as he slipped into the ensemble. Finally, he lifted the mask, its wooden surface painted with a mischievous, one-sided grin, and settled it over his face. The hat followed, casting a shadow over his already obscured features.

Satisfied, he slung his lute over his shoulder, his fingers trailing over the strings for the briefest moment. Then, with a grin hidden beneath his mask, he moved to the window. Without hesitation, he slipped through, landing with feline grace upon the street below. His boots barely made a whisper against the worn stone as he shut the window behind him and vanished into the night.

The city was alive with the sounds of revelry, raucous laughter, drunken shouting, the occasional clatter of a dropped tankard. Taverns would be the best place to start his search. If his quarry had any sense, they would be drowning their nerves in ale, clinging to the illusion of safety in the company of others.

Lindgurth moved through the streets like a shadow, his mind briefly drifting as he considered his surroundings. This world was a husk, drained of magic long ago, with only the rarest few capable of wielding the arcane arts. He had been to other places, lands where magic thrummed in the very air, but here? Here, the stories spoke of ancient sorcerers who had all but destroyed the world in their greed and hubris. The result? A near-endless expanse of desert, punctuated by struggling cities clinging to survival. He had no intention of being trapped here forever. One way or another, he would find a way out.

But first, there were loose ends to tie up.

He stopped outside a tavern, its entrance flanked by flickering torches. The din from within spilled into the street, a symphony of drunken merriment, clinking glasses, and a bard's mediocre attempt at song. Lindgurth hesitated, considering. His outfit was striking, and certainly memorable. Though his work had largely been conducted under cover of darkness, it would only take one sharp-eyed fool to recall his figure from the previous night.

A smirk tugged at his lips beneath the mask. Perhaps this was not a job for *The Grin.*

Reaching up, he removed the mask, slipping it into the hidden pocket of his coat. Then, with a mere thought, his form began to shift. His features reformed, his frame adjusting until he stood as a dashing young man, strong of jaw and confident of stance. His clothes remained the same, bold and ostentatious, but his identity? He was unrecognizable.

With the ease of a man who *knew* he belonged, he strode toward the tavern doors and pushed them open.

The moment he stepped inside, the room fell silent.

All eyes turned to him, the flickering candlelight casting dramatic shadows across his face. The bard, who had been mid-verse, faltered, his fingers stumbling over the strings of his lute. He recovered, barely, his expression twisting in displeasure as he eyed the instrument slung over Lindgurth's back.

"And who might you be?" the bard sneered.

Lindgurth grinned; a dazzling, almost arrogant expression. "Ah, my dear friends, you are fortunate indeed, for tonight you find yourselves in the presence of none other than *Devaultus*, bard extraordinaire!"

With a flourish, he bowed deeply, as though every soul in the tavern were a noble worthy of his utmost respect.

The tension in the room shifted, the murmurs beginning again, but not without a certain edge of curiosity. The bard at the front straightened, puffing up like a peacock. "Well, sir," he huffed, clearly affronted. "You are *not* needed here. I am Kontorious, the bard of this..."

Lindgurth, *Devaultus*, waved a hand dismissively before the man could finish. "It is of no consequence who you are," he said smoothly. "For I assure you, you are not nearly important enough for me to have heard of you."

Laughter rippled through the crowd.

Kontorious' face burned red, but he could do little more than grit his teeth and return to his song. His fingers, however, now shook slightly over the lute strings, and his performance suffered for it. Notes were missed, words stumbled over.

Lindgurth paid him no mind. His gaze flickered over the tavern's occupants, searching, watching. Then, like a gift from fate itself, the door creaked open once more.

There, stepping inside, was the human from last night.

A stroke of luck? Or had he been *too* predictable? No matter. There were only a handful of taverns along this street. The chances of running into the man were always high. What concerned him more, however, was the realization that this particular tavern was not just a drinking hole, it was a stronghold. The gang that ran it had deep ties to the city, and from the whispers around him, it seemed Lark, the man he sought, was quite popular among them.

Lindgurth exhaled slowly, considering his approach. If he moved against Lark here, the entire tavern would turn on him in an instant. That simply *would not do*.

Movement caught his eye. A tavern wench slipped into the back, her steps purposeful. *An opportunity.*

Rising from his seat, he followed her, slipping into the shadows, the hunt beginning anew.

The crisp night air wrapped around Devaultus like a familiar cloak as he followed the woman into the darkness, his boots barely making a sound against the cobblestone. He lingered in the shadows, watching as she paused near the outhouse, her laughter mixing with another woman's voice. They giggled, their words carrying easily in the still night. He listened intently, his sharp ears catching the hushed conversation. The woman spoke of her plans to warm Lark's bed that night, hoping to gain favor within the gang. A smirk played on Devaultus' lips. It seemed no one in this little underworld was worth saving. And yet, there was that thought again, that strange, nagging whisper in the back of his mind. The notion of being a hero. He scowled. Why did he care? He wasn't a hero, after all, nor did he intend to start now. He was in this for himself. Always had been. Always would be.

As the woman he had followed disappeared back into the tavern, her companion remained behind, chuckling to herself, whispering of her own intentions to seduce Lark for personal gain. Devaultus saw an opportunity and seized it. Emerging from the shadows, he moved with an effortless grace toward her.

"Good evening, milady," he purred.

The woman startled, but as she turned to face him, her expression quickly softened, hunger flickering in her gaze. He was, after all, a striking figure, a man of fine taste and finer appearances. She raked her eyes over him, already calculating the weight of his purse.

"I wish to perform for the tavern this eve," Devaultus continued, his voice smooth as silk. "And I could not help but notice you, easily the most enchanting maiden in sight. I would be honored if you graced my performance with a dance. There is very good coin in it."

She stepped closer, her hips swaying as she leaned in, a playful smirk curling her lips. "Oh, love, I could dance for you in private... or with a crowd," she teased, her fingers grazing the edge of his coat.

He chuckled, leaning in just enough to let her feel the heat of his breath. His hands found her waist, guiding her back against the side of the outhouse. "I do believe we have a deal then," he whispered, his voice thick with false desire. "I imagine you would look stunning in the fine silks I have waiting for you... or in nothing at all."

She let out a breathy sigh, excitement flashing in her eyes. This was it, her chance. If she played her cards right, she could take everything this man had. The weight of his wealth, the luxurious fabrics draped over his body, the ornate lute slung across his back, it all screamed opportunity. Without hesitation, she began to disrobe, letting her garments fall to the ground.

Devaultus captured her lips in a fervent kiss, his hands pinning hers above her head. She melted into him, but just as suddenly as the kiss had begun, it ended. Her eyes went wide. A strangled gasp escaped her lips as she felt the cold steel slide between her ribs. She shuddered, her breath hitching. The last thing she saw was his smirk before her vision faded to black.

With a practiced hand, Devaultus withdrew his dagger, its blade glistening with fresh blood. He wiped it clean on her disheveled hair before slipping it back into the cleverly concealed sheath along the edge of his lute. With barely a grunt of exertion, he dragged her lifeless form into the outhouse, positioning her just so, before shutting the door. A quick glance around confirmed no prying eyes.

Then, with the ease of a man who had done this before, he stripped out of his bard's attire and slipped into her discarded clothing. As he did, his body shifted, flesh and bone rearranging until he no longer resembled Devaultus. Instead, the curvaceous form of the woman – Andrea, he had heard her called – stood in his place.

Adjusting the dress, he let out a small laugh, mimicking her sultry voice. "Well then," he purred to himself, shaking out his hair. With a final glance at his hidden bard's attire, safely tucked into a nearby barrel, he sauntered back toward the tavern, every step mimicking the seductive sway of the woman he had just dispatched.

Inside, the woman he had originally followed stood chatting in the back, her laughter ringing through the air. As Devaultus approached, she turned to him with an easy familiarity.

"Don't forget, Andrea," she chided playfully. "We need to head to the other tavern and feed the slaves, or Lark will have our hides."

Devaultus, Andrea, nodded with a charming smile. "Of course, darling," he said, mimicking her mannerisms flawlessly. "I'll just fetch some more ale first."

He glided toward the back where the kegs were stored, his mind already working through the next step of his plan. A quick scan of the room revealed no prying eyes. Perfect. Reaching into his pouch, he retrieved a pinch of crushed herbs, dark and potent. With a practiced hand, he crumbled them into the next keg to be tapped. The cook, none the wiser, helped shift the keg into position before returning to his work. Devaultus watched, satisfied, as the tainted ale sloshed within its container.

Now, the trick was to ensure everyone drank their fill. And for that, he needed to be Devaultus again.

Slipping away, he retrieved his hidden bard's attire, his form rippling back into that of the dashing young man he preferred to present. He adjusted his lute, rolled his shoulders, and strode confidently through the front entrance of the tavern.

"Enough of this deafening racket!" he called out, his voice cutting through the noise.

All eyes turned to him. The bard on stage, Kontorious, if Devaultus remembered correctly, stopped playing, a sneer creeping across his face.

"Not you again," the bard sighed, his fingers tightening around the neck of his lute.

Devaultus waved a dismissive hand. "I do not care who you believe yourself to be. Give these folks a break from your screeching." He strode past him, stepping onto the stage, his fingers already plucking at the strings of his lute.

The room was tense, the crowd waiting for a response, but Devaultus merely leaned in close to the disgraced bard, his voice dropping to a whisper. "Step down, dear boy, before I grow cross with you."

Kontorious hesitated, eyes darting to the crowd. Finally, with a forced smirk, he stepped down. "Very well," he said. "Let's see if you can do better."

Devaultus smiled, strumming the first few notes. "Do allow me to tell you a tale," he began, his voice weaving its magic over the gathered patrons. "A story of a hero of old... And at the end of each verse, we shall drink to the man named Krest, the legend of old!"

He cast a glance toward the bar, where the newly tainted ale was already being poured into mugs. Soon, this tavern would be his stage, and the real show would begin.

With a charming yet sinister smile, Devaultus ran his fingers over the strings of his lute, his touch light as a whisper. The chatter quieted, anticipation thick in the air as he struck a haunting chord. He began to sing.

*Oh, gather 'round, ye weary souls, and hear a tale so bold,*

*Of Krest, the ghoul with piercing eyes and a heart so dark and cold.*

*Through misty streets and shadowed ways, where rogues and cutthroats creep,*

*He met them there, with sharpened spear, and sent them all to sleep.*

The patrons lifted their mugs, toasting the first verse with hearty laughter, their cheers blending with the melody. They drank deeply, the bitter-sweet ale sliding down their throats, its warmth spreading through their limbs. A few swayed in their seats, assuming the room was spinning from the drink alone. Devaultus continued, his voice weaving its spell.

*Spin and strike, the spear takes flight, a deadly waltz begun!*
*Step and sway, the fools must pay, Krest fights 'til there are none!*
*Through blood and dust, through bone and rust, his dance will never cease,*
*For in his hands, the spear commands, his art, a masterpiece!*

The chorus roused the crowd, feet stomping, fists pounding against the tables in rhythmic approval. More ale was poured, foaming over the rims of their cups. The first to fall was a wiry man near the hearth, his eyes fluttered, his grip on his mug slackening. His neighbor chuckled, thinking the man had simply overindulged. Devaultus watched, his lips curling as he transitioned seamlessly into the next verse.

*From alleys dark to crimson fields, his legend swiftly spread,*
*A warrior cursed, yet blessed with grace, who danced where mortals bled.*
*But whispers spoke of darker foes, of gods who reigned in flame,*
*And Krest, with but a smirk and bow, sought out the demon's name.*

A hush fell over the room, the hypnotic timbre of Devaultus' voice drawing the patrons deeper into the tale. Hands trembled slightly as tankards were lifted, the effects of the ale growing stronger. A burly mercenary, halfway through a boisterous laugh, suddenly slumped forward, his forehead hitting the table with a dull thud. The others barely noticed, too enraptured, too intoxicated. Devaultus played on.

*Spin and strike, the spear takes flight, a deadly waltz begun!*
*Step and sway, the fools must pay, Krest fights 'til there are none!*
*Through blood and dust, through bone and rust, his dance will never cease,*
*For in his hands, the spear commands, his art, a masterpiece!*

The once lively stomps grew sluggish. The clinking of mugs was now sporadic. A serving girl's tray slipped from her grasp, sending wooden goblets rolling across the floor. She tried to speak, her lips moving soundlessly before she crumpled onto the tavern's sticky planks. Devaultus did not falter, his melody flowing like liquid silk as he approached the tale's crescendo.

*Beneath a sky of shattered stars, the fiend arose in might,*
*A thousand voices screamed his name, his form eclipsed the night.*
*With claw and fang, with fire and hate, the demon struck with wrath,*
*Yet Krest just smiled, took a step, and danced upon his path.*

Only a few remained upright now, their bodies frozen in place, eyes glassy with the realization of their doom. Devaultus gazed upon them, relishing the slow collapse of the audience before him. He strummed the lute with purpose, the notes sharpening like blades.

*Like flowing silk, the spear did weave, through hellfire, fang, and claw,*
*Each thrust a note, each struck a chord, no god could match his awe.*
*A final twirl, a whispered breath, the ghoul took death's embrace,*
*His spear impaled the demon's heart, then vanished without trace.*

Silence gripped the tavern, save for the quiet, uneven breathing of the few still conscious. Devaultus let the last note linger, savoring the moment before delivering the final chorus like a death knell.

*Spin and strike, the spear takes flight, a deadly waltz begun!*
*Step and sway, the gods must pay, Krest fights 'til there are none!*
*Through myths and dust, through time and rust, his dance will never cease,*
*For in the wind, his song remains, his art, a masterpiece!*

Devaultus took a slow, deliberate bow. The last of the patrons slumped over, unmoving. The only sounds left were of the guttering flames, and the distant howl of the wind. He straightened, slinging his lute over his shoulder. He picked up the server who reminded him earlier of the slaves and began to dance with her paralyzed body. Her head hung limply as her eyes blinked at him. Swinging her in a circle he continued to hum the song to himself. He leaned in, giving her a kiss before dropping her paralyzed form to the floor. The herb now in her system unable to allow her to catch herself. Grinning to himself he strode toward the door.

Glancing down at Lark, he let his face flash to that of Lindgurth for only a moment, allowing the man to recognize him. He smiled at Lark and gave him a wink before his face changed back to that of the young man. Stepping over him, he paused and walked toward the keg of ale, tipping it over. The ale sloshed and began to cover the floor. A one-sided grin formed on his face as he put his mask on and took up one of the tavern's lanterns. He tossed it behind him, and it began to take light in the ale. Stepping out into the night. A silhouette of a man and a large painted grin on his face.

Behind him, the tavern lay still, its patrons caught in a paralyzed slumber they would never wake from. A blaze began to form in the windows. He hummed the melody under his breath as he disappeared into the night, leaving only the echo of his song drifting through the air like a whispered curse.

# CHAPTER 2

# FOLLOWER GAINED: THE HOT MESS EXPRESS

Devaultus stirred, stretching his arms above his head as the remnants of sleep clung to him like a stubborn mist. The small nap he'd taken before last night's... *festivities* had left him drained rather than refreshed. His muscles ached with a pleasant soreness, a reminder of his carefully orchestrated performance. With a slow roll, he slid off the bed, his bare feet touching the cool wooden floor. His keen eyes swept across the dimly lit room; everything was as it should be. His bard's outfit, hat, mask, and lute were all tucked away, safely locked in their rightful places. His form had reverted to that of the portly, unimposing young man known as Lindgurth.

Running a hand through his unkempt hair, he wiped the last traces of sleep from his eyes before pulling on his modest commoner's outfit. The drab fabric hung loosely over his frame, a far cry from the lavish attire he preferred as Devaultus. He dragged a brush through his hair absentmindedly, smoothing out the worst of the tangles before reaching for his shoes, just as a knock echoed at the door.

His brow furrowed. It was rare for someone to seek him out in this guise. Adjusting his posture, he strolled casually to the door and pulled it open.

Standing before him was Lacey, one of the serving girls. Her usual boldness had faded, replaced with a timid, almost nervous energy. She fidgeted with the hem of her apron, her voice unsteady as she spoke.

"Uhm... Lindgurth... There's a woman here to see you."

Devaultus paused, tilting his head in mock surprise. "A woman? For me?"

It wasn't unheard of for him to attract attention, but as Lindgurth? Unusual, to say the least. He studied Lacey's face, noting the hesitance in her eyes. Something about this unsettled her. Interesting.

"Yes?" she confirmed, though the word came out more like a question.

Devaultus found her uncertainty amusing but didn't press her on it. Instead, he offered an easy smile. "Very well, I'll be down shortly."

Lacey nodded quickly and scurried off, no doubt eager to be away from the strange encounter. As he shut the door, Devaultus pondered the implications. Who could possibly be looking for him? Someone from his past? That was highly unlikely, he was meticulous about covering his tracks. Perhaps an admirer? He chuckled to himself. No, he doubted anyone would go to such lengths simply for his company.

With one last adjustment to his tunic, he straightened his posture and descended the stairs with an air of relaxed confidence.

And there she was.

The woman from the previous night, the one he had rescued. Alone. No guards flanking her this time. A bold choice, and a foolish one, considering what had transpired the night before. She met his gaze, her expression unreadable, and then spoke in a smooth, controlled voice.

"Hello, Lindgurth. May we speak?"

As she spoke, her fingers absentmindedly brushed against the side of her head, and for the briefest moment, her eyes flickered with something: admiration, as though she were caught in a trance.

Devaultus tilted his head slightly, his curiosity piqued. "Very well, Miss...?"

A calculated pause. He needed her name. If she had found him this easily, she could prove to be a problem.

She blinked, seeming to pull herself from whatever reverie had momentarily claimed her. "I am Lorivelle Goldwynd." She motioned to a nearby private room. "Shall we?"

He smiled, concealing the many thoughts racing through his mind. The name Goldwynd was not unfamiliar to him. A prominent family, and if memory served, one of the few bloodlines still blessed, or cursed, depending on who you asked, with magic. This made her presence all the more intriguing.

"Very well," he said smoothly, gesturing toward the door. "Ladies first."

She strode into the room with the grace of nobility, every step poised and deliberate. But the moment they crossed the threshold and the door shut behind them, her entire demeanor shifted. With an almost theatrical flair, she all but threw herself onto a chair, sprawling out in a manner more fitting of a seasoned pirate captain than a highborn lady.

Devaultus leaned against the door, arms crossed as he studied her. Amusement flickered behind his indifferent expression.

Then, in a swift and unexpected movement, she dropped to her knees before him, clutching at his coat with trembling hands. Her breath came in uneven gasps, and a strange, feverish light burned in her emerald eyes.

"I was gone," she whispered, almost to herself. "Death was at my door... and from the shadows came a hero. No, a god, to my rescue."

Devaultus remained motionless, watching her with mild interest.

She giggled, the sound bordering on delirium. "A god of death, striking down his enemies with effortless grace. And I... I bore witness to his divine wrath." She clutched at her chest as though reliving the moment. "And now, this one humbly begs to be your disciple."

Devaultus exhaled slowly. This was... problematic.

She was clearly unhinged, a woman who had either shattered from last night's horrors or had always harbored the madness he now saw gleaming in her eyes.

"What of your family?" he asked, his voice even.

Lorivelle let out a small, amused sigh, her expression distant. "They believe me dead. The guards who were with me last night... are no longer a concern." A slow smile spread across her lips, one that did not quite reach her eyes. "I am yours and yours alone, my Lord."

Devaultus ran a tongue across his teeth, suppressing the urge to sigh. She was dangerous, but more importantly, she was an inconvenience. However... an opportunity lay in this chaos. A mind as broken as hers could be molded, twisted into something useful. If she became a burden, well, he had always been skilled with a blade.

He regarded her for a moment longer before allowing a slow, calculated smile to spread across his face.

"Very well," he murmured, reaching down to brush a strand of golden hair from her cheek. "I accept you as my disciple."

Lorivelle sprang to her feet with an almost childlike glee, skipping toward the door as if the weight of her past life had completely lifted from her shoulders. But Devaultus was quicker, stepping into her path and pressing a firm hand against the wooden doorframe to halt her.

"Hold."

His voice, calm yet commanding, sent a visible shiver through her, not of fear but of anticipation. She turned to him with wide, eager eyes, silently pleading for instruction, for purpose. At that moment, he could see it, her willingness to do anything he desired. If he so much as hinted at it, she would rush into the next room and slaughter everyone inside, all in the name of pleasing him. That was the depth of her madness, the extent of her devotion.

This... could be problematic.

Devaultus narrowed his eyes, considering how best to temper her instability without diminishing her usefulness. He had to ensure she wouldn't expose herself, or worse, him.

"We must, at times, wear masks," he said smoothly. "Not always physical ones, but those that deceive in other ways. You came here today wearing the mask of a noblewoman, a lady of grace and dignity. And I, in turn, wear the mask of a simple cook." He let that sink in, watching her expression closely. "When you leave this room, you will don that mask again. You will become Lorivelle Goldwynd, the highborn daughter of nobility."

Lorivelle blinked, then nodded frantically, her entire posture radiating excitement. "Yes, my Lord!" she nearly gasped, as if overwhelmed by the sheer joy of being given direction.

Good. That was one problem handled. For now.

He released the door, stepping aside to allow her through. As if on cue, she straightened her back, lifted her chin, and strode into the hallway with the grace of a queen, her steps slow and deliberate. Each movement sent a ripple through her finely tailored dress, drawing the eyes of those who dared glance her way. She was, without question, a vision of nobility.

Devaultus followed a few paces behind, casting a casual glance toward Fro'dovin, who stood by the doorway watching them with a mixture of curiosity and suspicion.

"I am needed to escort Miss Goldwynd to the market," Devaultus stated plainly.

Fro'dovin's brow furrowed slightly, his gaze flickering between the two of them. It was clear he found it strange that such a woman would take an interest in someone like Lindgurth, but he did not question it aloud. Devaultus simply offered a nonchalant shrug, as if he, too, had no explanation.

With that, the two stepped out into the bustling streets.

The marketplace was alive with the usual symphony of voices haggling over goods, merchants advertising their wares, and the distant clatter of wagon wheels against cobblestone. Devaultus kept a leisurely pace, observing Lorivelle carefully.

"We need to find you something less... conspicuous," he mused aloud. "If you continue to dress like nobility, you'll draw too much attention. And we both know what happened the last time you caught the wrong kind of attention."

For a brief moment, her noble facade cracked. A wicked little giggle escaped her lips, and she turned to him with eyes alight with something dark.

"I hope we do run into something like that again," she purred, almost wistfully.

Devaultus exhaled through his nose, his patience thinning. She was unstable, that much was clear, but perhaps, with the right guidance, she could become something useful rather than an outright liability. He would need to mold her, shape her into something more... controlled.

"Come along," he instructed, guiding her toward a shop with a sign displaying a needle and thread.

Lorivelle's posture wavered as they walked. One moment, she was the picture of noble poise, her back straight, her steps measured. The next, she was practically skipping like an overexcited child, unable to contain her enthusiasm.

Devaultus sighed. This would take work.

"Do you have any skills beyond standing at my side and looking decorative?" he asked.

She beamed. "Oh, yes! I'm quite skilled at many things!"

A long pause.

"...Such as?"

Silence.

She simply smiled, her expression unreadable, offering nothing more.

Devaultus clenched his jaw. This was growing tedious. Perhaps a test was in order. But first, proper clothing.

As they stepped into the tailor's shop, a small bell jingled above the door, announcing their arrival. An elderly woman, hunched with age but sharp in the eyes, looked them over with mild curiosity.

"Yes?" she asked.

"My friend here is in need of clothing that will help her blend in better," Devaultus said smoothly. With a practiced flick of his wrist, he slid a gold coin across the counter. "For your discretion."

The old woman's fingers closed around the coin, and she nodded knowingly. "Of course, dear. I have just the thing, though we may need to make some alterations."

She retrieved a measuring tape and stepped toward Lorivelle.

And that's when everything went wrong.

Lorivelle's expression darkened, her pupils dilating in an instant. Without warning, she spun to the side, snatching the tailor's scissors off the table in a fluid motion and pressing the sharp metal against the woman's throat.

The old woman let out a strangled gasp, frozen in place, her eyes wide with terror.

Devaultus didn't hesitate. Faster than a striking serpent, his hand shot out, gripping Lorivelle's wrist like a vise. His fingers dug into her flesh, his grip unrelenting.

"Easy," he murmured, his voice low and sharp as a blade. "She only wishes to measure you for clothing." He leaned in slightly, his eyes locking onto hers with quiet authority. "Now stand there and behave like a good girl."

For a moment, Lorivelle remained tense, her breathing uneven. Then, slowly, she relinquished her grip on the scissors and handed them to Devaultus without resistance.

She straightened her posture once more, the perfect noblewoman returning in an instant, as if nothing had happened.

The tailor, visibly shaken, looked at Devaultus with a mix of fear and gratitude. He gave her a single, reassuring nod.

"Continue."

The old woman hesitated for only a moment before cautiously resuming her work, though her hands trembled slightly as she took Lorivelle's measurements.

Devaultus watched, his mind already racing.

This was going to be more challenging than he had anticipated.

Devaultus knew he had to find a better way to temper Lorivelle's fractured mind, to mold it into something useful, something that aligned with his intentions. If left unchecked, her impulsive nature could spiral into chaos, and while he had no qualms with violence, unplanned bloodshed had a tendency to ruin well-laid schemes. He cast a glance at the old woman, who was still trembling from the near encounter with death.

"And do make it stain-resistant," he added smoothly.

The old woman swallowed hard, nodding so quickly that it looked as though her neck might snap. "Y-yes, my Lord! As you wish!" With that, she scurried off into the back of the shop, her hunched form disappearing behind bolts of fabric. "A few hours! That's all I need, mi'Lord!" she called over her shoulder.

Devaultus gave a satisfied nod and turned on his heel. "Come along," he ordered.

Lorivelle, hands delicately folded before her, followed in perfect step, her movements precise, controlled, yet the occasional flicker in her eyes betrayed the madness still simmering beneath the surface. They walked in silence, the crowd bustling around them, oblivious to the storm lingering between the pair.

As they reached a narrow alleyway between two weather-worn buildings, Devaultus veered inside, motioning for her to follow. The dimly lit space offered privacy, a brief reprieve from prying eyes. He turned to face her fully, his gaze sharp as he examined her with measured scrutiny. She straightened under his gaze, as though expecting an order, her emerald eyes glistening with unspoken devotion.

"You struggle to obey me properly," he mused, tapping a finger against his chin. "Not because you do not wish to, but because you do not fully understand what my will is."

She nodded fervently, eager, desperate, to prove herself worthy.

"We need a system," he continued. "A way for you to know what I expect without revealing too much to others."

Again, she nodded, hanging on his every word, her breathing shallow with anticipation.

"When I require you to act as a proper lady, graceful, noble, untouchable, I will call you 'Lorivelle.' When you are Lorivelle, you will not raise your hand in violence. You will be poised, elegant, untouchable. Do you understand?"

"Yes, my Lord," she breathed, her expression one of pure, unwavering devotion.

He studied her face carefully, looking for hesitation. Finding none, he continued.

"When I require a blade, a weapon to carve my will into this world, I will call you 'Scythe.' When you are Scythe, you will do whatever is necessary. There will be no hesitation, no mercy, no limits."

A flicker of something dark passed through her gaze. Excitement? Hunger? He ignored it and pressed on.

"And when there is no command, when there is no need for pretense or slaughter, you will be 'Vex.' In that form, you may be yourself... whoever that is."

Lorivelle's lips parted slightly as she repeated the names silently to herself, her fingers twitching at her sides as though inscribing the titles into her very skin. Finally, she lifted her gaze to him once more, a slow smile curling her lips.

"I understand," she whispered.

Devaultus held her stare for a moment longer, searching for comprehension in those striking green eyes. She seemed to grasp it. Or, at the very least, she would obey.

"Good," he said simply. Then, after a brief pause: "Lorivelle, you are dressed as a lady, so you will play the part."

At once, her posture straightened, her expression smoothing into something refined, regal. As though the erratic, manic creature from moments ago had never existed.

Pleased, Devaultus stepped back onto the main street, and she followed suit, the two moving seamlessly into the flow of the market. Vendors called out their wares, the scent of roasted meats and fresh spices thick in the air. Devaultus walked at a leisurely pace, pausing every so often to observe the goods displayed at various stalls. Lorivelle, ever the picture of noble perfection, matched his pace, her head held high, her steps measured.

A particular stall caught his attention, rows of skewered meat glistening with what appeared to be a sugary glaze, sprinkled lightly with aromatic herbs. He tilted his head slightly and turned his gaze to Lorivelle. She, too, was watching the food, her eyes lingering just a second too long.

"Do you wish to try one, Lorivelle?" he asked, his voice low, testing her discipline.

Her expression remained flawlessly neutral. "If it pleases my Lord."

A slow smile tugged at his lips. She was performing admirably. Still, he suspected she hadn't eaten since the night before, an interesting experiment in restraint. He turned to the vendor and held up two fingers.

The merchant, an older man with more gaps in his smile than teeth, grinned and handed over two skewers.

Devaultus accepted them, then passed one to Lorivelle, watching as she took it with careful fingers. Though she was clearly hungry, she maintained control, taking small, deliberate bites rather than devouring it in an unladylike manner.

Satisfied, he continued walking.

"Come," he said, once they had nearly finished their meal. "Let us check on your new clothing."

Lorivelle gave a delicate nod, keeping in step with him as they made their way back toward the shop. Whatever madness lurked beneath her skin, for now, she was Lorivelle. And that would do. Lorivelle moved with a noticeable lightness in her step, the meal having seemingly lifted her spirits. It was almost amusing. Devaultus wasn't sure if it was relief or concern that settled in his gut, but one thing was certain: he had no desire to find out what would happen if this woman became hangry. A dagger in his ribs seemed like a real possibility.

As they approached the tailor's shop once more, he paused at the entrance, pushing the door open and motioning her inside. The moment they stepped over the threshold, the old woman behind the counter stiffened. Her face lost what little color remained in her aged features, and her wrinkled hands trembled as they subtly reached beneath the desk. Devaultus didn't need to see to know that she had palmed the scissors she had been so eager to use for sewing, now clutching them as if they were a lifeline. Clearly, their last visit had left an impression.

Eager to be rid of them, she wasted no time. "M-mi 'Lord," she stammered, before regaining her composure, forcing a brittle smile onto her lips. "Right this way. Let's have the young lady try on her new attire."

She bustled to the back, retrieving a neat stack of carefully folded garments before returning to the counter, placing them down with a precision that suggested she wanted no further surprises.

Devaultus gave a satisfied nod and turned toward Lorivelle. "Try them on," he instructed.

The next moment was one that he should have anticipated, but somehow, he hadn't.

Without hesitation, Lorivelle's hands went to the fastenings of her current clothing, and before Devaultus could so much as blink, she was already halfway out of her top, stripping right there in the middle of the shop as if it were the most natural thing in the world.

"Wait...!" He took a sharp step forward, running a hand down his face in exasperation. "Not here. There are fitting rooms. Go change in one of those."

For a beat, she simply stared at him, blinking as though confused by the sudden correction. Then, with a small nod of understanding, she scooped up the new clothing, turned on her heel, and disappeared into one of the back rooms without so much as a second thought.

The tailor let out a shaky breath of relief, though Devaultus caught the way her grip remained tight on the hidden scissors, as if bracing for more unexpected chaos. He merely sighed and leaned against the counter, waiting.

A few minutes later, Lorivelle, or rather, Vex, reappeared, stepping lightly back into the room. The transformation was immediate and striking.

The outfit was a deep, inky black, tailored to fit snugly against her lithe frame. The fabric clung in all the right places while still allowing ease of movement, the cut designed for someone who needed to remain unnoticed yet agile. A hood rested lightly against her back, easily pulled up should she need to mask her presence, while a flowing cloak draped over her shoulders, serving the dual purpose of shielding her from both prying eyes and the harsh glare of the sun.

Devaultus took his time inspecting her, his sharp gaze sweeping over the ensemble. It was a perfect blend of utility and elegance.

"Is it comfortable, Vex?" he asked, purposefully using the name he had assigned for her in this role.

Across the counter, the tailor twitched slightly at the shift in name, her perceptive old eyes darting between the two of them with a mixture of curiosity and unease. But she wisely kept her thoughts to herself.

Vex beamed, nodding enthusiastically. "Yes, mi'Lord. It is very comfortable."

"Good." Devaultus gestured for her to gather the rest of her clothing before stepping toward the tailor. Leaning in, he lowered his voice just enough that only she could hear. "The other thing we discussed. Have it ready by tomorrow," he murmured, slipping a few more gold coins into her palm.

The woman swallowed hard but gave a swift nod, tucking the payment away without a word.

Satisfied, Devaultus turned sharply on his heel, striding toward the door. "Come," he commanded.

Vex practically skipped after him, her cloak swirling around her ankles as she fell into step beside him, her giddy energy a stark contrast to the quiet tension lingering in the shop they left behind.

# CHAPTER 3

# RECRUITING PSYCHOS: A BEGINNER'S GUIDE

The two made their way back to the Sweetwater Inn under the deepening hues of dusk. Before stepping through the door, Devaultus paused in a secluded corner and let his form ripple and shift until he looked once again like Lindgurth, his unassuming commoner guise. With a sigh of quiet exasperation, as if weary of having to hide behind yet another mask, he gathered himself and led Vex toward a vacant table. He gestured for her to sit down with a gentle command, his eyes betraying a hint of annoyance at having to play this role again.

Just then, he caught sight of Fro'dovin waving from across the room. Spotting Shell nearby, he called out, "Could you get her a bit to eat, my dear Shell?" His tone was warm yet brisk, and Shell's face lit up with a bright smile as she bounced off toward the back of the inn.

Turning to Vex, he lowered his voice conspiratorially, "I'll be right back. Behave yourself while I'm gone and do not harm anyone." Her large, expressive green eyes met his, brimming with trust and a trace of mischief, and she nodded obediently.

With a soft, resigned sigh escaping him, Devaultus strolled toward the bustling back room where Fro'dovin was waiting. Slipping on a well-worn apron, he joined Fro'dovin at a large wooden table cluttered with freshly picked vegetables and the tools of his trade. As he began to help chop the vegetables with practiced efficiency, Fro'dovin leaned in and remarked, "I find it odd that she'd want you to take her to the city. After all, Lindgurth, you're just a cook."

The comment spurred a brief flicker of thought in Devaultus' mind. He paused, considering how to spin the situation. Finally, he shrugged, his tone casual yet laced with a hint of wry humor. "Yes, it is a bit odd, but there's a strange sense of safety in my presence. You see, I ran into her being mugged last night," he explained, a wry smile tugging at his lips.

Fro'dovin scowled, his knife momentarily halting midair. "I hardly see how you, of all people, could make anyone feel secure," he grumbled.

Devaultus pondered this criticism, a part of him itching to prove his worth by demonstrating his capabilities. But then he chuckled softly to himself, realizing it was perhaps a testament to his extraordinary talent for assuming new identities. "Yeah, you might be right," he conceded. "But I suppose in a time of shock, one finds solace in whatever rock they can clutch in a storm."

Fro'dovin's chopping slowed as he mulled over those words, his eyes softening with reluctant understanding. "I suppose you may be right. Just be careful, lad. I dare say she seems like someone a person ought to keep at arm's length."

Devaultus flashed a knowing smile. "Of course, Fro'dovin. I'll be sure to be cautious, one never truly knows what a person is hiding beneath the surface." With that, he began to clean his knife meticulously and then removed his apron, his motions deliberate and calm.

"Is there anything you need from the village?" he inquired casually.

Fro'dovin paused, considering the question for a long moment before replying, "No, I believe you got everything I needed last time. Though tomorrow may bring a different tale."

Devaultus nodded thoughtfully. "Very well, Fro'dovin. I shouldn't make her wait any longer."

Fro'dovin's gruff voice broke the brief silence as he clapped him on the back, exclaiming, "Alright, lad. Best of luck!" The hearty slap, delivered with a force reminiscent of a stubborn beast in the stables, made Devaultus grimace internally. Despite the irritation, he accepted it as part of the routine, a small price to pay for the life he led.

With that, Devaultus stepped out of the back room, returning to his post to escort Vex into the wider world, each step laden with the silent promise of more intrigue and unexpected encounters.

Walking into the common room, Devaultus immediately spotted Vex finishing off the last remnants of her meal. Her delicate fingers swept across the plate, gathering up every crumb before she brought them to her lips, licking them clean with an almost childlike satisfaction. Across from her, Shell stood frozen, her expression caught somewhere between confusion and mild horror. Her gaze flickered between Vex and Devaultus before she quickly turned on her heel and scurried toward the back of the inn without a word.

Devaultus arched a brow, watching Shell's hurried retreat. "How odd," he mused internally. There was something peculiar about her reaction, had she noticed something strange about Vex? Or was she simply unsettled by the contrast between the noblewoman's stunning elegance and her downright feral table manners? He pushed the thought aside for now and stepped up beside Vex.

"Are you finished?" he asked, his voice laced with dry amusement.

Vex tilted her head toward him, still licking her fingertips clean. It was perhaps the least noblewoman-like thing he had ever seen, a far cry from the carefully curated grace she was supposed to possess. Then again, he had not instructed her to wear the mask of Lorivelle at this moment, and clearly, she had taken that to heart.

Suddenly, she sprang to her feet with an energy that made her golden hair bounce, nearly skipping toward the door like an overeager child.

"Do we get more treats from the market?" she asked, her voice bright with anticipation.

Devaultus narrowed his eyes slightly, watching her with quiet curiosity. How did she consume so much and yet remain so... perfect? Her figure, her complexion, none of it showed the effects of indulgence. Then again, he supposed he had no right to question it. He himself had spent years shifting his appearance at will, changing his face, his body, his presence, until even he had trouble recalling what his true form looked like.

"Perhaps," he said, his tone deliberately nonchalant, though he was already considering what their next move would be.

They stepped outside to where the bustling cobblestone streets of the market stretched before them, alive with the sounds of vendors hawking their wares, carts rattling over the uneven stones, and the occasional outburst of laughter from passing travelers. The air carried the scent of fresh-baked bread, spiced meats, and the ever-present aroma of ale from the nearby taverns.

As they walked, he turned his gaze toward her. "Do you sing or dance?" he asked, his voice casual but purposeful.

Vex considered the question, her delicate brows drawing together slightly in thought. Dancing was not a common skill for noblewomen, at least, not in the way he meant. Sure, they knew how to glide across a ballroom in a stiff, structured manner, but that was hardly the kind of performance he had in mind. Singing, however... She could sing, though the style of noblewomen's singing was leagues apart from that of a bard.

He nodded to himself, already forming a plan. "We'll need to work on your singing and dancing," he mused. "If you're going to stay by my side, you may as well learn to perform with me."

Vex's emerald eyes sparkled with something between excitement and mischief. "Oh," she purred. "That sounds fun."

Devaultus smirked. He had no doubt she would find a way to make it... interesting.

The two continued down the street, the noise of the market washing over them like the tides of an endless sea. Merchants called out their wares, the scent of spiced meats and roasted grains thick in the air. Devaultus walked with an air of ease, but his mind was a storm of calculations. After a few blocks, he abruptly veered into a narrow alleyway, pulling Vex along. Without missing a beat, he began the quick transformation into his more illustrious and enigmatic persona, Devaultus.

With swift precision, he shed the mundane skin of Lindgurth, replacing it with the effortless charm and charisma of the dashing rogue. His outfit shifted, the hat tilted just so, and in moments, the world would see him only as Devaultus. But one loose end still remained: a particularly troublesome, homicidal elf.

Today was the day he would begin his hunt.

There was a name he had heard the night before, a whisper on the lips of dying men. *The Plague.* He suspected that this was the gang Lark belonged to, and it was unlikely that the elf had merely been a wandering participant in the chaos. No, if they had been together, then the elf was also *Plague.* He would need to tread carefully, slipping his questions into conversation like a dagger beneath a cloak.

They reemerged from the alley and made their way toward the marketplace. Moving casually, pausing now and again to inspect trinkets and wares, playing the part of a young couple simply enjoying the afternoon. A smile here, a laugh there, each was another brushstroke painting them as ordinary in the eyes of those around them. Devaultus allowed himself to be momentarily distracted by a particularly curious leather hat, trying it on as he smirked at his reflection in a polished steel cap.

With a calculated flick of his fingers, he adjusted the brim and murmured to the merchant, "How do you manage to keep such fine wares with *The Plague* lurking about?"

The vendor, an older man with calloused hands, let out a dry chuckle. "Ah, they're not a problem if you know how to stay in line. Pay them what they think they're worth, and you'll find your shop still standing in the morning."

Devaultus laughed along with him, nodding as though in agreement. "A fair point."

They moved along, stopping at another stall where Vex's attention locked onto a set of ornate daggers. The blades gleamed like silvered moonlight, their craftsmanship leagues above the usual dull scrap found in this world. They were *metal*, a rare commodity so expensive that they might as well have been worth a sandship. Her eyes sparkled with an almost childlike admiration, her fingers twitching with the need to hold them.

Devaultus, however, had other business. He turned back to the vendor with a casual air. "I'm from out of town, supposed to meet up with someone, but he's been a no-show. Lark, heard of him?"

The vendor narrowed his eyes slightly, considering the question before nodding. "Yeah, I know Lark. Haven't seen him in a bit, though. He usually runs with two others, one's a big bastard named Oro, always looking like he wants to punch something. The other's some crazy elf called Leech."

Devaultus kept his expression neutral, filing the name away. *Leech. How fitting.*

The vendor continued, "Last I saw, Leech was at The Burning Breeches Tavern, but that was a couple of hours ago."

Devaultus flashed his best disarming smile. "Appreciate it. I'll see if I can track him down."

He gave a small nod before turning, moving fluidly back into the street, Vex trailing behind him like an eager shadow. She skipped along, entirely unbothered, seemingly lost in her own world. Meanwhile, Devaultus was already formulating plans of murder and mayhem.

As the twin suns began their slow descent beyond the horizon, the streets grew quieter. The market was still alive, but the atmosphere had changed. The daylight crowds were dispersing, replaced by those who thrived in the dim glow of lanterns. It was the time when honest folk retreated to their homes, leaving the night to creatures like him.

Devaultus took the opportunity to pry further into Vex's skillset, subtly testing what strengths she had beyond her appetite for violence. Their conversation danced between lighthearted and instructive, but his attention was suddenly pulled away by something unusual.

A sound. Faint, but distinct.

He tilted his head slightly, honing in on the noise coming from a side alley. It was the wet, sickening sound of flesh meeting force. The kind of sound that meant someone was getting *worked over*, and not in a friendly way.

He veered toward the alley without a second thought, slipping into the shadows. The scene before him was almost... *artistic* in its brutality.

Two robed figures stood over a man curled on the ground, his body a tapestry of fresh wounds. He tried to fight back, weakly clawing at his attackers, but they were relentless. Nearby, leaning against the wall with disturbing glee, was a third figure, a woman. Unlike the others, she wasn't participating in the violence. No, she was *enjoying* it.

Her hands clutched her own body as she shivered with excitement, squeezing herself as though the scene before her was some divine spectacle crafted for her pleasure. Her breaths were shallow, ragged, her lips curled into something between a grin and a sneer.

Devaultus watched her for a long moment, then slowly tilted his head to the side in thought.

Had he played *hero* today?

He didn't think so.

He exhaled a breath, his decision made.

His voice came low, smooth, and commanding.

*"Scythe."*

The word had barely left Devaultus' lips when Vex's entire demeanor shifted, as if a switch had been violently flipped. The playful glint in her eyes darkened, her body tensed like that of a predator scenting blood. In an instant, twin daggers materialized in her hands, their ornate designs unmistakable. Wait, when had she acquired those? Devaultus blinked, realization dawning that they were the very blades from the vendor earlier. He certainly hadn't seen her purchase them. Then again, did he truly know the extent of her resources? Or more accurately, her methods?

None of that mattered now. His lips curled into a knowing smirk as he pointed at the robed figures. "Bring me their ears."

Vex didn't hesitate. She moved like a phantom, vanishing from sight before reappearing midair, her feet silent as she launched off the alley wall. A blur of shadow and steel, she flipped over one of the attackers in an effortless arc, her dagger kissing his throat with a whisper of finality. By the time her feet touched the ground, the man was already collapsing, clutching at the crimson smile newly carved across his neck. She landed in a crouch, one knee pressing into the cobblestone, her free hand bracing her poised stance, hood drawn low over her eyes.

Then, without pause, she surged forward into a low, gliding slide. Her blade lashed out in a flash of silver, slicing across the Achilles tendon of the second attacker. The sickening snap of severed tendons was followed by an agonized scream as he crumpled onto his face, clawing uselessly at his ruined leg.

The third figure, a woman, froze in stunned horror before turning on her heel, panic overriding whatever cruelty had previously entertained her. She sprinted blindly, directly toward Devaultus.

He merely leaned against the wall, watching, unimpressed, hands tucked into his coat as if he had all the time in the world. This was Vex's test, and he would not intervene.

Vex, however, had no intention of allowing the woman an escape. With a flick of her wrist, she sent forth a cluster of crescent-shaped shadow blades. The projectiles sliced through the air with an eerie, whistling hiss, their edges imbued with darkness. One found its mark, embedding itself deep into the woman's knee, severing flesh and bone as if it were parchment. She let out a choked, gurgling cry as her legs failed her, sending her sprawling forward.

She landed at Devaultus' feet with a sickening thud, splattering a fresh spray of blood across his polished boots. He let out a sigh, his eyes dropping to the crimson-stained leather.

Taking his time, he pulled a silk scarf from his pocket and knelt slightly, meticulously wiping the gore away with quiet irritation. The woman's desperate whimpers filled the space between them, but he ignored them entirely. He had more pressing concerns, such as the state of his footwear.

Behind him, the alley was a chorus of gurgled death rattles and the dull, wet sound of steel meeting flesh. The remaining combatants barely had time to react before Vex's merciless dance ended their miserable existence. The symphony of slaughter was brief, efficient, and merciless.

Moments later, she emerged from the carnage like a satisfied predator, her movements eerily fluid, almost feline. A lazy grin stretched across her face as she held up her prize: a handful of severed ears. Eight, to be precise.

"Very good, Vex," Devaultus murmured, his voice smooth with approval.

Instantly, the bloodthirsty assassin dissolved into her more carefree persona. As if shedding her murderous skin, she wiped her hands clean and retrieved a meat stick from within her cloak, biting into it with an exaggerated moan of delight, her eyes rolling back in pleasure.

Devaultus, meanwhile, studied the collection of ears in her grasp. Eight? He frowned slightly and glanced down the alley. Four lifeless bodies lay strewn across the cobblestones, their faces grotesquely silent in death.

His frown deepened.

Ah. Even the original victim was missing his ears.

He exhaled through his nose, shaking his head slightly.

It would seem he would have to be more precise with his orders in the future.

Vex's eyes sparkled with exhilaration as she gazed up at Devaultus, her expression alight with something bordering on madness. "Did I do well, Mr. D.?" she asked, her voice carrying an almost childlike excitement.

Mr. D.?

Devaultus arched a brow, the peculiar nickname catching him off guard. That was certainly new. His lips twitched slightly in amusement as he reached out, running a hand over her wild locks in a patronizing pat. "You did well. Good girl," he murmured, his voice laced with approval.

Vex's entire face lit up at the praise, her lips curling into a delighted, almost manic grin. A bubbling giggle escaped her, a sound both airy and unhinged, before she eagerly set about cleaning her daggers with expert precision. The way she handled them was telling. It was clear now, she hadn't just stolen the ornate blades, she had claimed them, as if they had always belonged to her.

Devaultus noted this in silence. Now wasn't the time to interrogate her about where and how she'd acquired them. In truth, she hadn't been caught, and even *he* hadn't seen her do it. That meant she was significantly more adept at... *acquiring* things than he had originally given her credit for. That was both a useful and dangerous skill. One he would have to monitor closely.

"Come along, Vex. We have a missing elf to track down," he said smoothly, turning toward the darkened street ahead. "Word is, he was last seen in The Burning Breeches Tavern. We'll see if we can sniff him out there. I want you to be at my side. *Do not act until I tell you to.*"

Vex nodded eagerly, slipping into step beside him. "Of course, Mr. D.," she purred, as if she *relished* the idea of holding back until the perfect moment.

The two drifted through the night like shadows, slipping past the dim glow of flickering lanterns and the guttural sounds that spilled from the city's underbelly. The streets were alive with sin, moans of pleasure, cries of pain, and the occasional shriek that was swiftly muffled by unseen hands. It was a lawless hour, and the predators had begun their hunt.

Finally, they arrived at The Burning Breeches Tavern.

Devaultus stepped through the threshold first, letting his sharp eyes adjust to the dim, candle-lit filth before him. The air was thick with the scent of sweat, unwashed bodies, stale ale, and something far worse lurking beneath it all. This wasn't a place for respectable men, not that Devaultus had ever claimed to be one.

The tavern was as disgusting as he had imagined. In the darkened corners, men sat hunched over wooden tables, lost in their drunken stupors. More than a few of those tables had *women* beneath them, their heads bobbing up and down in a rhythm Devaultus chose to ignore. The floor was slick with spilled drinks, vomit, and unidentifiable grime, the combination of which made each step an exercise in restraint.

He moved through the filth without pause, slipping into the shadows to a vacant table. Vex followed, her sharp eyes darting around the room, scanning for threats, or prey.

A busty tavern wench sauntered over to their table, her hips swaying with practiced allure. She leaned in close, the scent of cheap perfume barely masking the musk of sweat on her skin. "What'll it be, love?" she asked in a sultry voice, her ample cleavage practically spilling into his personal space.

"Two ales will be fine," Devaultus replied smoothly.

The woman offered him a slow, knowing smile before turning on her heel to fetch his order, her gaze lingering on him longer than necessary. It was obvious she was used to men leering, and just as obvious that she didn't mind the attention, but Vex certainly did.

The moment the wench walked away, Vex tensed beside him. Her normally playful demeanor had shifted into something much darker, much more *dangerous*.

Her gaze snapped toward the woman's retreating form, her golden eyes narrowing with an intensity that would have sent lesser men running. Her fingers twitched, resting instinctively against the hilts of her daggers as she seethed.

Devaultus leaned back in his chair, stretching out comfortably as he propped his boots up on the table, surveying the tavern in search of the psychotic elf they sought. Meanwhile, Vex was glaring daggers at the tavern wench, her body practically vibrating with pent-up rage.

At that moment, the wench returned, placing two filthy mugs of ale onto the table with an exaggerated lean. This time, she got *closer*, her breath warm against his ear as she whispered, *"Anything else?"*

That was the moment Vex snapped.

Her foot had been idly shaking, trying to dislodge something sticky from her boot, but now she was deathly still. Her eyes burned with fury, her lips pulling back in a snarl.

"*Let me carve out her heart.*"

The words dripped with venom, her voice barely above a whisper yet so saturated with malice that Devaultus could *feel* the weight of it.

Her eyes flickered toward Devaultus, the hatred still present.

Was this... *jealousy?*

A slow realization settled over him. She wasn't just reacting to some tavern wench flirting, *she was furious because his attention wasn't on her.*

*Interesting.*

Terrifying. But interesting.

This was an unforeseen development. One that, if left unchecked, could spiral into chaos. He would have to handle this situation carefully. If she truly was possessive of him, it could cause unending problems down the road.

But, for now, he simply smirked and took a leisurely sip of his ale.

This... could be fun.

"Behave," Devaultus muttered under his breath, his voice low but edged with authority. His eyes flickered to the tavern wench, who still lingered, her chest practically spilling from her corset as she offered one last seductive jiggle, as if hoping to tempt him into some reckless indulgence. Instead, he gave her a polite smile, sharp as a dagger's edge.

"That will be all. Thank you."

The wench, seemingly pleased with herself, smirked and sauntered off, hips swaying in a deliberate rhythm as she turned her attention to another patron.

But Devaultus wasn't the only one watching her go. His gaze drifted sideways, catching the dark glint in Vex's eyes as she tracked the woman's every step, her expression unreadable, until one looked closer. Beneath that porcelain mask of stillness, barely restrained fury churned like a storm on the horizon. A promise of suffering, a thirst for retribution, all for the crime of daring to exist in Devaultus' proximity.

He exhaled through his nose, shaking his head slightly. "Easy, Vex. We are here for another." He leaned back against his chair, stretching his arms across the backrest in a casual, yet commanding posture. His voice was smooth but carried the weight of an iron-clad order. "Be calm. Pain and suffering will come in time."

Vex's piercing gaze lingered on the wench for a moment longer, her fingers twitching ever so slightly near the hilt of her daggers, before she finally, reluctantly, tore her attention away. When her eyes met his again, they had transformed, shifting from the simmering rage of a predator denied its kill to something softer, almost reverent. Admiration. Devotion.

"Of course, Mr. D." The words left her lips in almost a purr, a sharp contrast to the bloodlust that had clouded her features mere moments ago.

Devaultus lifted his ale, taking a measured swig. The moment the liquid touched his tongue, his lip curled in distaste. He stilled, feeling an odd sensation on his tongue. With a resigned sigh, he reached into his mouth, plucking out a few splinters of wood, their jagged edges scraping against his fingertips. His brows furrowed as he peered into the murky amber liquid, noting the tiny flecks of wood bobbing up and down like drowned insects.

His gaze shifted to the bar, his sharp eyes scanning the environment until he found the answer to his discontent. There, behind the counter, stood the bumbling tavern workers, their hands stained with ale as they clumsily poured drinks. The keg tap, in all their infinite wisdom, had apparently defeated them. Instead of properly affixing it, they had simply hacked a crude hole into the top of the barrel, letting the ale slosh out freely, wood fragments and all.

Devaultus sighed and shoved the mug aside. The ale wasn't worth it. He had tasted far better in his time.

His mind drifted for a moment, memories of a different kind of tavern, a different kind of drink. Now that had been *ale*. He once drank with a dwarven king, the finest, richest ale he had ever tasted filling his goblet. Of course, that particular night hadn't quite gone as planned. The king, Forforlug Iceforged, had been *enchanted* by Devaultus' presence, so much so that he had mistaken him for his long-lost, gushing dwarven bride. What was supposed to be a quick and clean theft of a ring for the Kar'Gromare King turned into a bloodied escape, running for his life as a lovesick, battle-hardened dwarf bellowed marriage vows in his wake. It had been pure chaos, dodging axes, barrels, and an entire wedding procession intent on seeing the union through.

Still, the ale had been worth the risk.

Then there was Marlogo, now *he* was a different kind of beast entirely. Pompous, massive, and brimming with arrogance, the towering brute bore a striking resemblance to a minotaur from other worlds. Standing at nearly ten feet tall, he was a presence that commanded attention, his deep, booming laughter shaking the very walls of whatever grand hall he chose to drink in.

Devaultus let a smirk ghost his lips at the memories, before shaking them away.

Now was not the time to dwell on past misadventures.

Now, there was a psychotic elf to find.

He was fairly certain he'd need to steer clear of that world for a long while, possibly forever. Still, the ring had been worth it. In fact, it was that very ring that had granted him the ability to travel between worlds in the first place. But fate, as always, had proven to have a cruel sense of humor. Upon arriving here, he had barely set foot on solid ground before being ambushed by a horde of bandits. Too many to fight off.

Normally, that wasn't a problem, escaping was what Devaultus did best. But luck had not been on his side that day.

One of those pathetic, unskilled brigands had gotten lucky. A single, well-placed slash, and just like that, his finger was gone. The finger that had once worn the ring.

The loss had been infuriating. He'd had to pay a significant sum of gold to have the finger regrown, an annoyance, but a necessary expense. The ring, however, was another matter entirely. That would take work to reclaim. Work and patience.

But that was a concern for another time. Right now, he had a more pressing issue: Leech. The psychotic elf needed to be dealt with. He turned slightly, preparing to instruct Vex to stay put while he maneuvered closer to their target. But as he shifted his gaze, he found that she was gone.

A spike of irritation, mixed with something dangerously close to panic, shot through him. His sharp eyes scanned the room, quickly landing on her across the tavern. She had wasted no time. She was already beside Leech.

Damn it, Vex.

He inhaled sharply, his hands curling into fists. She was going against the system, his system. When would she learn that the system was in place for a reason? He had plans.

Moving with fluid precision, he rose to his feet, weaving effortlessly between drunken patrons, shadowed figures, and the occasional unconscious form slumped over a table. He needed to get closer, fast. This place was a viper's nest of pain and betrayal. The Plague owned most of the underbelly of this city, and he had no illusions that this establishment was filled to the brim with its members. One wrong move, and this could spiral into chaos.

Meanwhile, Vex had already inserted herself into the situation, literally. She had pressed her chest against the back of Leech's head, the elf's gaze flicking upward as her arms draped around him in a sultry, deceptive embrace. His head nestled between the pillowy softness of her chest, his expression flickering between confusion and pleasure.

Vex's smile was the picture of playful mischief, but Devaultus knew better. That was not the look of a girl having fun. That was the look of a predator playing with her food.

Leech, none the wiser, seemed to be enjoying himself, until Vex's hand slowly, deliberately, slid downward. With a casual push, she pressed against the table, shoving it back just enough to reveal the tavern wench she had grown to hate over the course of the past few minutes kneeling beneath it. The wench, clearly eager to continue whatever sordid transaction had been taking place, looked up at the two excitedly, her expression one of intrigue rather than concern.

Devaultus clenched his jaw. This was spiraling fast. He needed to regain control, before the whole damn tavern went up in flames.

He continued to move with his usual grace, his footfalls as silent as a whisper against the grimy tavern floor. His mind raced, frustration bubbling beneath his carefully constructed mask of calm. How had he let Vex slip away like that? More importantly, had Scythe taken over, or was this truly Vex's own twisted desire? A dangerous question. One he didn't have time to answer.

He was nearly upon them when Vex made her move. With a sudden, vicious grip, she seized the wench's hair and yanked her head downward. The motion was brutal, unrelenting, and final. Her free hand shot over the man's shoulder, a flash of silver in the dim candlelight as she buried a dagger deep into the back of the wench's skull. The force of the strike drove the man's own member further down the woman's throat, an undignified, gruesome end. A strangled shriek erupted from Leech, the sound high-pitched and primal. Vex, her face a portrait of twisted delight, gripped his throat with an almost loving tenderness and turned his paling face toward her. She smiled, a cruel, delighted thing, before twisting with supernatural strength, snapping his neck like brittle kindling.

The entire tavern roared to life. Chairs scraped across the floor. Tankards slammed down. Weapons were drawn. A slow, collective realization settled over the room. One of their own had just been slaughtered in the filth-ridden heart of their den.

Devaultus exhaled sharply through his nose. For a brief moment, he considered simply stepping back into the shadows, letting her reap what she had sown. No one had connected him to her yet, at least, he hoped not. But no. As reckless as she was, she was still his. His wild, unpredictable, blood-soaked weapon. And weapons needed direction.

A mountain of a man lunged at Vex, his massive arms swinging with the force of a wrecking ball. But she was quicker. With a precise kick, she struck the inside of his knee, collapsing his leg and sending him toppling forward. His sheer weight and momentum carried him straight into the table, which exploded into a shower of splinters as his head crashed through it.

Devaultus sighed, plucking a dulled steak knife from an abandoned plate. With casual precision, he flicked it across the room. The blunt blade buried itself into another man's eye, causing him to scream and stumble backward, knocking into a group of his fellow thugs. All the while, Devaultus grumbled under his breath.

"I sneak in, I sneak out. No one sees me, no one knows I was ever here. That's how it's done. But no, of course not, along comes this woman and ruins everything." His fingers twitched, as he debated whether he should strangle her himself later.

Vex, oblivious, or perhaps all too aware of his frustration, had already moved on to her next victim. She crouched, snatching a dagger from Leech's cooling body, and, in one smooth motion, she drove it straight into another man's crotch. The pained howl that erupted from him was sickeningly satisfying. As he crumpled to his knees, she wasted no time, stepping onto his back and launching herself into the air. Her momentum carried her onto the shoulders of a larger thug, her weight forcing him to spin around just as another man lunged with a blade.

The steel meant for Vex found its mark instead, straight into the chest of the unwilling human shield she was balancing upon. A wet gurgle escaped the doomed man's lips as his own ally had unknowingly cut him down. Before his corpse could slump forward, Vex used him as a springboard, her lithe form flipping through the air. Mid-twist, she turned her body, her dagger flashing outward. The blade sliced clean across another assailant's stomach as she landed with feline grace, a wild, ecstatic grin stretching across her face.

Devaultus sighed again. Oh, how tiresome this was going to be. And yet, a small, almost imperceptible smirk tugged at the corner of his lips. She was chaos incarnate, but gods be damned, she was effective.

With a fluid twist, Vex redirected her momentum, her dagger plunging deep into the man's back. He let out a strangled gasp, his body seizing before crumpling forward. But she had already moved on. She was a storm of motion, wild and unpredictable, her strikes fueled by raw, primal instinct. Each attack was brutal, each cut a merciless carving of flesh as she dismantled her foes piece by piece. Blood splattered against the floor, painting the scene in crimson strokes of chaos.

Meanwhile, Devaultus moved among them like a phantom. He did not fight with savage force but with the elegance of a shadow slipping between flickering candlelight. Every attack against him met only air, his form seamlessly shifting just beyond reach. Where Vex tore through her enemies with unrelenting ferocity, Devaultus was a whisper of death, a fleeting presence that left ruin in his wake. His movements were precise, calculated, his blade never hacking, never overexerting. A flick of his wrist, and a thin red line would appear across an enemy's arm or leg, barely felt before the venom seeped into their bloodstream.

One by one, they faltered. Swords and daggers slipped from trembling fingers, bodies locked in paralysis as the poison took hold. Wide eyes filled with panic as those still standing realized they couldn't move, couldn't even scream as they toppled like statues, helpless to the effects of Devaultus' craft.

And still, Vex moved, a whirlwind of lethal grace, while Devaultus merely sidestepped and let his prey fall around him. They were opposites in battle, one a feral predator, the other a patient executioner. And yet, between them, the scene had become nothing short of a massacre.

It took just a few minutes for the only ones still breathing in the tavern to be Devaultus and Vex. The air was thick with the metallic scent of blood, mingling with the stench of spilled ale and death. The only sounds were the distant echoes of the city outside and the soft, satisfied exhale of Vex as she stood amidst the carnage, her chest rising and falling with exhilaration. A twisted, bloody grin spread across her face, her wild eyes gleaming with an almost childlike delight.

"That was... incredible," she purred, rolling her shoulders as if shaking off the last vestiges of a battle-high.

Devaultus, however, was far less amused. He straightened, brushing a fleck of blood from his sleeve with a look of mild irritation before shifting his gaze toward her. His expression was unreadable, though a storm of frustration brewed just beneath the surface.

"You and I most certainly need to work on our communication, Vex," he muttered, his tone sharper than any blade. "Why did you attack? I told you to stay put!" His voice carried a growing edge of annoyance, each word clipped with barely restrained vexation.

Vex merely tilted her head, her lips parting into an innocent smile as if she truly didn't understand his anger. "You said Vex does as she wants so long as she stays with you," she reminded him, her voice laced with amusement. "I wanted to kill them both."

Devaultus opened his mouth, only to close it again as her words settled in his mind. Damn. She had him there. He had told her that. He hadn't set out to mold a mindless puppet; after all, he wanted something more useful, something unpredictable but loyal. But he needed to find a way to keep her from dragging him into these unnecessary messes. There had to be a balance.

As he ran a hand through his hair in thought, a memory stirred in the back of his mind: the previous tavern, the murmurs of the patrons, the whispers of a hidden basement. Hadn't they mentioned something about this place? Or was it another tavern entirely? Either way, it was worth investigating.

"Vex," he said, his voice shifting from frustration to intrigue. "I believe there's a hidden basement in this tavern. Let's see if we can find it, shall we?"

Without hesitation, Vex's grin widened, and the two split up, wading through the river of blood and broken bodies strewn across the floor. Each step left a crimson footprint as they searched for whatever secrets lay buried beneath the filth of The Burning Breeches Tavern.

Devaultus stepped into the storage room, his sharp gaze sweeping over the shelves stacked high with barrels and crates. The air was thick with the scent of damp wood and stale ale, a stark contrast to the metallic tang of blood that still clung to the tavern outside. A few workers had tried to seek refuge here, but luck had not been on their side, not with Vex hunting them down like a cat playing with cornered mice. Their bodies lay crumpled against the walls, wide eyes frozen in terror, their lifeless fingers still curled as if in one last desperate plea for mercy.

With a sigh, Devaultus ran a hand through his hair, shaking off the frustration. He needed to focus. His fingers skimmed the walls, feeling for a lever, a switch, anything that might hint at a hidden passage. The rumors had led him here, and rumors were rarely without merit.

Yet, the walls were bare, unmarked by any telltale grooves or pressure plates. He was about to turn back, irritation rising, when something caught his eye.

A single droplet of blood pooled at his boot, seeping into a near-invisible crease between the floorboards. Then another. The slow, rhythmic drip of fresh crimson leaking downward.

Lowering himself to one knee, he traced a finger through the thick liquid, following the tiny rivulets to their source. His eyes narrowed. There, a barely perceptible seam in the floor. With renewed determination, he pressed his hand along the hidden groove, feeling for anything out of place. A small latch shifted beneath his palm. He gave it a sharp tug.

A deep, mechanical *click* echoed through the room, followed by the groan of wood and stone grinding apart. The floor near the center of the room shuddered, then lifted, revealing a set of descending stairs slick with fresh blood. The scent of decay and despair curled up from below, thick and suffocating.

"I found it, Vex," Devaultus called, his voice a hushed murmur of satisfaction. "Let's see what they were so desperate to hide."

They moved cautiously, each step down the treacherous, blood-slicked stairs requiring careful footing. The deeper they went, the colder the air became, and the darkness thickened like an oppressive veil. Most would struggle to see in such pitch blackness, but for Devaultus, the shadows were no obstacle. His nightsight flared to life, sharpening the details of the chamber as they reached the bottom.

The sight that greeted him made even his stomach turn.

Rows of iron-barred cages lined the underground chamber, their rusted hinges barely holding them together. Some were large enough to cram in four or five bodies, others were so small they barely held a curled-up child. Gaunt figures sat hunched inside, their eyes hollow and skin clinging to their bones. Their clothing, if it could even be called that, was tattered and threadbare, offering little protection from the chill that settled into their frail bodies.

Slaves.

Devaultus' jaw tightened as he stepped forward, scanning the chamber for keys. He needed to get them out. But before he could take another step, his vision erupted in a blinding flare of light. He recoiled instinctively, hand flying up to shield his eyes.

"What in the name of the gods...?" he hissed.

Beside him, Vex stood grinning, holding up a lantern so bright that it could surely be seen from the surface.

"Don't worry, Mr. D.!" she said cheerfully. "I found a light!"

Devaultus shot a sharp glare at Vex, his vision still struggling to recover from the blinding light she had so carelessly introduced into the dark, dank basement. Meanwhile, Vex, utterly undisturbed by the carnage around her, let out an excited squeal, her blood-streaked face lighting up with unrestrained joy.

"Oh! Are there puppies down here? There are puppies, aren't there? I *love* puppies!" she chirped, practically bouncing on her toes.

Devaultus, for a moment, simply stared at her in disbelief. Here stood a woman who had just carved her way through half a tavern without breaking a sweat, and yet she was now grinning like a child at the mere *idea* of small, fluffy creatures. He raised an eyebrow, his expression one of sheer exasperation.

"What? No, there are not puppies. There are *slaves* in the cages," he deadpanned.

Like a candle being snuffed out, Vex's joy vanished in an instant. Her bright, eager eyes dimmed, her lips pressing into a disappointed pout as she took in the caged prisoners around them. But Devaultus had a feeling her disappointment had little to do with the suffering of these people and everything to do with the absence of puppies.

Shaking his head, he sighed and motioned toward the cages. "Come, Vex. Let's free them."

A small smirk tugged at the corner of his lips. There it was. He was playing hero again. It wasn't intentional, but damn it all if there wasn't a sense of satisfaction in the act.

The two of them moved swiftly from one cage to the next, breaking locks, unfastening chains, releasing the captives. The terrified prisoners wasted no time scrambling up the blood-slick stairs, disappearing into the streets like rats fleeing a sinking ship. It was only when the last of them had fled that Devaultus finally turned, satisfied with their work.

That was when he noticed the girl.

She hadn't moved. While the others had seized their chance for freedom without hesitation, this one remained huddled in the corner of her cage, knees drawn to her chest, her thin frame trembling. She couldn't have been more than nineteen. Her raven-black hair hung in tangled locks around her face, her piercing blue eyes reflecting the lantern light in a haunting way.

Devaultus barely spared her a second glance.

"She's not our problem," he said dismissively, already turning toward the exit. "If she doesn't have the sense to run, that's on her."

Vex, however, didn't move.

"Mr. D..." she began, a note of protest in her voice.

"No, Vex." His tone was firm. "You're already trouble enough for me, I refuse to add *another* liability to my side."

Vex's arms crossed beneath her chest, her bloodied fingers drumming impatiently against her skin. She didn't look at him, she stared straight ahead, at the girl in the cage, her expression uncharacteristically serious.

Then, to Devaultus' surprise, she snapped.

*"No!"*

The word echoed through the basement, sharp and unwavering. It wasn't a plea. It was a *command*.

Devaultus pinched the bridge of his nose, already feeling the headache forming. This was a battle he wasn't going to win, and he knew it. With a weary sigh, he relented.

"Fine," he grumbled, rubbing his temples. "Let's just get out of here. We'll figure out what to do with *her* later."

Vex's expression immediately shifted back to giddy excitement as she *launched* herself at the trembling girl, wrapping her in a suffocating, blood-soaked embrace. The poor thing went rigid, wide-eyed with shock as Vex practically purred in delight.

"I'm going to call you *Puppy*," she declared happily, grabbing the girl's wrist and all but *dragging* her up the stairs.

Devaultus sighed as he followed. This was going to be a problem.

A very *big* problem.

# CHAPTER 4

# ERROR 404: THREAT LEVEL NOT FOUND

I n another part of town, deep within the lavish yet ominous chambers of a towering fortress, a monstrous figure loomed over a blood-soaked floor. Vera'Ala'Roja Bobalata'Cora, a hulking red-skinned behemoth, sat upon a throne carved from the bones of his enemies. His muscles rippled beneath his finely tailored suit, an odd contrast to the savagery that radiated from his being. Two massive horns curled from his forehead like a crown of war, his fiery eyes locked onto the battered and trembling man kneeling before him.

"What do you mean... another of my taverns is gone?" His voice was deep, slow, and weighted with barely restrained fury. "This wretched world is worth little to me, save for the commodities I extract, the people I haul off to serve in greater realms. And now, you stand here telling me that two of my establishments have been *destroyed*... and that The Plague, the very organization that *runs* this filth-ridden city, has no idea who is responsible?"

The broken man at his feet swallowed hard, his breath coming in ragged gasps. Blood dripped from his split lips onto the cold stone floor, his swollen eyes barely able to focus on the demon before him. "N-no one survived to tell us, my Lord," he stammered, his voice hoarse from pain and terror.

Vera'Ala'Roja Bobalata'Cora exhaled sharply through his nostrils, his patience fraying. "And yet... *you* are standing here. *You* survived, did you not?" He leaned forward, his massive hands gripping the armrests of his throne, claws digging into the bone. "So tell me, worm... *who* did this?"

The man flinched, his shoulders quaking. He knew his life hung by the thinnest of threads. "There were two, sir!" he blurted out desperately. "A man and a woman! The man was... he was dressed like a bard! We've never seen him before, and..."

"*The woman*," Vera'Ala'Roja interrupted, his voice like a blade against stone.

The man hesitated, the words catching in his throat. He knew the weight of what he was about to say. "Some say... she resembled Lorivelle Goldwynde."

The room fell into an unbearable silence. The air seemed to still, as if the fortress itself feared the reaction of the monster seated upon its throne.

Vera'Ala'Roja sneered, the very name igniting a deep, festering rage within him. The Goldwynde name, those wretched nobles, always a thorn in his side. "That's impossible," he spat. "Lorivelle Goldwynde is *dead*. She died days ago."

The man nodded quickly, still kneeling, head bowed so low it nearly touched the blood-stained floor. "Yes, sir! I... I thought the same! But rumors spread like wildfire in the streets. If she were truly dead... then *who* was this woman?"

Vera'Ala'Roja slowly rose to his feet, his imposing form casting a long shadow over the broken man before him. His tail flicked behind him, a slow, calculated movement that belied the rage simmering beneath the surface. He would need to speak with his informant within the Goldwynde family. *If there was a lie, he would carve the truth out himself.*

He turned his glare back to the man still trembling at his feet. "Is that *all* you have for me?" His voice, though soft, carried the promise of agony.

The man swallowed, his throat dry as sand. "Y-yes, my Lord... I barely escaped with my life..."

Vera'Ala'Roja exhaled in disgust before dropping back onto his throne, his gaze never leaving the groveling fool before him. With a flick of his wrist, he gave a silent command.

The man immediately fell forward, pressing his forehead to the cold stone in a deep bow.

*Crack!*

A monstrous boot slammed onto the back of his skull, driving his face into the floor with a sickening *squish*. Blood pooled instantly, mixing with the stains of those who had failed before him.

"Such a disappointment," Vera'Ala'Roja muttered, grinding his boot into the twitching corpse beneath him. "A man who runs instead of fights." He sighed, waving his hand in disinterest before looking toward his guards.

"Find out everything you can on these two. I want names. I want *faces*." His voice rumbled through the chamber like distant thunder. "Summon Tarus Goldwynde. I will have words with him."

One of his guards, a towering figure in spiked black armor, hesitated for a second before speaking. "Sir... shall we also summon The Puppeteer?"

At the mention of that name, a ripple of unease passed through the guards in the room.

All who were living feared The Puppeteer.

Vera'Ala'Roja's lips curled into a cruel smile. "Yes. Bring me The Puppeteer."

The guard shifted uncomfortably, his grip tightening on the hilt of his weapon. "Sir... the last time we used him, the mess was..."

Vera'Ala'Roja let out a deep, menacing growl, silencing the man immediately. His glowing eyes burned with deadly intent. "We *already* have a mess to clean up." His voice was like gravel and flame, unrelenting. "The *next* mess... will be *ours.*"

The guards bowed low, then hurried from the room, eager to be away from their master's wrath.

Alone in his throne room, Vera'Ala'Roja sat back, fingers steepled beneath his chin. His mind worked like a storm, calculating, shifting, adapting.

Whoever these two were... they had no idea what they had just started.

And soon... they would *beg* for the mercy he would never grant.

**One Week Earlier**

Lorivelle shot her father a venomous glare, her frustration barely contained beneath the icy mask of noble decorum. Tarus Goldwynde, at first glance, might have appeared to be the quintessential father of a highborn daughter, dignified, composed, a man of influence within the social hierarchy. But beneath the surface, behind the golden sigil of their house and the fine silks of his attire, lurked something far more dangerous.

Tarus was no ordinary noble. He was what the less refined called *Masha'Aldu*, a phrase borrowed from an ancient dialect, its translation carrying the weight of generations steeped in whispered fear. *The Bloodied Hand.*

To serve as Masha'Aldu was to be an instrument of death, a specter lurking in the shadow of a god. Tarus was bound not to a mortal king but to *Cojar* himself, a name that sent chills down the spine of those who knew its meaning.

Cojar was no mere ruler. He was a force of nature, a relic of the old world, a dragon, ancient and terrible, whose power stretched beyond the confines of a single realm. It was said that beings like him existed across countless worlds, moving between them as easily as one might step through a door. His magic, older than civilization itself, allowed him to transcend time and space, his existence a testament to the kind of dominion that mortals could never hope to challenge.

Unlike some of his kin, Cojar had little interest in masquerading as a man. He reveled in his monstrous form, soaring above cities with wings that cast entire districts into shadow, watching as fear took hold of those below. Mortals scattered like insects beneath his gaze, their panic a source of amusement, a reminder of their insignificance. He did not govern with politics or diplomacy. He ruled with sheer, unrelenting terror.

Yet, even gods had their limits. The affairs of men were beneath him, the struggles of rulers and warriors nothing more than meaningless noise. And so, when action was required, when defiance needed to be crushed, when order needed to be restored, Cojar sent his Masha'Aldu.

The Bloodied Hand.

To be marked by them was a death sentence. There were no negotiations, no trials, no hope of mercy. They wielded artifacts of unimaginable power, relics of the old world that bent the fabric of reality to their will. Those who opposed them vanished without a trace, their names erased from history.

And now, Lorivelle stood before one of the most feared men in the land, not just as a subject, not just as another pawn in Cojar's grand design, but as his daughter.

Her fists clenched at her sides. Her blood was noble, but it was also *tainted*, marked by the hand of a tyrant. And no matter how much she resented it, no matter how fiercely she longed to be free of his influence, Tarus Goldwynde was still her father.

But how much longer would she allow that title to mean something?

Mortals could only dream of the power wielded by the Masha'Aldu. Artifacts of immense strength, abilities that could turn armies to ash, one of them alone had been known to wipe entire cities from existence, leaving nothing but smoldering ruins in their wake. And

Tarus Goldwynde was no exception. Death and destruction followed wherever he set his gaze, and he was unaccustomed to being denied anything; unless, of course, the will of Cojar dictated otherwise.

Lorivelle, however, was cut from a different cloth. She had grown up under the shadow of her father's brutal legacy, trained from childhood to follow in his footsteps. But unlike him, she simply assumed the world would bend to her will, rather than forcing it to. Strength, cunning, and the dark teachings of the Masha'Aldu were all ingrained in her, shaping her into the formidable woman she had become. She was not her father's only daughter, though.

Kanashe Goldwynde, her elder sister, was a near mirror image of Lorivelle, though slightly taller, with an undeniable air of command. Where Lorivelle thrived in combat, Kanashe flourished in politics. She was the type to weave schemes with a practiced smile, to bend entire courts to her will without ever drawing a blade. She was destined to be a force in the city's future, a leader who would carve her name into history.

And then there was the youngest, Letty, the fiery-haired wild card. Unlike her sisters, she had no grand ambitions, no carefully plotted schemes. Instead, she threw herself into everything with reckless abandon, giving her all no matter the cost. Sometimes, her unrelenting determination worked in her favor. Other times, it led to spectacular disaster. But that was the way she was: passionate, untamed, and wholly unpredictable.

Kanashe had always believed she knew exactly where her future was heading. She had planned every step, every move, every alliance that she would forge. The city was meant to be hers, a throne waiting for its rightful ruler.

That was, of course, until that fateful meeting, the one that would change everything.

Lorivelle, Kanashe, and Letty were each caught up in their morning routines, preparing for yet another day, though none of them had the slightest inkling of how their lives were about to change forever.

Kanashe, as always, was meticulously assembling her appearance, ensuring that every garment, every jewel, and every thread was placed with perfection. She understood better than anyone that her image was a weapon, a means of earning the favor of the people. A single misstep, an unkempt strand of hair, or an ill-chosen fabric could send ripples through the opinions of the common folk, and she refused to allow anything to hinder her path to power.

Lorivelle, by contrast, was locked in battle with a comb, dragging it through the tangled chaos of her hair with the ferocity of a warrior wading into combat. How it had managed to transform into such a disaster overnight was beyond her, but after what felt like an eternity of effort, she had almost subdued the rat's nest atop her head.

Letty, the youngest, was in her own world, her fingers tracing over the delicate pages of her spellbook. She murmured to herself, lips forming silent incantations, etching every rune, every sigil into her mind with the precision of an artist painting a masterpiece.

Then, without warning, the heavy doors to their chamber burst open with a resounding crash. Tarus Goldwynde, their father, stood in the doorway, his presence commanding and urgent. His golden eyes, sharp as a blade's edge, swept across his daughters as he declared:

"Daughters, prepare yourselves. Lord Cojar has summoned you. This is an honor beyond measure, and I do not need to tell you what this could mean for your futures."

For a moment, stunned silence filled the room; then, all at once, the sisters erupted into movement, their excitement impossible to contain.

"A god, he wishes to see us?" Lorivelle gasped, clutching Kanashe's arm with both hands, her face alight with wonder.

Kanashe's expression was equally radiant, though she masked her exhilaration with practiced poise. "Stand tall, sister," she murmured, voice filled with unshakable determination. "An opportunity such as this comes once in a lifetime. We must carry ourselves with dignity. This could shape our destinies forever."

Lorivelle beamed, giving an exaggerated curtsy. "Of course, dear sister. Chin high, back straight, smile perfected. How's this?" She tossed her hair, striking a dramatic pose.

Letty, too, was practically vibrating with excitement, but her focus remained locked on the implications of such a meeting. A god. A being of ancient power, beyond mortal comprehension. The very idea sent a thrill down her spine.

Within half an hour, the three were dressed in their finest and ready to depart; record time, considering the usual pace of noble preparation.

Their journey took them far beyond the bustling city, across the sun-scorched dunes of the desert. As they rode, a massive structure rose above the horizon, its silhouette a testament to grandeur beyond mortal hands. The great stadium loomed before them, its vast stands empty of spectators.

But there, in the center of the coliseum, was Cojar.

The great dragon reclined, his massive form gleaming in the sunlight. His scales were the color of burnished bronze, each edge outlined with a golden glow, as if the very sun had kissed his body. His eyes, vast and ancient, regarded them with something unreadable, a being who had seen eons pass, who had watched empires rise and fall like waves upon the shore.

Tarus wasted no time. The moment they stepped foot inside the arena, he fell to his knees in reverence.

"Lord Cojar," he intoned, his voice steady but filled with deep respect, "I have brought my daughters, as you requested."

The three sisters stood before the god, their hearts pounding in their chests, knowing that whatever happened next would change their fates forever.

Cojar regarded them with an intense curiosity, his massive, golden eyes gleaming with something unreadable, like a scholar inspecting rare specimens or a predator evaluating potential prey. When he finally spoke, his voice thundered across the vast, empty coliseum, shaking the very ground beneath them.

"You have served me well, Tarus," the great dragon rumbled. "I am pleased with your unwavering loyalty. For your dedication, I offer you the position of Viceroy of the Masha'Aldu. Do you accept the rights of Lesh'raka?"

Tarus stood firm, his expression an unyielding mask of control. No joy, no sorrow, just the same stoic calm he had always carried. And yet, for those who knew him well, there was a subtle shift in his posture. A slight straightening of his spine, the barest flicker of something in his eyes. This was an honor beyond compare, a gift bestowed only upon the most trusted of Cojar's servants.

"I do, my Lord," Tarus responded, his voice steady and absolute.

Cojar let out a deep, satisfied hum, a sound that reverberated through the vast chamber. "Very well. Now that this is settled, let me see your daughters. The youngest first."

Without hesitation, Letty stepped forward, her movements swift, her resolve unwavering. She stood before the dragon, head held high, her spellbook still clutched in her fingers as though it were an extension of herself.

"My Lord, I am Letty, last-born of the Goldwynde family. I am here to serve you," she declared boldly.

Cojar lowered his massive head, his molten eyes sweeping over her like fire licking across parchment. He inhaled deeply, drawing in her scent as though unraveling the very essence of her being.

"You have potential, Letty," he mused, his deep voice reverberating around the empty stadium. "Now step back."

Without question, Letty retreated to her place, her heart pounding, but her expression unshaken.

Next was Lorivelle. She hesitated for a second before stepping forward, her movements less sure than her sister's. She swallowed hard, nerves catching in her throat as she spoke.

"I... I am Lorivelle, second-born of the Goldwynde family," she managed, her voice faltering.

Cojar's enormous head loomed closer, his fangs nearly triple her height, mere feet from her trembling form. He inhaled deeply, and the force of it sent her hair whipping around her face in wild, tangled strands. The rush of warm air from his nostrils washed over her, carrying the scent of fire and brimstone.

"You may step back," Cojar commanded.

Relief surged through Lorivelle as she hurried back to her place, feeling her heart hammering against her ribs.

Finally, it was Kanashe's turn. Unlike her sisters, she moved with complete confidence, her posture regal, her gaze unwavering. She strode forward, standing tall before the colossal dragon, meeting his gaze without an ounce of fear.

"I am Kanashe, first-born of the Goldwynde family," she proclaimed, her voice steady and authoritative.

Cojar studied her for a long moment, his piercing eyes flicking over every inch of her. He inhaled deeply, his massive chest rising as he took in her scent. Then, slowly, he turned his gaze toward Tarus.

"This one," he announced, his voice like a landslide of stone, "will do for the first part of the ritual."

Without another word, Cojar opened his enormous maw. A split second later, a stream of searing fire erupted from his throat, engulfing Kanashe in a brilliant inferno.

The flames wrapped around her like living serpents, licking hungrily at her body. At first, she stood firm, but then the agony set in. Her skin blistered, then cracked, then melted away entirely, dripping from her bones in thick, molten rivulets. Her screams tore through the arena, high, raw, filled with a pain so unimaginable it barely seemed human.

But it lasted only a moment.

As her vocal cords liquefied and her lungs burned away, the sound died, leaving only the crackling of fire and the scent of charred flesh hanging in the air.

Tarus remained as still as a statue, his expression unchanging, not even the slightest flinch betraying his emotions as his eldest daughter was reduced to little more than smoldering remains before him.

Cojar exhaled deeply, his breath sending the last of Kanashe's ashes scattering into the air like dust on the wind.

The ritual had begun.

Tarus had long understood the cost of power, the weight of servitude to a god, and the sacrifices required for ascension. He had known, from the moment Cojar summoned him and his daughters, what this ritual would entail. He had spent years preparing them, teaching them the histories, the traditions, and the inevitable fate of those chosen to serve the gods. In exchange for being elevated to Viceroy of the Masha'Aldu, an honor that came with immense wealth, unparalleled influence, and reverence from both mortals and deities alike, he had to surrender life in order to receive it.

Kanasha had been chosen to die.

Letty, however, had been chosen for something far worse.

She was to become the Ut'Matar, the breeding partner of Cojar.

Dragons were not simply born; their creation was an anomaly, a near impossibility. This was why their kind were worshipped as gods, why their numbers remained few, and why their power remained unchecked. One did not kill a dragon. It was unheard of. And just as one could not take the life of a dragon, one could not easily create one. Their reproduction was a brutal, merciless process. A ritual of destruction as much as creation.

Nothing about a dragon was gentle.

And there was a reason no living record existed of a human surviving the experience.

The odds of Letty making it through the night were less than one percent. Nearly nonexistent.

Tarus said nothing as his last remaining daughter was escorted from the great hall, her face devoid of emotion, her body trembling with the ghostly echoes of her sister's screams. Her hair was still singed, the acrid scent of burnt flesh clinging to her skin, a visceral reminder of what had transpired only moments before.

The guards led her through the corridors of the palace, past walls adorned with golden tapestries, past servants who dared not lift their eyes in pity. Not a single soul spoke a word as they entered her chambers and set her down upon the grand bed of silken sheets and intricate embroidery.

She remained there, unmoving.

For days, she did not speak.

For days, she did not eat.

She sat, staring into the void, unable to rid herself of the scent of burnt flesh and melted bone, unable to erase the image of her sister, her best friend, being reduced to nothing but ashes before her eyes.

And in the silence of her room, in the echoing emptiness that wrapped around her like a suffocating shroud, she understood the truth her father had always known.

Power was not given.

It was taken.

And the gods demanded their due.

Gods thrived on the devotion of their followers, but Lorivelle would be damned if she gave her allegiance to the very ones who had shattered her world so mercilessly. Cojar had ripped her life apart, burned it to ash before her eyes, and expected her to bow. No. She would find another to serve, one who stood against the gods. And in doing so, she would defy them all. She would unravel their power, strip them of their divine arrogance, and find a way to destroy them.

She would carve a new path, one written in the blood of those who had wronged her.

Her body trembled as she pushed herself up from her bed, her limbs weak from days without food, but her mind burned with purpose. Every movement sent a sharp ache through her muscles, but she forced herself onward. Slowly, she reached for her garments, the familiar weight of the fabric settling over her skin like armor. There was no time for fragility. No time for grief. Only resolve.

Stepping out of her chamber, she found her father going about his day as if nothing had transpired, as if Kanasha's screams had not echoed through the night, as if his own blood had not been reduced to a smoldering pile of charred flesh. Lorivelle's hands curled into fists at her sides. The callousness in which he carried on, the absolute disregard for the horror of what had taken place: it made her sick.

And then, it hit her again. That smell. The acrid stench of burnt flesh. It wasn't real, she knew that. Kanasha was long gone, and yet, the phantom scent lingered in her nose, taunting her.

Tarus barely spared her a glance before speaking. "Daughter. It is good to see you up and about," he said, his tone clipped and indifferent. His eyes held no warmth, no concern. In his mind, she was the only one not chosen by Cojar. The failure. The unworthy.

Lorivelle swallowed down the surge of rage bubbling in her chest and spoke, her voice hollow. "I will go to the market today, Father." He waved a dismissive hand. A gesture so small, so insignificant, as if she were nothing more than a passing thought. He didn't ask why. Didn't care. Instead, he offered a single guard, just one, a mere afterthought, before turning away entirely.

The chosen daughters of the Goldwynde family had been worth an army. But Lorivelle? She was just a ghost lingering in a house that had no place for her anymore.

The guard, a sturdy man clad in the dark armor of the household, rushed after her as she moved toward the waiting wagon. "I shall keep you safe, my lady," he said, offering his hand to help her inside.

Lorivelle climbed in without a word. The journey to the market stretched on in silence, the wheels of the wagon creaking against the dusty roads. She sat with her back straight, hands folded neatly in her lap, her expression unreadable. But inside? She was barely holding together the pieces of what was left of herself. The weight of her grief, her rage, her growing determination, it all simmered beneath the surface, waiting for the right moment to ignite.

Two hours passed in oppressive silence before they reached the marketplace. As the wagon slowed to a stop, Lorivelle took a deep breath and stepped out, ready to set her plan into motion.

The marketplace bustled with life, a chaotic symphony of voices, the clinking of coins, and the occasional bark of merchants hawking their wares. The rich aroma of roasting meats filled the air, mingling with the scent of fresh-baked bread and exotic spices. But for Lorivelle, the smells that once might have made her mouth water now only churned her stomach. Every time the smoky scent of charred meat reached her nostrils, she was dragged back to that moment, the flames, the agonizing screams, the way Kanasha's flesh had peeled away in molten drips. That scent lingered in her mind, suffocating her like a funeral shroud.

She moved through the market in a daze, her hands brushing over fine silks and polished trinkets, without her truly seeing them. She stopped at one stall, then another, feigning interest in their wares when in truth, nothing mattered. Not the delicate jewelry, not the fragrant perfumes, not the colorful bolts of fabric. It was all meaningless. A hollow existence. A cruel mockery of a life she no longer wanted to live.

Unbeknownst to her, a trio of figures lounged outside a nearby building, their eyes locked onto her like predators sizing up a wounded animal.

The largest of them was a monstrous brute, his sheer size enough to make most men reconsider crossing him. His head was shaven, revealing a thick network of scars that ran across his skull and face like a grotesque map of old battles. His few remaining teeth were stained yellow, jagged remnants of the brutality he had endured, and inflicted, over the years.

Beside him, an elf stood tall and wiry, his body a frame of sharp angles draped in ragged, unkempt clothing. His long, greasy hair hung in uneven strands, partially obscuring his gaunt face. When he grinned, it revealed a row of needle-like teeth, jagged and unnatural, as though he were more creature than elf.

The last of the trio was the most unassuming, a human man, lounging in his chair with an easy confidence, his boots propped up on the wooden table before him. There was a lazy hunger in his eyes as he watched Lorivelle, a smirk playing at the corner of his lips. He was a man accustomed to getting what he wanted, one way or another.

A small street boy darted past their table, weaving effortlessly through the busy crowd. The human's arm shot out like a viper striking its prey, his fingers clamping around the boy's neck. The child let out a startled yelp, his feet kicking up dust as he struggled.

"How'd you like to earn some coin, boy?" the man asked, his voice a purr of menace wrapped in false sweetness. His smile was anything but kind.

The boy swallowed hard, his wide eyes darting between the trio. He knew better than to refuse. You didn't say no to The Plague.

Leaning in close, the man whispered something into the boy's ear. A brief hesitation, a flicker of uncertainty, but then the boy nodded and took off, disappearing into the sea of people.

The hunt had begun.

Lorivelle was absentmindedly examining a selection of finely crafted hats at a vendor's stall, her fingers tracing the intricate stitching, when a sudden tug at her sleeve made her turn. A young boy stood before her, his chest heaving, his wide eyes brimming with fear. His small, dirt-smudged hands clenched into fists as he looked up at her with desperation.

"My lady, please, please help me," he gasped, his voice shaking.

Lorivelle arched a brow, regarding the boy carefully. She had grown wary of strangers, but there was something raw and genuine in his expression. "What is it, lad?" she asked, her voice steady but laced with caution.

Tears welled up in the boy's eyes as he spoke. "It's my sister... A man took her! He dragged her into the alley over there." He pointed a trembling finger toward the dark, narrow passageway between two buildings, his entire body quivering as if he was reliving whatever horror he had just witnessed.

Lorivelle hesitated. She had been trained well, but she was no longer under the protection of the Masha'Aldu, and the weight of that absence loomed over her. Still, she wasn't alone, her father had sent a guard to escort her, and surely he was more than capable of handling one rogue criminal.

She glanced at the guard, his stance firm, his hand resting lightly on the hilt of his sword. "You are well trained, aren't you?" she asked, as much for herself as for him.

The guard straightened. "Of course, my lady."

Lorivelle inhaled deeply, pushing aside the lingering hesitation gnawing at her mind. Finally, she gave the boy a nod. "Very well. Show me."

The boy's face flickered with relief as he turned and sprinted toward the alley, Lorivelle and the guard close behind, the shadows of the city swallowing them whole.

Lorivelle moved cautiously, her assigned guard keeping pace beside her, his head swiveling warily as they followed the ragged street boy through the narrow space. The deeper they ventured, the more the distant hum of the marketplace faded, replaced by the eerie silence of abandoned corridors and crumbling walls. The boy suddenly skidded to a halt, turning to face them with an innocent, almost sheepish expression.

"Well?" the guard demanded, brows furrowing in suspicion. "Where are they?"

The boy shrugged nonchalantly, but his gaze flickered toward Lorivelle. "Sorry, my lady," he said, his tone dripping with false regret. "A boy's got to eat, though."

Before they could react, a gleaming coin spun through the air. The boy caught it effortlessly, grinning as he pocketed his prize before darting off into the shadows. The realization hit too late: this had been a setup.

A slow, mocking clap echoed from the darkness, and two figures stepped into the dim light. The first was a towering brute of a man, built like a war machine, his head shaved close to the scalp, deep scars crisscrossing his craggy face. The second was a human, leaner but no less threatening, his smirk filled with cruel amusement.

The guard reacted immediately, steel rasping as he drew his blade, the tip glinting under the sparse light. The two men merely chuckled, their lack of concern sending a spike of dread through Lorivelle's gut.

Before she could react, something slithered behind her, a presence too close, too vile. Cold fingers, far too eager, wrapped around her waist. A sharp cackle broke the tense air as the elf revealed himself, his jagged, rotten teeth flashing as he pressed against her from behind. His breath was a putrid mix of spoiled meat and decay, hot against the nape of her neck.

"Ohh, now ain't you a fine little noble?" he purred, his hands roaming with deliberate cruelty, fingers squeezing, groping, making a show of his dominance. "All soft and delicate. Bet you taste real sweet."

Lorivelle's body stiffened in shock and disgust, but her mind, fractured, raw, was struggling to respond. The overwhelming scent of him, the feel of his damp tongue trailing up her skin, made her stomach churn.

Meanwhile, the guard, her only lifeline in this nightmare, was being toyed with like a cat playing with a wounded bird. The brute allowed him a few wild swings, easily sidestepping each one, grinning all the while. It was painfully clear her father had sent only a disposable escort, someone unskilled, someone who wouldn't be missed.

Growing tired of the game, the monstrous man lunged. He caught the guard's wrist, twisting it with sickening ease until the blade clattered uselessly to the ground. The guard barely had time to gasp before his arms were wrenched behind his back in an iron grip.

"You put up a good fight, lad," the human said, swaggering forward with a mocking grin. "But don't worry, we'll take real good care of the lady from here on out."

Before another word could be spoken, the dagger flashed. It was a clean, brutal movement, blade sinking deep into the guard's stomach, the hilt pressing against his gut. He gasped, blood bubbling from his lips as he slumped against his captor.

Leech, the filthy elf, barely seemed to notice. His focus was entirely on Lorivelle, his grip tightening, his body pressing against her in vile hunger. His excitement was evident, a grotesque bulge grinding against her as he chuckled, inhaling deeply against her hair.

"Struggle a little, sweetheart," he whispered, his fingers creeping higher, cruel in their possessiveness. "I like it when they..."

Lorivelle's breath hitched. The weight of everything, the betrayal, the loss, the horror, crashed down all at once. Her mind teetered on the edge of a dark Abyss, where every scream, every plea, every moment of helplessness threatened to consume her whole. Could she fight? Would it even matter? Was there anything left to fight for?

Then, a sound cut through the oppressive atmosphere, a slow, deliberate footstep.

A figure emerged from the mouth of the alley. He wasn't imposing in stature. In fact, he was quite the opposite, thick around the waist, not the sort of man one would expect to walk confidently into a den of predators. But something about the way he carried himself, the calculated pause before he spoke, sent a shiver through the filth-ridden air.

And just like that, the mood shifted.

Lorivelle's breath hitched as she locked eyes with the stranger, silently begging him to turn and leave. She didn't want to witness another senseless death. Not after everything. The weight of loss pressed down on her, paralyzing her limbs, making it impossible to move, let alone fight. Her guard, though well-meaning, was hopelessly outmatched; and this new man? He was broad but soft-looking, unarmed, and clearly no warrior. He had no chance against the brutes in front of him.

The two men sneered at the newcomer, their voices a garbled mess in her ears, words lost in the haze of her fractured mind. She should be thinking of a way out, searching for an opening, but her thoughts were sluggish, drowning beneath the suffocating memory of charred flesh.

The scent was back, Kanasha's burning body, the acrid stench of seared meat invading her senses. Her stomach twisted violently.

A force yanked her from her thoughts, sharp fingers digging into her arms before she was hurled through the air like a discarded doll. She barely had time to brace herself before she crashed against the stone wall of a nearby building. The impact knocked the breath from her lungs, pain exploding across her side. Then, darkness.

A moment later, she drifted back to consciousness, the world around her spinning and unfocused. Shapes blurred together, shadows bleeding into each other. Her head throbbed as she struggled to process what was happening. She was on the ground, her body aching from the brutal throw.

She was in trouble.

Her heart pounded in her ears, a frantic rhythm of survival instinct kicking in far too late. She blinked rapidly, her vision beginning to sharpen. A figure knelt in front of her.

The man.

He was alive?

She swallowed hard, her gaze flicking downward. His hands were drenched in blood. Thick. Dark. Fresh.

Her mouth went dry. "What... what happened to the men?"

The stranger smiled warmly, as if they were exchanging pleasantries at a market stall. "They thought guards were coming. They ran."

Her mind reeled. That didn't make sense. If they had simply run, why was there so much blood? The scent of iron was thick in the air, mingling with the dirt beneath her. She tried to glance past him, searching for the bodies, but the alley was just darkness and silence.

The man's expression remained calm, unreadable. He had saved her, that much was certain. And whether or not she wanted to admit it, he had done what she could not.

For the first time in weeks, something inside her clicked into place.

He was an enigma. Dangerous, perhaps, but powerful in ways she could not yet understand. And power was something she needed.

Slowly, she nodded. It didn't matter how or why, only that she was still breathing. He had given her that.

Finally, she found her voice. "We should leave."

The man nodded in agreement, his expression unreadable, as if this entire ordeal had been nothing more than a passing inconvenience. Just then, the pounding of heavy boots echoed through the alleyway, and a swarm of guards flooded in, her father's men, dressed in their pristine uniforms, their weapons gleaming under the harsh desert sun. Fashionably late, as always.

Lorivelle eyed them with cold suspicion. They weren't here to protect her. No, they had come expecting to find her lifeless body sprawled in the dust. It would serve her father's ambitions well, wouldn't it? His last remaining daughter slaughtered in a nameless alley, a tragic tale that would stir sympathy and, more importantly, bring forth desperate women eager to bear him new children. Perhaps this time he would get what he truly wanted: sons.

The guards closed in around her, a false show of protection, but her mind was elsewhere. She barely registered their presence, her thoughts consumed by the stranger. She could hear herself saying something to the guards. But her mind was elsewhere. It was as though her noble upbringing had spurred the response. Then the man had said something.

He was leaving.

No. He couldn't leave.

She had to follow him, to become his disciple, to learn whatever power had allowed him to make those men disappear so effortlessly.

She turned to him, desperation barely masked by the noble composure she had spent years perfecting. "Very well. Thank you, kind sir. But tell me, who might I call my hero?"

The man paused, as if considering the weight of the question. Then, with a small, knowing smile, he spoke. "I am called Lindgurth, ma'am." His voice was smooth, too smooth for a man of his rotund stature, carrying a strange, almost hypnotic quality that unsettled her in a way she couldn't quite explain.

"Very well, Lindgurth. I bid you farewell, and thank you again for your aid." She forced the words out, her tone measured and noble, the way she had been taught since childhood.

With an elegant bow, Lindgurth turned and sauntered away, moving with an almost unnatural grace, his steps light, his body swaying like a dancer performing a routine only he could hear. He disappeared into the shadows, leaving her standing there, her mind racing.

Then, a rough hand clamped around her arm.

"Come along, miss. We will bring you back to your father."

The guard's grip was firm, his tone laced with disinterest, as if she were nothing more than an inconvenience to be handled and escorted away like a misbehaving child.

Lorivelle's instincts flared to life, raw and sharpened by weeks of grief and rage. Before her thoughts even caught up to her body, she spun in a blur of movement. Her fingers closed around the hilt of the guard's bone dagger, yanking it from his belt in one fluid motion.

The moment was eerily silent.

Then, blade met flesh.

The dagger plunged into his throat, sinking deep, and a wet, choking gasp escaped his lips as blood spilled over her hand, warm and thick. His eyes widened in shock, fingers clawing at his ruined throat as he staggered backward, gurgling.

Lorivelle didn't flinch.

She simply watched as the man crumpled to the ground, a pool of crimson spreading beneath him like ink on parchment.

The other guards hesitated, exchanging uncertain glances. The girl they had dismissed as powerless, as a mere pawn in her father's grand game, had just executed one of their own without hesitation.

Lorivelle straightened, lifting her chin, her fingers still wrapped around the bloodied dagger.

"I will not be brought to my father like some disobedient child," she said, her voice cold and commanding. "And you will not be going back to speak to him."

Spinning with deadly precision, Lorivelle swept her leg out, striking the guard's knees with brutal force. He crumpled instantly, his balance lost as he tumbled backward. But she wasn't done. With a fluid motion, she planted one hand against the ground, using it as a pivot point to launch herself upward. Her legs coiled like a serpent around the neck of another guard, twisting with lethal grace. With a sharp motion, she hurled his struggling form over the ledge. His scream barely echoed before his body disappeared into the Abyss below, joining the countless corpses that had met the same fate.

As her feet touched the ground, she landed in a crouch, hair whipping across her face. Without hesitation, she sprang forward, her palm slamming into the next guard's chest. A surge of energy ignited from within her, and from her very flesh, jagged black blades erupted like a spray of obsidian quills. The man gasped, frozen in shock as the cruel spikes punched through his body from every direction. His mouth moved as if to speak, but only a strangled gurgle escaped before he collapsed in a lifeless heap at her feet.

She exhaled slowly, stepping over the body as she gripped the limp form and shoved him over the ledge, sending him to the depths below where the others had fallen. Straightening, she wiped the blood from her hands, her heart pounding with purpose. This was it. The past was dead, burned away like her sister in Cojar's fire.

Lorivelle had made her decision.

She would find Lindgurth. She would learn from him. Serve him. Become something greater. He had shown her kindness where the gods had only shown cruelty. And now, she belonged to him. He was her new master. Her new god.

Her everything.

# CHAPTER 5

# NEW CHALLENGER APPROACHES: BLIGHT

Fro'Dovin stared at Lindgurth, his thick brows knitted together in sheer disbelief. For nearly twenty minutes, he had been locked in this silent, unmoving stupor, eyes narrowed, lips slightly parted as if trying to form words but failing each time. The sheer absurdity of what he had witnessed had left him utterly speechless.

Devaultus, who had long since noticed Fro'Dovin's bewilderment, chose to ignore it, opting instead to enjoy his breakfast alongside the two women seated at Lindgurth's table. Still, the large cook couldn't shake the feeling that something was *off*. The entire inn was buzzing with speculation, hushed whispers trailing Lindgurth's every move like a ghostly presence.

How in all the infernal realms had *this* man, an overweight, awkward, utterly unremarkable individual, ended up with *two* women sleeping in his room last night? Not just any women, either. These were not the desperate, aging hags who loitered around the tavern's entrance hoping to catch the attention of lonely travelers. No, these were stunning, radiant women, elegant and striking enough to turn heads wherever they went.

Lindgurth himself looked exhausted, dark circles carved beneath his eyes, his posture slightly slumped as he absentmindedly picked at his breakfast. Had they kept him busy all night? His disheveled state sent a wave of stunned silence through the room, as one tavern patron after another made assumptions of what they thought had happened that night. The rumors spread like wildfire, tongues wagging about this mysterious man and the secret he must possess.

Fro'Dovin drummed his fingers against the wooden counter, his mind racing with possibilities. Maybe Lindgurth had stumbled upon some sort of enchanted artifact, something that made him *irresistible* to women. That, at least, made *some* sense. The alternative was simply *impossible*.

And yet... there was something else. A shift. A change in the way the women of the inn were beginning to look at Lindgurth. Their eyes lingered on him longer, their gazes softened with curiosity, as if they were trying to decipher what they had overlooked before. As if, perhaps, they too were starting to wonder if there was more to him than met the eye.

Just in case.

Devaultus cast a sideways glance at Fro'Dovin, the cook's lingering stare gnawing at his already frayed patience. He wasn't entirely sure what the hell the man was looking at, but given the way his gaze flicked toward the women beside him, Devaultus had a sinking suspicion. If Fro'Dovin was wondering how Devaultus had ended up with two women in his company overnight, he was welcome to trade places. At this very moment, Devaultus would have happily handed them both over in exchange for an hour of uninterrupted sleep.

The entire night had been a maddening ordeal. Vex, in her usual relentless fashion, had insisted on dressing their newest companion, Puppy. That name wouldn't do, of course. It was ridiculous. He needed to come up with something else, something dignified. But Vex was stubborn, and picking that battle seemed unwise, so he'd have to be more strategic about it. He'd make her believe it was her own idea to change the dark-haired woman's name. Eventually.

Meanwhile, Puppy had stood there like a silent doll, allowing Vex to fuss over her, draping her in different outfits as if she were nothing more than a plaything. She hadn't uttered a single word since they found her. Devaultus worried she was broken, another shattered mind he'd have to deal with. It was all becoming painfully tedious, and sleep was nothing but a distant dream.

His thoughts drifted, grasping at something, an old memory from another world he had once stumbled upon. What was its name? He couldn't quite recall, only that they had wielded something they called "technology" rather than magic. It had been a fascinating place, full of complexities and unknown variables. Too many for him to stay long. He had left, promising himself he'd return when he had the time to properly study it.

But there was one thing he did remember, something more important than anything else: their morning wine. They had called it "coffee."

Glorious, life-altering coffee.

He still remembered the way it burned down his throat, the way it jolted his senses awake like a divine elixir. With coffee, he had felt invincible, like he could stay awake for days, face an army single-handedly, bend reality to his will. Hell, if he'd had an army back then, he would have served them nothing but coffee and taken over everything, marching straight into the Abyss itself.

Now, slumped at this table, exhausted and on the verge of losing his patience, he longed for that miraculous brew more than ever.

Devaultus exhaled heavily, rubbing his temples as exhaustion weighed on him. What he wouldn't give for a steaming mug of that divine morning wine, the one called "coffee."

But now wasn't the time to get lost in wistful fantasies of forgotten worlds. He had a mission, and it was time to move forward. Sweetwater Inn had been a comfortable enough place, perhaps too comfortable. He was no closer to retrieving his ring, and wasting more time here was not an option. The ring had to be his priority. But coin was an issue, as it always was. If he was going to get anywhere, he needed information, and drunk men were the best source of that. Fortunately, drunk men also had a habit of spilling their secrets more easily when speaking to a beautiful woman.

That was where his new *companions* came in.

Finishing the last bite of his Chocka eggs, he dabbed the corner of his mouth with his sleeve, then pushed back his chair, rising to his feet with an air of finality. "Let's go, ladies. We have work to do."

Vex practically leaped up, eager and ready, her energy seemingly boundless. She thrived on movement, on purpose, even if she was currently little more than a thorn in his side. He cast a glance at the other woman, Puppy. That name still irritated him, but Vex had been insistent. He really would have to find a way to make her think it was her idea to change it.

Puppy blinked up at him with those wide, glassy blue eyes, hesitating for only a moment before standing. There was something unsettling about her, something unreadable in her silence. She hadn't spoken a single word since she had joined them last night, and Devaultus was beginning to suspect he had a knack for acquiring broken companions. Just what he needed.

Still, she followed them without resistance. That, at least, was convenient. She seemed to recognize that sticking with them was the safest option, though her sharp gaze lingered on Vex with a barely concealed skepticism. Devaultus could see it, the quiet assessment, the judgment. She thought Vex was a fool. Perhaps she was, that was yet to be determined, but Vex was not without her uses. If nothing else, she was a distraction.

Puppy, however... she was something else entirely. And he had yet to determine whether that was a good thing.

Stepping through the door, Devaultus emerged onto the bustling street, the morning sun casting long shadows against the uneven cobblestones. Behind him, Vex practically bounced in excitement, her every movement filled with an energy that was almost infectious, if one had the patience for it. Devaultus, however, did not. He rolled his shoulders and exhaled, bracing himself for the inevitable chaos she would bring.

Puppy, on the other hand, was the complete opposite. She trailed behind them with cautious, hesitant steps, her fingers twisting together as she cast nervous glances at the ever-moving crowd around them. Her big blue eyes darted from face to face, wary, as if expecting danger to lunge from the throng at any moment.

The city was alive today. Merchants shouted their deals from wooden stalls, the scent of freshly baked bread mingling with the less pleasant aroma of unwashed bodies and damp stone. Blacksmiths pounded away at their work in the distance, sending sparks dancing through the air. Lizard-drawn carts creaked under heavy loads, their wheels rattling against the cobbles. It was all a well-oiled machine, everyone playing their part to keep the city moving.

Devaultus turned on his heel, facing the two women. His sharp gaze flicked between them as he spoke. "Alright, listen up. I want you both to ask around, see if anyone has heard of a person possessing a ring that grants the ability to travel between worlds. Be subtle, don't be obvious about it. We'll split up and meet back here in an hour. Understood?"

Vex's grin stretched from ear to ear, her emerald eyes gleaming with mischief. She gave him a playful salute. "You got it, Mr. D.!" she chirped, already bouncing on her heels, eager to start.

Puppy, however, simply blinked, confusion clouding her face. She opened her mouth as if to speak, then closed it, lowering her gaze. Devaultus sighed. He didn't have time to explain it to her like she was a child, she would either figure it out or wander aimlessly until the hour was up. Either way, she wouldn't be his problem for a little while.

Turning, he strode down the street, his mind already focused on where he would begin his search.

Vex wasted no time, practically prancing off in the opposite direction, her long blonde hair swaying behind her as she disappeared into the crowd.

That left Puppy. She lingered there on the cobblestone street, blinking again in bewilderment as she watched them go. Her hands clutched at the hem of her tunic, her lips pressing into a thin line as she glanced around, unsure of where to start. She hesitated a moment longer; then, slowly, uncertainly, turned and wandered off in yet another direction, vanishing into the sea of strangers.

Vex sauntered down a dimly lit alleyway, her footsteps light, almost playful, as she whistled a carefree tune. The melody danced through the narrow space, contrasting sharply with the stench of stale ale and unwashed bodies that clung to the air. Ahead, a group of large, brutish men leaned lazily against a stack of crates, their thick fingers wrapped around clay jugs filled with whatever swill passed for liquor in this part of town. Their laughter was guttural, their voices slurred with intoxication, but their eyes, hungry, predatory, locked onto her the moment she stepped into view.

They raked their gazes over her body, slow and deliberate, practically peeling away the layers of her clothing with their stares. Most women would have turned and fled, or at the very least, made some attempt to avoid their lecherous attention. But not Vex. Instead, she pranced right up to them, hands on her hips, tilting her head with innocent curiosity.

"Hey, you guys got any rings?" she asked, as if she were inquiring about the weather.

The men paused mid-drink, lowering their jugs as they exchanged amused glances. Their scarred, filthy fingers were adorned with various rings, some stolen, some won in blood-soaked brawls. One of the men chuckled, displaying a row of crooked, yellowed teeth.

"Oh, we've got rings, sweetheart," he slurred, flexing his fingers so the bone rings shown in the dim light. "But you don't just take 'em. You gotta earn 'em."

The others laughed at that, a deep, rumbling sound filled with unspoken promise. They had no intention of parting with a single piece of jewelry. No, they were fairly certain this one would be good for far more than a few trinkets before they were through with her.

Vex considered this, her smile unwavering. She could gut them all in seconds, leave their corpses slumped in the grime like discarded trash. But... no. That wasn't Scythe's way. That was hers.

"How?" she asked sweetly, playing along.

A hulking brute stepped up behind her, his calloused hands gripping her backside with shameless entitlement. His breath, rancid with alcohol and rot, fanned against her ear as he chuckled. "Oh, don't you worry, girl. You'll find out soon enough."

For a moment, she merely stood there, as if contemplating his words. Then, barely above a whisper, she muttered to herself, "Do what you want, Vex."

And just like that, she did.

Without warning, she drove her elbow backward with brutal precision, feeling the sickening crunch of cartilage as she shattered the man's nose; no, not just shattered it, drove the jagged bone straight into his brain. He was dead before his body even realized it, crumpling to the ground in a heap.

Before the others could process what had happened, she was already moving.

Like a shadow with claws, she twisted into motion, weaving through them with a dancer's grace. A boot to the knee sent one man toppling. She snagged his wrist mid-fall, twisting until bone jutted through flesh, the ring sliding free from his limp fingers as he howled in agony. Another lunged for her, but she spun, dodging effortlessly before driving a dagger under his ribs, twisting it just to hear the choked gasp as the life left his eyes.

The alley erupted into chaos. But to Vex, it was nothing more than a game; one she played *very* well.

Puppy wandered aimlessly down the bustling street, her wide, unfocused eyes betraying the turmoil within. Ever since she had been thrown into that wretched cage, her existence had been reduced to a desperate struggle for survival, doing whatever it took to keep breathing, to avoid pain, to stay unseen. Now, even with the sun warming her skin and the sounds of the city buzzing around her, she still felt trapped, as though invisible iron bars still loomed just outside her peripheral vision.

She halted abruptly, her stomach twisting into a knot as her gaze locked onto two figures lingering near a side alley. They were short, unnaturally so, their bodies stocky but agile, their eyes sharp and filled with malice. Panic seized her lungs as realization struck her like a hammer blow. Halflings. No, no, no. Not them. Not here.

Puppy's entire being screamed for her to run, but her feet refused to move. Her mind raced with half-formed thoughts, tangled memories of whispered horror stories. Halflings despised all who weren't their own, and they didn't simply kill outsiders. They played with their food. They tore flesh while it still quivered, delighted in the taste of fresh, raw meat.

One of them slinked forward, his lips peeling back in what might have been a smile, if not for the jagged, shark-like teeth gleaming between them.

"Hey there, little lady," he drawled, his voice oozing with amusement. "Why don't you come with us? We've got something real special to show you."

The second halfling snickered beside him, his laughter high and cruel.

Puppy's gaze darted to the street behind her. Could she run? Would they chase her? Her breath hitched, every fiber of her being screaming for escape.

Then, before she could make a move, three figures emerged from the crowd, clad in dark robes. They moved with purpose, their hoods casting deep shadows over their faces. One of them, the tallest, stepped toward the halflings, his tone clipped and authoritative.

"You little savages," he sneered. "Have you seen a well-dressed man and a blonde woman in a black cloak?"

Puppy's breath caught in her throat. Wait, were they talking about Devaultus and Vex?

The halflings scowled, their expressions twisting from amusement to disgust. One of them turned his head and spat at the robed figure's feet.

"Be gone," he growled. "You're interrupting our fun."

The tallest robed man stiffened, his patience clearly thinning. "You will answer my inquiry."

Puppy had barely had time to process the unfolding situation when one of the halflings moved. In a flash, he lunged, his small frame launching through the air like a rabid animal. He collided with the robed man's arm, sinking his needle-like teeth into flesh. A guttural scream tore through the street as the man flailed, trying to shake the vicious creature off.

The second halfling wasted no time, snarling as he grabbed the leg of another robed figure, biting down with sickening ferocity. The man shrieked, clubbing the creature with his fist, but the halfling only clung tighter, gnawing like a starved dog.

That left the third robed man, still standing, still untouched.

Puppy's heart pounded. She could run. She should run. But then a terrible thought took root in her mind. If she fled now, she would have nothing. Devaultus wanted that ring. He needed information. If she failed to find anything useful, would he cast her aside? Would they leave her behind? She wasn't strong like Devaultus believed Vex was, wasn't quick with words like Devaultus. If she lost them, she'd be alone.

And if she was alone, they would find her again.

She could already feel the cold iron of the cage against her skin. Smell the stale, putrid air inside.

No. Not the cage. Never again.

Something in her snapped. A wild, frenzied look overtook her eyes as she surged forward, and her hand began to dig into the pouch at her waist. Her fingers curled around a smooth, clay sphere. Without hesitation, she hurled it against the ground at the feet of the last robed man.

The orb shattered with a sharp crack, releasing a thick, seeping cloud of yellow mist.

And then, all hell broke loose.

The robed man gasped, his body convulsing as the thick yellow mist filled his lungs. He wheezed, his vision blurring; and then, suddenly, he saw them. Dozens of her. A swarm of identical, pale-faced, wide-eyed women rushing at him from every direction. Panic overtook him. His breaths came in ragged, shallow gulps as he swung wildly, his blade cutting through nothing but illusions. His footing faltered, his mind slipping further into the fog of terror.

Puppy had moved swiftly, pressing a small herbal wad into her nostrils to filter out the gas. She darted through the shifting cloud of illusions, her body low and controlled. With a sharp exhale, she slammed her fist into his face. Pain shot up her knuckles like fire, she had never struck a man like this one before. The robed figure stumbled back, his eyes bloodshot, his expression twisting between rage and confusion.

Then, with a sudden burst of fury, his hand shot out and clamped around her throat. He had found the real one.

Puppy choked as he lifted her, his grip tightening like an iron vise. Her feet kicked uselessly at the air before he hurled her down onto the stone-paved street. She hit the ground hard, her body rolling from the impact. Through the haze of pain, her foot struck something. A lifeless bone dagger.

Her instincts roared to life.

She barely had time to think before she seized the weapon just as he lunged toward her again. He didn't realize his mistake until it was too late. The moment his weight pressed down on her, she drove the dagger deep into his chest.

A guttural gasp escaped his lips. He shuddered violently, his fingers twitching as the life drained from him. Puppy, still panting, shoved his corpse off her and rolled away, her heart pounding so hard that she could hear it in her ears.

Then, she froze.

The halflings were watching her.

Their beady little eyes darted between her and the three fresh corpses at their feet. Then, as if following some twisted ritual, each halfling leaned down and sank their razor-sharp teeth into their chosen kill. Flesh tore, blood dribbled down their chins, and they chewed with sickening satisfaction.

Puppy's stomach churned, and a cold dread seeped into her bones.

They weren't done.

She saw it in their eyes, the way they lingered on her, calculating, waiting. She knew what came next.

*She* was next.

Slowly, carefully, she began to rise. The halflings immediately stopped eating and mirrored her movement, their small bodies tensed and ready.

A test.

If she ran, they would pounce. They would tear into her like rabid animals, ripping flesh from bone before she could take another breath.

Survival instincts kicked in, sharp and unforgiving.

Puppy hesitated; then, without breaking eye contact, she crouched back down.

The halflings followed suit, hunching protectively over their kills.

She had to think fast.

Her stomach clenched as she looked at the corpse before her. Her lips trembled as she pressed them against the dead man's arm. The halflings tilted their heads, watching intently.

She squeezed her eyes shut.

And then, she bit down.

Warm blood coated her tongue. The taste was metallic, foul, and thick enough to make her gag. She chewed, her every instinct screaming at her to stop. But she didn't.

The halflings grinned, their jagged teeth glinting in the dim light.

Then, satisfied, they turned back to their feast, gnawing and tearing into flesh with animalistic fervor.

Puppy swallowed hard, forcing the bile down her throat. She had survived.

For now.

Devaultus leaned casually against the jeweler's polished wooden counter, his fingers absentmindedly tracing the edge of a velvet display case. He exhaled softly, casting an appreciative glance over the glittering assortment before him. "These are such fine wares," he murmured, his voice dripping with admiration. A slow, knowing smile curled on his lips as he lifted an ornate ring between his fingers, turning it in the light.

The jeweler, a stout man with keen eyes and a well-groomed beard, beamed with pride. "Do you like them, sir? I have traveled far and wide to procure only the most exquisite pieces."

Devaultus nodded, his expression thoughtful. "I can tell. Simply extraordinary craftsmanship." He let the ring rest between his thumb and forefinger for a moment before setting it back onto the display. His next words had to be chosen carefully. "Tell me, how often do you come across rings with... special properties?"

The jeweler squinted slightly, sensing intrigue in the question. "Special properties? What kind, exactly?"

Devaultus feigned casual curiosity, though every muscle in his body tensed with anticipation. "Oh, you know, the kind that can store things within them, or perhaps grant the wearer protection, shield them from harm. Or, dare I say, even allow one to travel between realms?"

The jeweler's bushy brows furrowed as he pondered the inquiry. "I've heard of such things," he admitted slowly, lowering his voice. "Most of those are the stuff of legend. But... the last one?" He hesitated, then leaned forward conspiratorially. "There is a Lord who is rumored to possess such a ring."

Devaultus forced himself to remain composed, though his pulse quickened. He had expected vague myths, hopeful whispers, but not a direct lead. "Truly?" He tilted his head in feigned curiosity, his fingers tapping the counter lightly. "I'd be most eager to meet such a man. Perhaps he would be willing to part with one for the right price."

The jeweler let out a hearty laugh. "Oh, he doesn't sell them, my friend." He glanced around, as if ensuring no unwanted ears were listening, before lowering his voice further. "Word has it that he's not merely collecting these rings, he's forging them. Crafting them in secret, preparing for something grand. They say he's building an army. A force he plans to send across realms."

Devaultus' mind spun. This was bigger than he anticipated. Not just a single ring, an entire operation. He masked his intrigue behind a charming smirk. "Fascinating. And tell me, if I were inclined to seek out this Lord, perhaps even serve him in this grand endeavor... how might one go about joining his ranks?"

The jeweler studied him for a moment before nodding slightly. "A strong young man like yourself? I don't see why you wouldn't qualify. Though..." He scratched his beard. "His name is a bit of a mouthful. What was it now?" He muttered under his breath, searching his memory before snapping his fingers. "Ah! Vera'Ala'Roja Bobalata'Cora. Strange name, isn't it? He's a Nor'tok, they're a race of warriors unlike any you've ever seen. Savage, disciplined, and incredibly dangerous. You don't often find their kind this far from their homeland."

Devaultus etched the name into his mind, committing every syllable to memory. It was cumbersome, but names held power, and this one would no doubt open doors, or, perhaps, serve as the key to tearing them down. He exhaled through his nose, nodding appreciatively. "How interesting. I believe I shall seek out this Lord and see if his army has need of me."

He paused, weighing the question. "You wouldn't happen to know where someone might find this man," he asked, casually. "You know... to join his army."

The man narrowed his eyes. Suspicion crept into his face like a slow frost.

He realized, too late, perhaps, that he may have said too much already. Still, no turning back now.

"I don't know exactly," the man said carefully. "Only that he's somewhere on one of the Sand Isles to the north."

With a practiced flourish, he pulled a gold coin from his pocket and set it on the counter with a soft clink. "For your time and your insight, my good man."

The jeweler grinned and bowed his head. "Safe travels, sir. And may fortune favor you."

Devaultus turned on his heel, his mind already racing with possibilities. This lead could be everything he needed, or a death sentence if he wasn't careful. Either way, he had no intention of turning back now.

The hour was drawing to a close, and the time for their rendezvous was fast approaching. Devaultus moved through the bustling crowd with practiced ease, his steps light, his presence nearly imperceptible as he leaned against the weather-worn wall of their meeting place. His sharp gaze flicked across the street, searching for any sign of his companions.

Puppy was nowhere to be seen. He exhaled slowly, wondering if she had actually followed his instructions or simply wandered off, lost in whatever fragile thoughts still clung to her mind. The girl didn't speak; hell, she barely reacted to anything. It was difficult to tell whether she was absorbing information or just drifting along, a leaf caught in a current she couldn't control. He hoped that would change soon. Then again, the idea of both women chattering endlessly through the night while he attempted to sleep didn't sound ideal either.

Not that it mattered. Either they proved themselves useful, or they were gone.

He considered this for a moment, arms crossed over his chest. He had always been a lone wolf, and yet... he had to admit, he was rather enjoying Vex's presence. She was unpredictable, reckless, and entirely too enthusiastic about violence, but she was entertaining at the very least. As for Puppy? She was an unknown variable, and Devaultus didn't deal well with unknowns. He had no intention of dragging around dead weight, no matter how pitiful or quiet it was. He wasn't some benevolent hero, he never had been, and he wasn't about to start now.

Just as the thought crossed his mind, a flash of blonde caught his eye. Vex.

She was practically skipping toward him, her movements light and carefree, her usual mischievous grin plastered across her face. What stood out, however, was the massive blood-soaked sack slung over her shoulder, bouncing against her back like a grotesque prize.

With a bright, almost childlike enthusiasm, she waved at him and called out, "Hey, Mr. D.! I gotcha lots of rings!"

The sack hit the ground with a wet thud, the fabric stained a deep crimson. Devaultus slowly turned his gaze downward, peering inside.

It was full of rings, alright. More than he could count at a glance. Some of them were still attached to fingers.

He exhaled sharply, his expression unreadable as he closed the sack and quickly shoved it into Vex's backpack before anyone in the crowd took notice. How many people had she maimed, no, outright butchered, for these? And more importantly... who exactly had she killed?

His jaw tightened. His fingers twitched slightly at his side.

"...Vex."

Devaultus started to speak, but barely got a single word out before a voice cut through the air like the edge of a well-honed blade.

"Hello, Lorivelle."

The words were smooth, yet heavy with malice, curling into the space around them with an unnatural weight. Devaultus stiffened, slowly turning toward the source. Vex turned as well, her expression shifting from playful to wary in an instant.

Before them stood a man built like a fortress, his towering form encased in dark armor that barely contained the massive muscles beneath. His mere presence exuded dominance, the kind that could silence a room without a word. But it was the man beside him who sent a chill creeping down Devaultus' spine.

Thin and wiry, the second figure wore a deep crimson robe that draped around him like the whisper of a phantom. His pencil-thin mustache curved with his smirk, his eyes gleaming with a sick, knowing amusement. He looked between them as if he already knew every secret they harbored.

"And who might you be?" the robed man asked, his voice as silken as a noose.

Devaultus felt it before he understood what was happening: something dark, something insidious pressing against his mind. A formless pressure slithered through his thoughts, threading its way into the very fabric of his consciousness like a writhing parasite. His vision blurred, the edges of the world smearing together into a haze of colors and shadows.

His fingers twitched. His hand lifted. Not by his own will.

What in the Abyss...?

His eyes dropped to his own palm, watching it turn over as if it belonged to someone else. The sensation was distant, foreign, like a marionette being controlled by unseen hands. His mind screamed to stop, to move, to fight back, but his body did not obey.

Somewhere, far away, he heard Vex's voice, her usual playful lilt replaced by something cautious.

"I'm Vex."

The voice, belonging to the robed figure, spoke deep, confidently through the space between them. "It is no matter, my dear. You and..." He turned his piercing gaze toward Devaultus, tilting his head slightly. "Devaultus, is it?"

A slow, cruel smile spread across the robed man's lips. "Ah... yes. That is your name." His voice dripped with satisfaction, like he had plucked it straight from Devaultus' mind.

The pressure tightened.

"You two will come with us. You are needed."

Vex's daggers flashed into her hands in an instant, the deadly gleam of their edges promising swift and violent retaliation. She crouched, ready to strike.

But Devaultus' hand shot up.

Not by his own command.

His mouth moved, the words slipping from his lips without his consent.

"No, Lorivelle. We will go with him."

Vex's body went rigid, confusion flashing across her face. Her fingers tightened around the hilts of her daggers before, just as swiftly, her posture shifted. The ever-present smirk she always carried faded, her demeanor replaced by the straight-backed elegance of a noblewoman, her movements suddenly refined, restrained.

The two strangers said nothing more. They merely turned and gestured toward a massive, iron-reinforced cart nearby.

Devaultus walked forward. Not by choice.

Vex hesitated only a fraction of a second before she followed.

Inside the cart, Devaultus sat motionless, his gaze locked forward, blank and empty. Vex settled beside him, but something was wrong. He wasn't looking around. He wasn't scanning the exits, the street, the shifting weight of their captors. He always knew what was happening around him. His senses were honed like a master's blade. His perception was razor-sharp, an unshakable presence in any situation.

But now?

Now he sat still.

Silent.

A puppet without strings.

Vex's chest tightened. This wasn't right. This wasn't him.

She would follow him into the Abyss if necessary. And together, they would carve their way back out.

But then a realization struck her, cold and sudden, lodging itself in her gut like a blade of ice.

Her breath hitched.

Where was her Puppy?

Puppy had barely managed to stomach a few bites, her body trembling as the taste of raw flesh lingered on her tongue. Meanwhile, her two twisted companions had devoured nearly an entire limb, tearing into it with the delight of true savages. When they finally stood, their faces slick with blood, Puppy braced herself, every muscle locking in terror.

This was it.

This was how she would die.

The two halflings sauntered toward her, and she scrambled backward, landing hard on her rear, her breath hitching in panic. But instead of pouncing on her like she was a fresh meal, one of them clapped her roughly on the back, nearly knocking the air from her lungs.

"You ain't so bad!" the first one declared with a grin, his sharp teeth still glistening with his last bite.

"For a human," the other added, his wicked smile stretching over bloodstained lips.

Puppy's heart pounded so violently, she thought she might be sick. She needed to run, to escape, but before she could so much as twitch, they grabbed her arms, yanking her up and practically dragging her along.

"I'd say this calls for a drink, wouldn't you, Kot?" the first halfling said, flashing a grin at his companion.

Kot let out a raspy laugh as he led the way, pulling Puppy along as though she were a dear friend rather than a walking meal. "I'd say so. For us and our new little friend here. You know, I've never much cared for humans," he added, his grip tightening, "but I can't bring myself to hate one who lends me a hand."

Dar, the other halfling, chuckled darkly before spitting out a chunk of flesh that had stuck between his teeth. "Yeah, there's something about that, isn't there?" His gaze flicked to Puppy, eyes glinting with amusement. "So, what's your name, female?"

Puppy's lips parted, but no sound came out. She willed herself to speak, but her voice betrayed her, swallowed by fear.

Dar let out a bark of laughter. "Ha! She's so full, she can't even talk."

Kot snickered. "I've been there before. Remember that time we found those lost children in that alley?"

Dar erupted into full-blown laughter, his mirth chilling. "Oh, that was a feast, wasn't it?"

A wave of nausea crashed through her, brutal and sudden. The very thought of what they were reminiscing about made her legs weak. She wanted to pull away, to run as fast as her feet would carry her, but their arms remained hooked around hers, as they led her forward with an unsettling camaraderie.

Then she saw it: the doorway.

Small. Shadowed. Unassuming.

The final threshold before escape became an impossibility. If they dragged her through that door, she knew she would never get out. Never find her way back to Devaultus and Vex. She would be swallowed whole by whatever horrors lay beyond.

Her breath came in short, sharp gasps.

But they didn't stop.

The door creaked open, and the trio stepped inside. Puppy's eyes widened in sheer horror.

The interior of a massive tavern stretched before her, packed wall to wall with halflings. At least thirty of them, maybe more. The air was thick with the scent of spilled ale and something more sinister, something metallic. Something that made her skin crawl.

A single gasp escaped her lips.

Two halflings had been terrifying enough.

But this, this was doom itself.

A tear traced a cold path down her cheek. She was trapped. Utterly and completely.

Dar, misinterpreting her expression, cackled gleefully. "Beautiful sight, ain't it?"

The tavern went silent.

Every halfling in the room turned, their predatory gazes locking onto her; a pack of wolves scenting fresh prey.

More than a few licked their lips.

Puppy's blood ran cold.

Kot's hand shot up, commanding the attention of the entire tavern. "Now hold up, everyone," he announced, his voice cutting through the murmurs and hungry gazes. "This one is with us." His sharp eyes scanned the room, daring anyone to challenge him. "Yeah, yeah, I know," he continued with an exaggerated sigh, as if already anticipating their protests. "She's a human. A mere cow, fit for slaughter. But listen up, she fought by our side, shared in the battle feast, and that earns her a place at our table."

Puppy, who hadn't even realized she had been holding her breath, finally exhaled, her lungs burning from the tension. The moment of relief was fleeting, however, as Dar wasted no time in dragging her toward a nearby table, practically throwing her onto the worn wooden bench.

"Oy! Ale!" Dar barked, slamming his hand against the table.

A curvy halfling woman with wild red hair and an attitude sharper than the knives at her belt swaggered over, balancing three oversized tankards with ease. She slammed them onto the table, frothy ale sloshing over the sides, and gave Puppy a lingering once-over before flashing a grin. "Try not to choke on it, human," she purred before sauntering off.

Dar wasted no time, grabbing his tankard and taking a long, deep swig.

"Come on, lass!" Kot encouraged, nudging Puppy's mug closer to her. "Drink up! You've earned it."

Puppy stared at the ale, her fingers twitching slightly as they wrapped around the handle. Was this a trick? Would they poison her, laughing as she choked and withered away, only to tear her apart afterward? The thought sent a shiver through her, but another part of her whispered, *If they wanted to kill you, they would have done it already.*

Steeling herself, she lifted the tankard to her lips and took a hesitant sip. The taste surprised her, a rich, bold flavor with a honeyed sweetness that lingered on her tongue. Her eyes widened slightly. It was... good. Really good. Before she knew it, she was drinking more, the warmth of the alcohol seeping into her bones. The weight of fear that had clung to her like a second skin began to slip away, just a little.

Laughter rumbled from Dar and Kot as they exchanged some joke, their voices barely registering in Puppy's ears. She was too caught up in the unexpected enjoyment of the drink. It had been so long since she'd allowed herself something simple, something that wasn't just about surviving the next moment.

Then Kot leaned in, eyes gleaming with a strange excitement. "Now then, lass. Who are you?" His grin stretched wide. "Allow me the honor of knowing the name of my battle pet."

The words should have stung, "battle pet," like she was some creature who existed only for their amusement. But in this moment, in this place, surrounded by monsters who had every reason to kill her but instead welcomed her as one of their own, well maybe not their own unless you were referring to their own pet, something inside her shifted.

Puppy's fingers tightened around the handle of her now-empty mug. She wasn't that scared, helpless girl anymore. She couldn't be. If she wanted to survive, if she wanted to carve a place for herself in this world, she had to become something new. Something stronger.

She placed the tankard down with slow deliberation, tilting her chin up ever so slightly. The name she had carried no longer fit her. She needed something else. A name that meant something. A name that *felt* like power.

"I..." She hesitated, inhaling deeply. No. No hesitation. No fear.

"I'm Blight."

Kot and Dar exchanged looks before their laughter roared through the tavern, loud and wild. "Blight, huh?" Kot smirked, slamming a hand down onto the table. "Well, ain't that a damn fine name?"

Dar grinned, lifting his tankard. "A toast, then! To Blight, the meanest, scariest little battle pet we ever did have!"

The rest of the tavern erupted in cheers, tankards clashing together, the air thick with the scent of ale, blood, and something that smelled like burning meat.

*Blight*, she thought to herself as she felt the name settle deep into her bones. *A new identity. A new path.* She wasn't sure where it would lead her, but one thing was certain.

She was no longer prey.

## CHAPTER 6

# STRINGS ATTACHED: TERMS AND CONDITIONS APPLY

The cart came to an abrupt halt, the sudden jolt snapping Vex from her thoughts as she braced herself against the wooden frame. Outside, the massive mansion loomed over them, its dark stone walls stretching high into the sky, illuminated only by flickering lanterns that barely pierced the thick night air. The building radiated an eerie presence, as though it breathed with a sinister life of its own.

Before she could fully take in the sight, the door of the cart was wrenched open, revealing the towering figure of the armored man who had captured them. His shadow swallowed the interior of the cart, his presence an oppressive force that made the air heavy.

"Out," he commanded, his voice deep, like stone grinding against stone.

Without hesitation, without a word, Devaultus stepped out, his movements unsettlingly mechanical. Vex hesitated, studying him carefully. Devaultus always had something to say, some quip, some dry remark, would always give some sign that he was thinking three steps ahead. But now, nothing. He was eerily silent, his expression void of its usual sharpness. A cold knot formed in her stomach.

Swallowing her unease, she followed him out of the cart, her fingers twitching at her sides, aching to reach for her daggers. But something told her to wait, to observe. The red-robed man emerged behind them, a smug air clinging to him like an unbearable stench.

The group moved forward, their boots echoing against the polished marble walkway leading to the mansion's grand entrance. Enormous doors flanked by imposing guards swung open as they approached, revealing a long, dimly lit corridor lined with statues of twisted, grotesque figures. Each one seemed to be watching, their hollow eyes following their every step.

Vex felt her heart hammer in her chest. Something was wrong. Something was very, very wrong. Devaultus wouldn't betray her, wouldn't give her up... would he? Would she even care if he did? Without him, she was nothing. A flicker of doubt crossed her mind, but she crushed it before it could take root. No, Devaultus would never do that to her. He was all she had, just as she was all he had. Right?

They reached a set of ornate doors, carved with intricate scenes of battles, suffering, and triumph. The guards stationed there moved in practiced unison, pulling them open to reveal an opulent chamber that reeked of excess and indulgence.

At the far end of the room sat an enormous man, though to call him merely "enormous" would be an understatement. He was gargantuan, his bloated flesh barely contained by the sheer silk draped over his massive form. Rolls of flesh jiggled as he reached out, plucking a piece of meat from a golden tray held by one of the twelve naked women scattered about the room. Another woman waved an oversized fan, crafted from the sinew of some long-dead beast, while another leaned in, placing morsels of food into his ever-hungry mouth. The sickening squelch of chewing filled the chamber, bits of half-masticated food tumbling down his chest to rest among the folds of his mostly bare body.

The armored man strode forward, his voice a low rumble that barely masked the disgust in his tone.

"Lord Rukarus, we are on a mission from Lord Vera'Ala'Roja Bobalata'Cora and request the use of your prison."

Lord Rukarus barely acknowledged them at first, continuing to chew noisily as he smacked his lips, his tiny, beady eyes gleaming with disinterest. Then, at last, he swallowed, wiping his greasy fingers on the nearest woman's thigh before waving a dismissive hand.

"And what, pray tell, is in this for me? Surely Lord Vera'Ala'Roja Bobalata'Cora does not expect me to grant access to my prisons out of charity?" His voice was high-pitched, nasal, entirely unfitting for a man of his size.

The red-robed man, the one who had been silent for most of their journey, finally stepped forward. His presence sent a shiver through the room, and for the first time, Vex saw something almost resembling fear flickering across Rukarus' gluttonous face. The robed man smiled, an expression filled with malice and satisfaction.

"Do you know who I am?" he asked, his voice like poisoned honey. "I am known as The Puppeteer."

Silence fell. The blood drained from Lord Rukarus' face, his once-carefree demeanor vanishing as he straightened ever so slightly. He swallowed hard, as though the very name had lodged itself in his throat like a bone.

"Very well," The Puppeteer said confidently. "I am not without mercy. If you lend us your prison, I shall have three hundred gold pieces sent to your coffers."

Lord Rukarus' grin widened, his jowls bouncing with the action. "That is more than kind," he said, his words dripping with condescension. "You may use my prison for as long as you need."

Rukarus exhaled in relief, his massive form sagging, the tension in the room dissipating ever so slightly. He nodded, eager to rid himself of their presence.

The Puppeteer turned, his gaze sweeping over Devaultus and Vex, a craftsman inspecting his tools. "I shall make sure they are... shall we say... tucked in." His grin widened further, showing too many teeth. "Then we shall discuss our time away."

Vex clenched her fists, her instincts screaming at her to run. To fight. To do anything but follow this path to wherever it led.

And yet, she walked forward.

The group turned, making their way toward the dark corridors that led to the prison below.

The cold, damp air of the prison clung to Vex's skin as they were led inside, the stone walls lined with rusted chains and the echoes of past suffering. Devaultus moved first, turning to face her, his expression unreadable. Then he spoke, his voice calm yet laced with something unnatural.

"Lorivelle, if you would be so kind as to hand over your weapons."

Vex's muscles tensed. The name Lorivelle did not belong here. It was a mask she wore when the situation demanded, but that was not now. Here, in this moment, they needed Scythe, the ruthless, calculated killer Lorivelle had become. Yet Devaultus had given a direct order, and despite the pit forming in her stomach, she obeyed. Without hesitation but with burning reluctance, she reached beneath her cloak, retrieving her twin daggers.

As she placed them into the guard's outstretched hands, she barely had time to react before the robed man stepped forward, a gleam of satisfaction in his eyes. In one swift motion, he latched something cold around her neck.

A collar.

Vex stiffened as an immediate, suffocating sensation washed over her. Her magic, it was there, but just out of reach, slipping through her grasp like sand in the wind. She clenched her jaw, her fingers twitching as though she could will it back to her. But it was gone.

Before she could fully process what had just happened, a rough shove sent her stumbling backward into her cell. The bars slammed shut behind her, and the lock clicked into place.

Across from her, the guard turned his attention to Devaultus.

Without so much as a struggle, Devaultus allowed himself to be seized, hauled unceremoniously into a separate cell. The brute stripped him down to his underclothes, then lifted him with ease, locking his wrists high above his head into a set of iron stocks. He now hung by his arms, exposed and vulnerable. He had made no move to resist. Not even once.

Vex's stomach twisted. Something was wrong.

Then, she saw it, the sudden flicker of clarity in Devaultus' eyes, the sharp inhale of breath as though her head were breaking the surface of deep water. The instant the cell door closed, he gasped, spitting on the stone floor with disgust.

"Bastard," he hissed under his breath.

His hands clenched into fists. His entire body pulsed with barely contained rage, his chest rising and falling in steady, controlled breaths. Devaultus did not fear captivity. He did not fear pain. But if there was one thing he loathed more than anything else, it was losing control. And they had stolen his control from him.

His head snapped up, eyes burning with fury as he fixed them on the two men.

"I do hope you both understand something," he said, his voice eerily calm. "I will get out of this. And when I do, the two of you will be nothing more than bloody remnants of my past."

The Puppeteer chuckled, shaking his head. "Oh, Devaultus. You act as if you matter. As if you are something more than a footnote in history." He stepped closer, a cruel smirk playing on his lips. "You think what I did to you was bad? You have no idea what awaits. When Lord

Vera'Ala'Roja Bobalata'Cora is finished with you, you'll beg to be back under my control."

Devaultus' lips curled into a grin, all teeth and malice. "I'll see you soon, puppet."

The Puppeteer's amusement flickered, replaced by a brief flash of irritation. He turned sharply on his heel, his robes billowing as he strode toward the exit. "I hope you do," he muttered. "I'll be waiting."

The heavy doors slammed shut behind him, leaving only the lingering tension and the towering figure of the armored guard.

The brute's gaze drifted toward Vex, his grin almost audible beneath the shadow of his helmet. "I did not properly search you." His voice rumbled like distant thunder. "Back against the wall."

Vex's heart pounded. This was bad. Very bad.

The guard moved toward her cell door, unlocking it with slow deliberation. As he stepped inside, he had to crouch slightly, his sheer size making the space feel suffocating.

Vex pressed herself against the far wall, each muscle in her body coiling like a spring. She had no magic. No weapons. And this man was built like a damn mountain.

Her mind worked fast. She couldn't let him get close.

The moment he took another step forward, she lunged.

Her fist swung toward his throat, aiming for the soft spot beneath his chin, but she might as well have struck stone. His arm lashed out like a whip, the hand catching her across the face with the force of a battering ram.

The world tilted.

Pain exploded through her skull as she was sent hurtling backward. Her body collided with the iron bars, the impact jarring every bone in her frame. A sharp gasp escaped her lips as she crumpled to the floor, the cold metal pressing into her cheek.

Distantly, she heard the guard chuckle. "Not much without your blades, are you?"

Vex groaned, her vision swimming. She tasted blood.

Her fingers twitched, digging into the stone floor beneath her.

No.

This wasn't over.

This was just the beginning.

He let out a low, rumbling laugh as the cell door clanged shut behind him, the sound reverberating off the cold stone walls. The dim torchlight flickered against his massive frame as he advanced, slow and deliberate, like a predator savoring the moment before striking.

Vex's pulse pounded in her ears. She refused to cower. Gritting her teeth, she lunged forward, aiming to sweep his legs out from under him, but the brute barely flinched. Her kick landed hard against his armored shin, sending a jolt of pain up her own leg instead. Damn it. She wasn't used to fighting without her magic. Every instinct screamed at her to call on her power, to ignite the force within her veins, but the collar around her neck kept her magic agonizingly out of reach.

The giant smirked, unimpressed. In a single, brutal motion, his meaty hand shot out and caught her by the head. His fingers clamped like a vise, shoving her downward with overwhelming strength. She hit the damp stone floor, barely catching herself on her hands and knees, her breath coming in ragged gasps.

No. No, she would not let this happen.

Snarling, she twisted, throwing her weight to the side in an attempt to break free, but he was too strong, too massive. The iron grip on her skull held her in place. She lashed out with her foot, aiming for his gut, but his armor absorbed the blow with a dull *thud*. It was like kicking solid rock.

Vex gritted her teeth, a flicker of panic creeping in. She needed a way out. Now.

Holding her in place, he reached down and freed his massive member. Eyeing Vex with a sinister grin.

Devaultus observed as the man closed the distance between himself and Vex, his every step deliberate, radiating a predatory confidence that sent a quiet ripple of tension through the air. A part of Devaultus wondered why he even cared. The Devaultus of old certainly wouldn't have. In fact, past Devaultus would have sat back with a bemused smirk, watching the scene unfold like a spectator at the theater, eager to see how the chaos played out. He had always relished a certain level of disorder; though, now that he thought about it, there was a difference between calculated chaos and reckless, unrefined mayhem. The former could be shaped, bent to his will like molten iron; the latter was nothing but a mindless storm, unpredictable and dangerous even to the one who conjured it.

He half expected Vex to explode into action, to come up with some wildly creative way to hack, slash, and dismember the man before he even got close. She was nothing if not unpredictable, and bloodshed was certainly in her nature. And yet... she didn't move. She just sat there, frozen in place. There was something in her eyes, something he hadn't seen before. Fear. Genuine, unfiltered fear. That certainly wouldn't do.

She was his.

For better or worse, Vex had become his responsibility, a force tied to him by fate or misfortune. Whatever she did, whatever mess she made, it would ultimately reflect back on him. His reputation, his plans, his ambitions, all of it could be affected by her actions. The realization settled in his mind like a stone dropped into still water, sending out ripples of understanding. Was that his way of saying he would protect her? Was that the line he was drawing in the sand?

Huh. Interesting.

Screw it, he thought.

Devaultus yawned loudly, stretching as if unimpressed by the show. Another guard, one of Lord Rukarus' men, stood outside the cells, watching with cruel amusement. "Hah! She won't last long," he sneered. "Haven't seen someone get dismantled this fast in a long time."

But his attention wasn't on Devaultus.

That was his mistake.

Devaultus' form shimmered and warped, his body shrinking down into that of a small child. The iron restraints meant for an adult were suddenly too loose, and he slipped free, silent as a shadow. His fingers snaked through the bars, dipping into the guard's pocket, and a moment later, he pulled out a rusted key. A grin spread across his face as he shifted back to his original form.

Glancing at the floor, he spotted the skeletal remains of the cell's previous occupant. He crouched, plucking a single, jagged finger bone from the pile.

Without hesitation, he reached through the bars and jammed it into the temple of the laughing guard.

The man's amusement turned to a choked gurgle as he staggered back, eyes wide in shock before he collapsed in a clattering heap.

The brute holding Vex paused, turning toward the sudden noise. "What the..."

Devaultus calmly picked up an entire skeletal arm and waved it mockingly, its fingers waggling as though in greeting.

The brute's eyes narrowed in fury. "Doesn't matter. You're still locked in there. You can watch while I break your friend in half."

Devaultus lifted the key between two fingers, a smug grin playing on his lips. "Oh, I don't think so."

The brute's face paled.

In a fluid motion, Devaultus unlocked his cell and stepped out, striding confidently toward Vex's.

Devaultus stood just outside his own cell, his expression alight with anticipation. His lips curled into a devilish grin, a glint of amusement dancing in his eyes as he observed the scene before him. The giant, still trapped within the cell alongside Vex, radiated pure fury, his massive chest heaving with each breath. He was a caged beast, an enraged lion pacing, waiting for the moment he could strike. And yet, Devaultus showed no hesitation.

With deliberate slowness, he stepped forward, his movements dripping with confidence, as though he were the one in control of this deadly game. The flickering torchlight cast along shadow over the dungeon walls, adding a haunting glow to the tension that thickened the air. The giant's surprise was evident, his brows furrowing in momentary confusion. What was this fool doing?

Devaultus' grin widened, stretching into something feral, something dangerous. His fingers, steady and sure, lifted the rusted key, twirling it between his fingers like a jester performing for his own amusement. Then, with an almost lazy motion, he slid the key into the lock of the giant's cell. The mechanism clicked. A simple sound, but one that sent a ripple of realization through the room.

The door swung open.

The beast was free.

And Devaultus? He merely chuckled, as if daring fate itself to entertain him.

The brute roared in fury, lunging at him. Devaultus waited until the last possible second before he feigned stumbling back, then propelled himself off the bars, slipping between the giant's legs.

In one swift motion, he leapt onto the brute's back, hooking the skeletal forearm across the man's throat and yanking tight.

The brute thrashed, slamming Devaultus against the walls, but Devaultus held on, pulling tighter on the forearm mercilessly. In a final, desperate move, the brute charged forward, accidentally slamming Vex's cell door closed just as she was about to step out.

The force knocking Devaultus off his back and onto the ground.

Seeing the opportunity, Devaultus ripped a skeletal finger from the arm he was still holding and stabbed it deep into the back of the brute's knee. Just between the plates of armor.

The beast let out a howl of pain, his leg giving way. He stumbled forward, his helmet slipping from his head just as his jaw connected with the stone floor with a sickening crack. Blood splattered across the cobblestones as a tooth skidded across the ground.

Before he could recover, Devaultus launched himself into the air and brought both feet down onto the back of the brute's skull.

The force was immense.

The sound was worse.

The guard's body jerked once, then went still.

Devaultus exhaled sharply, dusting himself off. He looked down at the bloody mess of hair and bone, then smirked as he bent down and used the skeletal hand to smooth out the brute's disheveled locks. "Had a hair out of place," he said, voice dripping with mock concern. "You're welcome."

Then, without another word, he strode over and unlocked Vex's cell.

Vex stood frozen in the dimly lit cell, her breath shallow, her pulse still pounding in her ears. The heavy iron door now gaped open, swinging idly on its hinges as if mocking the nightmare that had nearly become her reality. Just moments ago, she had been mere seconds away from becoming the guards' plaything, a helpless pawn in their cruel amusement. But now, everything had changed.

Across the room, Devaultus loomed over the massive, lifeless guard, absently toying with the corpse as though it were nothing more than a discarded piece of furniture. He hadn't struggled. He hadn't hesitated.

He had ended the man's life with such casual efficiency that it made her stomach twist. Not from fear. From realization.

Her mind drifted backward: to Letty. Her sister. The memories clawed at her, vicious and raw. She could still see Cojar's leering face, as she was taken. Vex had been powerless then, just a terrified girl caught in a cruel world she couldn't fight against. Was this her family's curse? To always be at the mercy of stronger men? To be prey, waiting to be devoured?

No.

That thought shattered as her gaze snapped back to Devaultus. He had made it look effortless, killing that guard like he was slicing through butter. He hadn't needed to save her, he could have ignored her entirely. But he had acted. And for the first time since Tarus Goldwynde, since she had watched her sister die in front of her, she felt something click into place inside her.

This only solidified her choice.

She had made the right decision in following him. He was her Lord. Her savior. Her everything.

Her fingers curled into fists at her sides as she stepped forward, her body moving as if drawn by an invisible force. Devaultus turned then, meeting her gaze with that familiar one-sided grin, his golden eyes gleaming in the dim light. He knew. He had always known.

And so had she.

She stepped out, her eyes locked on to him. "What happened? Why didn't you fight them before?"

Devaultus tilted his head, his expression unreadable. "The Puppeteer has a certain... skillset. He can take control of one's mind. Seems I wasn't as immune to it as I thought. A mistake I intend to correct."

Vex's stomach twisted. She could have helped him. But she hadn't even realized.

Devaultus sighed, already moving toward the door. "That's not our only problem. That collar of yours, only The Puppeteer has the key."

Vex clenched her jaw, gripping the daggers he had handed her.

Devaultus turned to look at her, his gaze sharp. "Until we leave this place, we'll need Scythe."

Her expression darkened, eyes glazing over as a twisted, sinister grin spread across her lips.

With a slow, deliberate creak, the heavy doors swung open. Devaultus stepped forward, his lips curling into a wild, wolfish grin as he entered the vast chamber. The scent of roasted meats, spiced wines, and something more primal, sweat and indulgence, clung thickly to the air. Lord Rukarus lounged at the head of a massive banquet table, half-buried beneath a gluttonous spread of food. Grease slicked his fingers as he tore into a slab of meat, while two nude women draped themselves over him, their hands wandering as they lavished him with whispered praise.

Across from him, The Puppeteer sat, his unnervingly thin fingers steepled as he conversed in hushed, amused tones with the Lord of the hall. The satisfaction in their expressions was unmistakable. They were pleased, no, thrilled, with their supposed victory, having ensnared both Devaultus and Vex in their web.

But their conversation came to an abrupt halt.

A sound filled the room, light, deliberate, mocking. The playful strum of a lute.

Devaultus tilted his head back and let his voice ring out, rich and unshaken, weaving melody into the air like a dagger wrapped in silk.

*I walked into the ring so wide, A giant stood, all clad in pride. His armor black, his stance was tall, But with one swing, I watched him fall!*

Lord Rukarus stiffened, his hand frozen over his feast. The Puppeteer's fingers twitched ever so slightly, the only sign of his immediate displeasure.

*The Puppeteer let out a cry,His prized brute gone, oh, how he sighed!He played his games, he pulled his strings,But I don't bow to coward kings.*

Devaultus moved further into the chamber, striding with the confidence of a man who owned the very ground beneath his feet. His hand trailed lazily over the golden goblets, the silk table runners, the jeweled platters. All of it was meaningless to him. He was here for something else.

*So drink, my friends, and hear me well,I sent his champion straight to hell.And now I turn with blade in hand.You're next, old fool, now make your stand.*

The final note lingered in the air, a haunting challenge wrapped in melody. Silence stretched taut in the room.

Then, Devaultus grinned wider, one hand resting lazily on the hilt of his blade.

"Well?" he mused, golden eyes glinting with mischief. "Shall we dance?"

The Puppeteer let out a low, irritated growl, his fingers twitching as he adjusted the folds of his elaborate robe. The amusement that had previously danced in his eyes faded, replaced by something cold and razor-sharp. "So eager to relive past failures, Devaultus?" he murmured, lips curling into a knowing smirk. "Very well, then."

Without warning, Vex's body stiffened, her muscles locking in place as if invisible chains had snapped around her. Her breath hitched, her pupils dilating as something slithered into the shattered cracks of her mind. His tendrils, unseen but suffocating, coiled through her consciousness, twisting into the darkened places left broken by everything she'd endured over the past few weeks. She had no walls left to keep him out.

"Lorivelle," The Puppeteer cooed, his voice thick with wicked amusement. "Be a dear and kill Devaultus for me."

Vex blinked. A tremor ran through her. Kill Devaultus? The words rattled in her head like they didn't belong there. No. No, that wasn't right. Lorivelle didn't kill. Lorivelle was a lady. But even as the thought formed, it unraveled into fog.

Lord Rukarus barked a sharp command. "Guards!"

The doors burst open. A flood of armored men poured into the chamber, weapons drawn, faces set like stone. Too many. Far too many.

Devaultus slung his lute behind his back with an easy motion, his fingers finding the familiar hilts of his daggers, only to grasp at one of them rather than both. His expression flickered. He tried again. Still nothing. A look of realization crossed his face.

"Hold up," he announced suddenly, raising a finger in a time-out gesture. "I seem to have misplaced my dagger."

His eyes darted around the room, scanning for the missing weapon. Where in the Abyss had it gone? That was one of his favorites. One of the two dipped in his own special paralytic poison. He let out a grumble of disappointment as he reached into his coat and drew another dagger, a lesser blade.

"I guess you'll have to do," he muttered, making a stabbing motion with it and testing its worth, sighing as if personally insulted by the substitution.

The moment was brief. Too brief.

Vex's foot snapped up, cutting through the air like a blade. She had grabbed two knives from Lord Rukarus' table and didn't seem opposed to using them.

Devaultus twisted, narrowly dodging as she came at him with terrifying speed, her fists flying in a flurry of attacks. Her strikes were relentless, her movements almost unnatural in their precision. She wasn't just fast: she was lethal. Even so, Devaultus moved with fluid grace, his own speed matching hers in a deadly dance.

Dagger met dagger. He parried her blows, redirecting each slash and thrust, sidestepping her wild swings with an almost casual elegance. But she wasn't holding back. Not even a little. Her strikes aimed for his throat, his ribs, his stomach, all places meant to end him quickly.

His mind flickered to the collar still locked around her neck. That was the only reason he stood a chance right now. Without it, a face-to-face fight might not end in his favor.

She lunged, slicing at his midsection. He batted the attack aside and launched himself into the air, spinning in a tight arc. His foot caught her in the chest, sending her staggering backward with a hiss.

Devaultus grinned.

This was fun.

Springing off the wall with a burst of speed, he propelled himself forward, slamming into Vex with enough force to send her flying. She tumbled, her body rolling across the polished floor before skidding to a stop, right at The Puppeteer's feet.

"Lorivelle?" The Puppeteer's voice slithered through the air like silk laced with venom. He leaned down, his fingers moving deftly as he unfastened the collar from Vex's neck. The heavy metal clattered to the floor, and for the first time today, she felt truly free. But as her lips curled into a grin, sharp, almost wicked, Devaultus' own smile wavered, just for a fraction of a second. This wasn't good. He had no magic to counter whatever hold The Puppeteer had over her. Unless, of course, one counted his devastatingly handsome face, but he doubted his charm would be much help here.

Then, the guards moved. A flood of steel and armor rushed toward him, weapons glinting under the flickering light of the torches.

"Alright then," Devaultus mused to himself, his grin snapping back into place. He was nothing if not adaptable.

With a graceful spin, he lashed out with his foot, sending a nearby brazier flying through the air. The fire within erupted, searing a group of guards as embers scattered like fallen stars. They reeled back, blinded by the sudden burst of flames. Without missing a beat, he dropped low, sliding effortlessly across the polished floor. His dagger found the back of a guard's knees, severing tendons in a single fluid stroke. A strangled scream filled the air as the man crumpled. Devaultus twisted, rolling onto his hands before launching himself into a handspring, flipping backward just as another sword slashed where he had stood a moment before.

Meanwhile, Vex had remained still, her expression unreadable.

Her mind snapped into clarity, a sudden and jarring shift from the fog of manipulation that had threatened to consume her. The tendrils of The Puppeteer's influence had been strong, but there were forces far stronger at play, forces that had anchored her to reality, pulling her back from the Abyss of control.

The first was her name. *Lorivelle.* The moment it left his lips, something within her stirred, hesitated. *Lorivelle does not kill.* It was a fact so deeply ingrained in her being that her mind was forced to reconcile the contradiction. It clawed through the layers of deception and control, struggling against the command that had been given to her. Devaultus had not called her Lorivelle. *Devaultus had called her Scythe.* A name was more than just a sound, it was identity, it was purpose. And she was not Lorivelle anymore. She was something else entirely.

The second, and perhaps the most powerful reason, was her devotion. Absolute, unwavering, as unshakable as the ground beneath her feet. Devaultus was her world, the axis upon which she spun, the tether that held her steady amidst the chaos of her shattered past. His voice, his commands, his very existence anchored her. The Puppeteer's powers, formidable though they were, could not force a person to slit their own throat. And in this moment, that was exactly what he had done. He had told her to kill Devaultus. To strike down the very man who had given her purpose, who had given her a reason to keep breathing.

And that? That was an order she simply could not follow.

Her breath hitched, her hands trembled, but her will solidified like iron in a forge. The haze lifted, the world sharpened, and in an instant, Vex was free.

Two guards flanked her, ready to strike alongside her, expecting her to move against Devaultus. Instead, she spun, her blade flashing as she lunged toward The Puppeteer himself.

The smug look on the man's face twisted into sheer horror as he stumbled back, his control over her shattered like brittle glass.

"What the hell?!" he sputtered, his voice quivering with disbelief. His tendrils of mental manipulation had dug deep into her fractured mind: she should have been his puppet! How had she resisted?

A shield intercepted her attack at the last moment, one of the guards barely managing to block the strike in time. The force of the impact sent vibrations rattling through her bones, but she didn't relent. More guards poured into the room, the metallic clang of weapons unsheathing filling the air. They converged on both her and Devaultus now, the previous plan to control her seemingly abandoned.

The Puppeteer, seeing his predicament unravel, made a snap decision: cowardice over confrontation. He turned on his heel and bolted toward a hidden exit, his robes billowing behind him like shadows fleeing the light. He wouldn't waste his energy on this; no, he thrived in the darkness, in manipulation and unseen strings. This direct battle was not his arena.

Devaultus scowled, watching the slimy man vanish into the night. "Oh, come now! I made a promise of pain and suffering, and I am a man of my word," he called mockingly after him, but there was no stopping the escape. Not yet.

Vex backed up, pressing her spine against Devaultus' for cover. The wave of enemies was closing in fast.

"I dare say we're a bit outnumbered," he noted casually, his voice almost amused despite the overwhelming odds.

"Then why are you smiling?" Vex asked, a flicker of bewilderment passing over her face.

"Because," Devaultus said, twirling his dagger, his grin widening, "I do love a good challenge."

And then, as if the gods themselves had decided to match his theatrics, the doors to the mansion suddenly burst open with a resounding crash.

The room was flooded with...

Little people.

Halflings.

The guards barely had time to react before the small, feral figures swarmed them like a living tide, launching themselves onto armored men with unnerving speed and unhinged savagery. The guards screamed, flailing desperately as the halflings tore into them, their razor-sharp teeth sinking into flesh. Limbs were wrenched free, throats were torn open, and the marble floors were soon slick with blood.

At the forefront of this nightmarish charge was...

"Puppy?" Devaultus' brows shot up.

She was barely recognizable.

Stripped down to a loincloth, a blood-streaked strip of cloth wrapped around her chest, her entire body was painted in crude, tribal designs, in what could only be blood. A brand was seared into her shoulder, identical to those some of the halflings bore. And judging by the wobble in her step and the wild glint in her eye, she was still thoroughly drunk.

Vex stared, stunned. "I... I don't know what happened to her, but I think we should ask after all this."

Puppy reached them, beaming like she had just found an old friend at a festival rather than stumbled into a slaughter.

The guards barely stood a chance. They were overwhelmed, ripped apart like meat thrown to a pack of starving wolves.

Across the room, Lord Rukarus floundered, his rotund form rolling onto his side in a pathetic attempt to escape. But Dar and Kot, the halfling duo leading the charge, weren't about to let that happen.

They descended on him with gleeful laughter, their small but strong hands latching onto his limbs. He thrashed and screamed as they sank their jagged teeth into him, tearing away flesh, ripping him apart one agonizing bite at a time.

He was still alive as they feasted. Still squirming.

For the halflings, that only made the meal taste better.

The carnage stretched on for what felt like half an hour before the last screams finally faded into silence. The mansion was nothing but a slaughterhouse now, corpses strewn across the floor in grotesque arrangements.

The halflings meandered through the aftermath, patting their full bellies, letting out satisfied belches. Blood dripped from their chins.

Dar and Kot strolled up to Puppy, who was still unsteady but grinning all the same.

"Aye," Dar chuckled, licking his fingers clean. "You were right, my dear Blight. Good meals were to be had here."

Puppy laughed, a strange glint in her eye, and for the first time since they met her, Devaultus wasn't quite sure what to make of her.

He tilted his head, his sharp golden eyes gleaming with curiosity as he took in the strange exchange before him. "Blight, is it?" he mused, a smirk creeping onto his lips. His tone was playful, but his interest had been piqued. The girl who had once been Puppy gave a small, shy smile in return, a faint blush dusting her cheeks.

Vex, however, was still wound tight like a coiled viper, her muscles tense and her gaze darting around for any lingering threats. Devaultus didn't miss the twitch in her eye, the barely restrained violence that lingered beneath the surface. He knew her well enough to recognize that she was still in fight mode, ready to cut down anyone who so much as breathed wrongly in her direction. With a calm, assured voice, he spoke.

"It's okay, Vex."

The effect was immediate. The tension bled from Vex's body as though someone had cut the strings holding her upright. Without hesitation, she sprang forward and threw her arms around Blight, squeezing her tightly.

"Puppy! I've missed you!" Vex's voice was filled with something rare: unrestrained joy.

Blight hesitated for a split second, considering telling Vex that she wasn't Puppy anymore, that she had been given a new name, a new identity. But... she liked the way Vex said it. The warmth in her voice, the familiarity: it made her feel safe. And safety was something she hadn't felt in a long time.

Smiling softly, she returned the embrace.

Vex pulled back, her violet eyes flashing with excitement. "How did you find us?"

Blight grinned and reached into her pouch. "Found this on the ground near where we were supposed to meet. Figured something went sideways." She held up a dagger, the silver blade catching the dim light.

Devaultus' expression shifted instantly. His mouth dropped open before spreading into a delighted grin. "Sheila!" he exclaimed, reaching out eagerly.

Blight extended the dagger handle-first, and to everyone's surprise, instead of simply taking it, Devaultus hugged it.

Actually hugged it.

Blight arched a brow, and Vex just sighed, clearly used to his antics. Devaultus eventually composed himself, well, as much as he ever did, and tucked the blade away, exhaling in satisfaction. Then, with the carefree confidence of a man who had just walked through hell and come out grinning, he turned back to the two women.

"Right then. I suppose our time here is limited." He took a moment to gather his thoughts before his lips curled into an expression of mild irritation. "Vera'Ala'..." He stopped mid-sentence, his brow furrowing in annoyance. "Ugh, how the hell did he say that ridiculous name again?" He waved a dismissive hand. "Who names their kid that? What happened to simple names? Like Jim. Or Kyle. Or even Jeff." He scoffed, shaking his head. "You know what? Screw it. Let's just call this pompous ass Bob. His name gives me a headache."

Vex and Blight exchanged glances, then nodded in agreement. Bob it was.

Devaultus clapped his hands together. "Anyway! First things first. We hit the Sweetwater Inn, grab my things, find a ship, and then..." He cracked his knuckles, his grin turning razor-sharp. "We go kill Bob. He's really starting to piss me off."

With that, the trio stepped out of the blood-drenched room, leaving behind the chaos and carnage, walking straight into whatever madness awaited them next.

## CHAPTER 7

# TAKEN: FANTASY EDITION

After a rather bizarre conversation, one in which Blight had to carefully and repeatedly explain to Dar and Kot that, no, Devaultus and Vex were not, in fact, an appetizer, the group finally parted ways with the halflings. Much to the disappointment of Dar and Kot, they had been quite set on claiming Blight as their own personal battle pet. The thought alone sent a shiver down Blight's spine. As much as she had grown strangely fond of their savagery, she had no desire to live among the chaos-fueled creatures. They were too unpredictable, too wild. She, on the other hand, preferred the safety and control that came with Devaultus and Vex.

Which, in hindsight, was hilarious.

Because Devaultus and Vex had done nothing but get themselves into insane, borderline catastrophic trouble since the moment she met them.

Blissfully unaware of the irony, Blight trudged along with her two companions, exhaustion creeping into her every step as they made their way toward the Sweetwater Inn. The night air was crisp, and the flickering lanterns lining the streets cast long, eerie shadows that danced with each passing figure. The trio moved in their usual manner, Devaultus striding ahead with his ever-present air of confidence, Vex bouncing beside him with a giddy, almost childlike energy, and Blight keeping slightly behind, quiet and ever watchful.

After a long stretch of silence, Blight finally spoke.

"Did you find your ring?" she asked, her voice soft but curious.

At once, Vex's face lit up, her expression brimming with excitement. "Oh! You bet I did! I found *lots* of rings."

Devaultus let out a slow exhale, pinching the bridge of his nose as he muttered, "We really need to talk about that."

Vex, completely unbothered, tilted her head and smiled at him as though she had done him the greatest favor in the world. "You wanted rings," she pointed out cheerfully. "I set out to bring you rings."

She beamed as if that settled the matter entirely.

Devaultus sighed. This was going to be a problem.

As much as he loved a good dose of chaos, it had to be carefully orchestrated, deliberate. Not this... *whatever the hell Vex had done.* He shook his head, deciding that this was a conversation for later. First, they had to figure out where to find Bob, or whatever the hell his real name was, and how they were going to reach him.

Nearly an hour passed before they finally arrived at the Sweetwater Inn, its familiar warm glow welcoming them like an old friend. But the moment they stepped inside, their path was abruptly halted.

A woman stood in their way.

She had thick curls of dark brown hair, caramel-colored skin, and eyes that gleamed with a sharp, no-nonsense authority. Though her stance was poised and refined, there was an undeniable ferocity to her presence, a weight of power that demanded attention. She wasn't just anyone.

Caralana Sweetwater.

Devaultus had encountered her once or twice before, though never in any personal capacity. He knew enough about her to be wary. She didn't bother with pleasantries, she had a way about her that revealed she knew far more than others believed her to.

He had a feeling he wasn't going to enjoy this meeting.

"You and I need to talk," Caralana said coolly, her voice smooth but firm. Then, her gaze flicked to Vex and Blight.

"And bring your friends."

Devaultus hesitated for only a moment before offering one of his trademark grins. This was unexpected... and possibly *very bad*. He knew better than to think she was just inviting them in for a friendly chat.

Still, there was no point in refusing.

"Very well, ma'am," he said smoothly, inclining his head before stepping forward.

Vex and Blight followed close behind, exchanging a brief but knowing glance.

Caralana led them into a private office, its walls lined with maps, ledgers, and various trinkets from distant lands. She stepped behind a large wooden desk, settling into her chair with practiced ease.

Then, with a single, commanding gesture, she motioned toward the three empty seats in front of her.

"Sit."

And just like that, the real game began.

Devaultus waited until both women were seated before he casually, yet deliberately, eased himself into his own chair. His posture was relaxed, but his mind was already calculating, analyzing the situation before him. He met Caralana's gaze with a sharp, curious glint in his eye.

"What seems to be the problem, Caralana?" he asked smoothly, his voice carrying an almost lazy amusement.

The woman before him, all sharp edges and knowing glances, rested her chin on her interlaced fingers, studying him with an intensity that set alarms off in his head.

"Let's cut to the chase, Devaultus," she said, her tone firm but unreadable.

Devaultus stiffened, though only slightly. His mind instantly latched onto the name she had used. Not Lindgurth. Devaultus. His real name. His true self.

Now, that was a problem.

His entire existence thrived on secrecy, deception, and careful manipulation of identity. He had killed entire villages before to protect what he was. He didn't just survive by shifting faces, he thrived in the shadows of anonymity. There were very few people alive who knew the truth, and even fewer who had been allowed to keep that knowledge.

His expression didn't change, but his fingers twitched toward his daggers.

She noticed. Of course, she did.

"Settle down, Devaultus," Caralana said smoothly, a small, knowing smile tugging at the corner of her lips. "I've known for some time. If I had any intention of revealing your little secret, trust me, the whole damn city would already know."

His expression remained cool, but his grip on the hilts of his blades beneath the table tightened.

"And what exactly is stopping me from silencing you permanently?" he asked, his voice dipping into something darker, laced with the subtle promise of violence.

Caralana barely reacted. She merely tilted her head slightly, amusement flickering in her eyes.

"I suppose you could try," she admitted, her tone almost inviting.

Devaultus didn't like that answer. His muscles coiled, as he prepared to spring. His daggers, though still sheathed, were already in his hands, ready to end the conversation in an instant.

But then, she continued.

"Though I wouldn't advise it," she said, her voice like silk wrapped around steel. "You see, I have a talent for obtaining information.

And right now, my people have informed me that you're looking for someone. Vera'Ala'Roja Bobalata'Cora."

Devaultus instantly grimaced, putting a hand up in protest.

"Yeah, yeah, no, we're not doing that," he interrupted, shaking his head as though the name itself physically pained him. "We call him Bob. Nobody in their right mind wants to waste time trying to spit out that abomination of a name."

Caralana chuckled, the corners of her lips quirking upward in approval.

"Very well. Bob, then," she conceded before continuing. "He is not a man who hides. In fact, he enjoys being found. He thrives on it. He takes pleasure in publicly humiliating those who come after him, watching them struggle before crushing them entirely. That is why I must insist, let this one go, Devaultus."

The smirk that stretched across Devaultus' lips was slow, dangerous, and utterly unconcerned.

"Oh, Caralana," he mused, leaning back in his chair, his voice laced with amusement and something far sharper. "You should know by now, that's not really my thing."

He leaned forward slightly, that sharp glint returning to his gaze, all humor vanishing in an instant.

"Bob is a problem," he said, his voice calm, yet carrying the weight of certainty. "Not just for me, but for plenty of people. And I don't particularly like problems that think they're untouchable." His smirk widened. "So, I think I'll just wander on over and kill him."

The air in the room shifted, tension crackling between them like an unspoken challenge.

Caralana watched him carefully, and for a moment, silence hung heavy in the space between them. Then, she exhaled through her nose, shaking her head slightly, almost in exasperation.

Devaultus only grinned wider.

Caralana exhaled sharply, the sound laced with exasperation as she leaned back in her chair. Her sharp eyes never left Devaultus. "You couldn't even defeat his lackey, The Puppeteer."

Devaultus' mouth parted as if he had an immediate retort, but then he hesitated, brow furrowing. He clicked his tongue in irritation. "I assure you, that particular annoyance won't be a problem for much longer. His time is running out."

Caralana arched an eyebrow, unimpressed. She ran a hand through her thick curls before giving him a pointed look. "Right. Of course, he will. Though I imagine it will have to be someone else who puts him down for good. Because let's be honest, you step into his web again, and he'll just pull your strings like a puppet."

A flicker of anger passed through Devaultus' eyes. He hated how smug she sounded. Hated even more how right she might be. But above all, what truly burned at him was the nagging question: how in the Abyss did she know so much?

His fingers twitched beneath the table, itching toward his daggers. She knew too much. That alone made her dangerous. Perhaps too dangerous to be left breathing. His gaze darkened, a storm brewing behind his smirk, but Caralana caught it instantly.

Her lips curled in amusement, as if she could hear his very thoughts. "Oh, don't give me that look, Devaultus. We already came to the understanding: if I wanted to spill your secrets, they'd already be out in the open. But instead, I'm offering you something useful."

With a deliberate motion, she reached into her desk and slid a small, unassuming pouch across the table toward him. "Consider this a loan. You've been a useful employee to me in the past, but not *that* useful."

Devaultus eyed the bag with mild suspicion before plucking it from the table. Loosening the drawstrings, he peered inside and immediately perked up. His expression shifted to one of intrigue as he reached in and pulled out a ring, rolling it between his fingers.

It was well-crafted, shimmering faintly in the candlelight with an unmistakable arcane presence.

A grin spread across his face, sharp and delighted, but the moment passed when he realized, this wasn't the ring he had been looking for.

Part of him had expected more from Caralana. With all her vast knowledge and the countless secrets she seemed to collect like trinkets, surely she would have known exactly which ring he sought. A part of him had even imagined her producing it with a smirk, sliding it across the table just to get him out of her hair. That would have been the efficient thing to do, the calculated move he had come to expect from someone like her.

And yet... she hadn't.

That left him with two possibilities: either she truly didn't know which ring he was searching for, or she did and had chosen not to give it to him. The thought gnawed at him. He had studied her every movement, every subtle shift of expression, but she had revealed nothing. No flicker of recognition, no smug satisfaction, no telltale hesitation.

Caralana had played the conversation with a masterful neutrality, leaving him uncertain whether she was ignorant or simply toying with him.

It irritated him more than he cared to admit.

Still, it was magical. And that made it interesting.

"What's the catch?" he asked, narrowing his eyes.

Caralana smirked. "No catch. Just a bit of insurance. This will help ward off mental attacks. It's not perfect, you won't be invincible, but it'll make things much harder for someone like The Puppeteer to get inside your head." She raised her own hand, tapping a ring on her finger identical to the one she had just given him. "I wear one myself, for obvious reasons."

Devaultus exhaled through his nose, staring at the ring with a mix of amusement and contemplation before slipping it onto his finger.

Caralana continued, crossing one leg over the other. "Now, if you're dead set on finding Bob, and I know you are, I know someone who can help. But nothing comes for free. You'll most likely have to prove yourself first. Maybe run an errand or two. She doesn't lift a finger without a price."

Devaultus let out a long, exaggerated sigh, tilting his head back dramatically. "Of course. Because nothing can ever be simple, can it?"

Caralana grinned. "Not in this world."

He smirked back at her, already rolling through possibilities in his mind. He despised getting sidetracked. But if this was what it took to get to Bob... then so be it.

"Her name is Al'Shandra," Caralana said, her lips curling into a knowing smile. "She is... well, you'll see soon enough."

She slid a slip of parchment across the desk toward Devaultus, the aged paper whispering against the wood as it moved. With a slow, deliberate motion, he picked it up, his sharp eyes scanning the address written in precise, elegant script. He committed it to memory instantly, burning the details deep into his mind.

Beside him, Vex and Blight sat in silence, their gazes flicking between Caralana and Devaultus, absorbing every word. The tension in the room was subtle but undeniable, like a thin wire stretched between two warriors just waiting to snap.

Caralana leaned back in her chair, watching them with the ease of someone who knew she had control of the situation. She gestured toward the door with an elegant flick of her wrist, silently dismissing them. "That will be all," she said.

Devaultus hesitated for the briefest of moments. Every fiber of his being screamed at him to end her. The fact that she knew so much about him, about his abilities, about his intentions, it made her a dangerous loose end. One that, in any other circumstance, he would have cut without a second thought. But... Caralana was a resource. A powerful one. And for now, she would remain untouched.

With a slow exhale, he turned toward the door. "Ladies," he called, his voice light, masking the storm within his mind.

Vex and Blight rose from their seats, moving in step behind him, but before they could leave, Caralana's voice stopped them.

"Wait."

The two women turned to face her.

Caralana's smile was gone now, replaced with something more serious, more knowing. Her gaze settled on them with an intensity that made Blight's breath catch in her throat.

"Keep him safe," she said, her voice low but firm. "I have a feeling he might be important in the near future."

Blight's eyes widened slightly, her face paling at the weight of those words. Slowly, she nodded.

Vex, on the other hand, simply grinned, throwing Caralana a playful thumbs-up as if the whole situation were nothing more than a game. "Don't worry," she said with a wink. "He's in good hands."

With that, the trio stepped out of the room, the door closing behind them with a finality that left an unspoken promise lingering in the air.

Once outside, Devaultus barely held back his frustration, forcing a smile as he turned to Fro'Dovin. "I'll send for my chest later," he said smoothly, offering a casual wave before stepping out the door. But the moment he was clear of the building, his composure shattered like glass.

"How *dare* she!" he erupted, his form shifting seamlessly back into his usual appearance. His hands curled into fists at his sides, his jaw tightening as his face turned a shade darker with irritation. Why did Caralana knowing so much *bother* him the way it did? He had walked away with everything he needed; more, even, so why did it feel like she had gotten the better of him?

Vex, on the other hand, was absolutely delighted. She let out a gleeful giggle, spinning in place with childlike excitement. "I *liked* her," she declared, throwing her hands in the air as if gesturing to an invisible display. "She had *so much cool stuff* in there!"

Devaultus arched an eyebrow, his sharp gaze flickering toward her hands, where, much to his complete lack of surprise, a few more rings now adorned her fingers. More than before. Oh, fantastic. Had she actually *stolen* from Caralana? Again? He sighed. He was starting to suspect that Vex had an incurable compulsion to take anything that wasn't nailed down. A problem for *tomorrow's* Devaultus, perhaps.

Shaking off his irritation, he straightened his coat and turned toward his companions. "Now then," he announced, regaining his usual flair, "to the northern docks."

Unlike the sprawling ocean harbors he had seen in other worlds, the docks here were an entirely different breed, built not for water-bound vessels, but for *sandships*. Massive contraptions designed to sail across endless dunes. It was an absurd concept to him, and frankly, he had *no idea* how they actually worked. Magic? Unlikely. This world had a frustrating scarcity of magic, so that couldn't be it. Perhaps some kind of mechanical ingenuity? He grinned at the thought. He did *love* learning new things. Knowledge was power, after all, and power was something he fully intended to hoard like a dragon with its gold.

With a newfound excitement for discovery, he led the trio toward the docks, weaving their way through the bustling marketplace. The air was thick with the scent of exotic spices, sizzling meats, and the unmistakable tang of hot sand. Traders shouted their wares, eager hands exchanged coin for goods, and the hum of a thousand voices layered into the background of their journey.

Whatever awaited them at the northern docks, Devaultus was ready. Or at least, he planned to *pretend* he was.

The marketplace was alive with frantic energy, the air thick with whispers and hushed conversations. News of Lord Rukarus' gruesome demise had spread like wildfire, infecting every vendor stall and street corner like a plague. The merchants spoke in hushed tones, their voices laced with both horror and morbid fascination as they described how the halflings had torn through the manor, leaving a wake of blood and carnage.

Devaultus, walking with his usual confident stride, looked annoyed by the gossip. His irritation only deepened as Blight, her voice filled with wonder, commented, "Well, at least nobody knows we were there."

He turned his head toward her, an exaggerated expression of disappointment plastered across his face. "How could you say that? Did you not see the one-sided grin I painted on the wall? The Grin was there! He did all of that and saved the day!"

Blight blinked, clearly confused. She tilted her head slightly, trying to recall any such presence at the mansion. "The Grin?" she echoed. "I've never heard of him. I didn't see him there at all. Where was he?"

Devaultus let out a grumble, rubbing his temples as though her words physically pained him. "Never mind," he muttered, sounding deeply put out.

The truth was, *he* was The Grin. His self-made persona, the phantom of justice, the lurking terror of villains, the shadow in the night, none of which seemed to have caught on. How, in all the Abyss, had people failed to talk about him? This was beyond frustrating. What was the point of crafting such an ominous and infamous identity if no one even recognized it?

Blight, still looking perplexed, replayed the events of the mansion in her head, scanning her memories for any trace of this so-called Grin.

No dark figure, no mysterious savior, nothing. The only people there were herself, Vex, Devaultus, and the raging halfling cannibals. Maybe Devaultus had simply been drinking too much ale again.

As they moved through the marketplace, dodging frantic townsfolk and weaving through stalls brimming with exotic goods, Devaultus' frustration over his ignored alter ego gradually faded. However, another concern was brewing: Vex, as usual, had acquired more *items* during their stroll, her pockets noticeably heavier than when they had entered. He decided to ignore it for now. Future Devaultus could deal with Vex's compulsive theft.

Finally, they made their way past the last of the marketplace's chaos and neared the docks.

And that was when Devaultus saw it.

A massive sandship loomed ahead, docked at the edge of the shifting dunes. His irritation evaporated instantly, replaced by childlike wonder. His eyes widened, a delighted grin stretching across his face. "Would you look at that," he breathed, barely containing his excitement. "How incredibly interesting."

The vessel looked much like a traditional sea ship, but with key differences: massive chains, carved from an unusual, dark stone, extended downward from its hull. These chains connected to immense sleigh-like runners that rested against the sand, giving the impression that the ship was meant to *glide* across the desert rather than sail on water.

His mind buzzed with curiosity. *How did it move? Was it propelled by wind? Some intricate system of pulleys? No, surely not magic.*

He *had* to learn more.

Vex, however, was less concerned with the ship and more with whatever shiny objects she could get her hands on. Blight, ever alert, simply took in her surroundings, her eyes darting between the dockworkers and the ship, scanning for any potential threats.

Devaultus, grinning ear to ear, took a few eager steps forward.

This was going to be *fun.*

Devaultus found himself utterly captivated as they made their way down the dock, his sharp eyes scanning every fascinating detail of their surroundings. The air was thick with the scent of sun-baked wood, mingled with the subtle aroma of oil and machinery from the massive sandship towering ahead. But what truly caught his attention, and that of many others, was the enormous, armored creature hanging at the far end of the dock.

It was a sandshark.

The beast was a monstrous seventeen feet long, its body covered in thick, jagged plating that seemed almost impenetrable. A natural armor against the relentless sun and whatever predators lurked above the dunes. Its massive, gaping maw bristled with rows of serrated teeth, and its dull, lifeless eyes still held a haunting presence. Devaultus had heard rumors of such creatures, whispered tales of ships being swallowed whole beneath the sands, of entire caravans lost to their insatiable hunger. But seeing one in the flesh, massive, imposing, and very, very dead, was something else entirely. He couldn't help but wonder how anyone had managed to take down something so formidable.

Filing away that curiosity for later, Devaultus returned his attention to the docks as they continued forward, moving steadily toward their destination. The towering sandship loomed closer, its intricate chains of an unknown stone connecting to sleigh-like runners buried in the sand. He had so many questions about how it functioned, how it could possibly glide across the dunes like a sea vessel upon the waves.

But then, he saw them.

A cluster of soldiers stood near the entrance to the ship, waiting. Their armor gleamed under the sun, polished and pristine, their stances rigid and disciplined. Immediately, Devaultus tensed, his instincts flaring with warning. Soldiers were rarely a good sign, and in his experience, when they gathered like this, it was never for a friendly chat. His sharp gaze flicked over their uniforms, as he recognized the insignia emblazoned on their chests. It was the same as on the guards he'd encountered before, the ones who had once been with Vex.

Slowly, his focus shifted to her.

She had changed.

All traces of her usual carefree mischief had vanished, her body stiffening as if she had just been plunged into icy water. Her vibrant energy dulled, drained away by something deeper than mere caution, something closer to pure terror. Devaultus had seen her fight with reckless abandon, laugh in the face of danger, and steal without a second thought. But this? This was different. Her wide, golden eyes were distant, filled with something raw and unspoken. It was as if the entire world was closing in around her, and she had nowhere to run.

"Vex...?" Devaultus called her name softly, but she barely reacted.

Then came the sound.

The rhythmic, deliberate clanking of armor from behind them. Devaultus' sharp ears caught the heavy footfalls of another unit moving down the docks, boxing them in. A glance over his shoulder confirmed it, more soldiers, moving with quiet purpose, their expressions unreadable. They were not in an offensive stance, but their presence alone made their intent clear. This was not a casual encounter. This was a retrieval.

A capture.

Then, Vex whispered something so faint, so broken, that it was barely audible.

"Father..."

The procession of soldiers came to a sudden halt.

And then, stepping through their ranks, came a man who could only be described as a living monolith.

He was massive, built like a war machine, his powerful frame encased in pristine armor that gleamed in the sunlight. A massive sword, easily the size of Devaultus himself, was strapped to his back. The weight of it alone should have been a burden, yet he carried it as if it were nothing. His presence radiated authority, his movements were sharp and precise, controlled in a way that spoke of absolute discipline. He held his helmet under one arm, his features carved from stone, stern, unreadable, yet undeniably commanding.

When he spoke, his voice was deep, unwavering, and laced with an unshakable power.

"Hello, Lorivelle."

Vex, no, Lorivelle, seemed to shrink at the sound of it, her usual fire utterly extinguished. It was not fear of battle that gripped her, it was something deeper, something personal.

Something inescapable.

Devaultus' fingers twitched toward his daggers.

This was about to get interesting.

Devaultus took careful note of her reaction, the way her body tensed, the way her expression twisted into something resembling fear. No, not just fear. Resignation. His sharp eyes flicked back to the imposing man before them, taking in every detail of the man's stance, his demeanor, the barely restrained authority in his voice.

The large man's piercing gaze shifted toward Devaultus, his expression dripping with irritation and disdain. "And who, exactly, might you be, that you should dare to accompany a noblewoman?" His deep voice carried the weight of someone who was used to giving orders, someone who expected obedience.

Devaultus, never one to shy away from theatrics, allowed a slow, amused smirk to spread across his lips. Without missing a beat, he gave a graceful, overly elaborate bow, sweeping his arm out in an exaggerated flourish. "Caster Anton, at your service, my Lord." His voice had shifted as he adopted an accent foreign to these lands, something from a place far beyond this one, dripping with the smooth charm of a seasoned trickster.

Somewhere along the way, his appearance had altered. His face now bore a jagged scar running down one cheek, a phantom wound from some fabricated battle of the past. One of his eyes, glazed over as though it had long since lost its function, only added to the illusion. Even his posture had changed, making him seem slightly hunched, as though years of hardship had weighed him down.

The man, Tarus, no doubt, narrowed his gaze at him, as if trying to see through the deception, then turned his focus back to Vex. His voice, though measured, carried an undercurrent of barely restrained anger. "You will come with me, Lorivelle. We have much to discuss regarding your whereabouts these past weeks."

Vex visibly paled, her hands clenching at her sides. "If you will allow me a moment to say goodbye to my escort," she said softly, her voice barely above a whisper.

Tarus gave a slight nod, and she stepped toward Devaultus. She hesitated only a moment before wrapping her arms around him, pressing herself close as she whispered urgently into his ear. "Don't come after me," she pleaded, her voice trembling. "He's too powerful. You can't fight him. I will always serve you, but we can't escape him. You can't win."

Devaultus simply grinned, winking his one "working" eye at her. "I'll see you soon," he murmured, the words carrying an undeniable promise.

As she pulled back, her eyes shimmered with unshed tears. She knew him. Knew how he was. Knew that telling him not to do something was the surest way to ensure that he would do exactly that. A sinking feeling filled her chest. He would come for her. She knew it. And she also knew that her father would have no hesitation in killing him where he stood.

Turning away, she forced herself to move forward, to follow Tarus as he led her through the sea of armored soldiers, away from Devaultus and into the unknown.

Devaultus stood motionless as he watched the procession of soldiers escort Vex away, his sharp gaze never leaving her retreating figure. A strange sensation twisted in his gut, an emotion he couldn't quite place, something between irritation and intrigue.

Then, like a whisper of silk against steel, a voice coiled around him from somewhere above. Smooth, teasing, and honeyed with amusement.

"Got yerself into a bit of a situation, did ya?"

His instincts flared, and he turned his head upward. There, leaning lazily over the railing of the massive sandship, was a woman who looked as if she had been sculpted from the very essence of temptation itself. A sinuous hourglass figure draped in dark leather and deep crimson cloth that did nothing to conceal her more... notable assets. Waves of fiery red hair cascaded over her shoulders, framing a face that was both wicked and breathtaking, the kind of beauty that men wrote songs about, and then died for.

Devaultus allowed his gaze to roam, unabashed in his appreciation, though his eyes never lingered long in one place. He knew better than to underestimate someone who commanded attention so effortlessly.

"And who might you be?" he asked, his voice cool, measured, and laced with curiosity.

The woman let out a sultry laugh, the sound rolling over him like the promise of trouble.

"I'm the ship's captain," she purred, tilting her head slightly. "That's all ye need to know for now."

Devaultus studied her, a smirk tugging at his lips. Mysterious, bold, and clearly amused by him, dangerous in all the best ways.

"I require passage for three," he stated simply, his tone as firm as it was casual.

The captain lifted a delicate hand, covering one of her piercing green eyes as if shielding it from the sun while she exaggeratedly counted the members of his party.

"I only count two, my dear," she said with mock concern, tapping a finger against her plush lips. Then, with a knowing smirk, she let her eyes flicker toward where Vex had disappeared. "I dare say ye should leave that blonde one be. Ye won't be seein' her again."

The words hung in the air like a challenge.

Devaultus' smirk didn't falter, but his fingers twitched at his sides.

He didn't take kindly to being told what he couldn't do.

The woman's laughter was rich and teasing, a sultry purr that curled around her words like smoke. "If you need someone to warm your bed, use the dark-haired one... or mine," she added with a slow, knowing smirk. There was no subtlety to her offer, no coyness, just raw confidence.

Devaultus arched a brow, mildly impressed by her forwardness. It wasn't often someone could match his own brazenness, let alone surpass it. Still, he had other matters to attend to. He cast a glance back at the dwindling figures of the soldiers disappearing into the streets. "When does the ship leave?" he asked, his voice even but his mind already calculating.

"Two hours' time," she replied with a lazy, catlike stretch that caused one of her ample curves to nearly slip free of the barely-contained fabric of her top. If the movement was accidental, she made no effort to correct it. Devaultus was beginning to suspect very little about this woman was accidental.

He nodded, filing the information away. "May my companion stay aboard in safety for a few hours?"

The captain tilted her head, giving Blight a slow, appraising look. It was the same expression a merchant might wear when inspecting a piece of jewelry, half curious, half indifferent. Then she simply shrugged, the motion causing yet another shift in her already precariously placed clothing. "Very well," she said, smirking. "But if you're not here to pay when we leave, we'll leave her here too."

Devaultus inclined his head slightly, acknowledging her terms. "Fair enough. I'll be back soon."

With that, he turned on his heel, his confident stride carrying him back down the dock. His mind, however, was razor-focused. Tarus had taken Vex. That much was clear. And though she had pleaded with him not to follow, Devaultus had never been the type to take orders from anyone, least of all someone he considered his own.

If they thought they could take something from him without consequence, they were gravely mistaken.

His pace quickened, his boots tapping against the wooden planks before shifting to the solid cobblestone of the street. The soldiers ahead marched with precision, their heavy footfalls a steady rhythm against the city's noise. Devaultus moved with purpose, veering into a narrow alleyway without hesitation.

When he emerged on the other side, his entire form had changed.

Gone was the rogue's sharp grin and casual posture. In his place walked a soldier of Tarus' personal guard, broad-shouldered, armored, with a grim set to his jaw. His movements were exact, his stride falling seamlessly in line with the other soldiers as they made their way through the bustling streets.

The city folk recognized authority when they saw it. People hurried to clear the way, stepping aside as the soldiers passed.

And Devaultus, hidden among them, was already planning his next move.

Devaultus moved in perfect rhythm with the guards, his every step mirroring theirs as they strode down the bustling streets. He kept his posture rigid, his face stern, just another soldier in Tarus' ranks, nothing more. But his keen eyes missed nothing. Every shift in the crowd, every glance exchanged by the officers, every subtle movement was cataloged in his mind.

It wasn't long before something particularly interesting caught his attention. A man, clad in the same uniform as the others, rushed forward with urgency, his boots clanking against the stone as he approached a lieutenant. The officer was distinguished by an odd-looking cape draped over one shoulder, the fabric embroidered with intricate patterns that suggested rank or prestige. Devaultus angled his head ever so slightly, his sharp hearing straining to pick up the rushed exchange between them.

A message. A runner delivering information.

Now that was something useful.

Vex had feared this man, her father, for a reason. A reason Devaultus did not yet fully understand. But fear? Fear was his domain. He was the shadow lurking in nightmares, the whisper in the dark that sent shivers down spines. Vex had underestimated him, thinking he would charge in with reckless violence. No, that was far too crude. While he did enjoy a bit of bloodshed now and then, there was a greater thrill in control. In standing amidst his enemies, unseen, unknown, holding their fates in his hands like a puppeteer with his strings.

This Tarus, this so-called god among men, had no idea Devaultus was already in his midst.

The thought sent a wicked thrill through him.

As the procession advanced, they neared a caravan of carts, each drawn by enormous, muscular lizards. Their scales shimmered in the sun, patterns of deep gold and russet rippling as they moved. Devaultus had seen many creatures in his time, but these beasts were something else: glorious, formidable, powerful. He made a mental note to look into them later.

Laughter rang through the air as a group of children sprinted past, their voices high and carefree. They threw a ball, crudely fashioned from the intestines of some unfortunate creature, back and forth with giddy excitement. Their innocence was such a stark contrast to the grim world of soldiers and war.

And then, in the blink of an eye, there was one less soldier in Tarus' ranks and one more child laughing and playing in the streets.

Devaultus had melted into his new form effortlessly, his body shrinking, his armor vanishing. He was now a wide-eyed child, his feet kicking up dust as he darted among the others. He whooped and hollered with the best of them, blending in seamlessly. Just another child in the street, chasing after a ball.

And just like that, he had disappeared.

Lorivelle followed her father in silence, her footsteps barely making a sound against the cobbled streets as he stormed ahead with a rigid, commanding presence. His heavy boots struck the ground with purpose, each step seething with restrained fury. The moment they reached the waiting carriage, he wrenched the door open without a word and climbed inside.

She hesitated for only a breath before stepping in after him, her body tense, as though bracing for an unseen blow. Sliding onto the bench opposite him, she folded her hands neatly in her lap, her fingers twisting together in an effort to suppress the rising tide of unease. Her gaze remained fixed on the floor, unwilling to meet his eyes, knowing full well the storm that raged behind them.

Then, the inevitable.

"What did you think would happen, Lorivelle?" Tarus' voice was a blade, sharp and unforgiving. "You vanish without a word and scurry about with street filth, dragging our name through the mud."

Her head snapped up, her mouth opening before she could think better of it. "They aren't..."

A single raised hand silenced her.

"Did you forget your place?" His tone was like ice now, measured, deliberate, cutting deep. "I have received reports. My men tell me you had a hand in the fall of Lord Rukarus. That you've slain countless Plague members. Do you have any idea what you've done? You've put me in a position of vulnerability, and I do not tolerate weakness."

He held her in his glare, his fury barely leashed, but there was something else there too. Calculation.

"At least," he continued, his lips curling slightly, "one good thing has come of this. Word of your... exploits has reached Lord Cojar. He wishes to reassess you."

Lorivelle's breath caught in her throat. The world around her blurred as memories flooded in, crashing into her like an unforgiving tide.

The acrid scent of burning flesh filled her nostrils. She could see the dust from Kanasha's body as the flames reduced her to nothing but ashes. Could hear the chains rattling as Letty was led away, her terrified eyes pleading for help that would never come.

No.

Panic twisted in her chest, coiling like a viper. "No, Father, please..."

"Silence."

Tarus' voice was final, unyielding. "You will fulfill your duty. Your purpose is to elevate this family above all others, just as your sisters have before you. You will not shame me further."

Lorivelle swallowed hard, her fingers clenching together until her knuckles went white. There was no escape. There never had been.

Then, three sharp knocks against the carriage door.

A runner stood outside, his posture rigid, his face void of emotion as he waited for Tarus to acknowledge him.

Tarus let out a slow breath, reining in his irritation before finally speaking. "Yes? What is it?"

The soldier saluted crisply before delivering his report. "My Lord. Our forces on the western front have been ambushed. We do not yet know the assailant's identity, but we believe they have a fighter of considerable strength."

Tarus' expression darkened. A flicker of something unreadable crossed his face.

And for the first time since she had stepped into the carriage, Lorivelle felt a sliver of hope.

"He's tearing through our brigade, my Lord," the soldier reported, his voice tight with urgency.

Lord Tarus' face darkened like a thundercloud before the storm, his lips curling into a sneer of pure contempt. "Who would dare strike at my men?" His tone was sharp, laced with outrage. But as quickly as his anger flared, it settled into something cold and decisive. "No matter," he muttered, stepping out of the carriage in a swift, purposeful motion. His sharp gaze flicked to his lieutenants, who snapped to attention.

Then, his eyes landed on Lorivelle, his expression a mask of ironclad authority. "You will remain here." The words were final, heavy with the kind of power that left no room for defiance. He turned and barked at the six guards standing nearby, "Do not let her leave unless I command it."

The soldiers thumped their fists against their chests in salute, their postures rigid with discipline. Without another word, Tarus spun on his heel, his thick cape billowing behind him as he strode toward the battlefield. His voice rang out like a war drum. "Let's go teach these street rats a lesson."

The carriage door slammed shut, leaving Lorivelle alone with the deafening silence of her own thoughts. She sat there, stiff and motionless, staring down at her hands as her mind raced with unwanted possibilities. She knew her father's strength, had witnessed it firsthand countless times. No one, not even Devaultus, could match him in combat. The thought of Devaultus lying bloodied and broken under her father's blade made her stomach churn.

She prayed it wasn't him.

Minutes dragged by, stretching into what felt like an eternity. Then, the sound of armored boots pounding against the ground reached her ears. Voices followed, her father's chief among them, his deep baritone heavy with irritation.

"Pathetic," Tarus growled, his voice carrying easily through the thick wooden frame of the carriage. "It wasn't even a challenge. I should never have had to lift my own blade." His disgust was palpable. "Surrounded by incompetents. Every last one of them."

The door handle rattled.

Lorivelle sat up straight, her breath catching as the carriage door swung open.

Tarus stepped inside, his presence filling the space with an almost suffocating weight. Blood spattered his once-pristine armor, smeared across his cheek like war paint. The scent of iron and sweat clung to him, a stark reminder of whatever carnage had just taken place.

His jaw clenched as he exhaled sharply, shaking his head in exasperation. "Now we wait for the rest of my brigade. They're handling the last of the clean-up." His fingers flexed as he opened a hidden compartment within the seat. From it, he retrieved a large, heavy pouch of coins, the leather bulging with wealth. He weighed it in his hand, the clinking of gold filling the tense air.

Lorivelle swallowed hard.

Her fate was sealed. And there was nothing she could do about it.

The guards exchanged uncertain glances, their unease apparent. Tarus never made casual decisions, and this sudden change in plans put them on edge. His voice, firm and commanding, cut through their hesitation.

"Lorivelle and I will get something to eat from that vendor while we wait. The sun is merciless today."

Vex furrowed her brows, confusion flashing across her face. Her father had never lowered himself to eating street fare. He had always demanded the finest cuisine, served on silver platters by trembling attendants. The very idea of him buying food from a common vendor was absurd.

Yet, without hesitation, Tarus stepped down from the carriage, his heavy boots striking the ground with authority. His cape billowed behind him as he strode forward, his presence alone causing pedestrians to scatter like frightened insects. A path cleared before him as he moved, his sheer presence demanding obedience.

Vex hesitated but followed, her arms folded tightly against her chest, her unease growing with every step.

"You should savor this," Tarus muttered, his deep voice laced with a chilling promise. "It will be the last decent meal you have for a long time. Consider it a kindness before your punishment," he said before adding, "You're welcome."

Vex barely had time to process the words before disaster struck. As they passed a vendor's stall, the heavy pouch of coins secured to Tarus' belt snagged against the corner of a wooden crate. The brittle leather tore apart in an instant, and the pouch burst open.

A rain of glimmering gold coins scattered across the dusty street.

For a heartbeat, silence hung in the air, the crowd frozen in wide-eyed shock. And then... chaos.

The starving and desperate lunged forward in a frenzied scramble, clawing at the dirt for their share of the unexpected fortune. The dry earth kicked up a blinding cloud of dust as feet trampled over one another, people shouting and shoving, some even coming to blows in their desperation.

The guards barely had time to react. By the time the dust settled and the last of the crowd had vanished, clutching their hard-won prizes, Lord Tarus and Lorivelle were gone.

# CHAPTER 8

# QUEEN OF THE HIGH SEAS (AND LOW STANDARDS)

V ex darted through the crowded streets, her breath quick and shallow, her pulse hammering in her ears. The market had erupted into chaos behind them, but she didn't dare look back. Devaultus was right beside her, now restored to his usual dashing self: tall, confident, and effortlessly composed even at a full sprint. They moved like whispers through the crowd, slipping between bodies with the grace of shadows, their footsteps barely perceptible against the uneven cobblestones.

The docks loomed ahead, the massive sandship rising like a beast of the desert, its towering masts stretching toward the sun. The scent of dust, spice, and hot, dry wood filled the air. Devaultus' sharp eyes caught the figure of the ship's captain standing at the edge of the deck, her presence commanding and knowing, as if she had anticipated their arrival before they themselves had.

With a flick of her wrist, she signaled to her crew. Ropes creaked, pulleys groaned, and a wooden gangplank lowered, but not fully. It hovered just out of reach, a taunting invitation rather than an easy escape.

Vex and Devaultus skidded to a halt at the dock's edge, their momentum sending up a spray of dust and grit. The ship rocked gently on its skates, the sunlight glinting off its weathered wood and metal reinforcements. Vex's chest rose and fell rapidly as she shot a glance at Devaultus, uncertainty flickering in her bright eyes.

The captain smirked from above, arms crossed over her ample chest. "Well now, ye best hope you can jump," she called, her sultry voice carrying over the wind.

The captain leaned casually over the railing, her smirk growing wider as she watched the two of them eye the just-out-of-reach gangplank. Her fiery red hair whipped in the wind, and her piercing eyes gleamed with amusement.

"I require payment," she purred, crossing her arms under her ample chest, making sure to flaunt her authority as much as her assets.

Devaultus barely glanced up as he steadied himself, urgency clear in his voice. "Allow us passage, and I shall pay as we shove off."

The captain feigned consideration, tilting her head before simply shaking it. "Five gold for each passenger," she declared with a devilish grin.

Devaultus' jaw clenched. He knew full well it was an outrageous price, borderline extortion. But what choice did he have? Time was not on their side, and Tarus was likely already tearing through the streets in search of them. His mind raced for an alternative, but the truth was painfully clear: they needed to be on that ship.

Sighing in resignation, he reached into his pouch and muttered, "Very well, you will have it."

The captain, however, wasn't finished. Her smirk deepened, her gaze narrowing in wicked delight. "And," she continued, drawing out the word like a cat toying with a mouse, "I will have two quests from you. Should you fail to fulfill them... well," she gestured lazily toward the side of the ship, where the open sands stretched infinitely below them. "The sharks will enjoy the company."

Devaultus grumbled under his breath, but there was no time for negotiation. "Fine," he said through gritted teeth. "As you wish."

Satisfied, the captain gave a small, triumphant nod and signaled to her crew. Within seconds, the wooden plank began its descent, extending fully to meet the dock. Devaultus and Vex wasted no time, dashing up it with the practiced speed of those who had spent too much of their lives running from danger.

They had barely set foot on the ship when the plank was yanked back with startling efficiency. Below them, the docks grew smaller as the vessel groaned to life. A strange mechanical clanking and grinding echoed through the hull as the chains anchoring the ship disengaged; and suddenly, with a violent jolt, they were in motion.

The ship didn't move like an ordinary vessel. Instead of the slow, gradual glide of a sea-bound craft, it *lurched* forward, as if propelled by an unseen force. Devaultus and Vex, unprepared for such a shift, stumbled back like drunken fools. Vex nearly lost her balance entirely, her arms flailing as she grasped at Devaultus for support.

"Gods, what is this thing?!" she gasped, breathless, as she struggled to plant her feet against the unnervingly smooth wooden deck.

Devaultus, equally unsteady, managed to catch her before she tumbled over completely. He shot a glare toward the captain, who remained effortlessly poised as the ship sped forward, her stance as steady as if she were standing on solid ground.

In the distance, Tarus stormed onto the docks, his furious strides sending soldiers stumbling out of his way like scattered leaves in a storm. His mere presence was enough to make hardened warriors flinch; but now, consumed by rage, he was a force of nature, reckless and unforgiving. Devaultus watched the chaos unfold with an amused gleam in his eye: soldiers scrambling to obey, some dashing off in search of a vessel to give chase, others desperately attempting to commandeer one from unsuspecting sailors. It was almost pitiful; their frantic movements like ants before a flood. Tarus demanded pursuit, and to fail him meant worse than death.

But Devaultus? He only smirked.

Locking eyes with the Masha'Aldu Lord, he let the moment stretch between them, tension thick as the sea air. Then, ever the showman, he reached up with deliberate slowness, fingers grazing the brim of his hat. With a devilish grin, he swept into a deep, theatrical bow, his hat dipping low in a mocking gesture of deference before he casually placed it back upon his head. The message was clear, undeniable: *You lost this round.*

Tarus' fury darkened further, his fists clenching at his sides, but Devaultus had already turned away. His coat billowed behind him as he strolled across the deck, exuding an air of absolute indifference. Not a glance spared, not a single acknowledgment of the storm brewing behind him on the docks. The ship had set sail, the first move in this deadly game had been made, and Tarus was left raging at the Sand Sea's edge.

Devaultus turned toward the captain, his expression shifting to one of intrigue as he met her piercing gaze. Al'Shandra, the infamous pirate queen, stood before them with an air of effortless dominance, her curvaceous form draped in a corset that barely contained her assets, red hair cascading in wild waves down her back. She looked at him and Vex as though they were new toys to be tested, her smirk laced with dangerous amusement.

"Welcome to my kingdom, loves," she purred, her voice rich and honeyed, yet carrying the edge of a blade. "I'm Al'Shandra." Her eyes flicked between them, assessing, weighing. Then, lips curling in a knowing smile, she added, "Now, let's see if you two are worth the trouble."

Devaultus studied the ship with the eager curiosity of a man who had always wanted to understand the impossible. He had long dreamed of unraveling the mysteries of these great vessels that sailed not on water, but across the endless sands. Now, finally, he had the chance to take a closer look. Of course, most of his time aboard had been spent waging war against his own stomach. It turned out that, while he admired the mechanics of the ship, he was far less enamored with the way it swayed and rocked beneath him. But after days of stubborn endurance, he was convinced he was getting his sea legs, or whatever one called it on a sand-bound ship.

Now, standing in the dimly lit belly of the vessel, he found himself face-to-face with one of the ship's engineers, a creature known only as "Leroy." Devaultus had encountered many strange beings in his time, but Leroy... Leroy was something else entirely. The hulking figure towered over him at nearly eight feet tall, his form seemingly sculpted from stone and dust, as though he had risen straight from the sands themselves. His movements were slow and deliberate, but there was an undeniable wisdom in his manner, an ancient patience that spoke of a lifetime spent tending to the ship's secrets.

Leroy's deep, gravelly voice rumbled through the chamber as he gestured toward the massive sleds beneath the ship. Devaultus followed his outstretched hand, noting the peculiar arrangement of angled plates mounted on enormous wheels. The plates, though appearing to be solid metal, seemed almost weightless, hovering just above the wooden frame of the ship.

With an almost lazy motion, Leroy grasped a nearby lever attached to an enormous wheel embedded within the ship's framework. With a grunt of effort, he began to turn it. Devaultus watched in fascination as the plates beneath the ship shifted ever so slightly, their angles adjusting in response. Suddenly, the massive wheels on the sleds spun to life, rotating rapidly as though caught in an unseen current.

Leroy explained in his slow, methodical way that the ship's motion was governed by an intricate system of magnetic forces. The large wheel Devaultus had seen was responsible for aligning powerful magnets beneath the vessel, which in turn interacted with the metallic plates on the sleds. As the wheel turned, the magnets adjusted their polarity, creating a force that both repelled and attracted in perfect sequence. This delicate balance of opposing forces allowed the ship to glide effortlessly over the sand, mimicking the way waterborne vessels rode the waves.

Devaultus leaned in, eyes gleaming with intrigue. The mechanism was ingenious, a seamless blend of raw power and precise engineering. He could already see ways to manipulate it, to improve it. If he had more time... But time was never on his side.

For now, it was enough to understand. And perhaps, one day, to use it.

The ship lurched forward with a surge of power, propelled by the intricate mechanism beneath its hull. Devaultus could feel the change immediately: the ship's speed outmatched that of any other vessel that dared traverse the Sand Sea. His eyes widened in amazement as he eagerly examined each component, his mind racing with possibilities. The engineering behind it was fascinating, a complex interplay of magnets and momentum, allowing the ship to glide effortlessly over the dunes like a phantom skimming the surface of another world.

Just as he was about to ask Leroy another question, a voice interrupted his thoughts.

"Devaultus."

He turned, spotting a crewman standing a few feet away. The man hesitated before speaking again. "The Captain wishes to speak with you."

Devaultus sighed, his shoulders sagging slightly. Of course, she did. He finally had a moment to himself, a rare chance to indulge in something genuinely interesting, and yet, somehow, she always managed to find him. It was as if Al'Shandra had eyes in every corner of the ship, always aware, always watching.

"Idle hands and all that, huh?" Devaultus muttered under his breath, mostly to himself.

The crewman furrowed his brow, clearly unsure of what Devaultus meant. The lack of comprehension made Devaultus sigh again, this time with dramatic resignation.

Sometimes, he wondered if he was wasting perfectly wonderful conversations on less-than-wonderful minds. He found himself reminiscing about another world, one he had stumbled into long ago, a place unlike any other, filled with wonders beyond imagination. There, they drank a glorious morning wine they called "coffee," and they entertained themselves with strange illusions that transported them to different realms.

He had watched a young man play what they called a "game," using an odd contraption that shielded his eyes. It was explained to him that within that visor, the man could see an entirely different world, an illusion so vivid that it felt real. Devaultus had assumed it was some sort of advanced illusion magic, though no one spoke of it that way. If only he could recreate such a thing in this world. But here? Here, they still marveled at the wheel as if it were the pinnacle of human achievement.

He chuckled at the thought, shaking his head. The people of this world had no idea how much they were missing.

The crewman was still staring at him, waiting expectantly for a response.

"Very well," Devaultus finally said, waving a dismissive hand. He turned back to Leroy, who had barely finished raising his hand in an agonizingly slow farewell. Devaultus had already disappeared into the corridors of the ship.

The young sailor leading Devaultus stopped just outside the captain's quarters, standing stiffly as he gestured toward the heavy wooden door. Devaultus barely suppressed a sigh. The formality, the exaggerated air of mystery: it was all so tiresome. Theatrics were his domain, his craft, his art. Watching others attempt to wield them against him was beginning to wear thin.

With little patience for pretense, he shoved the door open with a flourish, stepping inside like a storm rolling through the cabin. The room was dimly lit, the glow of lanterns flickering against polished wood. Al'Shandra sat at her desk, leaning back with a knowing smirk, as if she had foreseen his grand entrance. Her piercing gaze followed his every movement, the ghost of amusement playing at the corners of her lips.

From a small metal contraption on a nearby shelf, a slow, hypnotic melody drifted through the air. Devaultus tilted his head slightly. Now that was interesting. Another marvel of this world he had yet to decipher. How did the machine work? Was it mechanical? Magical? A fusion of both? He made a mental note to investigate later.

"About time, Devaultus," Al'Shandra drawled, her usual sultry voice edged with something unexpected: fatigue.

Devaultus strode toward the chair in front of her desk, settling into it with his usual swagger. He threw his feet up onto one of the armrests, lounging as if this were a casual fireside chat rather than an audience with the Pirate Queen herself. His yellow eyes gleamed with mischief as he lazily asked, "How can I be of service to you, Al'Shandra?" His tone was light, almost dismissive, as if he were already weary of whatever errand she was about to assign.

She smirked at his nonchalance, but her gaze held something deeper. Amusement, yes, but also calculation. "You still have two quests left to fulfill," she reminded him smoothly. "As luck would have it, we've found one Diego Stonewell. A flint dwarf. He's in possession of a particular crystal, one I require." She leaned forward slightly, eyes dark with intent. "You are to acquire it for me. By any means necessary."

Devaultus turned the name over in his mind. Diego Stonewell. He had heard of flint dwarves before, craftsmen, traders, sometimes mercenaries, but this one was new to him. His gaze flickered back to Al'Shandra, his curiosity piqued.

"And what exactly is so special about this crystal?" he asked, watching her closely. "Why do you want it so badly?"

For the first time since he'd met her, Al'Shandra hesitated. It was brief, almost imperceptible, but it was there. Her eyelids fluttered shut, as if she were searching for the right words. Then, without warning, a shudder ran through her body, so subtle yet so telling that Devaultus' sharp eyes caught it instantly.

He lifted an eyebrow, his usual smirk shifting into something more intrigued. Now that was interesting.

Devaultus had begun to suspect she was calculating the power that crystal could grant her, but his train of thought derailed when Al'Shandra nonchalantly reached under her desk. With a lazy flick of her wrist, she pulled out one of her overly muscular cabin boys, who had apparently been tucked away like a discarded trinket. The man, looking thoroughly unbothered, unfolded himself with a stretch, wiped his mouth with the back of his hand, and promptly scurried out of the room at her dismissive wave.

Devaultus arched a brow, his sharp mind piecing things together faster than he cared to admit. A slow burn of irritation simmered beneath his cool exterior. This was a blatant display of disrespect. He was Devaultus, after all, bard extraordinaire, charming rogue, master of wit and wordplay. To be treated with such flippancy, as though he were some common lapdog waiting for table scraps, was beyond insulting.

Al'Shandra, utterly unfazed by his reaction, gave a small shimmy as she tugged her leather pants back into place. The motion was as deliberate as it was teasing, a predator's smirk curling her lips. "What the crystal is," she said smoothly, voice rich with amusement, "is of no concern to you. Your job is simply to get it for me. When that task is complete, one of your quests will be fulfilled."

She took a languid step closer, mischief flickering in her gaze. "Now, unless you'd prefer to take his place beneath my desk..." she purred, trailing her fingers along the polished wood in invitation.

Devaultus clenched his jaw, resisting the urge to roll his eyes. He had half a mind to argue the absurdity of this so-called quest, but he also had no desire to be shoved into whatever role that unfortunate cabin boy had just occupied. Instead, he exhaled sharply, forcing himself to remain composed. He wanted this debt settled. The sooner, the better.

With an air of nonchalance, he pushed himself up from the chair, adjusting the cuffs of his sleeves before striding toward the door.

Behind him, Al'Shandra chuckled, clearly entertained by his restraint. "We arrive tomorrow," she called after him, her voice laced with satisfaction. "Be ready to disembark then."

Devaultus didn't spare her another glance as he stepped out, but his mind was already turning. This quest was going to be interesting... whether he liked it or not.

In another part of the ship, deep in the dimly lit alchemy lab, Blight was utterly consumed by her work. For the past few days, she had practically lived there, poring over ingredients, formulas, and strange concoctions, determined to absorb everything she could. If she was to be of any true use to Devaultus, she needed knowledge, real knowledge, the kind that could turn the tide of battle, earn her a place in this strange, shifting world, and most importantly, ensure she was never cast out. The mere thought of being forced to return to Kot and Dar as nothing more than their battle pet sent a cold shudder down her spine. That fate was not an option.

She adjusted the thick mask covering the lower half of her face, its enchanted fabric filtering out the acrid fumes curling from the beaker in her gloved hands. The liquid inside shimmered, shifting from deep violet to an eerie shade of green as she carefully poured it into another container. A thin, almost sentient wisp of vapor spiraled up from the mixture, and Blight leaned in, fascinated by the reaction. With quick, practiced motions, she jotted down notes in a small, worn leather-bound book, one of several gifted to her by Al'Shandra.

That, in itself, was an enigma.

Blight still didn't understand why the infamous Pirate Queen had taken such an interest in her. It was unusual, even suspicious. But she wasn't about to complain. Paper was a rare commodity, hoarded by the wealthy and powerful, especially in a land where trees were as precious as gold. Most writing materials came from leather, or worse, flesh. She had learned long ago not to ask what kind of flesh. Out here, nothing went to waste.

Across the room, hunched over a cluttered table, sat Non, the ship's alchemist, an old woman whose very presence seemed stitched together from years of hardship. Her body was a patchwork of wrinkles and sun-scorched skin, her face resembling weathered tree bark. Strands of brittle, gray hair stuck out at odd lengths, some long, some cropped short as if they had simply given up trying to grow. Her crooked nose twitched as she observed Blight's work, the single cloudy eye that peered out from under her sagging brow gleaming with approval.

Non's voice, hoarse yet laced with amusement, cut through the bubbling sounds of the lab. "That's a good mix, girl," she rasped, nodding toward the beaker in Blight's hands. "But it could be better."

Blight turned to her mentor, brow raised in interest. The old woman grinned, revealing a mostly toothless mouth, and pointed a gnarled finger at a small vial resting among the clutter. "Just a drop of that one, go on."

Blight didn't hesitate. With careful precision, she added a single drop of the mystery ingredient to her concoction. Instantly, the liquid flared with a brilliant burst of color before settling into a rich, deep amber. Her eyes widened with intrigue.

"What did that do?" she asked, glancing at Non.

The crone let out a cackle, tapping a crooked nail against the wooden table. "Oh, just a little something extra. That'll add a nice tinge of knockback to the mix. Along with its other effects... well, let's just say it'll make quite the impression."

Blight tilted her head, considering the implications. A slow, wicked smile spread across her lips. "Now that," she murmured, "is going to be very useful."

Non gave a nod of approval before waving a bony hand. "Good, good. Now then, let's get back to that other mixture you've been struggling with. You'll want to master it before we make port."

Blight nodded, rolling up her sleeves, determination burning in her eyes. There was still so much to learn, and she intended to learn it all.

Vex moved like a whisper through the bowels of the ship, her steps silent as a shadow. While Devaultus had been practically begging to get a closer look at the inner workings of Al'Shandra's prized vessel, Vex had been explicitly forbidden from setting foot anywhere near the engineering deck. Something about "not needing parts stolen or broken." As if! She never stole anything, things simply had a habit of finding their way into her bags. A mystery, really.

Now, stretched out on her back in one of the vents just above the engineering room, she smirked to herself. Technically, she wasn't in the engineering room. Loopholes were a beautiful thing. Holding a dagger between her fingers, she idly carved her name into the metal panel beside her, her delicate script a permanent mark of defiance against Al'Shandra's orders.

This ship was dull. Sure, it took her a little while to get used to the way it moved, but far less time than it had taken Devaultus or Puppy. At least she had some experience with ships; unlike them, she wasn't completely useless at the Sand Sea. But still, she never enjoyed it. The memory of another ship crept into her mind, her sisters laughing, the smell of burning, illusionary dust whipping through her hair. Her jaw clenched, and she shook her head, forcing the thought away.

Just then, something moved in the corner of her vision. She froze, her muscles coiled like a spring, and she turned her head ever so slightly. There, wobbling through the dim vent space, was a small, orb-like creature. It had the texture of shifting sand, but instead of spikes like a sand urchin, it sprouted short, jelly-like tendrils that wobbled with every movement. Vex's golden eyes widened in surprise.

What in the Abyss was that?

She had seen many strange creatures in her time, but nothing quite like this. A slow grin spread across her lips. This was interesting.

Suppressing a giggle, she reached out a careful hand. The creature hesitated for only a moment before eagerly clambering onto her palm, its shimmering form shifting with a strange, almost excited energy. Vex let out a delighted laugh.

"Oh, you are just so cute!" she cooed, lifting it up for closer inspection. It pulsed softly, as if responding to her voice.

She smirked, tucking the little thing close to her chest. "You can be my new friend. I don't get to spend enough time with my actual friends on this stupid ship."

At least now she had something to make things a little more interesting.

Devaultus is always so busy; and Puppy? She's holed up in that dreary lab all day. Vex huffed, crossing her arms as she lay sprawled in the narrow vent. It wasn't fair. She'd tried spending time with Blight, but the alchemists had thrown her out like she was some kind of menace. She rolled her eyes at the thought.

"You blow up one little lab, and suddenly they never want you back," she muttered indignantly, twirling the dagger in her hand. "I mean, it was really cool! The whole room went *boom*! And that crazy old hag Non? She flew so far! Like a wrinkly, screaming cannonball!" Vex snickered to herself, replaying the moment in her mind, complete with her own sound effects of explosions. "I kinda wanna do it again..." she added wistfully.

Her gaze flicked to the strange, wobbling creature now perched in her palm. It was small, round, and oddly gelatinous, like a sand urchin without the spikes, just short, wiggly tendrils pulsing with a strange rhythm. The little thing shimmered in her hand, almost as if it understood her words.

"You are just so cute!" Vex cooed again, lifting it up to eye level. "Yup, my new friend." She sighed dramatically. "Devaultus is always running around, being all important, and Puppy won't let me near her potions anymore. Like, come on, one explosion and they hold a grudge forever?"

The creature gave an excited little wobble.

Vex gasped. "You agree! See, you get me." She tapped her chin in thought. "You need a name. Something that screams... I'm adorable and slightly wobbly." The creature vibrated in her hand, as if waiting with bated breath. "Hmm... Jerry?"

The second she said it, the tiny orb wobbled so violently, it nearly bounced out of her grasp.

"Oh, you like that, huh?" She giggled, gently patting it with her finger. "Jerry it is, then."

Before she could continue, a long, echoing horn blared through the ship, reverberating through the walls of the vent. Vex immediately perked up, licking her lips in excitement.

"That's the dinner horn, Jerry! Are you hungry?"

The little creature wobbled once more before slipping into the folds of her hood, nestling itself away like it belonged there.

Grinning, Vex twisted around and began crawling her way out of the vent, expertly maneuvering through the ship's tight spaces. As soon as she reached open space, she dropped down onto her feet, dusted herself off, and skipped toward the ship's tavern. Not a mess hall, not a galley, Al'Shandra had been very clear on that. It was a *tavern*, and anyone who called it otherwise got an earful from the captain herself.

As soon as she entered, her sharp eyes landed on Devaultus, already seated with his usual air of casual self-importance. She grabbed a tray of food, her steps light and playful, and plopped down next to him without hesitation.

Just as she opened her mouth to introduce Jerry, Blight entered as well, gathering her own meal before settling at the table with them.

Before Vex could even get a word out, Devaultus leaned back, a slow smirk spreading across his face.

"So," he said, his voice carrying a weight of intrigue. "We have a mission tomorrow."

"We'll be disembarking at the next port," Devaultus said, his voice laced with the usual mix of confidence and mild exasperation. "Our mission is to track down a certain crystal for Al'Shandra." He leaned back slightly, swirling his drink absentmindedly before taking a slow sip.

Vex frowned, her lips pressing into a thin line. A crystal? This was starting to sound suspiciously like the whole *ring thing* again. What was it with Devaultus and finding random, shiny objects for other people? If all he needed was a crystal, she was sure she could find *plenty* of them! She didn't see the big deal.

More than that, though, she didn't like how distracted he had been. Ever since they boarded this cursed ship, he was always running off, talking to engineers, studying mechanisms, or, worse, spending time with Al'Shandra like she was the most interesting thing in the world. And *Puppy*, ugh, *Blight*, was just as bad, burying herself in the alchemy lab, obsessing over potions and poisons. Nobody had time for her anymore.

She missed how things used to be. Just the three of them. No ship, no crew, no arrogant pirate queen making Devaultus dance to her tune. Just them, getting into trouble, finding adventure, causing chaos.

Maybe this mission was *exactly* what they needed.

Maybe... maybe they just *wouldn't* come back to the ship afterward.

The thought sent a jolt of excitement through her. Yes! They'd find this crystal, *or pretend they couldn't*, and then the three of them, no, *four*, counting Jerry, would go off and find their own fun again. No captains, no rules, no ridiculous ships full of stuffy people who kept telling her she *wasn't* allowed to blow things up.

Lost in her daydream, she barely realized Devaultus was still talking.

She blinked, snapping back to reality just as his gaze settled on her, his lips forming a question she had completely missed.

Oh well.

She nodded quickly, grinning up at him, pretending she had been listening the whole time. His attention was on her, and really, that was all that mattered.

# CHAPTER 9

# DUNGEON RUN: CRYSTAL HEIST

The ship glided into port, its massive hull cutting through the golden sands of the sea like a blade. The crew buzzed with excitement, their energy almost tangible as they scurried across the deck, preparing for landfall. After over a week at sea, the sight of a bustling port was a welcome relief. The past few days had been especially grueling, Al'Shandra had pushed the ship to its limits, demanding full speed to put as much distance as possible between them and Tarus' relentless pursuit. The result had been a rough, bone-jarring ride, but they had finally managed to slip away, buying themselves precious time for this mission.

Devaultus stepped up to the deck, the dusty air mingling with the distinct scent of sand and engine fumes. He stood beside Al'Shandra, who leaned casually against the ship's railing, her piercing eyes scanning the lively port ahead. Dockworkers bustled about, their shouts and laughter rising above the creaking of wood and the clang of metal.

"Are you sure it's a good idea to take time to go after this crystal when Tarus is on our heels?" Devaultus asked, his voice edged with concern.

Al'Shandra rolled her eyes and turned to him, a smirk tugging at the corner of her lips. "It will be fine. Besides, how are you a pirate if you don't pirate?" she quipped with a wink.

Devaultus sighed, already regretting the conversation. He had prepared himself for this mission, but that didn't make the prospect of dealing with dwarves any more appealing. His past encounters with them had been... less than fortunate, and the thought of another run-in filled him with a sense of impending doom.

A soft rustle behind him signaled Vex's arrival. She moved gracefully, her form-fitting clothes hugging her lithe frame, the hood casting a shadow over her mischievous eyes. She leaned lazily against the deck rail, her gaze fixed on the chaotic flurry of dockworkers below. Her presence was like a breath of fresh air: wild, unpredictable, and always on the edge of trouble.

Moments later, Blight appeared on his other side, her entrance far more composed but no less intriguing. Devaultus' eyes immediately caught on to her changed attire. She had abandoned her usual garb for a new, peculiar ensemble: leather pants and sturdy boots that clung to her frame, and a snug top that revealed slender tubes running up her sleeves, an intricate design he wouldn't have noticed without a keen eye. Her neck was encased in a large, cumbersome collar that looked out of place, almost like it belonged to a different era. Around her hips, a belt supported an array of tubes filled with strange liquids, each glinting with an iridescent sheen.

Devaultus' curiosity was piqued and he couldn't wait to see what it all did. It would seem Blight had been busy.

Al'Shandra clapped her hands, breaking his train of thought. The crew sprang into action, letting down the gangplank with a heavy thud. She turned to Devaultus, her smirk deepening. "Remember, Diego Stonewell should have the crystal. And this time of day? Everyone's getting off work. Try a tavern. We know how much you love those," she teased.

Devaultus scowled, more annoyed by her accuracy than the jest itself. She seemed to know him far too well, a dangerous thing in his world. Once, he might've buried someone in the sand for that level of insight, but Al'Shandra... well, she was another challenge entirely.

Turning to his companions, he met Blight's calm, calculating gaze before shifting to Vex, who practically vibrated with excitement. There was a determined glint in her eye that both comforted and worried him.

"Are we ready?" he asked.

Both women nodded, Vex's enthusiasm nearly palpable.

The trio descended the gangplank, stepping onto the creaking docks. Devaultus inhaled deeply, taking in the mingled scents of sand, oil, and sweat.

This was a dwarven stronghold, no doubt about it. Flint dwarves with their ashen skin and jagged beards argued with mountain dwarves, who stood broader and prouder, their hair braided with runes. Dark dwarves with shadowy, obsidian-toned features lurked in the corners, eyeing passersby with suspicion. The diversity was staggering, and so was the tension. It didn't take long before Devaultus spotted a brawl breaking out in the middle of the street, two dwarves throwing punches, their companions cheering them on like it was the day's entertainment.

"Charming place," Devaultus muttered, sidestepping a rolling barrel that narrowly missed Vex.

She grinned, her perfect teeth peeking out from beneath her hood. "I like it already."

Blight, on the other hand, kept her head down, her hands tucked into the pockets of her alchemist's coat, though her eyes flicked around, taking in everything, the streets, the people, the potential sources of rare ingredients.

Devaultus led them deeper into the port city, the chaos of the docks fading into a tangle of narrow streets and crooked buildings. Now, all they had to do was find Diego Stonewell and secure the crystal. Simple, right?

Devaultus grimaced at the thought. It was never that simple.

They made their way slowly through the bustling streets, the noise of the port fading into the background as the tavern's crooked sign swung into view. Devaultus' mind, however, was elsewhere. Each step brought him deeper into his thoughts about Al'Shandra: more than just an annoyance, she was a necessary obstacle. As much as he hated to admit it, he needed her. He had dreams, wild and vivid, of captaining his own ship someday, leading his own crew under his command. But ships weren't just planks and sails; they were complex beasts, and he didn't yet know how to tame one. Al'Shandra, for all her infuriating quirks, was the key to that knowledge.

Still, the idea gnawed at him, her control, her power. From what he'd gathered, she commanded not just one ship, but a vast fleet. Hundreds, perhaps even thousands. Each vessel manned by a loyal crew not out of love, but out of sheer, bone-deep fear. No one dared to defy her. The thought of that much power slipping through his fingers made his hands clench into fists. He considered, for a brief and dangerous moment, if there was a way to take it all from her. Kill her, perhaps, and assume her form. It wouldn't be the first time he'd done something like that. But a bitter truth surfaced: wearing her face wouldn't grant him her knowledge. He'd still be fumbling in the dark, pretending to be a captain he wasn't.

Then again, when had lack of knowledge ever stopped him before?

His musings were abruptly shattered by a voice, a husky, teasing tone that sliced through his thoughts like a dagger.

"Aye, look at you!"

Devaultus turned, finding himself face-to-face with a stout dwarven woman, her round cheeks flushed from drink, or perhaps excitement. She smiled broadly, revealing a row of slightly crooked teeth, her eyes gleaming with mischief. "I certainly do like the tall type. A bit of coin and I'll climb you like a tree."

He blinked, momentarily dumbfounded. Trees were rare these days, nearly extinct in some regions, and he knew from experience that dwarves weren't exactly famed for their climbing abilities. But then the meaning of her words sank in, and his face paled visibly.

Memories, unwanted and vivid, flooded back. His last dalliance with a dwarven lover had been... catastrophic. They were anything but gentle, and the weeks that followed had been spent recovering, each step a painful reminder of his poor choices. He wasn't eager to repeat that experience.

"I... I do think I'm fine, my dear," he stammered, offering an awkward smile. "But thank you for the offer."

The dwarven woman wasn't so easily deterred. With a playful grin, she reached out and gave his backside a bold squeeze. "Well, if you change your mind, you know where to find me," she purred, licking her lips in a way that sent a fresh wave of unease through him.

"I... I'll keep that in mind," he muttered, his voice barely above a whisper.

Blight, trailing just behind him, couldn't hold back a soft giggle at his discomfort. The usually unflappable Devaultus, caught off guard: it was too good to pass up.

Vex, however, had a very different reaction. Her eyes darkened, a flicker of raw, violent intent flashing through them. Her hand inched toward the hilt of her dagger, her muscles tensing, ready to strike.

Devaultus noticed the shift in her almost immediately. "She's not a problem, Vex," he warned, his voice low but firm. "You will not harm her."

Vex scowled, her fingers reluctantly pulling back from the dagger. She grumbled under her breath, clearly displeased but unwilling to disobey.

The awkward encounter behind them, the group finally reached the tavern. Its wooden door creaked on rusted hinges as they pushed it open, stepping into a roaring sea of laughter, shouting, and the distinct smell of ale and sweat.

The tavern was alive: if there was one thing dwarves were known for, it was their ability to turn drinking into an art form. Long tables filled the space, packed with dwarves of all kinds: flint, mountain, and dark dwarves together, each one with a tankard in hand, sloshing frothy ale as they roared with laughter and banged their mugs against the tables. A group in the corner had broken into song, their deep voices blending into the kind of drunken harmony that only dwarves could pull off.

Barmaids bustled between the tables, their arms laden with more tankards than seemed physically possible. Their bosoms nearly spilled from their tops as they expertly navigated the crowded space, placing drinks on tables without missing a beat.

Devaultus led the way to an empty table near the back, weaving through the chaos. As they sat down, he couldn't help but glance around, his eyes sharp and calculating. Somewhere in this madness was Diego Stonewell, their key to the crystal. And he intended to find him before the night's end.

The tavern wench returned, her strong arms easily balancing three massive tankards of frothy ale. With a practiced thud, she set them down in front of the group, foam spilling over the rims and dripping onto the rough wooden table. The heavy scent of malt and something far stronger filled the air.

Vex eyed the enormous tankard in front of her, blinking in surprise at its sheer size. Curiosity piqued, she reached out, her slender fingers wrapping around the cold, clay handle. Lifting it to her lips, she took a generous swig, the strong, bitter liquid rushing over her tongue. Almost instantly, her eyes widened, nearly crossing as the overwhelming potency hit her senses like a sledgehammer. It burned going down, far stronger than anything she had ever tasted in her years of noble upbringing. The sharp contrast between her refined past and this fiery dwarven brew sent a ripple of amusement through her. She coughed once, setting the tankard down with a thud, blinking away the burn. "By the Abyss... what *is* this?" she muttered under her breath, her vision swimming slightly.

Blight, on the other hand, grabbed her tankard with both hands, as if she'd been waiting for this exact moment. She tilted it high, gulping down the warm ale with reckless abandonment. The amber liquid sloshed down her throat as though she hadn't tasted anything in days. Froth clung to her upper lip as she finally set the tankard down, now half-empty, and let out a tremendous belch that echoed through the noisy tavern. Her wide eyes stared at the tankard in confusion. "This... this isn't wine," she mumbled, the realization dawning on her as if someone had swapped her drink mid-guzzle.

Devaultus raised an eyebrow at her, amused. It was rare to see Blight in this state, but even rarer to see her wobbling slightly in her seat, her tiny frame swaying back and forth as the potent ale took hold faster than expected. He followed her line of sight and saw that a group of male dwarves at a nearby table had taken notice of the spectacle.

One particularly stout dwarf, his beard braided in thick coils adorned with rings, slid off his stool. His gait was uneven, he was clearly deep into his cups, but his eyes sparkled with admiration, or perhaps mischief. He staggered over, slamming a heavy hand onto the table near Blight's tankard.

"Aye, lass!" he roared, his voice booming over the din of the tavern. "Ye drink like a true dwarven woman! Strong of spirit and quick with the ale!" His grin revealed a row of crooked, ale-stained teeth as he swayed in place, clearly impressed by her feat.

Blight blinked up at him, still trying to process the strength of the ale she'd consumed. Devaultus smirked at the scene unfolding before him, leaning back in his chair, already predicting where this was headed. Vex, however, narrowed her eyes at the dwarf, her hand unconsciously drifting toward one of her daggers, ready in case things went a bit sideways.

The tavern around them buzzed with laughter, shouts, and the clinking of tankards. Somewhere in the background, a lute player struck up a raucous tune, but Devaultus kept his focus on the scene at his table, wondering just how out of hand this was about to get.

Blight's cheeks flushed a rosy pink, the warmth of the ale loosening her usual guarded demeanor. She giggled, her small frame swaying slightly as the potent drink worked its magic. "Do ya think so?" she asked, her voice lilting with tipsy amusement.

The dwarf let out a booming laugh that echoed through the raucous tavern. "Most definitely! A lass like you could be *loads* of fun to the right dwarven male," he declared, his grin wide enough to show his crooked, ale-stained teeth. With exaggerated flair, he spat into his calloused palm and smoothed down his wiry beard, clearly trying to make himself more presentable.

Blight squinted at him, one eye narrowing as she tried to focus on his fuzzy outline through her drunken haze. His words flew right over her head, their deeper meaning drowned out by her increasingly foggy thoughts. She clapped her hands together, her smile growing impossibly wide. "Ohhh, I *do* like fun!" she exclaimed, giggling again, swinging her legs beneath the table like an overexcited child.

The dwarf's grin broadened, his eyes gleaming with mischief as he inched closer.

Devaultus sighed heavily, resting his chin on his hand, already regretting this entire detour. The last thing he needed was a drunken Blight causing more trouble. He fixed the dwarf with a hard stare, his tone clipped but calm. "I dare say the lady's had a bit too much to drink," he began, swirling the amber liquid in his own tankard. "And I'm fairly certain her suitor, Diego Stonewell, wouldn't be too pleased with her enjoying your company."

The dwarf's jovial expression faltered for a beat as the name hit him. Diego Stonewell was well-known among the dwarves, someone you didn't want to cross lightly. He let out a nervous chuckle, raising his hands in mock surrender. "Ahh... didn't know she was spoken for," he muttered.

Blight tilted her head in confusion, blinking slowly. "Suitor? Who's that? He sounds nice," she giggled again, completely oblivious.

Devaultus rubbed his temples, wondering how this mission could possibly get more out of hand.

The dwarf's face flushed a deep crimson; he was caught between desire and shame. He scratched the side of his bushy beard nervously, but the lecherous grin never left his face. "Of course, that lowlife would have such a lovely lass," he grumbled, glaring into his now-empty tankard as if it had betrayed him. "But he's been holed up in that damned mountain for two weeks now. I could give you what you need, lass. A real taste of dwarven man. I'd ruin you for that worthless twig of a dwarf." He finished with a booming laugh, though there was a glimmer of hope in his eyes that his offer might be accepted.

Devaultus' brow arched slightly, the cogs in his mind turning fast. *So, Diego wasn't here at all. Hidden away in a mountain. That complicates things... but also simplifies them.*

Blight, meanwhile, blinked slowly, the dwarf's words bouncing around in her ale-fogged brain. "Ruin me?" she mumbled to herself, genuinely puzzled. "That... doesn't sound like fun." She furrowed her brow, her drunken mind trying to piece together the meaning but getting nowhere. In her distracted state, she noticed her own reflection shimmering in the golden ale remaining in her tankard. She leaned in closer, one eye squinting as she inspected her own face.

"What'er you lookin' at?!" she slurred, frowning at the liquid. Her tiny hand balled into a fist, which she awkwardly raised. "I'll punch ya right in yer ugly eye!"

Vex snorted, unable to help herself, though her hand still hovered near her blade, as she watched the dwarf for any sudden moves.

Devaultus sighed deeply, pinching the bridge of his nose before turning his attention back to the hopeful dwarf. "Listen, mate," he began, his tone conspiratorial, "she's been wanting to end things with Diego for a while now. She's just been too kind-hearted to do it." He glanced at Blight, who was now attempting to intimidate her with wild hand gestures. "But maybe... if you knew where he was, she could go... handle that business. Then come back here for another drink. With you, perhaps."

The dwarf's eyes sparkled with excitement, his beard twitching as a toothy grin spread across his face. "Aye! That'd be somethin', wouldn't it? Me, Smitty Darkstone, stealin' away the lass of that pointy-eared-loving bastard." He slapped his knee, nearly knocking over a nearby stool with his enthusiasm. "Well, he's been tucked away in Mount Fri'larja. Been there for weeks now. Tell Diego I said this..." He leaned in close, breath heavy with ale, and barked, "That his sweet lil' lass'll be warming my bed tonight!"

Smitty roared with laughter, slapping Devaultus hard on the back. The force nearly knocked the wind out of him, making him stagger forward a step. "Ah, you're a good lad!" Smitty chortled, clearly pleased with himself.

Devaultus forced a grin, rubbing his shoulder where the dwarf's massive hand had landed. "Of course, Smitty. We'll pass the message along."

Blight, still focused on her ale, hiccupped loudly before muttering, "Ohhh... a warm bed does sound nice."

Vex shook her head, muttering under her breath, "We need to get her out of here before she starts fighting the furniture."

Devaultus gave Smitty a final nod, scooping Blight up gently from her chair as she flailed lazily, still protesting at her reflection. "Time to go, love," he whispered, hoisting her over his shoulder as if she weighed nothing.

Smitty raised his tankard high, shouting after them, "I'll be waiting here when ya get back! And don't keep me waiting too long, lass!" His laughter echoed through the tavern as Devaultus, Vex, and a still-giggling Blight slipped out into the dusty street.

"Mount Fri'larja," Devaultus muttered under his breath. "Well, that's one step closer."

Vex shot him a sideways glance. "You really think she can survive a dwarven mountain drunk off her ass?"

He glanced at Blight, who was now softly singing to herself on his shoulder. "I suppose there is one way to find out."

Devaultus had intended to ask where Mount Fri'larja was, but the situation had spiraled faster than he anticipated. With Blight already incredibly drunk and Vex tightly wound, he worried things might spiral into a full-on brawl. He could almost see it: Vex lunging across the table, daggers out, and Blight haphazardly curled up on the floor fighting the Sheraka rug. He sighed, rubbing his temple. Keeping the two wildcards in check was becoming more of a challenge than dodging Tarus' ship.

But the immediate problem still lingered: finding the entrance to wherever Diego was holed up. Without a clear direction, they were effectively wandering blind. As they left the raucous tavern behind, the noise fading into a dull roar, they followed a dusty path that twisted along the edge of the cliffs. The air grew heavier, filled with the scent of minerals and dust, and soon they found themselves at a row of alcoves cut into the side of the jagged rock face.

Merchants, mostly dwarves, perched within the stone hollows, peddling their wares, gleaming weapons, strange trinkets, vials of brightly colored liquids, and plenty of questionable-looking food. The market buzzed with life, thick with the sounds of haggling, laughter, and the occasional cries of a drunken brawl.

Devaultus eyed the scene warily. They'd have to start asking around, try to pry loose some information about the entrance to Mount Fri'larja. But the idea of splitting up made his stomach twist. The last time they'd split up in a crowded area, chaos had reigned, Blight had made friends with halfling cannibals, and Vex had come within a hair's breadth of becoming a giant's plaything. Sure, they'd gotten out unscathed, but barely.

He glanced at the two women walking beside him. Blight was humming to herself, her steps swaying, clearly still riding the buzz from the tavern. She stopped at a stall selling odd crystal trinkets, poking at them like a curious child. Vex, on the other hand, walked with purposeful strides, her eyes sharp, scanning every shadow and passerby like they were potential threats. Her hand hovered near the hilt of her blade, her tension radiating like heat.

Devaultus sighed again, louder this time. "Alright," he muttered to himself. "We're not splitting up. Not this time. I'd rather face Diego alone than clean up another one of *those* disasters."

With that, he stepped forward into the market, motioning for Blight and Vex to stay close. It was time to start asking questions, carefully, and hope they could find the entrance to Mount Fri'larja without drawing too much attention... or setting anything else on fire.

The Puppeteer sat in a dimly lit chamber, his tattered robes stained with blood, both his own and others'. Shadows danced on the cracked stone walls as flickering lanterns cast a sickly glow over the scene. Servants scurried about him like frightened rodents, their hands trembling as they wrapped gauze around the jagged gashes that laced his arms and torso. The pain was sharp, but it was nothing compared to the searing heat of his humiliation.

It was quite unfortunate that during his escape he had run into a few of those halflings. Thankfully he had taken control of two of them and had them defend him. Though it wasn't until he had taken more than a few bites and slashes from them.

His jaw clenched tight, muscles twitching beneath his pale, sweat-slicked skin. The memory of the fiasco gnawed at him. This was supposed to be a clean operation, a simple trap, perfectly orchestrated. But no. Everything had unraveled, and it all pointed back to one name.

"Devaultus," he hissed, the name venom on his tongue.

The Puppeteer's mind raced, trying to piece together how it had all gone so catastrophically wrong. He had heard the whispers that spread like wildfire after his retreat from the mansion. Tales of Devaultus slipping through his fingers, leaving ruin in his wake. He slammed a fist into the wooden armrest of his chair, splintering it with the force.

"How?" he growled, his voice low and dangerous.

Vegas the Giant, his prized enforcer, was no common thug. The man had crushed warriors in the arena, snapping spines with his bare hands, leaving nothing but mangled corpses in his wake. He was a titan of muscle and rage, a near-unstoppable force. Yet, that fool had fallen to Devaultus. A *spinebug*. A weakling by comparison. It would have been laughable... if it didn't sting so deeply.

One of the attendants, a gaunt young man with shaking hands, dabbed a cloth soaked in medicinal salve against an open wound. The Puppeteer didn't even flinch. His mind was elsewhere, already calculating his next move. How could he turn this disaster into an advantage? Could he spin this to curry favor with the Lords? Probably not. He knew how they worked. They demanded perfection, any misstep was met with swift, brutal consequences.

And then there was *him*.

Lord Vera'Ala'Roja Bobalata'Cora.

The name alone sent a shiver down his spine. The cruelest of the Lords, known for his merciless punishments and twisted sense of humor. If word of his failure reached him, and it would, he wouldn't hesitate to make an example of him: his skin flayed, his bones shattered; perhaps he would be turned into one of his grotesque living dolls. He had seen what he did to failures before. It was never quick.

He wouldn't give him that satisfaction.

His eyes flicked open, filled with a cold, calculating fire. Somewhere out there, Devaultus was running, thinking he had won. The thought made his lips curl into a bitter smile. The Puppeteer wouldn't just hunt him down; no, he would tear apart everyone who had helped him, every soul who dared to stand in his way.

Perhaps he would start with the halflings, the two who led that rabble at the mansion debacle. He pictured them cowering in some dark corner of the world, thinking they were safe. He would find them, and when he did, their deaths would be slow. *Artistic.*

The Puppeteer exhaled slowly, forcing his body to relax, the pain in his wounds dulling into the background. His fingers drummed rhythmically against the armrest, his mind already weaving the next threads of his plan.

This wasn't over.

Not even close.

The door opened with a thunderous crash, splinters flying as if a bomb had gone off. A towering man strode into the room, his massive frame filling the doorway as though the space itself bent to accommodate him. His armor glinted under the dim light, each heavy footstep reverberating through the stone floor with a sense of absolute authority. Three soldiers flanked him, their faces hidden behind imposing helmets, weapons drawn and ready.

The Puppeteer shot to his feet, his heart racing as his wide eyes locked onto the colossal figure. His mind scrambled for control, for some semblance of leverage, but before he could speak, a deep, rumbling voice filled the room like the growl of an angry storm.

"Sit down, Puppeteer. I have need of you."

The command hit him like a physical blow, but pride flared in The Puppeteer's chest. He wouldn't be cowed so easily. With a flick of his wrist, three of his loyal servants rushed the intruder, their movements sharp and precise.

The massive man barely blinked.

With a brutal swipe, he backhanded the first servant, the force so immense that the poor creature's body flew like a rag doll, crashing through the stone wall in a gruesome explosion of blood, bone, and shattered masonry. Before the debris had even settled, his armored boot shot forward, smashing into the chest of the second servant. A sickening crunch echoed as ribs caved in, blood spurting from the servant's mouth before he crumpled lifeless to the floor.

The last servant didn't even have time to react. The man seized him by the head, massive fingers digging into the fragile skull. The Puppeteer could only watch in horror as he squeezed. There was a grotesque squelch, followed by a wet pop as the servant's skull gave way. Brain matter oozed from his nostrils and mouth before the limp body was flung aside like garbage.

The room fell into a suffocating silence, heavy with the stench of blood and fear.

The Puppeteer, now trembling, desperately reached out with his mind, attempting to weave his control over the towering brute. He focused, trying to infiltrate the man's mind, bend it to his will, but he was met with an iron wall, a force so strong that it nearly sent his consciousness recoiling.

The man smirked, as if amused by the pathetic attempt. "Your mind tricks won't work on me," he growled, spitting on the floor in disgust. His piercing eyes locked onto The Puppeteer with a cold, predatory glare.

The Puppeteer felt a bead of sweat trail down his temple, his heart pounding in his chest. This man was no ordinary thug.

The man took a step closer, the floor groaning beneath his weight. "Now that we've established the rules," he rumbled, his voice like grinding stone, "you will come with me. To my ship."

Recognition flared in The Puppeteer's mind. He swallowed hard, his pride shattered and survival instincts kicking in. He dipped his head, forcing a respectful nod despite the humiliation. "As you wish... Lord Tarus," he muttered, his voice barely steady, the weight of his failure heavy in the air.

Lord Tarus turned, his cape swirling behind him as he marched toward the door, leaving The Puppeteer to stumble after him, stepping over the mangled remains of his once-loyal servants.

Devaultus crashed through a precarious stack of oddly shaped fruits, sending them flying in all directions. Sticky juice splattered across his clothes as he tumbled through the mess, rolling onto his side before springing into a full sprint. His heart pounded as his boots pounded against the cobblestones. Behind him, Vex bounded over the shattered remnants of the fruit stand, a wild grin plastered across her face. A ridiculous hat, far too big for her head, bobbed with every leap. Her long blonde hair flailed behind her as she cackled, clearly having the time of her life.

"Wheee! Keep running, Devaultus! This is fun!" she called, her voice high-pitched and sing-song.

Trailing behind them, Blight stumbled over her own feet, nearly face-planting into the street before righting herself. Her tiny legs struggled to keep up, but the manic giggles spilling from her lips suggested she didn't mind one bit. She clutched a half-eaten fruit, the juice running down her chin as she giggled uncontrollably.

They barreled around a corner, Devaultus yanking them into a narrow alleyway. The shouts of dwarves echoed in the distance, their heavy boots stomping as they pursued. Devaultus slammed his back against the damp stone wall, chest heaving, gasping for breath.

"*What...*" he panted, "*was* that?!"

Vex blinked at him, her head tilting to the side in mock confusion. She twirled the absurd hat on her finger before plopping it back onto her head at a jaunty angle. "What do you mean?"

Devaultus glared, trying to suppress the mixture of exasperation and disbelief bubbling up inside him. "I mean," he gestured wildly, "*why* did you steal from that guy? We were *getting information*! It was going *fine*!"

Vex frowned, as if truly confused. "Steal? I would never steal! That's just rude." She crossed her arms with a pout, the massive hat drooping over one eye.

Devaultus let out a strangled groan and pointed at the hat. "You are *literally* wearing his hat. You took it right off his head while he was talking!"

Vex blinked, lifting the hat off her head and examining it as if seeing it for the first time. "Huh... well, *that's* weird. How'd this get here?" She tossed it up and caught it with a flourish, her grin returning full force.

Blight, still sprawled on the ground, burst into uncontrollable giggles. "I love your hat! It makes you look *so* important!" she squealed, clapping her hands together.

Devaultus pinched the bridge of his nose, letting out a long, frustrated sigh. They had managed to get a vague idea of where the entrance to Mount Fri'larja was, but thanks to Vex's chaos, the entire negotiation had ended with them being chased through half the city. Again.

"I swear," he muttered under his breath, "I'm going to lose my mind before this is all over."

Vex bounced across to him, playfully poking his nose with her gloved finger. "Oh, lighten up, Devvy! We had fun, didn't we? And now we have a souvenir!" She took his hat off his head and plopped the dwarf's hat onto his head, giggling as it flopped over his eyes.

Devaultus sighed again, but despite himself, the corners of his mouth twitched upward. Just a little.

Devaultus leaned against the rough stone wall, catching his breath, though his mind wandered far from the chaos they'd just left behind. He wouldn't admit it, not even to himself, but part of him missed being the wild one, the reckless force that charged headfirst into mayhem. Watching Vex twist and twirl through trouble, causing pure anarchy wherever she went, stirred something inside him. Despite the constant sighs and frustrated glares, he was growing to love it, love *her*. Her unpredictable nature, her gleeful descent into madness: it was intoxicating.

His eyes softened as he watched Vex crouch down in front of Blight, teasing the small, clumsy woman, her voice a playful melody. Blight giggled uncontrollably, completely enamored by Vex's chaotic energy. It was a strange scene, almost... familial. That thought twisted something deep in Devaultus' chest. Family. A concept that always felt jagged and broken to him.

His mind drifted into the dark recesses of his past. He remembered the cold halls of his childhood, filled with echoes rather than warmth. His father, Lord Sakatorious, one of the feared Lords of a group on that world named The Blood Brothers, was a towering figure, a man who took what he wanted and crushed anything in his way. Power and dominance were all that mattered to him. Devaultus had grown up in that looming shadow, a son born not out of love, but out of necessity.

And then there was his mother, or the creature who wore her face. Devaultus never truly knew her. She was a hag, a shapeshifter, deceiving his father with a flawless facade of beauty. She had been the envy of the entire kingdom, men whispering their desires, women sneering in jealousy. But beneath that perfect exterior lurked her true grotesque form. Hags were the only beings capable of birthing shapeshifters, and Lord Sakatorious had been blind to the trap he'd walked into.

It wasn't until after Devaultus was born that the truth unraveled. His father, having just secured favor from one of the gods, a monumental achievement, had burst into his wife's chamber, eager to share his triumph. But instead of the beautiful woman he'd married, he found the hag in her true, twisted form, her wiry limbs bent at unnatural angles, her sunken eyes reflecting malice.

Devaultus had been there, no older than three, playing with wooden toys on the floor, completely oblivious. He remembered hearing the roar, a mix of fury and betrayal, as his father's blade tore through the air. The hag barely had time to shriek before her body crumpled, blood pooling across the ornate rugs. Devaultus had sat there, wide-eyed, clutching a toy soldier, watching as his father stood over the corpse, breathing heavily.

That day marked him, stained him with a darkness he could never fully wash away. It wasn't long after that Lord Sakatorious began to view his son not as a child but as a potential threat, a reminder of his shameful mistake.

Lord Sakatorious' enraged gaze settled on young Devaultus. He was filled with a burning hatred that went beyond mere disappointment: it was loathing, a deep revulsion for the child born of deception. His pride had been shattered by the hag's trickery, and now that shame had a face: Devaultus.

The Lord's anger twisted into something darker. He would not be shamed by the creature his treacherous wife had birthed. Over the following months, the grand halls of Sakatorious' tower became a house of horrors for Devaultus. Cold, stone chambers that once echoed with the voices of nobles and priests now reverberated with the boy's muffled screams.

The "tests" began, though calling them tests was far too kind. They were tortures, methods designed to peel away any humanity left in the boy. Devaultus was strapped to cold stone tables, his limbs bound as runes flickered in the shadows. Acid was dripped onto his skin to see if it would heal. Searing blades sliced into his flesh, each cut measured carefully, as Lord Sakatorious observed with a cold, clinical eye. Pieces of his skin were peeled away, his bones cracked, his nerves exposed, all in the pursuit of discovering whether this "unnatural spawn" had any regenerative abilities or hidden powers. But Devaultus was nothing but a boy: wounded, terrified, and helpless.

In the beginning, Devaultus fought, screamed, and begged. But as the days stretched into weeks, his resolve hardened. The pain became background noise, a twisted lullaby that taught him that agony was simply life. Love was an abstract concept, something he had never known, never felt. His mother, a hag in disguise, was dead by his father's hand, her blood staining the very room where Devaultus had once played with simple toys, oblivious to the horror that loomed.

Sakatorious' patience waned. His fury grew as each test revealed nothing extraordinary. No divine gifts. No hidden strength. No miraculous abilities to heal or shapeshift. Just a boy: scarred, bloodied, and broken.

"You're nothing!" Sakatorious bellowed one day, his voice echoing off the cold stone walls. "A worthless abomination! I should have killed you the day you were born!" His massive form loomed over Devaultus, whose fragile body held together through sheer will.

In a final act of fury, Sakatorious gripped the young boy by the throat, his iron-clad hand squeezing until Devaultus could barely breathe. Without another word, he dragged him through the tower halls and onto a high balcony that overlooked the sprawling city below. The cold wind bit at Devaultus' torn skin as Sakatorious lifted him high above the railing.

"You'll be more useful dead," he spat. "At least then they'll pity me."

With a violent motion, he hurled Devaultus from the tower.

The fall seemed endless. The world became a blur of grey stone and cold sky. But fate, cruel as it was, had no intention of letting him die. Devaultus crashed into a wagon filled with cloth goods, the fabric breaking his fall just enough to keep him alive. Even so, the impact left him broken, bones jutting from torn skin, blood seeping through the colorful fabrics. He lay there, barely conscious, as the cart rumbled onward, its driver oblivious to the half-dead boy hidden among the wares.

But Devaultus wasn't alone.

Nestled deep within the cloth bundles, another boy watched with wide, sharp eyes, a young elf, scrappy and thin, with quick fingers that had long since adapted to surviving the streets. His name was Tristen. A street rat who had grown up in the shadows, Tristen knew the city better than anyone. He was a thief, a liar, a survivor.

Curiosity, or perhaps pity, drew him to the broken boy. Crawling over, Tristen poked Devaultus' bleeding form with a stick. "Hey... you still breathing?" he asked, voice low, almost amused. When Devaultus coughed up blood in response, Tristen grinned. "Well, guess you're lucky after all."

For reasons even Tristen didn't understand, he pulled the battered boy deeper into the cloth bundles, hiding him from view as the wagon continued its slow journey through the city. Over the next few days, Tristen nursed Devaultus back to life in his own rough way, stealing food, finding water, and teaching him how to mask pain.

Tristen became Devaultus' first taste of something akin to family, the two not bound by blood, but by survival. He taught him how to steal, how to run, how to talk his way out of trouble, and most importantly, how to never be a victim again. The two became brothers in all but name, navigating the underbelly of the city together.

For the first time, Devaultus realized there was more to life than pain. There was freedom in chaos, in defiance. And though the scars of his past would never fully heal, they hardened him into someone far stronger, a survivor molded by cruelty but tempered by friendship.

Devaultus blinked, his mind slowly returning from the depths of old memories. The haze of his thoughts lifted as he focused on the present, the dim alleyway, the soft shuffle of his companions, and the lingering adrenaline from their chaotic escape. He couldn't help but smile, just a little, as Blight yawned and curled up against the rough stone wall, her tiny frame swaddled in her oversized cloak. Her soft, contented breathing filled the silence, her innocence shining through even amidst the chaos.

Vex sat nearby, having kept his hat when she plopped the stolen one on his head. She had pulled the brim low over her wild eyes, a mischievous grin tugging at the corners of her lips as she leaned back beside Blight. She looked strangely peaceful, her legs stretched out in front of her, fingers absentmindedly twirling a few strands of Blight's raven-black hair. Even with the hat nearly covering her face, he could see the faint smudge of dirt on her cheek and the streak of blood along her knuckles from their earlier escapade. She didn't seem to care.

Devaultus tilted his head, observing them both. Was this... what a family looked like? A strange knot twisted in his chest. The word "family" had always been tainted for him, marred by the cold, cruel hands of his father and the haunting absence of a mother he never truly knew. But here, in this ragtag moment of peace amidst the chaos, he wondered... Could these two, Vex with her chaotic charm and bloodlust masked by affection, and Blight with her naive, wide-eyed view of the world, be his family?

They treated him better than any blood-relative ever had. That much was certain.

He exhaled slowly, his thoughts drifting deeper. Over the years of living on the streets, he had seen families, real ones. Parents hugging their children, lovers entwined in quiet moments, people sacrificing for one another. They spoke of family with reverence, like it was something to cherish, something worth fighting for. They spoke of *love*.

Love.

Devaultus frowned, his brow furrowing. That word had always eluded him, like smoke through his fingers. Every time he thought he grasped its meaning, it slipped away, intangible and confusing. Was this feeling, this strange warmth in his chest, as he looked at Vex and Blight... was this love? It didn't seem painful or sharp, not like the cold detachment he'd known all his life. It was... softer. Dangerous, maybe. But soft.

He rubbed his temple, frustration bubbling. He needed to understand this. If love was the glue that held people together, maybe... maybe he could figure it out. Maybe he could stop it from slipping through his fingers again.

His eyes lingered on Vex, who had now started braiding Blight's hair into messy loops, giggling softly to herself. She caught him staring and winked before flicking the brim of his stolen hat upward in mock salute.

Yes. More research was definitely needed.

Slowly, Devaultus pushed himself up from where he'd been resting, brushing the dust from his clothes with a sigh. "Alright," he began, straightening his jacket, "we know there's an entrance on the northern side of the mountain. We need to make our way through the city... without any more trouble. And by trouble, I mean stealing things," he added, turning a sharp gaze toward Vex.

Vex, crouched low with her arms draped lazily over her knees, widened her eyes in mock innocence. "Me? Steal? I'm offended!" she gasped, clutching her chest like he'd just accused her of murder; though, in her case, that would've been a compliment.

Devaultus didn't buy it for a second. He reached over and plucked his own hat off her head and firmly placed it back on his own. He tossed the oversized dwarven hat she'd stolen back at her. "At least steal something that fits next time," he muttered, shaking his head.

The massive hat landed on Vex's head sideways, completely obscuring her face. She giggled as she tilted it upright, making it sit lopsided. "I think it looks good on me," she declared, giving a playful twirl.

Meanwhile, Blight was sprawled out on the ground, snoring softly, her legs kicked out, like a napping puppy. Devaultus sighed, his patience wearing thin. He glanced at Vex, who was already nudging Blight's side with the tip of her boot.

"Wake up, Puppy," Vex cooed, giggling as Blight stirred.

Blight let out a massive yawn, stretching her arms above her head, her makeshift braid Vex had done earlier tangled and loose. Her eyes fluttered open; she was still hazy from the lingering effects of the ale. "Mmm... where are we?" she asked, groggy and innocent, like a child waking from a nap.

Vex's grin stretched even wider. "You were *so* drunk," she teased, her voice dripping with mischief, "you almost went home with that dwarf as his personal concubine."

Blight shot upright, her face flushing a bright crimson. "No! I didn't... did I?" she stammered, hands flying to her cheeks as if trying to wipe away the embarrassment.

Devaultus couldn't help the smirk tugging at the corners of his mouth as he watched Blight's horror unfold. "Oh, you definitely did," he said, folding his arms. "You were one hiccup away from calling him 'Master.'"

Vex burst out laughing, nearly doubling over as she clutched her sides. "But don't worry! Mr. D. and I saved you just in time," she added, giving Blight a teasing wink.

Blight groaned, burying her face in her hands. "I'm never drinking again."

Vex leaned in closer, still wearing the oversized dwarven hat, and whispered conspiratorially, "That's what they all say... until the next round."

Devaultus let out a long laugh, but despite himself, he felt a flicker of warmth. Chaos and all... these two were starting to feel like something dangerously close to family.

Devaultus tilted his head back, gazing up at the sky, its hues shifting from bright cerulean to soft amber as the sun edged toward its peak. "I suppose we should see about finding some lunch," he muttered, running a hand through his hair. "It wouldn't do us any good to be starving if we have to face Diego." Though the words left his lips, his heart wasn't entirely in them; he silently hoped they'd avoid a fight altogether. Maybe, just maybe, they could slip in, snag what they needed, and vanish without anyone being the wiser.

Before he could even finish the thought, Vex grinned and flicked her wrist with a flourish. A shimmering portal, no larger than a coin, snapped into existence, swirling with colors that defied logic. Devaultus blinked, taking a step back as Vex reached into the portal with gleeful abandon. One by one, she pulled out items that shouldn't have possibly fit: an elaborate checkered blanket, gleaming silverware, plates stacked high with cheeses, meats, fresh bread, and an assortment of colorful fruits. A pitcher of something sparkling and pink followed, and finally, an entire roast pheasant, still steaming.

Devaultus could only gape as the portal closed with a soft pop, leaving behind the most decadent picnic he'd seen in years. But that wasn't what had him completely dumbfounded.

His eyes locked onto the delicate ring on Vex's finger, glinting in the sunlight. It shimmered with a faint magical aura, subtle but undeniable. A Ring of Holding? His mind reeled, flashing back to that bizarre world, the one with those endless cups of bitter coffee. He remembered standing behind someone engrossed in that strange, blocky game. The player was obsessed, constantly muttering about needing a Ring of Holding to carry more loot. Devaultus had asked what it was, and another onlooker had explained, their excitement infectious. At the time, he'd scoffed, thinking the idea ridiculous.

But now? Seeing Vex effortlessly pull a feast from what was essentially thin air? Maybe it wasn't so ridiculous after all.

"Vex..." he began, pointing at the ring.

She popped a grape into her mouth, raising an eyebrow. "What? You said we needed lunch."

"Where... did you get that ring?" His voice was cautious, teetering between curiosity and the looming fear of what her answer might be.

Vex blinked, following his gaze to the ring. "Oh! This?" She twisted it around her finger. "No idea. Found it in my pocket this morning."

Devaultus' jaw tightened. Of course. She didn't even realize she'd stolen it.

Blight, who had been rubbing sleep from her eyes, finally noticed the spread before them. "Ooooh! Food!" she squealed, plopping herself down on the blanket with a delighted grin.

Vex winked at Devaultus and grabbed a slice of bread. "See? No need to find lunch. I've got us covered."

Devaultus sighed deeply, though he couldn't suppress the slight smirk tugging at the corner of his mouth. "One of these days, that chaotic luck of yours is going to get us all killed."

Vex grinned wider, raising a toast with her glass. "But not today, Mr. D. Not today."

Devaultus' mind raced, the possibilities unraveling before him like an endless tapestry. *If a Ring of Holding could exist here... what else from that game could be real?* His thoughts spiraled deeper: enchanted weapons, spells, artifacts beyond imagination. Entire mechanics could be pulled into reality. He barely tasted the food in front of him, his mind alight with wild ideas. This would take time, research, and precision... but if he could pull it off, it could change everything. He smirked at the thought. Devaultus, the architect of worlds.

A burst of giggles snapped him from his thoughts. Vex and Blight sat cross-legged on the ground, surrounded by the lavish picnic Vex had conjured from seemingly nowhere. Blight munched on a hunk of bread, crumbs dotting her lap, while Vex... well, she was being Vex.

Devaultus narrowed his eyes, watching as Vex kept reaching into her oversized hood, grabbing bits of food, only for them to vanish before reaching her mouth.

"What are you doing, Vex?" he asked, half-expecting some absurd answer.

Vex's eyes sparkled with excitement as she practically bounced in place. "Ohh! You haven't met Jerry yet, have you?" She grinned wide, her hands diving back into her hood.

Devaultus blinked. "Jerry?"

Vex beamed, pulling her hand out of the hood, empty again. "Yep! Jerry's my new pet!" She cupped her hands near her mouth, whispering into the shadowy depths of her hood, "Say hello, Jerry!"

A low, almost imperceptible *hiss* echoed back. Devaultus stiffened.

Blight's eyes widened in wonder, mid-bite, as she craned her neck to get a glimpse inside Vex's hood. "What is Jerry?" she asked, curiosity and concern mingling in her voice.

Vex gave Blight a wink. "Oh, don't worry, Puppy. You're still my favorite!" She shot Devaultus a mischievous grin before leaning back toward her hood and whispering, "I *had* to say that, Jerry. You'd make her sad."

There was another soft hiss from the depths of her hood. Devaultus rubbed his temples. *This is getting out of hand.*

But, oddly enough, he couldn't help but smile.

Devaultus cleared his throat, trying to bring Vex's scattered attention back to the moment. "What... exactly is a Jerry?" he asked, eyeing her with growing concern.

Vex's face lit up as though he'd just offered her the world's greatest gift. "Oh! I'm so glad you asked!" she squealed, bouncing slightly on the balls of her feet. She turned her head toward the depths of her oversized hood and cooed, "Come on out, Jerry! Say hi to Mr. D. and Puppy!"

Devaultus braced himself, though for what, he wasn't sure.

The shadows inside Vex's hood twisted unnaturally, swirling and rippling like dark water. Then, from the folds of fabric, a shimmering mass emerged, an orb-like creature covered in slick, writhing tentacles. The thing hovered in midair, its surface glistening as though coated in some kind of otherworldly slime. Small, unblinking eyes dotted its bulbous form, each one rolling in different directions, as if taking in every detail at once.

Devaultus stiffened, his mouth slightly agape. In all his travels, through cursed forests, forgotten catacombs, and twisted realms, he had never laid eyes on anything quite like this. "What... in the Abyss... is that?" he managed, backing up a step, instinctively reaching for the dagger at his hip.

Vex, completely unphased, tilted her head at him as if he were the one being strange. "What do you mean? It's Jerry," she replied matter-of-factly, as though she had just introduced him to a house cat.

The creature, Jerry, apparently, made a gurgling sound, a series of wet slurps and chirps that might've been a greeting. One of its tentacles waved enthusiastically.

Blight, who had been happily munching on a piece of bread, glanced up and let out a small, "Awwww!" before tossing a crumb toward Jerry. The tentacled orb snapped it out of the air with alarming speed, slurping it into what Devaultus now realized was a tooth-lined maw hidden among the tentacles.

Devaultus blinked, trying to process this madness. "Vex... where did you even find something like that?"

She grinned wide, spinning in place. "I dunno! He was just there one day. Followed me home after I accidentally, well, kinda set that one temple on fire. Remember? The one with all the screaming statues? Anyway, he seemed lonely, so I named him Jerry, and now we're best friends!" She glanced down into her hood and whispered, "Don't worry, Jerry. Mr. D.'s just being shy."

Jerry gurgled again, two of his tentacles reaching out toward Devaultus, as if inviting a hug.

Devaultus narrowed his eyes, mulling over Vex's vague response. *A temple?* He almost scoffed aloud. There was no temple, not one he knew of, at least. She was clearly hiding something, and it wasn't hard to guess why. Wherever she'd found Jerry, it was somewhere she wasn't supposed to be. That much was obvious. But he knew better than to push her now. Vex was like a cornered animal when she got defensive: push too hard, and she'd lash out or twist the truth even further.

*Fine,* he thought, watching her absentmindedly feed another scrap to Jerry, who wriggled in delight under her hood. *I'll press her later, when her guard's down. Maybe after a few drinks... or after she's distracted by something shiny.*

Still, the curiosity gnawed at him. Where had she really found that bizarre creature? And what else had she stumbled upon that she hadn't told him about? He filed the questions away, knowing that in time, Vex's chaotic nature would reveal more than she intended. It always did.

Devaultus exhaled sharply, trying to calm the whirlwind of thoughts in his head. First, the Ring of Holding. Now... Jerry. He wasn't sure which was more unsettling, the bizarre tentacled creature resting on her shoulder or the fact that Vex saw absolutely nothing wrong with any of this.

"Right..." he muttered, pinching the bridge of his nose. "Of course. Jerry."

Vex grinned wildly as she plunged her hand into the shimmering portal of the Ring of Holding, her arm vanishing up to the elbow as she rummaged around inside. With a triumphant "Aha!" she yanked out a hefty tankard of dwarven ale, frothy foam spilling over the sides. She thrust it towards Blight, her emerald eyes twinkling with mischief.

"Here, Puppy! A little hair of the dog!" Vex chirped, sloshing the mug in front of Blight's face.

Blight's skin turned an alarming shade of pale the moment she caught the potent, yeasty scent. Her cheeks puffed as she fought the urge to gag, clutching her stomach. "I don't... I don't ever want to *see* that again," she groaned, her voice trembling as she inched away from the offending tankard like it was cursed.

Vex cackled, tossing the mug back into the ring with a careless flick of her wrist. "Lightweight," she teased, snorting with laughter.

Devaultus couldn't help but smirk, the sound of Blight's suffering oddly endearing. For a brief moment, the tension that had followed them like a shadow melted away, replaced with genuine laughter echoing between them. In this insane world of chaos and danger, somehow, they had carved out a moment of pure, ridiculous joy.

The group lingered longer than they probably should have, basking in the rare moment of peace. The sun hung lazily overhead, casting warm rays across the small clearing where they sat. Devaultus found himself reluctant to break the calm, savoring the strange but comforting connection he was beginning to feel with his chaotic companions. He toyed with the thought a moment longer before finally speaking.

"Alright," he sighed, pushing himself to his feet, "I suppose we'd better get moving."

In truth, he hated the idea of ending this unique moment. It wasn't often he got to experience something so... normal. But the mission loomed, and time was not on their side.

Vex, who had been casually balancing a dagger on one fingertip, perked up immediately. With a few graceful motions, she swept the remnants of their picnic back into her Ring of Holding, humming a cheerful, off-key tune. Within moments, everything had vanished into the portal like it had never been there.

She clapped her hands together with childlike excitement. "So! We going to kill this guy?" Her eyes sparkled, her grin wide and wild, like a child on the verge of unwrapping a long-awaited gift.

Devaultus raised his hand, signaling her to slow down. "Now hold up." He fixed her with a measured stare. "Our goal is the crystal. If we can get it and escape without being seen, that's even better."

Vex's grin faltered, her shoulders slumping slightly as if he'd just denied her a favorite treat. She crossed her arms, pouting. "No killing? Not even a little bit?" she asked, her voice dripping with exaggerated disappointment.

Devaultus chuckled despite himself. "Not if we can help it."

It was always the same with her, every mission seemed to be a personal vendetta in her mind. It was as though she painted every target as someone who had wronged her, someone who needed to pay. And while that razor-sharp focus could be useful, he knew it could also lead them into chaos far quicker than necessary.

Still, he couldn't deny that a part of him found her twisted enthusiasm oddly endearing.

Blight listened closely, her head bobbing in agreement, though there was always that curious contradiction lingering around her. She preferred peaceful solutions, or so she claimed, always advocating for doing things without harming others. Yet, there was that nagging memory in Devaultus' mind: the time she had gleefully helped lead an army of cannibal halflings to devour an entire mansion full of people. That... didn't exactly scream pacifist. He frowned, the inconsistency gnawing at him for a moment, before he shook his head to clear the thought.

"Alright," he continued, pointing down the cobbled street ahead. "The entrance should be just a block away. I'm not sure what kind of security we'll run into, could be nothing, could be crawling with guards. We'll need to be careful."

Vex was crouched nearby, her legs bouncing with excitement. Her emerald eyes gleamed as she twirled a dagger between her fingers, clearly only half-listening until the word "guards" was mentioned.

Her hand shot up. "Ooooh! What if there *are* guards? Can we kill them?" she asked with the enthusiasm of someone suggesting a fun game, her wide grin practically infectious.

Devaultus groaned internally, pinching the bridge of his nose before responding. "No, Vex. No killing. That would trigger alarms long before we even got close to finding Diego. We need to be subtle, either distract them or sneak by unnoticed."

Vex let out an exaggerated sigh, dramatically flopping onto the dusty ground. "Booooring," she whined, twirling a lock of hair around her finger. "You never let me have any *fun*." But despite her complaint, there was still a glint of excitement in her eyes, the thrill of the game, even if it meant playing by someone else's rules... for now.

Blight, ever the quieter one, gave a soft nod. "I could try to lure them away... maybe make a sound or something?" she offered, brushing dirt off her skirt. Her innocent suggestion didn't quite match the dark memory Devaultus still held about her past deeds.

He sighed. "Let's just get there and see what we're dealing with first."

As they moved forward, Devaultus couldn't help but wonder if this plan had *any* chance of going smoothly, especially with Vex eyeing her daggers like they were candies she wasn't allowed to eat.

Vex slammed a hand against her chest in an exaggerated salute, her fingers splayed wide as if she were mocking some grand military tradition. "Rodger, Rodger!" she chirped, her voice filled with chaotic enthusiasm.

Devaultus froze mid-thought, brow furrowing as he shot her a sideways glance. "Now... who the hell is Rodger?" he asked, half-expecting her to yank another strange, tentacled creature from her sleeve and introduce it as her new "best friend."

But Vex simply grinned, saying nothing, her eyes twinkling with mischief. No odd critter this time. He let out a small sigh of relief and shook his head.

"Alright," he continued, gathering his thoughts again, "we'll need to find some common clothes, blend in, act normal, and get as close to the crystal as possible. Then, when the time is right, we snag it."

Vex's grin widened, but instead of her usual gleeful approval, she crossed her arms and gave him a mockingly stern look. "Devaultus! That is *so* rude. One should never steal. It's a terrible habit," she scolded, her voice dripping with seriousness.

Devaultus blinked at her, momentarily dumbfounded. *Was she serious?* This was the same woman who, without realizing, had swiped hats, rings, and entire coin purses right under people's noses. His jaw nearly dropped, but he quickly caught himself.

Blight burst into a fit of soft giggles, clutching her sides, clearly enjoying the absurdity of it all.

Vex, however, remained perfectly straight-faced, as if she had just delivered the most profound moral lesson of the day. Devaultus narrowed his eyes at her, still trying to gauge whether she was being sincere or just playing with him.

Finally, he shook his head with a sigh and said, "Well... it's a *good* thing this time. That crystal was stolen from Al'Shandra."

He had no idea if that was true, but he figured Vex didn't either. If there was one thing he'd learned about her, it was that her moral compass spun in circles, and sometimes, just sometimes, it pointed exactly where he needed it to.

Devaultus strolled boldly down the center of the cobblestone street, his boots echoing against the stone with each step. The sun filtered through iron-wrought balconies above, casting long shadows that danced along the bustling avenue. On either side, squat stone buildings rose up, carved directly into the mountainside, their heavy wooden signs swinging in the breeze. Market stalls overflowed with wares, polished gemstones, sturdy steelworks, and enough ale barrels to drown an army.

His companions flanked him, Vex practically bouncing along, her Emerald eyes wide with excitement, and Blight trailing more cautiously, her small frame nearly hidden beneath her cloak. Despite their attempts to seem casual, they were drawing attention. *A lot* of attention.

Devaultus wasn't surprised. The city was filled almost entirely with dwarves, stocky, broad-shouldered folk with thick beards and booming voices. His group stood out like a sore thumb. All three of them were significantly taller than the average dwarf, their silhouettes towering over the crowd. But rather than the suspicious glares Devaultus expected, the dwarves seemed... oddly fascinated.

He noticed it as they passed a group of burly smiths, their faces smudged with soot. They paused their work, leaning on their hammers to watch the trio pass. One even gave Vex an approving whistle. Across the way, a cluster of dwarf women huddled by a bakery's stone oven, giggling and whispering as they eyed Devaultus up and down. Blight, blushing furiously, tugged her hood lower over her face.

Devaultus muttered under his breath, "This is absurd."

Vex, of course, thrived on the attention. She winked at a group of armored dwarves leaning against a tavern wall, spinning once to make her cloak flare out dramatically. "Mr. D.! I think they *like* us!" she sang, throwing her arms wide.

He pinched the bridge of his nose. "They're staring because we stick out like a dragon in a chicken coop."

"But *why*?" Blight asked, her voice soft as she glanced around nervously. "We're not exactly inconspicuous."

Devaultus sighed, the corners of his mouth twitching into a reluctant smirk. "Dwarves have a... thing for tall folk," he explained. "Some believe if they mix their bloodlines with someone taller, they'll end up with kids who are both towering *and* strong as a dwarf."

Blight blinked, clearly baffled. "Seriously?"

Vex clapped her hands together. "Oh! That's *adorable!* I could be someone's *dream girl* here!"

"Let's not test that theory," Devaultus muttered, quickening his pace.

But the thought lingered. He couldn't entirely fault the dwarves' logic. Dwarves were already unmatched in strength and resilience, being warriors by nature. Pair that with the reach and agility of a taller race? It would create a truly formidable being. Still, it didn't help *his* current predicament.

Everywhere they walked, dwarves smiled, nodded, or outright waved. They might as well have been parading through the city center. So much for stealth.

"Y'know, Mr. D.," Vex piped up, sidling closer and draping an arm over his shoulder, "you *could* use this to our advantage."

He arched a brow at her. "How?"

She grinned. "Well, if they already love us, why not waltz through the front door? No one expects the bold approach."

Devaultus gave her a sidelong glance. "That *is* the plan."

She squealed with excitement. "See! We're already thinking alike!"

Blight giggled softly behind them, though she still looked somewhat uneasy.

Devaultus let out a breath, adjusting the brim of his hat. "Well, let's hope their fascination keeps them distracted long enough for us to get to that crystal."

"Or," Vex added with a mischievous grin, "we could just marry into the royal family and *own* the crystal."

"*No!*"

She pouted. "You never let me have any fun."

As they continued forward, dwarves parted before them like a sea of eager admirers, their whispered conversations trailing in their wake. Devaultus tried to ignore them, focusing instead on the towering fortress ahead, its stone gates looming large, guarded by armored sentinels.

He just hoped this insane plan of his actually worked.

Devaultus paused at the entrance, eyes scanning the stone archway guarded by a single female dwarf clad in sturdy armor. He took a breath, a sly grin spreading across his face. This was his moment. Time to put on the charm.

Turning to Vex and Blight, he gestured subtly with his hand. "Alright, when I get her to step away, you two slip inside. I'll find you on the other side."

Both women nodded, Vex barely containing her giggles while Blight focused, her expression determined.

Devaultus squared his shoulders and approached the guard with the confidence of someone who had done this a hundred times. "Aye, lass," he called out, his voice warm and smooth.

The female dwarf perked up immediately, her stern demeanor softening as her eyes met his. It wasn't every day a tall, mysterious stranger paid her any mind, let alone with that kind of smile.

Devaultus leaned casually against the stone wall, tilting his head just enough to make it seem unintentional. "I dare say, your captain has an eye for talent, posting someone as strong and capable as yourself to guard such an important entrance."

Her cheeks flushed beneath her bronze helmet, and she puffed out her chest with pride. "Well, they know I put my full attention into anything I do..." she purred, her voice dropping to a sultry tone, "and I do mean anything."

Devaultus grinned wider, locking eyes with her. "Oh, I don't doubt that for a second."

As she giggled, twirling a strand of hair that had slipped from beneath her helmet, Devaultus noticed Vex and Blight out of the corner of his eye, silently slipping through the entrance while the guard's attention was completely on him. Perfect.

# CHAPTER 10

# DON'T BE SUSPICIOUS, DON'T BE SUSPICIOUS

V ex exaggerated every step, lifting her legs comically high as if she were sneaking through a cartoonish heist. Her arms flailed out for balance, fingers splayed like claws, and with every step, her boots slapped the stone floor with an odd mixture of stealth and chaos. She moved like a child playing detective, fully immersed in her own performance, half spy, half jester. Blight trailed behind her, taking small, measured steps, doing her best to suppress the smile tugging at the corners of her lips. Watching Vex in her element, or at least, in *some* element, was always entertaining. It was clear Vex was reveling in the role, playing the part of a master sneak with all the subtlety of a fireworks display. Blight figured it was only a matter of time before Vex got bored of her self-appointed spy act, but for now, it seemed to be working... somehow.

Still, Blight's mind wandered to Devaultus. She hoped he was doing alright, though knowing him, she imagined him in the middle of some impromptu village celebration, probably surrounded by admiring townsfolk as he strummed his lute and spun tales of grandeur. He had a way of making even the most unlikely scenarios unfold in his favor. *Probably has a whole feast going in his honor by now,* she thought with a smirk.

Her attention snapped back to the tunnel ahead. The darkness pressed in thick around them, the only sounds being the exaggerated *clomp-clomp* of Vex's over-the-top steps and the occasional rustle of Blight's own careful movements. She squinted into the void ahead, trying to pierce the darkness. "Do you see…"

"Shhhh…" Vex hissed, spinning on her heel and dramatically pressing a finger to her lips. Her hat tilted slightly, casting her face in deeper shadow.

Blight sighed but relented. They pressed on, Vex leading with her absurdly high-kneed march, until Blight tried again, her voice a whisper, "I really can't see anything, can y…"

"Shhhh!" Vex interrupted again, this time even louder, waving her hands as though her shushing could physically push Blight's words away.

Blight huffed softly, biting her tongue. *How is she seeing anything?* It was pitch-black. Unless Vex had some hidden magical trick up her sleeve, there was no way she could navigate through this. Right as Blight was about to speak up again, the universe offered its answer.

With a loud *thud*, Vex's raised foot, mid-exaggerated step, collided directly with an unseen wall. The impact sent her sprawling backward, arms flailing, before she landed in a heap, clutching her nose. "Ouch!" she squeaked, voice muffled as she pressed her hands to her face.

Blight burst out laughing, unable to hold it in any longer. The sound echoed around them, filling the tunnel with warmth in the midst of all the darkness.

Vex, her nose slightly red but her pride intact, glanced up at Blight. "What's so funny?" she asked, her voice nasally from holding her nose.

Blight tried to stifle her giggles as she fished through her bag. "I was *trying* to tell you that I found a torch," she said, pulling out the dusty piece of wood and striking it to life. A warm glow filled the tunnel, illuminating the absurd scene, Vex still half-tangled on the ground, her hat slightly askew, and Blight standing over her with the lit torch.

Vex blinked against the sudden brightness, then sat up, dusting herself off. "Why didn't you say so?" she asked, as if the whole mishap had been Blight's fault.

Blight raised an eyebrow, fighting back another fit of laughter. "I *did*."

Vex grinned, unbothered by the incident. "Well, now we can really get sneaky," she declared, standing tall and adjusting her hat with a flourish.

Blight shook her head, torch in hand, and followed her unpredictable companion deeper into the tunnels, wondering what chaos would come next.

The two wandered down the dim, twisting path, their footsteps echoing off the stone walls. It was only now, in the eerie silence, that they both realized that they were faced with a glaring problem: they had absolutely no idea where they were going. Not a clue where this mysterious Diego was hiding, nor what the fabled crystal even looked like. For all they knew, it could be a massive, glowing gemstone the size of a grown man, or perhaps a speck small enough to fit beneath a fingernail. And what did the crystal actually *do*? Neither of them had the faintest idea. All of that information had been left to Devaultus, who, unsurprisingly, hadn't shared much before sending them off.

Blight sighed and broke the silence. "Hey, Vex... do you even know what this crystal looks like? Or where this Diego guy is?" she asked, her voice filled with growing concern.

Vex stopped mid-step, one foot still dangling in the air, and considered the question. After a beat, she shrugged. "Oh, I'm sure it won't be that hard."

Blight's eyes widened in horror. "Why would you *say* that?!" she gasped, clutching at the pendant around her neck as though to ward off impending doom.

Vex blinked, genuinely confused. "What do you mean?"

Blight threw her hands up in exasperation. "That's bad karma! You never say stuff like that. It's basically asking the universe to screw us over."

Vex tilted her head, repeating the unfamiliar word to herself. "Karma?" She let the word roll off her tongue, grinning. "Sounds exotic."

Blight sighed and started walking again, muttering, "Never mind. Let's just go."

They ventured further into the underground maze, the tension between them dissolving into the oppressive stillness. As they turned a corner, they stepped into a massive chamber, its high ceilings lost in shadows. Six doorways loomed ahead, each one identical and equally uninviting, leading into darkness.

Vex put her hands on her hips, surveying the choices. "Well... *karma!*" she blurted out, using the word like a curse.

Blight shot her an incredulous look. "I told you, it's *bad* karma! And that's not even how you use the word."

But Vex only smirked, folding her arms under her chest. "Puppy, I think I know exactly the karma I'm talking about."

Blight shook her head, though she couldn't help but grin at Vex's nonsense. Then, without hesitation, she began walking toward the far-left doorway.

Vex cocked her head, puzzled. "Wait, why that one? How do you know it's the right door?"

Blight paused and looked back. "Easy. In dungeons, you always go left. It's well-known."

Vex frowned, following behind her. "Dungeons? This doesn't *feel* like a dungeon."

Blight didn't stop. "Oh, it's a thing. Left is the way to go. Always."

Vex squinted suspiciously at her. "Where *are* you from, exactly?"

Blight hesitated for a beat before answering, her voice just above a whisper, "Somewhere where we know better than to say things like, 'It won't be that hard.'"

Vex chuckled, shaking her head. "Well, karma or not, this is going to be fun."

Blight hesitated at the doorway, cautiously raising the torch above her head to peer inside. It never crossed her mind that holding a bright, flickering light would make her an easy target, visible long before she could spot anyone lurking in the shadows. The warm glow danced across the cavernous room, revealing towering stacks of crates that reached all the way to the ceiling, forming a maze of shadowy aisles.

She took a cautious step forward, her boots crunching softly against the dusty stone floor. Vex appeared at her side, eyes sparkling with curiosity as they both scanned the labyrinth of crates. Blight bit her lip, whispering, "How do we know if it's in one of these crates?"

Vex's grin spread wide, a mischievous glint in her eyes. "Easy. I'll figure it out."

Before Blight could object, Vex sauntered over to the nearest crate, tracing a delicate finger along its rough wooden edge, pretending some hidden inscription would magically reveal the contents. After a few moments of this pointless inspection, she shrugged and reached into her Ring of Holding with a flourish, pulling out a massive dwarven blacksmith hammer.

Blight's eyes widened in shock. *Wasn't the dwarf just using that?* How Vex had managed to swipe it without anyone noticing was beyond her, but now wasn't the time for questions.

"Vex, wait, maybe we shouldn't..." Blight started, but it was too late.

With a gleeful laugh, Vex hefted the hammer over her shoulder and brought it crashing down onto the crate. The blow splintered the wood with a crack that echoed through the cavern like a thunderclap. Shards of wood scattered across the floor as the contents spilled out.

Blight cringed, her face draining of color. The echo still lingered in the air, bouncing off the stone walls. *If anyone was in here, they definitely knew now.*

Vex, however, seemed blissfully unaware of the racket she'd caused. She crouched by the opened crate, rummaging through it with excitement. "Oooh, look! Candles!" she exclaimed, holding up a fat, waxy pillar with pride. "See? I told you I could figure it out!" she beamed, completely oblivious to Blight's horrified expression.

Blight sighed heavily, pinching the bridge of her nose. "Vex... maybe don't open any more crates, okay? We don't want to..."

But her words trailed off as a faint scuttling sound echoed through the room. Out from beneath Vex's cloak, Jerry, the tentacled orb, slithered, his many limbs propelling him quickly across the stone floor. His bulbous body shimmered in the torchlight as he darted between crates, his curiosity leading him deeper into the warehouse.

"Jerry! Where are you going? That's the wrong way!" Vex shrieked, immediately giving chase. Her boots pounded against the floor as she weaved between crates, arms flailing as she tried to keep up with her bizarre pet.

Blight stayed behind for a moment, torn between laughing at the absurdity and screaming in frustration. Finally, she jogged after them, muttering under her breath, "We are so going to die down here..."

Blight jogged after Vex, her boots scuffing against the dusty floor as she called out, "You guys! That's backwards!" Her voice echoed through the cavernous space, laced with exasperation. Jerry, the inky tentacled orb, skidded to a halt in front of a weathered crate, his tendrils vibrating with excitement as he quivered in place.

Vex stopped so abruptly that Blight nearly collided with her. "What did you find, Jerry?" Vex crouched low, studying the crate. It looked identical to the dozens they had passed: rough wood, splintered edges, nothing remarkable. But Jerry was practically vibrating with anticipation.

Without a second thought, Vex yanked out the dwarven blacksmith's hammer from her Ring of Holding. Blight's eyes widened, a sinking feeling twisting in her gut. "Vex, no..."

But it was too late. Vex hoisted the hammer above her head with a gleeful grin, and with a thunderous *crash*, she brought it down, splintering the crate into jagged shards. The boom echoed through the cavern like a warning bell. Blight winced, covering her ears. "Why is *everything* so loud with you?" she muttered under her breath.

Dust billowed up from the broken crate, revealing a pile of coarse sand packed tightly inside. But what caught their attention were the glass orbs, half-buried in the sand, each one cradling a glowing, swirling light within. Jerry trembled with excitement, his tendrils dancing around one of the orbs.

Vex reached down, brushing sand off an orb and lifting it to eye level. The soft glow inside pulsed rhythmically, like a heartbeat.

"What is it?" Blight asked, stepping closer, her voice filled with curiosity and caution.

Vex squinted, bringing the orb closer to her face. Without warning, the glowing light inside lunged toward the glass, slamming against it as if trying to escape. Vex yelped and stumbled backward, dropping the orb. It hit the stone floor and shattered into a thousand glittering shards.

Jerry lunged forward, his inky form stretching and twisting. In an instant, he wrapped himself around the escaping light. The glow flickered, pulsing brighter for a moment before vanishing entirely into Jerry's swirling form. He hovered there for a heartbeat, then moved on as if nothing had happened.

"Did... did he just *eat* that light?" Blight asked, her voice a mix of awe and horror.

Vex tilted her head, watching Jerry. "Don't worry, he was just hungry." She giggled, kneeling to scoop up a few more of the glowing orbs and stuffing them into her Ring of Holding. "Snacks for later."

Blight's brow furrowed deeply. Her mind raced with questions. *What were those orbs? What kind of energy had Jerry absorbed?* She glanced at Jerry, who now floated contentedly beside Vex, his tendrils lazily curling in the air. He didn't *seem* dangerous, more like an overeager pet. But still... they didn't know what he was. Or what those lights had been.

*What if they were feeding him something they shouldn't?* Blight shivered at the thought but pushed it aside. Right now, they had bigger problems, like surviving this insane mission.

Blight paused at the next door and looked through. What kind of mess were the two of them going to find through here? Vex pushed forward past Blight. She seemed less cautious now as she nearly skipped forward.

The two women stepped into the next room, their footsteps echoing softly off the stone walls. This space felt different, warmer, more lived-in. A stout wooden table dominated the center, surrounded by heavy chairs, their legs scuffed and worn from years of use. Against the far wall, a fireplace crackled to life, the flames casting flickering shadows that danced along the stone. The scent of roasting meat hung in the air, mingling with the sharp bite of smoke.

At the table, a man sat comfortably, one booted foot propped on a chair beside him. He leisurely popped a piece of food into his mouth, chewing thoughtfully before glancing up at them. A smirk tugged at the corner of his mouth.

"You two seem to have taken your time," he remarked, his voice carrying a teasing edge.

The flickering firelight revealed his features as he adjusted the brim of his hat, tilting it back. It was Devaultus. His sharp features were softened by the warm glow, though his eyes still gleamed with mischief.

Vex gasped dramatically before breaking into an excited grin. Without hesitation, she sprinted forward and launched herself at Devaultus, nearly knocking him from his chair as she wrapped her arms tightly around him.

"Hey, Devvy! I missed you!" she exclaimed, her voice filled with genuine excitement. She leaned back just enough to meet his eyes, her own wide with hope. "Did you bring me a gift?"

Devaultus blinked, momentarily thrown off. "Why... would I bring you a gift?" he asked, his brow furrowing slightly in confusion.

Vex pouted, her lower lip jutting out in exaggerated disappointment. "Because we were apart for sooo long!" she whined, clinging to him a bit tighter.

Devaultus glanced over her shoulder at Blight, silently asking for help, but Blight only shrugged with a small, amused smile. She was getting used to Vex's antics, but today, Vex was being especially... Vex.

He sighed and tried to reason with her. "Vex, we were apart for maybe an hour."

Vex gasped, her eyes wide as if this was the most shocking revelation she'd ever heard. "Only an hour?!"

"Yes," Devaultus replied, trying to keep his voice steady despite her dramatics. "It wasn't that long."

Vex grinned mischievously, finally releasing him from her death grip. "Well, see? It didn't take that long after all!" She gave him a playful wink as if she had orchestrated the whole thing.

Devaultus exhaled sharply, rubbing his temples. He had definitely walked right into that one.

Deciding it was time to shift gears, he leaned back in his chair and asked, "So... have you found anything about the crystal?"

Vex twirled on her heel, pretending to consider the question seriously, while Blight chuckled softly behind her.

Vex straightened up, her posture exuding an air of exaggerated importance, as if she were about to spin an elaborate and undoubtedly ridiculous tale. But before she could get a word out, Blight, ever the voice of reason, cut in smoothly.

"Nothing on the crystal," she stated plainly. "But we did come across a massive warehouse. Though, in all honesty, there didn't seem to be anything particularly important there."

Vex, not one to let the conversation remain so dull, dramatically pulled out one of the glowing orbs and held it up triumphantly. "Except these! Jerry snacks!" she announced with childlike glee.

Devaultus furrowed his brow as he took the orb from her, turning it over between his fingers, examining the eerie, pulsing glow within the glass. He had never seen anything quite like it. It didn't radiate magic in any traditional sense, but there was something... unnatural about it. With a questioning glance, he turned to Vex. If anyone here had an extensive, albeit chaotic, knowledge of magical oddities, it was her.

"Vex," he asked, his voice tinged with curiosity. "Have you ever seen anything like this before?"

Vex nodded enthusiastically, as if she were the reigning expert on glowing orbs that apparently doubled as Jerry's food source. "Oh, plenty of times!" she declared confidently.

Devaultus squinted at her, his skepticism clear. It was hard to say if she truly had or if she just thought she had, which, for Vex, were often the same thing. Not that she would outright lie to him, Vex's reality was simply a flexible concept, dictated by whatever made the most sense to her in the moment. Still, she seemed so sure of herself, and that was at least somewhat reassuring.

Regardless, if they needed answers, there was always someone they could ask in town. Perhaps even Caralana. As frustratingly knowledgeable as she was, she had a habit of knowing people who knew things, and that was a useful trait. But for now, their focus had to remain on Diego.

"This looks like someone's living quarters," Devaultus mused, scanning the space. "Could be Diego's. Could be someone else's. Either way, let's search the place and see if we can find anything that tells us who lives here."

The group split up, each heading in different directions to rifle through the room's various belongings. Vex, naturally, skipped to the nearest box with a gleeful hum, prying open the lid with eager fingers. Inside, she found a set of small stone figurines, their craftsmanship impeccable. She turned them over in her hands, examining their details with an appraising eye. There were twelve of them in total, each depicting a different creature, though one in particular caught her interest.

It was a stout, muscular figure with oversized arms and a single lopsided eye, the other squeezed shut in what looked like a permanent wink. Vex grinned. He was ugly. She liked him. With a casual flick of her wrist, the figurine disappeared into her Ring of Holding.

Satisfied, she moved on, hopping over to another nearby box. Lifting the lid, she found an assortment of colorful stones, each one polished to a smooth finish. They were hoarded as if they were priceless jewels, yet to her trained eye, they seemed to hold no real value.

She huffed slightly, puffing out her cheeks. "Who collects rocks?" she muttered to herself, turning one over between her fingers before letting it clatter back into the pile.

Despite the odd collection, she wasn't convinced that they had found anything useful yet. But if there was something important hidden here, she was determined to find it.

Blight cautiously approached the enormous bed, its sheer size making her feel almost miniature. Whoever lived here clearly valued comfort, or at the very least, excess. She hesitated for a moment before gently sifting through the items scattered across the thick blankets, her fingers careful not to disturb anything too much. Every piece of clothing, every trinket, every personal belonging told a story, and she had no intention of disrespecting them. Still, she knew Devaultus wouldn't care about the sentimentality of it. They had a mission to complete, and as he'd made abundantly clear, failure wasn't an option. Their lives depended on this.

As she sorted through the belongings, something unusual caught her attention. Tucked between the folds of the heavy furs was a stuffed lizard, its scales eerily lifelike. At first, she thought it was a preserved specimen, but as she ran her hand over it, she realized it was stuffed with something soft, making it almost like a child's toy. It was made from real lizard skin; whoever owned it had gone through the trouble of having it crafted, rather than simply buying some ordinary doll.

Blight frowned, a quiet unease settling in her gut. This didn't fit the image she had of Diego, the supposedly fearsome and infamous figure they were hunting. Perhaps he had a child? That would complicate things. She chewed her lip, the thought unsettling. If things went south, if this mission turned violent, having a child involved would make everything infinitely worse. She could only hope the toy was nothing more than a bizarre indulgence and not a sign of something more personal.

Devaultus sifted through the countless parchments scattered across the desk, his fingers brushing over the worn edges of leather-bound scrolls and brittle sheets of paper. There was an odd assortment, some filled with neat, scholarly writing, others covered in almost childlike scribbles. He furrowed his brow, flipping through page after page, expecting to uncover something of significance: maps, coded messages, records of stolen treasures. But instead... stories. Simple, innocent children's stories.

He let out a slow, frustrated sigh, straightening the pile before tossing one of the parchments back onto the desk. This made no sense. The Diego they were after was supposed to be dangerous: a figure shrouded in mystery, power, and deception. Why, then, did his supposed quarters look more like the private study of a doting parent or a sentimental collector? Something was wrong.

Devaultus straightened, his mind racing through the possibilities. "I don't think..." he started, but before he could finish, the heavy wooden door to the room exploded open with a deafening *bang*.

The force rattled the shelves, a gust of air scattering loose parchments like startled birds. Instinctively, Devaultus reached for his weapon, his heart hammering against his ribs. The moment of quiet confusion had shattered. Whoever had just entered wasn't here for a bedtime story.

A massive figure had stomped into the room, his shadow swallowing the flickering firelight. It was a sand ogre, his hulking form disfigured in a way that made him all the more intimidating. One of his eyes drooped off-center, smaller and uneven compared to the other, which was large and bulging with alarm at the sight of strangers ransacking his home. His gut was immense, rounded, and his arms were as thick as Blight's entire body. The sight of him sent a wave of stunned silence through the group.

He was draped in a massive cloth that barely managed to cover all the parts they really didn't want to see, and his deep, gravelly voice rumbled through the room. "What you do in Bozz room? Not allowed in Bozz room!"

Devaultus instinctively took a step back, hand hovering near his weapons, though he kept them sheathed for now. Vex, for once, was caught off guard, stumbling back at the sheer size of the creature. But it was Blight who noticed something the other two had missed: the way the ogre's face twisted, not in anger, but distress. His massive, malformed mouth trembled slightly, and his large, wet eye glistened as if he were on the verge of tears.

Blight quickly put her hands up, offering the gentlest smile she could muster. "Oh! You must be Bozz!" she said, her voice bright and welcoming.

The towering ogre hesitated, his brow furrowing in confusion. "You know... Bozz?" His voice was still gruff, but there was an unmistakable note of uncertainty there, like he wasn't sure if he should be angry or touched.

Blight could feel the tension in the air, the way Vex and Devaultus were poised to react the second things went south. If Bozz so much as twitched wrongly, they'd dispatch him before she could say a word. She needed to act fast.

With an even softer smile, she took a careful step forward. "Well, no... but I want to! You seem very sweet."

Bozz blinked, his large, watery eye flicking between them, his expression torn between suspicion and something softer. The tension in the room held like a drawn bowstring, waiting to snap.

Bozz's already drooping eye narrowed with suspicion, his frown deepening. "Bozz not talk to strangers. Strangers bad," he grumbled, his voice a low rumble that vibrated the very air around them. His enormous arms crossed over his massive chest, his gut shifting with the motion as he loomed over the group. His presence filled the room, an immovable force blocking their only exit.

Vex's gaze flickered between the towering ogre and Devaultus, silently asking whether she could do something about this. Devaultus, however, gave her a subtle shake of his head, signaling for her to stay put. The last thing they needed was for Vex to provoke the creature, intentionally or otherwise.

Blight, on the other hand, let out a lighthearted giggle, as though completely unfazed by the situation. "Oh, I'm..." she hesitated for just a moment, clearly weighing her next words carefully before sighing in resignation. "I'm Puppy," she finally admitted, the name rolling off her tongue with clear reluctance. It was a ridiculous nickname that Vex had relentlessly insisted on using, but perhaps, in this moment, it would work to her advantage. "Now that you know me, we're no longer strangers," she added, flashing him her sweetest smile.

Bozz cocked his oversized head to the side, his wide, uneven eyes scanning her for any deception. His thick brow furrowed as his mind worked through her logic, trying to find a flaw. Eventually, however, a spark of realization showed on his face. His lips curled into an enormous grin, his jagged teeth peeking through.

"Bozz like Puppy," he announced, his entire demeanor shifting in an instant from guarded hostility to pure excitement. "Bozz show Puppy his toys!"

Devaultus, who had been tensed and ready for an attack, subtly released his grip on his daggers. Vex, despite her usual chaotic nature, wisely refrained from making a sarcastic remark, though the smirk tugging at her lips made it clear she was holding something back.

Before Blight could react, Bozz suddenly turned and lunged toward the side of the room. The ground shook slightly as he moved with surprising speed for a creature of his size. He snatched up something massive and soft, whirling back around to thrust it toward Blight with enough force that she had to brace herself to avoid being knocked off her feet.

"This Bonk!" Bozz announced with a deep, rumbling pride, thrusting the enormous, well-worn stuffed lizard toward Blight. She had caught a glimpse of it earlier, but now she could truly take in the details. The toy was crafted from real lizard skin, a fact she had noted before, but now she could see just how much time had worn it down. Its seams were barely holding together, stretched and frayed from years of handling. The once-intricate stitching had unraveled in places, leaving gaps in the rough fabric. One of its button eyes, which had likely been stitched on with care long ago, dangled by a single fragile thread, swaying slightly as Bozz moved. It was clear that Bonk had been cherished, hugged, and possibly even cried into over the years, its worn hide telling a silent story of companionship in Bozz's solitary life.

Blight blinked in surprise but quickly caught herself, her lips curling into an amused smile. "Bonk, huh? He looks... very loved."

Bozz beamed, clearly thrilled by her interest. "Bonk best friend. Bonk keep Bozz safe. Bozz keep Bonk safe." His large hands cradled the toy with a surprising amount of gentleness for a creature so large.

Vex leaned slightly toward Devaultus and whispered, "I swear, if we have to fight this guy, I'm stealing Bonk."

Devaultus shot her a warning look, but there was no stopping the glimmer of mischief in her eyes.

Blight let out a lighthearted giggle as she wrapped her arms around the enormous stuffed creature Bozz had thrust into her hands. The thing was massive, nearly as big as she was, and warn to the point of falling apart. Still, it was oddly soft, and she couldn't help but grin. "I love Bonk!" she declared, her voice full of enthusiasm.

Bozz's face lit up with pure joy, his lopsided eyes practically sparkling as he clapped his massive hands together. "Puppy love Bonk? Bozz love Bonk too! Bonk bestest friend!" His voice boomed with excitement, shaking some of the smaller trinkets on a nearby shelf.

While the two bonded over Bonk and the various odd trinkets scattered around the room, Vex slowly slinked over to Devaultus, her sharp eyes never leaving the hulking ogre. Her movements were careful, calculated, just in case things took a turn for the worse. Leaning in slightly, she murmured, "I don't think this is Diego."

Devaultus smirked, his arms crossing over his chest. "Weren't you listening? That's Bozz." He threw her a sideways glance, amusement flickering in his eyes.

Vex rolled her eyes but let out a small chuckle. "I caught that part, genius. But I mean, if this isn't Diego's room, then where is he?"

Devaultus hummed in thought, his gaze shifting back toward the odd pair. Bozz was positively beaming, showing off his collection of toys with the same pride a king would have for his treasures. And Blight, ever the gentle soul, was indulging him completely, examining each item with genuine curiosity, nodding along, and giggling at his excited explanations.

A thought crossed Devaultus' mind, and he arched a brow. "You know... Bozz might actually know where Diego is."

Vex's smirk widened. "Oh, you want me to ask him?"

Devaultus shot her a pointed look. "I was actually thinking Blight should, considering she's his new best friend."

Vex let out an exaggerated sigh, throwing her hands up in mock defeat. "Fine, fine. Let Puppy handle it."

The two of them turned their attention back to Blight and Bozz, watching as the unlikely duo continued their cheerful conversation, completely oblivious to the scheming looks being thrown their way.

Devaultus and Vex moved cautiously closer, their steps measured as they watched the towering ogre with wary eyes. Devaultus, ever the diplomat when necessary, gave a pleasant, if not slightly forced, smile as he addressed Blight. "Bli... I mean, Puppy, would you like to introduce your new friend?"

Blight beamed, clearly pleased with how things were going. "Oh yes, of course!" She turned back to Bozz, gesturing enthusiastically as though this were a formal introduction at some noble's gathering rather than a tense meeting with a massive ogre. "Bozz, these are my friends." She motioned toward Vex first. "This is Vex. She's very nice! I think you'll like her."

Vex, standing with her arms crossed, gave an exaggerated grin that did nothing to hide the mild irritation in her eyes. Nice wasn't exactly how she'd describe herself, but she supposed for Bozz's sake, she could play along.

Blight then turned toward Devaultus. "And this is Devaultus. He helps to protect Puppy."

Before either of them could react, Bozz let out an excited, rumbling laugh and lunged forward, his massive arms sweeping both of them up in an overwhelming embrace, one in each arm.

Devaultus immediately stiffened, his hands instinctively twitching toward his weapons, but he hesitated. This wasn't an attack, just an overly enthusiastic show of friendship. He felt his ribs compress painfully as the ogre squeezed them like treasured dolls.

Vex, on the other hand, had gone rigid, her eye twitching as she glared over at Devaultus. Her expression was clear: *Fix this. Now.*

Devaultus, however, had more immediate concerns, like the fact that he was being slowly suffocated in a vise of flesh, his face unfortunately pressed far too close to the overwhelming stench of Bozz's unwashed armpit. His mind repeated one desperate plea over and over: *Don't stab him, Vex. Don't stab him, Vex. For the love of all things, do not stab him, Vex.*

Finally, Bozz released them, dropping them unceremoniously to the ground. Devaultus hit the floor with a wheeze, gasping for air as he stumbled to his feet, resisting the urge to check if his ribs were still intact.

"Bozz be friends with Vex and Vaultus too!" the ogre declared proudly, beaming down at them like they had just been officially inducted into his personal circle.

Vex dusted herself off with a huff, giving Devaultus a long, unimpressed look. "I smell like ogre now," she muttered.

Devaultus, still gulping down fresh air, muttered back, "Could've been worse."

She raised an eyebrow. "Oh yeah? How?"

He shuddered. "Could've been a kiss instead."

Bozz suddenly grinned wider. "Bozz give puppy kisses?"

Blight clapped her hands together with a nervous laugh. "Oh! Maybe later, Bozz! For now, why don't we talk about Diego?"

Devaultus shot her a grateful look as Bozz's attention shifted away from potential ogre kisses and onto the topic at hand.

Devaultus exchanged glances with Blight before turning his attention back to Bozz. The towering ogre's innocent demeanor made it hard to tell just how much he actually understood about what was going on. If this truly was his home, then maybe he had valuable information, even if he didn't realize it.

Blight smiled warmly at Bozz, keeping her tone gentle and friendly. "Bozz, we're looking for someone named Diego. Have you heard of him?"

At the mention of the name, Bozz's lopsided expression shifted, his large, off-center eye widening slightly. He nodded enthusiastically. "Diego not like Bozz much," he admitted, frowning. "But Papa work with Diego. Diego Papa's boss."

Devaultus tensed at the revelation. If Bozz's father worked for Diego, that meant at least two more people were down here. He exchanged a brief look with Vex, who arched an eyebrow, clearly intrigued. This was the first real lead they'd gotten.

Taking a careful step forward, Devaultus spoke evenly. "Bozz, do you think you could show us where Diego is? We need to check on him... without him knowing we're here."

Bozz's face scrunched up in confusion as he tried to process what Devaultus was asking. "Check on him... but not here?" He frowned, deep in thought, before finally nodding. "Papa help you. Papa really smart."

That wasn't exactly the response Devaultus had hoped for, but it was better than nothing. If Bozz's father was involved with Diego, maybe he could offer some insight, or at the very least, lead them closer to their target.

"Very well," Devaultus said with a nod. "Bozz, could you take us to your papa?"

Bozz hesitated for a brief moment, as if working through the request in his mind. Then, with a decisive nod, he turned toward his bed, gently laying Bonk down as if tucking in a dear friend. He gave the stuffed lizard one final pat before lumbering toward the door.

The group followed closely behind, their senses on high alert. The air grew heavier as they stepped into the dimly lit corridor, the flickering torchlight casting jagged shadows along the stone walls. Vex and Devaultus exchanged knowing looks, both instinctively keeping their hands near their weapons.

Blight, however, walked with an air of quiet curiosity, her sharp eyes scanning each room they passed. Whatever lay ahead, one thing was clear: Bozz had just given them their next lead, and they had no choice but to follow it.

The group finally halted outside a sturdy wooden door, its surface scarred from years of use. Bozz grinned, his oversized teeth peeking out as he excitedly pointed. "Papa work in there! Bozz not allowed. Papa say Bozz break too much." His massive shoulders slumped slightly, as if the memory of past accidents weighed on him.

Blight offered him a reassuring smile, placing a gentle hand on his arm. "Alright, Bozz. Why don't you wait here, and we'll go talk to your papa?"

Bozz's face lit up with childlike excitement. "You come back to Bozz?" His wide, lopsided eyes sparkled with hope.

Blight giggled. "Of course, Bozz. We wouldn't leave without saying goodbye."

Bozz beamed, clapping his large hands together with enough force to shake the dust from the ceiling. Devaultus smirked at the display before stepping forward, placing his hands on the door. He pushed it open, striding in with the confidence of someone who belonged there. Vex and Blight followed closely, their senses sharp, ready for whatever, or whoever, awaited them inside.

Bozz, too big to slip in unnoticed, remained outside, happily peering in through the doorway, content that he had helped his new friends.

Devaultus expected to be met with another towering brute, perhaps a creature even larger than Bozz. Instead, his eyes widened at the sight before him.

A gnome.

The tiny figure bustled around the dimly lit room, muttering to himself, completely oblivious to the three intruders now standing in his workspace. Along the walls, massive glass tanks loomed like eerie sentinels, each filled with a thick, bubbling liquid. Suspended within were humanoid forms, some grotesquely large like Bozz, others smaller and more delicate. Some were human-like, others were monstrous hybrids of insect and flesh, their distorted limbs frozen in time within their eerie prisons.

Devaultus' grip instinctively tightened on his weapons as he took in the unsettling sight.

The gnome, standing barely three feet tall, was clad in an oil-streaked apron, its thick fabric draped protectively over his body. The lower half of his face was obscured by a mechanical mask that emitted a faint hiss with each breath. Strapped to his head was a bizarre contraption that magnified his vision, multiple lenses flipping in and out of place as he worked.

Something about him felt oddly familiar.

Devaultus narrowed his eyes, his mind flashing back to the Sweetwater Inn, where he had seen an apron like that before.

He cleared his throat, the sound cutting sharply through the hum of machinery.

The gnome stiffened. Then, slowly, he turned to face them, his mechanical lenses whirring as they adjusted, locking onto Devaultus with unsettling precision.

The gnome paused for a brief moment, as though it took him extra time to process that someone new had entered his lab. His wide, magnified eyes blinked behind the contraption strapped to his face before he waved a dismissive hand. "Eh... You're not allowed in here without proper gear. If you're looking for the outhouse, it's the second left." Without waiting for a response, he turned back to his work, muttering to himself as he scribbled notes onto a stained parchment.

Devaultus hesitated. This was... unexpected. He hadn't anticipated screaming or immediate hostility, but the sheer indifference to their presence was almost unsettling. The gnome had barely acknowledged them at all. Clearing his throat, he tried again. "Uhm... excuse me. Bozz, your son, said you could help us."

At that, the gnome stopped mid-motion. His shoulders shook, and for a moment, Devaultus thought he was about to hear some deep confession. Instead, the gnome let out a sharp laugh. "Bozz isn't my real son," he said with amusement. "You see, he was one of my experiments. Diego was quite unpleased with that one." His voice suddenly shifted to a deeper, gruffer tone as he mimicked someone else's voice. "'How about one with some intelligence?'" He scoffed and shook his head before turning back to his work.

"He wanted me to dispose of poor Bozz," he continued, his tone growing softer. "But I didn't have the heart. He's a sweet boy, even if he's a bit... slow. I'm sure you've noticed his mind hasn't developed like others have." He finally looked back at them, his eyes unreadable behind his thick lenses. "Perhaps it was a side effect of the experiment."

Devaultus exchanged glances with Vex and Blight before offering a slight nod. "That is indeed unfortunate. He seems like a delightful young man."

The gnome's hands stilled over his work for just a second before he muttered, "He is." Then, shaking off whatever thought had crossed his mind, he straightened and folded his arms. "Now then, what can I help you with?" His tone was clipped, impatient; whether from genuine annoyance or simple distraction, Devaultus couldn't tell.

Curiosity gnawed at him, though. His gaze swept over the strange tanks lining the room, each filled with murky liquid and the eerie, suspended figures of humanoid beings. "What kind of work do you do here?" Devaultus asked cautiously, his fingers twitching near his weapons.

The gnome's head tilted slightly as he regarded him, the lenses of his device reflecting the dim, unnatural glow of the tanks.

No doubt, this was a man who believed himself far more intelligent than he truly was, one of those minds so caught up in its own brilliance that it failed to recognize its own shortcomings. He likely assumed he needed to dumb things down for his audience.

"I am attempting to unravel the molecular strands that tether a being to its physical form," he explained, waving a hand dismissively as though this were common knowledge. "Even after one's unfortunate descent into the after-realm, I believe I have the means to reconnect those strands to their worldly vessel. With the proper amount of... tugging, of course." He paused, adjusting a set of dials on a nearby machine as he continued, almost speaking to himself rather than his audience. "If I can only determine how to make the spirit adhere properly, I should be able to forcibly anchor it back into the body, returning the individual to life. In essence, I could allow someone to dictate who lives... and who remains dead."

The gnome, if he had even acknowledged their presence fully, continued his work, flicking switches, turning knobs, and nodding in self-satisfaction. It was clear he had rehearsed these thoughts many times before, perhaps even convincing himself of his inevitable success.

"Mr. Stonewell believes this is a service that many Lords will pay vast sums for," he added, almost as an afterthought, as if the financial benefits were merely a footnote to his grand design.

Devaultus took in the information carefully, his mind running through the implications. "And how does it work? What exactly gives you the ability to do this?" he asked, watching the gnome carefully.

The small man hesitated, narrowing his eyes as if deciding just how much he was willing to reveal. "Oh, I'm not giving you that information," he scoffed. "The last thing I need is some self-important intruder waltzing in here and stealing my work." He chuckled to himself, shaking his head. "Not that it would matter. Even if you had the means, the technology would be utterly useless... without the crystal."

Devaultus hesitated for only a moment before shifting his gaze to Vex. She blinked, eyes wide with realization, before turning to Blight, who had already stiffened in recognition. Could it be...? Was this the crystal they had been searching for all along?

"What crystal is that?" Devaultus asked carefully, keeping his tone casual.

The gnome, Kalata, though they had yet to be introduced, grinned, as if he enjoyed holding onto knowledge others craved. "Ah, now that is something special," he mused, tapping the side of his mask. "It's incredibly rare. I haven't quite unraveled all of its secrets, but I do know it draws in the spirit and helps reconnect it to the body. Though, of course, it needs to be recharged frequently, an unfortunate limitation." He tilted his head in thought before adding, "Mr. Stonewell has a name for it, I believe... Ah, yes! He calls it the Lifeblood Core."

A heavy silence followed. Devaultus clenched his jaw, his mind racing. If this was truly the Lifeblood Core, then they were closer than he had dared hope. The trick now was getting to Diego without raising suspicion. His expression remained neutral, but his sharp eyes flicked to Vex with an unspoken signal.

"Mistress Lorivelle," he said smoothly.

Vex caught on instantly. She straightened, raising her chin with a noble air, adopting a posture of haughty elegance. "Yes, my dear guardian?" she asked, voice dripping with aristocratic charm.

Devaultus gestured toward the gnome, addressing him with a polite nod. "This is my mistress, Lady Lorivelle. She is quite interested in being among the first to invest in this service. It would be most beneficial for her to discuss the financial arrangements directly with Mr. Stonewell. Would it be possible for her to meet with him now?"

The gnome tapped his fingers against the workbench, clearly weighing his options. "Hmm... I suppose that would be acceptable. I've hit something of a standstill until the crystal is fully charged anyway." He waved a hand dismissively. "Very well. Come along, I'll introduce you."

Devaultus resisted the urge to smirk. Perfect.

As they exited the lab, Bozz immediately perked up, his wide grin returning as he spotted them. "Papa! New friends!" he rumbled excitedly, practically bouncing on his heels.

"Yes, yes, Bozz," the gnome muttered, leading them down a dimly lit hallway. Bozz happily followed, clearly pleased to be included.

They approached a heavy, reinforced door. The gnome didn't hesitate, pushing it open with surprising ease.

What lay beyond the threshold stopped them cold.

The room was thick with the heavy, cloying scent of incense, a feeble attempt to mask the stench of death that lingered in the air. It was large, lavishly decorated with the finest luxuries the dwarven city had to offer: ornate rugs, golden goblets, and velvet drapes that hung from the stone walls. But all the wealth in the world couldn't disguise the horror sprawled across the massive bed.

Two dwarven women lay motionless, their lifeless bodies a grim testament to Diego's indulgence. One had long since passed, her vacant eyes staring at nothing, while the other remained slumped over, a massive crystal stabbed deep into her chest. The Lifeblood Core pulsed with an eerie glow, its surface radiating with stolen energy.

Kalata's eyes widened in shock. He took a step forward, mumbling under his breath, his voice a mix of awe and horror. "Lifeblood Core... Could it truly be absorbing life force? Charging from the energy of living beings?" His fingers twitched as he reached out slightly, as though wanting to study it, to understand, but hesitation gripped him.

A voice, casual and unconcerned, cut through the room. "Yes, Kalata. It needs life force to function. That's how it works."

Diego sat across the room, entirely nude, lounging in a plush chair with an ale in his hand. He exhaled deeply, as if their presence was an inconvenience, and continued, his tone dripping with smug satisfaction. "It's simple, really. Each day, I find some desperate woman, whether through charm or coin, bring her back here, have my fun, and charge the crystal. I get to relieve stress, you get your research, and everyone's happy." He smirked, taking a slow sip from his mug.

Blight's expression twisted in disgust, her hands clenching into fists at her sides. "I'd say they don't seem all that happy," she spat, her voice shaking with anger.

Diego simply chuckled at her outrage, lifting his mug in a mock toast. "They don't matter," he said nonchalantly. "No one even misses them."

Kalata, who had been frozen in shock, suddenly looked sick. His hands trembled at his sides, his mind racing between the horrors before him and the moral implications of his work. "I... I cannot be a part of this, Mr. Stonewell," he stammered. "I signed on to create life, not steal it!"

Diego leaned forward, his smirk widening as if he were entertained by Kalata's sudden crisis of conscience. "You *are* creating life," he countered smoothly. "We're simply trading the less useful for the more useful. Think about it, if a few nameless whores have to die so we can build something that will provide an endless water supply, isn't that a fair trade? What do you think is more important? The lives of a handful of expendable women, or the future of our people?"

Kalata's face went pale, his breathing unsteady. His mind fought against the logic Diego presented, yet no matter how he tried, the sight of the dead women on the bed made it impossible to accept. His voice wavered as he shook his head. "N-no... I refuse to be a part of this."

The weight of his words hung in the air like a death sentence.

Diego pushed himself to his feet, stretching leisurely as if the conversation bored him. Then, with a dangerous smirk, he stepped closer to Kalata, his voice dipping into something cold and final.

"I don't think you understand, Kalata," he murmured, his tone laced with amusement, but his eyes gleamed with a predator's edge. "You *are* a part of this. If I go down, you go down with me. You will continue your work, whether as my partner... or my slave."

Kalata's face drained of all color. His small frame trembled, his hands curling into fists at his sides. "No..." he breathed, barely able to force the word past his lips. Then, slightly louder, his voice shaking but resolute, "I won't."

Diego's expression darkened, his amusement vanishing in an instant. His fingers flicked toward the side, and without warning, he thrust his hand forward with a sharp motion. A set of sharpened kitchen knives, clearly repurposed for something far worse than cooking, whipped through the air, cutting through the thick incense-laden atmosphere like deadly arrows.

"Then I have no need for you," Diego sneered.

Devaultus reacted in a blink. His daggers spun into his hands, a blur of steel as he deflected two of the knives midair with sharp, precise strikes. The clang of metal rang through the room. But he wasn't fast enough: two more slipped past him.

Kalata barely had time to gasp before the knives found their mark, slamming into his small body with sickening force.

His tiny form slowly crumpled to the ground, a weak gurgling sound escaping his lips as blood bubbled up from his mouth. Blight was at his side in an instant, her knees hitting the floor with a painful thud. Her hands trembled as she reached for him, pressing against the wounds in a desperate attempt to staunch the bleeding.

"Kalata, I'm going to try to heal you," she said quickly, her voice cracking. She wasn't a healer, she knew that, but she had been working on mixtures, on alchemical solutions that could mend flesh, restore strength. If there was ever a time for them to work, it was now.

Kalata gasped, his body shuddering as his small, bloodstained fingers curled into the fabric of her shirt. "P-please..." His voice was weak, barely a whisper. "Take care of the boy... Find him... somewhere... safe..."

Blight shook her head violently. "No, you can take care of him yourself! Just stay still!" She fumbled through her bag with frantic hands, nearly spilling its contents in her panic. She found the vial, uncorked it with her teeth, and poured the shimmering liquid over the wounds. It hissed and sizzled on contact, sealing the torn flesh, but the bleeding didn't stop completely. She grabbed another vial, this one meant to stabilize internal injuries, and forced it between his lips.

"Drink, damn it!" she pleaded, tilting his head back as she tried to coax the potion down his throat. His breath hitched, his body convulsing as he weakly swallowed.

For a moment, just a moment, she thought it was working. His breathing steadied, his fingers twitched against her sleeve, and hope flared in her chest. But then his body tensed, a sharp, shuddering gasp escaping him before his grip slackened. His chest rose once more, then fell. And didn't rise again.

Blight froze. "No..." she whispered. She reached for another vial, her fingers shaking so badly, she almost dropped it. She uncorked it with trembling hands, but the moment she tilted it toward his lips, she realized he was gone.

She let out a sharp breath, staring down at him as the truth sank in. Her hands, stained with his blood, hovered over his lifeless form as if she could will him back. But there was nothing left to heal.

A cold, hollow feeling settled in her chest. She squeezed her eyes shut, pressing her forehead against his as tears slipped down her cheeks. "I'm sorry," she whispered.

Behind her, Devaultus exhaled sharply, his blades still glinting in the light. The tension in the air thickened as he slowly turned to face the murderer, his expression dark and unreadable.

Diego, standing with an air of casual arrogance, sighed as if this entire ordeal had inconvenienced him. "A waste," he muttered, shaking his head. "He had potential. But sentimentality always gets in the way of progress."

Blight's hands curled into fists. The grief in her chest burned into something hotter, sharper.

Diego turned his gaze on them, utterly unfazed. "Now then," he said, a smirk playing at his lips. "Shall we discuss what happens next?"

## CHAPTER 11

# TODAY IS A GOOD DAY TO DIE

D iego let out an unimpressed sigh, swirling the ale in his hand as though this entire situation bored him. Devaultus didn't look away from him, his gaze remaining locked on the man who had so carelessly discarded life. He couldn't see Vex, but he knew better than to assume she was gone: no, she was waiting, watching, deciding when to strike.

Then Bozz stumbled into the room, his massive form shaking with every heaving sob that tore from his throat. "Papa?" His voice was fragile, uncertain, as he dropped to his knees beside the lifeless gnome. Tears splattered against the bloodied fabric of Kalata's apron as Bozz reached out with trembling hands, cradling the small, unmoving body.

Blight shifted uncomfortably, hovering nearby, her fingers twitching at her sides. She had fought; she had tried, she had been so close. "I... I tried, Bozz," she whispered, her voice barely audible over the giant's muffled sobs.

She had seen death before. Everyone in this world had. But this was different. This was a failure. She had never watched the life drain from someone she was actively trying to save. Never felt the helplessness of pouring her knowledge, her resources, her very soul into a person, only to have them slip away regardless.

Bozz sniffled loudly, his massive fingers brushing against Kalata's limp arm as if the touch alone could bring him back. "What do I do,

Papa?" His voice cracked, thick with pain, as he clutched the gnome's body against his chest, his entire frame trembling with sorrow.

There was no answer.

Devaultus fixed Diego with a wild, lopsided grin, the dim light of the room catching the glint of his teeth. His body swayed ever so slightly, a predator gauging his prey, though there was an undeniable edge of exhilaration in his stance. His fingers curled around the hilt of his blades, his grip firm but playful.

"There's nothing to discuss," he murmured, his voice laced with a chaotic amusement.

His sharp eyes never wavered from the dwarf, but in the back of his mind, he noted an absence. Vex. Where had she gone? Had she slunk off to plunder something shiny, pilfering trinkets from Diego's gaudy collection? Or was she already lurking in the shadows, waiting for an opening to strike? It didn't matter, this fight belonged to him, and once again, he found himself forced into direct combat rather than the methodical, unseen approach he preferred. He was beginning to resent this shift in his tactics.

Diego merely smirked, unbothered, and reached for a pair of pants, slipping them on with a casual ease. As he fastened them, he retrieved two more knives, their wicked edges glinting as he twirled them experimentally between his fingers. His smirk widened into something menacing.

"Very well," Diego mused, stepping forward. His stance was balanced, confident; he was hungry for blood. "Then come. Let's introduce you to the Abyss."

Devaultus wasted no time. With a burst of speed, he dashed forward, his blade slicing low toward the dwarf's calf. But Diego, nimble despite his stout frame, lifted his leg just in time, effortlessly avoiding the attack. The dwarf twisted midair, bringing a blade down toward Devaultus' exposed back in a ruthless counterstrike.

Instinct roared through Devaultus' veins, and he ducked, the sharp edge of the knife slicing just close enough to sever a single feather from his hat. The severed plume fluttered to the ground as he rolled away, smoothly transitioning into a crouch before rising to his feet.

Diego let out a hearty laugh, his confidence unwavering. The two men began to circle each other, eyes locked, testing for weaknesses in each other's movements. The tension in the air thickened, an electric charge building between them.

This time, Diego struck first. He lunged forward, his knife flashing downward in a brutal overhead stab. Devaultus knew better than to meet the attack head-on: the dwarf's sheer strength would drive the blade through flesh and bone alike. Instead, he deflected the strike to the side, redirecting its force.

Diego's smirk didn't falter. He used the momentum to spin, bringing his other knife in a vicious backhanded slash.

Devaultus twisted, narrowly evading the brunt of the attack, but the blade still kissed his side, slicing through cloth and skin. A thin, warm line of blood welled along the wound.

Diego grinned victoriously, his dark eyes gleaming. "I draw first blood."

And then, before either could move again, a scream, shrill and unhinged, like a wild banshee's wail, pierced the air.

Blight stormed into the fray, her eyes alight with fury. Devaultus had a brief moment of unease, something foreign, something he wasn't accustomed to feeling. Worry. Not for himself, but for Blight. The old Devaultus would have welcomed another body between himself and a blade, would have used any distraction to his advantage. But now? Now, he wasn't so sure. Blight didn't seem like a warrior, and that made him anxious. Would she survive this?

That moment of distraction was all Diego needed. The dwarf lunged forward, his powerful leg striking Devaultus square in the chest. The force of the blow sent him flying backward, his body hurtling through the air before crashing into the kitchen table, the wood splintering beneath him. A groan escaped his lips as he lay in the wreckage.

"Ohh... yeah, that hurt," he muttered, wincing as he attempted to roll onto his side. "I think... from now on... I'm going to avoid that. This is exactly why I prefer the whole 'stabby stabby in the dark' routine."

Diego wasn't an easy kill. That much was clear.

Meanwhile, Blight had already thrown herself into action. She skidded across the ground, her hands working with practiced precision as she hurled a small glass orb at Diego's feet. The moment it shattered, a thick gas erupted from within, swirling into the air. Devaultus recognized the acrid scent immediately, some sort of chemical concoction.

Blight, however, was prepared. Her fingers found a switch on the cumbersome collar around her neck, pressing it with a sharp click. A mechanical hiss sounded as part of the device shifted, a section rising to cover her mouth and nose, filtering the air.

Diego coughed, hacking as the gas filled his lungs, but he didn't slow. Instead, he surged through the haze, swinging wildly at Blight. She reacted just in time, raising her arm, a thick bracer intercepting the strike. The force rattled through her, but she held firm. Diego's expression twisted in frustration, his lips curling in a snarl.

Blight didn't give him a moment to recover. With a flick of her fingers, the glove on her outstretched hand flexed open, and from one of the tubes running along her arm, a thick stream of viscous gas hissed out, aimed directly at Diego's face.

He snarled at Blight, his teeth bared in frustration as he pivoted on one leg, twisting his body with practiced precision. His hands found purchase on a heavy wooden chair, and with a guttural roar, he hurled it toward her with all the force of a battering ram. Blight reacted in an instant, her instincts razor-sharp. Dropping onto her back, she kicked up with both legs, sending the airborne chair flipping over her head, where it crashed into the floor behind her with a splintering crack.

But Diego had already anticipated her move. The moment her defenses were occupied, he lunged, his daggers raised high, both poised for a vicious dual-stab meant to skewer her where she lay.

Devaultus, still struggling to regain his bearings, saw the attack unfolding but knew there was no way he could reach her in time. His fingers tightened around his weapons, frustration mounting, until a new thought struck. His voice rang out with urgent desperation.

"Scythe! We need you!"

The thick haze of incense hanging in the air seemed to ripple as a shadowed figure emerged from the swirling smoke. A delighted grin stretched across Scythe's face, her eyes gleaming with wicked amusement. She moved like a phantom, weightless and deadly, launching herself into the fray with an acrobatic burst of speed.

Her foot connected with Diego's side midair, the impact enhanced by her magic. The dwarf twisted violently, as he was sent spinning across the room before slamming into the ground with a heavy thud. Dust kicked up from the impact as he groaned, momentarily winded.

Scythe landed smoothly, her expression brimming with excitement. She had torn strips of cloth and stuffed them into her nose, an improvised defense against the lingering fumes of Blight's concoctions. Without hesitation, she flicked her wrists, sending two shimmering ghostly blades hurtling toward Diego.

The dwarf barely had time to react, instinctively diving to the side, wary of what sorcery the spectral daggers carried. He tucked into a roll and sprang back to his feet, only to find himself face-to-face with Scythe once more.

Her grin widened as she lunged, two gleaming daggers clenched in her hands, their points aimed straight for his chest.

He threw his hands up, crossing his blades in a defensive block just in time to stop Scythe's daggers from plunging into him. Their faces were inches apart, eyes locked in a heated clash, yet what unsettled Diego wasn't the attack itself, but the sheer exhilaration glimmering in the emerald depths of the blonde woman's gaze. She was enjoying this.

Diego snarled and lashed out, kicking toward her stomach in an attempt to knock her back. But she was faster. In a movement that defied reason, she twisted midair, almost as if rolling up along his leg. With a flick of her wrists, her daggers spun, slashing toward his throat. He barely reacted in time, jerking backward to avoid the gleaming edges. The proximity was too close for finesse now. He did the only thing he could: lunged forward and grabbed her.

With a grunt, he hurled her across the room. She slammed into the stone wall with a force that would have broken a lesser fighter. But instead of expressing pain, or anger, Scythe only laughed. A wild, delighted sound, like a child unwrapping a long-awaited gift. She rolled her shoulders, dusting herself off as she stood, then turned toward Diego with an expression that was nothing short of manic glee.

Devaultus, across the room, spun his daggers between his fingers, his ever-present lopsided grin deepening. He stuffed fabric into his nose, a precaution against the lingering gas, and tilted his head. "Ready to end this?" His voice was taunting, confident.

Blight, however, wasn't smiling. Unlike the others, there was no playfulness in her stance. No thrill of battle, no amusement. Her fury radiated from her in chaotic waves, her chest heaving with unspent rage. She stood with her arms spread wide, fingers twitching in anticipation, waiting, daring Diego to make his move.

Devaultus smirked, eyes gleaming. "You could barely handle us one at a time. Your end is near."

But Diego? Diego grinned. Of all things, he grinned. With a slow, deliberate motion, he reached into his belt, retrieved a small vial, and poured its contents into his mouth. He winced as it slid down his throat, his muscles tensing, veins darkening ever so slightly beneath his skin. His voice rasped, thick with something more than pain.

"You think Kalata was only working on that one project for me?"

His body convulsed violently, veins bulging beneath his skin like writhing serpents. A sickening crack echoed through the room as his flesh peeled away, replaced by jagged plates of flint that erupted across his body forming a natural armor. Diego's roar was guttural, raw with agony, his form twisting and distorting as his muscles swelled, stretching his frame to monstrous proportions. Shards of flint jutted from his forehead in wicked angles, giving him the appearance of some ancient, stone-forged demon.

Scythe shot a quick glance at Devaultus, her usually amused expression replaced with something far more calculating. The entire group shared the same unsettled look, the weight of what was happening pressing down on them like a coming storm.

"What the hell was that?" Scythe hissed, her hands tightening around her daggers.

Blight's voice was measured, though tension crackled beneath it. "Some kind of alchemical fiber-manipulation serum."

Devaultus tilted his head, his one-sided grin faltering slightly. "So is this permanent? Or do we just have to wait it out?"

Blight exhaled sharply, frustration lacing her words. "I wouldn't know without studying the serum. Could last minutes, could be irreversible."

Diego's transformation was complete. He stood nearly two feet taller than before, a towering beast encased in razor-edged stone. His grin was maddening, wild with confidence. "Well then," he rumbled, voice distorted by his warped anatomy. "Let's end this."

Without hesitation, Scythe exploded into motion, vanishing into a blur as she dashed toward him, aiming for his Achilles' heel. Devaultus was right behind her, spinning his blades and slashing upward, forcing Diego's attention toward his chest. Blight lunged from the opposite side, her wrist snapping forward, revealing a gleaming needle meant to pierce through flesh and deliver whatever concoction she had prepared.

Diego moved unnaturally fast for something of his size, stepping up just enough to make Scythe's attack miss by mere inches. Devaultus barely had time to react before Diego's arm swung, deflecting his daggers with brutal strength, sending jolts of pain up his arms as if he had struck solid steel.

Blight's needle found its mark, only to shatter uselessly against the hardened flint plating of Diego's side. Her eyes widened slightly, her mind already racing for another approach.

Diego's grin only widened. "You'll have to do better than that."

Diego's massive hand swung out in a brutal backhand, catching Blight with full force. She barely had time to brace herself before she was sent hurtling through the air, crashing hard onto the stone floor. A pained gasp tore from her lips as she tumbled to a stop, her body aching from the impact. Before Devaultus could react, Diego's clawed fingers snatched his wrist in an iron grip.

With an effortless heave, Diego flung him like a rag doll straight into Scythe. The two collapsed in a tangled heap, groaning from the force of the collision.

"Well, that didn't work out at all," Scythe muttered, rubbing her head as she pushed Devaultus off her.

"Can we even pierce that armor?" Blight wheezed, forcing herself upright. Her breath came in ragged gasps, her limbs shaking.

The three of them struggled to their feet, forming a shaky but determined front. Diego loomed before them like an unbreakable wall of stone and fury, his monstrous form unscathed. It felt hopeless. But before anyone could make a move, the room trembled.

A massive, meaty fist came out of nowhere, slamming into Diego's skull with a sickening *crack*. The behemoth of a dwarf was launched sideways, crashing straight through the wall as dust and debris exploded outward.

There followed a furious roar. A sound full of unrelenting rage and raw grief.

Bozz.

The giant of a man burst through the hole he had just sent Diego flying through, his face twisted in unbridled wrath. His massive frame heaved with heavy breaths, his normally kind eyes darkened with pure hatred.

Devaultus, Blight, and Scythe could only stare in shock before rushing toward the gaping hole, peering through the dust and rubble.

Diego was barely conscious, trying to drag himself up, but Bozz was already on him. He grabbed the dwarf by the head with both hands and slammed it into the ground. *Once.* A loud *crack* echoed through the ruined room.

He lifted him and did it again. *Twice.* A spiderweb of fractures spread through the flint-like plating on Diego's skull.

*Thrice.* The cracks deepened, shards of flint flying from the force of the impact.

A sickening, wet *crunch* rang out as Bozz drove Diego's head into the stone one final time. Blood splattered outward, seeping into the cracks of the floor. The once-monstrous form twitched, then fell limp.

But Bozz didn't stop.

He let out a guttural wail, his grief twisting into something feral, something uncontrollable. His knuckles, already slick with blood, slammed into what remained of Diego's skull, turning it into nothing more than a pulped mess on the floor. Over and over again, until there was nothing left to break.

"You hurt Papa... You *not* hurt again," he sobbed through gritted teeth, his voice thick with anguish.

The three barely had time to process what had just happened before a deep, ominous rumbling shuddered through the foundations beneath them. The entire structure groaned in protest, its integrity compromised by the ferocious battle that had shattered far too many of the supporting pillars. Dust rained down in thick clouds as the walls trembled, and massive chunks of rock began to dislodge from the ceiling, crashing down with deafening booms that sent shockwaves through the chamber.

Blight's sharp eyes darted to Bozz, whose bloodied hands still twitched with the remnants of his raw fury. She wasted no time: grabbing his wrist, her fingers slipping against the fresh blood coating his skin, she yanked him toward her and shouted over the chaos, "We need to go, now!"

Bozz hesitated, his wide eyes locked onto what remained of Diego. The lifeless, pulverized form of the dwarf lay unrecognizable, a grotesque mess of shattered flint and crushed flesh. The raw weight of what Bozz had done held him in place for a moment too long. But then, with a deep, shuddering breath, he tore his gaze away and pushed himself up, his massive form moving to follow Blight.

The group sprinted toward the exit, weaving between falling debris, their path an unpredictable gauntlet of collapsing stone. Each step was a gamble as jagged chunks of rock smashed into the ground with bone-rattling force. It was chaos, uncontrolled and merciless.

Then, Devaultus suddenly stopped. His body tensed, his head whipping around as a single thought cut through his panic like a dagger. *The crystal.*

His heart hammered as he turned back, eyes darting toward the place where it had last been. *If this place goes down, the crystal will be lost forever.*

He wasn't about to let that happen, not when Al'Shandra's debt hung over him like a noose. He refused to owe anyone anything.

Blight saw him pivot, saw the reckless determination in his face, and she cursed under her breath. "Devaultus, we need to go! It isn't worth it!" she screamed, but she already knew he wasn't listening. His mind was set, and nothing short of dragging him out would get him to move.

"Bozz, bring him!" Blight ordered, and, in one swift motion, Bozz scooped up Devaultus as if he weighed nothing.

Devaultus snarled, thrashing in his grip. "No, damn it! Let me go!" he snapped, struggling against Bozz's iron-like hold, his arms swinging wildly. But the giant wasn't having it. Without so much as a glance, Bozz tightened his grip, securing Devaultus under one arm like an unruly sack of grain, and kept running.

Behind them, the cavern gave one last, sickening groan before the true collapse began.

He had half a mind to stab the man's hand to break free, but after everything Bozz had done to help, Devaultus couldn't quite bring himself to do it. Instead, he gritted his teeth and let himself be carried, frustration burning in his chest as they charged through the collapsing tunnels.

The stone above them groaned like a dying beast, the passage shaking with every step. Dust filled the air, choking their lungs as massive chunks of rock shattered against the ground behind them. Their legs burned, each stride a desperate attempt to outrun the impending doom that threatened to bury them all.

Bozz was gasping, his massive form unused to such prolonged exertion. His breath came in ragged, pained wheezes, but he didn't stop. He couldn't. Vex's sharp eyes locked onto the exit ahead, a shrinking gap of light that was rapidly filling with debris. She pushed herself harder, arms pumping as she broke ahead of the others.

The collapsing ceiling rained death in front of her. There wouldn't be time.

With a final burst of speed, she dove forward, her body sliding across the dirt and through the narrowing opening just as the ceiling gave way behind her. A second later, Bozz hurled Devaultus forward with a surprising amount of strength. He tumbled through, hitting the ground in a graceless roll before springing up, cursing under his breath.

Bozz was right behind him, his hulking form lunging toward the exit. His massive hand shot out, shoving Blight through the gap at the last possible second. She hit the ground with a grunt, skidding to a stop.

She turned just in time to see the boulder come down.

The sound was deafening, a thunderous crash as the massive slab of stone slammed down, crushing Bozz's arm beneath its unrelenting weight. More rocks followed, slamming into his back, his legs, his chest. He let out a choked gasp, his enormous body pinned under the avalanche.

Blight's scream ripped through the cavern.

She scrambled toward him, clawing at the debris as if she could somehow free him. Dust and blood streaked his face, but through the agony, he managed to give her a weak, lopsided smile.

"Bozz... helpful," he wheezed, each word a struggle.

Blight's breath hitched, tears burning in her eyes as she reached for him. But there was nothing she could do.

Even Vex, wild and chaotic as she was, had gone silent. Slowly, she stepped up beside Blight, her expression uncharacteristically solemn. A single tear slipped down her cheek, catching in the dim light. Without a word, she reached into her Ring of Holding, her fingers brushing against something familiar.

She pulled out Bonk.

Gently, she pressed the beloved, bloodstained stuffed Lizard into Blight's shaking hands.

Apparently, she had swiped it at some point. Blight hadn't realized it. Typical.

Blight crouched down beside Bozz, her hands trembling as she gently placed Bonk next to his face. The worn stuffed creature rested against his cheek as if it belonged there, as if it could somehow save him. Bozz's lips curled into a faint, final smile before the light in his eyes flickered out like a candle in a storm.

A raw, broken wail tore from Blight's throat, a sound so full of anguish it seemed to shake the very earth beneath them. Her fingers clutched at his lifeless hand, nails digging into his massive palm as if she could anchor him to the world, keep him from slipping away. But there was no saving him now. He was gone.

He didn't deserve this.

Bozz had been kind, too kind for the cruel world that had taken him. All he ever wanted was to help. To be useful. To protect the people he cared about. And this was how the world repaid him? Crushed beneath the weight of a life that had never given him a fair chance? It was wrong. It was so damn wrong.

Blight's body shook as sobs wracked her frame, her face buried against Bozz's unmoving chest.

Then, something unexpected happened.

Vex crouched beside her, silent for a moment before she wrapped her arms around Blight. She didn't speak. She didn't offer empty words or meaningless comfort. She just held her.

It was strange seeing Vex like this: soft, vulnerable. She never showed sadness, never seemed to truly care about anything beyond her own desires. But now, here she was, holding onto Blight as if she felt her pain as deeply as her own.

Because, in that moment, she did.

Somewhere, somehow, Blight had become a part of her.

Devaultus crouched on the cold, unforgiving stone, his elbows braced against his knees, fingers threaded through his disheveled hair. His chest ached, not from exhaustion, nor from battle wounds, but from something deeper. The crystal was gone. His lifeline, his leverage, his mission. He knew he should feel more grief for Bozz, but the truth was, he hadn't shared much with the man. Not the way Blight had. Not enough for it to hurt like it did for her. But still... something gnawed at him. A hollow, twisting sensation buried beneath his usual self-interest. Was it sadness? No, not quite. It was an ache, a strange, unfamiliar pain that clawed at his ribs. A different kind of agony.

He sucked in a breath and forced the feeling away. It had to be the crystal. That was what really mattered. His failure, his debt. That was what burned in his chest. Nothing else.

A soft shuffle of footsteps pulled him from his thoughts. Vex. She moved with an easy, fluid grace, though her expression was unreadable. She stopped beside him, tilting her head slightly. "That was close," she murmured, her voice softer than usual. "I was worried for you."

Devaultus let out a slow breath and reached up, pushing the brim of his hat back just enough to look at her. His usual grin was absent, replaced by something quieter. "Thank you for your help, Vex," he said. The weight in his voice was new, unfamiliar even to him.

The wild, dangerous tension that made her Scythe melted away, fading into something softer. The shift in her stance, the way her lips curled just slightly; it was Vex again. Just Vex.

She reached into her Ring of Holding and, with a slow, deliberate motion, pulled out the crystal. The glow of it bathed her fingers in an eerie light, and for a moment, the dust-filled air around them seemed to still.

Devaultus' eyes widened in utter shock. "How?" he breathed, his voice barely above a whisper.

Vex grinned, mischief dancing in her emerald eyes as she held the precious artifact between her fingers. "I stole it," she said, her voice light, almost teasing, as if she hadn't just revealed something monumental.

Blight, still trembling from grief, snapped her head toward Vex, her breath hitching. Then, as if realizing the weight of the moment, she surged forward, desperation in every movement. "Bring him back," she demanded, her voice shaking. "Bring Bozz back!"

Devaultus didn't answer immediately. Instead, he exhaled, rubbing his thumb along the edge of his dagger before giving her a solemn, almost pitying smile. "We can't."

Blight's fingers tightened around his arm like a vise, her body wracked with sorrow. "Please, Devaultus. Please," she choked out, her voice breaking as fresh tears carved tracks through the dust on her face. Her chest heaved with silent sobs, her grief raw, unbearable.

His expression softened, and for the first time in a long while, something unfamiliar twisted in his chest. Guilt? Pity? He wasn't sure. "His body is destroyed, Blight," he said gently. "We don't have a body to bring him back to."

Blight's breath hitched, her grip on him weakening as the weight of his words settled over her like a crushing tide. She shook her head, unwilling to accept it. "There has to be a way. There has to be something..."

Vex stepped closer, her usual playful demeanor subdued. "It would be a horrible thing," she murmured, her voice uncharacteristically soft, "to bring him back to such pain... only for him to die again."

Blight's shoulders slumped. Her arms fell uselessly to her sides, and she barely managed a whisper. "I know..." The words came out broken, shattered by grief, as she stared at the ground, her body trembling with quiet, pained acceptance.

She leaned forward, her arms wrapping tightly around Devaultus. He stiffened, his entire body going rigid as if she had struck him rather than embraced him. This... this was unfamiliar. Foreign. Unnerving. He had faced blades, fire, death itself, and never once had he hesitated. But this? This made him falter.

His hand twitched, hovering uncertainly over her shoulder, fingers curling slightly as if unsure whether to make contact or recoil. His eyes, usually sharp and calculating, now held something unrecognizable: fear. Not of pain, not of death, but of something far worse. A sensation that threatened to unravel him.

Would this single act of compassion be his undoing?

Slowly, hesitantly, his hand drifted downward. It loomed over her, frozen in indecision, before finally coming to rest on her shoulder. A small, hesitant touch. Barely there, but enough.

Blight's form shuddered against him as her sobs wracked her body, her tears mixing with the dust and blood that clung to her skin. She held him, not for warmth, not for comfort, but because grief had hollowed her out, and he was the only thing solid in this moment.

Devaultus stared down at her, his own existence feeling strangely fragile. His instincts screamed at him to pull away, to slip back into the safety of detachment. But he didn't move.

For the first time, he simply let someone hold on to him.

Vex watched the two.

She would not be a victim of fate any longer.

Vex's fingers curled into fists at her sides, her nails biting into her palms, but the pain was distant, irrelevant compared to the storm inside her. Her rage was a living thing, wrapping around her ribs, whispering promises of vengeance in her ear. She could almost hear the screams of those who had wronged her, who had wronged them all. And yet, as she watched Blight sob against Devaultus, she realized something else.

Devaultus had no idea what to do with this. His hand hovered uncertainly over Blight's trembling form, his expression unreadable, but his eyes, the way his eyes darted, searching, confused, spoke volumes. He didn't understand how to comfort someone. He didn't know how to process what he was feeling.

Vex tilted her head, studying him as a predator might study prey. Was it possible he felt the same confusion she did? She knew her own emotions well enough, knew that she adored him, worshipped him, wanted to follow him into the Abyss if that was where he chose to walk. But Devaultus... he was still figuring it out. He didn't understand love, not yet. But he would.

Her gaze dropped to Blight again, and for the briefest moment, something flickered in her chest, something foreign, something akin to pity. Blight was drowning in grief. And Vex? Vex was too burned out to cry. Maybe she had already lost too much. Maybe she was too broken for sorrow. All that remained in her now was a hunger for something greater.

She had always been chaos incarnate, a storm that stole what it pleased, killed when it felt right, laughed in the face of morality. Unlike Lorivelle, who was weak. But now, she wanted more than just carnage. She wanted change. A world reshaped in her image. A world where none of them would have to suffer like this again.

It didn't matter how much blood she had to spill to get there.

Blight looked up at Devaultus, her tear-filled eyes searching his face. She could see it, how deeply uncomfortable he was, how stiffly he held her, as if one wrong move could send the entire world crumbling around him. One arm hung awkwardly at his sides, hesitant, uncertain. It wasn't rejection, nor was it cruelty. It was something far worse. Devaultus simply didn't know how to hold her. How to comfort. As though the very act of human closeness was foreign to him.

She wasn't sure what kind of life had forged him into this. What pain had left him so utterly detached that a mere embrace could shake him to his core? For a moment, despite her own anguish, she felt sorry for him. She had known sorrow, yes, but she had also known love, kindness, and passion. She had been cared for. But Devaultus... she wasn't so sure. He was a perfect killer, a blade honed to precision, feeling nothing when he drove his daggers into flesh. Had he ever felt anything at all? Had he ever even been given the chance?

The smaller group moved toward the entrance of the mountain, their steps heavy with exhaustion. The battle, the loss, the weight of everything pressed down on them. No one in the city stopped them as they passed, no guards called out, no merchants tried to sell them wares. Perhaps they saw the grief written on their faces, or perhaps even the cruelest among them knew that now was not the time.

Al'Shandra stood waiting as they ascended the gangplank, her sharp gaze assessing them. She said nothing at first, but when her eyes met Devaultus', she raised an eyebrow ever so slightly.

Ever the performer, Devaultus shifted in an instant. His lips curled into a grin, and he swept into a half-hearted bow, as if the weight of everything hadn't been on his shoulders mere moments ago. "Your crystal," he said smoothly, presenting it with a flourish.

Al'Shandra returned his smile, though hers was far more satisfied. "Well done," she purred. "It seems your first mission is complete. Go. Get some food and rest."

Without another word, Devaultus turned and strode toward the ship's tavern. He slipped inside, ordering an ale and whatever meal was hot, settling into a quiet corner. He played his part well, acting as if there was nothing on his mind, as if this was just another mission, another job completed. But Vex saw through him.

She didn't say a word as she approached, sliding into the seat across from him. The two sat in silence, eating their food, sipping their drinks.

No words were spoken, but Vex didn't need them. She could feel it, even if Devaultus himself didn't fully understand it yet. Something was different now. Something weighed on him.

And that, more than anything, intrigued her.

Blight lingered at the entrance of the ship's tavern, watching as the only two people she could truly call friends sat in silence, their meals barely touched. There was an air of discomfort between them, as if the weight of everything they had endured still clung to their shoulders, pressing them into their seats. The thought crossed her mind to join them, to sit with them like the dysfunctional family they had become, bound by blood and survival. But something in her hesitated. She wasn't hungry, not for food, not for conversation.

Instead, she turned away, slipping through the dim corridors of the ship, her footsteps light, almost ghostlike. She needed space, time to herself, though she wasn't sure what good it would do. When she reached her small quarters, she pushed the door open and stepped inside, closing it behind her with a soft click. The familiar space felt suffocating tonight, the walls too close, the air too thick with the echoes of everything she had lost.

With a trembling breath, she moved to her bed and curled up atop the thin mattress, tucking herself into a ball as if making herself smaller would make the pain hurt less. But it didn't. The grief clawed at her, tearing past her defenses, until the sobs wracked her body in violent, gasping waves. She pressed her face into the pillow, muffling the sound, but it didn't stop the ache deep in her chest.

She hated this world. Hated how cruel it was. How everything in it seemed to be built on anger, suffering, and destruction. No matter how hard she tried, no matter how much she fought, it never seemed to change. The unfairness of it all crushed her, and she wished, just for a moment, that she could escape it, to a place where kindness wasn't a weakness, where people like Bozz didn't have to die just for trying to help.

Her exhaustion weighed her down, pulling her deeper into the bed, into the darkness that wrapped around her like a shroud. Her sobs softened, fading into quiet sniffles, until finally, her body gave in. Sleep took her, dragging her down into restless dreams, back to the world she had left behind.

## CHAPTER 12

# FORGOTTEN REALMS: BLIGHT'S LOST LIFE

T wo weeks earlier, in a world far away.

Cassandra giggled, her heart fluttering with anticipation. She and Thomas had been together for over a year now, and, unlike all the worthless men she had encountered before him, the ones who only ever saw her as a prize, who wanted far more than just her company, Thomas treated her like she mattered, like she was more than just a pretty face.

She had grown up in the bustling city of Denver, Colorado, a place teeming with opportunity, yet filled with distractions that made it easy to lose oneself. But Cassandra had never lost sight of what she wanted. She had thrown herself into her studies, dedicating nearly every waking moment to pharmaceutical research. Well... that wasn't entirely true.

In reality, she had another passion, one that consumed what little free time she had. She was a gamer, through and through. And not just any gamer: she was a dedicated streamer, carving out a small but loyal following in the digital world. Massive Multiplayer Online games, or MMOs, were her true love. She adored the thrill of stepping into another existence, of leaving the mundane behind and embracing the extraordinary. Taking on a persona that was anything but ordinary, embarking on perilous adventures, surviving against the odds, completing quests: it was exhilarating.

Cassandra smiled to herself at the thought. If only real life could be as thrilling as the virtual one.

But when she wasn't immersed in a fantastical world, she had another obsession: alchemy. Not the kind from games, with bubbling cauldrons and magical elixirs, but the real-world chemistry of creating compounds, of testing formulas and pushing boundaries. She loved experimenting, seeing if she could stumble upon something new, something groundbreaking. Maybe, just maybe, she would create something extraordinary.

She wasn't oblivious to her own appearance. She had always possessed the kind of beauty that turned heads, though she never deliberately played into it; at least, not in public. Her piercing light blue eyes contrasted strikingly against the deep raven-black of her hair, a feature that often drew lingering stares. Her body, naturally curvaceous in all the ways that made men glance twice, could be a weapon if she wanted it to be. But Cassandra preferred comfort; jeans and a T-shirt were her go-to, practical and simple.

That said, she wasn't above a little strategy when it came to her streams. The tightness of her shirts, the way the fabric clung just enough to accentuate her figure, ensured engagement. A well-placed cut in just the right spot, a teasing glimpse of cleavage, it was all part of the game. Not that she needed to do it, but why not use every advantage?

She reached up, threading her fingers through her silky black hair, exhaling softly. Life was good. But something told her life was about to drastically change.

Her raven-black hair shimmered under the afternoon sun, each strand catching the light like silk as she walked. The warmth of the day kissed her skin, and a smile spread across her face the moment she spotted him, a towering figure of strength and comfort. Thomas stood by his truck, arms crossed, his broad shoulders stretching the fabric of his flannel shirt. Worn jeans and sturdy boots completed his rugged look, but it was the way his face lit up at the sight of her that made Cassandra's heart race.

Without hesitation, she rushed forward, her excitement bubbling over as she practically launched herself into his waiting arms. He caught her with ease, holding her as if she weighed nothing at all, their bodies fitting together in a way that felt natural, perfect. Their lips met in a kiss, soft but filled with a familiar passion, a warmth that spread through her like wildfire.

Thomas let out a chuckle, his deep voice rich with excitement. "Are you ready for this weekend?" he asked, his eyes searching hers for that same anticipation.

Cassandra practically beamed, her blue eyes sparkling with eagerness. "I am! Did you talk to Dina and Anthony as well?"

He smirked, the corners of his mouth tilting up in that charming way that always made her stomach flutter. As much as he was looking forward to spending the trip alone with Cassandra, there was something about having their best friends along that promised even more fun. "I did, and they're both in. It's gonna be a weekend to remember." His voice dipped slightly, turning just a bit teasing. "You're still sure about us sharing a tent, right?"

His question carried both excitement and restraint. He wanted this, wanted her, but he was a good man, raised right. If she changed her mind, he wouldn't push. His mother would have his hide if he did.

Cassandra giggled, her cheeks flushing a delicate pink. "Yes, I haven't changed my mind," she assured him, her voice playful but firm.

Thomas grinned, obviously pleased with her answer, but before he could say anything more, she sighed and glanced at the time. "I have to get to class," she said, her voice tinged with reluctance. "I'll see you after, and we can go get our stuff."

She gave him one last quick kiss, her fingers brushing through his short hair before she pulled away. With one final smile, she turned and hurried off, already counting down the hours until their trip began.

The day dragged on, each lecture feeling longer than the last as Cassandra did everything she could to make time pass faster. She tapped her pen against her notebook, checked the clock a hundred times, and even attempted to focus, but the excitement bubbling inside her made it impossible. Finally, after what felt like an eternity, the final bell rang.

Barely containing her enthusiasm, she bolted from her seat, weaving through the halls to her locker. She shoved her books inside, grabbed her things, and practically sprinted for the exit. A few classmates waved her way, calling out well wishes for the weekend. She flashed them a bright smile and waved back, but she didn't stop.

The moment she spotted Thomas' truck idling by the curb, she quickened her pace, her heart racing with excitement. She yanked open the door, tossed her bag inside, and lunged across the cab, pressing her lips against his in a quick but eager kiss. Thomas let out a low chuckle, his strong hands settling on her waist for a brief moment before he shifted into gear and pulled away from the campus.

The road stretched before them, the city gradually giving way to long stretches of highway lined with towering trees. Behind them, Dina and Anthony followed in their own truck, their headlights flashing every so often as they played around on the road. The four of them had been planning this trip for weeks, and now that they were finally on their way, the excitement was almost overwhelming.

Anthony had been the one to suggest their destination, a secluded spot deep in the mountains that he had stumbled upon during one of his solo hiking trips. He had gone on and on about how breathtaking it was, swearing it was like stepping into another world. Cassandra hadn't fully believed him at the time, but as they finally pulled into the clearing, she realized he hadn't exaggerated one bit.

The sight before her stole her breath away. A waterfall cascaded down smooth, moss-covered rocks, spilling into a crystal-clear pond that shimmered under the golden evening light. The water was so pristine, she could see straight to the bottom, where smooth stones glowed beneath the rippling surface. Lush trees framed the clearing, their emerald leaves swaying in the breeze, casting flickering shadows over the soft earth.

Cassandra gasped, her eyes wide with wonder. "This is incredible..." she whispered, unable to tear her gaze away from the view.

Dina let out an excited squeal, grabbing Cassandra's arm as they exchanged thrilled looks. Meanwhile, the guys wasted no time getting to work, unloading the trucks and setting up the tents in the perfect spot. The steady sound of hammering stakes into the ground mixed with the gentle rush of the waterfall, created a soothing, rhythmic background noise.

Once the tents were up, they turned their attention to building a fire. Sparks crackled as the flames caught, sending a warm glow flickering across their faces as the night deepened. The scent of firewood and charred meat filled the air as they cooked their food over the open flame, the juices sizzling as they laughed and chatted, soaking in the peaceful isolation of their hidden paradise.

With full bellies and a few drinks in hand, they lounged in their chairs, the warmth of the fire licking at their skin. Above them, the sky stretched endlessly, stars twinkling like scattered diamonds against the deep black expanse. Cassandra leaned back, completely content, the soft hum of the night surrounding them.

This was going to be a weekend to remember.

Finally, Anthony and Dina, who had been growing increasingly absorbed in each other, disappeared into their tent, leaving Cassandra and Thomas alone by the crackling fire. Cassandra smirked, already guessing what their friends were up to.

Thomas turned to her, a playful glint in his eyes. "Hey, you wouldn't want to go for a swim, would you?"

Cassandra arched a brow, amusement flickering across her face. "I'd love to," she said, her lips curling into a knowing smile.

Feeling mischievous, she stood, stretching just enough to make sure he noticed before reaching for the hem of her shirt. With a smooth motion, she pulled it over her head, letting the firelight dance over her skin before tossing it aside. Then, with a slow, deliberate movement, she slipped out of her shorts, casting a glance over her shoulder before stepping into the water.

The coolness sent a shiver through her, and she gasped, laughing softly. Behind her, she heard the sudden shuffle of movement, Thomas moving a little too quickly, nearly tripping over himself in his eagerness to follow. Another laugh bubbled from her lips as he rushed in after her, the night air humming with anticipation.

She turned to him, pressing close, her hands tracing over his shoulders as their lips met. The cool water contrasted with the warmth of his touch, sending a pleasant shiver down her spine. In the distance, soft murmurs and laughter drifted from the nearby tent, a reminder that they weren't the only ones enjoying the night.

As their foreheads rested together, breath mingling in the still air, Cassandra's lips curled into a knowing smile. "Let's go to our tent," she whispered.

Thomas didn't hesitate. With a grin, he lifted her into his arms, her laughter soft against his ear as she curled into his embrace. The world outside faded away as they disappeared into the tent, the glow of the fire flickering against the canvas. Inside, they tumbled onto the blankets, their voices lowering to whispers, the quiet rustle of movement filling the space.

Tonight, they had only each other, and nothing else mattered.

In the nearby tent, the air was thick with heat and the scent of smoldering embers. Low murmurs and the shuffle of bodies stirred the fabric walls, a rhythm in tune with the night's steady pulse. Dina's fingers curled against warm skin, her breath hitching as strong hands held her close. There was no need for words, this was a dance they knew well, an unspoken language of movement and intent.

The fire outside crackled, casting faint shadows against the tent as she let herself be lost in the moment. Her world narrowed to the warmth surrounding her, the closeness, the steady rhythm that sent a pleasant hum through her nerves.

Then...

A sickening thud.

The weight above her shifted, sudden, unnatural. Before she could process what had happened, something warm splattered against her skin. Dina's eyes fluttered open, a lazy, satisfied smile still lingering on her lips.

"That was a big one," she murmured breathlessly, still lost in the haze of the moment.

But something was wrong.

Anthony was still.

Dina's breath hitched, the warmth of the moment vanishing as an unnatural chill settled over her. Her gaze drifted downward, as she expected to see his familiar smirk, the teasing glint in his eyes. Instead, a terrible stillness had taken hold of him. Her pulse pounded in her ears. The dim light revealed something slick pooling beneath him, dark and spreading, staining the tent floor.

A shadow loomed over her.

She barely had time to register the hulking figure crouched beside her, a monstrous thing with sickly green skin and a grotesque, toothy grin stretched across its twisted face.

Terror struck her like a bolt of lightning.

Her mouth opened to scream, but the sound never came. A massive hand clamped around her throat, squeezing, cutting off her breath. Her limbs flailed, grasping at nothing, strength abandoning her in the face of something far greater, far crueler.

The last thing she saw before the darkness swallowed her whole was the gleam of jagged teeth as the creature leaned in, its breath hot and rancid. It was savoring the moment, relishing her fear, drawing it in like the scent of a fresh meal before the feast began.

Cassandra lay back against the blankets, breathless, her heart pounding, not just from the closeness of the moment, but from something deeper, something unspoken between them. The warmth of Thomas' touch lingered as they held onto each other, lost in their own world. She felt the rise and fall of his chest, the steady rhythm of their breathing, the comforting weight of his presence.

Outside, the night had grown eerily silent. Even Anthony and Dina, who had been anything but quiet earlier, seemed to have settled. Cassandra smirked, curling closer to Thomas, letting the glow of the moment keep her safe from whatever lay beyond their tent.

Then, a shadow shifted.

The movement was so subtle, so silent, that Cassandra might have missed it if not for the faint glint of steel in the darkness. Her breath caught in her throat, her body frozen for just a second too long. A shadow emerged behind Thomas, tall, lean, and unnervingly precise.

The blade flashed.

Thomas stiffened, his entire body locking up before a choked, wet gasp escaped his lips. His breath hitched, his fingers convulsing as a dark crimson stain bloomed across his throat. Cassandra barely registered what was happening before the warmth of his blood spilled onto her, soaking into the blankets beneath them, trickling against her skin like molten fire. His eyes, once so full of life, flickered with fading recognition before his body slumped forward, heavy and unmoving.

Panic surged through her veins. Cassandra struggled to push him off, but the weight of him pinned her down. Her hands scrambled for leverage, her breath coming in ragged gasps, but before she could free herself, a clawed hand clamped around her wrist: strong, unyielding.

She barely had time to turn her head before she was yanked from beneath Thomas' corpse and thrown outside the tent.

The impact sent a sharp jolt of pain through her side, knocking the air from her lungs. She gasped, dirt clinging to her skin as she pushed up on trembling arms. But as soon as she lifted her head, her blood ran cold.

Dina lay bound beside her, gagged and trembling, her wide, terror-stricken eyes glistening in the dim firelight. Dark streaks covered her skin, the horror in her expression more telling than words could ever be.

Above them, a towering figure loomed, its grin stretched too wide, too unnatural. It crouched low, watching them with gleeful, hungry eyes, its breath coming in slow, measured inhales, savoring the fear that hung thick in the air.

Cassandra's scream tore into the night.

But no one was coming to save them.

The two creatures laughed, a deep, guttural sound that sent icy dread slithering down Cassandra's spine. The larger one loomed in the firelight, a hulking mass of thick, corded muscle, his sickly green skin marred with scars and crude tribal markings. Compared to him, Thomas had been nothing more than a brittle twig, easily snapped. His very presence radiated something raw and primal, a force of nature that knew nothing of mercy.

But it was the other one that truly set her blood to ice. Lean and wiry, he moved with an unnatural grace, his sinewy frame built for speed and precision. His ears, though long and pointed, were jagged, as if something had gnawed at them. When he grinned, his teeth gleamed, razor-sharp, filed to wicked points, turning his smile into a predator's promise. He wasn't just some warped version of an elf. He was something out of a nightmare.

Then she saw what he was holding.

A piece of raw, bloody flesh dangled from his grasp, dark and glistening in the fire's glow. Cassandra's stomach twisted violently. A gleam of metal caught her eye, a ring, barely visible beneath the slick crimson.

Thomas' ring.

The breath in her lungs turned to stone. A strangled sound caught in her throat, her body locking up as realization sank its claws into her mind. They had killed him. They had butchered him.

The elf met her gaze and grinned wider, his lips curling as he raised the flesh to his mouth. With a slow, deliberate motion, he bit down, tearing into it with relish.

Cassandra let out a shaky sob, her limbs trembling as she curled into herself. Panic pressed against her ribs, crushing the air from her lungs. The firelight flickered, their laughter warping in her ears, twisting into something distant and surreal.

A sharp ringing filled her head.

Then, darkness swallowed her whole.

She woke to the dying glow of the fire, shadows dancing eerily across the clearing. Her breath came shallow and uneven, her thoughts sluggish, as though she had been drowning in some terrible dream. But the nightmare was real. Her body ached, her skin was cold with sweat.

Somewhere close by, beneath the crackling of embers, she heard something else: heavy, rhythmic movements. A deep, guttural breath. The sound of something working, relentless, unbothered by the horror it had created.

And then she realized she wasn't alone.

She turned her head, her pulse hammering. A towering green form loomed over a smaller figure: Dina. Her caramel skin glistened in the firelight, her wrists bound, her body limp beneath the sheer power of the orc. He moved over her like a predator claiming its prize, his massive hands keeping her pinned effortlessly.

Dina barely reacted. There was no fight left in her. Her breath came in shallow, ragged exhales, her gaze unfocused, as if she were somewhere far away. Anthony was gone. Everything was gone.

The orc chuckled low in his throat, his grip tightening as he whispered something against her skin. Cassandra wanted to look away, but her body refused to move. A strange numbness crept over her limbs, the world growing distant, like she was sinking beneath the surface of icy water.

She heard the elf's voice, smooth and mocking, somewhere beyond the pounding in her ears.

"Try not to break her," he said lazily. "Lord Vera'Ala'Roja won't be pleased if you ruin the goods before we deliver them. She'll fetch quite the sum back home."

The orc only grunted in response.

Cassandra's vision blurred. The crackling fire, the shadows shifting, the gleam of jagged teeth; it all faded, swallowed by the heavy fog creeping into her mind. She didn't want to see. She didn't want to know.

Darkness took her.

When her eyes fluttered open, the fire had burned low, its embers casting a dull glow over the camp. The air was thick with sweat and smoke, and the world felt cold despite the lingering heat against her skin.

Dina lay beside her, motionless. Her expression was empty, her stare fixed on nothing.

Nearby, the orc stretched with a satisfied groan, rolling his shoulders as he cracked his knuckles. His grin was smug, victorious, as he glanced down at the two of them like a beast surveying its conquered prey.

Cassandra's stomach twisted violently. Her mouth went dry.

The orc's deep voice rumbled through the night, thick with amusement.

"Now... your turn."

Before she could react, the elf beside him sighed, wiping his hands on his tunic as he glanced toward the sky. "Not tonight, Toos," he muttered, almost bored. "We're already behind schedule, and by the look of things, I'd say you've pushed that one a little too far." He gestured lazily toward Dina, whose vacant stare made it clear she had retreated somewhere deep within herself.

Toos scowled, clearly displeased, but after a moment, he let out a heavy sigh. "Fine. We'll finish this later," he grumbled, cracking his neck.

With little effort, the orc bent down, grabbing both women as if they weighed nothing. Cassandra cried out, thrashing in his iron grip, but it was useless, he was too strong. Dina, on the other hand, remained limp, her breathing steady but distant, as if she was somewhere far away.

The elf flicked his wrist, and a shimmering portal of swirling darkness crackled to life before them. Without another word, Toos stepped forward, hauling the two women through.

On the other side, they emerged into a dimly lit dungeon, the air thick with the scent of damp stone and unwashed bodies. Cages lined the walls, filled with other captives, some watching in silence, others too broken to care. A man in fine yet worn robes sat at a desk, his piercing gaze sweeping over the new arrivals.

He stood, stepping toward Cassandra first. She recoiled as he reached out, grabbing her chin and tilting her face side to side as if inspecting livestock. A slow, cruel smile stretched across his lips.

"She's in good shape," he muttered. His fingers pried at her lips, checking her teeth. "Strong. This one will fetch a fine price."

Tears stung Cassandra's eyes as she clenched her jaw, refusing to give him the satisfaction of breaking down.

The man turned his attention to Dina, who had been unceremoniously dropped to the ground. He barely gave her a glance before sighing. "And this one?"

The elf shrugged, a smirk tugging at the corner of his mouth. "Both of them were with males when we found them," he said smoothly. "But Toos... well, let's just say he ruined this one." He gestured toward Dina, his tone more amused than apologetic.

The man's expression soured, his displeasure clear. "A shame. Could've been worth more." He waved a dismissive hand. "This one is of no value."

Toos' grin widened, his tusks catching the flickering candlelight. "Then I'll take her." He reached down, gripping Dina by the arm and hoisting her up like a rag doll. She didn't resist, not even a flinch. Her eyes remained distant, as if she was staring at something beyond the walls of the dungeon.

The man barely acknowledged the exchange, already losing interest. "Put the other in a cage," he instructed.

Toos was already moving toward the door, hauling Dina's limp form along with him. Cassandra's stomach twisted as she watched, her breath catching in her throat.

The elf clicked his tongue, rolling his eyes as he followed after Toos. "You aren't keeping this one all to yourself this time," he warned, his voice carrying a hint of amusement.

Their voices faded as the door shut behind them, leaving Cassandra alone in the dimly lit chamber. She shivered, her mind racing as she tried to grasp what was happening, what would happen next.

Tears burned in her eyes, but she forced them back. She had to stay strong. Had to think. Had to find a way out of this.

Had to survive.

Cassandra lay curled in the cramped confines of the cage, her body shivering despite the suffocating heat of the room. The pen was small, barely large enough to stretch out, though the overwhelming stench of filth and decay made movement unbearable. Feces and urine stained the floor, trickling through the cracks between cages, seeping into the very air she breathed. She had long since lost track of time: hours, days, maybe even longer.

Each time the door creaked open, her heart leapt with desperate hope, only to sink like a stone when unfamiliar figures entered. None of them were Dina. None of them brought salvation. So, eventually, she stopped looking, stopped hoping. She curled into herself, knees drawn to her chest, arms wrapped tightly around her shivering form. It was easier to shut out the world.

Until one day...

*Bang!*

The door burst open with a force that sent a gust of putrid air through the dungeon. The sudden chaos snapped Cassandra's eyes open. This wasn't the slow, creaking entrance of the slavers. This was different.

Two figures strode inside, their presence an anomaly in the dark hellhole. The first was a woman, strikingly beautiful, with golden hair that seemed to glow even in the dim torchlight. She moved with an energy that clashed against the misery of the room, bouncing on the balls of her feet as if she could barely contain her excitement. The second was a tall, lean man, his sharp features partially shadowed by the wide brim of his hat. He exuded an air of cool detachment, his every movement calculated and precise.

The air was thick with something else; metallic, raw. Blood. Cassandra smelled it before she saw the faint smears on their clothing. The people upstairs were dead. She was certain of it.

The other captives sensed it too. A cacophony of cries and frantic whispers filled the room as the prisoners rattled the bars, pleading, sobbing, reaching for salvation. The blonde woman moved quickly, unlocking the cages with an almost gleeful urgency. One by one, prisoners surged forward, scrambling into the open, gasping as if they had been drowning.

Cassandra watched them, unmoving.

A corpse lay in the cage just a few feet away, pale, lifeless, curled up as if death had crept in silently and stolen the last breath before freedom arrived. The woman had been nude when she died, her thin body covered in filth and bruises. Cassandra gasped sharply, her stomach twisting.

But it wasn't Dina.

She exhaled in relief, though shame followed close behind. That woman had been someone's Dina. Someone who mattered.

Her mind flickered back to Thomas, to the final, horrific moments when his eyes had locked with hers as his life drained away. The weight of his body, the heat of his blood soaking her skin... the helplessness, the horror. Her chest tightened, and a sob clawed its way up her throat, but she swallowed it down. She wouldn't cry. Not now.

A voice pulled her from the depths of her grief.

"She's not our problem."

Cassandra looked up, her vision blurred with exhaustion and unshed tears. The man in the hat stood over her cage, gazing down at her with a cold, assessing stare. His expression barely shifted as he turned away.

"If she doesn't have the sense to run, that's on her," he added dismissively, already moving toward the exit.

The blonde woman hesitated, her torchlight flickering across Cassandra's hollowed face. But she said nothing.

They were leaving.

Cassandra's fingers curled against the filthy floor. She was here, in this strange, cruel world, alone.

And if she didn't move, she would die here, too.

The blonde woman, however, spoke up, her voice firm despite the chaos surrounding them.

"Mr. D..."

But the man cut her off sharply. "No, Vex. You're already trouble enough for me, I refuse to add another liability to my side."

His tone was final, but the woman didn't waver. She crossed her arms beneath her chest, the fresh blood on her fingers smearing against her skin as she tapped impatiently. She didn't even glance at him. Her piercing gaze remained locked on Cassandra, expression unreadable but intense.

Then, suddenly, she erupted.

"*No!*"

The single word rang out like a gunshot, raw and filled with unshakable conviction.

The man exhaled slowly, pinching the bridge of his nose as if trying to ward off an oncoming headache. His annoyance was palpable, shoulders tensing as he stood there, unmoving, weighing his options.

"Fine," he muttered at last, exasperation lacing every syllable. "Let's just get out of here. We'll figure out what to do with her later."

Cassandra barely had time to process his reluctant agreement before the blonde woman let out an excited squeal, her entire demeanor shifting from deadly serious to outright giddy in an instant.

"I'm going to call you *Puppy!*" she declared with a delighted giggle, clapping her bloodstained hands together as if she'd just been given the best gift imaginable. With that the woman grabbed Cassandra's wrist and pulled her to her feet.

Puppy?

Cassandra blinked, stunned. What kind of ridiculous name was that?

But she didn't have the fight in her to argue. Not now. Not after everything.

She swallowed hard, stealing one last glance toward the cage across from her, toward the lifeless body of the woman she had feared was Dina. It wasn't, but that did little to ease the suffocating weight in her chest.

Thomas flashed through her mind next, his wide, terrified eyes as the life drained from him, the warmth of his blood as it spilled over her skin.

No. She had to focus. She was still alive. And she would stay that way.

Cassandra inhaled shakily and lowered her head in submission. If these two were offering her a way out, safety, even temporary safety, then she would take it.

She would be whatever they needed her to be.

She wouldn't be a liability.

She would survive.

# CHAPTER 13

# DEAL OR NO DEAL: PIRATE EDITION

A knock echoed through the cabin door before Devaultus stepped inside. He always approached Al'Shandra's quarters with a degree of caution, not out of fear, but because experience had taught him that he could never quite know what he'd walk into. It wasn't beyond her to be engaged in something... lewd. But today, luck was on his side. She was poring over her books, a deep, contemplative frown marring her otherwise unreadable expression. That was unusual.

Pausing in the doorway, he watched her, waiting for acknowledgment. Normally, when he was in his usual Devaultus mood, he'd saunter in like he owned the place, throw himself onto her couch, and kick his boots up on her desk, just to piss her off. But he knew to, every once in a while, play the role of the obedient crew member. You know, just to keep up appearances.

Finally, she spoke, her voice cool and sharp. "Come in, Devaultus. Stop standing there like an idiot."

He huffed, mostly to himself. This was exactly why he preferred to just be himself. No point in playing nice when it only got him insults anyway. With a signature swagger, he strolled into the room and dropped into one of the large chairs, making himself comfortable despite her clear irritation.

"What seems to be the problem, Captain?" he asked, his voice laced with casual amusement.

Al'Shandra studied him for a moment, like she was sizing him up, weighing whether or not to trust him. That was another thing about her: she didn't trust easily, not even her own crew.

"I haven't told you the full reason for this voyage," she admitted, folding her hands together on the desk. "It isn't just a convenient escape from your dear friend Tarus Goldwyne."

Devaultus let out a short laugh, leaning back lazily. "Ah, yes. The man does seem to have it out for me."

Al'Shandra ignored his quip, continuing with a rare hint of seriousness in her tone. "He's part of the reason we're pushing so hard, but he's not the main reason. I have a much larger prize in mind. A ship, Devaultus. One so powerful, the gods themselves would tear the world apart to claim it."

That got his attention. He straightened slightly, eyes narrowing with intrigue.

She continued, her voice lowering. "I need a few things to get it running. The crystal you acquired for me? That was just the first."

Devaultus tilted his head, waiting. She hesitated, something he wasn't used to seeing from her. That meant this was important.

Sighing, she finally added, "There are two more pieces I need. And I intend to get them."

A slow smirk crept across Devaultus' face. "Well, well, Captain. Now you've got me interested."

Devaultus leaned back in his chair, his sharp eyes scanning her as he mulled over her words. "What makes this ship so special? Is it magical?" His voice carried a skeptical edge, as if he half-expected her to be exaggerating. After all, the ship they were on now seemed perfectly fine. It got them from point A to point B without crumbling to pieces. What more could a ship possibly do?

Al'Shandra met his gaze with an almost amused glint in her eye, though the concern that had darkened her expression earlier hadn't fully lifted. "In a manner of speaking, yes. But magic manifests in different forms across different worlds. This ship..." she paused, drumming her fingers against the desk, "...this ship has the ability to travel distances far beyond what you've ever imagined. It is unlike any other vessel you've encountered. If you secure the remaining pieces for me, I give you my word, I will take you and your people away from this wretched place."

Devaultus tapped a finger against his chin, considering her offer. He hated this place. Hated the endless struggle, the constant chase, the damn noose tightening around his neck with every step he took. But at least he understood it. He knew the rules, even if they were written in blood and betrayal. Stepping into the unknown, trusting Al'Shandra to lead him somewhere better: it felt like a gamble.

And yet, what was the alternative? Stay here, forever running, forever looking over his shoulder for Tarus Goldwyne and whatever other nightmare lurked in the shadows? No, that wasn't a future he wanted. Wherever Al'Shandra planned to take them, it couldn't possibly be worse than this.

He let out a breath and straightened in his seat. "Very well," he said, his voice steady despite the nagging feeling that he was about to throw himself into the fight of his life. "I'll find these pieces for you."

Al'Shandra's lips curled into a knowing smile, and in that moment, Devaultus swore he saw the glint of something ominous behind her eyes, like she had just set a grander game in motion, and he had willingly placed himself right in the center of it.

Devaultus leaned back in the chair, drumming his fingers along the armrest as he studied Al'Shandra. There was something about the way she looked at him, something calculating, something amused. He knew that look. It was the same look she had right before she sent him into the jaws of death with nothing but a smirk and a promise.

"Now then," he said, rolling his shoulders as if to shake off the weight of what was surely coming. "Where and what is this next piece?"

Part of him almost regretted asking. Almost. He had long since learned that Al'Shandra had a gift, a downright *delightful* habit, of throwing him and his crew into the worst situations imaginable. And yet, here he was, still playing along. He mentally shrugged. Maybe, when all of this was said and done, he'd put a dagger in her back and take the ship for himself. It *would* be fitting, wouldn't it? A true pirate's ending.

But the more he told himself that, the less convincing it sounded.

His lips pressed into a thin line as he sat there, considering. He had already risked himself more times than he could count for Vex and Blight. And not just for his own gain, either. He had pulled them out of trouble, shielded them when he didn't have to, made decisions that put himself in the line of fire just to keep them breathing.

He frowned.

No. He wasn't dying for them. He was *not* dying for them.

...But he hadn't exactly let them die, either.

"The next item is a metal rod. It's being hoarded as some prized artifact by Casterland Orthcog, a gnome Lord on another continent," Al'Shandra explained, her lips curling in amusement as she leaned back in her chair. The candlelight flickered over her exposed collarbone, tracing the smooth curves of her form. "Metal is rare in this world, so naturally, he believes it to be a source of immense wealth. In a way, he's not wrong, just not for the reasons he thinks."

Devaultus scoffed under his breath. Of course, it had to be a gnome. He hated gnomes. Arrogant, insufferable little creatures who always thought themselves the smartest beings in the room. Granted, most of the time, they actually were, but that just made them even more intolerable. What a pain this mission was going to be. It wasn't just about breaking into some Lord's estate, it was about slipping into an entire gnome settlement, a place built for beings half his size, filled with paranoid little bastards who probably had more traps than they had furniture. And with his current crew? That was going to be damn near impossible.

Vex would never let him go in alone, that much he knew. She'd argue, she'd insist on tagging along, and then she'd get distracted looting everything that wasn't bolted down. And Blight? She wasn't fully herself yet. The loss of Bozz had hit her hard. Devaultus still didn't quite understand why, Bozz had been with them for only a short time. But grief was a strange thing. Maybe it wasn't just Bozz. Maybe it was everything. The weight of this brutal world pressing down on her. Maybe there was more to the story than he knew.

He ran a hand through his hair, exhaling through his nose. "And I suppose you have some grand plan for how we're going to do this? Or do you just enjoy throwing me into the fire and watching me figure it out?" He smirked, but there was an edge to it, a frustration lingering just beneath the surface.

Al'Shandra chuckled, the sound sultry and full of promise. "Oh, Devaultus, my dear," she purred, standing up and sauntering toward him with slow, deliberate steps. She placed a finger under his chin, tilting his face upward as she leaned over him, her golden eyes gleaming with mischief. "Where would the fun be in handing you all the answers?"

"We're only a day's time from our destination," Al'Shandra purred, stretching like a satisfied feline as she leaned back in her chair. Her corset, laced scandalously tight, emphasized every curve, and the dim lantern light flickered over the sheen of her exposed skin. "We won't be able to stop, but I do have a way to get your team to shore... though it won't be pleasant."

Devaultus exhaled sharply, already regretting whatever madness he had just signed himself up for. "Of course it won't be," he muttered under his breath, rubbing his temples as if bracing for an inevitable headache. He could already feel the weight of another absurdly dangerous, convoluted plan pressing down on him like a boot to his throat.

Al'Shandra smirked, her lips curling in that knowing, devilish way of hers. She thrived on this, on watching people squirm, on having them dance in the palm of her hand. "Go gather your team, inform them of what's to come, and get some rest." The way she said it, all honey and steel, told him that rest was something he'd be dearly missing once this all began.

Devaultus pushed himself up from the chair, his movements slow, deliberate. He sauntered toward the door, the weight of Al'Shandra's gaze pressing against his back like a knife waiting to sink in. Something about the way she watched him unsettled him. He knew better than to trust her, she was too much like him. Cunning, unpredictable, and entirely too comfortable with playing the long game.

Pausing at the threshold, he turned his head just enough to glance at her over his shoulder. Their eyes met, a silent challenge exchanged between two predators, neither willing to look away first.

Then, without a word, he stepped out and closed the door behind him.

Al'Shandra chuckled, licking her lips as she leaned forward, elbows on the desk. "Oh, Devaultus," she murmured to herself, her grin spreading like wildfire. "You'll learn soon enough just how out of your element you truly are."

Devaultus moved through the ship's dimly lit corridors with the lazy confidence of a man who always expected to be in control, even when he wasn't. The wooden planks creaked beneath his boots as he stopped outside a door, rapping his knuckles against it without preamble.

"Let's find Blight. We need to talk," he said. That was all. No explanation, no pleasantries. Just an order wrapped in indifference.

From inside, Vex blinked in confusion, tilting her head like a mischievous cat caught in the middle of something she shouldn't be doing. But after a beat, her lips stretched into a grin, and she sprang to her feet, skipping after him with a light bounce in her step.

They arrived at Blight's quarters, where Devaultus paused for the briefest moment before knocking. "May we come in?" he asked, though it was more of a formality than a question.

Inside, Blight sat at her desk, quill in hand, the flickering candlelight casting deep shadows across her face. She had been writing something, though at their arrival, she carefully closed the book as if tucking away a secret.

Vex, never one for patience, didn't wait for permission. She all but pranced inside, arms outstretched, and flung herself at Blight in a dramatic embrace. "Hello, Puppy! Did you miss me?" she chirped, her voice thick with amusement and affection.

Blight stiffened for a split second, caught off guard by the pet name. Of all the things she had come to expect from Vex, being called "Puppy" still felt absurd. Yet, she found herself hesitating before offering a careful, "Yes, of course, I did, Vex."

That was all the encouragement Vex needed. She giggled in delight, spinning slightly as if drunk on her own excitement.

Meanwhile, Devaultus pushed the door shut behind them with a quiet *click* and strode toward the bed, dropping down onto it without a care. His fingers tapped idly against his knee before he finally spoke, his voice carrying the weight of something significant.

"I've made a deal with the captain. A proper escape from this forsaken world. But there's a catch." He let the words linger, savoring the way Blight's expression darkened and Vex's eyes sparkled with curiosity.

"We need to retrieve a couple more artifacts to make this happen."

Blight's reaction was immediate. Her posture stiffened, a flicker of unease passing through her eyes. She had seen enough of this world's horrors to know that any plan involving them would be a brutal one.

Vex, on the other hand, looked positively thrilled. "When do we leave?" she asked, practically bouncing in place like an overexcited child about to open a present.

Devaultus held up a single finger, silencing her with an expectant look. "Not so fast. The captain expects me to take the *entire* team." His voice dipped into something almost mocking. "But that *won't* be happening."

For the first time, both Blight and Vex looked genuinely confused.

He fixed Blight with a sharp, assessing look, his voice leaving no room for argument. "You will be staying here this time."

Blight's expression was a war of emotions, relief flickering through her features only to be quickly overshadowed by something else. Guilt. Uncertainty. She bit her lip, as if she wanted to protest but wasn't sure she had the right to. Part of her was glad she wasn't being thrust into another deadly mission, yet another part of her recoiled at the idea of being left behind, of not proving herself useful. Not proving she wasn't just dead weight.

"No, Devaultus. You have to take me. Please," she said, though even she seemed to hear the hesitation in her own voice. It wasn't a demand, not really. More of a plea for reassurance.

Devaultus, of course, saw right through her. He simply lifted a hand, silencing any further argument before it could leave her lips. "I do not completely trust our dear Captain, Blight," he said, his voice low and edged with the usual cynicism. "I need assurances that when this mission is through, this ship will be waiting for me so I may escape."

Vex, who had been bouncing on her heels in quiet anticipation, nodded as if this made perfect sense, her usual chaotic energy momentarily stilled in understanding. Of course, she could always be counted on to follow his lead, until she got distracted by something more fun, or bloody.

Then, just as quickly, Devaultus turned his piercing gaze toward her. "You will be staying as well, Vex."

It was as if a fuse had been lit. Vex's entire demeanor shifted, her body going rigid before practically vibrating with outrage. She looked ready to explode, her eyes burning with disbelief and fury.

"I most certainly will not!" she snapped, her voice rising as she stomped a foot like a furious cat preparing to claw someone's face off. "Where you go, I go. That is not up for discussion. There is no other choice!"

Her anger was wild, untamed, a storm ready to tear through anything in its way. She wasn't pleading like Blight had been. No, she was making a demand, one that could very well end in bloodshed if he dared push her further.

Devaultus let Vex unleash her full fury, arms flailing, voice rising and falling in an erratic, chaotic stream of protests, curses, and outrage. He simply stood there, expression unreadable, waiting her out. She needed to get it out of her system before he could force her to listen. When her words finally sputtered to a halt, leaving her chest rising and falling with the force of her frustration, he spoke, calm, direct, cutting straight through her whirlwind of emotion, his voice sharp and direct.

"You and I both know the best chance I have of getting out of there is Blight," he said, his tone leaving no room for argument. "She's the most intelligent out of all of us. If something goes wrong, I need her thinking, not fighting, to make sure I make it back. And I need her alive, Vex. The only way to guarantee that happens is for you to stay here and protect her."

This response served a dual purpose, both calculated and necessary. First, it was meant to bolster Blight's confidence, something he suspected she desperately needed. Whether she realized it or not, she was the most intelligent among them, and Devaultus knew that a sharp mind could be just as dangerous as a sharp blade. If she started believing in her own abilities, she might stop seeing herself as dead weight.

The second reason was far more manipulative. Vex was unpredictable, chaotic, and utterly relentless when it came to her attachment to him. But she had one undeniable weakness: her fierce, almost obsessive desire to protect him. If she truly believed that keeping Blight alive was the only way to ensure his safety, then maybe, just maybe, she'd follow orders instead of rushing into danger without thinking. It was a gamble, but one he was willing to take.

He had no illusions about what he was: self-serving, opportunistic, always looking out for himself first. But he wasn't stupid. If he wanted to survive, he needed his team in one piece. Even if that meant playing the part of a leader... a hero, even. The thought almost made him sick.

Still, for now, the pieces were in place. He would just have to see how the game played out.

Vex's face twisted, her mind visibly battling itself. She wanted to call him a liar to distort the truth in her favor, find some loophole to justify ignoring him, but she couldn't. The logic was too sound. Too airtight. Her mouth opened, but the only thing that came out was a soft, pained, "No..."

"Yes." Devaultus' voice hardened, forcing her to look at him. "I demand it. Do as you're told, or you put me in danger."

That hit her harder than she'd expected. Vex always followed orders, always. But the thought of being apart from Devaultus made her chest constrict, her hands twitch with frustration. She had not left his side since that day, the day everything changed. And now, he was pushing her away.

Her lips pressed together into a thin line. Her fingers clenched, then released. Then, without another word, she stood and stormed out, boots slamming against the wooden floor with every step. She barely made it out of the room before she reached up and wiped a single tear from her eye.

Fine. If he wanted her to stay, she would stay. But she would make damn sure Blight lived, even if it meant tearing through every last soul on this ship to do it.

Blight sat still, watching the door swing shut behind Vex. A strange mixture of relief and guilt flickered across her face. Slowly, she turned back to Devaultus, something hesitant in her eyes. Then, finally, she mouthed two words: *Thank you.*

Devaultus smirked, the corner of his lips tugging up in that signature, one-sided grin. He pushed himself to his feet, stretching his shoulders as he made his way toward the door.

"Keep an eye on her," he said, giving Blight a sidelong glance. "She's... a bit of a handful."

Then, without another glance back, he slipped out of the room, heading for his own quarters, the weight of leadership pressing just a little heavier on his shoulders.

The morning arrived sooner than Devaultus would have liked, the horizon still painted in the pale hues of dawn as he stepped onto the deck of the ship. The dusty sea air carried the distant screeches of odd birds, and the ship rocked gently beneath his feet, a steady reminder of the world he was still trapped in. His eyes immediately found Al'Shandra, lounging near the ship's helm like a predator basking in the sun.

She cocked her head at him, lips curling into a smirk. "Where is your team, Devaultus?" she asked, voice dripping with amusement, as if she already knew the answer.

Devaultus returned her smirk with a confident grin of his own. "They're staying behind. I'll be handling this mission alone." His tone left no room for debate, his posture one of unwavering confidence, as if he had already succeeded before even beginning.

Al'Shandra let out a soft, throaty chuckle, taking a slow, deliberate step toward him. "A bit full of yourself, aren't you, Devaultus?" she purred, her sultry voice teasing. "Do you really think you can pull this off by yourself?"

Devaultus gave a casual shrug, his smirk widening. "I don't think, I know. I have absolute confidence in my ability." His gaze flicked over her, challenging. "You should consider yourself fortunate to have me on your ship, Al'Shandra. Let's not forget that."

She laughed at his audacity, his voice a rich, husky sound that sent a shiver of something dangerously close to amusement through him. "Oh, I suppose we'll find out soon enough just how 'fortunate' I am."

It was then that Devaultus noticed the contraption waiting for him on the deck: a wooden frame, bent into a circular structure with a ramp leading up to it. The craftsmanship was foreign, unlike anything he had encountered before. His brow furrowed in suspicion.

"What in the Abyss is this?" he asked, eyeing the strange device.

Al'Shandra's smirk widened as she handed him something equally peculiar: an odd bundle of straps that resembled some kind of backpack. "That," she said, gesturing toward the contraption, "is how you'll be reaching the continent."

Devaultus narrowed his eyes as he inspected the item she had handed him. It felt oddly weighted, the straps sturdy, but it was the small, corded lever attached to the shoulder that caught his attention.

"And this?" he asked, already feeling a sense of foreboding.

"You'll need it," she replied smoothly. "When you're at your peak, pull that lever."

Devaultus exhaled sharply. "That seems rather vague."

She merely grinned, stepping aside and motioning toward the ramp. "Well, off you go." Then, with a wicked gleam in her eye, she added, "And Devaultus? Try not to die."

Devaultus gave her a slow, deliberate smirk as he stepped onto the ramp, turning slightly to meet her gaze. "Oh, Al'Shandra," he said with a teasing lilt, "you're about to witness firsthand just how incredible I truly am."

He winked at her, his grin sharp and full of reckless arrogance. "You're welcome."

And with that, he strode forward, stepping through the ominous wooden circle without another word.

# CHAPTER 14

# CREATE-A-CHARACTER GONE WRONG

T he moment Devaultus stepped through the circle, reality twisted. A force unlike anything he had ever felt before wrenched him forward, launching him into the sky at an impossible speed. It felt as though his body had been turned inside out, his organs compressed, his skin stretched and peeled by the sheer velocity. Air resistance hit like a wall of knives, the dust and sand in the atmosphere shredding across him like a thousand tiny razors.

He barely had time to register the world spinning around him before the true horror of his situation set in: he was hurtling toward the continent with absolutely no control. His fingers scrambled to locate the lever on his shoulder strap, but the rush of wind made even moving his arms a battle. Sand stung his eyes, blinding him, making it impossible to gauge his altitude. He had no idea how close he was to the ground or how much time he had left before impact.

Finally, his fingers found the lever. He yanked it.

With a mechanical pop, wooden arms snapped outward on either side of him, followed by folded cloth meant to function as wings. For a brief, glorious moment, he felt the resistance against the air, slowing his descent. But then...

A jolt. A shift.

His left wing didn't open properly.

Devaultus cursed, his hands fighting to free the caught mechanism, but the damn thing refused to comply. His body lurched violently as he spun into an uncontrollable spiral, the sky and land twisting in a blur of chaos.

His stomach turned. The world was a whirlwind of color, a storm of motion he couldn't break free from.

He yanked the lever again, harder this time, desperate. The wing finally released, but at a cost. A loud rip tore through the air as the cloth shredded, rendering the contraption only half-functional.

"I hate you, Al'Shandra!" he roared into the wind, his voice snatched away by the storm of his own rapid descent.

The torn wing flailed wildly, the wind ripping it further apart. Devaultus stretched his arm out, trying to catch the fraying cloth before it was lost entirely. His fingers grasped at empty air again and again, frustration mounting. Finally, he snagged a piece and clenched it tightly, but by then it was almost too late.

The ground was approaching, fast.

Too fast.

"Oh, this is going to hurt," he muttered, trying to adjust his trajectory. He pulled up, struggling to level himself out, but, with only one stable wing, he could barely control his descent. He was still coming in too quickly.

Then, impact.

His left wing clipped the ground first, sending him into a brutal tumble. His body slammed against dirt and rock, flipping violently, every collision sending fresh bursts of pain through his already battered form.

The last thing he saw before darkness swallowed him whole was the blurred shapes of trees and the shattered remains of his so-called 'safe landing' device.

Then, nothing.

His eyes fluttered open, his vision swimming as he struggled to focus. The world around him felt like it was spinning, disoriented shapes bleeding into one another. He could hear voices; high-pitched, excited, and coming closer. Not good. His body ached as though he'd been thrown off a cliff and battered against every jagged rock on the way down.

"This isn't good," he muttered under his breath, trying to push himself upright, but his limbs refused to cooperate. He needed to...

His vision flickered, then went dark again.

A moment later, at least he hoped it was just a moment, his eyes cracked open once more. The world was clearer now, and standing above him were two gnomes, one male, one female, their eager faces peering down at him with unconcealed curiosity.

"I do not believe you stuck the landing," the male gnome observed with a voice as sharp and high as a rusty gear grinding against metal. "Though, I must say, the contraption itself was magnificent in its structure!"

The female gnome giggled in delight, nodding in agreement, as though his near-death experience was merely an interesting footnote to whatever marvel of engineering they had just witnessed.

Devaultus groaned internally. Of course, they were more interested in the damn glider than the man who had just crash-landed right in front of them. Gnomes. They were all the same: tiny, excitable creatures obsessed with machines, gears, and devices, and utterly blind to anything that wasn't mechanical genius.

Wait. Why weren't they panicking? Why weren't they losing their minds at the sight of him? Gnomes despised taller folk. Their entire society was built around their deep-seated distrust of anyone who could tower over them; and yet, here these two were, happily chattering away as if he were one of their own.

A cold chill ran through him as he slowly, carefully glanced down at himself.

The breath he had been holding released in a slow exhale of relief. Instead of his usual form, what met his eyes was that of a short, balding man with a neatly trimmed beard, dressed in a pair of well-worn brown pants held up by suspenders, a dusty shirt, and a pair of thick goggles that rested over his eyes.

A gnome.

Devaultus grinned to himself. That had been far too close.

He groaned as he pushed himself up into a sitting position, every muscle in his body screaming in protest. His vision blurred for a moment before sharpening on the two gnomes still utterly engrossed in his broken contraption. They ran their hands over the damaged frame, fingers tracing every joint and seam, muttering to each other in rapid, excited tones. No doubt they were already scheming how to reverse-engineer the damn thing and make a small fortune selling knockoffs. Typical gnomes. Opportunistic little bastards.

He quickly composed himself, slipping seamlessly into his gnomish disguise, his voice adopting the telltale lilt of the gnome dialect, layered with a rich Irish accent. "Ah now, and who might ye two be, eh? Don't reckon I've seen the likes o' ye about before."

The male gnome, clearly more interested in the contraption than the broken pile of flesh that had just crash-landed near him, took a moment before even glancing Devaultus way, his nose still buried in the glider's ruined mechanics. When he finally did turn, it was with the air of someone remembering an afterthought. "Oh! Well, name's Zeff, lad! And this 'ere's me wife, Spar."

Spar, a wiry thing with wild, grease-smudged curls, waved absently, her sharp green eyes darting between Devaultus and the glider as though deciding which was the more fascinating discovery. Spoiler alert: it wasn't him.

Devaultus suppressed an eye roll. He could already tell he'd have to fight for their attention. With a sharp grin, he thrust out his hand for a firm handshake. "Pleasure's all mine! Name's Zigglespot," he said, his mouth curling into a smug half-smile.

Zeff gave his hand a firm shake, while Spar merely squinted at him, clearly trying to place whether or not she'd ever heard the name before. Devaultus ignored her scrutiny, rising to his short, stubby feet, rolling his shoulders and stretching each aching limb. Everything seemed to be in working order, though every movement sent sharp spikes of pain through his body. Functioning? Yes. Pain-free? Not even close.

With an exaggerated huff, he reached down and scooped up the battered contraption, cradling it protectively in his arms. This thing might just save his ass in more ways than one. If these gnomes wanted to get their grubby hands on it, they'd have to work for it.

"Well, now," he said in a high-pitched, nasal whine, feigning deep annoyance as he eyed the wreckage. "This just won't do at all! Not at feckin' all!"

"What will I do indeed," Devaultus muttered under his breath, his tone laced with feigned frustration.

Zeff and Spar, who had been fixated on the broken remains of the glider, finally tore their attention away from it to glance at him with curiosity. Spar tilted her head, gears practically turning behind her bright, inquisitive eyes.

"And what d'ye mean by that now?" she asked, her voice carrying that distinct Irish lilt.

Devaultus let out an exaggerated sigh, his expression one of utter exasperation. "Ah, it's just a terrible mess, truly. I was meant to be presentin' this grand contraption to none other than Lord Casterland Orthcog himself, wasn't I?" He shook his head, rubbing his temples as though the stress of the situation was weighing on him. "And now, look at it! Ruined! Smashed to bits! And I've only till tomorrow to fix the blasted thing, or I'll be in for it, I tell ye."

The two gnomes exchanged glances, their eyes lighting up with an almost childlike enthusiasm. This was their chance. If they could get their hands on the mechanics of the device, tinker with it, perhaps even improve upon it, oh, what a discovery it would be!

Zeff puffed out his chest and spoke up first, practically bouncing on his feet. "Ah now, lad, no need to be despairin' just yet! Suppose ye use me lab, eh? A fine setup I've got, all the tools ye could be needin'!"

Spar eagerly jumped in, nodding so quickly, her short curls bobbed around her face. "Aye, aye, right up indeed! We help ye fix it up proper, better than before even!"

Devaultus barely held back the grin that threatened to split his face. Oh, they were taking the bait so easily. These gnomes were just as gullible as he'd hoped. They thought they were getting an opportunity, but in truth, they were handing him exactly what he needed: a workshop, time, and a way into Lord Casterland's circle.

Feigning relief, he let out a breath and plastered a grateful smile onto his gnomish face. "Oh, bless yer clever little heads! Ye've no idea how much this means to me," he said, voice still high-pitched and tinged with that gnomish brogue.

Gathering up the battered remains of the glider, he fell in step behind Zeff and Spar as they eagerly led him toward their workshop. His mind, however, was already working far ahead, piecing together his true plan.

Fools. This was almost too easy.

The small band of gnomish inventors bustled down the narrow cobblestone path, their short legs moving with surprising urgency. Every so often, Zeff or Spar would stop abruptly, reaching out with nimble fingers to disable yet another hidden trap before proceeding. Devaultus noted how natural this seemed to them, their paranoia of outsiders momentarily overshadowed by their overwhelming curiosity; more specifically, their greed. The prospect of reverse-engineering his glider outweighed their deeply ingrained mistrust, granting him rare access to their most sacred space, their laboratory.

Trailing behind them, Devaultus moved with deliberate caution, eyes sharp as he silently committed everything to memory. Every trap, every pressure plate, every nearly invisible tripwire; they were all cataloged in his mind. He studied how the gnomes worked, the specific methods they used to conceal and disarm their defenses, their little quirks and habits. No system was perfect, and in their confidence, they were showing him the weaknesses in theirs. A smirk tugged at his lips. This information would prove useful.

After a winding descent through the intricate maze of their defenses, they finally arrived at the heart of the workshop. The lab was a chaotic masterpiece; gears, blueprints, and half-built contraptions cluttered the space, the air thick with the scent of oil and burning wood. Devaultus set the damaged glider down on one of the many workbenches, the gnomes immediately swarming around it like scavengers descending on a fresh kill.

Their hands were already moving, prodding at the torn fabric, assessing the fractures in the wooden frame. Devaultus joined them, feigning a shared enthusiasm as they set to work repairing the broken masterpiece. In reality, he was already thinking ten steps ahead.

Blight burst out of her lab, stumbling into the corridor as her eyes burned with tears. Her breath hitched, coming in desperate gasps as she choked on whatever noxious fumes still clung to her lungs. Right behind her, Vex staggered out as well, her own face streaked with tears, coughing and wheezing like she'd just inhaled a cloud of poison, because she had.

Blight whirled on her, her usually calm demeanor shattered by raw frustration. "What did you do?!" she shrieked, her voice rasping as she wiped at her watering eyes.

Vex gagged, waving her hands wildly as if trying to clear the air itself. "I was helping you!" she croaked, blinking rapidly to rid herself of the chemical-induced tears.

Blight let out a furious cough, her glare cutting through the haze of lingering fumes. "You weren't supposed to mix those two! Together, they become ridiculously potent!"

Vex gritted her teeth and wiped her sleeve across her face, her expression twisting between exasperation and sheepishness. "Well, I *know* that now, don't I?! Would've been nice to know *before* I mixed them! Why in the hells would you keep them right next to each other if they weren't supposed to be mixed?"

Blight groaned, rubbing her temples, her voice thick with irritation. "Because *I* know not to mix them, Vex!"

The two of them collapsed onto the ground just outside the lab, still wheezing, still trying to catch their breath. Vex let her head thump against the wall behind her. "Well, that knowledge didn't exactly help *me*, now did it?" she muttered, her voice still raw from the coughing fit.

Blight shot her a murderous glare, barely resisting the urge to throttle her. "You weren't supposed to mix *anything*! Especially *not that*!"

They sat there for nearly half an hour, letting the lab air out, neither of them eager to re-enter the scene of the near-disastrous mistake. Eventually, they exchanged wary glances and, with mutual reluctance, crept back inside.

Blight's sharp gaze scanned the lab, noting that, somehow, nothing had outright exploded. The damage, while present, wasn't as catastrophic as she'd feared. Glassware had been knocked over, some of the liquid had burned holes into the wooden worktable, but overall... nothing too devastating. No worse for wear, all things considered.

But then, she noticed something.

A chill ran down her spine.

One of her petri dishes sat completely *empty*.

She took a step closer, heart pounding as she racked her memory. She had been cultivating something in there, something rare. Something... dangerous.

Ophiocordyceps unilateralis.

A fungus with an insidious nature, known to infect and control its host. Al'Shandra had claimed it came from *another world*, an oddity she had acquired during one of her many bizarre escapades. Blight had found it *fascinating*. She had studied it, carefully contained it, kept it in a controlled environment.

And now, it was gone.

But fungi didn't just... *disappear*.

Blight's breath hitched.

A fungus does not simply get up and walk away.

...Does it?

Blight's breath hitched as a sinking feeling settled deep in her gut. Her mind raced through possibilities, her hands fumbling over the worktable as she searched frantically. Could the two mixtures Vex had so carelessly combined have somehow reacted with the Ophiocordyceps? Could it have mutated; worse, moved?

"Not good. Not good," she muttered under her breath, her pulse hammering as she shoved aside vials and scattered notes, searching for any sign of the missing fungus. It had been contained in a petri dish, sealed and monitored; there was no way it should have just vanished. Unless...

"Whatcha looking for?" Vex asked, her tone light, almost amused, as she peeked over Blight's shoulder.

Blight's movements became more frantic, her words spilling out in a sharp, clipped rush. "The Ophiocordyceps unilateralis: it's gone. I need to find it. It could be dangerous."

Vex blinked, tilting her head like a confused puppy. "Sooo... this Orphy-uni-whatever is dangerous how?"

Blight stopped just long enough to glare at her before pushing a shaking hand through her already-messy hair. "In the world it came from, it had the ability to infect living creatures, take control of them, override their will. It turned them into mindless, zombie-like husks." She turned to Vex, eyes wide with unfiltered dread. "If it's loose on the ship, I have no idea how it will react to the physiology of creatures from this world. If it infects the wrong thing, if it adapts..."

Vex stared at her blankly for a moment. Then, her lips curled into a grin. "And... that's bad?"

Blight let out an exhausted, exasperated groan, dragging her hands down her face. "Yes, Vex. That's very bad. We could all be killed."

Vex, entirely unfazed, waved a dismissive hand. "Oh no we won't! I'm here to protect you. We'll find your Orphy, put it back in its little fungus cage, and then get ready to help Devaultus when he gets back!"

Blight wasn't sure Vex had fully grasped the sheer horror of the situation. But despite her reckless tendencies, she was right about one thing: finding the fungus had to be their top priority before it spread.

Taking a steadying breath, Blight scanned the lab again, forcing herself to think. Where could it have gone? The room was sealed, no vents were large enough for anything to slip through. She crouched, checking along the floor, her sharp eyes catching something: a narrow gap between two warped wooden planks. A perfect escape route, leading straight into the dark, damp underbelly of the ship.

Her stomach twisted.

"We need to go below," she said, her voice grim. She pointed at the small opening. "That's the only place it could have gone."

Vex clapped her hands together, practically bouncing with excitement. "Ooooh, a fungus hunt! Sounds fun!"

Blight had a feeling she was going to regret this.

The two crept down the dimly lit corridor, their footsteps muffled against the worn wooden planks. The air smelled of oil, dust, and the faint musk of neglect. At the far end of the passage, the door to the ship's underbelly loomed, cast in shadows, as though it belonged to another world entirely. Blight swallowed hard. Her mind conjured images of clawed hands and slimy tentacles writhing beneath the door, grasping, searching for something, or someone, to pull into the darkness. She clenched her fists, forcing herself to shake off the irrational fear, but it lingered, curling in the pit of her stomach like a sickness.

Vex, on the other hand, let out a delighted giggle. "You'd think they'd at least throw a few lanterns up, huh?" she mused, not the least bit concerned by the ominous atmosphere.

Before Blight could stop her, Vex sauntered forward and, without hesitation, grabbed the handle and shoved the door open. A wave of stale air rolled over them, thick with dampness and something vaguely metallic.

Blight let out a sharp breath through her nose, biting back a curse as she reached for the various belts and pouches strapped to her body, tightening them, making sure every tool, vial, and weapon was within reach. She needed to be ready. For what, she wasn't entirely sure, but her imagination supplied a long list of things she very much did not want to encounter.

That was just her paranoia, right? Surely there weren't actual tentacle monsters down there. Right?

She hesitated at the threshold, casting a wary glance at Vex, who handed her a torch with a lopsided grin before skipping inside as if she were heading into a festival rather than the dark and potentially infested underbelly of a ship.

Blight scowled. How could she be so damn fearless?

No, Blight corrected herself. It wasn't bravery, was it? No, Vex wasn't fearless. She was just... foolhardy. She didn't consider the consequences, the dangers, the very real threats that lurked in the shadows. She wasn't immune to fear, she was simply too reckless to acknowledge it. To Vex, everything was just a grand adventure, a game where the stakes were never quite real.

Blight sighed, gripping the torch tightly as she followed her friend into the Abyss.

Blight took a deep breath, steeling herself before stepping through the doorway and pulling it shut behind her with a quiet *click*. Every part of her wanted to leave it open, to have an easy escape route, but if that thing had already gotten past them, the last thing she needed was to let it spread to the rest of the ship. She refused to be *that* idiot in a horror story, the one who left the door open and doomed everyone.

The wooden steps groaned under their weight as they descended, torches casting flickering shadows against the damp walls. Blight wasn't entirely sure they even *needed* their torches. Dim lanterns dotted the lower deck, providing just enough light to see the silhouettes of pipes, crates, and machinery lining the ship's underbelly. And beyond that, she could hear them. *Voices.* The rhythmic thudding of tools. The low murmur of workers going about their duties.

At least... she *thought* they were workers.

She *hoped* they were workers.

Blight swallowed, her grip tightening around her torch. She hadn't actually *seen* anyone down here yet, and that nagging little voice in the back of her mind whispered: *What if they aren't workers? What if it's already spread?*

Vex, of course, didn't share her concerns. The rogue skipped ahead without a care in the world, her head swiveling from side to side, eyes glittering with curiosity. Blight highly doubted she even knew *what* they were looking for. More than likely, she was just shoving every shiny, expensive-looking thing into her pockets with the full intention of stripping this place clean before the day was over.

Blight sighed, rubbing her temples. By the time they were done, she'd be lucky if Vex left *enough* of the ship intact for it to still be seaworthy.

They stood at the edge of the massive storage area, Blight's wide, uncertain eyes flitting from one shadowy corridor to the next. The underbelly of the ship stretched far beyond what she had imagined: a maze of wooden beams, stacked crates, and hanging lanterns that flickered with an eerie, swaying glow. Her fingers tightened anxiously around her torch as she swallowed hard.

"Where do we even start?" she murmured, her voice barely above a whisper, as if speaking too loudly might wake something lurking in the dim recesses of the cargo hold.

Vex, in contrast, had none of Blight's hesitation. Folding her arms beneath her chest, she gave a casual glance around before her gaze landed on a crate labeled in bold, blocky letters: *RUM*. With a delighted grin, she crouched down, pried open the box, and pulled out a glass bottle with a look of childish fascination.

"How about this one?" she mused, turning the bottle over in her hands. The glass was smooth and clear, the amber liquid inside sloshing slightly with each tilt. Her brows knitted together as she examined it, as if she were trying to unravel some grand mystery. "Looks safe. But how can we be sure?"

Before Blight could even open her mouth to protest, Vex had already freed the cork with a satisfying *pop* and taken a deep, greedy swig. She pulled back with a sharp inhale, her emerald eyes widening in surprise as the burn hit her throat.

"Oooh... that's new," she coughed, licking her lips. "That isn't ale. What is that?"

Blight's fear momentarily took a backseat to her scientific curiosity. Her torchlight flickered across the label of the bottle, and her stomach twisted as recognition struck her. Her world's language. Her world's branding.

The bottle was sealed with an all-too-familiar image: an old, well-known brand from home, depicting a sailor with one foot propped up in a heroic pose.

Her thoughts raced. How? How in the name of science and logic did they have liquor from *her* world here? The ingredients to make alcohol weren't anything special, and yes, they had glass in this world; after all, she used beakers and flasks all the time in her lab. But *this*? This was something else.

Blight's fingers ran hesitantly over the print, her mind spinning in circles. There was no way this was a coincidence. Something about this world... about how she had ended up here... but *why*...

Vex took another swig.

Blight scowled, yanking the bottle from her hands. "Stop drinking it! We don't even know if it's safe!"

Vex pouted. "You just said it's from your world. How dangerous could it be? You're like a timid baby Scorch beetle."

Blight groaned, pinching the bridge of her nose. They had much bigger problems right now; like a rogue, possibly murderous zombie fungus skittering around in the dark. She needed to focus. But the bottle of rum in her hands told her something she wasn't ready to confront.

She might not be as far from home as she thought.

Blight yanked the bottle from Vex's hands, bringing it to her lips and taking a deep, thoughtful sip. The warmth of the liquor spread through her, but more importantly, the taste was unmistakable. Her world. It had come from her world. A sensation twisted in her gut: excitement, fear, maybe even hope. Could Al'Shandra have been telling the truth? Could the pirate queen really travel between worlds? If that were true, then Blight had a chance; no, a *way* to get home. Back to her warm bed, back to the safety of her family's embrace. Back to a world where she understood the rules, where she wasn't constantly in danger or fumbling in the dark.

Her fingers tightened around the glass. This changed everything.

"Is this your Orphy?" Vex's voice yanked her out of her spiraling thoughts.

Blight turned to see Vex holding something up: a furry creature's head, complete with pointy antlers. It was large enough that Vex had to grip it with both hands, and she held it aloft as though it were some grand discovery. Her grin was wide, triumphant; she seemed completely unaware of how ridiculous she looked.

Blight blinked, then let out a sigh. "No, Vex. That is definitely not it."

Vex turned the mounted deer head over in her hands, examining it with keen interest. "Weird-lookin' thing," she mused, running her fingers over the coarse fur. "Why's it got so much hair? Nothin' here has that much hair; well, 'cept for that barkeep at The Split Cock Canteen." She shuddered dramatically. "That was one hairy dwarven woman."

Blight couldn't help but let out a small, breathy laugh, though her mind was still racing. She could see the genuine confusion on Vex's face as she studied the taxidermied head. Of course, Vex had never seen a deer before; why would she have? Creatures from Blight's world didn't belong here.

Blight swallowed hard. "It's an animal from another world," she murmured, her voice quieter now, more uncertain. Her gaze lingered on the glass bottle in her hand, on the familiar logo stamped into the glass. "From my world."

The weight of those words settled heavily in her chest. She had been thrown into this brutal, unfamiliar place, constantly struggling to understand its dangers. But this: this was proof. Proof that her world wasn't as far away as she'd feared. Proof that, maybe, just maybe, she could find her way back.

Vex tilted her head, studying the mounted deer head with an almost comical level of scrutiny, her fingers absently poking at the glassy, lifeless eyes. "How does it get around without any legs?" she asked, her voice filled with genuine curiosity. "Does it crawl like an eeltok?"

Blight opened her mouth, ready to explain, but instead, the mental image of a deer dragging itself across the ground by its antlers hit her, and before she could stop herself, she burst into laughter. It was the kind of unrestrained, tear-bringing laughter that she hadn't allowed herself in a long time. She doubled over, clutching her stomach, wiping at the corners of her eyes. "No, no," she finally managed between giggles, taking in a deep breath to calm herself. "It doesn't crawl! It's just a trophy. Someone killed it, stuffed it, and mounted the head to hang on their wall."

Vex's eyes went wide, her expression lighting up with sudden understanding. "Ohh... I get it now!" she said, nodding sagely. Then she frowned. "Though that seems like a terrible waste of the eyes and horns."

Blight blinked. "The... eyes and horns?" she echoed, her laughter quickly fading as her brain caught up with whatever bizarre thought process Vex was working through.

"Oh, absolutely," Vex said matter-of-factly, finally setting the deer head down and moving along, seemingly losing interest. "The eyes are quite delicious on most animals, I've been told on most everything, really. And as for the horns? What better way to make a stock of some kind?"

Blight stared at her, her stomach twisting in equal parts horror and reluctant fascination. It wasn't that she hadn't already learned that most things in this world were used to their fullest extent, nothing was wasted, not when food was so scarce. She had heard in her prison cell how certain races didn't even bury their dead. They were simply... consumed. But hearing it stated so casually, as if it were the most natural thing in the world, sent a fresh shiver down her spine.

"Right," Blight murmured, nodding absently as she followed after Vex, suddenly hyper-aware of just how much she still didn't understand about this world, how much she might never truly be ready for.

As the creature stepped into the dim torchlight, an unnatural chittering echoed through the underbelly of the ship, setting Blight's nerves alight with fear. Vex stilled beside her, her usual carefree expression replaced with something more serious, more focused. The thing that rounded the corner was no ordinary monster. It was a nightmare stitched together from death and rot, its very presence sending a shudder down Blight's spine.

The Cordyphage was grotesque in every way, an abomination born from a terrible alchemical mistake. It stood hunched, its gaunt, elongated frame covered in brittle, armor-like fungal plating that pulsed with eerie bioluminescence. Patches of blackened, necrotic flesh peeked through the fungal growth, as if something human had once been part of its creation, though whatever it had been before was long lost to decay and mutation.

Its head was an unsettling fusion of insect and fungus, a warped skull covered in chitinous plating that cracked open along the center like a rotting fruit. Beneath the split shell, a cluster of undulating fungal tendrils writhed and twisted, oozing a thick, sticky substance that reeked of damp earth and decomposition. Where eyes should have been, two pits glowed with a spectral green light, shifting and pulsating as though they were alive: watching, calculating.

The Cordyphage's limbs were impossibly long, its bony fingers tipped with jagged, spore-ridden claws that dripped with viscous black fluid. The creature's torso heaved unnaturally with every movement, as if the fungal mass inside it was constantly growing, shifting, searching for a new host to consume. Its legs bent at unnatural angles, its steps silent and unsettlingly smooth; it was like a predator that had learned to stalk rather than stumble.

But what made Blight's blood run cold was the way the fungus on its back moved. Thick, pulsating cords of fungal tissue jutted from its spine, writhing like hungry tentacles. At their tips, swollen sacs bulged, filled with twitching spores that seemed to shimmer in the low light, as though they were just waiting for the perfect moment to burst and spread their infection.

And then, it stopped. The glowing pits of its "eyes" locked onto them. The fungal tendrils in its split maw twitched, tasting the air, as if recognizing them not as threats, but as something... useful.

Blight's throat went dry.

Vex, however, tilted her head, an unsettling grin creeping across her face.

"Oh-ho," she murmured, her voice laced with unhinged amusement. "That's new."

Vex's grin stretched wide as she drew her daggers, the dim torchlight glinting off their wicked edges. Her gaze flicked toward Blight, a silent, questioning look in her eyes, as if asking if this was just another one of her world's horrors. Blight swallowed hard, tightening her grip on her own weapons.

"No, Vex," she said, her voice tense, her breath coming in short, panicked gasps. "That... that is not from my world. I think that's my Orphy."

Vex's smirk curled with amusement. "They grow up so fast," she said with a playful gleam in her eyes, as if they were watching some fledgling beast take its first steps rather than standing in the presence of something that shouldn't exist.

Blight shuddered, trying to fight the icy dread crawling up her spine. "Don't let it touch you, Vex," she warned. "I don't know what will happen if it does."

Vex cast another glance at the creature, her eyes flickering over the writhing, glistening tendrils sprouting from its back, the slick, fungal plating of its skin, and the faint, eerie mist of spores leaking from its joints like a broken pipe, releasing toxic fumes. Then, with a slow blink, she turned back to Blight, a lopsided grin forming.

"Yeah…" she drawled, the sarcasm thick in her voice. "Because letting it touch me was the *first* thing I planned on doing."

Blight, despite the icy panic in her chest, found herself smiling for just a fraction of a second. But then the Cordyphage's gaze locked onto her, its grotesque mandibles twitching; that hollow, sunken stare full of something awful, something *hungry*.

It wasn't interested in Vex. Not at all.

It wanted *her*.

Blight froze, a rabbit caught in the eyes of a predator. It could *feel* her fear. It was drawn to it, feeding on it, reveling in the way her breath hitched in her throat. Every movement, every shiver of terror only seemed to fuel its focus.

Vex, meanwhile, vanished into the darkness like a ghost, her form blurring between flickering shadows. She slipped soundlessly through the rows of shelving, darting between crates and barrels, circling the creature with deadly precision.

Blight forced herself to move, her fingers trembling as she reached into her pack. She retrieved two metal rods, each with intricate tubing attached to them. Swiftly, she connected the hoses, her hands working on instinct even as her mind screamed at her to *run*. Her thumbs brushed over the buttons lining the rods, and at the press of one, a sharp, electrified *crackle* filled the air. Blue sparks flickered along the rods, illuminating the fear in Blight's wide eyes.

This was bad. This was *so* much worse than she had imagined.

Her hands tightened around her makeshift weapons.

She was not ready for this.

She wished Devaultus were here. He would know what to do.

Or, no. No, he really wouldn't. Devaultus would *pretend* he knew what to do, charge in headfirst with some reckless, borderline suicidal plan, and by some infuriating twist of fate, he'd *win* anyway. He'd crash through the problem like a wrecking ball, leaving chaos in his wake, and somehow, against all odds, come out on top.

She wished Devaultus was here even more.

Blight barely had time to process the thought before the Cordyphage lunged forward, moving with a speed that *should not* have belonged to something so grotesque. Its elongated arms shot forward, fungal tendrils twitching with unnatural life. Blight's breath hitched as she scrambled backward, just in time to avoid the creature's clawed fist as it came crashing down. A deafening crack echoed through the storage hold as the blow shattered an entire shelf, splintering thick wooden beams as if they were nothing more than kindling.

Blight paled. *That strength, how?!* The Cordyphage should have only been able to control whatever host it had infested, *not* amplify its power to this level. No creature, *nothing*, was supposed to be *that* strong.

Fear clawed up her spine, turning her limbs to ice.

Then, a blur of movement: Vex burst from the shadows, her form a streak of motion as she *dove* low and slashed at the Cordyphage's leg with a vicious flick of her dagger. The keen edge of her blade cut through the fungal flesh, slicing deep.

For the first time, the creature reacted.

A sickening, inhuman sound escaped from within its mass, a gurgled, agonized *cry* from something trapped deep beneath the layers of rotting tissue and parasitic growths. It was muffled, strangled, *smothered* beneath the infestation that had overtaken its body.

Blight's stomach churned. There was something still *alive* inside it. Something suffering.

*Screech*, the sound wet and garbled as if it were being choked beneath layers of fungal growth. A shudder ran through its towering form, but the Cordyphage did not collapse, did not falter; it merely turned its pulsating, fungal-infested head toward Blight with renewed hunger.

Blight's breath caught in her throat. *Why isn't it going down?!* She had expected resistance, but this thing wasn't reacting the way a normal creature should. Even the most hardened beast should have staggered from a direct electric shock, let alone a puncture wound to the leg. Yet the Cordyphage remained upright, its body swaying unnaturally, movements jerky like a puppet being yanked by invisible strings.

The mutated monster swung wildly again, its elongated, clawed arms tearing through the air. Another shelf exploded into splinters as Blight threw herself to the side, rolling over broken crates and scattered glass. Her hands stung as she scrambled to her feet, mind racing. *Think, think, think! It's not just one creature, it's a host. Killing the body might not be enough!*

Vex, ever the opportunist, used the moment of chaos to dart in, her form flickering through the shadows like a specter. She appeared just long enough to drive her daggers into the Cordyphage's exposed back. The twin blades sunk in deep, their edges slicing through the thick layers of fungus and decayed flesh.

For the first time, the Cordyphage *screamed*.

It wasn't just a cry of pain, it was a chorus. A grotesque, overlapping cacophony of voices, some deep and guttural, others shrill and inhuman. It was like the fungus itself was wailing.

Vex twisted her daggers, grinning wickedly. "Oh-ho, now that's interesting." She yanked one of her blades free, coated in viscous, oozing mycelium. "Blight, whatever this is, it's got *friends* inside of it."

Blight swallowed hard. "That's... that's horrifying."

Vex cackled, effortlessly dodging a retaliatory swipe. "*Right?!* Gods, I love my job."

Blight didn't know what disturbed her more: the Cordyphage's unnatural resilience, or the absolute glee in Vex's voice as she carved into the abomination like it was nothing more than a particularly interesting science experiment.

The Cordyphage lurched forward, seemingly intent on her now. Blight could feel its fixation like a weight pressing against her chest. It wanted her, drawn to her fear like a predator smelling blood in the water.

She gritted her teeth and adjusted her grip on her weapon. Fine. If it wants me, it can have me. But it won't like what it gets.

She thumbed another switch on her rod, the device humming ominously as its energy reserves surged to their peak.

The fight wasn't over yet.

She found it nearly impossible to think as the Cordyphage hunted her with relentless precision, its grotesque limbs swinging wildly, shattering crates and demolishing shelves in its frenzied pursuit. Every near miss sent splinters flying past her face, every impact a thunderous reminder of its monstrous strength. Her breath came in frantic gasps as she darted between obstacles, her mind racing just as fast as her feet.

Vex, unfazed and disturbingly gleeful, clung to the creature's back like some kind of psychotic parasite, her daggers plunging into the fungus-covered flesh again and again. She carved her way upward, slicing through the pulsing cords of sinew and spore-ridden tendrils, her path leaving behind a thick, oozing mess. Yet, despite the ferocity of her assault, the creature barely seemed to register her presence, its focus locked entirely on Blight.

Blight's own weapon crackled uselessly in her grip, the electricity arching harmlessly over the creature's fungal hide. No matter how much power she fed into it, the effect was negligible at best. She gritted her teeth, frustration bubbling beneath her panic. This was a problem; a solvable one. She just needed to think. She needed to apply logic.

Her mind scrambled for an answer as she threw herself aside, narrowly avoiding the monster's crushing blow. The impact sent another shelf toppling, smashing into a crate labeled *RUM*, which promptly exploded in a spectacular shower of golden liquid, shattered glass, and splintered wood. The scent of alcohol filled the air.

Blight's eyes widened. Electricity wasn't working because, damn it... it was *grounding out*. If the creature was more plant than flesh, then the electricity likely dispersed too easily. But *fire*? Fire was different. Fire *devoured* plant matter.

A new plan snapped into place.

She scrambled to her feet, hand flying over the buttons on her weapon. The static hum of the electricity died out with a sputter, replaced by the telltale *whoosh* of igniting fuel. A long, searing flame burst from the end of the rod, flickering like the torch of a vengeful god. The sight of it sent a twisted surge of confidence through her chest.

For the first time since the fight began, she felt like she had a *chance*.

The Cordyphage's hollow eyes flicked toward the flame, a strange, unsettling hesitation rippling through its grotesque form.

Blight tightened her grip.

"Oh, you *don't* like this, do you?" she muttered, her voice barely above a whisper.

Good.

Then *burn*.

The Cordyphage hesitated, its grotesque form shifting backward as if, for the first time, it was second-guessing its dominance. The flickering flames cast writhing shadows across the room, illuminating the uncertainty in its posture. Fire: this was something it feared. The revelation sent a shiver of anticipation through Blight. She had found its weakness.

Vex, however, was having the time of her life. She cackled, her wild grin illuminated by the growing firelight, as she drove her daggers into the Cordyphage's back in rapid, brutal succession. Each stab was met with a muffled, otherworldly wail, an eerie, discordant screeching that rose from deep within the corrupted body, layered with unsettling clacks and chirrs that seemed almost insect-like. The ship's belly echoed with the inhuman chorus, the sound bouncing off the wooden walls and mixing with the crackle of growing flames.

Blight seized the moment, her fear overridden by an urgent need to act before the creature regained its confidence. With a determined shout, she lunged forward, thrusting the now-blazing rod directly into the Cordyphage's chest.

The reaction was instantaneous.

The monster went up like dry tinder, its fungal flesh crackling as the flames devoured it from within. Its shrieks reached an agonized crescendo before cutting off entirely, but the fire didn't stop there. Blight's stomach lurched as she realized the blaze was spreading; too fast. The floor, soaked in the rum from the shattered bottles, ignited in an instant.

Her breath caught in her throat.

"Oh no, no, no..." she whispered in dawning horror, watching as the fire eagerly licked its way across the floorboards. "Al'Shandra is going to be *so* angry."

Vex, quick as ever, leapt from the back of the burning corpse just before it collapsed in on itself, fungus curling and blackening as the inferno consumed it. And then, as the fire stripped away the monstrous growths, what remained beneath became horrifyingly clear.

The Cordyphage had not simply been a beast: it had once been a *man*.

A giant, to be precise. Now lying lifeless on the scorched floor, his body riddled with gaping holes where the fungal parasite had replaced his flesh. The pieces that had been consumed by the Cordyphage were gone entirely, leaving charred, gaping wounds in their place. His massive, calloused hands twitched once before falling still. His eyes, once flickering with something resembling understanding, stared up at them, clouding over as the last traces of life slipped away.

Blight's breath was ragged, her mind racing.

They had killed the monster. But at what cost?

Blight's fingers fumbled over the controls of her weapon, her mind racing as she twisted dials and clicked through the various buttons. "Okay, okay... reverse wind," she muttered to herself, her voice shaking slightly as she locked in the settings. "That should, should suck the air out instead of feeding the flames."

With the final flick of a switch, the device hummed to life. The gears within whirred violently as the rods twisted and pulled at the air, drawing the oxygen away from the hungry fire. The flames, once roaring and threatening to spread, sputtered and choked before finally vanishing, leaving behind only the charred remains of their destruction.

Blight let out a breath, shoulders sagging as she surveyed the damage. The hull was blackened, scorched, and undeniably weakened. She grimaced. "Yeah... Al'Shandra is going to be so mad at us," she murmured, running a nervous hand through her hair.

Vex, standing beside her, sheathed her daggers with a dramatic sigh. "Yeah, I think we can agree on that," she said, a grin tugging at her lips despite the situation.

As if summoned by their guilt, the unmistakable sound of heavy boots echoed through the ship. Then, from around the corner, Al'Shandra strode into view, her every step radiating fury. Her tight corset-style top, half-unbuttoned as usual, did little to contain the heaving rise and fall of her chest as she took in the chaos before her. The pirate queen's hips swayed with dangerous intent, her wild mane of crimson hair framing an expression of pure wrath.

Behind her, several crew members peered in, eyes wide with shock.

"What in the Abyss is goin' on here?" Al'Shandra's voice was a venomous growl, dripping with both anger and exasperation.

Blight opened her mouth, but before she could even attempt an explanation, Vex stepped forward, grinning ear to ear.

"Well, you see..." Vex began, holding up her hands as if recounting a harmless tale. "I was helping, yeah? And then Blight mixed that pink stuff with the green stuff; bad idea, by the way; aaaaand poof! Gasses everywhere, a lot of yelling, so we ran, and then boom, Orphy escaped and bolted down here. Obviously, we couldn't let that stand, so we came after it, and then there was a whole lot of boom, bang, wham! Aaaand..." She gestured grandly towards the wreckage, the still-smoking remains of their battle. "Here we are."

Silence.

Al'Shandra's piercing eyes burned into them, her lips pressing into a thin line as she inhaled deeply through her nose.

Blight gulped.

Vex just kept grinning.

Al'Shandra's eyes narrowed, her expression twisting into something between frustration and sheer disbelief as she ran a hand through her wild mane of dark curls. Her hips cocked to one side, the dramatic curve of her form only accentuating the exasperated shake of her head.

"What in the Abyss are you even talking about?" she demanded, her voice thick with irritation and disbelief. "What you've just said is one of the most insanely idiotic things I have ever heard. At no point in that rambling, incoherent response did you come even remotely close to anything that could be considered a rational thought."

Blight blinked, her lips parting slightly as she considered those words. That... sounded oddly familiar. She furrowed her brow, racking her brain, but the memory remained just out of reach. Had she heard something like that before?

Before she could dwell on it further, a sharp, chittering clack echoed through the air. It was not just one sound, but many, layered, rhythmic, and drawing closer. The hair on the back of her neck prickled as she turned her head toward the source.

Emerging from behind the towering shelves, their grotesque fungal forms illuminated by flickering lantern light, came five more Cordyphage. Their milky, spore-covered eyes locked onto the group, their twisted, pulsating limbs twitching as if eager to latch onto something living, something warm.

Blight's stomach dropped into a pit of ice.

Al'Shandra's sharp gaze snapped to the creatures, her full lips parting in a mixture of shock and fury. "What did you do?" she hissed, her voice dripping with accusation before her narrowed gaze flicked between Blight and the monstrosities before them. Her expression darkened further, dangerous and scalding. "And what in the name of the drowned gods is that?!"

# CHAPTER 15

# ORIGINS UNLEASHED: DEVAULTUS' DARK PAST

**T**wenty-Three Years Ago

Devaultus' eyes fluttered open, his vision swimming with hazy shapes and muted colors. A blurred figure loomed over him, shifting, moving, speaking. He tried to make sense of it, but his thoughts were sluggish, tangled in the throbbing pain coursing through his body. Everything hurt. Every breath burned, every twitch of muscle sent fire lancing through his nerves. What had happened? Why was he like this?

Instinct told him to push the pain away. Bury it. His father had taught him well: pain was weakness, and weakness invited more suffering. If he let it show, if he whimpered or groaned, then the punishment would only get worse.

A soft rustle pulled his scattered attention back. The figure was draping something over him. A blanket? A coat? But then, instead of walking away, they dropped down beside him, covering themselves as well. A voice, thick with urgency, broke through the haze.

"I know you must be gravely injured. Please. Just hold on. I know someone who can help you."

The words barely registered before a jolt rocked his body. Movement. The world trembled beneath him, sending waves of agony rolling through his battered form. His instincts screamed at him to stay silent, to keep his suffering locked behind clenched teeth. If he cried out, if he showed weakness, he knew exactly what would happen.

He fought to stay aware, to make sense of what was happening, but the pain was relentless, dragging him under like a riptide. Voices murmured above him, more than one now, but their words were muffled, distant, like they were speaking through water. Hands pressed against him, lifting, shifting, carrying. Each touch sent fresh bursts of torment through his limbs.

He wanted it to stop. Wanted it all to end. If death meant freedom from this suffering, then maybe... maybe he should just let go.

But some stubborn, buried part of him clung to consciousness, grasping at the frayed edges of awareness. He fought against the darkness clawing at him, tried to hold onto something, anything,

And then, just as quickly as he had surfaced, he lost the battle.

The world faded. The voices disappeared.

Unconsciousness swallowed him whole.

Devaultus had no idea how long he had been unconscious, how many hours, days had slipped past while he lay still and broken. But something felt different now. A softness cradled his aching body, the faint scent of hay and aged wood filling his senses. Wait... soft? That wasn't right.

A bed.

His bleary eyes fluttered open, struggling to focus as the dim room swam into view. It was small, cluttered with mismatched furniture and the scent of something vaguely herbal hanging in the air. His gaze drifted, landing on a boy, no bigger than himself, slumped in a chair beside the bed. The kid couldn't have been older than twelve, his gangly form swallowed by clothes that were far too large. His pants, cinched at the waist with a tattered leather strip, looked as if they'd been salvaged from a leathersmith's scrap pile. His shirt, once white, now clung to his wiry frame in faded shreds. But it wasn't just his ragged attire that caught Devaultus' attention.

Pointed ears. Sharp, pointy teeth peeking from between his lips.

An elf.

Devaultus stiffened instinctively, his mind racing through every story he had ever heard. Elves were supposed to be vicious, wild creatures lurking in the forests, waiting to sink their teeth into unsuspecting flesh. And yet... this one wasn't trying to gnaw his arm off. If anything, he looked bored. Tired.

Until their eyes met.

Devaultus quickly looked away and down. He wasn't allowed to meet someone's eyes or he was likely to be beaten.

The boy jolted upright as if struck by lightning, his face lighting up with excitement. "Master! He's awake!" His voice cracked from the sheer force of his yell as he sprang from his chair, nearly knocking it over in his rush to Devaultus' bedside.

Devaultus inwardly flinched as he waited for the strike. Not showing it outwardly.

He beamed, rocking on his heels with barely contained energy. "Hey, I saved you! Pretty sure you'd be dead if I hadn't found you. You were beat up real bad, looked like someone tried to turn you inside out."

Devaultus blinked sluggishly, his thoughts moving through a fog, thick and heavy. Words felt distant, disconnected, but they slowly began to arrange themselves into something comprehensible.

"The... tower..." his voice rasped, his throat dry as sand. He wanted to ask more. He wanted to know how he was alive. He remembered falling. But he knew what would happen if you spoke without being spoken too.

The boy's head bobbed so fast, it was a wonder his neck didn't snap. "How did you fall from there? You flew like a stark snout, you did! I saw the whole thing, flappin' your arms like you thought you could sprout wings and take off." He grinned wide, showing off those sharp teeth. "And then *bam!* Face-first into the wagon I was hiding in."

Devaultus let out a weak, breathy groan: big mistake. The pain that followed was immediate and searing, shooting through his ribs like hot iron. His breath hitched, a groan turning into a hacking cough that rattled his bones and made the whole world tilt. Abyss take him, that hurt.

Devaultus wanted to say how he didn't feel so well. How he just wanted to sleep and let the pain go away. But he was used to hiding the pain. So, he kept quiet.

The elf boy just grinned wider, rocking on his heels. "You really don't look so well. A bit pale, if you ask me."

"I don't doubt he does."

The voice was smooth, refined, carrying the effortless authority of someone accustomed to command. A slender, well-dressed man strode into the room, his presence exuding confidence and control. His attire was a striking combination of black and gold, the fabric rich and well-tailored, marking him as someone of wealth, or at least someone who knew how to present himself as such. His jet-black hair was parted precisely down the middle, the sides slicked back with meticulous care. A pointed goatee, reminiscent of that of a nobleman or perhaps a devil in disguise, framed his sharp features, blending seamlessly into a thin, pencil-like mustache that curled ever so slightly at the ends.

"You took quite the tumble," the man continued, his dark eyes scanning Devaultus with the keen interest of a scholar examining a rare specimen. "And from what I can tell, you shattered quite a number of bones. Frankly, I'm not sure how you remained conscious for as long as you did. Most men would have passed into the Abyss well before I found you." He folded his arms, his expression unreadable. "I had a rather skilled healer mend you, but make no mistake, it will take time before you feel whole again. For now, you must rest. Let your body do the work it was meant to do."

He then shifted his gaze toward the young elf standing nearby. The boy had been watching the exchange with wide, eager eyes, clearly invested in the conversation.

"Tristen," the man said smoothly, "you will continue your studies. There will be plenty of time to familiarize yourself with our guest when it is appropriate."

The elven boy, who looked no older than twelve, gave an enthusiastic nod. "Yes, Master," he said, his tone laced with obedience. Without hesitation, he turned on his heel and hurried out of the room, leaving Devaultus alone with the enigmatic figure who had apparently saved his life.

The man took the recently vacated seat beside the bed, crossing one leg over the other with effortless grace. He studied Devaultus for a long moment, as if weighing something in his mind. Then, at last, he spoke again.

"Now then, lad. What is your name?"

Devaultus hesitated, looking at his covered feet. He wasn't sure what to make of this man, but the fact remained: he had saved him. Perhaps he wasn't so bad. Then again. His father had saved him from near death plenty of times only so he could torture him further.

"I'm Devaultus, sir," he replied, keeping his tone polite, though a trace of uncertainty lingered beneath his words.

The man gave him a warm smile, one that almost seemed like it could ease the years of pain Devaultus had buried deep inside. "Well, Devaultus," the man said, his voice smooth and rich, "allow me to introduce myself. You can call me Donovine Octaviane." Donovine wasn't his real name, of course. But it would do for this purpose.

Devaultus blinked, taking in the name, feeling the weight of it, like it meant something more than just simple introduction. His voice, barely more than a whisper, cracked as he answered. "Yes, sir."

Donovine stood up, his movements graceful and purposeful. He went to a nearby table, where he poured a glass of water; clean, clear water that shimmered in the light like something precious. To Devaultus, it might as well have been gold. He stared at it for a moment, his mouth dry, as though he hadn't tasted something this pure in his entire life. In fact he had only had clean water once. That was a trick of his father's. He played it off as a gift from his loving father. But it was poisoned. His father wanted to see if he had any resistance to poison. Devaultus had nearly died that night. Over the course of the next couple years, he was poisoned multiple times; each time though, the poison did just a bit less too him.

The man handed him the clay mug, his fingers brushing against Devaultus' for a moment, the touch surprisingly gentle. Devaultus looked at the water warily. He knew waiting this long to do as he was told would end in a lashing from his father. He sighed a bit to himself, lifted it to his lips and drank deeply, the water feeling like a cool embrace, like it could wash away all the suffering he had endured.

"Now, slow down," Donovine said, a quiet chuckle in his voice. "There is more where that came from."

Devaultus, still thirsty and confused, tried to slow himself, but the sensation of the water was almost intoxicating. He'd never slept in a bed before, never felt something so soft beneath him. Never had clean water, or anything clean, really. It felt too much like a dream.

Donovine watched him carefully, a flicker of something, maybe concern, maybe curiosity, passing through his eyes. "Now then, Devaultus," he began, leaning forward just a little, "tell me what happened. How did you end up in such a state?"

Devaultus froze for a moment, a feeling of fear as the man leaned toward him. His mind raced. If he said the wrong thing, if he let anything slip about the tower, about his father, they'd throw him back. They'd throw him right back into that hell, with nothing but cold stone and the smell of rot to keep him company. The fear gripped him again, like an old, familiar shadow.

He forced himself to take a breath. "Sir," he began, his voice shaking slightly, "I'm an orphan. I thought... maybe there'd be food up there. A place to sleep. So I climbed up and... I lost my footing."

The lie came out more easily than he would've liked to admit. He kept his eyes on the table, on the mug of water, on anything but Donovine's piercing gaze.

Donovine's expression didn't change much, but Devaultus could feel the weight of his stare, as though the man was seeing through him. There was a subtle shift in his posture, a slight narrowing of his eyes. Donovine didn't buy the story, not completely. But he didn't press him on it either.

The man let out a quiet sigh, almost like a patient parent. "You'll tell me when you're ready, lad," Donovine said softly, his voice carrying the weight of understanding. "I'm not here to force answers out of you."

For a moment, Devaultus felt something in him relax; just a little. But only for a moment. Because he knew lying was a terrible sin. One that would come with horrific repercussions. His father once had one of his fingers sawed off with a dull saw for lying. Only to have the healer come over and fix it. Part of Devaultus felt that something would happen to him while he slept.

"Well, lad. Get some rest. When dinner's ready, I'll bring it up to you." Donovine's voice was calm, his words kind but direct, the sort of tone someone used when there was a quiet understanding between the two of you. He stood up from his chair, moving toward the door with a purposeful step. Devaultus watched as the man reached for the handle, the door creaking open slightly before Donovine closed it behind him.

And then, the silence settled in.

Devaultus lay there, his mind racing as he stared at the wood of the door. He expected the familiar sound that had haunted him his whole life: the sharp thud of the drawbar. The click of imprisonment. But instead, there was nothing. The door remained closed, but there was no drawbar, no sound that kept him trapped in this place. It was an unsettling quiet. The absence of something that had always been there before, like a chain that wasn't wrapped around his wrist.

It was an unfamiliar feeling. Freedom? Or something close to it. He didn't know how to handle it, how to embrace it. All he knew was the soft bed beneath him, the clean air that didn't reek of rot and neglect, and the soft pillow cradling his head like a new luxury he'd never known.

But he had to get out of there before the torturing began again. He had to hide somewhere. He tried to push himself up. Pain shot through his body as set bones attempting to mend shifted. He was used to pain. But this was too much. Darkness took over as he passed out from the pain.

A few hours passed, and they seemed like an eternity.

The soft, hurried sound of footsteps woke him from his light sleep. His eyes snapped open; disoriented, for a moment he wasn't sure if it was real or just a remnant of a nightmare. But the voice that followed soon confirmed it.

"Eh, Devaultus?" Tristen's voice was bright and a little too casual for the situation. "Master wants me to bring you some food."

Devaultus blinked, still groggy, his senses slowly returning to him. He watched the boy approach, his small, eager figure crossing the room with a purpose that spoke of someone used to moving quickly. Tristen settled into the chair next to the bed and handed him a bowl. The warmth of the stew wafted up to his face, and Devaultus' stomach growled audibly in response, the ache in his belly too familiar. It had been days since he'd eaten properly, days of hunger and pain, each moment of it gnawing at him.

He grabbed the bowl with trembling hands and dug in, ignoring the shooting pain from the reaching motion. Barely able to hold back his hunger as he wolfed down the stew. It was rich and thick, unlike the thin scraps he had grown used to, and each bite felt like it was healing a part of him he didn't even know was broken. His ribs, which had been so painfully exposed, finally seemed to settle as the food filled him. He hadn't realized how much his body had been starving for something more than scraps.

When he finally took a breath and swallowed, he glanced at Tristan. "Thank you," he said in a voice that felt more somber than he intended. He was trying to sound grateful, but it came out quieter.

Tristen watched him carefully, eyes sharp for someone so young. The boy tilted his head, scrutinizing Devaultus' every move like he was looking for something beneath the surface. "You don't get much to eat, do you?" Tristen asked, his tone light but with an edge of curiosity. "You must not be very good at stealing."

The words hit Devaultus like a gust of desert air. He froze, his spoon halfway to his mouth. Tristen's blunt observation stung more than he expected.

*Stealing?*

It was true. He had never been good at sneaking around. He had spent his entire life locked away, chained in that tower, the only contact with the outside world being his father's cruel orders. *Stealing*, if he'd ever tried to, had always been an afterthought, something he was too terrified to attempt. The only thing he'd ever "stolen" was scraps, and even then, they'd been taken from him, and he had been beaten within an inch of his life.

He swallowed slowly, the taste of the stew now turning to ash in his mouth. How could he explain that he had spent his entire existence in the dark, forced to survive in ways that left no room for things like stealing or scheming? All he'd ever known was the cold stone of the tower and the coldness in his father's eyes.

"I... I don't steal," Devaultus mumbled, avoiding Tristen's gaze as he focused on the stew again, suddenly embarrassed by the vulnerability the boy had exposed.

Tristen raised an eyebrow, sensing that there was more to the story, but he didn't press it. Instead, he just nodded, as if satisfied with the silence that fell between them.

Devaultus didn't know how to respond to that kind of openness. It was heavy. In some ways, Tristen's innocent curiosity was harder to deal with than anything his father had ever done to him. But there was something else beneath it. A part of him that, deep down, wanted to reach out to the boy and share the truth, just a fraction of it. Just to know what it was like to have a friend. But the walls he'd spent so long building up around himself had never felt thicker.

So, he continued eating, the words stuck in his throat. It was too soon to tell anyone what had really happened to him. Too soon to trust anyone with the darkness that clung to him like a shadow.

For now, the stew was enough. And in that small moment, Devaultus allowed himself to feel a flicker of something new. It was brief, but it was there, a sense of hope, fragile and raw, as he tried to forget what had come before and focus on this fleeting moment of peace.

Tristen's words hung in the air, soft but warm. "Don't worry. I won't say anything." His eyes suddenly twinkled with excitement, "Hey, I found some good parchments today. Want to look at them with me while you eat?"

Devaultus let out a breath he didn't realize he was holding. It wasn't frustration, no. It was relief. Relief that the boy wouldn't turn him in for lying about being an orphan, relief that he wasn't pressing him for more information.

He feigned a smile knowing that was what the boy wanted. That was what normal people did in this instance. Wiping a bit of stew off his lip, he suddenly felt a little embarrassed. "I can't read," he muttered, his face flushing slightly.

Tristen didn't seem fazed at all. He just grinned, that familiar mischievous twinkle in his eye. "That's alright. I'll read it to you. The Master taught me to read. Maybe he can teach you, too."

Devaultus' heart seemed to leap in his chest, fluttering like a bird caught in a cage. Could he? Could he really learn how to read? The thought of it, the thought of learning something, of being more than just a broken thing in a tower; well, it stirred something deep inside of him. For a moment, the excitement was so overwhelming, he felt like he might burst out of bed, like he could run through the walls and fly through the air.

Could this really be his life now? Could someone teach him, show him things he never thought he'd have access to? The world, so huge and daunting, suddenly felt a little less unreachable.

Tristan flipped through the parchments, his eyes scanning each one with a look of deep disappointment. "Boring, boring, boring," he muttered, tossing each page aside as if it was little more than a piece of useless scrap. "I'll bet these are just ledgers for some traders and shopkeepers. The thri... I mean Donovine will probably make use of these." He let out a soft sigh, clearly deflated. None of the parchments were anything exciting.

"Well, I was hoping to find something magnificent," he said, the words heavy with regret. "Like the one I found a year ago..."

Devaultus' curiosity piqued at the mention of the mysterious find. His curiosity always outweighs his need to not speak out of turn.

Finally, he spoke up. "What did you find a year ago?" he asked, his voice rising slightly, the question hanging in the air.

Tristan didn't miss a beat, and his eyes lit up like a spark had been struck inside him. He leaped to his feet, his energy suddenly pouring out of him. "Oh, let me get it and show you!" he exclaimed, before darting out of the room in a blur of excitement.

Devaultus, still not fully used to the new world around him, lay in the bed and waited. His eyes flicked to the door, as he wondered if Tristan would return soon. Minutes stretched on before the boy burst back into the room, a shiny, intriguing piece of paper clutched in his hand.

Tristan practically bounced over to the bed, his eyes wide with joy, and thrust the paper toward Devaultus. It was covered in images, images that seemed to jump off the page, more vivid and lifelike than anything Devaultus had ever seen.

"What in the Abyss is that?" Devaultus asked, his voice full of awe and confusion.

Tristan's smile only grew wider, if that was even possible. He seemed so proud, like he had just discovered some hidden treasure. "I found a caravan with so many things I'd never seen before," he began, his voice growing animated with excitement. "Magical items, or so they had to be, because they were just so amazing. Your mind can't even put together what they could've been used for. One of the chests I opened had these parchments in them."

He took the parchment in both hands and turned it toward Devaultus, pointing to the top left corner with enthusiasm. "It says here it's called a 'comic,'" he said, practically glowing as he spoke the word, like it was something sacred.

Devaultus' eyes traced the intricate details of the images on the page, his mind racing. "A comic?" he whispered, the word feeling foreign, like a taste he had never known, yet one that filled him with a strange hunger to understand. What was this world, this strange new place he was in, and why did it hold so many wonders he had never even dreamed of?

Tristan leaned in closer, eager to share his discovery. "It's like a story," he explained, "but with pictures. And these pictures are more real than anything I've ever seen." His voice dropped into a conspiratorial whisper. "I bet it's magic. The way it makes you feel, like you're in the story."

Devaultus, unable to look away from the comic, felt a deep stirring inside him. Magic, stories, pictures... These were things he had never even dared to imagine, yet they seemed so real now, and they were right before his eyes.

Devaultus watched, wide-eyed, as Tristan flipped through the comic with the same energy and excitement he'd seen in the boy since he'd arrived. He couldn't help but feel his own excitement rising inside, a mix of curiosity and awe. He had never seen anything like this before, these strange pages, filled with vivid images that were both captivating and intimidating. Each page turned revealed a world he didn't even know could exist; a world so different from the cold stone walls of the tower.

The first page showed a sprawling village, so vast that Devaultus felt like the buildings reached up to touch the sky itself. The architecture was like nothing he'd ever seen. The tower he had been locked in seemed like a mere speck compared to these towering structures. But the man standing at the center of it all was what drew Devaultus' attention. He wore a dark mask with empty eyes and a grin that looked almost unnatural, as if it had been carved into his face. His cloak billowed around him, almost alive, and in his hands were two shining daggers. A wide-brimmed hat rested on his head, casting shadows over his features. He stood tall and confident, a figure of mystery and power.

Devaultus couldn't tear his eyes away. There was something about this man, the way he stood, the way he seemed to command attention, that made Devaultus feel something inside. A sense of awe. A longing. Looking at this "comic" made him briefly forget his fears, his worries about beatings and pain. He would let them beat him if it meant he could look at this "comic."

"That's *The Grin*," Tristan said, his voice filled with excitement. He pointed at the character in the comic, his finger tracing the lines of the drawing with a familiarity that made Devaultus feel even more distant from it. "This guy is my hero. He's going to fight all the bad guys, save his friends, and escape from the world he's stuck in. When I'm older, I'll be just like him."

Devaultus glanced down at the page again, feeling something strange in his chest. The Grin... who was he? What did he do? There was a sense of power in the character, an assurance that Devaultus could almost feel through the page. But he still didn't fully understand. The words danced across the pages, but they were meaningless to him.

He shifted uneasily, feeling the weight of the silence between them before he finally asked, "What does it say? About him, I mean."

Tristan's smile softened as he nodded, understanding exactly what Devaultus was asking. "It says The Grin doesn't give up, no matter what. He's been through everything, fighting, running, hiding, but he always comes out on top because he fights for what's right." Tristan paused, looking up from the page to meet Devaultus' eyes. "He fights for the good, for the people who can't fight for themselves. He doesn't let anyone tell him what he can or can't do. He's the kind of person who doesn't let the world hold him down, no matter how tough it gets."

Devaultus felt a deep pull in his chest, a flicker of something, something unfamiliar but bright. A part of him wanted to leap off the bed and follow that pull, to understand more about The Grin, about this world that seemed so far beyond him.

"You'll be like him someday," Tristan said with such certainty that it almost made Devaultus believe in himself. "You just have to keep fighting. Don't let anything keep you down. You'll be strong, just like The Grin."

Devaultus was quiet for a moment, his mind whirling with possibility. Could he really be like The Grin? Could he leave this place, this life of pain and confinement, and become someone better? A hero, even? His heart raced at the thought, but fear quickly followed. How could someone like him, someone so broken and lost, ever become anything close to that?

But for the first time in his life, the thought didn't seem so impossible. Maybe there was a chance for him, after all. Maybe, just maybe, he could fight for something more than survival.

He looked at the comic again, at the man called The Grin, and for the first time, a small flicker of hope stirred inside him.

Tristan's grin stretched wider, almost mischievous, as he leaned back in his chair. "Well, you'll have to come up with your own name, Devaultus. The Grin is all mine. It's taken." He winked at him, teasing in the way only a boy with too much energy could.

Devaultus for the first time in a long time gave him a genuine smile; the act felt foreign but warm. He smiled at Tristan, meeting his eyes.

"I think it's fitting for you," Devaultus said, his voice almost shy but sincere. He couldn't help it: the boy's grin, so full of mischief and warmth, seemed like it belonged to The Grin in the comic. There was a spark of something alive in Tristan, a fire that made Devaultus feel like maybe, just maybe, there was hope for him too.

Tristan rolled his eyes but didn't lose the smile. "Yeah, I know. It's perfect," he said, giving a small dramatic sigh, as though he were the hero of his own story already. "But come on, you need a name. How else are you going to fight the bad guys?"

Devaultus didn't answer right away. The idea of being a hero, of fighting back against something, was still new to him. He thought about the comic, about the hero The Grin, and wondered what it would be like to step into a world so full of possibility. Maybe he could be something more than the boy trapped in a tower, the boy who never had a name, never had a purpose. Except for the one he created for himself. Devaultus. He had come up with that name. His father only called him 'welp'.

The thought lingered in his mind, a seed planted in the fertile soil of his dreams. A name. A hero's name. Could he be someone else? Someone better? It was a question he'd never dared to ask before, but now, looking at Tristan and the comic, the world suddenly felt just a little bit bigger.

"I'll think of something," Devaultus said, his voice quieter now, more thoughtful. "Something... fitting." He looked away, lost in the thought for a moment. The possibility was strange but exciting, like a door opening to a world he could hardly imagine. A world where he could choose who he was.

The moment the door creaked open, a figure stepped into the room, the soft click of the door's hinge punctuating the silence. Donovine stood in the doorway, his presence as commanding as ever. With a warm, almost playful smile, he asked, "What are the two of you up to?"

Tristan, ever the energetic one, jumped from his chair, a spark of excitement in his eyes. "Master, Devaultus wants to train with me!" His voice was filled with a mixture of pride and amusement, as though he had just made the best suggestion ever.

Donovine's gaze shifted to the young boy, his expression unreadable for a moment. His eyes flicked to Tristan, then to Devaultus. Training another apprentice hadn't been in his plans. Tristan was enough of a handful, wild, untamed, and in constant need of attention. But Devaultus, though different in his quiet desperation, was equally in need of something more. Something he hadn't had in his entire life: guidance. The world was harsh, and if he wasn't careful, the boy would be lost to it, a fragile thing destined to be crushed under the weight of it all.

He gave a small sigh, exhaling through his nose, before asking, "Is that so, Devaultus?" Donovine's voice carried a note of curiosity. He could see it in the boy's eyes: the pleading, the raw desperation. The hunger to belong. To learn.

Devaultus' heart thumped in his chest. His hands, still trembling from the stew, curled into fists at his sides. "Yes, sir," he said, his voice soft and meek, yet insistent.

For a moment, Donovine's gaze softened. It was clear the boy didn't truly understand who he was, what he had done, and what he represented. To the untrained eye, Donovine was a mere rich bureaucrat, a man in fine clothes who could make things happen with a snap of his fingers. But beneath that polished exterior, he was 'The Thren'. An assassin. A fixer. A killer-for-hire in a world where death was just another tool to wield.

Devaultus had no idea of the darkness hidden behind that well-groomed mask. The boy didn't know that the very skills he was begging to learn were steeped in blood.

Donovine took a moment, letting the weight of the decision settle in. The boy was right about one thing: if he was cast into the world unprepared, he'd never survive. He'd be a victim, a pawn in a much larger game.

Donovine looked down at him, his lips curled into a thin, almost reluctant smile. "Very well," he said, voice low but steady. "It will not be easy. Are you sure?"

Devaultus' eyes widened, a flicker of excitement mixed with uncertainty. But there was determination there, a resolve that had never been allowed to fully bloom until now. "Yes, sir. Nothing has ever been easy for me. I can learn. Just give me a chance."

For a moment, Donovine simply stared at the boy, weighing his words. He knew the boy had no idea what he was asking for, but something in his plea resonated with him. Life wasn't kind. No one ever got the chance to learn if they didn't fight for it.

He stood there in silence, his mind weighing the consequences, the dangers of dragging another child into this world, his world. But Devaultus had already been broken by the cruel hands of his past, and perhaps, in some twisted way, this was the only chance he had.

"Very well," Donovine said at last, his voice carrying finality. "You start next week." He turned and walked towards the door, but not before offering one last glance. "Prepare yourself."

As the door closed softly behind him, leaving Devaultus in the stillness of the room, the weight of what had just happened settled heavily on his chest. He was no longer just some boy, no longer a nameless orphan. He had been given a chance. A chance to learn, to grow, and to survive.

Tristan, wide-eyed and brimming with excitement, practically bounced in his seat. "We're going to be like brothers, you and I," he said, his voice filled with uncontainable enthusiasm. "You wait and see. Nobody will stand up against us."

Devaultus could only smile in response, a smile laced with a mix of disbelief and cautious optimism. Perhaps this was the beginning of something more. Something better. Something that would take him far from the shadows of the tower and into a world he could finally begin to understand.

And maybe, just maybe, he could learn to become someone he could be proud of.

Eight years later...

The wind howled through the city as Tristan launched himself off the edge of the bridge, his body twisting midair before he crashed onto the back of a large, creaking cart. The weight of his landing sent a thud echoing through the street, and a moment later, Devaultus dropped from above, landing smoothly beside him. The two shared a breathless laugh, their eyes alight with the thrill of the chase.

"I didn't think you'd make it, brother," Tristan teased, his grin wide and proud.

Devaultus smirked, his face framed by the cool wind of the city's heights. "Oh, I assure you, if you can do it, I can do it just as well." He paused, letting the challenge sink in, but it was more than just words between them. It was a bond forged in years of shared struggle, training, and mutual understanding.

With a devilish grin, Tristan flung himself off the side of the cart. His hands gripped the rigging tightly as his feet scraped the cobblestone road, the harsh friction making his skin burn. His mind raced, adrenaline coursing through him as he dragged along, laughing under his breath. He glanced over his shoulder, looking for Devaultus, only to turn and find himself face-to-face with him, his adopted brother, moving with unnatural speed.

In the blink of an eye, both of them released the rigging simultaneously, and the cart rumbled over them like a heavy storm passing, leaving the two young men sprawled out on the cold, gritty cobblestones. They lay there for a moment, their laughter drowning out the drumbeat of their own hearts. The familiar taste of danger hung in the air: this part of the city was a place no one dared to tread lightly.

The road, worn and littered with decay, followed a well-known ledge that dropped down into the lower districts. It was a place few ventured, a dark corner where shadows stretched longer than the sun ever dared to shine. People disappeared in this part of the city. Murmurs of whispers about things better left unsaid. But for those like them, those with a different view of the world, this was the perfect place to gather information, rumors, secrets, or items that needed to vanish into the right hands for the right price.

Without a second thought, Devaultus propelled himself off the ledge, his body hitting the roof of a nearby building with practiced ease. Tristan was close behind, his footwork flawless as he tumbled in a roll and came up into a crouch beside him.

The two of them rushed forward, their movements fluid, crossing the gap between the buildings and landing on another roof. Tristan skidded to a stop, his arm shooting out to grab Devaultus' shoulder, pulling him down swiftly. The urgency in his touch was enough to make Devaultus freeze. They crouched low, peering over the edge of the building into the alley below.

The figures in the alley were cloaked in shadows, their movements slow but purposeful. Something about them didn't sit right with Devaultus. Their bodies were almost too still, too composed, as if they were waiting for something, or someone.

"Who are they?" Devaultus whispered, his voice low but sharp, his instincts already alert to the possible threat below.

Tristan's eyes narrowed as he studied the figures. A soft chuckle escaped his lips, but it was laced with something darker, the thrill of the unknown. "That, my friend, is the question of the hour."

A hint of danger hung between them.

Devaultus slid down the side of the building, his boots barely making a sound on the cobblestone below. The cool night air was thick with the scent of oil and damp stone. His mind was sharp, focused on the mission, but something lingered at the back of his thoughts, an unease he couldn't shake. He and Tristan had come this far, and now was the time to prove they could do it alone, without Donovine's help. Without relying on anyone but themselves.

The guards had wandered into the next building. Their attention drawn to a keg of ale that seemed to beckon them.

He crept closer to the crates, eyes scanning the surroundings, calculating his next move. His fingers twitched as he reached for one of the steel blades. The weight of it was just as he imagined, cold and heavy in his grip. But before he could lift it fully from the crate, something caught his eye, a glint of metal from the corner of his vision. He froze. Guards. Two of them, on patrol, heading straight for him. It would appear not all had ventured into the building.

Devaultus' heart skipped. He had to act fast. He knew the Thren's training well; too well, perhaps. His first instinct was to slip away, to vanish into the night like he had done countless times before. But tonight... tonight felt different. There was a challenge in the air, a pull that made him question everything he'd learned.

A thought sparked in his mind. If he could get caught with this dagger in hand, if they could chase him down, maybe he could lead them away from Tristan. Give him the space to do what he was best at. The plan was reckless, but it was the only one he had.

Without hesitation, Devaultus slipped one of the blades into his cloak, making sure they saw him, and stood up straight, his movement loud enough to alert the guards. He needed to be seen. The guards spotted him instantly, their eyes narrowing.

"Hey! Stop right there!" one of the guards shouted, his heavy boots echoing against the stone as he started toward him. Devaultus didn't need any more prompting. He turned, running as fast as his legs could carry him, darting through the alley and around a corner.

Behind him, he could hear the guards giving chase, their footsteps quickening. He led them deeper into the maze of alleys, keeping just enough distance between himself and them to make the game exciting. The thrill was building inside him, the adrenaline pumping through his veins. It was dangerous, and he knew it. But for once, he felt alive, like he was really living.

Meanwhile, Tristan had slipped off the roof with an agility that only he could manage. The moment he landed, he was on the move: quick, silent, and determined. He wasn't interested in the chase. He was focused solely on the weapons. He grabbed as many as he could, stuffing them into his bag, his heart racing with each new blade he added to his haul. This was his kind of mission. Sneak in, take what was valuable, and slip away without anyone even knowing he was there.

But just as he hefted another crate, a voice pierced through the stillness of the night. Low, but sharp.

"Looks like we've got ourselves a little thief."

Tristan froze, the hair on the back of his neck standing up. He turned slowly, eyes scanning the shadows. And that was when he saw them: two men standing just a few paces away. One was large, a hulking figure with a broad chest and arms like tree trunks. The other was smaller, quicker-looking, with sharp eyes that seemed to take in everything in an instant.

"Should've known someone would be around here," the larger man muttered, cracking his knuckles.

Tristan's heart pounded; his mind was racing. He wasn't exactly built to fight these guys head-on, especially with how much gear he was carrying. But if there was one thing Tristan knew, it was that he could talk his way out of almost anything. And if that didn't work, well... he'd improvise.

He smiled, trying to keep the edge of panic out of his voice. "You know, I was just thinking about how much I love your city. So full of surprises."

The smaller man smirked. "You've got a funny way of showing it." He took a step forward, hand reaching for the knife at his belt.

Tristan's grin widened, but his pulse was hammering. He wasn't ready to get caught. Not now, not when they were so close to having everything.

Tristan lept back as the large man swung at him, his massive fist barely missing him. The other man dashed forward, sliding across the ground and slashing at him. Tristan followed his backstep with a backflip, ducking the fist, then springing back. This wasn't going well; he had found himself in a bit more then he had bargained for. He spun to the side, kicking sand into the eyes of the smaller man. The man fell back, hopping up angrily. The large man grabbed a smaller crate nearby, throwing it at Tristan. "No..." he said as he dove to the side. The small man recovered and launched himself at him. Slashing forward. The tip of his blade clipping Tristan's shoulder. Ripping both fabric and flesh. Tristan screamed out in pain. Lunging to the side, kicking out his foot, meeting the smaller man's chest and kicking him away. The large man swung out his massive fist, punching hard into Tristan's stomach. Tristan gasped in pain, feeling ribs cracking and breaking.

Devaultus' heart pounded as he sprinted through the dark, Tristan's scream echoing in his mind. His thoughts raced. What had gone wrong? Were there more guards than he had realized? He couldn't afford to stop and question it. He had to get away, lose the guards, and get back to Tristan.

Without hesitation, he scaled a nearby wall, his hands and feet finding purchase with ease. Leaping down onto the other side, he vanished into an alleyway, his movements fluid and silent. No armored guard could keep up with him, not the way he was trained.

His instincts guided him as he dashed forward, slipping beneath the shadow of a broken-down wagon. The cool night air stung his face, but it only spurred him onward. He reached the building where he'd last seen Tristan. A pit formed in his stomach as he spotted his friend on his knees, the two men standing over him.

Devaultus' mind went blank for a moment. What had happened? Tristan was one of the sharpest people he knew. Yet here he was, kneeling, struggling to stay conscious while the smaller man seemed to toy with him, poking at his body with a dagger, deliberately avoiding anything vital. The larger man was grinning, clearly enjoying the scene, the cruel laughter echoing through the alley.

"No, no, no..." Devaultus whispered in panic, his breath catching in his throat. He couldn't let this happen. Not to Tristan.

He moved faster than his thoughts, launching himself from the roof with a fluid grace. Landing in a roll to absorb the impact, he quickly sprang to his feet. His eyes darted around, spotting a nearby crate with several steel daggers glinting inside. He grabbed two, one in each hand, their weight comforting as he gripped them firmly.

Without wasting a second, he rushed toward the large man, his movements like lightning. With a slash of the steel blades, he carved across the man's neck, his strikes so precise and brutal that the larger man crumpled to the ground without a sound, the life draining from him in a second.

The smaller man's furious shout ripped through the air as he spun around, eyes wild with rage. "You little shit!" he snarled, his dagger raised and ready to strike. Devaultus stood his ground, ready for whatever came next.

Devaultus slid low, narrowly avoiding the incoming attack. His boots ground across the stone as he used the momentum to spring back into a perfect kip-up, landing on his feet, heart pounding in his chest. The larger man was already swinging again, his blade cutting through the air with deadly force, but Devaultus was ready. With a swift flick of his wrist, he deflected the strike, his other hand seizing the opportunity to plunge the dagger into the man's eye socket. The sickening squelch of steel meeting flesh echoed in the tense silence.

The man staggered back, eyes wide in confusion. How was this kid so fast? Before he recovered, Devaultus was already moving. His legs shot out, one, two, three kicks to the chest, sending the man stumbling further back. The moment the man's chest opened up in a ragged breath, Devaultus shoved the other dagger into his stomach, ripping upwards, and feeling the warmth of his insides spilling onto the ground.

With a savage twist, Devaultus yanked the dagger from the man's eye and drove it into his throat. The man's body jerked, and Devaultus lept, kicking off the man's chest, still holding both daggers, the body crashing into the dirt in a lifeless heap.

Devaultus' gaze immediately shot over to Tristan. "No, please..." His voice broke as he rushed to his side, desperation clawing at his throat. "Don't die on me, man. You're all I've got. You're my family."

Tristan spat up a mouthful of blood, a weak smile stretching across his face despite the obvious pain. "Ah, man... I think I'm tapping out. But..." He coughed violently, more blood spilling from his lips. "Just think... Now you get to be the hero. You get to be The Grin." The words were strained, each one forcing its way out of his lungs.

"I don't want to be The Grin," Devaultus whispered, his heart breaking. "That's you."

Tristan's smile grew wider, though it was tinged with pain. "Not anymore, man. Get off this world for me," he said with a grim chuckle, his body convulsing violently as the last breath left him.

Devaultus' hands trembled as he reached out, pressing them to his friend's chest, trying to hold on to the last bits of life slipping away. "No... no, I can't..." His voice cracked. Tears streamed down his face as the pain of loss seared through him. He didn't want this. He didn't want to lose another person.

The darkness of the world, the suffocating loneliness of the tower; it had been so much easier to be alone, to not care. But now, with Tristan gone, it felt like an unbearable weight crushed his chest.

He covered Tristan's eyes gently with the back of his hand, his voice breaking under the weight of grief. "I'm sorry, my brother. I'll make things right. I'll get off this planet. I'll be The Grin... but I'm not the hero. I won't be. I'll make them all pay. For taking everything I've ever had. They'll know the name of Devaultus. I promise you that."

# CHAPTER 16

# THE GRIN BORN AGAIN

Zeff and Spar had it. They were absolutely sure of it. That all-too-trusting, wide-eyed little fool of a gnome, Zigglespot, had just handed them the key to their fortune on a silver platter. Now all they had to do was get there first, before he even had a chance to realize he'd been played. If they moved quickly, they could sell this invention to Lord Casterland, rake in a fortune, and maybe even secure an exclusive contract with his army. A deal like that would put them in the annals of history, their names whispered in the same breath as the greatest inventors of their time.

Because gnomes didn't covet gold, not really. Oh, coin was nice, but it was fleeting. Fame, recognition, the eternal glory of their creations living on beyond them: that was what truly mattered.

Devaultus watched the two, his keen eyes drinking in every smug twitch of their mouths, every greedy glint in their eyes. He'd seen it before, this very look, this quiet, scheming calculation that meant betrayal was already in motion. Zeff and Spar were working through the details of their plan at that very moment, ticking through each step like clockwork. And Devaultus would have bet every coin in his purse that they thought no one had noticed.

They really were idiots.

Zeff finally spoke up, his voice dripping with false sincerity. "I sure am glad we got to help out such a good guy," he said, flashing a too-wide grin, all teeth and deception.

Devaultus nearly rolled his eyes. This was the best they could do? Amateurs.

Zeff turned to his partner. "Spar, why don't you go get the wagon and the leech lizard? I'll help Zigglespot get this loaded up."

Spar, ever the obedient fool, gave an eager nod. "Of course." Without a moment's hesitation, she turned on her heel and disappeared out the door, leaving Zeff alone with the prize.

Perfect.

Devaultus took a slow step forward, the dagger already warm in his grip, its edge gleaming faintly under the lantern light. He could feel the sharpness of it, the weight balanced just right.

Zeff bent down, hands gripping the edge of the glider, preparing to lift it. And in that single, vulnerable moment, Devaultus struck.

The blade sliced cleanly across the tendons of both his Achilles heels. The reaction was immediate. Zeff's body jerked, his knees buckling as the strength drained from his legs in an instant. A strangled, guttural scream tore from his throat, but Devaultus was faster. He clamped a hand over the man's mouth, stifling the sound, pressing down hard enough to smother it into a pitiful whimper.

Devaultus leaned in, his voice a whisper of amusement against Zeff's ear.

"Gnomes really are the kick-me creatures of this world."

Zeff's entire body convulsed in pain, hands grasping helplessly at the glider, fingers scraping against the wood. But Devaultus wasn't done. Not yet.

Devaultus let out a long, exasperated sigh, shaking his head as he muttered, "Oh, shut up. Let's not pretend you don't have a little contraption tucked away with my name on it, just waiting for the right moment." His voice dripped with disdain, his grip tightening as he hoisted Zeff higher, forcing the gnome to meet his gaze. "You insufferable little rodents always think you're the smartest ones in the room." His expression darkened, annoyance flaring in his eyes. "Where is Lord Casterland's manor?"

Zeff dangled helplessly, his body limp except for the trembling that wracked his frame. The once-cocky gleam in his eyes had been replaced by a look of sheer terror. His legs, useless now thanks to Devaultus' precise, merciless handiwork, twitched feebly, unable to support even their own weight. He gasped, his breath shuddering as Devaultus' grip shifted.

"Answer me before I start cutting pieces off," Devaultus added, his voice low and impatient, like he was already bored of the conversation. His free hand tightened around his dagger, the threat hanging thick in the air.

Zeff whimpered, his words tumbling out in a panicked rush as soon as Devaultus' hand moved from his mouth. "T-to the north! A large building, you can't miss it!"

Devaultus chuckled, the sound devoid of warmth. "See? That wasn't so hard." He leaned in slightly, his tone shifting into something almost teasing, a cruel smirk on his lips. "You know, I could've killed you and your little partner long ago." He tilted his head, studying Zeff like he was nothing more than an insect pinned to a board. "But I let you have your moment. Let you think you were winning. Let you taste that little sliver of joy, that rush of discovery." He let out an exaggerated sigh and offered a mockingly sincere smile. "You're welcome."

Then, with a sudden, brutal efficiency, he drove his dagger straight into the gnome's chest. Zeff's breath hitched, a soft, strangled sound, before his body convulsed and then stilled. Devaultus gave the blade a slight twist before yanking it free, wiping the blood off on Zeff's own shirt with practiced indifference.

"Oh yeah," he muttered, voice low and gravelly. "I'm not a good guy."

With that, he grabbed the lifeless body and dragged it across the floor, the limp form leaving a faint, smeared trail of blood in its wake.

Spotting a linen basket nearby, he unceremoniously hoisted Zeff up and dumped him inside, the corpse folding in on itself like laundry.

He took a step back, hands on his hips, admiring his work for a moment before rolling his eyes and muttering, "I really, really hate gnomes."

Devaultus strolled out the door, moving with an almost lazy confidence as he navigated the labyrinth of traps set throughout the workshop. He stepped over tripwires, sidestepped pressure plates, and ignored the faint click of deactivated mechanisms as he made his way toward the stables. His movements were fluid, practiced, almost mocking in their ease; he'd seen this sort of paranoia before, and frankly, it bored him.

His eyes locked onto Spar, the second half of the gnome duo, just as she entered the pen where her prized leech lizards were kept. The creatures were grotesque, nearly the size of a small horse, their bodies covered in slick, leathery skin that glistened in the dim torchlight. Their lamprey-like mouths sucked at the air with a sickening wet noise, nostrils flaring as they sensed movement.

Disgusting.

Leech lizards were prized for their endurance, their uncanny ability to sense carrion, and most notably, their complete disinterest in feeding on the living, so long as that living thing remained standing. Fall asleep in their pen, however, and you'd wake up anemic, if you woke up at all. Devaultus curled his lip. He despised the creatures almost as much as he despised gnomes. The two species deserved each other, in his opinion: overly clever, opportunistic little parasites.

Slipping a thin, gleaming needle from his sleeve, he twirled it between his fingers, considering his timing. Spar moved deeper into the pen, her attention fully on the creatures, unaware of his approach.

Perfect.

With a flick of his wrist, the needle sailed through the air in a whisper of metal, piercing the back of Spar's neck with pinpoint precision. The effect was nearly instant, the paralytic poison seeping into her bloodstream like an old friend. She stiffened, her hand flying up, fingers brushing the thin shaft as she yanked it free. Her breath hitched as the realization hit, her small frame turning slowly, fighting against the rapidly encroaching numbness.

Her eyes found his.

Devaultus smirked, lifting a hand in an exaggerated wave, his grin widening as her vision swam.

"Evenin', Spar."

Spar's body crumpled into the dirt of the pen, her limbs giving out as the paralytic took full hold. She twitched, her breath coming in shallow, uneven gasps as she struggled in vain against her failing muscles. Her eyes, wild with fear, darted about as she realized what was coming. The leech lizards, sensing her stillness, lifted their broad, slimy heads. Their nostrils flared, forked tongues flicking out to taste the air. One took a cautious step forward, then another, until the entire herd lurched toward her in a slow, grotesque shuffle.

They latched on greedily, their wide, lamprey-like mouths sealing over any exposed skin. Dozens of tiny, needle-like teeth sank into her flesh, and her pupils shrank in terror. She could feel it, her blood being drawn, her strength leaving her, but she couldn't scream, couldn't move, couldn't fight back. Her own breath betrayed her, coming out in short, wheezing pants as if her body was already mourning its loss of life.

Devaultus leaned against the wooden fence of the pen, watching the slow, inevitable draining with an air of detached amusement. He idly flicked a bit of dust from his sleeve before meeting Spar's terrified gaze with his own calm, knowing one.

"You shouldn't have tried to backstab me," he said smoothly, as if he were scolding a misbehaving child rather than a dying woman. He tilted his head, considering. "You had a choice, you know. Could've been a good person. But you weren't." His lips formed a half-smile. "And now? Now you've met someone worse. You've learned your final lesson, Spar." He tapped a finger against his temple. "And I? I am your teacher."

He grinned wider. "You're welcome."

With that, he turned on his heel and strode back toward the house, leaving the gurgling, half-conscious gnome to her fate. Inside, he moved with precise efficiency, rifling through their supplies, taking only what was useful. He worked quickly and methodically. Then, with the same cold patience, he knelt beside Zeff's body and carved a twisted, one-sided grin into the gnome's slack face. Blood welled up, sluggish and thick, trickling down like war paint.

When he returned to the pen, the lizards had done their work. Spar was nothing more than a pale, shriveled husk, her once-vibrant flesh reduced to a sickly, waxen white. He crouched beside her and, with a steady hand, carved the same grotesque smile across her lifeless features. Bloodless. Hollow.

Standing, he dusted off his hands, took one last glance at his grim handiwork, and then sauntered north down the road.

Lord Casterland was next.

Devaultus had only made it about a mile down the dusty, uneven road when the rhythmic creaking of wooden wheels and the slow, labored breaths of a beast of burden reached his ears. A leech lizard-drawn cart rolled up beside him, its driver a hunched, weathered old man wrapped in a tattered cloak. His sun-creased face bore the weight of countless years, but his eyes still held a sharp glint of awareness. He tugged lightly on the reins, bringing the sluggish lizard to a stop.

"Well now, lad, ye look like ye been walkin' a fair spell. Need a lift?" The old man's voice had the slow, deliberate drawl of someone in no hurry to get anywhere.

Devaultus hesitated, sizing him up with a practiced glance. The man's gnarled hands rested easy on the reins, his posture relaxed, unconcerned. No twitchy fingers reaching for a hidden dagger, no sly glance measuring his worth in coin or blood. Still, Devaultus had learned long ago that the most dangerous liars were the ones who didn't seem like liars at all.

He forced a pleasant smile. "Much appreciated, sir," he said smoothly and climbed into the back of the cart. The wooden planks creaked beneath his weight as he settled in, stretching his legs out across a pile of burlap sacks that smelled faintly of grain and something vaguely metallic: rust or dried blood, it was hard to tell.

Truthfully, part of him wanted to wave the old man off and continue walking. He preferred to keep his own pace, keep control of his own movement. But another, louder part of him, the one that despised this tedious, never-ending trudge of a journey, was sick of the monotonous crunch of gravel underfoot. If some fool wanted to drag him closer to his destination for free, who was he to refuse?

Still, his muscles stayed coiled like a wound spring as he cast a suspicious glance toward the back of the man's head. So far, there was no sign of deceit, no nervous shifting, no careful maneuvering to get the jump on him. The man was either exactly what he seemed, an old traveler willing to help a stranger, or he was playing a much longer game.

Devaultus leaned back, resting his hands behind his head, and let his eyes drift shut, feigning the slow, even breaths of sleep. But he remained hyper-aware, listening for the hitch in the old man's breathing, the shift of weight that meant a blade was about to be drawn. He half-expected to feel the prick of a dagger at his throat, to hear the telltale rustle of a thief trying to pilfer his belongings.

But nothing came.

The cart rumbled along, the steady plodding of the leech lizard's clawed feet scraping against the dirt road. The sun inched its way across the sky, and still, the old man simply drove.

As the cart rolled to a stop before the looming city gates, Devaultus cracked an eye open. A pair of guards approached, spears in hand, their sharp eyes scanning over the cart with the bored efficiency of men who had done this routine a thousand times before.

"State your business," one of them droned, already looking unimpressed.

Devaultus remained still, watching, waiting. If things went sideways, he wanted to be ready.

The old man gave Devaultus a gentle shake. "Lad, we're here."

Devaultus cracked one eye open, feigning the sluggishness of deep sleep before forcing a yawn. "Mmh, right... thanks." His voice held the perfect blend of drowsy gratitude as he stretched, rolling his shoulders before standing. It was an act, of course: he hadn't actually slept a wink. Trusting strangers had a nasty habit of getting people killed.

As he stepped down from the cart, he was immediately greeted by the city guards. They barely spared him a second glance, their scrutiny passing over him like he was just another gnome traveler, some harmless tinkerer with a heavy pack and a docile demeanor. If only they knew. His hands were still metaphorically stained with the blood of the last gnomes who had underestimated him.

The cart swayed forward, its leech lizards trudging dutifully through the gates before the old man pulled it over to the side. "Well, lad, this is my stop," he said, stretching his aged limbs before turning to Devaultus. To his surprise, the man reached into his coat and handed him a small pouch. "Wind's rollin' in shortly, lad. Get yourself some shelter, have a bite on me." His grin was wide, revealing teeth that had clearly seen better days.

Devaultus hesitated for a moment, his sharp instincts warring with something else, something almost foreign to him. Perhaps he had misjudged the old man. Perhaps not everyone was plotting some form of treachery. He gave the man a nod, sliding the pouch into his pack without checking its contents. "I appreciate it," he said smoothly, then smirked. "Name's Zigglespot. Take care of yourself, old man."

The man's eyes crinkled with amusement at the name, but he said nothing about it. Instead, he tipped his hat in farewell before turning his attention back to his cart.

Devaultus turned away, his expression shifting back to something unreadable. Enough procrastination; the manor was now in sight.

Devaultus sauntered down the bustling street, his keen gaze flitting from one passerby to the next, weighing his options with every step. The city churned with life, its people moving like cogs in a massive, chaotic machine, but he had no interest in any of them. His goal was clear: get to Casterland's manor, secure the rod that Al'Shandra needed, and get the Abyss out before this place became another stain on his patience.

Devaultus halted just before reaching the guards, slipping into a side alley with practiced ease. With a sigh, he drew one of his daggers and dug a small hole into the crumbling wall. Carefully, he nestled his weapons inside, covering them as best he could to keep them hidden. He hated this: leaving his daggers behind felt almost unnatural.

Not that he lacked other ways to kill a man, far from it, but still, it just wasn't right. He was fairly certain Sheila, one of his favorite daggers, hadn't entirely forgiven him for the last time he abandoned her.

"I'll be back for you, my dear," he murmured, running a finger along the hilt before flashing a wide grin. Then, with a confident saunter, he made his way toward the gate.

He adjusted the weight of his pack, rolling his shoulders back as he approached the towering gates of the estate. The stone-crafted bars stretched high, their tops curved into wicked spikes as if taunting anyone foolish enough to try scaling them. Two gnomish guards stood at the entrance, their armor polished but dented in places, a sign that they'd seen some action but probably preferred to sit on their asses most of the time.

The shorter of the two, with a thick red mustache that nearly consumed his face, squinted up at him. "An' what do ye want?" he demanded, his thick accent turning the words into a gruff challenge.

Devaultus didn't hesitate. "I have an invention to present to Lord Casterland." He kept his tone smooth, confident; too much arrogance and they'd get suspicious, too little and they'd dismiss him outright.

The guards exchanged looks, amusement passing between them before the other, a stocky gnome with a nose that looked like it had been broken one too many times, gave a scoffing laugh. "You an' everyone else in the damn city," he said, crossing his arms over his chest. "What makes yours so special, eh?"

Devaultus allowed a slow, knowing smirk to creep onto his face, his fingers idly tapping against the strap of his pack. "Oh," he drawled, letting the anticipation build, "because mine is something you have never seen."

Devaultus' eyes gleamed with the thrill of deception, the pure joy of spinning a tale so grand, it could make men forget their senses. This was where he thrived, where words became weapons sharper than any blade. With a dramatic flair, he spread his small arms wide, his voice weaving a vision so vivid, it demanded belief.

"Have you ever longed to soar through the sky? To feel the wind cradle you, lifting you above the world?" His voice took on a mesmerizing cadence as he stepped lightly on his feet, mimicking the weightless grace of flight.

The gnomish guards exchanged glances, but Devaultus didn't give them time to question him. He swept forward, his voice rising with intensity.

"Imagine an army unstoppable! A force so powerful, their enemies can do nothing but tremble! No more brutal, drawn-out sieges. No more useless battering against walls. Instead, Lord Casterland's soldiers, rising like gods, blotting out the sun with their numbers. Walls? Worthless. Fortresses? Helpless. Just one or two elite warriors, descending like shadows in the night, striking down an enemy leader before anyone even knows they're there!"

His movements became a performance, a masterful dance of illusion. He leaped forward, twisting through the air as though soaring on invisible wings. With a flick of his wrist, he mimed drawing a blade, slashing through an unseen foe. The imaginary enemy spun, their silent, tragic demise playing out before an audience entranced by the show. The roar of triumphant soldiers filled the air, if only in their minds.

The guards' eyes glowed with excitement. Devaultus could see it: the spark of belief. The seed of greed. The longing for something beyond the lives they led now. One of them, a gnome with a thick red mustache, turned toward his companion, his voice tinged with something close to awe.

"And... ye can really do this?"

Devaultus let the silence stretch just long enough. Then, ever so slowly, his signature one-sided grin curled across his lips. His gaze held a challenge, a promise wrapped in mystery.

"I can. And I have."

The mustached gnome hesitated, then gestured to his companion. Without a word, the second guard disappeared inside the gates. Devaultus barely resisted the urge to smirk outright. He had them. He was in.

It took only a few moments before the heavy doors groaned open, revealing a man standing beside the guard who had retreated earlier. His posture was rigid, his gaze sharp, scrutinizing them with the practiced indifference of a man who had seen one too many supposed "geniuses" fail to deliver on their extravagant claims. Still, there was a flicker of interest in his eyes, half excitement at the prospect of something truly groundbreaking, half weary skepticism, already bracing for yet another crackpot to waste Lord Casterland's time.

He straightened his coat, clearing his throat as he regarded Devaultus with an air of superiority, as though everything before him was beneath his notice. "And whom shall I tell Lord Casterland has come calling?" His voice was clipped, precise, and utterly insufferable.

Devaultus arched a brow at the man, his fingers twitching with the barely restrained urge to draw a dagger. Patience was not his strong suit, and people like this, smug, pompous, and wrapped so tightly in their own self-importance, made it very difficult to resist the temptation to simply remove them from existence altogether.

Before he could act on that impulse, Zigglespot Cogglesworth the Third stepped forward with a grand flourish, his oversized goggles slipping slightly down the bridge of his nose. "Ah, yes! It is with the greatest pleasure that I, Zigglespot Cogglesworth the Third, have arrived to present my revolutionary invention: The Bird of Prey Artificial Flight Mechanism!"

The man blinked, his lip curling ever so slightly at the name of the contraption. "Is that so?" he said dryly, his tone teetering between disinterest and barely restrained annoyance.

There was a moment of silence before he sighed through his nose, waving them forward. "Very well. Come along, then. Let's see how you intend to disappoint my Lord today."

The sheer audacity of the man's tone made Devaultus' fingers tighten at his sides. Oh, how easy it would be to slide a blade between his ribs, to watch the arrogance bleed from his face as realization dawned.

But no. That wasn't part of the plan. Not yet.

With an exhale that sounded more like a growl, Devaultus followed the man inside, forcing his hands to remain at his sides.

*Very, very hard indeed* to keep from putting a dagger in his back.

Devaultus pressed his fingertips into the palm of his hand, a silent effort to quell the violent impulse surging beneath his skin. This man, this insufferable, self-important worm, was testing him. And why? Why was he letting such a pathetic excuse for a lackey push him to his boiling point? He was better than this. Usually, he could suffer fools with a smirk, letting them play their little games, only to exact retribution when they least expected it. But this time, it gnawed at him. It itched under his skin like an old wound torn open.

He inhaled slowly, holding the breath in his chest, forcing himself to focus. He was control incarnate. He never let emotions dictate his actions. That was the point of always being three steps ahead, having contingencies stacked upon contingencies. Chaos was his domain, but he wielded it like a scalpel, not a club. Losing control was for lesser men. He would not let it happen again.

His grip on his frustration locked away, Devaultus followed the servant through the lavish halls, each corridor dripping with excess. Opulent tapestries, polished marble, and statues carved in the image of Lord Casterland himself, each piece a monument to a man who clearly loved himself more than his people. The wealth of this estate could have fed a starving city, but instead, it had been funneled into indulgence. Typical.

They entered the Lord's meeting hall, and Devaultus took in the man before him. Lord Casterland was shorter than Devaultus' current form by a few inches, but his width more than made up for it. The man was a walking testament to gluttony, his heavy frame stuffed into fine silks that strained at the seams. He lounged in his gilded chair, more akin to a throne, stuffing his face with whatever delicacies had been brought before him.

The servant beside him straightened, clearing his throat with a sniff of self-importance before making the grand announcement.

"Lord Casterland, allow me to introduce Commoner Zigglespot Cogglesworth the Third. He wishes to..."

Casterland barely lifted his gaze before waving a meaty hand, cutting the man off mid-sentence.

"Yes, yes, Ingsly, that's enough of that," the Lord muttered, his voice thick with disinterest as he popped another morsel into his mouth, chewing lazily. He swallowed, barely concealing a belch before turning his gaze to Devaultus. "What do you have, lad?"

Bored. Dismissive. Another pompous fool who thought himself untouchable. Devaultus offered him a sweeping bow, the very picture of false deference, his mind already weaving through the countless ways this man could be disposed of should the need arise.

Devaultus took a measured step forward, his posture exuding confidence, though his mind worked furiously beneath the surface. "My Lord," he began, his voice smooth and persuasive, the tone of a man who knew exactly how to sell an idea. "I bring to you my greatest invention yet, The Bird of Prey Artificial Flight Mechanism." He spread his arms wide, as if unveiling something grand, his movements theatrical, deliberate. "A device of my own design, capable of granting a man, your men, the power to soar over enemy walls undetected. To infiltrate cities with ease. To steal priceless secrets, sabotage supply lines, and, should you desire, assassinate rival Lords, all in *your* name."

He let the words hang in the air, his voice dipping into something almost conspiratorial. "With this, *you* will be the most feared and powerful Lord of all time."

As he spoke, he wove the scene with his hands, painting a picture in the Lord's mind, shadows slipping over castle parapets, silent assassins gliding like specters through the night, striking unseen before vanishing into the darkness. He described every intricate detail of the device, how it functioned, how it could be mastered, how it would revolutionize warfare. His words were a masterful blend of truth and embellishment, a melody of promise and persuasion.

Lord Casterland leaned forward, intrigued, greed flashing in his small, beady eyes. His fleshy fingers drummed against the arm of his chair before he gave a slow, calculating smile. "Yes, yes," he murmured, swallowing a mouthful of food before jabbing a thick finger toward Devaultus. "But does it *work*?" He gestured vaguely with his other hand, dismissive yet expectant. "I've seen too many charlatans parade through these halls, spouting big ideas and grand promises. All of them fall flat the moment I ask for proof." He smirked, leaning back in his chair. "So, show me. Fly."

Devaultus resisted the urge to sigh, though irritation prickled at the edges of his carefully maintained composure. He had known this moment would come, but he had hoped, perhaps foolishly, to avoid it. Testing the device before an audience wasn't the issue, it was the landing that posed the problem. Even with his skill, surviving a demonstration unscathed was far from a guarantee.

"Of course, my Lord," he said smoothly, inclining his head. Then, after a calculated pause, he added, "I would love nothing more than to provide a proper demonstration... but, regrettably, I have an urgent meeting with Lord Sprocketstone in mere moments." He let that name linger, watching as Lord Casterland's mouth twisted into a scowl. "You see, my Lord," Devaultus continued, lowering his voice just enough to make it feel like a whispered confidence, "*he* is *very* interested in this invention. In fact, he made it clear he's eager to fund its full production. And, as you might imagine, I cannot afford to keep him waiting."

Lord Casterland's expression darkened instantly. The rivalry between the two Lords was no secret: years of scheming, backstabbing, and blood-soaked betrayals had turned their feud into one of legend. The mere *thought* of Sprocketstone gaining such an advantage over him was enough to make Casterland's meaty hands clench into fists.

Devaultus saw the greed in the man's eyes and knew he had him.

Lord Casterland let out a deep, satisfied chuckle, his thick fingers drumming against the armrest of his chair. "Oh, you most certainly will not be making that meeting," he declared, a smug glint flashing in his beady eyes. "I will fund the production of your invention for my own army. And as an incentive to cancel your dealings with Lord Sprocketstone, I'll add an extra ten percent to the price."

The words were spoken with the weight of finality, an offer not so much proposed as dictated. The portly Lord leaned forward, grinning, bits of food clinging to the corners of his mouth as he watched for Devaultus' reaction, confident in his own generosity.

Devaultus returned the smile with one of his own, practiced, polished, hiding the sharp edges of his true intentions. "As you wish, my Lord. With such a generous offer, I find myself with no need to keep my appointment," he said smoothly, inclining his head in a gesture of false deference.

But inside, he was already calculating. The excuse to avoid a demonstration had evaporated with that agreement, and he could feel the weight of expectation settling back onto him. Lord Casterland's gaze had not yet sharpened with realization, but it was only a matter of time before his greedy mind circled back to the one thing he had yet to see: the machine in action.

Devaultus needed a distraction, and he needed it fast.

"My Lord," he said, shifting the conversation with an effortless pivot. "I must say, you have impeccable taste. And not just in weaponry." He gestured vaguely at the lavish feast spread before Casterland, plates piled high with roasted meats, exotic fruits, and decadent pastries, the wealth of a kingdom laid out for one man's indulgence. "In fact, I happen to have a dear friend, a well-regarded importer of rare and exotic goods. They once procured for me a liquor unlike any I've tasted before. A true treasure of flavor, smooth as silk and potent enough to bring a warlord to his knees."

He let the words settle, let the seed of curiosity take root. Then, with the perfect measure of hesitation, he added, "As a celebration of our newfound business partnership, I would be honored to retrieve a bottle for you myself." His voice lowered ever so slightly, slipping into a tone of conspiratorial reverence. "A drink fit for a ruler such as yourself. That is, of course, if you would permit me the honor?"

The bait was set. Now, he only had to watch the gluttonous Lord take it.

Devaultus let the words settle, watching as Lord Casterland mulled them over, his beady, greedy eyes flickering with excitement. The promise of something rare, something no other Lord in the region could boast about, was too tantalizing for a man like him to resist. His plump fingers drummed thoughtfully against the armrest of his chair before his lips curled into a wide, self-satisfied grin.

"That would be to my liking, Mr. Cogglesworth," he said, his voice dripping with anticipation; he was already savoring the idea of indulging in some exclusive delicacy while his rivals could only dream of such luxuries.

Devaultus returned the smile, though his own was laced with something far sharper beneath the surface. "My Lord, might I make a request? It would put my mind at ease if I could store my invention in your treasure room. After all, I wouldn't want another Lord, say, Lord Sprocketstone, to catch wind of it and attempt to steal its secrets. In your esteemed vaults, I know it would be safe."

Lord Casterland's expression shifted instantly, his delight deepening into something far more devious. The wheels in his mind were turning. If the fool was willing to place his invention in *his* treasury, then should anything happen to him... oh, what a terrible, tragic accident that would be... well, the device would still be in his possession. His, and his alone.

"Oh, of course," the portly Lord said, barely concealing his glee. "Insly, show Mr. Cogglesworth to the treasure room."

The smug little advisor, Insly, inclined his head obediently before motioning for Devaultus to follow. The entire exchange was almost too easy. Lord Casterland thought himself so very clever, so utterly cunning in his silent scheming. He had no idea that he was being played just as skillfully as a grandmaster played the pieces on a chessboard.

Devaultus exhaled slowly, forcing down the dark satisfaction creeping into his thoughts. This was a step forward, another piece falling neatly into place. But even now, he felt the familiar strain pulling at him, a reminder that he was walking the razor's edge. He was no hero, and he certainly wasn't here to *save* anyone. He had his own agenda. And yet...

No. He shoved the thought away, stepping forward to follow Insly. The time for self-reflection would come later. For now, he had a vault to infiltrate.

Following the insufferably smug little gnome down the winding corridors toward the treasury, Devaultus moved with the silent, calculated ease of a predator studying its prey. Each turn, each step, he memorized, committing every detail to memory like a painter studying a canvas before leaving his mark. His sharp eyes flicked over the guards stationed at key points, taking in the thickness of the walls, the flickering torchlight that cast shadows deep enough to hide in.

"You must be quite proud of yourself," came the gnome's self-satisfied voice, thick with condescension. Insley barely reached

Devaultus' waist in his normal form, yet he carried himself with the swagger of a king addressing a peasant. "It is not every day a nobody such as yourself gains the attention of such a *magnificent* Lord as Lord Casterland."

Devaultus forced a placid smile, though his fingers itched to silence the pompous little creature. "Yes, you are correct," he responded smoothly, layering his voice with just the right amount of reverence to sound convincing. "I am *quite* fortunate to find myself in Lord Casterland's esteemed graces." He let his tone drip with feigned awe, even widening his eyes slightly as if in admiration. Inside, however, he was calculating how many ways he could kill the gnome before anyone noticed.

At last, they arrived before the towering treasury doors, their gilded engravings gleaming under the flickering torchlight. Two armored guards stood watch, each armed with halberds, their expressions unreadable behind thick visors. With a curt nod, they heaved the massive doors open, revealing the dazzling sight within: piles of gold, precious gems, artifacts humming with barely-contained power. Devaultus' eyes flickered with interest.

"We will only be a moment," Insley announced haughtily to the guards. Then he turned to cast a scrutinizing look at Devaultus. "Please, close the doors behind us, just in case *Mr. Cogglesworth* here gets any ideas about lining his pockets. One can never be too careful around the *lesser folks*, after all."

Devaultus gritted his teeth, his hands twitching at his sides as a storm of irritation threatened to rise within him. He did *not* lose control. He was precise, methodical, *calculating*. But, oh, how easy it would be to paint the treasury floor red with the gnome's blood.

The doors groaned as they shut behind them with heavy finality.

Devaultus let his gaze drift across the grand expanse of the treasure room, his fingers itching, not with rage, but with the anticipation of opportunity.

Devaultus let his gaze wander, drinking in the wealth that surrounded him. His sharp eyes flicked from one glittering artifact to the next, cataloging each with the quiet precision of a predator assessing its prey. The treasury was a hoard of wonders: metals so rare that they were whispered about more than seen, some nearly mythical in their scarcity. He noted how the nobility, particularly these gnomes, seemed to have an unnatural abundance of such materials.

Fine silks and lavish brocades spilled from open chests, shimmering under the golden glow of lantern light. There were quills, crafted not from mundane feathers but from some yellowish metal that he suspected was gold. Then again, he had never actually laid eyes on real gold before. The cities were full of forgeries, wooden coins dipped in deceptive hues, merchants spinning lies as skillfully as spiders wove silk. But here, within these vaults, the riches were undoubtedly genuine. His attention snagged on a crown, resplendent with gemstones and metals whose names eluded him. The craftsmanship was beyond anything he had ever seen. *How incredible*, he mused.

A smirk curled Insley's lips, his tone practically dripping condescension. "I bet ye've never seen anything so shiny as what's in this room. Not a speck o' dirt like ye're used to, eh?" The gnome's smug gaze raked over him, relishing his supposed inferiority.

Devaultus did not respond, merely arching a brow.

"Just put yer little contraption down somewhere," Insley continued with a dismissive wave. "Try not to get dung and filth on anythin' important."

Grinding his teeth, Devaultus crouched down, setting the device carefully on the polished floor. As he stood, he stretched, rolling his shoulders lazily, as though entirely unbothered by the gnome's prattle.

Insley folded his arms, scrutinizing him as though he were nothing more than a particularly clever dog who had, against all odds, learned a trick. "Good. Looks like ye can follow directions after all," he sneered. "Perhaps ye're not completely worthless."

Devaultus tilted his head. *Worthless?*

Then, in the span of a heartbeat, a needle shot from his hand with deadly precision, embedding itself deep into Insley's temple.

The gnome's eyes widened in stunned disbelief, his mouth parting in a silent, strangled sound. His fingers trembled as they reached for the needle jutting grotesquely from his skull, as if his mind still struggled to comprehend what had just transpired.

Devaultus leaned in slightly, voice silk-smooth. "I don't like you. You're an annoying little man." He placed a firm hand on Insley's forehead, fingers pressing against clammy skin. "I think I can handle things from here." With an effortless shove, he sent the gnome toppling backward. Insley crumpled to the floor, his body twitching once before stilling completely.

Devaultus exhaled slowly, the corners of his lips tugging into a satisfied smirk. "That," he murmured to himself, "that is so much better."

He half wondered how long it would take before the guards noticed something was amiss in the treasury. No doubt Insley's absence would eventually raise suspicion, but that was a problem for later. Right now, he had an opportunity, and he wasn't about to waste it. His sharp eyes scanned the room, searching among the treasures, and when he caught sight of the ring cases, he felt a flicker of anticipation.

His fingers moved quickly, sifting through the collection with growing irritation. He had hoped, perhaps foolishly, to find *his* ring among them. But it wasn't there. He clenched his jaw, suppressing the urge to curse. Of course, it wouldn't be that easy. He knew better.

For a moment, he considered how much easier this would have been if he had Vex's ring. *That* little trinket would've made looting this place effortless. But then again, he wasn't a thief. That was *her* thing. Not that he had any moral objections to stealing, far from it. He simply knew that lifting valuables, especially from a noble's treasury, came with more complications than it was worth. More often than not, theft led to unnecessary problems, and he had enough of those already.

Still, curiosity gnawed at him. What were all these rings for? Surely they weren't just decoration. Without much thought, he grabbed a handful and slipped them into his pocket. Immediately, the soft chime of metal against metal reached his ears. He let out a low sigh. *Of course.* There was no way he'd be able to walk past the guards with them jingling like a damn wind chime.

He considered his options. He could slip them onto his fingers, but that was an easy way to get noticed; and worse, he had no idea what these rings did. The last thing he needed was to put one on and find himself cursed or glowing like a beacon. No, best not to take that risk.

With a final exhale, he forced his mind back to the mission. Taking the rings from his pocket, he tossed them into the pile of coins. All but one ring for each pocket. He hoped they were the most important rings here. Though there was no way of knowing till they were appraised. There was no time to linger. He had what he could take, and now it was time to move.

The rod. That was the prize. That was what he had come for.

Devaultus scanned the room, his sharp gaze flitting over the countless treasures until it landed on an object that matched the description he had been given. Across the opulent chamber, resting atop a pedestal adorned with velvet, sat a rod unlike any he had ever seen. It was entirely metal, an absurd rarity in this world, worth more than some small kingdoms.

As he approached, he studied its design. It was an intricate thing, composed of an inner rod encased within a broader metal cuff. Curious, he turned the inner piece in a circular motion, noting how the cuff remained stationary. It had the mechanical complexity of a wagon axle, though clearly intended for something far beyond mundane transportation.

What in the Abyss could Al'Shandra possibly want with this?

He doubted she was after it for its material worth alone. No, there was something more to it, something he didn't yet understand. And while he had little patience for mysteries, this one gnawed at him.

Shaking off his musings, he forced himself back to the pressing issue at hand. How in the Abyss was he going to get out of here with this? The weight of the rod alone meant smuggling it out unseen would be difficult, but that wasn't the real problem.

No, the real problem was Insley.

The man's corpse lay sprawled across the golden floor, his lifeblood pooling in rich crimson rivulets across the wealth he had once lorded over. Devaultus had acted without much thought, driven by his own irritation and distaste for the smug bastard. But now, in the wake of that moment, he had to acknowledge the consequences.

Had he let his emotions get the better of him? Had he made a mistake?

A slow smirk tugged at his lips. No.

Insley's death was a delight, a thing to be savored. The man was an obstacle, one that now no longer existed. Besides, there was no way Devaultus would have gotten this rod out of the treasury with Insley standing there, watching him like a vulture. This changed nothing.

Still, that didn't mean he was eager to carve a bloody path through the entire estate just to make his escape. Slaughter was fun, but a mindless massacre was *work*, and more work than he cared to do tonight.

Perhaps, just this once, a little *planning* might make things easier.

He tapped his fingers against the rod, his mind running through possibilities. *How to play this?* How to get out without raising immediate alarm? How to carry something this rare, this *impossible*, through the halls unnoticed?

He exhaled slowly, rolling his shoulders.

One thing was certain: this night was far from over.

A sharp knock echoed through the chamber, drawing the attention of the two guards stationed at the door. One of them stepped forward, pulling it open to reveal Insley standing in the hallway, his face twisted into a mask of barely concealed irritation. He exhaled sharply, as if the mere act of addressing them was an unbearable chore.

"I simply cannot deal with this insufferable common country bumpkin any longer," he announced, pinching the bridge of his nose in frustration. "Keep an eye on him, and for the love of the gods, check his pockets before he leaves. I wouldn't put it past him to try and smuggle something out."

With that, Insley turned on his heel, striding out of the treasury, the metal rod gripped tightly in his hand. One of the guards hesitated, his eyes narrowing as they locked onto the object.

"Uh... sir?" he ventured, pointing at the rod. "That thing..."

"Yes, yes, I know." Insley cut him off with an impatient wave of his hand. "Lord Casterland insisted I bring it to him. Something about selling it to fund an attack on Lord Sprocketstone. Tedious business, but not my concern. Either way, you know who I am. You know where I live. It's not as though I could run off and do anything untoward, now, is it?" He heaved a theatrical sigh before adopting a tone laced with exasperation. "If you simply must, when you're finished dealing with our guest, go verify the request with Lord Casterland himself."

Before the guards could formulate a response, Insley turned and walked away, his footsteps echoing down the corridor. The two men exchanged glances before shifting their attention to the treasury's occupant.

The gnome.

There he stood, on the far side of the room, his pockets bulging with what was unmistakably stolen treasure. Gold and jewels weighed his coat down, the outline of pilfered valuables pressing against the fabric like tumors of greed. The audacity of this insignificant commoner, this thieving little rat, thinking he could steal from Lord Casterland's treasury!

"Hey! You!" one of the guards bellowed, both men surging forward, hands already reaching for their weapons. They stormed toward the gnome, prepared to beat the wretched thief senseless if need be...

Then they stopped dead.

Their breath caught in their throats as they truly saw what stood before them.

Insley.

Not the gnome. Insley himself, his lifeless body propped up against an armor display, his sightless eyes staring into the void, his mouth slightly ajar as if he had been caught mid-protest. The blood had already begun to pool beneath him, dark and glistening against the golden floor.

The guards' heads snapped toward the door, realization dawning in a sickening wave of horror.

There, in the doorway, stood another Insley. The very same man who had spoken to them mere moments ago.

He grinned.

Then he raised a hand, waggled his fingers in a mockingly cheerful wave, and winked.

Before the guards could react, the door slammed shut, sealing them inside.

Tying a sturdy cord to each end of the rod, Devaultus slung it over his shoulder, letting it rest against his back like an impromptu satchel. The weight of the metal was an unusual burden: precious, rare, and more valuable than most kingdoms, but he carried it as though it were nothing more than a trinket. His gait was casual, his expression unreadable; he was the very essence of a man who belonged exactly where he was. To anyone watching, he was no more than Insley, the sniveling noble lackey, carrying out some errand at his master's bidding.

And if everything went according to plan, that was exactly what they would believe.

Devaultus strolled down the hallway with ease, resisting the urge to whistle. Confidence was key. He had played the part of countless men before: kings, beggars, merchants, fools. Insley was just another mask, another skin to slip into. As long as he didn't draw attention to himself, he could simply walk out the front door, make his way down the street, and climb aboard Al'Shandra's ship. By nightfall, they'd be halfway to whatever hellhole she had planned to drag them too next.

A smirk tugged at the corner of his lips. *Too easy.*

And then, because he was *Devaultus*, and the world never allowed him the satisfaction of an easy escape, fate shoved its hand straight down his throat and twisted.

Turning the corner, he nearly collided with Lord Casterland himself.

The nobleman stood regal and imposing in his deep crimson robes, the heavy gold chains of his station glinting in the torchlight. His face was a mask of perpetual disapproval, his beady eyes sharp and searching. *Not good.*

Beside him, flanking his every step like a personal wall of doom, were four guards. *Even worse.*

For a fraction of a second, Devaultus considered his options. *Play it cool, act the part.* He straightened his shoulders and let out an exaggerated sigh, as if deeply inconvenienced by having to explain himself to a man who should already know what was happening.

"Ah, my Lord," he drawled in his best Insly impression, adding just the right amount of nasal contempt. "You did say to fetch this, did you not?" He gave the rod a pointed little bounce against his back, making sure it caught the noble's eye. "Frankly, I don't see the value in it, but I suppose that's why you're in charge and I'm merely your loyal servant."

He offered an almost lazy bow, inwardly preparing for whatever fresh disaster was about to unfold.

Lord Casterland's beady eyes flicked over Devaultus with a slow, deliberate gaze, his lips curling into an unsettling smile. "No, Insley. I did not ask for that," he murmured, his voice carrying an eerie calm that sent a ripple of unease through the air.

Devaultus stiffened. Something was wrong. The bloated Lord should have been livid, should have been barking orders, demanding blood. But instead, he stood there grinning, his thick fingers clasped behind his back like a man watching an amusing stage play.

Devaultus had seen that look before, the kind a predator gives when its prey has already stumbled into the trap. His instincts screamed at him. He forced himself to remain still, his eyes subtly scanning the corridor, taking in every detail, searching for the missing piece. There was something here, something he hadn't accounted for.

And that smile... That damned smile meant trouble.

Devaultus had seen a lot of over-compensation in his time, but Lord Casterland truly excelled at it. The guards flanking him were absolute mountains of flesh: broad-shouldered brutes, or at least huge for gnomes, so they struggled to fit within the narrow corridor, forced to march in pairs just to squeeze through. It was almost comedic. Almost. Because at the moment, those walking slabs of muscle stood between him and his freedom.

"Well... nope." Devaultus muttered under his breath, already pivoting on his heel. A new plan was in order. Walk away, double back, change his disguise, and find a nice window to slip out of. Simple. Clean.

Except it wasn't.

As soon as he turned, he was greeted with an equally unwelcome sight: another five guards, effectively boxing him in. His stomach twisted in irritation. That was fast. Too fast. Sure, he expected them to catch on eventually, but how the hell had they figured something was amiss this quickly? This wasn't adding up.

Lord Casterland took a measured step forward, his round face flushed with barely-contained rage. "We found out about ye," he spat, his voice sharp. His tone carried no doubt, no hesitation, only cold certainty.

Devaultus barely resisted the urge to roll his eyes. Oh, fantastic. Another genius noble who thought he had unraveled the grand mystery of the century. He forced an exasperated sigh, feigning annoyance rather than concern. "Oh, did you now?" he drawled, raising an eyebrow.

"We know ye've been skimm'n' off me coffers fer quite some time now, Insley," Lord Casterland declared, his voice drippin' with smug satisfaction.

Devaultus barely kept himself from laughing. His jaw tightened, as he fought the reflex to gape at the sheer ridiculousness of it. *Of all the rotten, miserable luck.* The old bastard wasn't on to him at all; he thought Insley had been robbing him blind.

Devaultus could have played it safe. Could have denied it, could have wormed his way out of the accusation like a professional. But he was Devaultus. And he was petty.

His lips curled into a slow, wolfish grin. "Oh, that's not all I've been stealing," he said smoothly. Then, just to make sure there was no possible way to talk his way out of this later, he added with a wink, "Ask your wives."

Oh, how he hated gnomes. Every single one of them was an insufferable little rat, but Insley? Insley was particularly loathsome. If given the choice between getting skewered by a dozen swords or lifting a single finger to save that sniveling sack of filth, Devaultus would gladly bleed out with a smile. Not that Insley needed saving, he was already sprawled across the treasury floor, lifeless eyes staring up at the ceiling in dumb surprise.

Lord Casterland's face turned an impressive shade of crimson, his cheeks puffing like a bloated corpse left too long in the sun. Devaultus had seen boils less ready to burst. He half-expected the man's head to pop like overripe fruit, spraying the walls with his privileged, highborn juices.

"Kill Insley an' bring me his head!" Casterland bellowed, spittle flying from his lips like foam off a rabid hound.

Well, that escalated quickly.

The guards surged forward from both sides, their armor clanking as they closed in. The sheer bulk of them nearly blotted out the torchlight, and Devaultus realized with mild annoyance that Casterland had gone out of his way to hire the largest, most slab-chested brutes he could find. An inhuman wall of muscle, pointy things, and idiocy.

Okay, that did not go how... actually, no, let's be honest. That went *exactly* how he thought it would. But there was that tiny flicker of hope; for a moment he imagined they'd all stop, nod in agreement, and laugh about what a terrible little bastard Insley was before skipping off merrily into the night. Alas, reality was rarely so kind.

With a resigned sigh, he reached for his daggers, ready to carve his way out, only to find *Shiela* missing from his belt.

"Oh... yeah..." he muttered, eyes going wide.

That was *not* good.

The first guard lunged with a pike, the deadly tip whistling through the air toward his chest. Devaultus twisted, narrowly avoiding being skewered, and swept his leg out to trip the man. Or at least, that was the plan. Instead, his stubby little gnome leg thudded harmlessly against the brute's shin, accomplishing precisely nothing. The guard barely noticed.

"Wait, hold up," Devaultus said, hopping back to avoid the next thrust. He glanced over his shoulder, quickly assessing the distance of the guards behind him. Not great. His odds of walking out of this weren't exactly looking promising.

His mind raced. *Alright, think. Talk your way out. Distract them. Turn them against each other.*

"We can share his wives!" he blurted, throwing his hands up in an exaggerated display of generosity. "I heard one fancies you, after all." He pointed at the nearest guard, whose grip on his weapon faltered just slightly.

There was a beat of hesitation.

Then the guards surged forward again.

Yeah. He *really* should've just kept running.

The guard's grip tightened on his spear, his knuckles going white as he swung in a vicious, slashing arc. Devaultus barely managed to duck under it, feeling the air part just above his head. He let out an exaggerated sigh. "Alright, but this is really going to be difficult on the kids!"

The sound of boots thundered behind him. The other guards were closing in fast, their heavy steps pounding against the stone floor. He could feel them like a storm at his back. "Think of the kids, damn you!" he snapped, twisting just in time to avoid another pike lancing toward his ribs. He let his momentum carry him, using the spin to mask his next move. A flick of his wrist, a blur of movement, and his fingers found the needle laced into the fabric of his sleeve.

With a sharp, deliberate thrust, he drove it deep into the eye of the lunging guard. The man howled, dropping his pike as his hands flew to his face, blood leaking between his fingers. Devaultus didn't pause. "Well, this is definitely going to make the work holiday party quite awkward," he muttered as he bent down, fingers curling around the hilt of the wounded man's short sword, yanking it free from its scabbard.

The clink of armor and the hiss of shifting chainmail alerted him to another attack. A guard behind him lunged, the long steel tip of a pike thrusting forward. Devaultus smirked. "Ah," he chuckled darkly, twisting just out of reach, "this really isn't the best weapon for the job, now, is it?" The hallway was grand, yes, but not quite grand enough for polearms to be wielded effectively. With a deft parry, he smacked the pike aside and surged forward, his eyes locked on Lord Casterland.

But the guards were learning. He saw it in the way they adjusted their footing, their grips tightening with grim determination. This time, two of them struck in tandem. He managed to bat one pike away, sending its wielder stumbling, but the second guard had anticipated his move. Devaultus barely registered the flash of wood and bone before the spear plunged deep into his shoulder.

Pain exploded through him, white-hot and electric. His vision blurred for half a second, but he clenched his teeth against the agony. "Oh," he grunted, glancing at the embedded weapon, "well, this is not good at all."

Gripping the sword tightly, Devaultus braced against the searing pain tearing through his shoulder. With a sharp exhale, he swung the blade down in a brutal arc, cleaving clean through the wooden shaft of the pike still lodged in his flesh. He had seen warriors pull this move in the arenas before, shattering weapons mid-combat, making it look almost effortless. Turns out, though, when the weapon is already buried in your body and you suddenly jolt it loose, the pain is a whole new kind of hell, like scrubbing an open wound with a vinegar-soaked rag while a pack of gecko cats use you as a scratching post.

"Ouch! Son of a..." He clenched his teeth, the searing pain nearly buckling his knees. "Wait, time out!" he barked, throwing up his free hand.

The words, of course, meant absolutely nothing to the oncoming guards, who surged forward, weapons at the ready, undeterred by his plea for mercy.

"You know what? Screw this." Devaultus scowled, his form shifting in an instant, the illusion peeling away like snakeskin to reveal his true self: the towering, dashing, and unmistakably non-gnomish Devaultus.

One of the charging guards, a younger recruit, by the look of him, stumbled back with a gasp, the color draining from his face at the sight of the transformation.

Devaultus wasted no time. With a vicious grin, he reeled back and delivered a powerful kick, sending the stunned gnome skidding backward like a tossed rag doll. The poor bastard barely had time to yelp before slamming hard against the stone wall, crumpling in a heap.

Another guard lunged at him, pike thrust forward in a desperate attempt to pierce his chest. Devaultus twisted, his movements smooth despite the throbbing wound in his shoulder, and smacked the spear aside with his stolen sword. Before the guard could reset, Devaultus drove a fist straight into his face, feeling the satisfying crunch of cartilage as the man's nose caved under the blow. The guard stumbled back, dazed, clutching his face as blood gushed between his fingers.

Now this was more like it.

"I..." Devaultus started, his voice a low snarl as he twisted his body, his blade whistling through the air in a vicious arc. The edge bit deep, severing the legs of the unfortunate gnome in his path. Blood spattered the stone floor, and the shriek that followed was an unholy mix of shock and agony. "Hate gnomes," he growled, his voice laced with raw contempt.

As he turned, he felt the rush of air from a pike stabbing forward, just narrowly missing him. The sharpened tip found an unintended target instead, plunging deep into the chest of the guard ahead of him. The man let out a strangled gasp, his eyes bulging in horror as crimson bloomed across his armor. Devaultus barely spared him a glance.

With fluid, predatory grace, he lashed out with his foot, driving his heel backward with bone-crushing force. The solid impact landed squarely between the legs of the gnome behind him. There was a sickening pop, followed by a high-pitched screech that could have shattered glass. Gnomes already had irritatingly shrill voices; this one was now hitting a frequency that made Devaultus' ears ache.

"But... I... really..." His hand shot forward, seizing the dying, impaled guard and using the poor fool's momentum against him. With a grunt of effort, Devaultus spun, hurling the body like an inhuman projectile toward the remaining guards. They barely had time to react before the corpse slammed into them, knocking them off balance in a tangle of limbs and armor.

"Hate being... stabbed." The words were a growl from deep within his chest as he threw himself into a roll, his body tucking tight as he vaulted clean over the next incoming pike. The spearhead whizzed just below him, missing by mere inches as he landed in a low crouch, right beside none other than Lord Casterland.

The air between them was thick with tension. Blood dripped from Devaultus' blade, his breath came in steady, measured draws, and a slow, wicked grin crept onto his lips as his eyes met Casterland's.

"Well," he mused darkly. "That worked out nicely."

Lord Casterland's face was a mask of fury, his chest rising and falling with ragged breaths. Devaultus, on the other hand, looked as nonchalant as ever, tilting his head slightly as he regarded the enraged gnome.

"You come here often?" he quipped, his tone dripping with amusement.

The remaining guards, still loyal despite their employer's outburst, tensed, gripping their pikes as they advanced in unison, the sharp tips of their weapons now pointed directly at Devaultus. However, in their haste, they had positioned themselves poorly, their weapons now aimed squarely at Lord Casterland as well.

"What in the name o' the bloody ancestors are ye eejits doin'?!" Casterland roared, his face turning an even deeper shade of red. "Point them damn spears at him, not me, ye witless gobshites!"

The guards hesitated, scrambling to adjust their attack without skewering their employer in the process. Their disorganized shuffle gave Devaultus just the opening he needed. Smirking, he leaned in close to the furious gnome, his lips nearly brushing his ear as he whispered, "I dare say you should've hired smarter guards."

With a sudden forceful shove, Devaultus shifted Lord Casterland directly into the path of the nearest lunging guard. The gnome let out a sharp yelp as a pike tip met his side, slicing through fabric and skin alike. The guard who had landed the unfortunate blow froze in horror, his face turning ghostly pale as his eyes locked onto his master's livid expression.

"*I'll have ye impaled on me front lawn, ye useless, clumsy sack o' shite!*" Casterland bellowed, clutching his wounded side. His rage-filled shriek echoed off the stone walls like a banshee's wail.

The guards looked at one another, uncertainty flickering in their eyes. Lord Casterland was now an unwilling human, or rather, gnome, shield. With their employer standing squarely in the way, their movements grew clumsy, uncertain.

And Devaultus? He grinned. This was getting fun.

Devaultus arched an eyebrow, his lips curling in amusement. "So, how shall we proceed with this delicate situation?" He tapped his chin as if mulling it over, then snapped his fingers. "Oh! I know. His wives are still waiting, after all. I can pretend this whole mess never happened. Just go ahead. I'm sure they'll be absolutely thrilled to see you."

The guards exchanged uneasy glances, their brows furrowing. Devaultus could see the slow grind of reluctant gears turning in their skulls. He tilted his head slightly, giving them an encouraging nod. "Think about it. If you stick around, he's just going to yell at you again." He gestured toward Lord Casterland, whose face was now a lovely shade of puce.

One of the guards, a gnome with a particularly receding hairline, exhaled sharply and lowered his head. "Aye... he's got a point," he muttered.

Devaultus clapped his hands together. "Excellent! Off you go, then."

Without another word, the two guards dropped their pikes, turned on their stubby heels, and marched straight toward the chambers of Lord Casterland's wives.

"Wait! Where are you going? Stop listening to him, ye bloody fools!" Lord Casterland shrieked, his rage hitting a fever pitch.

Devaultus spun the rotund man around to face him, gripping his arms firmly. "Now, listen. I can understand mistaking me for Insley. Honestly, I'm flattered. I truly am a master of my craft." He straightened the man's disheveled collar with mock care, smoothing out the fabric as if tending to an old friend. "I can even understand sending your guards after him. He was a miserable, insufferable excuse for a man." Devaultus leaned in just slightly, his smirk widening. "Or... well, he *was* anyway."

With that, his fingers curled around something that had tumbled from Lord Casterland's head in the scuffle: a weighty, ornate crown.

He lifted it, turning it in his hands, eyes gleaming as he inspected the craftsmanship.

"Well, well," he murmured. "Would you look at that? Actual gold."

The absurdity of Lord Casterland's crown was almost comical: massively long, gleaming spines jutted upward, an ostentatious attempt to make the squat little gnome feel taller than those around him. Devaultus had heard the rumors, but seeing it up close made it all the more ridiculous. He let out a low chuckle and shoved the gaudy thing into the gnome's pudgy hands.

"But I really hate being stabbed," he murmured, his voice cold and sharp as a blade.

With a sudden, brutal kick, Devaultus drove his foot into the crown with the full force of his weight. The metal spikes crunched inward, spearing straight into Lord Casterland's chest like a grotesque array of golden daggers. The gnome gasped, a strangled, wet sound, as his eyes bulged in disbelief. He trembled, his fingers twitching feebly at the band of the crown now embedded deep in his flesh. Blood bubbled at the corners of his lips, dribbling down his chin as he let out a shuddering breath.

His knees buckled. He collapsed, convulsing violently on the marble floor, each tremor sending fresh rivulets of crimson seeping from his wounds. By the time Devaultus turned his back on him, Lord Casterland had gone still. Silent.

Without a second glance, Devaultus strode from the corridor, stepping over the gnome's cooling body. On his way out of the mansion, he spotted a length of cloth, snatching it up and wrapping it around the gilded rod to conceal its wealth. No need to invite more trouble than he already had.

Moving swiftly, he wound through the darkened streets, his pace quick but casual; no sense in drawing attention. The city's familiar filth clung to the air, a mixture of sweat, spice, and decay. He was nearly at the designated meeting place when something caught his eye.

He stopped short. His head tilted slightly, brow furrowing.

The ship.

Al'Shandra's ship.

It was burning.

The flames licked hungrily at the hull, golden tongues dancing against the night sky as the grand vessel slowly sank into the Sand Sea. Parts of it had already disappeared beneath the shifting dunes, while the rest crackled and hissed, fire consuming what remained.

Beyond the wreckage, more ships loomed in the darkness, Al'Shandra's fleet. The imposing vessels floated like specters around the destruction, their dark silhouettes stark against the fire's glow.

And then, on the deck of one of the intact ships, he saw her.

Al'Shandra.

She stood with her arms folded beneath her breasts, the dim firelight casting flickering shadows across her flawless, sun-kissed skin. Her usual playful seduction was gone, replaced by something colder, sharper. The smoldering intensity in her eyes wasn't just fury: it was a promise.

Devaultus exhaled slowly through his nose, his hands clenching at his sides.

"What did you do, Vex...?" he muttered under his breath.

# CHAPTER 17

# SHIPWRECKED IN QUARTERS

Tarus strode into the massive hall, his armored boots thudding against the polished stone floor with the weight of a storm rolling in. His eyes burned with anger as they locked onto the man seated before him. His jaw tightened, his nostrils flared.

"You are not Lord Casterland," he snarled, his deep voice rumbling through the chamber like distant thunder. His patience was already razor-thin. "Where in the Abyss is he? I informed him I wished to meet him immediately, and yet here I am, looking at you!"

Beside the towering, battle-hardened warrior stood an old man, his posture eerily straight despite his thin, wiry frame. His hooked nose, an unfortunate relic from what some suspected was dwarven ancestry, curved slightly over his pencil-thin mustache. Wisps of stringy white hair hung down the sides of his gaunt face, stark against the deep crimson of his robes. There was an unnatural stillness to him, an ever-present readiness coiled beneath his brittle exterior, an unspoken threat.

This was *The Puppeteer*.

His piercing eyes held a glint of ruthless calculation as he studied the man before him, fingers twitching subtly at his sides, prepared to take control at a moment's notice.

The man seated on the throne swallowed hard, his face paling as he shifted uncomfortably under their combined scrutiny. His hands trembled where they rested on the gilded armrests. "L-Lord Tarus...

I... I am merely filling in. Lord Casterland..." his breath hitched "...was murdered. Yesterday."

A deep, guttural growl rumbled in Tarus' chest, low and dangerous. His fingers flexed over the hilt of his massive sword, the veins in his forearm pulsing with restrained fury. "*Who?*"

The man licked his dry lips nervously, his voice barely above a whisper. "M-my Lord, we do not know who it was. No one saw him enter the city. Trust me, if they had, he *would* have been spotted." His voice grew increasingly frantic, as if speaking faster might save him from whatever wrath was brewing beneath Tarus' heated glare. "After the massacre... and Lord Casterland's murder, he just *walked* through the city, bold as anything! A human, or at least, he seemed to be. He was wearing fine clothing, a long-brimmed hat. He was *covered* in blood. And on his back..." The man hesitated, as if he could barely believe his own words.

"*A lute.*"

Silence hung in the air for the briefest moment. Then...

A *roar* of fury.

Tarus' massive sword was in his hands before anyone could blink. With a swift, brutal motion, he lunged forward and buried the steel deep into the chest of the nearest gnome. A wet, sickening crunch echoed through the hall. The gnome barely had time to gasp before the blade was yanked free, blood spraying across the floor in a violent arc.

But Tarus wasn't finished.

With a snarl, he hacked into the corpse again. And again. Flesh tore. Bone snapped. Blood splattered in thick streaks against the marble. The remaining guards stood frozen, weapons half-drawn, their hands shaking as they watched their companion reduced to a pile of butchered meat.

By the time Tarus stepped back, his breath was ragged, his body heaving with exertion. His armor was slick with blood, his blade dripping red onto the ruined corpse at his feet.

The entire journey had been spent unraveling the mystery of the man who had dared to take what was his, his daughter, stolen away in the dead of night like some common prize. His spies worked tirelessly, slipping through the underbelly of cities, bribing, threatening, and gutting those who did not comply. Name after name whispered through the dark corridors of his mind, each one a useless thread in a tangled web. But one name remained constant, lingering like the stench of blood after battle.

A bard.

Unlike most who skulked in the shadows, this man did not cower or conceal himself. He did not whisper his name in hushed tones, did not fear discovery. No, he flaunted it, as if daring the world to challenge him. Wherever he went, his presence was a spectacle, an announcement carved into the very bones of the city. It was as if he wanted to be found.

His lip curled. His voice came out as a growl, low and seething with unrelenting hatred.

"*Devaultus.*"

He exhaled sharply through his nose, his fingers tightening around his sword hilt as if he were already wrapping them around the bastard's throat.

"*I'll find you.*" His teeth bared in something between a snarl and a promise.

"*And I'll kill you.*"

He turned on his heel, blood trailing in his wake.

"*Be sure of that.*"

Tarus' furious gaze snapped to the man on the throne, who all but shrank into the plush cushions, his face pale with fear. He looked as though he wished to vanish into the fabric itself, to be anywhere but under the warlord's scrutiny.

"Show me where this massacre took place," Tarus commanded, his voice thick with barely restrained rage. "I wish to see everything this bard took."

The man hesitated for only a moment before nodding hastily and stumbling to his feet. With hurried, shuffling steps, he led them through the grand hallways, his head low, his shoulders hunched as though he were expecting a blow at any moment. Tarus and the two towering figures at his side followed, their heavy footfalls echoing ominously against the stone walls.

As they entered the site of the slaughter, the stench of blood and death hung in the air. The carnage remained untouched, bodies sprawled in unnatural positions where they had fallen. Other gnomes, smaller and shrouded in the garb of investigators, picked through the remains with grim determination. The once-grand hall was painted in blood, thick, dark rivulets crusting along the walls and pooling in the crevices of the uneven floor. Thin strands of gore dangled from the ceiling, torn remnants of the violence that had erupted here.

Tarus let out a slow breath through his nose, his expression unreadable.

"Why was he here?" he asked, his voice quieter now, but no less dangerous.

The man beside him swallowed hard before answering. "A guard claimed he had something from our treasury strapped to his back."

Tarus turned his head sharply, his piercing gaze locking onto the man who had yet to earn the right to a name in his eyes. "I wish to speak with this guard."

The man visibly flinched. "My Lord... he was dismissed from duty and imprisoned for his failure to prevent this... for running from the fight."

"Bring him to me," Tarus growled, his tone leaving no room for argument.

The man stiffened before quickly bowing. "Y-yes, my Lord."

With a frantic motion, he gestured to the guards, who rushed off down the corridor. Moments stretched, the silence filled only by the distant murmurs of those still working through the wreckage. Then, after several tense minutes, the guards returned, dragging a shackled figure between them. The defeated man stumbled forward, his chains clinking against the stone.

Tarus did not speak immediately. He simply stared down at the pitiful wretch before him, his expression unreadable but his intent clear.

The interrogation was about to begin.

The guard's face drained of color the moment his eyes landed on Tarus, the massive figure looming over him like an executioner ready to pass judgment. He swallowed hard, his shackles clanking as he trembled.

"What did the man take?" Tarus' deep, rumbling voice echoed through the grand chamber, each syllable carrying an undeniable weight. The walls themselves seemed to shrink at the sound.

The guard stammered, his words tumbling over each other in his panic. "H-he took some metal rod," he blurted, voice quivering. He kept his answers clipped and to the point, as if he knew the wrong word could spell his end.

Tarus narrowed his eyes. "What does the rod do?"

"I... I'm unsure, my Lord," the guard stuttered, licking his lips anxiously. "In truth, Lord Casterland never knew. He only kept it because it was made entirely of metal and worth a fortune."

Tarus' gaze darkened. That answer did not satisfy him. Wealth alone would not have drawn Devaultus to such an item. From what he had uncovered of this man, riches were not his primary motivation. He took what he wanted, through wit, deception, or force, but always with purpose. A rod made of solid metal was little more than a prize. There had to be something more.

His massive shoulders shifted as he turned, striding toward the exit, his cloak billowing behind him. But he hesitated at the doorway. Without looking back, he inclined his head toward the wiry old man at his side. The Puppeteer met his gaze, understanding the silent command instantly.

And then, chaos erupted.

Every guard in the chamber lurched forward at once, steel flashing as swords were drawn in unison. Serving girls, seemingly harmless just moments before, lunged forward with butter knives clutched in their hands, their faces twisted into masks of lethal intent. They fell upon the shackled guard in a perfect, nightmarish symphony of violence.

The guard barely had time to scream.

Blades plunged into him from every angle. Blood spurted into the air in thick, wet arcs, splattering against the walls and staining the once-polished marble floors. The man convulsed, his body jerking as knives and swords ripped through flesh, muscle, and bone. The frenzy did not stop, did not slow. Each stab, each slash, turned what was once a man into something unrecognizable.

By the time Tarus and The Puppeteer stepped beyond the threshold of the chamber, the killing was done.

Behind them, the guard no longer resembled a person. His remains were a shredded pile of meat and splintered bone, nothing more than a grotesque heap of red ruin pooling in the center of the chamber.

Tarus did not look back.

He had what he needed. Now, there was only one thing left to do.

Find Devaultus. And kill him.

Devaultus lay sprawled across his bunk, his long-brimmed hat tilted over his face, shielding his eyes from the dim lantern light swaying from the ceiling. For once, he could sleep without worrying about a blade sliding across his throat in the dark. It was a rare luxury, this fleeting moment of peace. Here, in the shared quarters of his crew, he could, at least in theory, let his guard down. Not that he trusted them entirely. Oh, they wouldn't kill him on purpose. But accidental injury? That was practically a certainty.

Across the cramped quarters, Blight lay curled on her bunk, her pale fingers smudged with coal as she meticulously scribbled notes. The parchment in front of her, part of Al'Shandra's latest collection of documents, was filled with symbols and writings far older than most could decipher. She studied them in silence, her eyes flickering with quiet curiosity, lost in the endless riddles of the world. Every so often, she'd pause, biting her lip in thought before marking something down on a separate page, her mind a storm of theories and calculations.

Then there was Vex.

She lay sprawled across her bunk on her back, one leg propped up over the other, idly tossing a knife straight into the air. The silver blade gleamed as it spun, flipping end over end before she caught it effortlessly by the handle, time and again. Each time, she let it rise just a little higher, push the edge just a little further. The last throw brought the blade dangerously close to her nose before she snatched it midair with a satisfied grin. She didn't seem the least bit concerned that if she missed, the knife would end up lodged somewhere very inconvenient.

Devaultus sighed beneath his hat. This was his team. A shy scholar unraveling the secrets of the world, a reckless thief toying with death like it was a game, and him, a man who had never planned to be anyone's hero, yet somehow kept ending up in situations that required him to pretend otherwise.

He should have known peace wouldn't last long.

The three had been banished to their quarters until further notice, a punishment that, given Al'Shandra's rage, was likely the only thing keeping them from being thrown overboard into the merciless Sand Sea. The pirate queen had been a breath away from ordering their execution, until Devaultus had presented her with the metal rod.

The shift in her demeanor had been instant. Her smoldering fury had been replaced by something else entirely. The way her fingers traced the length of the rod, the way her breath hitched just slightly, betrayed the immense value she placed on it. Even so, she had forced herself to remain composed, inhaling deeply through her nose as though steadying herself. Devaultus had watched the internal war play out in her eyes before she finally pointed to one of the crew members.

"Take them to shared quarters. Lock them in," she had ordered, her voice tight with restraint. "I'll talk to them when I'm good and ready. And when I'm certain I won't kill them."

The crewman had nodded, giving them a look that was equal parts amused and pitying before ushering them away. Devaultus had briefly considered arguing; being locked up like some unruly child did not sit well with him, but something in Al'Shandra's expression told him it was best not to press his luck. So he had gone quietly, retreating to his bunk without protest.

That had been three days ago.

Since then, they had been left to rot in their quarters, forgotten; or at least, that was how Devaultus felt. Food was brought to them in regular intervals, but beyond that, they saw no one. No explanations. No updates. Just isolation. And it was starting to get to him.

Devaultus was growing restless, his fingers twitching with the need for action. Vex, predictably, was even worse, pacing like a caged animal, tossing knives at the walls, muttering under her breath about how she was "this close" to burning down another ship, just for the entertainment of it. The only one who didn't seem the least bit bothered was Blight.

The girl had buried herself in her studies, poring over the research Al'Shandra had sent her way; at least, whatever research wouldn't result in an accidental explosion or sudden inferno. She scribbled notes in coal, flipping through pages with an intensity that bordered on obsession. It was, at the very least, a welcome distraction from the madness of their confinement.

Devaultus, however, was nearing his limit. If they didn't let him out soon, he was going to find a way to let himself out.

Just when Devaultus thought he would finally snap from the sheer monotony of their confinement, a sharp knock echoed through the room. The sound was almost foreign after days of isolation, a break in the endless cycle of waiting, pacing, and Vex threatening to set something, or someone, on fire.

Vex's head whipped toward the door in anticipation, her attention completely overtaken by the interruption. The knife she had been tossing in the air was forgotten, and it plunged down, embedding itself deep into the straw mat beside her face with a solid *thunk*. She barely blinked, her eyes instead locked on the door as it creaked open.

A man stood in the doorway. He was of medium build, with a clean-shaven head but a thick, shaggy beard that made him look somewhat unbalanced, as if he had only committed to grooming halfway. His arms were crossed, but there was an uncertainty in his stance, like he wasn't entirely sure whether opening this door had been a good idea.

"Devaultus?" he called, his voice gruff but cautious. "Al'Shandra wishes to see you."

Before he even finished speaking, Vex launched herself off the bed in a blur of motion, rushing straight for the door.

The man jolted back a step, wide-eyed, clearly not expecting this action.

Devaultus, having long since learned to anticipate Vex's unpredictability, simply lifted a hand and caught her mid-motion. She skidded to a stop inches from Ed, her glare sharp enough to slice through bone.

The man hesitated before adding, "Devaultus only, please."

Vex's eyes narrowed dangerously. "What's your name?" she demanded.

The man blinked at her, clearly caught off guard. "It's Ed, ma'am."

Vex huffed, arms crossing tightly over her chest. "I might stab you while you sleep, Ed," she said flatly.

Ed visibly paled.

"That's enough, Vex," Devaultus muttered, rubbing his temples. "Just sit down. I'll see if I can't get us out of here."

Vex exhaled heavily, dramatically throwing herself back onto her bunk in frustration. From the depths of her hood, Jerry slithered out, his pulsating, ink-like form quivering in irritation. One of his slick tentacles emerged and wagged menacingly at Ed, as if seconding Vex's threat.

Ed swallowed hard. "I'll, uh… take you to the captain now," he mumbled with a cautious step back.

Devaultus sighed, straightening his coat and hat before stepping forward. Whatever Al'Shandra wanted, it was bound to be either an opportunity… or a disaster. With her, there was rarely an in between.

Devaultus watched as Ed practically fled down the corridor, the man moving with a haste that bordered on fear. Good. He should be afraid. Working for Al'Shandra was dangerous enough without throwing Vex's threats into the mix. With a sigh, Devaultus pulled the door shut behind him, ensuring the little menace stayed put. The last thing he needed was for Vex to slip out and cause some catastrophe that would land him in even deeper trouble.

For once, Devaultus wasn't inclined to take his time. He usually enjoyed the walk through the ship, the scent of sand and wood, the sway beneath his feet, the occasional glimpse of a scandalously dressed crewmember, but not today. Ed's hurried steps kept him at a brisk pace, and he followed without protest, irritation simmering just below the surface. Three days locked up. Three days of pacing, listening to Vex throw knives, and watching Blight scribble away like their situation didn't bother her at all.

Finally, they arrived at Al'Shandra's quarters. Ed knocked, and from within came her sultry voice, rich with amusement. "Come in."

Ed stepped aside, and Devaultus entered, shutting the door behind him. His gaze immediately settled on Al'Shandra, lounging behind her desk, exuding confidence and temptation in equal measure. Her clothing, as always, was strategically draped to emphasize every curve, her long legs crossed, her lips curled into that infuriatingly smug smirk.

"You've summoned me?" His voice carried his irritation, and he didn't bother to hide it as he strode forward and sank into the chair opposite her. He made himself comfortable, sprawling slightly, but the sharp edge in his gaze told her exactly how he felt about being kept locked up for days.

Al'Shandra's smirk only deepened, her yellow eyes glittering with amusement. "Oh, don't look at me like that, Devaultus. You're upset, I know. It's understandable." She leaned forward, resting her chin on her hand as she studied him. "But let's not forget, your little band of misfits burned down my second favorite ship."

He arched an eyebrow at her, his fingers drumming against the armrest. "You do realize I wasn't even here for that? I was off on a mission. For you."

Her smirk didn't waver. "Mmm. Yes. But those two are your problem. And what they do? That falls on your shoulders." She leaned back, stretching like a lazy cat, her barely-covered chest rising with the motion. "I suggest you learn to rein in your team."

Devaultus scowled. That was a responsibility he had absolutely no interest in.

He had long since learned to recognize when arguing was a pointless endeavor, and this was clearly one of those times. So, with a reluctant sigh, Devaultus relented, settling back in his chair with the air of a man resigned to his fate. "What is it you summoned me for, Al'Shandra?" His voice carried a clear note of irritation, though he kept his tone measured, unwilling to give her the satisfaction of seeing just how much being locked up had grated on his nerves.

Across the desk, Al'Shandra was watching him with barely contained amusement, her sultry lips curving into a smirk. The glint in her eyes was one of pure enjoyment; she was a cat toying with a mouse that thought it still had a chance to escape. She stretched languidly, the movement entirely unnecessary, but clearly designed to flaunt her curves as she leaned forward just enough to make sure he noticed. "We are still a ways from retrieving the final piece I need," she began, her voice a purr of calculated seduction, though her words carried an edge of seriousness. "In fact, at our current pace, it may take a few weeks to get there. And now that my faster ship has been reduced to smoldering wreckage, the one I am currently forced to grace with my presence has very little chance of outrunning Tarus."

At the mention of the name, Devaultus tensed slightly. He had known this was coming, but that didn't make the reality of it any more pleasant.

Al'Shandra's expression didn't falter. If anything, she seemed amused by his reaction. "Which means," she continued, "we will have to confront him, sooner rather than later. I see no way around it. That being said..." She leaned back, draping one leg over the other, her fingers drumming idly on the desk. "I do have a plan that should buy us a bit more time. However, that will only be delaying the inevitable."

Devaultus had never been under any illusions that he could avoid Tarus forever. That man was relentless, and sooner or later, their paths would cross once more. He had simply hoped that when that moment came, it would be under much more favorable circumstances, preferably, when Tarus was fast asleep, unaware of Devaultus slipping into his chambers, a blade whispering across his throat in the dead of night. But, from the way things were unfolding, it seemed fate had something much messier in mind.

He sighed again, rubbing his temples before giving her a sideways glance. "And this plan of yours?"

Al'Shandra's grin widened, turning almost mischievous, her eyes dancing with wicked delight. "Oh, darling, you're going to love this," she purred, shifting forward once more, her voice dropping to a conspiratorial whisper. "Let me tell you exactly what we're going to do."

# CHAPTER 18

# UNHOLY ALLIANCE: BLOOD FOR BLOOD

Tarus stood like a dark specter at the bow of his ship, his long, obsidian hair whipping around in the wind as if it, too, shared his frustration. His gaze was fixed forward, unblinking, willing the horizon to deliver Devaultus and his ragtag crew into his sight. Every fiber of his being itched for the moment he could see their broken bodies sprawled at his feet. He wanted them all dead. Every last one of them. The fools who dared to defy him. Hell, at this point, he wouldn't hesitate to snuff out his own daughter, if she were still alive; the world could burn, for all he cared. He could always breed more, create more chaos with his own twisted seed. He was the puppet master, and the strings ran long.

A dark presence slipped into the silence behind him, and Tarus didn't need to turn around to know who it was. The voice was unmistakable. A low, gravelly whisper that cut through the tension in the air. "My Lord," the figure said, the words weighed down by the ever-present gloom that clung to them. "I have word on what you wished me to check on."

Tarus didn't acknowledge him right away, his eyes remaining locked on the distant line of the ocean, as though he could will his enemies into existence by sheer force of will. He could already hear the sound of their bones cracking under his boots. But, in time, the voice of Silus cut through, once again. A reminder that his work never paused. "Speak," Tarus growled, voice low, dangerous.

Silus, ever the shadow, stepped up beside him, his presence a chill in the already cold air. Tarus didn't have to look at him to know the man's face, sharp angles, a thin nose, eyes as cold as the winter winds. What Silus lacked in size, he made up for with quiet brutality and unmatched precision.

The Seeker.

That's what Tarus called him, though others might've called him a tracker. Silus could find anything. He could hunt a whisper, track down the faintest sign of blood or a broken branch. He was a creature of the shadows, and he'd found something new to dig his teeth into. He'd been tracking the elusive, unrelenting Devaultus, a pain in the ass Tarus couldn't get rid of no matter how many resources he poured into hunting him down.

Silus was, after all, one of the rare shadow elves, an ancient breed, shorter than the normal elves, but far more lethal. Tarus had only crossed paths with a handful of them in his time, but none of them had left an impression like Silus had. While regular elves would tear into you with their claws, gnawing and tearing flesh straight from the bone in a brutal, savage fashion, shadow elves had a different way of doing things. They weren't mindless animals. No, they were sadistic, cruel to the core, but efficient in how they chose to torture their victims. They didn't eat their prey immediately. No, they captured you, tore you apart, slowly, methodically, cooking your pieces in front of you. Then, the ultimate cruelty: they fed you your own flesh while they ate alongside you. They savored it, unlike their more brutal cousins who tore and chewed with reckless abandon.

Yes, this particular shadow elf was a rarity. As dangerous as they came.

Silus had a way of keeping quiet, of being nearly invisible even in plain sight. He was as much a part of the darkness as Tarus himself, a tool that never broke, never faltered. His cold stare could freeze the blood in your veins.

Tarus exhaled through his nose, finally glancing sideways, his lips curling into a near imperceptible sneer. "And what have you learned?" he asked, his tone like ice, though inside he was bubbling with frustration and anticipation. The storm was coming, and he would break Devaultus. He would make them all pay.

The shadow elf turned toward him, his expression unreadable in the moonlight. "Devaultus... It's not just the ship, my Lord." He paused, letting the weight of the words settle between them, the silence heavy. "There are rumors. He's more than a simple rogue. More than just a thorn in your side. Something more dangerous."

Tarus' eyes narrowed. His mind whirred, trying to process this new information. "Go on," he demanded, his patience wearing thin.

Silus continued, his voice a whisper in the wind. "The man has ties to the forbidden, the Abyss itself, some say. The stories don't match. Some say he wields an ancient power, one that can revive the dead, control the very forces of life and death. Some say he's a hero. Others... a monster. Either way, he's not just some mercenary anymore. He's a force to be reckoned with."

Tarus took in the words, his gaze turning colder. A force of nature. That was exactly what he wanted to destroy. Devaultus was more than an annoyance. But he'd be the one to tear him apart. No one else could do it. He had the power to destroy him. He would grind him down, piece by piece, until there was nothing left but ash and blood.

The last thing Tarus wanted was to play into the rumors of this new, formidable enemy. But he couldn't ignore it. He would take Devaultus and rip him apart; but it seemed there were far more layers to this war than he'd anticipated. And with those layers came new dangers, new threats.

But he was ready. Always ready. And he was already planning his next move.

Silus stood with the grace of a predator, his white hair slicked back, tight and flawless, as if nothing could ruffle him. His pointed nose gave him a sharp, almost hawkish appearance, and his near-black eyes gleamed with an unsettling intensity. His athletic build and quick reflexes made him a nightmare to outrun: many had tried, but few had succeeded. He was a perfect match for the brutal world of Tarus, a relentless hunter in a sea of prey.

Tarus, standing tall on the bow of his ship, turned his steely gaze to Silus, the faintest flicker of interest crossing his face. His voice was low, but the weight of authority carried it. "Is there anything else?" he asked, though his tone implied he'd already been anticipating this news.

Silus, always precise, nodded slowly. "It seems this Devaultus is somehow tied to one Sakatorious. The details remain... murky, but anyone who may have known the full story is either dead or disappeared. It's a tangled mess, my Lord, one I've yet to untangle fully."

Tarus' sharp brow arched at the mention of Sakatorious. "Sakatorious..." He mulled the name over, savoring the potential implications. His mind worked quickly. "Interesting. Have a message sent to him. I want to speak with him directly. After all, he's one of The Blood Brothers, a faction we've long been allied with. If there's anything worth investigating here, surely the two of us can strike a deal."

Silus gave a curt nod, his cloak fluttering in the cool breeze as he spun to issue the orders. His voice rang out, sharp and commanding, as he called for a missive to be dispatched to Sakatorious without delay. "As you wish, my Lord," he said, the words almost formal, as though he'd said them a hundred times before.

Tarus remained on the bow, his gaze locked on the horizon, thoughts churning beneath the surface. He was not a patient man, but he could make the ship move faster with his mind if he willed it, urging it forward with a deep, unwavering will. He had always known his enemies would come; it was only a matter of time before the ship he was hunting would come into view. His thoughts went to Devaultus, and he grinned. The time would come when they would meet, he would make sure of it.

Two days passed, and in that time, Tarus had grown restless, the quiet hum of anticipation filling his every thought. Now, seated in the dim light of his private quarters, he idly chewed on a piece of stone bread. Normally, he would never deign to partake in such humble fare, but today, he was only after something that would suffice. His focus was razor-sharp, he could feel the distance between his ship and Devaultus shrinking with every passing moment. The hunt was drawing near its climax, and Tarus' sword, as always, thirsted for blood, specifically the blood of Devaultus. And Tarus was a man who never denied his blade its due.

As the ship's creaking and the wind's howls filled the air, there came a sharp knock at his door, disrupting his reverie. "Enter," he called, his voice a low rumble like distant thunder.

The door swung open, revealing Silus, his tall, lean figure darkening the doorway. His usual quiet confidence was in place, but there was something about his stance that told Tarus the news was important.

"Lord Tarus," Silus began, his voice smooth, almost too calm for Tarus' taste. "Sakatorious will be boarding in moments."

Tarus didn't hesitate. His fingers tightened around the stone bread, crushing it into a ball with unspoken frustration. He downed the last of his ale in one swift motion, the bitter taste matching the growing tension within him.

"Very well," Tarus said, his voice a cutting edge. "Let us have words with him, then." His eyes narrowed, locking onto Silus with a glint of determination. "Ready the crew. Just in case something goes wrong."

Silus gave a quick nod, his cloak swishing around him as he turned on his heel, stepping out with the same silent grace that marked his every move.

Tarus stood, his muscles coiling; a beast ready to spring. He strode toward the corridor, the sound of his boots echoing off the walls. The air on the ship was thick with tension as he made his way to the deck. Each step was deliberate, each movement calculated.

When he reached the ship's edge, Tarus paused, his eyes scanning the horizon. The sea stretched out before him, dark and foreboding, as though it could feel the weight of what was about to unfold. His fingers gripped the rail tightly, and for a moment, he stared down into the swirling waters, his mind racing with the possibilities. Sakatorious. One of The Blood Brothers. If anyone could be of use in his pursuit of Devaultus, it was him.

But even as he stood there, his gaze fixed on the distant shore, a cold, uneasy feeling crept up his spine. The hunt was almost over. And yet, something told him that the real challenge was still ahead.

It was said that the Bloody Hand was more than just a symbol, it was an army unto itself. And Sakatorious embodied that very image. Standing tall at the back of a massive, scaled lizard, the creature glided effortlessly across the Sand Sea, its sleek body moving like a shadow beneath the scorching sun. The beast's leathery hide shimmered as it sliced through the dunes, a perfect companion to the imposing figure of Sakatorious.

The man himself was a sight to behold. His massive frame, already towering over most, was cloaked in intimidating armor that seemed forged to enhance his sheer presence. The plate was intricately designed, the gleam of its polished surface reflecting the harsh sunlight like the edge of a blade. He looked every bit the part of a warlord, a titan of destruction. The heavy armor didn't just add to his stature, it made him seem even more colossal, as if his very form could swallow the world. His helm, an artful piece crafted to mimic the fearsome visage of a dragon, completed the intimidating look. The dragon's eyes seemed to stare into the horizon, unblinking, as if daring any who stood in his path to challenge him.

A long, blood-red cloak billowed behind him, fluttering wildly in the wind, the fabric snapping like a flag of war as it trailed in the wake of his movement. His massive hand, calloused and scarred, gripped the reins tightly, the leather almost groaning beneath the pressure. His focus remained unyielding as he glared ahead, scanning the vast, empty horizon with the calm, calculating gaze of a man who had conquered more than his share of challenges. His expression, dark and unwavering, betrayed nothing: he was a force of nature, prepared to crush anything that dared to stand in his way.

Sakatorious was not alone, though. The company he kept was just as intriguing as the warlord himself. A woman rode alongside him, her figure impossible to ignore. She was the embodiment of an hourglass, ample in the chest, narrowing to a slim, toned waist before flaring out into full, well-rounded hips that swayed with each movement of her mount. Her curves were emphasized further by the way she carried herself: an effortless, natural grace that made her look both delicate and deadly at the same time.

Yet it wasn't just her figure that caught Tarus' eye. There was something else, something odd about her face. Perched on her nose was a strange contraption, unlike anything he had ever seen before. It wasn't a mask, at least not in the traditional sense. It was made of crystal, clear as ice, but cut and shaped in a way that allowed it to rest on her face without obscuring it completely. The structure framed her sharp eyes, and the way the sunlight hit its surface sent tiny, prismatic reflections dancing across her features. It was as though she peered at the world through a thin sheet of frozen glass, yet it didn't seem to hinder her sight in the slightest. If anything, it made her gaze all the more piercing, as though she could see things others could not.

And then there was her hair, a deep, rich red that cascaded down her back like a river of fire, catching the light in a way that made it seem almost alive. It was a striking contrast against her fair skin and the crystalline lenses that adorned her face. The fiery strands shifted in the wind, untamed yet elegant, much like the woman herself.

She was an enigma, a contradiction. Small and delicate, yet strikingly voluptuous. Beautiful, yet otherworldly. A stark contrast to the hulking form of Sakatorious, yet she moved with a quiet confidence that suggested she was no mere accessory to his power: she was a force of her own. Tarus watched her closely, narrowing his eyes. There was something about her, something more than just her unusual appearance. And Tarus did not like mysteries.

On Sakatorious' other side, a man, a human, by the looks of him, rode in silence, shrouded by a dark cloak that obscured his features completely. Tarus couldn't make out his face, but that didn't bother him. There was something about the man's demeanor that told Tarus that looks didn't matter. The cloak seemed to hide more than just his identity. Perhaps this was a man of hidden power, one who preferred to remain in the shadows. But aside from his lack of distinguishing features, there was nothing remarkable about him. He appeared... ordinary. Yet, in a world where nothing was ever truly ordinary, that might mean everything.

Tarus' eyes narrowed as he took in the trio's approach. The Sand Sea stretched out in every direction, its golden waves rolling like a vast, barren ocean. The wind whipped against his cloak, the sound of it mingling with the distant cries of the creatures that called this desert home. Despite the endless expanse of the sand beneath them, the arrival of Sakatorious felt almost... monumental. It was as though this moment was the beginning of something larger, something Tarus could feel creeping in the air.

The time for words had come. And Tarus was ready. He would have his audience with the warlord.

Sakatorious boarded the massive vessel with the unshakable confidence of a man who had nothing to fear. Each step was measured, deliberate, and the wooden deck groaned faintly beneath his weight as he moved forward, his towering frame casting long shadows in the dim light. His companions followed closely behind, their presence nearly as intriguing as the warlord himself.

He came to a stop directly before Tarus, the two men standing eye to eye, twin monoliths of power and command. Tarus was not accustomed to looking another man in the eye like this. He was used to being the most imposing force in any room, the figure that drew silence and submission with his sheer presence alone. But Sakatorious was different. The air around him was heavy, filled with a quiet but undeniable menace, as though the weight of countless battles clung to him like a second skin.

"Lord Sakatorious," Tarus greeted, his voice carrying the authority of a man who expected respect but would not offer it freely.

"Lord Tarus," came the reply, Sakatorious' voice a deep, rumbling growl that seemed to resonate in the very bones of the ship.

There was no unnecessary posturing, no wasted words. These were men who understood power, who had spilled enough blood to know that respect was earned through action, not conversation.

"Let us find somewhere to talk. In private," Tarus offered, his gaze never leaving Sakatorious as he turned, leading the way toward the ship's meeting hall.

Sakatorious followed without hesitation, his companions moving in sync behind him. The woman with the crystalline lenses walked with an effortless, almost feline grace, her fiery red hair catching the light as she moved, while the cloaked man beside her remained eerily silent, an indistinct presence wrapped in shadows.

The meeting hall was a grand chamber, its centerpiece a large, heavy wooden table, scarred and worn from years of use. Around it sat numerous chairs, each one carved with intricate designs that spoke of wealth and power. The air here was thick, carrying the scent of salt, old parchment, and the faint metallic tang of blood, perhaps just a lingering trick of the mind, or perhaps something more real.

As the group entered, the tension in the room was palpable. This was not a gathering of allies, nor was it yet a meeting of enemies. It was something in between, a moment balanced on the edge of a knife, waiting to tip one way or the other.

The tension in the meeting hall thickened as the powerful figures took their seats. Lord Tarus sat on one side of the grand table, his large form imposing even in stillness. To his right sat Silus, ever the shadow at his master's side, sharp-eyed and unreadable. On his left sat The Puppeteer, a figure whose very presence was an enigma, a whisper of something unsettling beneath a composed exterior.

Across from them, Lord Sakatorious settled into his own chair, his presence no less formidable. To his right sat the red-haired woman, her hourglass figure poised yet relaxed, her striking features framed by that strange crystalline device that clung to her face like a second set of eyes. The glass-like lenses caught the light, shimmering faintly as if alive with some hidden energy. To his left sat the cloaked man, still silent, still unreadable, as though he existed just on the edge of reality itself.

Sakatorious regarded Tarus with measured curiosity, his deep-set eyes scanning the warlord as if peeling back the layers of his intent. "Now then, Lord Tarus," he said, his voice as steady as a rolling storm, "what was the reason for this requested audience?"

Tarus exhaled slowly through his nose, his fingers tapping idly against the wood of the table. He wasn't certain how this conversation would unfold, and that uncertainty gnawed at him. What if Devaultus was an ally to Sakatorious? The wrong word here could make an enemy of the Bloody Hand, and that was a mistake Tarus had no interest in making.

"My Lord," Tarus began carefully, choosing his words with the precision of a man navigating a battlefield of unseen dangers. "I was wondering if you may have heard of one known as Devaultus?"

The reaction was instant and violent.

Sakatorious shot to his feet with a force that sent his chair toppling backward, the heavy wood slamming against the floor with a deafening crack. His powerful frame loomed over the table, his fists clenched as a roar of fury erupted from him, shaking the very walls of the chamber.

"You will never speak that name in my presence again!" he bellowed, his voice a force of nature, raw and filled with venomous rage.

Tarus did not flinch, but there was a flicker of wide-eyed concern in his gaze; not of fear, but of calculated wariness. This reaction was more intense than he had anticipated, and that alone made him rethink his approach. Across the table, the two companions who had followed Sakatorious into the meeting looked outright shaken by his sudden outburst. The red-haired woman tensed, her lips parting slightly as though she wanted to speak but thought better of it. The cloaked man remained still, though even he seemed unnerved, his posture shifting as if he expected further violence.

Tarus lifted a hand, a gesture of calm. "My apologies, my Lord," he said smoothly, his tone even, steady. "I meant no disrespect. You see, he is the one I pursue. My people understand that you have a connection to him, and I wished to ensure that my slaying him would not anger the Bloody Hand."

His words hung in the air like the blade of an executioner's axe, as he waited for the next move to determine whether it would fall.

Lord Sakatorious narrowed his eyes, suspicion flickering across his face like the shadow of a blade. How in the Abyss had this man come to suspect a connection? He had made certain, painstakingly, ruthlessly certain, that anyone who so much as whispered of it had been silenced. Snuffed out. Reduced to nothing but bloodstains and forgotten screams. Yet here Tarus sat, prying at something that should have remained buried.

For a moment, Sakatorious entertained the simplest solution: gutting Tarus where he sat, painting the ship's walls with his entrails, and reducing every soul on board to lifeless husks. It would be easier. Cleaner. No loose ends. No lingering questions.

And yet...

His fingers drummed against the table as a far more enticing thought slithered into his mind. Tarus wanted Devaultus dead. He had no idea what the fool had done to earn the man's wrath, but for once, it wasn't his own problem. Perhaps, for the first time in years, he wouldn't have to dirty his own hands with that particular nuisance. Devaultus had been like a curse upon his existence, returning again and again when he should have rotted away in some forgotten plane. No matter how deep he was cast into the Abyss, no matter how thoroughly Sakatorious thought he had rid himself of that failure, he always clawed his way back.

But now?

Now, here sat Tarus, an unwitting blade poised at Devaultus' throat. Sakatorious slowly leaned back into his chair, his lips curling into something that wasn't quite a smile. Let Tarus chase him. Let Tarus kill him. And when the deed was done, he would personally see to it that Tarus met the same fate. There would be no trace of their connection left in the world. No lingering shame.

Sakatorious exhaled slowly, his momentary rage tempered by cold calculation. "Very well," he said, voice now smooth as steel drawn from its sheath. "Tell me, Lord Tarus... how exactly do you plan to kill Devaultus?"

Tarus leaned forward, his grin widening as he looked Sakatorious dead in the eye. There was a wicked gleam in his gaze, a deep, insatiable hunger for the suffering he was about to describe. He wanted Sakatorious to know, to feel every twisted detail of what he had planned.

"I won't just kill him, my Lord," Tarus said, his voice laced with dark amusement. "No, that would be too simple, too merciful. A man like Devaultus doesn't deserve an easy end. He deserves pain, drawn out over days, weeks if I have the time. I will break him, body and mind, and when there is nothing left but a hollowed-out husk, I'll carve the last breath from his throat."

He leaned back, tapping a finger against the table as though savoring the thoughts before continuing.

"First, I'll take him alive. That part is important. He'll be bound, shackled with iron so heavy it digs into his flesh, so tight it grinds bone against bone. I want him to feel his own strength wane with every passing second. And then, I'll suspend him in the brig, his arms stretched above his head, his toes barely touching the floor, just enough so that every breath, every twitch, is agony."

Tarus exhaled, tilting his head slightly, his expression almost dreamy. "Then the real fun begins. I'll carve into him, small cuts at first, thin slices with a razor's edge. Just enough to make him bleed, to make him feel his own flesh part under my hand. And when the pain starts to dull, I'll bring out the salt. I'll rub it into every wound, let it sink into his skin, into his bones. Maybe I'll use vinegar instead, just to watch the way it burns."

He chuckled darkly. "Of course, physical pain is only the beginning. No man truly breaks until he watches everything he loves crumble before him. That's when I'll bring in his companions, one by one. The pirate queen... Al'Shandra, isn't it? Oh, she'll be a fun one to break. A woman like that, so full of fire, so used to being in control... imagine what she'll look like on her knees, begging me to stop. I'll strip away that confidence, that strength, until there's nothing left but a sobbing, desperate wretch."

He licked his lips, savoring the thought. "And then, there's the little black-haired one. There's something delicate about her, something... innocent. I'll make sure Devaultus watches as I rip that innocence away. He'll scream, he'll fight, but he won't be able to do a damn thing to stop me. And that... that will break him more than any knife ever could."

Tarus' grin stretched wider, his fingers drumming against the table in anticipation. "And when he's nothing but a shattered remnant of himself, when his spirit has been wrung dry and his body can barely hold itself together... then, and only then, will I kill him. Maybe I'll flay him alive, strip the skin from his bones inch by inch. Or maybe I'll crucify him against the mast of my ship, let the sun and the wind and the sand finish what I started. If I'm feeling especially creative, I might even send him back to you in pieces. A finger one week, an ear the next. His tongue, maybe, just so you know he won't be spewing any more nonsense. And finally, his head, preserved just enough so you can see the exact moment he realized he was nothing."

Tarus exhaled deeply, satisfied, his grin never faltering. "That is how I will end Devaultus, my Lord. Slowly. Painfully. Completely."

Sakatorious exhaled sharply through his nose, the weight of his own history pressing against his chest like a vise. With a slow, deliberate motion, he settled himself back into his seat, fingers drumming against the armrest. His gaze, cold and calculating, locked onto Tarus.

"Devaultus was a failed experiment," he said, his voice laced with venom and something deeper, something dangerously close to regret. "I thought I had removed that blemish from my life long ago. Yet, like a festering wound, he lingers." His lips curled in disdain. "You have my blessing to destroy him in any way you can. I want there to be nothing remaining of him. Burn his name from existence. Kill everyone who knows him. Any friend, any ally, any family: wipe them from this world. Make them disappear."

Across the table, Tarus grinned, his teeth flashing like those of a predator who had just scented fresh blood. This was better than he could have hoped. He had entertained the idea that Sakatorious might join him in the hunt, but this? This was just as satisfying. The mighty Sakatorious, a warrior feared across the sands, was so desperate to distance himself from Devaultus that he was willing to let another man handle it for him. That spoke volumes.

"Very well, my Lord," Tarus purred, leaning forward slightly, his massive hands pressing into the table's surface. "I'll see to it personally."

Sakatorious stood without another word, his movements fluid, his cape sweeping behind him as he strode toward the door. The tension in the air shifted, crackling like a storm waiting to break. Just as he reached the threshold, he hesitated, turning his head slightly to glance back over his shoulder.

"Send me his head when you're through, Tarus."

And with that, he was gone, leaving only the weight of his command hanging in the air like a death sentence.

As Lord Sakatorious turned to leave the ship, he paused, his imposing presence casting a shadow over the deck. He glanced back at Zen with a cold, calculating look. "Zen, you will stay and lend your knowledge. You know what we are dealing with." His words were clipped, commanding, as if the very idea of asking her opinion was a chore for him.

Zen felt the weight of his gaze like a physical force, pressing down on her shoulders. She hesitated for a moment, her hands instinctively fidgeting with the fabric of her cloak as the wind whipped around them. Despite the heavy armor of confidence she had built for herself, there was something unnerving about being in his presence. She swallowed hard, trying to steady herself, forcing her voice to stay steady despite the knot in her chest. "As you wish," she murmured, her words tinged with a hollow emptiness she couldn't quite hide.

Lord Sakatorious gave a curt nod before turning, his cloak billowing behind him as he strode purposefully toward the gangplank. His companion followed close behind, their movements swift and silent, leaving Zen standing alone on the deck. The ship's wooden boards creaked under the wind's pressure, but it felt as if the air itself was heavier, pressing down on her with the force of the command she had just been given.

She watched as the two men departed, leaving her with nothing but the harsh sounds of the Sand Sea and the oppressive weight of her own thoughts. The cool sea breeze was a far cry from the warmth of the ship's interior, and Zen's heart skipped a beat at the thought of the isolation she was left with. Her hands wrung together nervously as she turned to face Lord Tarus.

"Where are my quarters?" she asked, her voice barely above a whisper, betraying the anxiety that churned inside her. Tarus, ever the obedient servant, nodded with a slight bow and motioned for a man nearby to lead her to her designated room.

The guide led Zen through the ship's labyrinthine halls, their footsteps echoing in the otherwise quiet space. The ship had an oppressive feel, the walls close and unyielding, as though the very vessel was closing in around her. Zen felt trapped. She could hear the muffled laughter and conversation of the crew in the distance, but it all felt so far away, so out of reach.

Finally, they arrived at her quarters, and the door swung open with a creak. Zen stepped inside, her eyes scanning the small room. It was one of the nicer quarters, but that was little consolation. The bed was made neatly, a small desk sat against one wall, and the only real decoration was a lone painting on the opposite wall. Nothing particularly special, yet to Zen, it felt cold and empty, just like her.

She nodded politely to the man who closed the door behind her, the creek of the hinges echoing in the quiet room. For a long moment, Zen just stood there, staring at her reflection in the glass of the small window, the moonlight illuminating her features. She reached up and pushed a few strands of her red hair behind her ear, her fingers trembling slightly as they brushed the locks back into place. Her glasses, perched delicately on her nose, slid a little down, and she quickly adjusted them, but the action felt automatic, as if she was trying to maintain some semblance of control over the chaos within her.

Once the door clicked shut, the illusion of strength she had been carefully constructing throughout the day crumbled. The confident woman, poised and in control, was a mask she wore for Sakatorious and the others. It was a lie, a facade that kept her alive, kept her from being broken by the power she was forced to serve. Zen slouched, the weight of the act lifting, and for the first time since she'd stepped aboard the ship, she allowed herself to feel.

The tears that had been threatening to fall all day finally made their presence known, welling up in her eyes. She bit her lip, trying to hold them back, but the strain was unbearable. Her hands clutched at the edge of the table near the window, the rough wood scraping against her skin as if it could offer her some comfort. The sharp chill of the night air seemed to seep into her bones, matching the icy emptiness she felt inside.

Her breath hitched, but she quickly steadied herself, her heart pounding in her chest. No. She couldn't break down. Not now, not here. Not when she had to keep up the illusion. Sakatorious' words, *You will lend your knowledge*, rang in her ears like an unspoken command. She was more than just a tool for him; she had to be. She couldn't afford to slip, to let him see the cracks, the fear that lurked behind her fragile composure.

Zen blinked back the tears and lifted her chin, forcing herself to stand tall once more. She adjusted her glasses again, this time with more force, as if the simple act of correcting them could correct everything else. The brokenness inside her felt all-consuming, but she couldn't let it show. She had to be the strong, capable woman everyone expected her to be.

With a deep breath, Zen squared her shoulders and turned toward the small bed, willing herself to move forward. She was trapped in this role, this life. And she had to play the part. She had no choice. The weight of her isolation, of her fear, was something she would carry silently. For Sakatorious. For everyone else.

*Stay strong, Zen.* She repeated the words in her mind like a mantra. It was the only thing that could keep her from completely shattering.

Zen stood alone in the dimly lit quarters, the creak of the ship's wood the only sound in the otherwise silent room. She glanced at the door one last time, ensuring it was securely shut before allowing the mask of confidence she'd worn all day to slip away. Her breath caught in her throat as her fingers gently traced the scars across her back. The lash marks were deep, jagged reminders of the cruelty Lord Sakatorious had forced on her. They were like a map of her torment, a map that stretched across her body and psyche.

The fresh air from the open porthole barely touched her as she stood, motionless for a moment. The silence in her quarters was suffocating. This place, these walls, had become more of a prison than a sanctuary. She hadn't been free for a long time, not since the day Lord Sakatorious had taken her. He made her wear confidence like armor, forcing her to act like someone she wasn't. It was exhausting. And, in the dead of night, with only her thoughts to keep her company, she could no longer hide the truth: she was broken.

Zen's fingers gently caressed the lacy fabric of her sleeping silks, a fragile semblance of comfort that was the only thing she could hold onto in the vast, unforgiving world she was trapped in. She had learned the art of hiding her fear, but tonight, tonight, her heart could no longer bear the weight.

Her mind drifted to Shade. She hadn't been able to look at him the same since she'd been forced to study him, forced to watch as he, too, had been shaped and broken by Sakatorious. She shuddered, a cold tremor running down her spine at the thought. Shade was a man, a shell of a man, molded by years of torment, now little more than a puppet. His mind was shattered, his will nothing more than the dust Sakatorious had left behind, ready to be reshaped at the whims of their sadistic master.

Zen swallowed the lump in her throat. She couldn't think of him. She couldn't think of any of it. The nightmares were still fresh, those nights where she saw things she would never speak of, where the memories of her 'studies' left her lying awake, drenched in sweat. But she was trapped. What could she do? Sakatorious had her bound in invisible chains, chains that made her both a slave and a soldier, both broken and forced to act whole.

With a deep, shaky breath, Zen slipped under the covers of her bed, the silky fabric barely covering the coolness of the sheets. She had to sleep, or the demons of her past would swallow her whole. But even as her body tried to relax, her mind was racing, flooded with fears she couldn't escape. The mere thought of Devaultus made her shiver. His name had caused such a stir on the ship, so much anger from Lord Sakatorious. And though she didn't know who he was, only that he was something Sakatorious despised, there was something about him that intrigued her.

Maybe it was the idea of someone who could stand against the very man who controlled her. Maybe it was the mystery, the chaos that surrounded him. Or perhaps it was the faintest sliver of hope that, just maybe, he could end it all. Could he free her from the clutches of Sakatorious?

She shook her head, burying the thought deep inside. There was no freedom. Not for people like her. Not for people like Dust. And certainly not for anyone who dared to cross Lord Sakatorious.

Zen closed her eyes, pulling the covers tight against her chest, her thoughts swirling into a chaotic storm as she tried to drift off into what would surely be an uneasy sleep.

Zen lay in her bed, the faint creak of the ship's timbers the only sound breaking the silence. The sheets were cool against her skin, but her mind refused to settle. She tossed and turned, unable to escape the weight of her thoughts. It wasn't even late enough to be in bed, but here she was, restless and tangled in the quiet of her quarters.

She hadn't heard much about Devaultus, but what little she did know unsettled her. All she had were the vague whispers, the passing comments from Lord Sakatorious and the others. They spoke of him with such disdain, such loathing. Tarus, especially, seemed to have a particular vendetta against him. Zen had only heard bits and pieces, nothing concrete, but the hatred between them was palpable. She had never been told exactly what Devaultus had done, but whatever it was, it had left a deep scar. The way Tarus spoke of him, if you could even call it speaking, was venomous. It was as if Devaultus had done something unforgivable, and the rage that Tarus carried with him was almost overwhelming. And Lord Sakatorious... well, he barely even mentioned the name, but there was a sharpness in his tone when he did. That alone was enough to tell Zen that whatever connection they shared, it was nothing short of toxic.

She tried to focus on that. Tarus was dangerous, she knew that much. A man like him, so full of rage, so intent on destruction, was not someone you wanted to get in the way of. And yet, for some reason, he wanted to hunt down and kill Devaultus. But why? Why was this man so hated? What could he have possibly done to earn such disdain from two of the most powerful men she'd ever known?

Zen shifted under the covers, her thoughts slipping and sliding like the ship beneath her. She didn't know the details of Devaultus' crimes, if there were any, but the way Tarus and Sakatorious acted, the way they spoke, it was as if he was more than just a target. It was as if he were a symbol of something, something far more dangerous than just one man. What had Devaultus done to earn that kind of enmity?

She couldn't push the questions away, no matter how much she tried to ignore them. And that uncertainty gnawed at her. Was there something more to this situation? Something she was missing? She closed her eyes, trying to clear her head, but the lack of answers made sleep impossible. Every time she thought about the looming confrontation, the fear of the unknown crept in. What if Devaultus fought back? What if he survived? Or worse, what if he wasn't the monster they all seemed to think he was?

Her mind wouldn't quiet, not even for a moment. She could feel the weight of the unknown pressing against her, and the dark waters of the coming conflict loomed larger than she could ignore. She wanted to be far from all of this, away from the endless schemes, the hate, the violence, but she knew she was trapped. There was no escaping the chaos Lord Sakatorious had thrust her into. With a frustrated sigh, Zen turned onto her side, clutching the pillow tightly to her chest. Maybe, just maybe, sleep would find her eventually. But for now, she was alone with her thoughts, and they weren't letting her rest.

# CHAPTER 19

# WHAT LURKS IN THE HEART OF MAN

Tarus stood at the bow of his ship, his gaze fixed on the vessel ahead. They were closing in fast. Around him, his crew moved with practiced urgency, securing weapons, tightening ropes, and preparing for battle. The air crackled with tension, the scent of salt and steel mingling as they neared their prey. Tarus grinned to himself, his fingers tightening on the hilt of his sword. Today, Devaultus would pay for every insult, every setback, every moment he had been a thorn in his flesh.

A small red-haired woman stepped up beside him, her posture rigid, her expression unreadable as she stared at the enemy ship. She was an enigma, this woman; two days aboard his ship, always watching, always listening. There was something unnerving about her, though he hadn't yet decided if it was caution or curiosity that made him wary.

"So this is your... white whale?" she murmured, her voice calm but carrying the edge of something unspoken.

Tarus turned his head slightly, eyeing her with a raised brow. "What in the Abyss is a whale?" he asked, irritation creeping into his tone. This woman had a habit of spouting nonsense, and his patience for it was wearing thin.

She didn't answer, only continued to watch the ship ahead. Tarus exhaled sharply, shaking his head. "I grow tired of the gibberish you spew," he muttered. "When will your owner be back to claim you?"

Her head snapped toward him, her green eyes flaring with sharp disapproval. "You will watch your tongue," she warned, her voice as cold as the sea beneath them. "If things do not go as Lord Sakatorious wishes, he will be more than happy to remove it... and feed it to you."

Tarus smirked at her, unbothered by the threat. "I'd like to see him try."

The woman said nothing more, only turned her gaze back to the ship ahead. Tarus chuckled to himself. This was going to be an interesting battle.

Tarus wasn't sure if this small red-haired woman held any real sway over Lord Sakatorious, but the way she spoke, so unwavering, so assured, made him wary. There was no hesitation in her voice, no trace of doubt, only a quiet authority that carried the weight of something dangerous. He studied her for a lingering moment, his mind turning over the possibility that she was more than she appeared. But whatever game she played, it would have to wait.

Without another word, he turned sharply on his heel and stalked across the deck, his heavy boots thudding against the worn planks. His sharp gaze swept over his crew, men who had fought and bled at his side, who knew the taste of battle as intimately as they knew the sea.

"Ready your weapons!" Tarus bellowed, his voice a crack of thunder over the wind-whipped deck. "We fight within the hour!"

Lord Tarus, like many of the ruling Lords, understood the power of metal in a world where it was a rare and valuable commodity. From the moment he claimed dominion over his lands, he made it his mission to acquire and hoard as much iron and steel as possible, knowing that control over these materials meant control over warfare itself.

Unlike lesser Lords who squandered their resources, Tarus saw beyond simple greed: he saw strategy. He bought out every blacksmith, every smelter, every scrap of metal he could find. He sent his soldiers to confiscate weapons from villages, melting them down and reforging them for his own army. Even farming tools were seized when necessary, their iron repurposed for war. If anyone dared resist, they were made an example of, ensuring that no peasant questioned his right to rule.

Most Lords followed a similar practice, not only to equip their forces but to keep the common folk weak, ensuring they never had the means to rise up against their masters. A blade in a farmer's hands was a threat, but a blade in Tarus' armory was power. By keeping the supply of metal strictly in the hands of the nobility, rebellions were crushed before they could ever begin. The people toiled in servitude, unarmed and helpless, while Tarus' warriors strode the land clad in steel, enforcing his will with iron fists.

Through this iron-fisted rule, Tarus ensured that when battle came, his forces would be the best equipped, his enemies would be at a disadvantage, and his people would remain obedient: too starved, too afraid, and too unarmed to even dream of resistance.

The ship exploded into motion. Men scrambled to their positions, loading weapons, sharpening blades, and securing armor. The scent of salt and iron filled the air, the promise of bloodshed looming on the horizon. Tarus grinned, the anticipation of battle sending a wicked thrill through him. Today, Devaultus would finally pay.

Zen gasped softly as Tarus stepped away, her chest rising and falling rapidly, as though she had been holding her breath in anticipation of a blow that never came. Her body remained tense, muscles coiled as if still expecting pain, but none arrived. Perhaps the painful lessons Lord Sakatorious had beaten into her had some use after all. Fear kept her in line, but it also kept her alive.

She leaned forward against the ship's railing, her grip tightening as her mind raced. What had she gotten herself into? The chaos of the battle ahead loomed over her like a storm, and she found herself drowning in the hopelessness of it all. The thought of throwing herself over the railing into the endless Sand Sea flickered in her mind, but she dismissed it just as quickly. That particular weakness had been beaten out of her long ago. She was his. Only his. No matter how far she sailed, no matter whose company she kept, she would always belong to Lord Sakatorious. The brand on her soul burned hotter than any iron ever could.

A lump rose in her throat, her vision blurred, but she blinked rapidly, forcing the tears away before they could spill over. Weakness had no place here. It was a dangerous thing to show among men like Tarus, men who smelled fear like blood in the water. She inhaled deeply, steadying herself, then exhaled with a sigh, forcing her spine straight, her expression remaining calm.

"Very well then," she murmured to herself, her voice barely more than a whisper against the desert wind.

But what was her purpose in all this? What role was she meant to play? Sakatorious had forbidden her from fighting, from even holding a weapon. She was to be an observer, nothing more. But how could she be of any use like this? She clenched her hands into fists at her sides, frustration bubbling beneath the surface.

She knew nothing of this Devaultus, nothing of why Sakatorious and Tarus hated him so deeply. His was a name whispered in malice; he was a man spoken of only in rage and with disdain. But beyond that, she was blind. Sakatorious had kept her in the dark about so much. And yet, she had the sickening feeling that before long, she would learn exactly what sort of monster had captured their wrath.

The ship surged forward, cutting through the Sand Sea like a beast on the hunt. Tarus stood at the helm, his eyes locked onto the vessel ahead, his bloodlust rising with every second. The air crackled with tension as his crew scrambled to obey, pushing themselves and the ship to their very limits.

"Ready the planks for boarding!" Tarus roared, his voice carrying across the deck like the tolling of a war drum. His grip on the railing tightened as he counted down. "Launchers in three... two... one... Fire!"

A deafening twang split the air as the ballistae loosed their massive bolts. The deadly projectiles screamed through the sky before slamming into the enemy ship's hull, splintering wood and tearing through the side like it were mere paper. The force of impact sent a violent shudder through the vessel.

Chaos erupted within the targeted ship. Tarus watched with satisfaction as shadows darted back and forth, their movements frantic. His sharp eyes caught the glint of weapons, blades hastily drawn, their crew scrambling to mount a defense; but they had been caught off guard.

A slow, satisfied grin spread across his face. "Good," he murmured, gripping the hilt of his weapon. "This should be over shortly."

The planks clattered across the gap between the two ships, the harsh sound like thunder on the storm-tossed deck. The crew, drunk with bloodlust, surged forward like a wave crashing against the rocks, their eyes wild with the thrill of the coming battle. Steel clanged against wood, and the scent of sweat and salt filled the air. Tarus stood tall, watching as his men crossed the planks, weapons drawn and ready. It wasn't long before two of them arrived at a large, reinforced door, their axes raised to hack furiously at the thick wood.

Then, with a tremendous crash, the door exploded outward. A hulking form ripped through the debris, the sheer force of its movement sending splinters flying. It was a Cordyphage, a creature like nothing Tarus had ever seen. Towering at nearly eight feet, its body was a grotesque fusion of muscle and sinew, thick, mottled gray skin stretching taut over its bulging form. The creature's head was an unnatural blend of human and monstrous, with deep-set eyes glowing a sinister green. Jagged, dark horns twisted from its skull, curving upward like blades aimed at the heavens, and a thick mane of black, wiry hair ran down its back. Its mouth opened wide, showing rows of serrated, sharp teeth, dripping with venomous saliva.

With inhuman strength, the Cordyphage grabbed one of the men by the head, its clawed fingers digging into his skull. It slammed him with brutal force against the nearest wall, the sickening crunch of bone and flesh barely audible over the battle cries that echoed through the ship. The other man, trembling with fear, turned and bolted, desperate to escape, but the Cordyphage was faster. It extended a spined hand, sharp like a weapon, and thrust it through the fleeing man's shoulder. The poor soul let out a strangled scream before being launched like a rag doll across the gap, his limp form crashing onto the deck of Tarus' ship.

More figures emerged from the wreckage of the doorframe. Another eight Cordyphages, each more terrifying than the last, their hulking forms filling the narrow corridor of the ship. They snarled and growled, their bloodshot eyes scanning the deck, seeking fresh prey. Their claws clicked against the floor with each step, a horrible, dissonant sound like metal scraping against stone.

Tarus stood frozen, his heart pounding in his chest. His hand gripped the hilt of his blade so tightly, his knuckles turned white. He had encountered many creatures in his time, pirates, beasts, and horrors from the Abyss, but this? This was something new. Something far more dangerous.

"What in the Abyss are they?" Tarus' voice rang out, filled with disbelief, and a hint of fear. His men rallied around him, weapons raised, but the air bristled with the sense of impending doom. There was no way to prepare for something like this.

The sudden shift in Tarus' demeanor was palpable. For a moment, the air on his ship thickened with the tension of uncertainty. His previously bold and commanding presence faltered: a crack in the veneer of arrogance. As the injured man groaned in agony, clutching his shoulder where the Cordyphage's spined hand had pierced, the crew scrambled to drag him away, the ship's medics rushing to stabilize him. But the damage was done: the once resolute front of Tarus' crew was now shattered.

Tarus' eyes locked onto the chaos unfolding on the other ship. His men were fighting desperately, but the Cordyphages were relentless. With monstrous speed and strength, they cut through them, their near invincibility rendering every weapon useless. It was as though the creatures were forged from death itself, unstoppable in their fury. A bone-chilling realization crept into Tarus' mind. Their assault was doomed.

His voice, once booming with confidence, now trembled slightly. "Withdraw the planks!" he barked, the words leaving his mouth like a forced command, desperate in its tone. Panic clawed at the edges of his mind, but he tried to suppress it, pushing for the retreat he knew was the only option. His eyes darted to the other ship, watching as his men fell, shredded by the relentless onslaught of the Cordyphages. They were losing. Losing badly.

Zen, standing nearby, couldn't help but feel the stark contrast between his usual ruthless authority and the fearful man before her now. Her gaze hardened as she turned toward him, her voice sharp. "You will leave your crew on the ship to fend for themselves?" The words hung in the air like a challenge.

Tarus' glare shot back at her, seething with irritation, though his eyes betrayed his inner turmoil. "They are lost. This was unexpected. We lose them, or we lose them and more," he growled, the weight of the decision pressing on him. He knew that what he was saying was the cold truth, but the admission left a bitter taste in his mouth. It was a captain's duty to protect his men, yet here he was, condemning them to die to save his own skin.

Zen, however, didn't turn away. She stood still, her gaze locked onto the brutal, bloody spectacle unfolding on the other ship. Her mind reeled with the uncertainty of what was happening. The men she had watched Tarus command so proudly were now scattered, falling one after another beneath the Cordyphages' relentless assault. Her heart fluttered with fear, but she did not show it. She simply watched, transfixed by the carnage, her thoughts swirling.

The planks were swiftly retracted, their connection between the ships severed. The ship, now in retreat, lurched backward, pushing away from the nightmarish scene on the other vessel. The distance between them grew, but this did little to ease the tension. Zen stood still, her heart racing in her chest. She wasn't sure whether the retreat would save them or simply delay the inevitable. It was all a blur, a cruel, unrelenting fight for survival that no one seemed ready for.

The quiet aftermath was just as unsettling. The ship moved further from the chaos, but the haunting image of the Cordyphages' monstrous forms stayed etched in her mind.

The battle on the other ship was a nightmare come to life, a horrifying dance of death and destruction that unfolded in gruesome detail. On the deck, the once-proud crew of the ship had been reduced to little more than frantic, desperate souls fighting for their lives against an enemy that seemed to defy everything they knew about combat.

The Cordyphages, grotesque creatures from the Abyss, were the embodiment of terror. Standing at nearly seven feet tall, they were hulking, twisted figures of sinewy muscle, their bodies a sickly gray hue, like dead flesh stretched too thin over bone. Their skin was spiked with jagged protrusions, each sharp and deadly, capable of slicing through armor like it was paper. Their faces were barely human, half covered in an almost crystalline, translucent membrane, their hollow eyes glowing with a sickly green light. Their jaws were elongated, filled with rows of needle-like teeth, and their spined hands seemed to grow sharper with each strike.

The first wave of Cordyphages tore into the defending soldiers in a torrent of destruction. One of the creatures reached out with its massive, clawed hand, grabbing a soldier by the arm and yanking him off his feet, throwing him across the deck with such force that the man's body slammed into the side of the ship with a sickening crunch. Another Cordyphage lunged at a group of three soldiers, its spined hands cutting through their ranks like a scythe through wheat. One of the men managed to get a sword up in defense, but the Cordyphage easily swatted it aside, and with a swift, brutal motion, it impaled the man through the chest with its massive claws, lifting him into the air before tossing him aside with a flick of its wrist.

The soldiers fought valiantly, but the odds were stacked too heavily against them. Their weapons, swords, spears, and axes, were no match for the Cordyphages' monstrous strength and near invulnerability. When a soldier swung a sword at one of the creatures, it barely left a scratch. The Cordyphage responded with a devastating counterattack, slicing through the soldier's defenses and leaving him gurgling in a pool of his own blood. The ship was quickly becoming a slaughterhouse, with body after body piling up in grotesque heaps.

In the chaos, a few soldiers attempted to flee, but the creatures were fast. One Cordyphage jumped onto the railing, its spiked body scraping against the wood, and landed in front of a group of fleeing men. With a screech, it swung its massive arm, knocking the first man off his feet and sending him careening toward the edge of the ship. The second man, desperate, swung a sword at the creature, only for it to break on the creature's armored skin. The Cordyphage responded with a horrifying roar, slamming the soldier into the deck, its claws digging deep into the man's chest and pulling him apart with sickening ease.

On the far end of the ship, a group of soldiers tried to barricade themselves in the captain's quarters, hoping to hold out until reinforcements arrived. But before they could even set their defenses, another Cordyphage burst through the door with terrifying speed. The wood splintered under the force of the creature's entry, and in moments, it was upon them, tearing through their fragile resistance. The screams of the soldiers were drowned out by the creature's eerie growl as it slaughtered them one by one, its claws raking across their bodies with surgical precision.

Amidst the carnage, the rest of the Cordyphages continued to pour onto the ship, moving with unnatural coordination, a well-honed pack of killers. They surrounded the few remaining soldiers who had fought their way to the front, their weapons now stained with the blood of the fallen. As one of the soldiers raised his sword in a futile last stand, a Cordyphage lunged at him, its spined hand plunging deep into his gut, lifting him into the air before tearing him apart. His scream echoed across the deck as his life was drained in mere seconds.

The deck, once full of vibrant life and the bustle of seafaring labor, was now a battlefield soaked in blood. The sound of steel scraping against bone, the squelching of flesh being torn apart, and the guttural cries of the dying filled the air, mingling with the ominous groans of the ship as it rocked with the struggle. The few remaining soldiers, their will to fight rapidly fading, tried to regroup, but their movements were sluggish, and their morale shattered. Each wave of Cordyphages that charged at them felt like the death knell, and the soldiers' once-bright eyes now reflected only fear and the inevitability of death.

Amidst the chaos, there was no hope. No rallying cry. No salvation. The ship, once proud and defiant, was now a floating tomb, its crew reduced to broken bodies scattered across the blood-soaked deck. And as the last soldier fell, gasping for breath, the Cordyphages moved on, leaving behind only carnage, their thirst for blood seemingly unquenched.

From Tarus' ship, Zen and the others could only watch in horrified silence as the slaughter continued. There was nothing they could do. Nothing they could offer that would change the course of this horror. The Cordyphages were unstoppable.

As Tarus stood there, his fists clenched tightly, the blood-soaked deck beneath his feet seemed to mirror the rage and disbelief coursing through his veins. "What in the Abyss were those things?" he bellowed at his crew, his voice strained with frustration and terror. The once-vibrant chaos of battle had turned to horror as his crew members, their faces frozen in terror, gaped at the twisted remains of their comrades. Shreds of torn flesh and broken bones littered the deck, a gruesome testament to the brutality of the creatures they had just encountered. Tarus' eyes swept over the scene, but no words came. The sight was too much. His men were frozen, slack-jawed in disbelief at what they had just witnessed, unable to comprehend how they had been so easily outmatched.

Zen stood beside him, her usual air of forced confidence unraveling before his very eyes. The proud and poised woman now looked like a shattered doll, her face pale and her eyes wide with shock. She had seen battle before, had been forced to witness horrors that would break lesser people, but nothing could have prepared her for this. The sight of the grotesque, dismembered bodies, her comrades' blood staining the deck, ripped away the veil she had so carefully maintained. The fear in her eyes was raw and unmistakable. She was no longer the composed woman she had been mere moments ago.

Zen turned her gaze back to the ship ahead, her breath catching in her throat as her mind reeled. How had this happened? How had Devaultus done this? Her heart pounded in her chest, her thoughts spiraling. The crew had been completely unprepared, overwhelmed by something so horrific that they had never even imagined it could exist. The monstrosities, the Cordyphages, had appeared like a nightmare out of the Abyss itself, tearing through the crew with relentless brutality. The sight of those monstrous, spiny creatures, almost inhuman in their grotesque form, was enough to strip away any semblance of composure.

Zen's gaze shifted back to Tarus, her heart sinking as she saw the fear that had replaced his once-confident exterior. He was no longer the invincible Lord he had once seemed. Devaultus had outwitted him, baited him into a trap, and destroyed nearly half of his men in one fell swoop. The realization hit her like a ton of bricks. Tarus, for all his rage, was no longer the biggest threat in this war; Devaultus was. The very man who had made enemies of so many was proving to be more dangerous than any of them had imagined.

A cold shiver ran down Zen's spine. Maybe, just maybe, this Devaultus was the true monster everyone had whispered about in the shadows. She swallowed hard, her mind racing. She had to get this down, had to record every detail of this disaster for Lord Sakatorious. It was clear that the battle was far from over, and Lord Sakatorious would need to know what had transpired. Every moment, every horror had to be documented. Devaultus was one step ahead of them, and Zen had to figure out what that meant for her survival. She closed her eyes for a moment, steeling herself for the task ahead.

Tarus turned away, barking orders at his crew to regroup, but Zen's mind was elsewhere. The image of the blood-streaked ship, the body parts scattered across the deck, and the fierce creature tearing through her comrades was now burned into her memory. It was a nightmare she couldn't escape, and the thought of what came next, of facing Devaultus, was almost more terrifying than the chaos they had just witnessed.

The chaos of the battlefield still hung heavily in the air as Zen moved across the ship's deck, the sounds of panic and grief echoing all around her. The once pristine ship now bore the scars of a brutal attack, blood staining the wood and bodies scattered like discarded toys. Zen's hands trembled slightly as she gripped the small booklet, her quill flying across the pages in frantic scribbles, desperate to capture every detail of the destruction. The crew, however, was falling apart around her.

Tarus, still seething with rage and shock, bellowed orders to his men, his voice cutting through the air like a whip. But his words were empty echoes, and the crew paid little heed. They had been shattered, broken by what they had seen. Tarus' commands to regroup, to focus on recovery, did little to steady their nerves. His soldiers, once fierce and loyal, now stumbled about aimlessly, eyes wide with horror, faces pale as the realization of their loss set in.

Zen's own stomach churned as she walked among them, hearing their cries, their broken mutterings.

One man leaned heavily against the side of the ship, his face ghostly white and his eyes bloodshot, the vacant look in them haunting. He mumbled to himself, his words barely audible, but Zen caught them. "Me wife told me not to take this job. But we needed the coin. Lil' Lars needed food, she said." His voice cracked on the last words, as if even speaking them brought the grief flooding back, drowning him in guilt and sorrow.

Nearby, another man sat in a stupor, his glazed eyes unfocused as he stared at nothing, as though his soul had fled the vessel that now carried his broken body. Zen knew better than to interrupt him. His mind had already fled to some darker place, where the horrors he had witnessed would follow him, gnawing at him for the rest of his days.

But it wasn't just the men who had broken: there were tears on every face she passed. The captain's crew, hardened soldiers who had seen their share of battle, were now reduced to shadows of their former selves. A man sat on the ground, shoulders shaking with each sob that racked his body. His hands were clasped in a prayerful pose, though there was no god to hear him now. "Dale was over there," he whispered, his voice cracking like dry wood. "I watched that creature rip him in half... Oh, Abyss, what am I going to tell his wife? They were expecting..."

The words hung in the air, sharp and bitter. Zen's heart twisted in her chest, but she couldn't allow herself to feel it, not here, not now. These men were lost. She had to finish her task. She had to get this all down for Lord Sakatorious. But the sight of their mental pain, the torment in their eyes, was almost too much for her to bear. The grief was palpable, thick in the air like smoke, and it clung to everything. She had never seen such raw despair, and it rattled her more than she cared to admit.

Her steps faltered for a moment as she walked towards the stairs leading below deck, the weight of their suffering pressing heavily on her shoulders. Each sob she heard seemed to echo in her chest, each tortured whisper a reminder of the price they had all paid. And she couldn't even offer them comfort. Her role here was to report, to relay the carnage to Sakatorious. It wasn't her place to console them, not when her own confidence was so fragile, so carefully constructed to keep the cracks from showing.

She needed to finish writing. To finish this. But the suffering of the crew, the toll the battle had taken on their minds, lingered in her thoughts. She heard the cries of one of the men echo in her head, a constant reminder of the helplessness that now suffocated the ship.

Zen quickly wiped her eyes, forcing the tears back down. She had to do this for Sakatorious. She had no other purpose.

Zen's feet moved quietly on the wooden steps as she descended below deck, her thoughts swirling around the chaos that had unfolded above. Devaultus, the name that had haunted her ever since she'd been thrust into this cruel world, had actually done the unthinkable: he had held his own against Tarus, and in that moment, Zen felt the weight of the horror settling in her gut. She couldn't remember a single instance where anyone, let alone someone so chaotic, had stood up to the brutal Tarus. The thought of Lord Sakatorious' reaction to this defeat made her stomach churn. He wouldn't take this news lightly.

Her legs carried her aimlessly through the darkened corridors, the wooden floor creaking beneath her. As she passed one open door, something caught her attention. The faint scent of antiseptic and blood hit her nose. She paused. The medic's station. The sight that greeted her inside was something she hadn't been prepared for, though in this cursed world, there was little left that could truly shock her.

It was there that she saw him, lying on one of the tables: the man who had been hurled across the ship, the same one she had seen fall to the creatures' savage attack. "Wait... that's right, one escaped," Zen muttered to herself under her breath. The thought that at least one of Tarus' men had survived brought a flicker of relief to her, though she knew it was only a temporary comfort. Perhaps not all was lost... but the dread still gnawed at her. What now? What did it mean that one had survived? How many others would still be left unburied?

She stepped closer to the table, her eyes studying the man. The doctor was bent over him, her hands moving quickly but with frantic uncertainty. His face was pale, slick with sweat, and his breath came in labored gasps. Every exhale was a soft groan of pain. His eyes flickered between unconsciousness and agonized awareness, as he no doubt struggling to process the immense pain from his injury. Zen's gaze shifted to the man's wound. It was a gruesome sight, an enormous hole torn in his shoulder, the flesh shredded as though it had been gouged by a twisted, brutal force. But it was the oozing black substance that made Zen's stomach tighten. The tendrils spreading from the wound like some unholy vine, cracking the skin, and forming pus-filled pockets. It was like nothing she had ever seen before, the very air around the injury seemed to pulse with something dark.

The doctor was muttering to herself, working as quickly as possible, but Zen could tell by the way the woman's brow furrowed in confusion that she didn't have the answers. "I just don't understand," she murmured under her breath, her voice thick with disbelief. "What is happening? It's spreading..."

Zen couldn't bring herself to look away. The wound, this corruption, was spreading like a plague. She had seen death, suffering, and torment, but this... this was something different. She had heard whispers of the horrors Devaultus left in his wake, and she couldn't help but think that this, this unnatural affliction, was yet another example of the terror he wrought. She shuddered involuntarily, her mind racing with questions she had no answers to. What was it that Tarus and his men were truly up against? What had they unleashed by trying to fight him? And what of the survivors? How many would be able to withstand whatever nightmare this was?

As the doctor continued to work in frantic silence, Zen stood rooted to the spot. Her fingers tightened around the book in her hand as a wave of dread washed over her. She had to report everything. She had to make Lord Sakatorious understand the severity of this, whatever this *thing* was that Devaultus had brought upon them. But with every passing moment, Zen felt a sickening truth settling in. She didn't think they were going to win this.

Zen stood frozen in place, her eyes wide with horror as the man on the table screamed in agony. His cries twisted into something else, a horrid, guttural sound that was almost inhuman. The pain tore through the air like a thunderclap, and Zen's stomach churned at the sight. The wound in his shoulder, already an abomination of dark, oozing tendrils, seemed to writhe with life of its own. The wound, as though it were hungry, pulsated with unnatural movement, spreading across his flesh like a dark stain. His flesh trembled, the texture shifting in ways that didn't seem possible for a human body.

Zen's chest tightened as she watched his body twitch and jerk, unable to look away. Each ragged breath the man took sounded like it was breaking his ribs. But then, a new noise emerged, a sharp, unsettling clacking sound that reverberated through the room. Zen's heart raced. Her eyes darted nervously to the soldier outside the door, the one who had dared to peer in. He took a cautious step forward. "Everything alright in here, Candace?" he asked, his voice uncertain, but too calm for the situation.

Candace, the doctor, didn't even seem to hear him at first. Her focus was on the man on the table, whose body was now trembling uncontrollably. The bloodshot eyes of the soldier flicked between the doctor and the writhing, suffering man. Candace's face had gone pale, her brow furrowed in her desperate attempt to understand what was happening. She whispered under her breath, "I don't know. Something isn't right. Come help me restrain him."

Zen instinctively took a small step back, her hands trembling at her sides. She had been in the midst of battle before, seen horror and violence, but this? This was something else entirely. She had never seen anything like this before. Her mind raced as she watched the soldier push past her, all but shoving her aside. He grabbed hold of the man's arms, pinning him down with brutal efficiency.

Candace continued to clean the wound, but it was clear from her increasingly frantic movements that she was losing control of the situation. Then, a faint yet unmistakable clicking sound filled the room. It was too loud, too sharp, and it seemed to come from deep within the man's body. Candace froze, and her hand hesitated over the wound. Slowly, her eyes widened with dawning terror. She reached up, trembling, and slowly opened the man's mouth. What she found made her blood run cold.

There, between his lips, something new had taken root. His teeth had become jagged, extending into sharp, cruel points, but that wasn't the worst part. What was truly horrifying were the mandibles that now protruded from his gums, twitching and clacking together as if alive. The doctor's voice quivered as she stumbled back, her words coming out in a panicked whisper, "No... no, no..."

Zen's heart dropped, a cold sweat breaking out across her skin. The transformation had begun: what had been a man was now something else, something monstrous, something dangerous. Candace's voice rose in desperation, fear surging through her, "Kill him! Kill him now!"

The soldier, now visibly stunned, looked from Candace to the man. For a brief moment, hesitation flickered in his eyes, but the weight of the situation was clear. This wasn't just an injury, it was a threat. Slowly, he released the man's arm, his hand fumbling at the hilt of his dagger. The blade gleamed in the dim light before he plunged it into the man's chest with a sickening, wet sound.

Zen recoiled as the man's body gave one last, horrible shudder. The soldier's dagger thrust had come too late, his actions dictated by the horrific change the man had undergone. The man's body convulsed, spasming violently as if resisting death itself. Then, there was silence. The room was heavy with it, thick and suffocating.

Zen stood there, heart racing in her chest, unable to fully comprehend what had just happened. She could hear her own breathing, too fast, too shallow, and it echoed in her ears. This was no simple wound. This was no ordinary sickness. Something far darker was unfolding, and Zen wasn't sure if they were ready for it.

As she stood there, the lingering sense of terror clung to her skin, reminding her that in this new world of chaos, monsters didn't always look like the beasts you expected. Sometimes, they were hidden inside the bodies of men.

The black blood oozed from the wound in thick, viscous strands, bubbling and foaming around the dagger that had been plunged deep into the man's chest. His body trembled violently as the last remnants of life slipped from him, but it wasn't death that came next. No, it was something far worse. His body contorted in unnatural ways, muscles spasming as his hand shot up, fingers curling like claws, and, with terrifying speed, he gripped the soldier's throat. His fingers tightened, the sickening crunch of bone and the soft gurgle of crushed windpipe echoing through the cramped room.

Zen's breath caught in her throat as she took a fearful step back, her heart pounding against her ribcage. She whispered under her breath, almost in denial. "No... Please, no..." The words felt foreign on her tongue, useless in the face of the horror that was unfolding before her. She turned on her heel, desperate to escape, to get away from the nightmare that was consuming everything around her.

But before she could even reach the door, a surge of blood erupted from the creature's body, splattering across the walls, the ceiling, the floor, coating everything in its grotesque, pitch-black essence. The stench was overpowering, thick with death and decay. Zen's eyes widened in panic, her feet scrambling to gain traction as she fled the scene, but the ground seemed to slip beneath her.

The door slammed open just as the doctor, in a state of near hysteria, rushed toward Zen. She shouted a warning, a scream of terror. "Run!" But Zen's legs faltered as she heard the sickening sound of flesh tearing and the scrape of something unnatural. She froze, eyes wide, heart hammering against her chest.

Then, without warning, a hand shot out from the bloody mess, grasping the doctor's hair with brutal force. With a sickening yank, the creature pulled her back into the room, the doctor's shrill scream cut off as she was dragged into the Abyss of horrors. Zen could only stand there, paralyzed, her mind screaming in terror as the last traces of humanity in the room were ripped away by the monstrous presence that now lurked in the shadows.

Zen forced herself forward, her heart hammering in her chest as she sprinted down the dimly lit corridor. The smell of blood clung to the air, thick and suffocating. Behind her, wet squelching noises echoed as crimson liquid seeped from the ruined medical bay, pooling out into the hall like the ship itself was bleeding.

Then, with a sickening crunch, the doorframe splintered as the three monstrous Cordyphages exploded from the room. Zen barely had time to glance back before sheer horror gripped her lungs. The soldier and the doctor, just moments ago human, were gone. Their twisted, infected forms now shambled with the same grotesque, insect-like movements as the others. *That fast.* The infection took them *that fast.* Her stomach lurched at the realization. If even the slightest scratch could do this... *How the Abyss were they supposed to fight this?*

Her blood-slicked feet betrayed her, sliding out from under her as she hit the floor hard. Pain jolted up her side, but she had no time to register it. The clacking sound of mandibles snapping together echoed closer; too close. *Move!* She scrambled up, hands slipping in the warm blood coating the floor, and bolted toward the stairs.

Behind her, a guttural screech filled the hall, not one of pain, but of rage. The three Cordyphages had clogged the narrow space, pushing and clawing at each other in a frenzy to reach her first. Razor-sharp mandibles snapped, tearing into flesh, *their own flesh.* Their hunger, their *need* to kill overwhelmed them, and they turned on each other in a violent, frenzied struggle for dominance.

One Cordyphage slammed another into the wall with bone-shattering force, causing wood to crack beneath the impact. Another lashed out with jagged, clawed fingers, raking deep wounds across its rival's abdomen. Black ichor splattered the walls as they tore and snapped at one another, mandibles clattering in a vicious battle to be the first to *feed*.

Zen didn't dare look back again. She could still hear them. Still hear the crunch of tearing flesh, the screech of something being ripped apart, the clacking: gods, the clacking, like a thousand insect legs scuttling in the dark.

Her feet hit the stairs, and she didn't stop. She *couldn't*. Not when death was fighting over who would get to take her first.

Zen exploded onto the deck, her eyes wild with terror. "They're on the ship!" she screamed, her voice cracking with panic.

Tarus spun toward her, his face hardening as his hand instinctively reached for his sword. Beside him stood Silus, the shadow elf, his presence as unsettling as ever. There was something about him, something unnatural in the way he moved, in the way his piercing gaze seemed to see too much. Every time Zen looked at him, an involuntary shiver ran down her spine.

Silus didn't hesitate. The moment the words left Zen's lips, his twin blades whispered free of their scabbards, gleaming even in the dim torchlight. Tarus followed suit, drawing his massive sword with a metallic rasp that sent a thrill of fear and anticipation through the crew.

Zen didn't slow until she was behind them, her chest heaving, her pulse pounding in her ears. The crew, still reeling from the horror they had just witnessed, paused their grieving. Bloodshot eyes lifted from trembling hands; men who had just lost their friends now forced to pick themselves up, to ready themselves for yet another nightmare.

And then... silence.

Every breath was held. Every movement stilled. It was as though the entire ship had been frozen in time, every soul aboard waiting, dreading, what would come next.

The only sound was the deep, eerie groan of the ship as it carved its way through the endless desert, the sand shifting like waves against its hull.

All eyes were locked on the stairs.

Waiting.

The wooden doorframe exploded into splinters as a monstrous figure lunged through, its body writhing with grotesque fungal growths. Spore-covered tendrils extended from its shoulders, pulsating and releasing a fine, sickly-sweet mist into the air. Its milky, fungus-infected eyes locked onto the nearest crew member. Then, with a grotesque *clack-clack-clack*, its mandibles snapped open and shut, jittering with inhuman hunger.

Before the sailor could react, the thing struck, jagged fingers, warped and twisted by parasitic growth, latched onto his skull. His screams filled the air as the infection spread in seconds, pale filaments snaking into his ears, eyes, and mouth. His body convulsed violently, his skin rippling as something inside him *grew*. Then, with a final, shuddering gasp, his face *burst* apart in a shower of fungal matter, his twitching corpse falling limp before the thing discarded him and turned its attention to the others. Its mandibles twitched, *clacking* together in a horrible rhythm, as if excited by the fresh carnage.

Two more of the Cordyphages followed, their bodies grotesque parodies of what they had once been; twisted, spore-infested husks of the men and woman they used to be. Their flesh was riddled with bulbous growths, some pulsating, others *bursting* open to release a wave of writhing fungal tendrils that sought out new hosts. As they moved, their mandibles clicked and chattered, a maddening, ceaseless *clack-clack-clack*, like a horde of starving insects on the hunt.

The deck erupted into chaos.

Crew members scattered, panic taking hold. Some drew weapons in desperation; others simply ran, knowing in their hearts that fighting these *things* was suicide. A young deckhand barely made it two steps before a tendril lashed out, wrapping around his ankle and *yanking* him off his feet. He hit the deck hard, screaming, as the fungal growth rapidly spread across his leg. He tried to crawl away, clawing at the wood, but his fingers stiffened, curling unnaturally as the infection overtook him. His scream turned into a sickening gurgle as fungal stalks *burst* from his throat, his eyes rolling back as his body went still.

Another sailor, an older man who had seen his share of battles, roared and swung his cutlass with all the strength he had left. The blade severed a Cordyphage's arm, sending a spray of spore-laden ichor into the air. But before he could celebrate his success, he realized that the creature barely seemed to notice. Instead, a new limb *grew* in its place, sinewy tendrils twisting and knotting into the shape of an arm. The old sailor's expression turned from defiance to horror, then he gasped as a fungal tendril *shot* from the creature's chest, impaling him straight through the stomach.

His body convulsed, veins blackening, flesh rippling with unnatural movement. The clacking of mandibles filled the air as his face twisted in agony, his features warping as fungal plates began to form over his skull. In mere moments, *he* was one of them.

Tarus moved then, his massive sword cleaving through the air with merciless power. His first strike carved through the nearest Cordyphage, slicing it from shoulder to hip, its two halves collapsing in a twitching heap. A second later, he stepped into another swing, hacking a creature's head clean off. But even as it fell, the fungal mass inside the corpse began to *move*, reassembling itself. Tarus snarled, undeterred, and swung again, obliterating the writhing remains before they could take shape. His movements were raw, brute force, unstoppable: a whirlwind of carnage that kept the horrors at bay.

Silus, by contrast, was a flickering shadow, darting between the creatures with almost inhuman speed. His twin daggers flashed in rapid succession, slicing into weak points, severing tendons, puncturing swollen fungal sacks before they could erupt. He *vanished* into the darkness, only to reappear behind them, his blades carving through spines before they could react. One of the monsters lunged at him, mandibles snapping furiously, *clack-clack*, but it met only empty air. Silus was already behind it, severing the back of its neck before slipping away again. His attacks were relentless, precise, and deadly. But no matter how many he felled, more took their place.

Zen cowered behind a stack of crates, her entire body shaking. She had seen death before, but not like this. This wasn't battle, this was an *infestation*. There was no fighting these things. Every strike, every wound, only seemed to feed their grotesque rebirth. She hugged her knees to her chest, pressing herself against the wood, praying they wouldn't see her.

Beside her, The Puppeteer had stepped forward, his normally eerie composure shattered by sheer panic. His hands flickered with power as he seized control of the minds of nearby crew members. Those frozen in terror suddenly lurched forward, their faces blank, their bodies forced into action as he sent them to fight. But it was *pointless*. As soon as they reached the creatures, they were torn apart, infected in mere moments. One barely had time to scream before his own arms turned against him, his body *twisting* unnaturally as the Cordyphage overtook him.

The Puppeteer's breath came in ragged gasps, his fear plain. He was losing control, every new puppet he raised was dead before they could even lift a weapon.

The deck was slick with blood and spores now, the air thick with the stench of decay and death. The creatures advanced, clicking their mandibles, their bodies pulsating with grotesque growths that yearned to spread further.

This wasn't a battle. This was a *plague*.

The three quickly realized this was a losing battle. The creatures were relentless, and for every one they cut down, another took its place, clacking its mandibles in eerie anticipation. Tarus snarled in frustration before roaring, *"Enough of this! To the skimmers!"* His deep voice cut through the chaos, snapping Silus and Zen into motion.

Without hesitation, Tarus sprinted toward the ship's edge, his heavy boots pounding against the blood-slicked deck. Silus followed in a blur of shadow and speed, moving so fast he seemed to flicker in and out of existence. Zen, her breath ragged and hands trembling, forced her legs to move, terror gnawing at the edges of her resolve.

One by one, they vaulted over the rail, plummeting down toward the awaiting skimmer lizards below. The creatures, sensing the urgency, shifted restlessly, their reptilian eyes darting toward the growing sounds of carnage above.

Zen landed hard, gripping the reins of her skimmer with white-knuckled fingers. Instinct forced her to glance back. She couldn't see the slaughter directly, her angle only offered a glimpse of the ship's towering side, but the sight was enough. Thick, dark blood seeped through the cracks in the wood, running like veins down the hull, dripping in heavy splashes onto the sand below. It was more than just a massacre: it was a complete annihilation.

Her heart clenched, nausea rising. *So many dead. So many gone.*

# CHAPTER 20

# WHO'S A GOOD BOY?

D evaultus strolled through the dimly lit corridor of his ship, the wooden floor creaking faintly beneath his boots. The scent of salt, aged wood, and a faint trace of Al'Shandra's signature exotic perfume filled the air as he paused outside the captain's quarters. He didn't bother knocking, there was no need. She always knew. How she managed to keep an unseen hand on every moment that transpired aboard this vessel was a mystery he never quite solved.

"Come in, Devaultus," came her voice, a sultry purr that practically slithered through the door.

He sighed to himself before pushing it open, stepping inside with his usual air of arrogant confidence. The room was a blend of chaos and luxury, silken red drapes hung from the ceiling, candlelight flickering off gilded trinkets and well-worn maps spread across the desk. The scent of rum and something sweet, something distinctly hers, lingered in the warm air.

Al'Shandra lounged across a plush chair, her long legs draped over one of the armrests, a half-empty goblet of deep crimson wine dangling from her fingers. Her outfit left little to the imagination: an open, gold-trimmed corset that barely held her ample chest, sheer silks draped over her hips, and thigh-high boots that accentuated every curve. Her fiery hair cascaded over one shoulder, her smirk a mix of amusement and warning. She was a vision of temptation wrapped in a deadly package, and she knew it.

Devaultus didn't hesitate, strolling in like he owned the place, settling into the chair opposite her and throwing his feet up on her desk with a smirk.

Al'Shandra arched a perfectly sculpted eyebrow at him as he began to speak. "Well? Did it work? Are we free to continue our journey?"

Instead of answering right away, Al'Shandra let the moment hang, watching him with that infuriating knowing look of hers, like she had everyone eating out of the palm of her hand.

She set her goblet down with a click and gave him a slow, dangerous smile. "First off, get your damned feet off my desk before I rip them off you and beat you over the head with them."

Devaultus chuckled but, for once, relented, dropping his boots back to the floor with a small thud.

"Secondly," she continued, swirling her wine as she leaned forward, "yes, the diversion worked. They chased the ship far off course. It'll take them time to realign their pursuit." She paused, letting the weight of her words settle. "We've bought ourselves a few days, at the least."

She took a slow sip, licking a stray drop from her lips before tilting her head at him. "So, darling... how do you intend to use our borrowed time?"

Devaultus smirked, his lips curling into a half-amused, half-dismissive grin as he brushed aside Al'Shandra's words with practiced ease. He had long grown accustomed to the games she played, each one as blatant as the last. Her intentions were as obvious as the stars in the sky, and yet, he couldn't help but find amusement in how effortlessly she tried to coax him into her web. She was a master of seduction, a true pirate queen who wore her desires as openly as she wore her provocative attire.

Her yellow eyes shimmered with a calculated gleam, and the way her full lips parted slightly as she spoke, there was no mistaking it. She wasn't after strategy or information; no, she wanted more than that.

She wanted him in her bed, tangled in sheets. The thought should have ignited some spark of desire in him, but it didn't. Not this time.

Devaultus leaned back in the chair, the quiet creak of it under his weight a subtle declaration of indifference. He could smell her perfume, sweet and intoxicating, like forbidden fruit. He let her words hang in the air for a moment, watching her closely, her red hair flowing loosely over her shoulders, her figure framed perfectly in the low light of the room. Even with the heavy tension in the air, he remained unmoved.

His attention was brought back to his initial question. That of the diversion of Tarus.

"Good," he said, ignoring her question completely. His voice oozing with casual confidence. He leaned back in his chair, stretching his arms behind his head in an effort to appear completely unbothered by the undeniable tension between them. "Perhaps this is exactly what we need, to push forward and find the final piece."

Al'Shandra nodded, her gaze never leaving him as her slender fingers toyed with a lock of her fiery red hair. It fell in soft waves down her back, the dark auburn strands catching the low light of the room, giving her a flame-like aura that matched the predatory gleam in her sharp, golden eyes. Her posture was casual, but there was nothing relaxed about the calculated way she studied him.

"Yes, it will help," she said, her tone laced with a quiet amusement that made him wonder what she was really thinking. She uncrossed and then recrossed her legs, the hem of her skirt riding up higher, revealing a glimpse of her smooth, tanned thigh. The fabric of her shirt clung to her curves, the top button undone just enough to leave her neckline tantalizingly exposed. "Though I dare say it won't be enough. We won't make it before they catch up to us again."

Her voice dropped to a lower, more dangerous register as she leaned forward, her yellow eyes flashing in the dim light. "Our best bet would be to stop over at Deshara. Gather supplies. Perhaps see about getting this ship moving a bit faster."

Devaultus thought for a moment, a small frown crossing his face. He was always planning ahead, but there was something undeniably tempting about Al'Shandra's suggestion. There was something in her tone, something in the way she carried herself, like she knew exactly what they needed, and how to push him to take it.

"Very well," he said after a cautious beat, his voice cool but edged with sarcasm. "Let's stop off at Deshara, then. It might do the crew some good to step off the ship for a bit. Let them drink, fight, and do whatever it is a ship's crew does at port." None of this was really any of his concern. He somehow felt she was playing with him by telling him all this. Like he had some say, some power.

Al'Shandra's lips curled into a sly smile, one that didn't reach her eyes but still managed to send a shiver down his spine. She leaned back, draping herself across the chair in a way that made every inch of her body look like it was sculpted to perfection. "I agree," she purred, her gaze never wavering from him. Then, her smile grew wider, as she leaned in just a bit more, her voice dropping to a teasing whisper. "And, Devaultus... this time, you take your friends with you."

Devaultus sighed to himself. Al'Shandra always had a way of making everything more complicated, and this time was no different.

Devaultus exited Al'Shandra's office, his mind already drifting toward their next destination: Deshara. The name alone sparked a flicker of intrigue within him, yet he couldn't quite push down the unease that followed. Deshara had always been a place of whispers and rumors, and from what he'd heard, it was far from a paradise for someone like him. The city was ruled by women; yes, powerful, capable women, which he had no issue with, except for the minor inconvenience that the men in the city were little more than slaves. That was the part that made Devaultus' gut twist. While he wasn't a stranger to domination and power struggles, being on the wrong side of that equation...? Not so much his cup of tea.

He scoffed under his breath, shaking his head. He could practically hear Al'Shandra's laughter from the other room. Oh, she'd be in her element there, wouldn't she? He could already picture her strutting around, claiming the attention of every woman in the room with that provocative, teasing air of hers. She reveled in control, in being the one others desired, and perhaps that was part of the reason she found him so... amusing. He was, in some ways, her foil.

Devaultus couldn't deny that he felt a bit of curiosity. Deshara wasn't just a city, it was a playground for the strong and the cunning. Still, the thought of the men being subjugated didn't sit right with him. He'd been born to lead, not follow, and that made him uneasy. Sure, he had the ability to transform himself, to take on the appearance of a woman if it served his needs, but he knew the limits of his powers. For short periods of time, he could make it work, decently enough to play the role, but for anything longer? His true nature always slipped through. His words, his mannerisms, his gestures: they would betray him, and there was no hiding that.

He walked through the halls of the ship, the weight of the looming mission pressing on his mind. Deshara had to be navigated carefully. Devaultus wasn't a man who took kindly to being controlled by anyone, and he wasn't about to start pretending to fit into their carefully constructed world, no matter how tempting the notion of infiltrating their power structure was. But first, he had to deal with the immediate reality that lay ahead, gathering his companions for what would surely be an adventure filled with its own set of dangers.

It seemed that, as always, Devaultus was about to step into a world where control was a fleeting illusion, and power had a way of shifting from one hand to the next. He had learned long ago not to be naive about such things.

Devaultus' thoughts wandered as he paced the narrow hallway, contemplating the options that lay before him. The idea of pretending to be someone's slave, especially Vex's, made his stomach churn. The very thought of being at her mercy, however brief, sent a shiver of dread down his spine. Vex wasn't the kind of person to take things lightly. She had a habit of turning every situation into a chaotic mess, and her enjoyment in causing destruction would likely escalate any situation into something... far worse than he could manage.

Then there was Blight. Her quiet, curious demeanor made her seem far too timid to pull off anything as bold as this. She might be a key to blending in, but her shy and fearful nature might draw suspicion rather than deter it. Yet there was something strangely appealing about the thought. If he could push her to be more assertive, it might be worth considering, though how he might manage that was anyone's guess.

Devaultus wasn't the type to relinquish control, not ever. Control was everything to him, it was the foundation upon which his entire existence rested. Every decision, every move he made was calculated, meticulously crafted to ensure that he stayed at the helm, directing the chaos in a way that worked to his advantage. Even in moments of unpredictability, he held onto his ability to steer the ship, figuratively speaking, through stormy seas. He'd constructed an elaborate web of contingencies, always thinking two steps ahead, anticipating every possible outcome and preparing a response.

To surrender even a sliver of that control, to place trust in someone else, felt like a betrayal of everything he had built. Trust wasn't a luxury he afforded others, not when it left him vulnerable. Vulnerability was a weakness. It opened doors to things he didn't want to face, things that would make him falter in his pursuit of power. Trusting anyone enough to follow their lead was something that simply didn't sit right with him.

Yet here he was, in a position where that was exactly what he would have to do. The very thought of it made his jaw tighten, a wave of discomfort washing over him. How could he possibly maintain the illusion of strength if he wasn't in control? How could he keep others in line if they weren't following his lead?

His mind raced with questions, but deep down, he knew he had no choice. The situation was beyond his usual control, beyond any carefully orchestrated plans. And that... was what bothered him the most.

No, these were the best options, but each one came with its own set of complications. As his mind churned through every possible scenario, the complexities of each choice grew clearer, and he realized that navigating this would be far more treacherous than he had initially thought.

Still, he wasn't one to back down easily. If there was one thing Devaultus knew for sure, it was that he could handle almost anything thrown his way... or at least, make a good show of it.

He took a long breath, trying to prepare himself for whatever was to come next, and his thoughts turned to the bigger picture: what would it take to actually succeed in this strange and dangerous place?

Devaultus stood outside the quarters for a moment, his boots tapping softly on the wooden floor of the ship. The slight sway beneath his feet was a familiar sensation, but there was an unfamiliar tension in his chest. He wasn't used to this. Nervousness. A rare, unwelcome feeling. He ran a hand through his dark hair, exhaling a sharp breath, then straightened his posture, pushing the door open with a quiet creak.

Inside, Blight was fast asleep at her desk, her delicate body swaying gently with the rhythm of the ship. The soft sound of her snores filled the air; a gentle reminder of the quiet moments that passed in the chaotic world they traversed. A book lay splayed open across her chest, a half-read passage forgotten as she slipped into a peaceful slumber.

And then, there was Vex. She was looming over Blight, her posture tense and impatient. The chaos in her eyes was unmistakable, and her usual playful grin was absent, replaced by a look that was almost dangerously close to frustration. She held a pillow in one hand, gripping it tightly as if it were a weapon. Her eyes flicked to Blight, then to Devaultus as he entered.

"Vex?" Devaultus' voice was calm, though his curiosity was laced with a hint of confusion. What in the seven hells was going on?

Vex's eyes snapped to him, and for a moment, she seemed thrown off guard, as though she hadn't expected him to arrive just then. She fumbled with her words, her usual cocky demeanor faltering. "Oh... uh... Hello, Devaultus," she stammered, but the frustration still lingered in her voice, the pillow clutched like a lifeline.

Without any further preamble, she leaned down, roughly grabbing Blight's hair and yanking her head up from the desk, causing the smaller woman to stir. Blight's face scrunched up in discomfort, eyes fluttering open to meet the blurry vision of Vex looming over her. She blinked, disoriented, her voice thick with sleep. "Uhm... was I snoring again, Vex?"

Vex's face softened, her rough exterior cracking just slightly. She sighed, her lips curling into that familiar mischievous grin. She dropped Blight's hair, but not before giving it one last tug, as if making sure she had the small woman's attention. The playful pat on Blight's forehead followed, each one getting a little rougher, expressing a little more annoyance. "Oh, you're fine. Just, y'know... try not to do that again."

Blight, her eyes still groggy with sleep, let out a small, embarrassed laugh. She wasn't fully awake yet, but the strange interaction and Vex's forceful antics were enough to make her more alert.

Devaultus, however, stood there in the doorway, shaking his head. His mind quickly ran through the possibilities, Blight's snoring, Vex's behavior, the chaos that seemed to follow them wherever they went, but one thing was clear: This wasn't a situation he was ready to handle, and he wasn't sure either of them was his ideal candidate for the Deshara plan.

A subtle sigh escaped his lips, the weight of the situation pressing down on him. He stepped further into the room, closing the door behind him, but his thoughts remained focused on the idea that was still gnawing at him. What were the odds any of them, Vex, Blight, or anyone else, could pull off being convincing as a fake owner on Deshara? They certainly had their... peculiarities.

Vex's chaotic energy, Blight's innocent curiosity, and even his own internal battle between keeping control and giving up control... He'd have to think this through.

Devaultus suddenly had an idea, one that curled at the edges of his mind like smoke. He let it sit for a moment before he spoke.

"Blight?" he called; then, after a short pause, added, "Lorivelle?"

At the sound of that name, Vex's spine went rigid, her posture snapping into something unnaturally perfect. That reaction had become less predictable as of late. In the beginning, "Lorivelle" was an unshakable trigger, pulling her into sharp focus. Now, it was less certain, less absolute. He never knew which version of her he was going to get when he used it. These days, it seemed like Vex was always there, riding in the passenger seat of her own mind, grinning at the wheel, waiting for an excuse to take over.

"Alright," he continued, setting his thoughts aside, "here's the plan. Looks like our next job takes us to Deshara."

His gaze flicked to Blight, curiosity narrowing his eyes. He didn't know everything about her past, but there were... oddities. Moments when she seemed utterly lost in conversations about things that should have been common knowledge. She wasn't stupid, far from it, so he'd always assumed there was a reason for it. Something hidden. Something deliberate.

"Do you know about Deshara?" he asked, watching her reaction closely.

Blight hesitated. She hated revealing too much, feared that if they saw her as a liability, they might abandon her. But this? This felt like something important. Something where honesty mattered.

"No," she admitted, her voice steady but quiet.

Devaultus exhaled, a slow sigh, not of frustration, but of calculation. How exactly should he explain this? Deshara wasn't just another city. It was a place that carried weight, a reputation that clung to it like a heavy perfume.

"Deshara is a city entirely run by women. Every single race, every single background," he said, then hesitated, his jaw tightening. "The only males there are..." He trailed off, as if the words themselves left a bitter taste in his mouth.

Finally, he forced himself to say it.

"Slaves."

The women exchanged glances, an unspoken understanding passing between them. Vex tilted her head, curiosity glinting in her emerald eyes. "Alright then, how do you plan to get in? Or will you just shift into something a little more... appealing to the locals?"

Devaultus leaned back, resting his chin on his hand as if weighing the thought. "I did consider it," he admitted, his voice carrying the reluctant air of someone forced to acknowledge an inconvenient truth. "But I dare say, I'm unsure if I could maintain the necessary traits well enough to fool them. When I take on a feminine form, it's usually to get close for a kill, an assassin's tool, not a long-term disguise. And, more often than not, my targets are men." His lips curled into a smirk, though there was little humor in it. "Men are fools for a beautiful woman. They don't notice the little imperfections, the tiny slips in behavior. But in a city of women? They'd see through me in an instant."

A pause, heavier than the last. His fingers drummed once against the table, and for the first time, hesitation crept into his expression. "So," he said at last, "I will enter Deshara as Blight's... slave."

The words hung in the air, thick with meaning.

Blight stiffened, horror flashing across her face. "I would never!" she blurted, recoiling from the very thought.

Devaultus raised a hand to calm her before she could spiral further. "We will be in and out," he assured her, his tone even, controlled. "Get what we need and leave. Nothing more." His gaze locked onto hers, dark and unwavering. "I will not be your actual slave. It will be an act, a necessary deception to keep us safe." Then, his voice dipped, something quieter, more dangerous slipping into his words. "I am placing a great deal of trust in you, Blight. More than I ever have."

Blight swallowed hard, his words cutting through her like a blade. Trust. It wasn't a word Devaultus threw around lightly, nor was it something she took for granted. But the weight of it, the gravity of what he was asking her to do, made her hesitate.

For the first time since joining him and Vex, she wasn't sure if she could meet his expectations.

All she wanted, more than anything, was to be truly accepted by this group. Not that they treated her poorly or made her feel unwanted, but there was a bond between them, a familiarity forged in blood and chaos that she had yet to fully become a part of. They had been together longer. They had survived together. She was still finding her place, still figuring out where she fit among them.

But this... this was her chance.

More than just proving her worth, this was about trust. And Devaultus, everyone knew, was not a man who gave trust lightly. He guarded it as fiercely as a dragon hoarding gold, and the fact that he was offering even a shred of it to her meant something. Something big.

Blight swallowed hard and straightened her back. "Okay," she said, her voice stronger than she felt. "I'll do it, Devaultus."

His golden eyes locked onto hers, unreadable, yet she swore there was a glimmer of approval in them. He gave her a single nod. "Thank you, Blight."

To the side, Vex frowned, clearly put out by being left out of this little arrangement. Arms crossed, she pouted in that exaggerated way of hers, pursing her lips. Devaultus smirked at her reaction, amused but not unsympathetic. "Don't worry, Lorivelle," he said smoothly. "You'll be there with us. We need your expertise in... well, in the finer things. Do you still remember all that from your previous life?"

Vex instantly perked up, grinning wildly. "Of course, my Lord." She gave him a dramatic bow, sweeping an imaginary hat off her head as if she were some noblewoman at court.

Devaultus shook his head with a chuckle, then wagged a finger at both of them. "Starting now, we practice. The moment we step foot in that city, I am no longer Devaultus. I am a slave. And you two will treat me as such."

Blight hesitated, glancing at him uncertainly. The very idea of treating Devaultus, of all people, like a slave made her stomach twist. But she nodded, pushing down her discomfort.

"We'll be in Deshara within the hour," he continued, producing a slip of parchment from his coat and unfolding it. "This is what we need, a special cloth for a sail. It must be procured and delivered to the ship. That's our primary objective."

Both women nodded, accepting the mission.

It was at that moment that Al'Shandra made her entrance, striding into the room with the effortless sway of a woman who owned any space she stepped into. Her lips curled in a knowing smile, golden eyes gleaming with amusement as she took them all in. The way her barely-there corset and thigh-high leather boots hugged her curves was almost distracting, but that was Al'Shandra in a nutshell: always walking that fine line between commanding and temptress.

"Do you have your plans for this little excursion, then?" she asked, voice as smooth as honeyed rum.

Devaultus turned to her, offering a sharp nod. "I do, Captain. I think we're ready. Though, as always, more time to prepare would be useful, especially given the circumstances."

Al'Shandra chuckled, shaking her head. "Oh, sugar, if we always waited until we were ready, we'd never do a damn thing." She leaned in slightly, her voice dropping into something almost sultry. "Besides, I've got faith in you."

Devaultus exhaled through his nose, glancing at Blight and Vex. No going back now.

The game was about to begin.

"Well, prepare on the way. The ship is here," Al'Shandra purred, her lips curving into that oft-present smirk.

Devaultus had long since suspected that she found great amusement in throwing him headfirst into the fire, watching him scramble and adapt just to survive. This time was no different. He exhaled sharply and began stripping away his gear, the weight of his weapons and armor lifting from his body but settling like a stone in his gut. He handed his daggers off to Vex, who accepted them with a gleeful grin, spinning one experimentally before tucking them away at her sides. The rest of his armaments were left on the bed, useless to him now.

He hated this. Hated the idea of walking into unknown territory unarmed, vulnerable. But there was no choice. He would be searched the moment they set foot in Deshara.

As if reading his thoughts, Al'Shandra sauntered closer, her hips swaying with deliberate exaggeration. She let something drop onto the bed with a casual flick of her wrist.

"You'll be needing this," she said, the amusement in her voice unmistakable.

Devaultus didn't have to open the bundle to know what it contained. Still, he unwrapped the cloth with a resigned sigh, his suspicions confirmed the moment he saw the wretched garment inside: the unmistakable attire of a male slave.

The others had already begun to filter out, heading for the deck to prepare for departure, but Devaultus lingered. For a moment, he simply stared at the outfit in his hands, his grip tightening. The fabric was thin, barely more than an insult to dignity. A simple loincloth, little more than a strip of fabric meant to remind the wearer, and everyone who saw him, exactly what he was supposed to be. Some slaves carried packs for their mistresses, meant to haul goods like beasts of burden, but that wasn't their primary purpose.

They were meant to be entertainment.

Devaultus clenched his jaw.

"You can do this, Devaultus," he muttered under his breath. "It's only an act. One you know well."

The words tasted bitter as he forced them out.

With another heavy sigh, he stripped down and pulled the garment on, the familiar sensation sending a wave of unease rolling through him. He ignored it. There was no time for hesitation.

By the time he stepped onto the deck, the others were already gathered. The crew had arranged for a smaller vessel to ferry them to shore; at least they wouldn't be launched onto shore again.

Small mercies.

But the moment the wind hit his exposed skin, Devaultus knew one thing for certain.

He fucking hated Deshara already.

Al'Shandra ensured no men remained on deck when the smaller vessel docked alongside theirs. The moment the gangplank lowered, a handful of women strode aboard with the casual arrogance of those who knew they held absolute power in Deshara. Their sharp gazes swept over the assembled party, immediately honing in on Devaultus. He stood with his shoulders hunched, gaze lowered, the very picture of subservience. It was an act, one he loathed playing, but one he had perfected long ago.

One of the women, a hardened enforcer with a jagged scar running down her cheek, stopped in front of him, eyes narrowing. "This your property?" she asked, her voice edged with lazy authority.

Blight hesitated for only a second before nodding. "He is."

The woman didn't ask permission. She simply grabbed a fistful of Devaultus' dark hair and wrenched his head up, forcing him to meet her scrutinizing gaze. He didn't flinch, though his jaw tightened. Her hands roamed over him with an impersonal efficiency, searching the thin scrap of fabric he wore. The examination wasn't for weapons, everyone knew a slave wouldn't be armed. This was for dominance, for humiliation.

Satisfied, she released him with a grunt. "He'll need shackles before he sets foot on Deshara," she said bluntly. "Law's the law. Pets need leashes."

Devaultus swallowed, the words striking something deep inside him. His fingers twitched, his breath coming a fraction too fast. His mind flashed back to the tower, the cold, unyielding bite of steel around his throat and wrists, the suffocating weight of control stripped away. He forced himself to remain still, to smother the panic clawing its way up his throat.

The woman motioned to her companion. "Get the extras."

A younger enforcer stepped forward, holding a pair of iron shackles. She snapped one around Devaultus' right wrist with practiced ease. The moment she moved for the other, the world seemed to tilt. The weight of memory pressed against him like a vise. The sharp scent of metal, the finality of the lock...

*Click.*

His breath hitched. A ghostly echo of past captivity threatened to break through, but he swallowed it down, forcing his body to obey, forcing himself to be *here, now.*

And then came the collar.

*Click.*

The woman smirked. "Good dog."

Something primal burned in Devaultus' chest, but he kept his expression neutral, schooling his features into submission. *It's just an act.* He repeated the words in his mind, gripping them like a lifeline.

The enforcer turned away, already bored, and waved toward the skiff waiting below. "Everyone on. Time's wasting."

The group stepped aboard, the vessel rocking slightly as they took their places. Al'Shandra remained on deck, watching the scene unfold with a glint in her eye. Whether it was intrigue, amusement, or something else entirely, Devaultus couldn't tell. But there was something undeniably feline about the way she tilted her head, lips curled in a knowing smirk.

And as the skiff pushed off toward the shore, Devaultus exhaled slowly, bracing himself for what came next.

# CHAPTER 21

# RULE NUMBER ONE. DON'T TALK ABOUT BLIGHT CLUB

The skiff sliced through the sand of the harbor, its hull bumping against the dock with a hollow thud. The docks of Deshara were a controlled storm of movement, slaves toiling under the watchful eyes of their mistresses, the crack of whips punctuating the air as enforcers disciplined those too slow or too weak to meet the relentless demands of their owners. Men scurried like vermin beneath the boots of their female overseers, lifting crates, hauling supplies, and tending to the ships without a moment's rest. Those who faltered were met with swift, merciless correction.

Devaultus let out a slow exhale, his eyes sweeping the chaos before him. This was going to be a challenge. Keeping his mouth shut had never been a strong suit, and in a place like this, speaking out of turn would earn him more than just a beating. It could mean death, or worse.

The skiff rocked slightly as it came to a full stop, the sand covered ropes groaning as they were secured to the pier. He remained motionless, waiting for Blight to take the lead. Her hesitation was nearly imperceptible, but he caught the flicker of uncertainty in her eyes before she tugged sharply on the chain connected to his collar.

"Come along, slave," she said, her voice steady but lacking the venom of a true mistress.

Devaultus clenched his teeth but followed, stepping onto the dock barefoot and stripped of everything that once made him dangerous. His movements were slow, deliberate, communicating that he was too proud to shuffle like a broken thing, but cautious enough not to invite suspicion.

Vex trailed just behind them, her posture unnervingly perfect, back ramrod straight, shoulders rolled back with an effortless grace that screamed of nobility. Every step she took was precise, calculated. She didn't acknowledge the slaves around her, didn't spare them a glance. To the world, she was a woman of power, a mistress who expected obedience without question. She was playing her part beautifully, but Devaultus knew her well enough to see the telltale glimmer of amusement lurking beneath the mask. She was enjoying this, maybe not the circumstances, but the sheer ridiculousness of the role.

Blight, on the other hand, was still finding her footing in this game. She turned her head slightly, casting a glance toward Vex. "We must find these sails," she said, her tone carefully measured.

Vex flicked her gaze over the dock, considering their options. As a male slave passed by, his arms loaded with supplies, she reached out and grabbed him by the collar, her fingers curling around the rough fabric like she'd done it a thousand times before.

The man froze, his breath catching in his throat as he was yanked to a stop. Panic flared in his eyes, sweat already forming at his brow.

"Where would one find sails?" Vex asked, her voice level but holding an unmistakable note of command.

The man swallowed hard. "S-south side, Mistress," he stammered. "O'Malley's is the name."

Vex nodded, releasing him without another word. The man hesitated for a moment, as if expecting something more, perhaps a blow, perhaps a cruel remark, but when none came, his confusion was palpable.

His gaze darted between Vex and Blight before he hurried away, disappearing into the throng of laboring men.

Devaultus smirked slightly, lowering his gaze before anyone noticed. Oh, this was going to be interesting.

"Less nice," Blight muttered through gritted teeth, her fingers tightening around the chain in her grasp.

Vex didn't need to be told twice. With a sharp shove, she sent the trembling man stumbling away from her. "Get back to what you were doing," she ordered coolly. He didn't hesitate, bolting away as if he had narrowly escaped a death sentence, eager to lose himself in his assigned labor once more.

The two women moved forward, their pace unhurried but purposeful, dragging Devaultus along with them. He felt the tug of the chain fastened to his collar, a bitter reminder of the role he had agreed to play. His gaze remained lowered, taking in the smooth stone streets beneath his feet, each slab carved and placed with meticulous care. This city, it seemed, had been built not just for function, but to be a testament to wealth and dominance.

The grandeur was impossible to ignore. Towering structures flanked either side of the street, their facades adorned with intricate carvings, each more elaborate than the last. The artistry in the stonework told stories of conquest, power, and indulgence. Balconies overlooked the streets below, occupied by lounging women draped in silks, their skin kissed by the golden sun. Slaves hovered at their sides, slipping bits of fruit between their lips, fanning them lazily, or rubbing fragrant oils into their skin. It was a kingdom of queens, where men were nothing more than property, tools to be used and discarded at their mistresses' whims.

Devaultus forced himself to keep his eyes averted, resisting the temptation to take in the spectacle more fully. Meeting the gaze of a woman here, especially as a man in chains, would not end well. He had played roles before, worn masks of deceit and deception, but this was an entirely different battlefield. Here, he wasn't the one in control.

The trio turned down another street. Judging by the sun's position, this had to be the south side of the city.

Vex strode with unwavering confidence, her posture perfect, her presence commanding, as if she had walked these streets her entire life. Blight trailed just a step behind, gripping Devaultus' tether with a firm hand. Every step felt unnatural to her, but she didn't falter.

Devaultus had just settled into the rhythm of their movement when Blight came to an abrupt halt. He barely had time to stop himself from colliding into her back. His instincts screamed at him: something was wrong. But when he followed her gaze upward, he found her frozen, staring in wide-eyed shock at one of the balconies above.

Something, or someone, had caught her attention.

Blight's breath hitched, her throat tightening as if invisible hands had wrapped around it. Her wide, misty eyes locked onto the woman lounging above, a figure she had long since assumed lost to the world, or at least, lost to her. She barely registered the flow of foot traffic around her or the pull of the chain in her grip. Everything else blurred into nothing, leaving only that caramel-skinned woman basking in luxury, draped in silks, her every whim attended to by a small flock of slaves.

Vex, realizing Blight was no longer keeping pace, slowed to a stop and turned on her heel, following her friend's gaze up to the balcony. She cocked her head, scrutinizing the woman as she was delicately fed a piece of fruit by a trembling, near-naked man. The scene would have seemed absurdly theatrical, almost comedic, if not for the way Blight's entire body had gone rigid with shock.

Vex meandered back to Blight's side, her voice dropping to a hushed, playful whisper. "What's up, Puppy?"

From behind them, Devaultus muttered under his breath, his tone edged with irritation. "Call her Mistress Blight."

Vex shot him a scathing look, her lips curling in exasperation. She was really taking this roleplay a bit too seriously. As she always did.

Blight barely heard either of them. Her fingers twitched around the chain, her pulse hammering. "That's... that's Dina..." Her voice trembled as the words stumbled out. "The girl I came here with..."

Dina, who had seemed completely at ease just moments ago, now straightened, stepping forward to the balcony's edge. Her keen eyes swept the street, locking onto the small group staring up at her. A flicker of curiosity crossed her face, followed by something colder: suspicion.

She squinted, her lips parting as though she were trying to place a long-forgotten memory.

"...Cassandra?"

The name barely reached Blight's ears before Vex let out a relieved chuckle, clapping Blight on the back hard enough to make her stumble forward a step.

"Oh, good, she doesn't recognize you," Vex chirped, ever the optimist. She grinned, her voice light and teasing despite the weight of the moment. "Your name is Puppy... or, as Devaultus calls you, Blight."

Blight swallowed hard, but she couldn't tear her gaze away from Dina's piercing stare.

The moment stretched unbearably, the gap between them a chasm that could either be bridged or broken completely.

Blight waved awkwardly at the woman, her heart beating faster as she saw her long-lost friend. "I used to be called Cassandra," she said, her voice soft but tinged with a nostalgic edge. "Just like you had a different name before." The words hung between them like a secret, an unspoken connection that reached back through time.

Dina's eyes lit up as the woman waved back at her, and she grinned, her excitement contagious. "Stay where you are," she said in a voice that was both commanding and playful. "I'll be down promptly." Without waiting for a response, she spun on her heels and vanished into the house, her slaves parting like the Red Sea as she moved through them with practiced grace.

The brief moments that followed felt like an eternity, each second stretching out until Dina returned, practically throwing herself at Blight in a whirlwind of movement. "I have so missed you!" Dina exclaimed, her voice catching in a breathless laugh. She clung to Blight, her caramel skin soft against Blight's, as though no time had passed at all.

Blight couldn't help but smile, her eyes lighting up with genuine joy at seeing her friend again. "I was so worried about you, Dina," Blight admitted, the weight of the worry she'd carried now lifting slightly. She motioned to Vex, who stood a few steps behind with her usual exaggerated air of disinterest, and then to Devaultus, who looked about as out of place as a lion in a den of rabbits. "This is my dear friend Vex," Blight said, her voice laced with affection, "and my slave, Devaultus." She didn't miss the discomfort that passed over Vex's face when she mentioned the word "slave," but the woman seemed to take it in stride, as she always did.

Dina's gaze shifted first to Vex; and then, as if noticing Devaultus for the first time, she barely gave him a glance before turning her attention back to Blight. She smiled at Vex, her lips curling in a playful, flirtatious manner as she kissed Vex's hand in an exaggerated show of grace. "It is a pleasure to meet you, Vex," Dina purred, her tone low and sultry, the words practically dripping with charm.

But when her gaze landed on Devaultus, it was as though he ceased to exist for her. She didn't acknowledge him: no glance, no word. It was almost as if he were invisible, his presence was so entirely dismissed.

Vex rolled her eyes with exaggerated boredom but didn't protest, instead watching the exchange with a mix of amusement and mild confusion. Blight, for her part, took in Dina's every word, her heart swelling with a bittersweet mix of joy and apprehension.

Dina's next words came out in a melodic laugh that held both mischief and hospitality. "Please, you must join me for wine and a bite to eat. I really must find out what you have been up to!" Her tone was one of genuine curiosity, but there was something almost predatory in her eyes, something Blight couldn't quite place.

The invitation hung in the air, as enticing as it was dangerous. Blight found herself drawn in, the possibility of reconnecting with Dina overwhelming her, even though she knew the path to this moment had been long and fraught with pain. What had she gone through and how did it affect her? Was she the same person? She was so broken when they had last seen each other.

The soft call of the woman's voice, the lingering warmth of a friendship long lost, tugged at Blight's heartstrings, but something deep inside her, something instinctual, whispered that not everything was as it seemed.

Dina's voice, light and sweet, lingered in the air as she beamed at Blight. "I really must find out what you have been up to." The words sounded innocent enough, but there was an undercurrent of something more, something Blight couldn't quite place. She hadn't seen Dina in so long, and the sight of her now, in this new world, made Blight's heart race. Her old friend had changed. Blight had changed, too. But the words felt foreign on her tongue, as if this whole encounter wasn't real; and yet here she was, standing in front of her.

Devaultus, despite himself, had a strong urge to step in and steer the conversation in a different direction. He knew full well how easily things could slip out of control. His mind raced with a thousand lies, a dozen different stories, each one feeling more ridiculous than the last.

Trying to come up with something convincing on the spot was not his forte; and yet, as much as he wanted to speak up, he couldn't risk saying something that would reveal too much. Not when they were this close to danger.

Blight, oblivious to his internal turmoil, was still locked in a gaze with Dina, her expression softening as her friend's words sank in. There was a shimmer of something in her eyes, an eagerness, a hope that maybe, just maybe, things weren't as broken as she thought they were. She hadn't been sure what she expected, but certainly not this... not Dina. And for a moment, Blight almost forgot the world around her, the chaos, the danger, the brutal reality of everything they'd left behind.

Vex, noticing the excitement in Blight's eyes, could see the spark of familiarity lighting up her face. It wasn't often she saw Blight like this: vulnerable, caught in the grip of past emotions. It was almost too easy to play the part of the outsider, observing the scene while the others lost themselves in the reunion. She gave a small, almost playful shrug, her voice light and teasing. "We'd love to, Dina. Thank you for having us," she said, her tone dripping with feigned sincerity. Her words hung in the air like a sweet promise, even as her eyes darted around, searching for anything that might throw the situation off balance. Vex was never one to settle into anything too easily, but she could tell Blight was happy, even if it made her feel a little uneasy.

As the group began to move toward the door, Dina's house looming just ahead, another voice broke the fragile bubble of ease that had formed between them. A sharp, commanding tone. The kind that made even the most seasoned of men stand at attention.

"No need to sully the mistress's home with your slave," a woman called out, her words cutting through the air. She stood in the doorway, her posture rigid and imposing, her eyes cold and calculating. "I'll take him to the stables with the other beasts."

Devaultus froze for a second. A surge of anger and frustration bubbled up inside him, but he bit it back before it could break free. He hadn't anticipated this. *Of course they'd treat him like this. He was a slave. Nothing more than an animal in their eyes.* But that didn't make it any less infuriating. Irritation crossed his face, and for a moment, he felt the overwhelming urge to lash out, to do something, anything, to show them just how wrong they were.

Blight looked up at the woman, a faint frown creasing her brow. She opened her mouth, as though to protest, but then stopped herself. Her gaze flickered over to Vex, uncertain. This was all too much for her. Too much too soon. The world she had been thrust into was nothing like the one she had known, and every time she thought she could keep up, the rules seemed to change.

Vex, however, took it in stride. She stepped forward with a grin, eyes dancing with amusement. Her fingers twitched, a mix of boredom and curiosity running through her veins. "Oh, I'm sure you've got your hands full with that. But tell me, what exactly do you mean by 'beasts'? You wouldn't be so kind as to show me where these... 'other beasts' are kept, would you?" Her voice was light, laced with a tone that suggested she might just be willing to go along with it for the sheer fun of it.

The woman's glare could've cut through stone, but Vex wasn't intimidated. She was too chaotic, too unpredictable for anyone to get under her skin, and she loved it. The woman's jaw clenched, and she looked down at the leash in Blight's hands, her gaze flicking between Devaultus and Vex. "I'll take care of him," she said again, her voice more forceful this time, but Vex was already losing interest in her. The threat of authority didn't seem to phase her.

Blight hesitated, torn between wanting to protect Devaultus from this woman, and the odd sense of duty that weighed heavily on her shoulders. She didn't want him to be treated this way, but at the same time, she wasn't sure how to stop it. Her eyes flickered to Vex for a moment, silently asking for help. Vex simply smiled, an unpredictable glint in her eye.

"Well, if we must," Vex said with a shrug, "but don't think we won't come looking for him if he doesn't make it back in one piece." Her words were light, but there was something more dangerous beneath them, an unspoken threat that she was more than capable of carrying out.

The woman gave a curt nod, but Blight wasn't sure if she believed it. There was so much at play here and she had a feeling that Dina's home, this place, wasn't the sanctuary she'd heard rumors of in her past. There was something else here. Something Blight couldn't see yet. Dina seemed off. She couldn't put her finger on it, but it was there.

As the woman led Devaultus away, Vex and Blight exchanged glances, both silently agreeing that they needed to be cautious. Dina's kindness might have been genuine, but something about this place, about Dina, was just not right.

The woman led Devaultus away, her grip firm and her posture stiff with authority. Vex watched them disappear across the yard to the stables, her sharp eyes etching the route into memory. She didn't trust these people; hell, she barely trusted anyone. But Devaultus? He was hers to torment, not theirs. A sly smirk crept onto her lips as she turned back toward the others, making a mental note of exactly where she would find him later.

With a bounce in her step, she followed Blight inside, where Dina had already made herself comfortable, lounging with effortless grace, a knowing smirk playing at her lips. She leaned forward, resting her chin against her knuckles, her caramel skin glowing in the soft candlelight.

"Now then, my dear," Dina purred, her voice rich with curiosity. "Do tell, what have you been up to?" That mischievous glint in her eye hadn't dulled with time. If anything, it had only sharpened.

Blight practically beamed, her earlier nervousness melting under the warmth of familiarity. "Well," she started, tucking a strand of raven hair behind her ear, "I was fortunate to have been rescued from that slaver's pit by Vex here and... and her friend." She faltered, realizing she had nearly let Devaultus' name slip.

Vex grinned wickedly but said nothing, watching the exchange with amusement.

"They rescued everyone," Blight added, her voice filled with admiration.

Dina's lips curled into something between a smirk and a frown. "Well, dear," she murmured, tilting her mug slightly, watching the liquid swirl inside. "Not everyone."

Blight hesitated, the weight of guilt pressing on her chest. Her face flushed. "Yes, well... we tried. We looked for you. Where did they take you? We searched everywhere."

Dina's expression shifted, her gaze darkening as she stared into her drink as if it held the ghosts of her past. She hesitated, her fingers tightening around the mug, knuckles whitening.

"Those two took me away to their place..." she finally murmured. The air in the room seemed to still. "They forced me to do many horrible things. For them and for..." She shook her head abruptly, cutting herself off before the memories could drown her. A slow, deliberate breath passed her lips before she looked up again, that carefully crafted mask slipping back into place. A teasing smile played at the edges of her mouth, as if she hadn't just pulled back from the edge of something deep and dark.

"But enough about me," she said smoothly, her tone light once more, as if the moment of vulnerability had never happened. "We were talking about you. What else have you been up to?"

The shift was so seamless, it was almost unnerving. Blight could see it now: this wasn't quite the Dina she had known before. There was something sharper in her eyes, something carefully hidden beneath layers of charm and ease.

"Well, we found ourselves in a bit of trouble," Blight admitted, her voice light but carefully measured. She gestured toward Vex with a tilt of her head. "Her father... let's just say, he's not too pleased with us at the moment. So, we thought it best to put a bit of distance between us and him."

Vex's posture stiffened, and she shot Blight a look: sharp, almost panicked. Why was she bringing that up? Lie. Keep it vague. Keep it simple. The last thing they needed was to get tangled in a web of half-truths.

Blight caught the unease in Vex's gaze and quickly backpedaled. "Eh, no worries, it's nothing serious," she added, perhaps a little too hastily. "We just figured we'd take the opportunity to find some new sails, make our trip a little faster."

Dina's face lit up with delight, practically buzzing with excitement. "Oh, then ye must go to O'Malley's! She's the finest in the trade, hands down. But you'll have to wait till tomorrow, she's out for the day."

Vex seized the moment, her eyes flicking between Blight and Dina, trying to steer the conversation away from dangerous territory. "Oh, we really wouldn't want to impose," she said, her tone casual, but with an undercurrent of tension. "Besides, we've got our slave down there, and we wouldn't want him to be a bother to you and yours."

Dina giggled, a rich, musical sound that carried a hint of amusement. "Oh, it's no bother at all. He'll be just fine down there with the others," she assured them with a dismissive wave of her hand. "Now, I won't hear another word about it! Let me show ye where ye'll be stayin'. The two of ye must be absolutely exhausted from your travels."

She grinned, all warmth and hospitality, but there was something else beneath the surface, something harder to read. She had a look Blight couldn't quite place, but before she could dwell on it, Dina was already leading them deeper into the house.

Vex really didn't want to do this. Every fiber of her being screamed that this was a bad idea. Her mind kept circling back to Devaultus, locked away in the stables like some common beast, and it gnawed at her like an itch she couldn't scratch. This wasn't good. Not at all.

Blight, standing beside her, mirrored her unease, her gaze flickering between Vex and the floor as if searching for some reassurance in the polished wood beneath them. "He should be fine down there," she said, though her voice lacked conviction. "A night in a real bed would do us good. Besides... where else would we stay?"

Vex exhaled sharply, knowing Blight had a point. They had no other options, no inn, no safe house. But that didn't make her feel any better about leaving Devaultus. He wasn't the type to tolerate submission, not even as an act, and she had no doubt that every second of this charade was chipping away at his already unstable patience. She could only hope he managed to keep his temper in check long enough for them to get what they needed and leave.

Their quarters were extravagant, a stark contrast to the rough conditions they were used to. Everything in the rooms was tailored to a woman's comfort: silken drapes, embroidered pillows, and furniture carved with delicate floral designs. The air smelled of lavender and jasmine, an almost sickeningly soft aroma compared to the blood and sand she was accustomed to.

Vex drifted toward the window, her fingers twitching as she pulled back the curtain just enough to peer outside. The stables loomed in the distance, shrouded in darkness, their faint lantern glow flickering in the night. Her stomach twisted. If Devaultus lost control, if he snapped... She wasn't sure what would happen, but she knew it wouldn't be subtle. His issues ran deep, just as deep as her own, maybe deeper. But where her chaos was wild and reckless, his was a storm waiting to break, all wrapped up in that sharp-edged arrogance he wielded like a weapon.

Maybe, someday, he'd tell her what had made him this way. Maybe, someday, she'd understand. But right now, none of that mattered.

Because if something happened to him, if they dared harm him, she would burn this entire city to the ground and laugh while it turned to ash.

In the next room over, Blight curled up in the plush bed, her small frame sinking into the softest mattress she'd felt since arriving in this world of brutality. It was a strange comfort, one that almost felt unnatural after all she had been through. But exhaustion overtook her quickly, and soon, she drifted into a dreamless sleep, cocooned in the warmth of something that, for once, felt safe.

The morning came too soon. Vex had barely slept, her nerves too frayed, her mind too restless. Every hour or so, she had crept from her bed, padding silently to the window, peering out at the stable where Devaultus had been dragged off the night before. The darkness outside had offered no answers, just the unsettling quiet of the early morning hours. She had stood there, waiting, listening, hoping for a sign that he hadn't done something reckless. But the night had remained silent, and eventually, she had forced herself back into bed, though sleep never truly came.

Blight, on the other hand, had slept like the dead. The plush bed had cradled her in a comfort she had long forgotten, and for the first time in what felt like forever, she had woken up feeling... safe. She stretched lazily, her arms reaching above her head as she soaked in the softness of the room around her. It was a stark contrast to the harshness of the world she had been thrown into. Just as she began to pull herself from the blankets, a knock came at her door.

"Come in!" she called out, her voice light and cheery, still half-drenched in the comfort of a good night's sleep.

The door swung open, and Vex slipped inside, her face tight, her shoulders rigid with tension. Blight blinked at her, instantly realizing how much worse Vex had fared through the night. The dark circles under her eyes, the irritated twitch of her fingers: it was obvious she hadn't rested at all.

"Let's go," Vex said flatly. "We need to get Devaultus and get out of here."

Blight's smile faltered, her heart sinking. She cast a longing glance around the room, at the luxurious bed, at the fine silks, the fresh smell of clean linens. "Are we sure we need to leave so quickly? It's so nice here..."

Vex's glare was sharp enough to cut through the walls. "Maybe for you," she snapped. "I'm sure Devaultus is thinking otherwise."

Blight swallowed hard, heat rising to her cheeks as she looked away, embarrassed. "Yes... You're right. I'm sorry."

Vex sighed, the sharpness in her gaze softening just a little. "Come on. Let's find our host and figure out how to get to O'Mally's."

With that, the two slipped out into the corridor, their footsteps soft against the polished floors. The hall stretched before them, leading toward the grand balcony where they had first seen Dina the night before.

Sure enough, there she was, lounging like a queen upon a cushioned chair, her posture lazy yet undeniably commanding. One of her slaves knelt beside her, offering her fresh fruit, while another held a goblet in one hand, waiting patiently for her next sip. She looked every bit as untouchable as she had the night before.

Vex and Blight continued forward, their pace steady; but then, just before stepping out into the open, they hesitated.

The slave's foot slipped, a slight misstep, but enough to send the goblet of wine tilting too far. A deep crimson splash spilled across Dina's chest, staining the fine silks draped over her like a queen's robe. For a moment, everything was still. The man's breath caught in his throat, his face blanching in sheer terror. Then Dina's eyes flashed, a predatory gleam of unbridled rage.

"You *worthless* male!" she snarled, her voice a whip crack of fury.

Before the slave could stammer out an apology, Dina lunged from her chair, hand snapping out with the precision of a viper. The silver fork in her grasp became a weapon, plunging into the man's face with a bloody stabbing motion. He screamed, staggering back, but she was on him, her movements wild, feral, utterly merciless. Again and again, the fork drove into his flesh, each strike fueled by pure, unrestrained wrath.

The man gurgled, hands weakly grasping at the ground as he tried to crawl away. Blood dripped from his ruined face, his body jerking with each brutal stab. Dina wasn't finished. She straddled his back, her knees pressing into his ribs as she drove the prongs of the utensil into the base of his skull. A sickening crunch, a final spasm, then stillness.

The fork clattered from her fingers, bouncing once against the stone floor. Dina exhaled sharply, as if shaking off a mild inconvenience, then lifted her hand and rang a small silver bell.

From around the corner, a handful of maids appeared, their expressions neutral, almost bored. They barely spared the body a glance before exchanging a few quiet words and setting to work. One retrieved a mop. Another fetched fresh linens. Not a single one looked surprised.

Vex blinked, eyes flicking from the lifeless corpse to Blight, whose face had paled considerably. "So... was Dina always a little *cray cray* back when you knew her?" she asked, voice dry but tinged with a note of genuine unease.

Blight swallowed, still staring at the blood pooling across the floor. "Yeah, but... not *that* cray cray."

Vex ran a hand through her hair. This wasn't just some misplaced aggression, this was something else. Something darker. Something rotten. *Great. Just what we needed.*

She shook herself from her thoughts and turned on her heel. "I'm getting Devaultus. You say your goodbyes."

"Yeah..." Blight murmured, hesitantly stepping toward Dina, though there was a stiffness in her posture now, a wariness she hadn't felt before.

Devaultus was led through the heavy wooden doors of the stables, the oppressive atmosphere settling over him like a thick, suffocating fog. The air was stale, tinged with the musk of unwashed bodies and old blood. Only a few dim lanterns flickered along the stone walls, casting long, wavering shadows that danced like specters against the damp, aged wood of the stalls. His keen gaze swept the corridor as he was marched down the central hall, noting the figures within each enclosure: men, every last one of them, in varying states of despair and mangled mess.

One wept softly in the corner of his stall, shoulders shaking as he cradled his hands against his chest. Devaultus' sharp eyes caught the source of his misery: his fingernails had been torn clean from his fingers, leaving raw, tender flesh exposed. Another unfortunate soul sat stiffly against the wall, his once well-kept hair hacked away in uneven chunks. Deep, jagged scars marred his face, forming crude words that had long since healed but left behind a permanent testament to his suffering.

The grim procession didn't slow. Before long, rough hands shoved Devaultus forward into an open stall, the stench of damp straw and sweat assaulting his senses as he stumbled. His instincts flared, muscles tensing, but he forced himself not to retaliate. *Play the part,* he thought. He hit the ground hard, palms scraping against the rough floor as the guards sneered down at him.

"Keep your mouth shut and stay put," one of the women snapped, voice laced with disdain. She loomed over him, her expression twisted with cruel amusement. "Unless you want a lesson I doubt your mistresses teach you often enough."

Devaultus clenched his teeth so hard, his jaw ached. The words he wanted to spit at her burned the back of his throat, but he swallowed them down. This was temporary. He'd be out soon.

Slowly, he pushed himself upright, back pressing against the cold wooden boards behind him. He forced himself to regulate his breathing, steadying the chaotic storm churning within him. This was fine. This was manageable.

A quiet voice hissed through a small hole in the wall beside him. "Oi. Mate. You alive over there?"

Devaultus turned his head slightly, crawling toward the hole. "I'm here," he murmured, keeping his tone neutral. "Why is everyone in here so..." he glanced toward the weeping man again, "...broken?"

A bitter chuckle filtered through the hole. "Because we belong to Mistress Dina. And Mistress Dina... she ain't like the others. She's got a hatred for men I ain't never seen before. The ones that end up in her house? A week. Maybe two. That's all they last."

Devaultus exhaled slowly, his fists tightening against his thighs. His situation had just gone from uncomfortable to outright dangerous.

"She beats and kills her own slaves enough," the man whispered through the small hole in the wall, his voice hollow, drained of all hope. "But then she'll rent them out, let other mistresses do whatever they please. Some use them for pleasure. Others for pain. Some just to break them, leave them worse off than before."

Devaultus remained still, absorbing the words, letting the weight of them settle like a stone in his gut. He had felt something wrong the moment he set foot in this place. That gnawing, crawling sensation under his skin, like he had just walked into a slaughterhouse, and the scent of blood hadn't even faded yet. But he had dismissed it, convinced himself it was just the nature of the role he was forced to play, just his personal distaste for submission skewing his judgment. But now? Now, there was no mistaking it. This place wasn't just a prison. It was a slow, rotting grave for men.

His bindings were nothing to him. He could tear through them in a heartbeat. He could melt through the bars, leave this wretched stable behind, leave these broken men in the dirt. But the sails. The ship. Tarus.

If he left now, he would doom them all.

So, he stayed put.

The hours stretched on, each one longer than the last. The cell was cold, but not unbearably so, just enough to creep into his bones and make the silence even worse. He wasn't sure how long he had been there, but it had been far too long. This was supposed to be quick. An hour, maybe two at the most.

So where were they?

Had they abandoned him?

No, Vex wouldn't do that. She was reckless, but she wasn't disloyal. Blight wouldn't leave him either, not if she had a choice.

But Dina?

That bitch could have changed the plan the second she got Blight alone.

His jaw clenched, and a dark seed of rage began to root itself in his gut. He swallowed it down, but the bitterness remained, coating his tongue like ash.

"Hey," he called out, his voice firm despite the unease settling in his chest. "I need to see my Mistress."

The man in the next cell sucked in a sharp breath. "What the hell are you doing? Keep your mouth shut. I don't think they're coming back for you. Just lay low."

Devaultus didn't answer. He just waited.

And then, footsteps.

Slow, deliberate, with the unmistakable air of someone savoring the moment. A shadow stretched across the floor as she approached, the dim lantern light catching the sneer on her face before she even stopped in front of his cell.

The guard.

She didn't just look pleased. She looked hungry.

She grinned, a slow, cruel thing, her teeth flashing in the darkness.

She had power here. And she was about to make damn sure he knew it.

Opening the cell door, the guard sneered down at him, her lips curling into something between amusement and disgust. "You don't get to make requests, you worthless creature."

She stepped inside, the flickering torchlight casting jagged shadows across the filthy walls. From the rack beside the door, she grabbed a long whip, the leather coiling like a serpent in her grip. She ran her fingers along its length, savoring the moment before snapping it taut with a practiced flick of her wrist.

"I'll teach you your place," she purred, raising the whip high above her head, her muscles tensing as she prepared to bring it down.

Devaultus forced himself to stay still. Every instinct screamed at him to act, to strike first, to dismantle her piece by piece before she could take another breath. One sharp kick to the knee would crumple her stance, and by the time she realized what had happened, his knee would already be crushing her windpipe. It would be easy. It would be satisfying.

But it would also ruin everything.

He clenched his fists, nails biting into his palms as he exhaled through his nose. Stick to the plan. He would kill her in time. That was a promise.

The whip came down.

And stopped.

A hand, firm and unyielding, had caught it mid-swing.

Vex.

She stood just behind the woman, fingers clamped tight around the guard's wrist, her grip like iron. Her usual playful mischief was gone, replaced by something cold and dangerous. Her eyes gleamed with an intensity that sent a shiver through the dimly lit cell.

"You dare punish my slave without my permission?" Vex's voice was smooth, but it carried a threat that settled thick in the air.

The woman sneered, attempting to yank her arm free, but Vex held firm.

"I'll do whatever I damn well please in this house," the guard spat. "You will do nothing but sit there and watch."

Vex's expression didn't change. If anything, she grew eerily still, the flicker of candlelight reflecting off her emerald eyes like a predator sizing up prey. "I am not one of your slaves," she said, voice barely above a whisper. "And you will watch your tone with me, or I'll cut out your tongue and ensure you don't have one anymore. Do you understand me?"

The woman's lips curled, her patience snapping like dry twigs. She was bigger than Vex, muscled from years of hard labor, and confident in her strength.

"You little..."

She never finished the sentence.

Vex struck like lightning, her fist slamming into the woman's throat. The guard staggered back, eyes widening as she gasped, her body betraying her with a desperate fight for air. She collapsed to one knee, coughing violently, her hands clawing at her neck as if she could physically pull the pain away.

Vex, unfazed, ripped the whip from the woman's weakened grip.

She took a step back, the leather unfurling with a deadly grace.

Then she lashed out.

The whip cracked across the woman's back, splitting the silence with a sound like thunder. The guard screamed, her body jerking from the force of the strike, but Vex didn't stop. She was relentless, her arm moving in fluid arcs as she lashed again, and again, each strike landing with merciless precision.

"Keep talking, you little stable whore," Vex taunted, her voice laced with mockery as she readied another strike. "I promise you won't be spending much time on your back when I'm through with you."

The woman choked on a sob, her body trembling beneath the onslaught, and still, Vex did not let up. The madness in her grin gleamed like a blade in the darkness, and Devaultus, watching from the cell floor, couldn't help but smirk.

Chaotic. Unhinged. Unpredictable.

Vex was at her best.

The fury in Vex's voice was unmistakable, a sharp edge cutting through the damp, musty air of the stables. Devaultus could see it in her stance: the way her shoulders squared, the way her fingers twitched like she was itching to keep going, to paint the floor with the woman's blood. It was chaos humming beneath her skin, and she was barely keeping it in check.

He needed to break through to her, but subtly. The last thing he wanted was to draw attention to himself in a way that would make things worse. A slight shake of his head was all he offered, a barely perceptible movement, but he saw the shift in her eyes as she caught it.

For a second, she hesitated, her nostrils flaring as if she might ignore him altogether. But then, with an exaggerated huff, she let the whip slip from her fingers, letting it coil lifelessly on the ground like a discarded snake.

"Come, slave. We leave," she barked, her tone still thick with irritation, but at least now it was directed forward instead of at the crumpled woman at her feet.

Devaultus didn't hesitate. He stepped over the whimpering, gasping figure, his eyes barely flicking downward as he moved. His restraint burned like a coal in his gut. Oh, he would kill her. Not today. Not in this moment. But he would remember her face. The weight of her whip. The sick satisfaction she had worn just moments ago.

He followed Vex out of the stables, his mind already calculating their next move.

Standing outside Dina's home, Vex waited, arms crossed, glancing between Blight and Dina with a flicker of confusion in her eyes. Dina had cleaned up: no longer smeared with the blood of her servant, her expression calm, almost too composed.

Blight spoke first. "Dina says O'Mally's is a bit out of the way, and she wishes to show us how to find her place."

Vex gave Blight a questioning look, but the girl merely shrugged. With a short huff, Vex relented. "Very well. We best get going."

Dina nodded and waved for a carriage. Two large men pulled it up to the curb, their expressions unreadable as they waited. The three women climbed in without hesitation, but Devaultus was given no such luxury. Instead, he was leashed to the bumper, forced to walk behind like an animal.

The city rolled past them, its outer layer vibrant and filled with laughter as women moved freely, their voices high with excitement. But beneath the surface, the undercurrent of the city whispered a darker tale. Slaves moved through the streets like shadows, their eyes downcast, their faces empty. The weight of the world pressed heavy upon them, resignation etched into every movement.

The carriage veered down an alleyway, then onto a narrow country road.

Vex frowned slightly, turning her gaze to Dina. "O'Mally's isn't in the city?"

Dina let out a soft laugh, as if amused by the question. "No, my dear. There would not be room for sails that size in the city."

Vex considered this for a moment before giving a nod. It made sense.

The carriage finally pulled to a stop before a large building. The door swung open, and Dina smiled brightly. "Here we are," she said cheerfully.

The door to the carriage opened, and Dina stepped out first. Vex hesitated, looking at Blight.

Blight smiled at her. "Relax," she said. "Dina has always been my best friend."

Vex exhaled, stepping out of the carriage alongside Blight.

Then Dina stopped. Not to admire the building, not to take in the night air, but as if she were waiting for something.

The building's door creaked open.

Out stepped Tarus.

A smug look crossed his face as he regarded them. His eyes settled first on Dina, then on Devaultus, and a slow, satisfied grin lit his face as he recognized Devaultus.

"Hello, my dear daughter..." he said, his voice dripping with amusement.

His gaze flicked to Devaultus.

"...And Devaultus." He nearly spat the words out.

## CHAPTER 22

# MAXIMUM CARNAGE

V ex's daggers were in her hands before anyone could blink, her muscles tensed, a wicked grin playing on her lips as she practically vibrated with excitement. She lived for chaos; and this? This was pure, unfiltered madness.

Blight, on the other hand, spun to face Dina, her wide eyes filled with something raw: betrayal, confusion, maybe even a sliver of hope that this wasn't what it looked like. "What have you done?" Her voice trembled, a soft plea against the rising tide of violence that was about to crash down on them all.

Dina's expression was maddeningly calm. "Oh no, Cassandra, I'm not betraying you," she purred, as if the very idea was offensive. "He has promised to leave you alone. All he wants is his daughter... and Devaultus." Her lips curled in satisfaction. "He's offered me many male slaves in return. It will be fine. I'll simply gift you a few in payment for him."

Blight's breath caught in her throat. She turned slowly, her gaze settling on Devaultus. He stood there, unreadable, his presence a looming storm on the horizon. This was her out, wasn't it? She could stay. Live peacefully. Build a life with Dina. She didn't have to keep running, fighting, fearing the unknown.

Devaultus exhaled, barely more than a sigh, but his mind was spinning. He knew that look in Blight's eyes. He'd seen it before in others, a quiet battle, the temptation of an easier road. "She isn't who you think she is, Blight," he said, his voice a low, measured growl. "She kills her slaves without remorse. She has changed."

A chuckle drifted through the tense air. Tarus. That smug bastard was enjoying every second of this. Devaultus didn't have to look to know the expression he wore.

And then, from the shadows, he stepped forth: The Puppeteer. His long, spindly fingers twitched with anticipation as he moved to Tarus' side. That sharp, unnerving grin stretched across his face, filled with unrestrained glee. Oh, how he savored the sight of Devaultus standing on the precipice of ruin.

Blight's head snapped toward Dina, her hesitation shattering as she strode forward. "Dina, don't do this." Her voice was desperate now, but firm. "Help us fight. Come with us. Devaultus will keep us safe."

Dina's laughter rang out, wild and unhinged, like a song sung by a woman who had long since stopped caring about the weight of her own sins. "No, Cassandra," she spat, eyes flashing with something dark, something broken. "I will never be near another male. I will kill them. One after another." Her breath hitched, her grin spreading into something terrifying. "I will flay their skin from their bones..."

The air crackled, thick with tension. This wasn't a woman to be reasoned with. This was something else entirely, a storm that had already decided its path of destruction.

Dina's laughter twisted and cracked, a jagged, hollow sound laced with madness. It wasn't just laughter, it was a wail, a feral, broken thing that crawled up from the depths of her suffering. Tears streamed down her face, but they did nothing to soften the wild hysteria in her voice.

"They passed me around the camp," she choked out between breaths, her shoulders trembling. "I was used by everyone. I was nothing more than their toy, their entertainment. But I'll have my revenge. I'll purge this world of them." Her fingers curled into claws, as if she were already ripping them apart in her mind. "And when I'm done, I'll purge the next world, and the next. I'll burn them all, I'll flay them to the bone, and I'll laugh while they beg for mercy."

Blight took a hesitant step forward. Her heart pounded against her ribs, fear coiling in her stomach like a viper, but she forced herself closer. Her voice dropped to a whisper, gentle but pleading. "No, Dina. There is still good." She reached out, barely touching the edge of Dina's sleeve. "We've already lost too much. Don't be a part of the problem. Please... be the good in this world."

Dina's smile was slow, eerie in the flickering light, the grin of a woman who had already decided she was too far gone. And yet, she leaned in, wrapping her arms around Blight, her embrace warm, almost tender.

"The only good in this world," Dina murmured against her ear, "can be found when they are all dead."

Blight's breath hitched. She let herself sink into the embrace for a brief moment, savoring the last flicker of warmth between them. Then, with steady fingers, she slipped a small needle into Dina's side.

Dina gasped, her body jerking as the sting of the puncture registered. Her eyes went wide with betrayal, her foot kicking out in blind panic as she shoved Blight backward. But it was too late. The damage was already done. One of Blight's vials now sat empty at her hip, its contents already seeping into Dina's bloodstream.

"What did you do?!" Dina's scream was raw, frantic, as she staggered, clutching her side.

Blight wiped at her tear-streaked face, her voice trembling but resolute. "I released you," she whispered. "From all this pain. From all those memories." Her lip quivered, but she held Dina's gaze. "I love you, Dina."

The world felt unbearably still. A heartbeat stretched into eternity. And then Dina swayed, her knees buckling as the vial's contents took hold.

Dina staggered, her body betraying her as the sensation drained from her legs. Her breath hitched, a shuddering gasp as she crumpled to the ground, her limbs no longer her own. Her fingers clawed weakly at the dirt, but her strength was fading fast, her body shutting down piece by piece. A final breath rattled from her lips, and then... nothing. The fight left her. The anger, the vengeance, the suffering, all of it faded into the stillness.

Blight stood frozen, staring down at her fallen friend. Dina had been so much more than a name in this world: she had been a storm, a force of nature, wild and untamed. And now, she was just another corpse in the endless tally of the dead. Blight swallowed against the lump in her throat. This had been mercy. The only mercy she could give.

A whisper of movement cut through the heavy silence.

Blight's instincts flared just in time. A figure lunged from the darkness, blade flashing in the dim light. She jerked back, her wrist snapping up. A burst of thick smoke hissed from the hidden canister strapped beneath her sleeve, billowing out in a dark, curling cloud that swallowed the attacker whole.

The figure coughed, hacking as the acrid vapor wormed its way into his throat. "What in the Abyss..." he snarled, staggering back.

The smoke began to clear, revealing the sharp, predatory grin of a shadow elf. Silus. His silver hair clung to his face, damp with sweat, his dark skin barely visible against the gloom. His tongue darted out, tasting the remnants of the smoke still clinging to the air. He grinned, teeth gleaming like a wolf about to feast.

"Oh," he purred, his voice thick with amusement. "I'm going to enjoy this. Killing you. Cooking your flesh."

Blight's eyes locked onto his. No hesitation. No fear. Just a cold, simmering rage that was slowly taking root, twisting deep inside her like thorned vines.

"I don't know who you are," she said, voice low, steady. "But you do not want a piece of me right now."

Silus chuckled darkly. "Oh, but you are nothing," he sneered. "You're not even on our radar. Do you really think you can survive me?"

Blight tilted her head, a smirk playing at her lips. Something dangerous gleamed in her eyes, something new. The timid, frightened girl who had stumbled into this brutal world was fading. Piece by piece, she was being burned away, reforged into something sharper, something deadlier. Dina's death had sealed it. There was no going back. Devaultus' path, Vex's path: it was hers now.

Silus watched her, amused. "I'll give you a chance to run," he said, as if speaking to a cornered animal, his voice filled with the sick pleasure of the hunt. "I do love a good chase."

Blight exhaled slowly, rolling her shoulders back. Her fingers flexed, her body coiling like a spring ready to snap. "I will not run," she murmured.

Silus cupped a hand to his ear mockingly. "What was that? I didn't quite hear you."

Blight's jaw clenched. The weight of everything crashed down at once. Dina's body still warm on the ground. The choice she had made. The new path she walked. A scream ripped from her throat, raw and unrestrained.

"*I will not run!*"

And then she moved.

She launched herself at him, hands a blur as she struck out. Rods slid from her wrist guards with a metallic snap, catching the dim light as she swung them in sharp, brutal arcs. Silus reacted fast, his blades flashing as he met her blows, parrying each one with practiced ease. Their weapons clashed, sparks flying, the rhythm of battle swallowing them whole.

Blight launched herself into the air, her rods slicing through the darkness like falling meteors. She brought them down with deadly precision, aiming to break bones, to end this fight before it could truly begin.

But Silus was fast, unnaturally fast. He twisted, his body moving with an eerie fluidity, slipping between her strikes like smoke through fingers. One moment he was there, the next, gone. Blinking in and out of existence, his form melted into the shadows, only to reappear behind her, his blade slashing toward her back.

Blight barely twisted away in time, the dagger grazing the fabric of her clothing but missing flesh.

This wasn't going to work. He was too fast, too unpredictable.

Her hand shot to her bracer, fingers finding a small switch. She hesitated for half a heartbeat. The serum in her hidden vial was untested. She had no idea what it would do to her body, whether it would save her or kill her.

But right now, she didn't care.

She pressed the button. A thin needle hissed from the bracer, stabbing into the soft flesh of her arm. A sharp sting shot through her veins as the serum flooded into her bloodstream.

For a moment, nothing.

Then everything hit at once.

A surge of raw, electric energy exploded inside her, setting every nerve on fire. Her breath hitched as her heart slammed against her ribs, beating at a rapid, almost unnatural pace. Her limbs trembled, not with weakness but with power: raw, unfiltered power. Her muscles felt lighter, stronger.

Faster.

A grin spread across her lips as she shot forward.

Silus barely had time to register the change before she was on him.

Her speed had doubled; no, tripled. She moved in a blur, her rods flashing through the air faster than before, striking with newfound aggression. One swung for his ribs, the other for his knee. He twisted to dodge, but she was already ahead of him, sweeping her leg in a lightning-fast arc.

His footing broke.

For the first time, a flicker of panic crossed his face.

Devaultus watched Blight struggle with the weight of what she had just done. The anguish in her eyes, the way she trembled ever so slightly; she was too damn good for this world. Too soft. Too trusting. It would get her killed. He had been certain this was it. That she would hesitate, that she would betray him in some desperate attempt to cling to her old life.

But then she slid the needle into her friend's side.

His breath caught.

For a moment, he wasn't standing in this hellhole anymore. He was somewhere else, someone else, back in the nightmare of losing Tristan. But how much worse would it have been if he'd been forced to be the one to kill him? To be the hand that severed the last thread?

He suddenly understood Blight.

She had made her choice.

Him. And Vex.

There was no doubt anymore: she was theirs. She was family.

Vex was already ahead of him, always was. She had a wild grin plastered across her face, her eyes glinting with unhinged excitement as she tossed his daggers through the air without a second thought.

"Catch, Mr. D.!" she cackled.

The blades spun end over end, slicing through the dim light like falling stars. Devaultus snatched them from the air with fluid ease, the familiar weight settling into his grip like an extension of himself.

Vex gave him a wink, but then, with a casual flick of her blade, slashed through his leash.

He still had the collar to deal with, but that could wait. Right now, there was only one thing on his mind.

Tarus.

His gaze locked onto the bastard, but before he could take a step, Vex's voice cut in.

"I'll deal with my father." Her tone was different now, deadly serious, though the smirk never left her lips. "We have some family business to discuss."

That was fine by him.

Devaultus turned to face The Puppeteer.

This was personal.

Nobody took control of him and got away with it. Nobody crawled inside his head and walked out unharmed. He had promised this man pain, and Devaultus never broke a promise.

But before he could move, an unbearable pressure crashed into his skull.

His vision blurred, his thoughts shattered under the force of something massive and foreign, clawing its way into his mind.

The ring Caralana had given him flared against his finger, struggling to absorb the onslaught, but it wasn't enough.

Devaultus fell to a knee, gripping his head as agony seared through his skull.

The Puppeteer's laughter slithered into his ears, dripping with amusement.

"I'll pop your little brain like a pea," the bastard purred.

Devaultus gritted his teeth, muscles trembling as he fought to keep his consciousness from slipping.

Footsteps echoed closer. The Puppeteer sauntered toward him, three female field workers flanking him, their movements eerily stiff, their faces blank. Puppets. Their eyes were lifeless; they were empty shells of people who once had names.

He, on the other hand, wore a broad, delighted grin.

"This," he said, stretching his fingers as if preparing to pluck the last string of his masterpiece, "is the moment you finally learn what it means to cross The Puppeteer."

Suddenly, a slow, wicked grin spread across Devaultus' face, sharp and knowing, a predator toying with its prey. His golden eyes gleamed with something dark and triumphant. The Puppeteer's breath hitched, his confidence cracking like old glass as realization dawned: he didn't have the control he'd thought he did.

The old man's face twisted with sudden panic, his bony fingers twitching as if trying to grasp at strings that were no longer there. He staggered back, his eyes wide with fear.

"No! No, that's not possible...!" His voice broke into a shriek as he flung out his hands, his desperation turning to fury. "Kill him! Kill him now!"

The three women at his side, blank-eyed, slack-jawed, snapped into motion like puppets yanked forward by invisible threads. Their movements were eerily synchronized, their bodies lunging in unison: arms reaching, clawing, their speed unnatural, their faces void of emotion.

Devaultus didn't flinch. If anything, his grin only widened.

Vex sauntered forward, every step dripping with deliberate defiance, hips swaying like she was walking a catwalk in the Underworld. Her grin was crooked, unhinged, and painted with mischief. Her eyes locked on the mountain of a man who dared to call himself her father.

"You really think this ends well for you?" she purred, voice slick with venomous charm.

Tarus sneered, crossing his thick arms over his barrel chest. His towering form loomed, just as it always had; foreboding, oppressive, a wall meant to keep her caged. "You are a stain, Lorivelle," he spat, twisting the name like it tasted sour on his tongue. "The weakest of my blood. A walking humiliation. You never deserved the name, nor my legacy. You're not my daughter. Just a failed experiment I'd prefer to forget."

Vex's laughter rang out, high-pitched, erratic, with that signature manic edge. "Oh, Tarus," she said, rolling her eyes so hard, they nearly fell out of her skull. "I'm not *Lorivelle*. That girl died choking on your lies. I'm *Vex* now. And I'm not your daughter, I'm your reckoning."

Her voice sharpened like a blade. "You talk about failure? You're the damn blueprint. You couldn't kill Devaultus, what, three times now? Four? How many tantrums does it take before even Cojar stops returning your blood sacrifices with a 'I'm sorry, new magic ball, who's this,' missive?"

That struck home. She saw the flicker, just for a breath, where his smug mask cracked. A twitch in the jaw. A shift in his weight. A flare of shame behind the fury. Good.

"You threw your own daughters to Cojar to earn favor with a god who doesn't give a damn," she went on, smile curling with madness. "And now you stand here, pretending to be important. You're not. You're *nothing*, Tarus. I'm the chaos you couldn't control."

His posture stiffened, but the aura of dominance was thinning like old smoke. His pride, the one thing he cherished, had been struck like a gong.

Then Vex caught movement behind him. Her eyes, sharp and predatory, zeroed in on a flash of red hair peeking from a window above. A woman; no, a girl. Pale face, wide eyes trembling with disbelief. Something glinted on her face, odd translucent lenses perched on her nose like fragile armor. She looked Scared.

Interesting.

Jerry stirred beneath her hood like a restless shadow. The pulsating, ink-slick creature wriggled silently, tentacles twitching with focus. Not at Tarus. Not at the redhead. No, Jerry's strange and stubborn attention was locked elsewhere.

Blight.

Vex's lips twitched into something almost affectionate. Almost. Things were about to get messy.

Vex's lips barely moved as she whispered, "Go... help Puppy if you can."

Jerry didn't hesitate. He never did when it came to her. One second, the pulsating ink-like mass nestled against her shoulder, and the next, he was gone, vanishing in a slick blur of writhing tendrils. A blink later, he was perched on Blight's shoulder, a dark smear slipping into her hood unnoticed while Blight was fighting for her life.

Her father snarled at the quiet exchange, his rage igniting like a match to oil. The ground seemed to tremble beneath his boots as he stormed toward her, each step deliberate, every muscle in his hulking form ready to bring violence onto the world. The massive broadsword strapped to his back was in his hands before she even saw him move. The blade gleamed, wicked and heavy, as he pointed it straight at her heart.

"I'll correct the mistake I made years ago," he sneered, voice thick with venom. "And when I'm finished with you, I'll start fresh. A new daughter. A better one. Maybe with a woman who isn't a gods-forsaken disappointment."

Vex twirled her daggers, the motion as casual as that of a bored noble playing with their wine glass. But there was nothing casual about her grip, about the way her muscles tightened beneath her skin. These weren't just daggers, not like Devaultus' quick, efficient blades. No, hers were longer, nearly short swords, their edges slightly curved, made to bite and tear rather than just pierce.

She exhaled slowly, then grinned; a sharp, reckless thing.

"Some bloodlines are better left to die," she mused, rolling her shoulders. "If our wretched little family tree ends here, with the two of us, I'll die happy knowing Devaultus never has to deal with our filth again. But..." Her smirk widened, flashing teeth. "If I win, maybe I'll build something better. Maybe I'll start a new line, one not cursed with your miserable legacy."

Her father's lip curled, his grip on the broadsword tightening.

"But let's be real," she purred, taking a single step forward, her daggers glinting in the dim light. "If you win, there won't be a bloodline left. Because you? You're nothing. A sad, bitter relic. And compared to Devaultus?" She laughed, wild and untamed, a sound that sent a shiver through the air.

"You don't even deserve to stand in his shadow."

With a roar that shook the walls, Tarus lunged. His massive frame was a battering ram of pure fury, the weight of his broadsword carving through the air with lethal intent. The sheer force behind his strike could have cleaved through steel, let alone flesh and bone.

Silus darted back, his boots skidding against the stone floor as he took cover behind a pillar. A second later, a rod slammed against it with a deafening crack, shattering the stone like brittle wood. His eyes widened in disbelief as the rod didn't just strike, it tore straight through, barely missing his head by a breath. Jagged fragments rained down, cutting into his skin like tiny razors.

"What in the Abyss did you do to yourself?!" he shouted, his voice edged with panic.

Something was wrong. This wasn't the same woman he had been briefed on. Blight's pupils were blown wide, her bloodshot eyes filled with raw, unhinged fury. Her veins pulsed, dark and swollen, running like rivers of something unnatural beneath her skin. Whatever she had injected herself with, it had transformed her.

"I'll kill you! I'll kill you! I'll kill you!" she shrieked, her voice ripping through the air like a war cry.

For the first time in a long time, Silus felt something creeping into his chest, something he rarely felt these days: fear.

This wasn't the weak, powerless girl they had dismissed. She wasn't just some insignificant pawn. The mission dossier had labeled her as a bargaining tool: expendable, harmless, not even worth considering a threat.

They were wrong.

They were so, so wrong.

Blight was a nightmare in motion.

Silus barely had time to react as she lunged, her rods striking again. He vanished into the shadows, just as one slammed into the floor where he had stood. The impact sent shockwaves through the stone, cracking and splintering it apart. A chunk of rock the size of a man's head blasted into the air, ricocheting off the walls with enough force to dent steel.

He reappeared a few feet away, panting. He had fought assassins, mercenaries, monsters, but this? This was like facing a force of nature gone rogue.

Blight whirled around, wrenching her rod free from the stone with a violent tug. The ground trembled at her strength, and debris scattered like shrapnel.

Silus darted backward again, desperate to stay ahead of her rampage, but no matter how quickly he moved, she was faster.

She was relentless.

And she wasn't going to stop until one of them was dead.

Everything about her was faster. Stronger. More violent. The raw power coursing through her veins turned her into a storm of destruction, her every movement cracking stone, shattering wood, and tearing through the air with lethal intent.

Silus barely had time to register the shift before she was on him again. One of her rods whistled through the air, smashing into the pillar behind him. The force of the blow cracked the stone clean through, sending deep fissures splintering across its surface before the structure groaned and collapsed, spilling debris across the floor. Silus barely managed to slip away, blinking into the shadows just as another rod came crashing down in the exact spot he had stood a moment ago.

He reappeared across the room, crouched low, heart hammering in his chest. *What in the Abyss had she done to herself?*

She stood in the middle of the destruction, her breath coming fast and ragged. The veins along her arms bulged unnaturally, pulsing with some unknown energy. Her pupils were blown wide, bloodshot and furious, like a predator that had locked onto its prey and would not stop until the kill was made.

"I'll kill you!" she howled. "I'll kill you! *I'll kill you!*"

She lunged.

Silus barely dodged as her rod slammed into the floor where he had just stood. The stone shattered on impact, sending jagged shards flying in every direction. He threw his arms up, feeling a sharp sting as a few of the smaller pieces cut into his skin. He didn't have time to react further; she was already moving again.

Another strike. Then another.

Each strike pushed him back further into a nearby building. He hadn't noticed, but through the battle they had progressed to this point. Now they seemed to be far from the others.

Each blow was wild yet impossibly fast. The floor cracked and caved beneath her relentless attacks. The walls bore deep scars where her rods had struck. A nearby wooden support beam splintered as she swung wildly, missing Silus by a breath, the sheer force of the impact sending a shockwave through the air.

*Damn it!* He was being driven back, unable to gain even a second to counter.

He vanished into the shadows once more, appearing behind her, but she anticipated it. Her foot lashed out, sweeping toward his legs. He barely leapt back in time, but her rod was already following, swinging up in a vicious arc. Silus twisted, arching his body back just enough to avoid having his skull caved in.

A sudden explosion of force sent him flying.

She had struck the floor mid-motion, and the ground beneath them *buckled*. The sheer impact cracked the stone deep enough that a crater formed, sending another wave of debris outward. Silus landed hard, rolling to recover as dust filled the air.

For the first time since the fight started, he began to believe he was going to lose this.

This wasn't the same woman they had deemed harmless. She was supposed to be an *unimportant bargaining chip*, a *pawn* to lure in bigger players. And yet here she was, torn from their reports, rewritten in blood and violence, *a living nightmare on the battlefield.*

She shouldn't be this fast.She shouldn't be this strong.

But she was.

And she was winning.

Silus gritted his teeth. It would take a miracle for him to survive this.

And then it happened.

Her step faltered. Just slightly. A microsecond of hesitation.

Then her entire body *seized*.

She stumbled forward, her knees buckling, her weapon slipping just an inch in her grasp. Her breath hitched; shallow, ragged, panicked. Her eyes, still blown wide, flickered with something new.

*Fear.*

The serum was *wearing off*.

The monstrous strength that had fueled her destruction drained away like water slipping through her fingers. But it was worse than that: her body had been forced beyond its limits, and now it was breaking under the strain.

Pain erupted through her limbs as she collapsed onto one knee, her muscles *screaming in protest*. She had pushed too hard, too fast, *she had torn something.*

Silus straightened slowly, wiping the sweat from his brow, a slow smirk forming on his lips as he took a cautious step forward.

"Well," he exhaled, rolling his shoulders. "That was *impressive*."

She struggled against the weight in her hands, her fingers barely managing to keep their grip on the rods that had, just moments ago, sliced through solid stone like it was wet parchment. Her breath came in ragged gasps, her chest heaving as sweat dripped from her brow.

"No..." The word slipped from her lips, barely more than a whisper, tinged with disbelief and growing panic. Her body trembled, muscles locking up from the brutal exertion she'd forced upon them. The serum had worn off too soon, far too soon.

Silus, several feet away, paused. He was breathing hard himself, sweat clinging to his temples, his stance still tense from the prolonged fight. He had spent the last several minutes dodging her relentless onslaught, every strike of hers threatening to turn him into a smear on the ground. But now, she was hunched over, her arms quivering under the unbearable weight of the rods still hung attached to her gauntlets.

He narrowed his eyes. Was this a trick? A final ploy to lure him in?

Slowly, carefully, Silus took a step forward, his movements cautious, calculating. He watched for any shift in her posture, any sign that she might lash out again. When she didn't move, when she just sat there gasping, he took another step.

Then, with a swift motion, he kicked out. His boot slammed into her ribs with a sickening crack.

She screamed, her body folding around the pain as she was sent rolling across the stone ground. The impact jarred her arms, and the rods dragged behind her, now dead weight attached to her gauntlets. She came to a stop, curled up slightly, her fingers twitching weakly against the rock.

Silus watched as she tried to push herself up, but her arms failed her. Those once-burning, bloodshot eyes had dulled back to their normal, striking blue, though now, instead of fury, they were filled with something else. Fear.

She had miscalculated. The serum hadn't lasted as long as she had thought, and now, she was paying the price for it. If she survived this, she would make sure never to make the same mistake again.

Silus took his time as he strolled toward her. There was no rush now. She wasn't going anywhere.

A cruel chuckle laced Silus' words as he strode toward her, his confidence swelling now that she was broken. "Well, guess you ran out of steam, didn't you?" He tilted his head, watching her struggle to keep herself upright. "I won't lie, for a moment there, you had me worried. Thought you might actually be more than just dead weight."

Before she could even muster a response, his hand shot out like a viper, gripping her throat with ironclad fingers. Then, with effortless brutality, he hurled her across the stone floor. She hit the ground hard, her body skidding and tumbling like a discarded rag doll. The impact sent shockwaves of agony through her already shredded muscles. She barely had the strength to even attempt to catch herself, and the moment her arms tried, white-hot pain lanced through them. A raw, gut-wrenching scream tore from her lips.

This was it. She was finished. She knew it. Her body wasn't going to listen to her anymore. Vex had her own battle. So did Devaultus. No one was coming.

Boots scraped against the stone as Silus advanced once more, his slow, deliberate pace almost mocking. He wasn't in a rush. He wanted to savor this. He crouched down, his fingers tangling into the front of her clothing, yanking her up just enough to slam her back down onto the ground. Dust kicked up around them, swirling in the dim light. Then, in one smooth, practiced motion, he climbed on top of her, straddling her with his full weight, ensuring she was pinned and helpless beneath him.

His fingers wrapped around her throat once more, but this time, there was no theatrics, just the cold, methodical pressure of death tightening against her windpipe. "I'll kill you slowly," he murmured, his voice low, almost intimate in its menace. His face hovered mere inches from hers, his breath warm against her skin, drinking in the sight of her suffering.

Blight fought. She clawed weakly at his arms, her battered muscles screaming in protest, but it was useless. Her body refused to obey her. The world around her started to blur at the edges, dark spots dancing in her vision. Her lungs burned. Panic gripped her, but her limbs felt heavier and heavier, her struggles weaker. The light in her eyes flickered, dimming...

Then, out of nowhere, a blur of inky black shot from her hood.

It was so fast, so sudden, that even Silus didn't have time to react before it slammed into his face with a sickening squelch. He jerked backward, his hands instantly releasing her throat as he let out a garbled, choking noise. His eyes bulged in horror as the thing forced its way down his throat.

Silus reeled, clutching at his own neck, his fingers digging desperately into his flesh as if trying to rip whatever had invaded him back out. He staggered off of Blight, his body convulsing as muffled, wet gags escaped his lips. His knees buckled, his back arching unnaturally as Jerry, silent, merciless, and utterly in love with chaos, began his work from the inside.

Blight gasped, each breath a ragged, wheezing struggle as the weight of what had just happened settled in her bones. Tears blurred her vision, but she barely noticed them. She was trembling, not just from pain, but from the raw, visceral shock of nearly dying.

Her wide, fearful eyes locked onto Silus as he staggered like a marionette with its strings cut. His fingers clawed at his throat, his movements frantic yet oddly uncoordinated, as though he wasn't entirely in control of his own body. Then, without warning, he simply... stopped.

He stood eerily still, swaying slightly, his eyes glazed over with a vacant stare. His breath was shallow, mechanical, like he was nothing more than a husk. Then, in slow, deliberate movements, his hands drifted downward, brushing against the hilts of the daggers strapped at his waist, daggers he had wielded with deadly precision just moments before. But now they seemed alien in his grasp, as if he were touching them for the first time.

Leaning against a nearby wall for support, he stared at his own arm as though it belonged to someone else. A flicker of awareness crossed his empty face, but before Blight could even process what was happening, his other hand snapped up, dagger in its grasp.

Then, in a single, brutal motion, he drove the blade into his own wrist.

Blight's breath hitched as she watched in horror. He didn't hesitate, didn't grunt in pain or flinch. He just... kept hacking. The sickening sound of metal tearing through flesh and tendons filled the air. Blood splattered onto the cobblestone beneath him, painting it in slick crimson strokes. His wrist, no, his entire forearm, was a ruined mess of torn sinew and shredded skin, yet still he kept cutting, his movements disturbingly methodical.

And then, with a final, stomach-churning slice, his hand dropped to the ground with a wet *plop*.

Blight wanted to scream, wanted to look away, but she was frozen, paralyzed by the sheer insanity of what she was witnessing.

Then something changed. The blankness in his gaze wavered, and his face contorted as his body finally caught up with what had just happened.

Silus stared down at the stump where his hand had been, realization dawning in his widening eyes. And then, at last, he screamed.

"What the Abyss, what the actual Abyss?!" he howled, his voice ragged with agony. He stumbled backward, his breathing rapid and uneven as he clutched at the gory mess that had once been his wrist. The shock, the confusion, it was all-consuming.

But the nightmare wasn't over.

A sound, deep and unnatural, echoed from within him. A cracking. A shifting.

His screams turned into a gurgle as blood bubbled up between his lips. His chest heaved violently, spasming, his ribcage distorting. His sternum bowed outward, his bones groaning under some unseen pressure. His entire body arched as the grotesque transformation reached its peak.

And then, with a sickening, wet *crack*, his chest *burst* open.

Blight could only watch, eyes wide, as the nightmare unfolded before her.

Jerry landed with a sickening squelch, his inky form glistening with blood and torn viscera, a grotesque masterpiece of his own creation. The lifeless husk of Silus crumpled beside him, the last shudders of his desecrated body twitching before going utterly still.

Blight let out a strangled, shuddering breath, half sob, half disbelieving laugh, as relief flooded her. Tears welled in her wide, fear-stricken eyes, spilling freely down her cheeks. "Jerry? Oh, Jerry!"

Her voice trembled, thick with gratitude and exhaustion. "Thank you... thank you for saving me."

At her words, Jerry gave an eager, delighted wriggle, his pulsing, tentacled mass shifting like a creature utterly pleased with itself. Without hesitation, he slithered up her battered form, the warm slickness of him seeping into her torn clothes as he nestled into the crook of her neck. His ink-black body, still drenched in gore, oozed into her hood, curling against her skin in what she could only assume was a form of comfort.

Blight wanted to move, wanted to stand, wanted to run, but her body had other plans. Every muscle screamed in protest, every fiber was torn and strained past its limits. She felt as though she were made of lead, pinned to the battlefield by sheer exhaustion and pain.

But maybe, just maybe, she and Jerry had done something right. Maybe one less enemy on the field would be enough to turn the tide. Maybe Vex and Devaultus had the edge they needed now.

Her fingers curled weakly against the blood-slick stone, and she forced herself to breathe. Whatever happened next... she had to believe this had made a difference.

Devaultus spun backward, bare feet skidding slightly across the blood-slick cobblestones. Gods, he hated fighting in nothing but a loincloth. It was hard to feel like an epic force of darkness, or salvation, when you were one breeze away from full exposure. No flowing cape, no intimidating armor, just muscles, blood, and a mild draft. So much for theatrics. Still, he was here, but unfortunately, *so were they*.

What was worse was The Puppeteer, for all the defenses Devaultus had against him. Still, he had managed to make him see a thick fog around him. He couldn't force Devaultus to do his bidding due to Caralana's ring, but he had been able to ever so slightly invade his mind with an image of fog. This was annoying to say the least.

A woman lunged out of the fog like a mad banshee, shrieking through cracked lips and wielding a wooden pitchfork like it was forged by the gods themselves. She thrust the crude weapon toward his chest, aiming to skewer him like a pig. Devaultus sidestepped with a twist of his hips and lashed out with his foot, catching her in the shin. Her legs buckled, and she crashed face-first onto the stone path with a sickening crack.

The impact wasn't merciful.

Her teeth burst from her mouth like white shrapnel. Blood splattered in tiny arcs as her lips tore apart, ribbons of red fluttering as she groaned and pushed herself up, slowly, methodically, her eyes dead and unblinking. Pieces of shattered teeth clung to her chin like grotesque jewelry. Her face was a ruined landscape: torn skin, flaps of meat where lips used to be, blood drooling down her throat, and yet... she rose.

They always rose.

They wouldn't stop. Not until he was a corpse cooling on the stones. And then, the voice. Mocking. Cruel. Unseen.

"You won't win this, boy," came The Puppeteer's voice, oily with glee. "Trying to play the hero, are you? Heroes don't kill the innocent. Or has that little detail slipped your morally ambiguous mind?"

Devaultus clenched his jaw, that bitter truth cutting deeper than any blade. He didn't *want* to be a hero. He wasn't born with a shining sword and a list of virtues. He was chaos wrapped in a man's skin, shoved into a role he didn't understand. Every strike he made tasted like compromise. Every kill, a contradiction.

Another woman lunged at him from the left, a flash of steel in the moonlight, a rusted sickle arcing toward his throat. He ducked low, hair whipping in his eyes as he surged up under her guard. His blade sliced through the tender hollow beneath her arm, tearing into the muscle with a wet *snap*. She screamed, a sound more beast than human, and dropped the sickle as her arm went limp, flopping uselessly against her side.

Devaultus backed away, breathing hard, his skin gleaming with sweat and splattered red. The villagers weren't fighting like people. They were puppets. Possessed. Broken things with soft faces and a butcher's strength.

And he, the reluctant hero, was caught in the middle.

Devaultus chuckled, the sound low and sharp as he shoved another thrashing villager aside like an unruly drunk in a tavern. They moved like dolls with broken strings, violent, relentless, and utterly hollow behind the eyes. He raised his voice above the chaos, taunting the source of this madness.

"Are you really that thick?" he called, his smirk growing as he yanked a dagger from his belt. He spun, caught a woman by the hair as she lunged, and, without hesitation, buried the blade deep into her temple. There was a sickening *crack*, then the telltale *shluk* as he wrenched the dagger free, grey matter and blood clinging to the blade like some morbid trophy.

"I'm not your hero..." he growled, flicking the gore off casually, "and I'm sure as hell not your villain."

The Puppeteer, an oily man with eyes like festering wounds, stumbled back, his lips parting in sudden unease. Something had shifted in the air. Devaultus wasn't playing anymore.

But he didn't have time to savor the fear.

Two more women charged at him, field hands from some gods-forsaken backwater. Their hands gripped crude tools: one brandished a pitchfork that looked more rust than metal, the other a serrated knife used for gutting livestock. Their dresses were stained with dirt, blood, and the scent of death, but their faces were eerily calm, deadpan, as if they weren't aware of their own bodies anymore.

And worse, they didn't feel pain.

The first woman lunged with the pitchfork, jabbing at his gut with surprising speed. Devaultus twisted away, barely dodging the prongs. As he pivoted, the second came in low, slashing at his thigh. The knife scraped against his skin, biting in just enough to bleed.

He hissed, "Cute."

He surged forward with a roar, slamming his shoulder into the knife-wielder. She staggered but didn't cry out, not even when he elbowed her face hard enough to split her nose and send bone fragments flying. She simply righted herself, eyes vacant, mouth slack, and slashed again.

Devaultus danced back, his dagger weaving through the air in fluid arcs. He ducked another pitchfork thrust, then grabbed the handle mid-attack and yanked the weapon from the woman's hands. With a vicious spin, he drove the pitchfork back into her stomach, *through* her, and slammed her down onto the cobblestones like a sack of meat.

She didn't scream.

She just kept writhing, trying to stand with the fork still buried in her torso.

"Oh come *on*," Devaultus snarled, kicking her in the ribs. "You're not even trying to be dramatic!"

The knife-wielding woman leapt onto his back, her arms wrapping around his throat in a strangling embrace. She hissed and gnashed her teeth near his ear like some feral thing, slicing at him with the blade in her hand. Devaultus grunted, stomping backward into a stone wall to crush her, once, twice, *three* times, until her grip loosened and she slid down him, boneless and twitching.

He turned and drove his dagger straight into her chest, twisting.

"Stay. Down."

The pitchfork woman, impossibly, was crawling toward him, dragging the long, wooden shaft of the weapon still buried in her gut behind her like a macabre tail. Blood smeared the stones beneath her as she moved, inch by inch.

Devaultus let out a breath, exasperated. "You're worse than bad songs at a bard's funeral."

He stepped forward and stomped down hard on her head, once, *crunch*, then again for good measure. Her body stilled.

Silence, save for the ragged sound of his breathing.

The Puppeteer didn't laugh this time. Didn't gloat. He only stared, pale and quiet, as if he'd just glimpsed something buried beneath Devaultus' skin, a force that wasn't good, wasn't noble, but was *necessary*.

Devaultus wiped the blade on a dead sleeve. "Still think I'm trying to be a hero?" he muttered.

Devaultus turned his head slightly, his grin sharp and mocking as he locked eyes with The Puppeteer. His voice dripped with slow, deliberate amusement.

"Oh, look at that, we're alone now," he murmured, his steps lazy, almost careless, as he strolled toward the man. His movements had a casual sway, but his eyes... his eyes told another story. Cold. Calculating. Dangerous.

"You twist into the minds of others, make them dance like marionettes," he continued, his voice carrying an eerie calm. "Always lurking behind the curtain, never stepping into the fire yourself. Never feeling the agony you inflict."

His daggers hung loosely in his grip, their edges dark and wet, blood dripping in slow, steady patters onto the bodies sprawled at his feet. He tilted his head slightly, watching The Puppeteer, waiting.

"You thought to invade my mind." A soft chuckle rumbled from his throat. "I wouldn't wish that Abyss on anyone. But lucky for you..." His grin widened into something more sinister, something inviting and full of malice. "I'm better at keeping control now."

He spread his arms slightly, exposing himself, daring The Puppeteer forward. "Go ahead," he offered. "I'll even leave the door cracked, just a sliver. Take a peek. If you're so desperate to see."

The Puppeteer's lips curled into a wild, hungry grin. Fool. Did Devaultus really believe he could control what happened once the invasion began? Did he think he could push him back out of his mind? He would break the threads that held his mind together and leave the man a heap of broken spirit on the ground.

With a forceful, violent shove, The Puppeteer dove into Devaultus' mind. The sheer impact of the intrusion was like a battering ram to the skull, nearly driving Devaultus to his knees.

The Puppeteer observed the scene unfolding, his fingers twitching with anticipation. A younger Devaultus knelt over an elven man, his body tense with emotion, his face shadowed with something that looked an awful lot like grief. The Puppeteer smirked. Oh, this was good. This was rich. He had forced men to their knees in horror before, made them weep and wail like children lost in the dark, but this? This was something else.

Devaultus wanted him to see this moment. That much was clear. But why?

Still, The Puppeteer indulged the display. If nothing else, he could use it against him, twist the knife further into his psyche. No one had ever resisted him this deeply, this effectively, when he dug his claws into their minds. That alone was enough to warrant patience.

He crouched beside the young Devaultus, studying his expression, the shimmer of tears in his eyes. Broken. Splintered at the core. The sight sent a thrill down The Puppeteer's spine.

Then, Devaultus moved.

His fingers curled into fists as he rose, his face hardening, the grief bleeding into something colder, sharper: pure, unfiltered rage. His voice, when it came, was low and steady, each word etched with venom.

"Everyone who matters to me is gone." His breath was slow, measured, deadly. "I am unleashed. Anyone involved in taking my joy will be erased."

There was no hesitation, no sluggishness of spirit. He rolled his shoulders back, straightening as though something inside him had locked into place. His path was deliberate as he turned and strode toward a nearby building.

The Puppeteer's gaze flickered to the elf sprawled on the ground. Recognition didn't strike immediately, but it didn't need to. He didn't need to know who the elf was, only that he mattered. And oh, how The Puppeteer would make that face a phantom in Devaultus' mind, a specter whispering guilt and regret at the worst possible times.

Devaultus reached the door, placing his hand against the worn wood.

Slowly, deliberately, he pushed it.

The door groaned open, revealing the dimly lit interior of the rundown warehouse. Torchlight flickered against the damp stone walls, casting jagged shadows over the crates and barrels stacked haphazardly around the room. The air reeked of unwashed bodies, old blood, and ale gone sour.

Devaultus stepped inside, his black cloth armor clinging to him like a second skin, hood pulled low over his eyes. He moved without hesitation, his steps measured, deliberate. A lone wolf stepping into a den of jackals.

The bandits lounging around the room barely spared him a glance at first, too wrapped up in their own arrogance. They were men who had never known real fear, only the fear they inflicted on others.

One of them, a thick-necked brute with a dented breastplate and a smirk full of rotten teeth, let out a rough chuckle. "Oi, look at this one.

Hooded little shadow thinks he's scary." He jabbed his friend in the ribs, nudging a man with a scar running from cheek to jaw. "What do ya think, Finn? Think he's lost?"

Finn exhaled through his nose, unimpressed, as he leaned against a crate filled with stolen blades. "Nah. I think he's *stupid*."

The others laughed, some knocking their mugs together, others palming their weapons lazily, like they didn't even think they'd need them. A mistake. A *final* mistake.

Devaultus didn't speak. He didn't need to. His answer came in the form of a dagger leaving his fingers in a blur, embedding itself deep in Finn's throat. The laughter died with a wet gurgle. Finn dropped his mug, clutching at his neck as blood pulsed between his fingers. He crumpled against the crate, his legs twitching.

For a moment, the room hung in stunned silence.

Then, chaos erupted.

Chairs scraped back. Steel flashed.

A bandit with a rusted cutlass lunged at him, but Devaultus was already moving. He sidestepped cleanly, twisting behind the attacker and slamming a dagger up under his ribs. He wrenched it free with a sharp *twist*, and the man collapsed, clutching his side and screaming.

Another charged, swinging a heavy mace down at his head. Devaultus ducked, feeling the rush of air as it missed by inches. He rolled forward, slashing as he came up, cutting through the man's thigh. The bandit bellowed in agony, stumbling, and Devaultus drove his dagger into the back of his knee, severing tendons. The man hit the ground hard, howling.

Now they felt fear.

Now they *understood*.

"Shit, get him!" someone barked.

Two came at once. One had a cleaver, the other a short sword. Devaultus spun between them, his movements smooth, fluid, like death made flesh. He caught the cleaver-wielder's wrist, twisting until bone snapped, then used the same man's broken arm to deflect the short sword coming for his ribs. The blade bit deep into flesh, just not his own.

The man with the short sword gasped as he realized he had just gutted his own friend.

Devaultus didn't give him time to process it. He kicked him square in the chest, sending him crashing into a stack of crates.

The last three bandits hesitated now, weapons clutched tight in shaking hands.

"You, you *bastard!*" one of them snarled, spitting at the ground. "You have *any* idea who you're dealing with? We own this district! You're *dead*, you hear me? *Dead!*"

Devaultus tilted his head slightly. Then he smiled.

"You talk too much."

And then he was *on* them.

He moved like a wraith, a streak of shadow and steel. One went down screaming, his stomach split open in a red spill of entrails. Another tried to run, but Devaultus grabbed him by the collar, yanked him back, and slit his throat so deep, it was nearly a beheading.

The last one dropped his sword, hands raised, face pale with terror.

"Wait! *Wait!* Please, I..."

Devaultus didn't wait.

His dagger buried itself in the man's chest. He held it there, twisting it slightly, watching the light drain from his eyes. Then he pulled it free, and the body slumped to the ground with the others.

Silence.

The only sound left was the quiet drip of blood pooling beneath the corpses.

From the doorway, The Puppeteer had gone rigid. He had thought he knew the extent of Devaultus' ruthlessness. Thought he understood his capacity for violence.

He had been wrong.

This wasn't just a man killing enemies. This was a predator culling prey.

The Puppeteer watched Devaultus, his back rigid, his posture eerily still. The room was thick with the scent of blood, of death, yet Devaultus stood unmoving, staring ahead as if lost in something deeper than the carnage around him.

For a long moment, he didn't move, didn't react, like a puppet with its strings cut. Then, slowly, almost absently, he took a step back. Then another. His breath came shallow, his fingers twitching at his sides. His lips moved, words slipping out in a hushed, broken murmur.

"You took something from me..."

The Puppeteer leaned forward, straining to catch the words.

"...The feeling of safety."

Another step back, his boots scraping against the blood-slick floor. His shoulders trembled, but not with fear. No, this was something else. Something brewing beneath his skin, something rising like a storm about to break.

"The feeling... of having a real family."

The Puppeteer's stomach twisted. Devaultus wasn't speaking to anyone in the room. He was talking to the ghosts in his head, the memories that never left him.

"I won't make that mistake again. You have nothing to take if nobody is close to me," he said somberly.

A chill curled up his spine. He had seen broken men before, shattered minds, twisted souls, but this was different. Devaultus wasn't *broken*. He was *unleashed*.

And then, Devaultus stopped.

The moment stretched, a breath held between life and death.

Then, without warning, he *snapped around*, his eyes locking onto The Puppeteer with a sharp, predatory intensity.

The Puppeteer recoiled, his breath hitching. He wasn't supposed to *see* him. No one ever *saw* him inside their own mind. It wasn't possible. It wasn't...

Devaultus grinned, but it was wrong. The expression carved itself into his face like something *forced* there, one side of his mouth twisted unnaturally. His eyes weren't just filled with anger, they burned with something *cold*, something primal and untamed.

His voice was no longer a whisper. It was a *declaration*.

"Gods help anyone who tries to do that to me... *or my family!*"

The Puppeteer's world *lurched*. His stomach turned violently as the illusion shattered around him. His mind *rejected* the reality unfolding before him, panic gripping his chest like a vise. If Devaultus could *see* him inside his mind, then...

*What the Abyss was happening in the real world?!*

He jolted awake in his body, gasping, eyes darting wildly. The room spun, his breath ragged. Where was he? Where was Devaultus...

A whisper of steel.

Then *pain*.

He barely had time to react before the blade traced a thin, merciless line across his flesh. His hands flew up instinctively, gripping his throat as warmth spilled between his fingers.

Blood. *His* blood.

He staggered, choking, gurgling, his legs giving way beneath him.

Above him, Devaultus loomed, stepping over his dying body, a grin splitting his face, this time, fully, truly.

*Wild. Unhinged. Triumphant.*

And then...

Darkness.

Zen crouched low behind the shattered frame of a second-story window, fingers clenched so tight around the ledge that her knuckles had turned bone white. Her breath hitched in shallow bursts, barely audible over the chorus of screams and steel outside. Her eyes, wide with horror, drank in the carnage below, and she couldn't look away.

She'd seen death before. Plenty of it. From the safe distance of palace shadows and silk-curtained lies. But never like this. Never this close. Never raw, and brutal, and alive.

The urge to run surged up like bile, burning her throat. Her entire body screamed at her to turn and flee, to throw herself down the narrow hallway and out the back, toward Deshara. Toward the city. Toward safety. Or at least the illusion of it.

She could be safe. Couldn't she?

But that thought crashed into a brutal memory. Her last attempt to escape. The guards who caught her. The beating. The blood. The slow, crawling hours where pain was her only companion and her limbs refused to obey. The taste of iron and failure still haunted the back of her throat.

No. There was no safety. Not for her.

Not in running.

Not in hiding.

Fear gripped her like a cold chain wound tight around her ribs. It wasn't the chaos of the battle that terrified her most. It wasn't even the fire or the screams or the monsters fighting monsters. It was the men.

One man in particular.

Tarus.

She spotted him amidst the chaos. Towering, unflinching, his armor smeared with blood like war paint. A name spoken in hushed terror behind doors in Deshara. Tarus the Harsh. Tarus the Butcher. Tarus the One Who Breaks.

He moved through the battle like a god of violence, and Zen couldn't tell if he was there to destroy the enemy or to destroy everyone. The others seemed like ants in comparison: scurrying, dying, meaningless. He was more than a man. He was a force.

And yet... something else stirred in her gut.

A different fear.

One not clad in iron or soaked in blood.

Devaultus.

She couldn't see him yet. Not from where she knelt. But she felt him. Felt the weight of his presence like a storm building behind the clouds. He was chaos given form. Unpredictable. Dangerous. A knife that might save you, or slit your throat while humming a tune.

She trembled.

Not knowing who to fear more.

Tarus, the known beast.

Or Devaultus, the wolf trying to wear a hero's skin, and failing with every drop of blood spilled in his name.

Zen knew what she was. A mask. A tool. A woman sculpted by terror and duty, forced to smile through the ache in her soul.

And as the world outside the window burned, she knew one thing with blistering certainty.

She wasn't ready for whatever came next.

He wasn't alone.

With him stood The Puppeteer.

Zen's breath hitched. The name alone sent a chill skittering up her spine like frost crawling across glass. She had heard whispers of The Puppeteer since she was a child, half-forgotten stories told in hushed tones when the lamps flickered low and even the boldest dared not laugh too loudly. The tales were never the same, but they all shared one thing: a darkness that could not be reasoned with.

The Puppeteer didn't need chains or blades. He didn't need to be near you. He would crawl into your mind like a spider, silk-wrapped and quiet, and twist your thoughts into something unrecognizable. He made you see things, awful things, things no one should have to witness. Your greatest fears turned real in front of your eyes. Faces of the dead, shadows that moved when they shouldn't, the sound of your own screams coming from someone else's mouth.

But that wasn't the worst of it.

He could take you.

Not just your thoughts. Not just your senses. He could seize your will, marionette your limbs, and force you to dance in your own skin while you watched in horror. He could make you kill, make you betray the ones you loved, make you beg and laugh and burn and smile through it all like a doll with a broken jaw.

And you might never even see him coming.

Zen swallowed hard. She'd always thought the stories were just that: stories. Just old ghost tales to keep street kids in line. Every child caught sneaking an extra heel of bread, every brat who'd thrown a rock at a guard's helmet; they all had the same excuse.

"It wasn't me," they'd say, lip quivering. "The Puppeteer made me do it."

She had laughed then. Even used the excuse herself once, long ago.

But now, staring down at the man in the distance, seeing the way the air seemed to shiver around him like it didn't quite know how to behave, she wasn't laughing.

He was real. The myths were real.

And he was here.

Then there was Silus.

She didn't know much about him. Not really. Not beyond the scraps she'd picked up during the past few days stuck on the same ship, breathing the same stifling air. What she had learned, though... it had teeth.

He was brutal. He carried the kind of violence in his walk that didn't need to be spoken aloud. *Rough* didn't begin to cover it. He didn't ask. He didn't flirt. When he wanted a woman, he took her. Whether it was for pleasure or for hunger, Zen couldn't tell. Maybe it didn't matter. Either way, it was monstrous.

She'd heard the screams. Late at night, echoing through the wooden walls like ghosts clawing to be remembered. Screams from his room that didn't stop until they fell into silence, the kind of silence that rang louder than sound. Tarus never seemed to care. He barely acknowledged it. Monsters don't notice the screams of other monsters.

Silus was no rumor. He was real and raw and terrifying.

But what twisted her gut tighter was the question she kept coming back to, over and over.

Why?

Why did these monsters, Tarus, Silus, even the bloody Puppeteer, seem afraid of *him*?

Devaultus.

He wore nothing but a loincloth and chains. A prisoner. Filthy. Beaten. His body bore the marks of hard travel and harsher treatment. And yet... when they looked at him, it wasn't with pity or amusement.

It was with caution.

And maybe a sliver of fear.

He didn't stand tall or speak loudly. But there was something about him. Something coiled beneath the surface. A thing waiting to be unshackled. He traveled with two women who looked far too delicate for a world this savage. One of them, a dark-haired beauty, was unsure of herself like she was just learning to be... her, she didn't belong on a battlefield. The other, blonde and wild-eyed, had that twitchy, manic energy that made Zen uneasy. The kind of energy that smelled like blood and laughter at the wrong time.

But wasn't everyone a little mad in this place?

This world was rotten. Drenched in cruelty. And if Zen had learned anything since her fall from the life she once knew, it was this:

There are more monsters here than people.

And she had never been given a choice about which monster to follow.

Until now.

Now, with the screams still echoing in her memory and the silence of that strange man ringing louder than any howl, she had a sliver of a chance. A moment to choose one devil over another. Maybe even slip through the cracks.

Maybe find refuge.

Or, at the very least... an ending.

Vex launched herself forward with a feral screech, her twin blades flashing like silver fangs under the blood-colored sky. Her movements were fast, erratic, beautifully chaotic, each step less like a fighter and more like a dance choreographed by a lunatic. She struck high, low, feinted left, and twisted right, slashing at her father in a frenzy of motion that would have shredded any lesser man.

But Tarus wasn't just any man.

He stood like an iron statue amidst a storm, his massive broadsword held lazily in one hand, as though it were a child's toy. The blade caught her attacks effortlessly, *clang, clang, clang,* his arm barely shifting under the weight of her rage. Sparks erupted from their blades, but his face remained maddeningly calm. Bored, even.

"You always were loud," he said coolly, stepping back just enough to let her lunge and miss. "But noise doesn't make up for incompetence."

Vex growled through gritted teeth, flipping backward and springing into another wild assault. Her foot lashed out, a dagger arcing toward his side. Tarus sidestepped like he was dodging spilled ale, and, with a single swing of his blade, he sent her crashing back against a crumbling wall.

"You think fury can fill the void where talent should be?" he sneered. "You're not a warrior, Vex. You're a tantrum wrapped in skin. All your stealing, your killing, your petty chaos, none of it makes you powerful. Just... pathetic."

That did it.

Vex's eye twitched. She leapt back to her feet, face red with rage and embarrassment. "*Pathetic?* You stone-faced son of a bitch, I'll carve your lungs out and wear them like earrings!"

She attacked again, even more erratic, more furious, the kind of madness that only someone truly unhinged could muster. Her attacks blurred, becoming a whirlwind of metal, a rabid storm in woman's form. But Tarus deflected every strike like he was brushing off raindrops. He yawned, *yawned*, mid-fight, and twisted to slam his boot into her chest, sending her skidding across the ground like a discarded doll.

"You're not even worth the energy to kill," he said, voice dripping with contempt. "You were a mistake. A loose thread. And I've finally come to cut it."

Vex coughed, spat blood, and pushed herself back up on shaky arms. She was battered, bruised, and absolutely fuming. But still grinning. That unhinged sparkle in her eye never dimmed.

"Big talk for a man who can't take a beating from his *adorable* little girl," she wheezed, staggering to her feet, blades trembling in her hands. "Go on, Daddy. Keep underestimating me. I *live* for this shit."

And she charged again.

Vex spat blood to the side and grinned through the crimson smeared across her lips. She charged again, reckless and wild, her dual blades shimmering with fury. Tarus swung, but this time she ducked under the arc, slashing along his side with a satisfying *shhhhhk* of steel tearing flesh.

"Guess *someone's* not invincible after all!" she cackled.

He grunted, more surprised than hurt, and twisted to block her next strike, but not fast enough. Her second blade jabbed up, scraping across his pauldron and nicking his shoulder.

"You bleed, old man," she hissed, eyes wild. "Looks like you're just as mortal as the rest of us. Kinda disappointing, really. I expected *more* from my absentee daddy."

Tarus' eyes narrowed.

"Oh, did I touch a nerve?" she cooed, mock pouting. "Was it the part where I called you a disappointment, or the part where I reminded you I exist?"

The calm cracked. His muscles tensed, lips curled into something feral. "You insufferable little brat..."

*Wham!*

His gauntleted backhand landed like a thunderclap. Vex was flung across the square again, skidding through stone and sand, slamming into a stack of crates that shattered on impact. She groaned, blood dribbling from her mouth as she dragged herself up onto one knee.

Her grin didn't fade.

"You hit like a baker with arthritis," she wheezed. "Gonna have to try harder, dearest Dad."

Tarus stalked toward her now. No games. No taunts. Just murder in his eyes.

She reached into her cloak with shaking fingers and pulled out a small, grimy jar, filched weeks ago from a shady alchemist's stall. *She hadn't known what it did. But it had a label on the side with a small picture of a flame: fire sounded fun.*

With a flick of her wrist and a whispered, "Oops," she hurled the jar at his feet.

*Ka-foooooom!*

The explosion erupted like a vengeful dragon. Fire roared outward, devouring the crates, and half the alleyway. Screams echoed from nearby buildings as the inferno swirled to life. Tarus stumbled back, swatting at flames licking up his cloak and armor.

The world became firelight and smoke.

And then, like a whisper from a nightmare, a laugh slithered through the heat. It wasn't joyful. It wasn't sane. It was the kind of laugh that knew death personally and sent it birthday cards.

The flames parted just enough to reveal a silhouette.

A man walking through the fire as if it bowed to him.

He wore nothing but a loincloth. Twin blades glinted at his sides, one dragging against the side of a burning building with a *shhhhhhhtk* as he approached. His face obscured by darkness, save for that smirk: a sharp, one-sided, and absolutely unhinged grin.

Devaultus.

If the Lord of the Abyss had someone to fear, it was him.

He stopped just outside the blaze, cocked his head, and flashed that grin, cut from madness and spite.

"You know," he said, voice low and smooth like venom in silk, "I've heard a lot about you, Tarus. Big bad war daddy. Makes your daughter cry. Swings that oversized toothpick like it's supposed to impress someone."

He glanced at Vex and gave her a wink.

"Tell me something, though." His eyes snapped back to Tarus, glowing faintly from the light of the fire. "Do you *always* get your ass handed to you by tiny, unhinged women with parental issues... or is today just special?"

Tarus blinked through the haze, barely able to register the absurdity in front of him.

The man stepping through the blaze wore nothing but a soot-smeared loincloth and enough swagger to drown a kingdom. Muscles slick with sweat and blood, his body bore the kind of scars that whispered stories no one survived long enough to retell. The fire painted him in dancing gold and red, an infernal god come to collect.

And gods, did he look pissed.

Devaultus tilted his head, that cocky grin still tugging at the corner of his lips like he knew exactly how terrifying he looked. One hand rested lazily on the hilt of his dagger, the other still trailing one of his blades against the stone, sparks hissing beneath it like the world was catching fire just to keep up.

"You know..." he began, his voice cutting through the roar of flame like a blade through silk, "I was having the *worst* day. Some dead-eyed puppeteer thought he could rummage through my memories like a drunk at a whorehouse. Then I hear *you*, Tarus the Terrible, the big bad brute who thinks yelling at his daughter is fatherhood."

Devaultus clicked his tongue and took another step forward. "I bet the holidays are so much fun!" The fire behind him flared higher, framing his silhouette in near-supernatural glow. His eyes gleamed like something unholy had taken residence behind them.

"I'll give you this," he said, gesturing vaguely with his dagger. "You *look* tough. Real intimidating. Sword the size of a coffin. Chest puffed out like a rooster on performance potions. But then... I feel like you might be compensating..."

He gestured at Vex, still on the ground, wiping blood from her busted lip and flipping Tarus off.

"...also, you let her get in two hits. Two. Do you know how chaotic her technique is? She once stabbed herself mid-spin."

"*It was a learning moment!*" Vex shouted from the floor, waving a fist.

Devaultus chuckled darkly. "Anyway, point is, you're not scaring anyone, Tarus. Especially not me."

Tarus growled, lifting his sword. "I'll cleave you in half, worm."

"Oh gods, *please do*," Devaultus said, arms wide in an open invitation. "I'd turn into two Devaultus' just to spite you."

He grinned wider, stepping over the broken remnants of a barrel, blade in each hand now. "But before we tango, let's set some ground rules. First, no hitting below the belt. Second, no talking about each other's mom... oh, wait, I don't know mine. Never mind. Anyway, third..."

He vanished in a blink, appearing just to the side of Tarus with that wolfish grin inches from his ear.

"...never, *ever*, mistake my lack of pants for lack of danger."

Tarus swung.

Devaultus moved.

And the real carnage began.

Vex lay half-curled on the cracked stone floor, smoke licking the air like tongues of judgment around her. Her vision pulsed from the sting of a fresh bruise flowering across her ribs, her breath shallow, ragged. And yet, her eyes never left the battlefield.

She watched, spellbound, as Devaultus collided with Tarus in a clash that shook the very air. Blades screamed with each strike, steel whirling in a blur so fast she could barely track it. Devaultus wasn't fighting like a man, he was fighting like something unchained, something feral, his twin daggers carving deadly arcs through the space between them. A storm of violence wrapped in sinew and smirks.

Tarus, for all his brute strength, no longer looked composed. He grunted with effort now, his enormous broadsword intercepting strike after strike with grinding precision. Gone was the casual arrogance. He was locked in.

Matched.

Just then, a soft voice to Vex's side pierced through the din like an errant memory.

"Are you alright?"

Vex turned her head, wincing at the pain that shot down her side. Her hand tightened around her dagger, lifting it instinctively in a shaky grip.

The woman standing next to her wasn't armed. Or armored. In fact, she didn't look like she belonged anywhere near a battlefield.

Tall and statuesque, the woman had an hourglass figure poured into a dark, form-hugging corset that managed to be both conservative and infuriatingly alluring. Her fiery red hair spilled over her shoulders in waves that looked unfairly perfect given the flaming war zone they were currently surviving in. Square glasses rested on the bridge of her nose, giving her a studious air that contrasted with the slight tremble in her hands and the haunted look in her eyes.

"You," Vex hissed, blade still poised, "I saw you with *him*. With *Tarus*. So why the hell would you care if I'm breathing?"

The woman blinked rapidly, her pale cheeks flushing. She looked away from Vex and back to the raging battle, her eyes full of conflict. "I'm not... with him. I mean, I sort of am. But only as an observer. Sakatorious sent me. I didn't have a choice. I'm his."

Vex narrowed her eyes. "Being sent by Sakatorious was even worse." Every instinct screamed at her to not trust this woman. But she wasn't lying, her shoulders were hunched slightly like she was trying to fold into herself. Her posture screamed *not a fighter*. No weapons that Vex could see. No aggression. Just an air of... self-doubt wrapped in silk and silence.

Still, it didn't stop the snarl in Vex's voice. "Why are you watching us then? Why are you following *him*?" She nodded toward Devaultus, who had just locked blades with Tarus in a flash of sparks and grit.

The redhead, Zen, studied the scene for a long moment, her lips twitching like words were dancing on the edge but refusing to come out.

Zen blinked a bit. "Again, observer. It's literally all I'm allowed to do, is watch you." She paused, looking back at Devaultus. "Why do you follow that monster?"

"He saved us," she growled, sitting up straighter despite the pain. "All of us. You think he's a monster? Maybe he is. But he's *our* monster."

There was pride there, sharp and untamed.

Zen blinked at her, surprised by the heat in her tone. "He doesn't... charge you? For his protection?" she asked, voice tinged with confusion rather than judgment.

Vex tilted her head. "Charge us? What? He's not running a battle harem here?"

Zen looked sheepish. "I mean... That's how Lord Sakatorious does it. Protection, power: everything has a cost. I've never seen someone fight so hard for others for... nothing."

Vex snorted. "Yeah, well. Devaultus does a lot of things people 'never see.' Like survive with just a loincloth and rage."

Zen gave a tiny, startled laugh. Just a breath of one. And for a moment, there was something almost... human in her.

But Vex still didn't take her hand off her blade.

Just in case.

The ground trembled beneath them as Tarus drove his sword into the earth, the sheer force of the impact sending out a shockwave that shattered the stone like glass. Dust erupted upward, momentarily veiling the two figures locked in their deadly dance.

And through the swirling smoke, Devaultus emerged, grinning.

Not just any grin. A wicked, sideways slash of a grin that didn't belong on a sane man's face. He moved like a phantom, weightless and fluid, as if gravity itself wasn't entirely sure how to handle him. He weaved around Tarus' monstrous swings with an elegance that mocked the brute's strength.

"You swing that thing like you're trying to build a house," Devaultus quipped, sidestepping a blow that cratered the cobblestones. "But I'm not some nail you can hammer into place, Daddy dearest."

Tarus snarled, eyes blazing with fury. The veins in his neck bulged as he lifted his broadsword for another punishing strike. "You think this is a game, boy?" he roared, voice thick with disdain. "I carved men stronger than you in half before you grew your first pube."

"Probably the highlight of your romantic life," Devaultus purred, sliding under the blade with barely a breath of space between steel and skin. "But let's talk about your form: very caveman chic. *Rawr, smash.* Love it."

Tarus' fighting was raw, savage, like a hammer made of pure hate. Each attack was a declaration of dominance, meant to crush bones and flatten will. But every swing only met empty air or the whisper of Devaultus' footsteps. The rogue's style was a masterclass in contrast: precise, predatory, impossibly fast. He flowed like water, bled like poetry, moved like a dancer with a vendetta and a blade in each hand.

And he never stopped smiling.

Tarus lunged forward with a two-handed overhead cleave, aiming to split Devaultus down the middle. Devaultus spun on his heel, the strike missing by inches as his blade slashed across Tarus' forearm, drawing blood.

Just a nick. But a *visible* one.

"Oops," Devaultus said, spinning away again. "You're leaking. I didn't think we were hitting each other yet. Should I try?"

Tarus bellowed in rage, the sound primal and wild. "Enough of your damn jokes!" he thundered, swinging with renewed fury. His attacks grew more desperate, heavier, as frustration gnawed at the edges of his technique.

And Devaultus... laughed.

"Come on, Tarus," he taunted, flipping back onto a fallen beam with a flourish. "I'm giving you the show of a lifetime here, and all I'm getting is red-faced rage? At least buy me dinner before you try to kill me this hard."

He darted back in, blades flashing, slicing shallow cuts across Tarus' legs and side, a slow bleed strategy. Death by a thousand elegant cuts. Tarus tried to catch him, to grapple, but Devaultus slipped from his grasp like a shadow made of silk and spite.

"You were never the storm," Devaultus whispered, circling him. "You were the thunder. Loud. Obvious. Easy to dodge."

Tarus turned, blood trickling down his arm, chest heaving. "And what the hell are *you*, then?"

Devaultus stopped just outside his range. His grin dropped. Just a bit. "I'm the lightning."

Then, without warning, he shot forward, blades a blur, feet dancing, the wind itself seeming to follow his movements.

Zen stood still, the hellish glow of the fire painting her pale skin in strokes of orange and red. Her red hair was wild in the rising heat, her glasses slightly fogged, but her wide eyes never blinked. She couldn't tear her gaze away from him.

Devaultus.

The name had been little more than a whisper where she came from. A half-spoken myth. A bogeyman for the brave. No records, no reports. No one who had met him survived, or so Sakatorious had told her, with a smile that didn't quite reach his eyes.

And now, here he was.

Not some mindless beast tearing through flesh like a rabid animal... but a creature of *purpose*. Of *grace*. Of absolute *control*.

He danced across the battlefield in nothing but a torn loincloth and leather bracers, gliding through flames and blood like a phantom dipped in chaos. Where Tarus struck with brute force, every swing of his massive broadsword capable of flattening a building, Devaultus *flowed*. He ducked, twirled, dodged with elegant ease, then struck like a serpent, quick and precise. His blades were an extension of his soul, whispering promises of pain with each deadly arc.

And it was working.

Tarus, the monstrous juggernaut who'd nearly killed Vex moments ago, was bleeding.

Bleeding *and* furious.

Zen's lips parted slightly. "That's... that's him?"

Vex stood beside her, practically glowing with a strange kind of pride. She was bruised, battered, probably concussed, and still looked like she'd just seen the hottest damn thing to ever crawl out of the Abyss.

"He's not what you expected?" Vex said, not looking away.

Zen slowly shook her head. "No. I thought he'd be... mad. Savage. Like a wild dog off its chain."

Vex laughed, a breathless, exhausted sound. "Oh, he *is*. But he's *our* wild dog." She looked up at Zen with a feral grin. "He's the storm. You don't leash a storm, you let it tear your enemies apart."

Zen furrowed her brow. "But... Sakatorious never told me anything about him. Just that people who *knew* about Devaultus died. That no one should ever speak his name out loud. Not even him."

Vex shrugged, still staring at her favorite blood-soaked war god with heart-eyes. "That's because Sakatorious is smart. You don't *know* Devaultus. You survive him. Or you don't."

Zen's pulse quickened. Something deep inside her, a place that had only ever known fear and performance and hollow strength, shivered. It wasn't just that Devaultus was deadly.

It was the fact that he *chose* not to be that made him ten times more terrifying.

He was a monster not because he couldn't be anything else.

But because the world had taken everything he loved... and this, this divine chaos, was what he gave it back.

The clang of steel echoed like thunder. Sparks rained from each clash, each parry, as Devaultus and Tarus wove a tapestry of death and defiance in the inferno.

Tarus snarled, muscles bulging as he brought his broadsword down with the weight of a collapsing mountain. Devaultus slid under the arc, pivoted like a dancer mid-spin, and slashed a line of crimson across Tarus' ribs.

The big man grunted, but barely flinched. His face twisted in something between rage and respect.

"You move like a ghost," he growled, breath huffing like a bull's. "But even ghosts bleed."

Devaultus blinked at him. "What does that even mean? No, ghosts don't bleed! You are just terrible at this."

Tarus smirked and pointed to his side. "You do."

Devaultus twirled away, blood trailing down his side from a minor cut that had gone unnoticed. He smirked, panting slightly. "Funny. I thought you'd be more talk, less wheeze."

Tarus roared, and that was the moment everything shifted.

Feigning another heavy downward swing, Tarus *missed on purpose*, his sword carving through air just to bait Devaultus in. And the rogue bit, stepping into what should've been an opening.

That's when the dagger flashed.

A hidden blade, short and jagged, drawn from beneath Tarus' armored belt. It came up quickly, jamming deep into Devaultus' side with a sickening *shhhk*. The rogue's body jerked mid-motion. His breath caught.

"Got you," Tarus hissed, breath hot on Devaultus' face.

Devaultus staggered, boots scraping against the cracked stone beneath them. For the first time, his rhythm faltered. His steps were no longer a dance: they were survival.

The world around them pulsed with heat and flame, and somewhere off to the side, Vex screamed his name.

Tarus yanked the dagger free, letting Devaultus stumble back, blood painting the ground like a morbid signature.

"Not so elegant now," he said, twirling the blade. "You're just a man after all."

Devaultus clutched his side, the wound angry and wet. And yet... his grin stayed. Slower now, more blood-stained and feral. His eyes locked with Tarus' like a predator deciding whether to pounce or play dead.

"Yeah..." he muttered, coughing slightly, blood on his teeth. "Just a man."

He spat. The saliva hit the ground between them like a challenge.

"But let's see how many *gods* it takes to kill one."

Vex groaned, rolling onto her side, every nerve in her body howling in protest. Her ribs ached with every breath, her lip was split, and her temple throbbed from where Tarus had backhanded her and sent her flying as though she weighed nothing. She blinked smoke out of her eyes and stared at the battlefield through the flames licking the edges of the ruins.

Devaultus was hurt: she saw the blood. That bastard Tarus had drawn it. Her eyes narrowed.

"Don't," Zen's voice cracked beside her, quiet but desperate. She knelt next to Vex, her red hair soaked with sweat, glasses slightly askew, her eyes wide with fear. "Please... don't go out there. You can't stop him. Tarus is too strong. You'll just..."

"Die?" Vex spat, pushing herself to one knee, blade in hand. "He's our apocalypse, not yours. If he falls, we all fall."

Zen reached out, gripping Vex's wrist. "But you're hurt. You can't..."

"I've *always* been hurt," Vex snapped, eyes blazing with that feral spark that never quite went out. "But he's still my monster. And we dance better together than any of you could dream."

Zen's hand slipped away, useless in the shadow of that conviction.

Vex stood fully now, shaky but upright. She limped toward the battlefield, then broke into a sprint.

Devaultus ducked another strike, barely deflecting a hammer-like blow from Tarus. He stumbled, pain making his balance slip for a half-beat.

That was all Vex needed.

She came in from the left like a dagger thrown by fate itself, sliding low and fast, her curved blade scraping across Tarus' leg just below the knee. A bellow escaped the brute's throat as he turned toward her.

But Devaultus was already moving.

He launched forward with a spinning arc, blades slicing toward Tarus' exposed right. The two moved in perfect tandem, like twin serpents dancing in a blood-red waltz. Vex dropped as Devaultus leapt. He vaulted over her crouched body mid-swing, his heel catching Tarus' jaw with a savage back-kick.

Steel clanged. Sparks burst. Vex twisted behind Tarus, cutting at the tendons behind his ankle while Devaultus distracted him from the front. Tarus tried to turn, to counter, but they were already gone, one step ahead, like ghosts whispering around him.

"*You cheating, bitch!*" Tarus roared.

"Damn right it is," Vex grinned through bloody teeth. "But you raised me. You expected *honor*?"

Devaultus flashed a crooked grin, blood still dripping down his side. "We're monsters, remember?"

The two rogues circled like sharks now, blades ready, energy electric. They didn't speak to each other; they didn't need to. When Devaultus stepped in with a feint, Vex already knew where to strike. When Vex pivoted to the right, Devaultus was already ducking low to open a vein.

To Tarus, it was like fighting smoke and mirrors, if the mirrors had daggers and a shared grudge.

And somewhere behind them, Zen could only watch, awestruck, disoriented, and questioning *everything* she'd ever been told about this so-called monster who fought like vengeance had taken human form.

Tarus bellowed again, but this time... it lacked the force. There was still power behind his swing, of course there was, but his movements were starting to falter. A half-second too slow here, a misjudged step there. The rhythm of battle was no longer his.

His chest rose and fell like a forge bellows on overdrive. Blood leaked from dozens of cuts, thin lines at first, but now enough to paint his torso in streaks of red. His left leg twitched unnaturally from a well-placed tendon slice. His right hand trembled, ever so slightly.

Then he froze. Just for a moment. Eyes widened.

The poisons.

Devaultus had laced his blades earlier, as he always did, not for a quick kill, but for the long game. Most men fell to their knees after one gash. But Tarus? The walking mountain? He simply slowed... subtly, but unmistakably. The slight paralysis had started creeping in, his fingers clutching the hilt of his massive broadsword like iron trying to bend.

"You're... cheating," Tarus snarled, spit laced with crimson.

Devaultus, ever the picture of death in motion, smirked. He rolled his wrist, twin blades catching the glow of firelight behind him. "You raised a thief, old man. What did you *expect*? A duel?"

Vex laughed from behind him, wild and breathless. "I once poisoned a turkey leg just to avoid having dinner with a noble. This is us being *nice.*"

Tarus roared and charged again, sloppy, desperate, a wounded bull throwing all its weight into one last charge.

Devaultus sidestepped like wind through trees, smooth as silk.

Vex dropped low, slashing behind his knee again.

And Tarus... stumbled.

The blade in his hand wavered. He tried to lift it again but his arm gave out. It dropped with a metallic thud, sinking into the dirt. His other hand clutched at the wound in his side, where dark veins spidered out around a jagged cut.

Breathing heavy, body trembling, Tarus staggered one more step, and then dropped to his knees.

The warlord, the monster of myth, the man who had broken empires and crushed rebels underfoot, now sat hunched forward, unable to lift his sword, barely able to lift his head.

Devaultus stepped forward, casually, blade still glinting in one hand. The blood covering him made him look like something that had crawled out of a divine massacre; shirtless, barefoot, and every bit a nightmare incarnate.

Vex followed at his side, limping, eyes burning with satisfaction.

Tarus looked up at them, hate still boiling in his eyes. But there was something else now. Fear. Confusion. And just a hint of regret, buried deep.

Devaultus crouched in front of him, tipping his head to the side.

"You know what the best part of this is?" he asked, voice low and dark.

Tarus said nothing.

Devaultus leaned in, lips near the man's ear. "You didn't lose to a hero. You lost to your own creation."

Then he stood, and the silence that followed was thick enough to drown in.

Zen stood frozen.

Her delicate red brows were drawn tight, lips parted in silent disbelief as she stared across the battlefield. The fire crackled hungrily around her, casting shifting shadows across the carnage. Bodies, burned, slashed, unrecognizable, littered the ground like forgotten puppets. Blood mixed with soot. Smoke curled into the sky like black prayers.

And there, at the center of it all, stood *him*.

Devaultus.

No armor. No gleaming hero's blade. Just blood-spattered skin, a tattered loincloth, and those infernal eyes that burned like twin suns behind a stormcloud.

He wasn't what she'd been told. Not by Sakatorious. Not by the whispers that slipped between shadows like fearful rumors. She'd been told Devaultus was a monster. A devourer. A man who left no witnesses because death followed in his wake like a hungry lover.

And yet...

There he stood, not gloating, not smiling. Just *watching*.

Vex dropped to her knees beside Tarus' still body, her breath ragged as the weight of what she'd done, what she *had* to do, sank into her bones. Her sword hung limply from her hand now, forgotten. Her shoulders trembled, first from adrenaline, then from sorrow. The sob hit her like a punch to the gut, and then another, until she was crying openly; ugly, painful sobs ripped from a place so long buried, she didn't even know it still existed.

Zen took a step forward... then stopped.

She wanted to speak. To say something. Anything.

But what words could reach someone who had just killed their own father?

And then Devaultus moved.

He stepped over the fallen wreckage of what used to be a warlord, stopped beside Vex, and crouched low. His voice was low, rough with smoke and something harder to define, like gravel scraping across glass.

"We don't do this for us," he said.

Vex didn't respond, but she was listening.

"We do this for the ones who are already gone. The ones whose names are written in blood and silence. And for the ones who *would be* gone if we let him live to draw another breath."

He looked up. At Zen.

Not accusing.

Not angry.

Just... *real.*

"Heroes don't leave scenes like this behind," he muttered, motioning to the flames and ruin around them. "They don't carve trails of corpses through cities. They don't walk out of fire with smoke in their eyes and blades in their hands."

He stood slowly, his silhouette framed by dancing flames like some war-god pulled from a myth darker than most dare speak.

"We're not heroes," he said. "We're something else."

A pause. The fire popped, like it was agreeing.

"We're what the world really needs."

He looked down at Tarus' smoldering corpse.

"Because sometimes... *people just need killing.*"

Zen didn't speak.

She couldn't.

Because deep in her core, behind all the rules and obedience and training, she felt it.

The truth.

And it terrified her.

Zen stared at Devaultus.

She clenched her hands at her sides, pressing her nails into flesh as if to anchor herself. This wasn't what she'd been told. This wasn't what *anyone* had told her. He was supposed to be an inhuman force of destruction, a shadow that left nothing behind but death. But the man standing there, bathed in the glow of fire and ruin, wasn't a monster. He wasn't mindless rage or senseless slaughter.

He was *something else.*

And for the first time, she saw a path that wasn't chains disguised as duty.

Sakatorious would never let her leave. That collar wasn't just around her neck, it was around her soul. But *Devaultus?* Maybe... just maybe, he could break it.

Maybe *he* was the only thing in this world that could truly save her.

She swallowed thickly, forcing herself to breathe. Her decision was made.

A sharp sob shattered the air.

Vex.

She was still standing there, her shoulders wracked with trembling grief, her face hidden behind bloodied hands. The sword had long slipped from her fingers, forgotten, like the weight of her father's presence had died with him.

And then Devaultus did something that *no one* could have predicted.

He stepped forward.

And *hugged her.*

Vex stiffened. Her breath caught, her mind reeled, her body refused to move.

This wasn't something she knew. This wasn't something she had *ever* known. Her father had never held her, never whispered reassurances, never offered even the smallest scrap of warmth.

Love had always been something outside her reach, something she had to *fight* for.

But here, now, she didn't have to fight.

The warmth of Devaultus' arms around her was *foreign*. Strange. Unnerving.

But... safe.

And so, she broke.

Her fingers dug into his back, clinging to him as the sobs tore through her. She hated crying. Hated the weakness it showed. Hated that she wasn't laughing in the face of this pain, making some obscene joke to cover the gaping wound in her heart. But she couldn't. Not this time.

Devaultus stood still, stiff at first, his hands uncertain where they should rest. This wasn't something he *did*. Affection wasn't part of his nature, it was something distant, something he had never truly understood.

And yet...

He held her tighter.

Maybe just this once.

A shuffle of movement caught their attention.

Blight.

She emerged from the wreckage, leaning heavily on a stick, her body weak but her gaze filled with awe and exhaustion. At her side, Jerry pulsed, his inky tendrils shifting like a creature torn between smug satisfaction and the exhaustion of dragging her broken body across this battlefield.

Zen reacted instantly.

She ran to Blight, steadying her before she could collapse fully.

"You're hurt," Zen murmured, her voice softer than she expected.

Blight looked at her, her blue eyes wide, confused, but not fearful. Not of *her*. Not of *this*.

"It's over," Blight whispered.

Zen glanced back at Devaultus and Vex, still standing in the embers of the past, wrapped in something neither of them truly understood.

"Yeah," Zen murmured.

The sun dipped beyond the horizon, its golden light fading against the backdrop of burning ruin. Smoke curled toward the darkening sky, carrying the echoes of blood and fire into the night.

And as the flames dimmed, the world faded to black.

Far away, high atop a jagged cliff shrouded in dusk, three silhouettes stood against the fiery backdrop of the setting sun. The wind whipped around them, carrying with it the distant scent of smoke and blood.

The first was massive, monstrous even, gleaming scales catching the light like molten gold. A dragon, its wings folded, its serpentine tail lazily curling behind it. Beside the beast stood a towering figure clad in blackened armor, the very sight of him enough to make lesser men drop to their knees. Sakatorious. His arms crossed, jaw tight, eyes locked on the burning battlefield below. At his side stood a smaller, shadowed figure, cloaked and silent, a young man whose presence alone seemed to make the air colder. Shade.

"Well, my Lord," Shade said smoothly, his voice a touch too calm, like the edge of a razor before it cuts. "That certainly didn't go as planned. Shall I go now? Bring this to a close? It wouldn't take long."

The dragon, Cojar, shifted, his deep golden eyes gleaming with amusement. The corners of his massive mouth curled upward into something resembling a grin. "No. Leave them."

Sakatorious stiffened. His lips pressed into a thin line. His stare remained on the fading chaos below, but something in his posture betrayed the boiling impatience within. "We could end it. Now."

But Cojar did not seem troubled. In fact, he seemed entertained.

"Tarus was a brute," the dragon rumbled. "His death was… instructive." He squinted down at the tiny figures below. "Devaultus isn't the problem. Not the real one. There's something else among them. Something far more dangerous… and I intend to find out what."

Sakatorious did not speak. He didn't need to. The tension in his shoulders spoke volumes.

"Keep watch," Cojar continued, beginning to unfurl his colossal wings. "Measure the danger. Let me know what you discover." He paused and thought about it for a moment. "I suppose keep that insufferable Vera'Ala'Roja Bobalata'Cora up to date as well. As much as I disdain him, he could prove to be useful."

"Yes, my Lord," Sakatorious replied, though his jaw clenched tightly enough to grind bone.

With a single beat of his wings, Cojar leapt from the cliff, his form cutting through the sky like a streak of shadow, staying low, hidden from the ragged band of survivors far below.

The armored warlord turned slowly, fixing his gaze on the young man beside him.

"Shade," he said, voice low and cold, "you will go down there. You will observe them. And when the moment is right... It's time to show him how little power he actually has."

He stepped closer, lowering his voice to a whisper as the smoke of battle coiled upward toward the cliff.

"This is what I want you to do..."

# CHAPTER 23
# THE FINAL ACT OF WAR

Devaultus rested on the ship, his body still aching from the battle, but his mind refusing to grant him peace. The rhythmic sway of the vessel should have lulled him into a rare moment of relaxation, but instead, it left him staring at the wooden beams above, thoughts swirling like a storm-tossed sea.

Vex and Zen had gone to pick up the sails. A necessary errand, but more than that, it gave him space to think. Zen had finally explained her situation, or at least, as much as she understood of it herself.

It seemed they were collecting broken people. Strays, lost souls, those who had no ability to help themselves. The thought nearly made him laugh. When had that become his role? He was no hero. He wasn't someone who lifted others up. Or at least... he hadn't been.

Yet none of them had had the ability to fight for themselves before they met him. Vex had been little more than a simpering noble woman, she had no idea of her place in the world, she was only prey for those who would take advantage of her. Blight, wide-eyed and fragile, would have been devoured by the world had they not found her. And now Zen, so conditioned to servitude that she barely knew how to exist outside of it.

He sighed, rubbing his temple. He would train her. Somehow. But how do you train someone who has been raised to be nothing?

She refused to wield a weapon. At first, he thought it was fear, but the more he watched her, the more he realized, it was something deeper.

She recoiled from the very idea of violence, like a beaten dog flinching before the strike even came. Was it his father's doing? Some twisted lesson beaten into her, that she was never meant to fight, only to serve?

Devaultus scowled. He despised Sakatorious more with every passing day.

She didn't know how to be without direction. She followed orders because she had no concept of making her own choices. Without someone telling her what to do, she seemed lost, and she felt afraid to make her own choices.

He'd seen that before. In himself.

He pushed himself up with a sigh, stretching out his muscles. He would find a way. He always did.

Because if there was one thing Devaultus was good at, it was taking broken things... and turning them into something dangerous.

A few rooms down from the deck, tucked away in the quiet belly of the ship, Blight lay curled on her bed, barely more than a lump of tangled sheets, aching muscles, and silent reflection.

Every inch of her body throbbed. The serum she had injected mid-battle, the one she hadn't even tested properly, had done its job... and then some. It had turned her into something terrifying, something *capable*. And now, her reward was an entire body screaming in protest, like her tendons were trying to file formal complaints with her bones.

She groaned softly, shifting just enough to let the candlelight spill across her bruised face. Her potions were working, slowly knitting torn muscle fiber and repairing the internal damage, but it wasn't instant. No flashy magic glow and a "Ding, you're healed!" No. This was the *real* kind of healing, slow, raw, and earned through fire.

It would take a full day to recover. Maybe longer.

Blight sighed and rested her head back against the pillow. The real pain, though, the one potions couldn't fix, was lodged somewhere deeper.

*Dina.*

She saw her face every time she blinked. Heard her voice. Felt the weight of the needle in her hand, the final whisper of goodbye.

It had been necessary. It had been mercy.

But gods, it hurt.

Still... there was something else too. A strange, quiet sense of closure. She wasn't that girl anymore, the one who trembled and begged. The one who was passed around like a forgotten thing. That version of her had died in the fire.

And something else had taken her place.

She sniffled softly, trying to ignore the sting behind her eyes. And then... she felt something move.

Blight peeked down beneath her arm.

A shape shifted beside her. Small, curled close like a particularly judgmental shadow. Pitch black fur, soft and velvety like smoke given form. A long tail ended in a sharp little spike that flicked lazily back and forth. Four glowing eyes blinked at her, all at once, their expression unreadable but oddly... affectionate?

Jerry.

Or... what used to be Jerry.

After the battle, somewhere between survival and sleep, he had *changed*. Evolved, maybe. Or grown. Or possibly just decided that "tentacle sludge" was out, and "demonic murder-cat" was in.

Blight watched his tail flick. He yawned, revealing too many teeth and a tongue shaped like a question mark. Then, with a low grumble of contentment, he curled tighter against her side and nuzzled into her ribs.

She smiled, weakly.

"Definitely cuddlier than the blob," she murmured.

He responded with a deep, throaty purr that made the bed vibrate just enough to distract her from the ache.

Blight closed her eyes.

For the first time in a long time, she felt... safe. Not entirely whole. Not healed. But safe.

And maybe, just maybe, she wasn't alone anymore.

Jerry snuggled up closer, nestling against Blight's ribcage like an unusually ominous cat. His tail flicked lazily, and he let out a low, almost mechanical *chortle*, a sound somewhere between a purr, a snicker, and a bubbling kettle.

Blight chuckled through her teeth and reached a trembling hand down to stroke the top of his fuzzy, four-eyed head. He was warm now. Not gooey or slimy like before. Just... warm. Solid. Comforting.

"Thank you, Jerry," she whispered, her voice cracking a bit more than she meant it to. "I really needed you as a friend."

She paused, swallowing the lump in her throat. "Seems I'm bad for my friends," she added with a bitter little huff. "They all keep ending up dead."

It wasn't true.

*Not really.*

But the thought still sat at the back of her mind like a parasite, chewing away at her confidence when she wasn't looking. Guilt, always ready to slither in and claim the cracks.

Blight lay there in silence, her fingers curling gently in Jerry's new fur. He didn't speak, he never did, but he didn't need to. His little chortling purrs said enough. He was here. He had *chosen* to stay.

And that meant more than she could ever put into words.

Still, a whisper of doubt flickered in her chest. *He stayed for Vex.* That was always the assumption. Vex was chaos and fire, glory and blood. Vex was larger than life, the kind of person people followed just to see what she'd burn down next.

Blight? She was the quiet one. The weird one. The one with shaky hands and a trauma cocktail that could knock out a rhino.

She sighed and pulled Jerry a little closer, burying her face in his fuzzy side. "Maybe you're just here for her," she muttered, half to herself, half to him. "And I'm just the sad pit stop."

Jerry let out a disgruntled *glarble* and shifted his mass aggressively until he was almost on top of her, like a living weighted blanket with too many eyeballs. One of his tails, he seemed to have two now, wrapped protectively around her wrist.

She blinked.

"Okay. That felt intentional."

Jerry made another chortle-purr-noise and nuzzled her jaw.

Blight let out a soft, broken laugh. "Alright, alright. I get it. You're *my* creepy abomination now."

It didn't fix the hurt. But it dulled the edges.

She had a companion. A friend. A weird little mutant creature who understood her better than most people ever had. That was enough, for now.

She sighed and let herself drift back into the pillows, pain dulling into a distant hum.

And for the first time in a long time... she didn't feel quite so alone.

In the heart of a city that reeked of perfume, rot, and stale beer, Vex leaned against the weather-worn wall outside of O'Mally's, arms crossed, eyes flicking back and forth like a wolf waiting for a reason. Beside her stood Zen, red hair tucked behind one delicate ear, glasses slightly askew, her hands clasped in front of her like she might shatter if the wind blew too hard.

Vex still didn't trust the woman. Not even a little. She had the calm, polite energy of someone who knew too much and wasn't letting you in on the secret. But right now? She was all Vex had to work with.

Blight was a wreck, curled up somewhere licking her emotional and very literal wounds. And Devaultus? Well, the last time she saw him, he had a dagger sticking out of his ribs like a decorative brooch and a look on his face that said, *I will murder a small continent if anyone brings this up again.* He made it pretty damn clear he wasn't coming back to this city. Called it a leash, said it felt like trying to stuff a hurricane into a teacup. He didn't do "leashed." Vex respected that. Sorta. She wouldn't mind being leashed if it was by him. She blushed at the thought.

So here she was, stuck walking through a city she hated with a woman she didn't understand, hunting down a stupid sail. They'd just finished talking to the grizzled old broad who ran O'Mally's, she had more facial hair than Vex preferred to think about, and she'd promised to have the sail delivered to their ship right away. Task done.

Now they wandered awkwardly down the cobblestone street toward the docks, the smell of fish guts and cheap perfume dancing on the air like it was trying to seduce someone with no self-respect.

Conversation was... not happening.

Vex chewed her lip. She was a lot of things: killer, thief, chaos incarnate in hot leather pants, but she was not what one would call *a small talk person.*

Zen walked with her head slightly down, feet careful, movements precise like someone who'd been trained to take up as little space as possible. She hadn't said a word since they left. Vex could almost hear her thinking. Probably calculating the risks of breathing near her.

What the Abyss were they supposed to talk about?

Vex liked knives. Zen didn't. Vex liked stabbing. Zen looked like she might cry if someone broke a teacup. Vex would probably *be* the reason someone broke that teacup.

Seriously, what else was there?

"Hey?" came a voice, low and hushed, slithering out from a nearby alley like it knew it didn't belong.

Both women stopped.

Vex's hand was instantly on her blade, body tense, eyes narrowing into slits. Zen stepped slightly behind her out of pure instinct, her hand going to her chest like she was expecting her heart to leap out and flee for safer territory.

They turned their heads slowly.

The alley yawned dark beside them, like a mouth that had just whispered a secret.

Someone was in there.

And suddenly, this boring sail-fetching chore got a whole lot more interesting.

It was Devaultus.

Of *course* it was Devaultus.

Vex blinked once, then again, just to be sure her brain wasn't playing tricks on her. Nope. That unmistakable silhouette was real. He stood at the edge of the alley like a painting that had swaggered off the canvas, head tilted, wide-brimmed black hat leaving his eyes in shadow, the feather dipped in purple like it had stabbed a grape on the way over. His bard's coat, deep violet and shadow-black, clung to him like sin itself, stitched with silver thread that caught the dying light like a threat. And of course, his lute slung across his back like an afterthought, or a weapon. With Devaultus, it could go either way.

Why the Abyss was *he* here?

Actually... knowing him? Probably looking for trouble. Trouble, blood, or the occasional performance review from Death herself.

Respect.

Vex threw a glance over her shoulder toward the street. Nobody seemed to have clocked him. Yet. She darted into the alley like a thief slipping into a lover's bed; swift, fluid, and halfway expecting violence.

He was already leaning against the stone wall like it owed him money. That smirk curled on his lips like smoke from a burning tavern.

"What in the Abyss are *you* doing here?" Vex hissed, keeping her voice low but sharp enough to shave stone. The last time she'd seen him, he'd had a knife sticking out of his side and was having a philosophical debate with gravity.

Still, the man looked no worse for wear now, except for the usual aura of "someone's definitely going to die near me today."

Devaultus shrugged lazily, the brim of his hat tilting as he looked her over. "Got word where we're headed next," he said. "Al'Shandra said I needed to find you both immediately."

At that name, Vex snorted. "Of course she did. That horny wench in heat couldn't whisper a message without groping a few lives in the process." Her tone was exasperated, but there was a little warmth there too. Al'Shandra was chaos incarnate, but she *was their* chaos.

Still, Vex sighed. "Fine," she muttered, not quite hiding the twitch of a grin. "I wasn't really enjoying this painfully normal walk with Miss Nervous over here anyway."

She turned to head out of the alley just as she caught the shift in Zen's face. Wide eyes. Pale skin. Jaw slack in fear.

Vex spun.

Too late.

Devaultus moved.

A flick of the wrist, so fast it was almost imperceptible, and a dagger was flying through the air. Vex dove instinctively, the blade whistling past her and burying itself in Zen's shoulder with a wet *thwack*.

Zen gasped, her red hair cascading as she stumbled back, hand clutching the dagger hilt. Her glasses were askew, one lens cracked. Her lips parted in pain and confusion, no words finding their way out.

"What the actual abyss was that?!" Vex snapped, half drawing her sword, but Devaultus was already gone from where he'd been. His coat flared behind him as he strode forward, steps silent and exact.

Chaos wrapped in velvet. That was Devaultus.

Zen crumpled.

The moment the blade sank into her shoulder, her legs gave out beneath her like they'd forgotten how to exist. She hit the cobblestone hard, her breath stolen by the pain, and then by something far worse. A cold numbness began to crawl outward from the wound, spidering through her body with unnatural speed. Her limbs grew heavy, her fingers slack. She tried to cry out, to warn Vex, but her lips wouldn't move.

She was frozen.

Eyes wide and terrified, she could only watch.

Vex, still standing, immediately went into full murder mode.

"Oh *hell* no."

She lunged, twin daggers flashing like the fangs of a beast unleashed. The man, Devaultus? No, not quite... met her strike with the fluid grace of a dancer and the precision of a seasoned killer. He moved like Devaultus, yes... the same elegant economy of motion, the same knowing smirk, but polished. Sharpened. *Perfected.*

Where Devaultus fought like the wind, graceful, unpredictable, and wild, this man was the storm *with purpose.*

Every one of Vex's strikes was deflected, redirected, or simply *missed.* She snarled, twisting midair, bringing her foot up in a desperate roundhouse kick that might've taken someone's jaw off, only to find her leg caught mid-spin, body slammed into the wall, then hurled to the ground.

She rolled, bleeding from her lip, fury blazing in her mismatched eyes. "Who the Abyss *are* you?!"

The man didn't answer.

He just stepped forward, calmly, pulled a tiny silver needle from his belt, and flicked it toward her with surgical precision.

Vex instinctively moved to dodge. Too late. It embedded itself just beneath her collarbone.

She staggered back, ripping it out, but the poison was already in her bloodstream. The world tilted. Her limbs turned to molasses. She dropped to one knee, then to both, and finally collapsed beside Zen, her eyes blinking sluggishly as she tried to curse through a tongue that wouldn't move.

The man knelt beside Zen.

His face shimmered.

Shifted.

Morphed.

Until what stared down at her was something familiar, yet wrong. A younger face. Sharper cheekbones. The same devil-may-care grin, but this one was cruel, not charming. A mirror image of Devaultus if you squinted, but darker in every sense.

Shade.

Zen's pulse hammered in her ears.

"Master is... disappointed in you," he whispered, voice like silk laced with arsenic. "But perhaps... not without use."

He leaned down closer, his grin widening as he turned his gaze briefly to the paralyzed Vex, then back to Zen.

"Tell Devaultus..." he said with a venom-laced chuckle, "his *brother* says hello."

He stood, his coat billowing slightly as he turned and disappeared into the shadows, gone before the sun had even finished setting.

And Zen?

Still couldn't scream.

Devaultus stood upright with a wince, fingers brushing the still-tender stab wound along his ribs. It pulsed like a second heartbeat, hot and annoyed with every breath. He grumbled low under his breath. Pain was fine, it reminded him he was alive. But pain *this early in the day*? That was just rude.

A ruckus echoed from the deck above: panicked voices, hurried steps, the telltale ripple of something *wrong*. He grabbed his gear without flair, belt, lute, coat, and ascended the steps, boots thudding softly against the wood.

The moment he stepped onto the deck, he saw the crowd.

Crew members were clustered around something, or someone, like crows around a fallen meal. Murmurs carried on the wind, worried and hushed. He pushed through the ring of bodies, his presence enough to part the mass like a ripple in water. And then he saw it, red hair.

Zen.

Sprawled on the deck, her skin pale, her eyes swimming with confusion and fear. Blood stained her shoulder where a blade had found its home.

Devaultus froze, that stab of icy dread clawing up his spine.

"Where is Vex?" he asked, voice sharper than he intended. The words sliced the air, more command than question.

No answer.

He stepped in closer, gaze dropping to the wound. It wasn't the blade that made his jaw tighten, it was the *style*. The cut was clean... but not elegant. Familiar in all the wrong ways. The weapon that had done this bore craftsmanship eerily close to his own, a mimicry of his favorite daggers. But slightly... off. A warped echo.

Jagged. Crude. Deliberate.

The crew worked swiftly, patching the wound, bandaging Zen's shoulder. She flinched, gasped, cried out as the cloth pressed in. Her fingers trembled, lips quivering with pain and something deeper; betrayal, maybe.

Devaultus dropped to one knee beside her, brushing damp strands of hair from her face. "What happened?" he asked, this time softer.

Zen blinked at him, her eyes wide, glassy.

"We didn't see him coming," she whispered. Her voice was fragile, like it would shatter under its own weight.

Devaultus' stomach clenched.

"Who?" he pressed.

She hesitated. Her lip trembled, her fingers curled into the deck as if holding onto something real. Then she looked up into his eyes, horror reflected in her own.

"It was you," she said, voice barely audible. "He looked *just* like you. I didn't know... Devaultus, I didn't *know* he was your brother."

The color drained from his face. For a moment, the world tilted on its axis.

His brother.

That word hit like a thunderclap inside his skull.

He thought back. The words of his father, like an old wound torn open: *At least the other one might be worth something.* He had dismissed it. Buried it. Thought it just another of his father's cruel barbs.

But now? The wound, the imitation, the cold precision of the attack. Zen's haunted eyes.

His brother was real.

And he had found them.

The beat of silence stretched too long.

Then Devaultus stood, slowly, like a man bearing a weight no one else could see. His face, usually so full of playful arrogance or chaotic smirks, was blank. Cold.

Something deep had stirred in him, and it wasn't joy. It was a memory with teeth.

The past... had just caught up.

"He took her," Zen choked out, her voice hoarse and trembling. "And told me to tell you something..."

Devaultus turned back toward her, the brim of his black hat casting a shadow over his eyes. His heart thudded, slow and heavy.

"Your brother says *hello*."

The words hit harder than any blade.

Devaultus didn't reply at first. He just stood there, jaw clenched so tight, the muscle in his cheek twitched. Slowly, without a word, he turned toward the gangplank, boots striking the deck like war drums, one heavy footfall after another.

Zen's voice called after him, sharp and desperate. "It's too late! I've been paralyzed for over an hour. He's *long* gone."

Devaultus paused at the top of the gangplank. Wind tugged at his coat, his hat, the ends of his scarf flapping like battle flags.

"But I know who has her," Zen continued, forcing the words through gritted teeth. Her hand clutched her bandaged shoulder, tears streaking down her cheeks. "Someone called *Lord Sakatorious*."

Devaultus didn't move. Not even a twitch.

"Your brother's name is Shade," she added, barely above a whisper.

The word *brother* echoed in his skull like a blade dragged across stone.

He didn't understand it. Not really. People kept calling Shade his brother. Tossing it out like some casual truth, as if it didn't shatter something every time he heard it. Devaultus searched his memories, the ones he hadn't buried so deep, even *he* couldn't find them.

A memory surfaced, uninvited.

He had been young, young enough that his hands hadn't yet known the weight of blood. Standing outside a thick wooden door, just barely cracked open. His father's voice, deadly as a blade dipped in poison.

"I hope the other one turns out more useful than *this* one."

Devaultus had assumed, back then, it was about some other Lordling. Some spoiled brat in the tower above him. But what if it wasn't? What if the "other one" wasn't just a rival... but a sibling?

Shade.

His hand clenched at the rail, veins bulging as the wind howled past him like a scream from the gods themselves.

Could it be true?

Was *he* the first failure?

Was Shade the upgraded model, crafted in the same hell-forge, but somehow... better?

He snarled under his breath, low and barely audible.

If Shade was his brother, then Sakatorious had crafted them both to be weapons. Pawns in some divine game. But only one of them had broken the board.

And Devaultus had no intention of being outplayed now.

He would simply have to kill his brother and take him off the board.

A long silence followed.

Devaultus stood at the bow of the ship, cloaked in shadow as the city glimmered in the distance like a dying star. The wind caught his coat, whipping it around him like a second skin. He watched the skyline with narrowed eyes, his thoughts were dark.

Were the Lords truly united? Or was it all theater?

He turned, and his gaze fell on Zen like a weight. She froze under the sudden scrutiny, her body going still like prey spotted by a predator.

"Are the Lords working together?" he asked, voice quiet, but no less dangerous for it. "Who are they working for? I know the gods... but is it all of them, or just one?"

Zen blinked rapidly, lips parting in surprise. His intensity was suffocating, and she knew one wrong word could paint a target on her spine.

"I... I don't think they're working together," she stammered. "It felt more like competition than cooperation. They all serve the gods, yes... but this region, this city? It's Cojar's territory. Most of them report to him."

Devaultus' expression didn't shift, but the way his fingers flexed against the railing gave away the wheels turning in his mind.

"He lets them fight each other. Keeps things messy on purpose," Zen continued, her voice quieter now. "It's... entertainment for him. Chaos with a leash."

She hadn't been told any of this directly. She was just a slave. A pawn. Nothing. But she'd served the Lords enough to be invisible in their presence, just another warm body in the corner. And warm bodies heard things when no one was paying attention.

Devaultus stared through her now, gaze unfocused as his thoughts spiraled down darker roads. The Lords weren't united. That made them weak. Predictable. And ripe for exploitation.

"I see..." he murmured.

The Lords didn't matter much to him. Not directly. But their squabbling could be used. If they were busy tearing each other's throats out over pride and petty power plays, they'd never notice the knife slipping in under the ribs.

And Devaultus had always been very good with knives.

A smirk ghosted across his lips. Chaos wasn't just a tool.

It was home.

And he said, quietly, deliberately, like every syllable was a vow chiseled in stone: "Then we gather an army..."

He reached back and tightened the strap of his lute, as if preparing for war.

"...and we burn them all to the *ground*."

His gaze was wildfire. Controlled. Purposeful. But underneath it, just barely, was a hint of something else.

Something *personal*.

"You don't mess with *my family*."

"It's time I remind people of that."

Zen and Blight slipped quietly into the ship's tavern, the air still heavy with smoke and something far heavier: guilt. Zen's eyes darted around like a cornered animal's, haunted and hollow. Her fingers shook as she reached for a mug, the wood clinking softly against her nails. She brought it to her lips with trembling care, taking a sip that did nothing to settle her nerves.

Blight watched her closely, head tilted slightly. Her voice was soft, but it didn't bother pretending. "Are you alright, Zen?"

Zen didn't answer immediately. Her throat clenched, jaw twitching as she fought off the tears, until she didn't.

"No," she whispered, the word cracking as she collapsed into quiet sobs. "I'm not alright, Blight. I didn't help her. I couldn't. I just stood there while they took her, and now..." Her voice faltered. "Now I'm sure Devaultus blames me. For being weak. For not stopping them."

Blight frowned, unsure. Devaultus wasn't exactly a vault of forgiveness, but he wasn't subtle either. If he'd truly blamed Zen, wouldn't he have said something? Or, more likely, done something violent and poetically cruel?

But instead, he'd gone quiet. Too quiet.

Blight had seen the flickers behind his eyes: the coiled rage, the wild magic building like a storm beneath his skin. He was holding back. But for how long?

She glanced toward the door they had just come through and swallowed hard. "I don't think he blames you, Zen," she said at last. "I think he's blaming himself. And that's a much more dangerous thing."

Then there was the matter of Devaultus and his so-called army. That didn't track, not with the man she knew. He barely tolerated people on a good day. Half the time, Zen was sure he didn't even like *existing* near them. An army? It felt like a lie. Or worse, a joke only he was in on.

She stared into the murky swirl of her ale, heart thudding like a warning drum. Was he planning to kill them all? Was she going to die at the hands of Devaultus?

The tavern door creaked open.

A figure stood silhouetted by the flickering firelight, still as a shadow. Devaultus.

"I need to speak with you, Blight," he said, voice flat. "In my quarters."

Then he turned and vanished into the hallway like a phantom that decided not to kill... this time.

Zen's face drained of color, her freckles stark against her pale skin. "He's going to kill me," she whispered.

Blight rose without a word, placing her mug down gently. "I'll talk to him," she said, and followed the storm into its eye.

Inside his quarters, the air felt heavier, tighter, like the room was holding its breath. Devaultus sat at the edge of a table, hands folded under his chin, eyes fixed on the wall like he could will it to bleed.

Blight hovered near the door. "What can I do for you, Devaultus?"

He didn't look at her. Just stared through stone and time.

"You and I are taking a trip," he said. "I'm going to find out where they took Vex."

Blight's heart kicked. "To build your army?" she asked, hesitating.

His gaze snapped to hers. No glow. No madness. Just pure, focused intent.

"No, Blight," he said, voice low and calm, and so much worse because of it. "I don't give a damn about that army. It's a smoke screen. Something for the Lords to chase while I do what actually matters."

Blight blinked. "But... people will die. You know that, right? Retaliation like this, it won't just be you who bleeds."

Devaultus turned his eyes to her, dark, tired, sharp.

"I know."

"I'm not the hero, Blight," he said simply.

Blight didn't argue. She didn't need to. Devaultus wasn't the hero, never had been. She saw him clearly, where others squinted through their delusions. He was the storm in a crumbling world.

Terrifying. Relentless. Capable of destruction on a scale few could imagine. But in the wasteland left behind, that same storm brought rain. Hope. Life. He was chaos wrapped in purpose.

She nodded once, slowly. "Then... what about Zen?"

Devaultus' eyes flicked to her. Cold. Sharp. That gaze could cut glass. "She stays behind."

Blight straightened. "You can't just abandon her. You know Sakatorious won't let that slide. She betrayed him, he'll kill her."

"I don't care," Devaultus said, voice like frost. "I won't have useless people with me."

That hit hard. Blight flinched, but didn't back down. Her fists clenched at her sides.

Useless? Zen wasn't a fighter, no. But she had helped. Quietly. Constantly. Blight thought of the night she'd been wounded, barely able to breathe from the pain, and Zen had sat beside her for hours. Mixing herbs, applying salve, holding her hand while she screamed into the pillow. She hadn't fled. She hadn't hesitated.

They'd grown close. Closer than Blight had expected. Closer than she'd wanted to admit.

"Please, Devaultus," she said softly. "For me? Let her stay. Just for now."

His jaw tightened, his stare burning holes through the wall behind her. Then finally, he exhaled through his nose like a dragon trying not to roast the room.

"She stays. With Al'Shandra," he said, voice low and clipped. "And she learns to be useful. Fast."

Blight nodded, holding in the sigh of relief that threatened to break her resolve. She didn't thank him. She knew better. But the look she gave him was enough, a mix of gratitude, loyalty, and something heavier.

He didn't respond. He was already thinking three steps ahead, planning blood and fire.

And somewhere on the deck above, Zen remained unaware she'd just been granted the thinnest thread of mercy, because Blight had dared to care.

"We leave tomorrow, Blight. Ready yourself. This won't be easy." Devaultus' voice was calm, but carried the weight of war behind it. "Then again... nothing on this world ever is."

Blight gave a slow nod, emotions colliding inside her like mismatched waves. There was a quiet pride rising in her: Devaultus trusted her. He *really* trusted her. Maybe she hadn't failed as badly at Deshara as she thought. Maybe, in his chaotic mind, she'd finally earned a place.

But underneath that pride was sorrow. Leaving Zen behind twisted something in her chest.

Zen had stayed by her side after the injuries. Fed her, tended to her wounds, kept her grounded when Blight felt like slipping into the void. And the way Zen talked, the little slips, the odd phrases, Blight had a growing suspicion they were from the same world. Two strangers tossed into a nightmare with only each other to cling to.

It wasn't fair. Not to Zen. Not when she was finally starting to open up.

But it was done.

"I'll be ready," Blight said quietly as she rose to her feet.

Devaultus gave a simple nod, then walked her to the door. No more words, just a subtle gesture of respect, one he didn't offer often. He watched her step into the hallway, then turned away.

Blight allowed herself the smallest of smiles.

She felt useful. Needed. Like she'd become something more than just a survivor.

But her thoughts wandered back to Zen, quiet, trembling Zen, left behind in a world full of wolves. She wasn't far from what Puppy had been at the start. Lost. Afraid. Untrained. But there was potential buried in that mess of trauma and red hair.

She just needed someone to believe in her.

Blight would be that someone.

Even if she had to do it from afar.

# EPILOGUE

Marko sighed, the sound barely louder than the hearth's crackle. His fingers toyed with the frayed hem of his coat, the same one he'd worn for gods only knew how long. Dust clung to it like an old friend. His boots were scuffed, one sole flapping with every step like a loose tongue trying to speak. He looked like a man who'd walked a thousand miles just to remember why he started.

But when he spoke?

The room listened.

Now, he sat hunched forward at a crooked table near the fire, the last words of his tale still floating like smoke in the air. That part, the end, always hit differently. Sometimes it stirred cheers, sometimes fists. Sometimes tears. But this time?

This time it was quiet.

Too quiet.

Marko scanned the room through heavy lids. He expected fire. Righteous fury. At the very least, some drunken oath to stab a Lord through the teeth. But instead, he saw hesitation. Eyes shifting, not toward him, but between each other. Subtle glances passed like whispered secrets. There were no cries of allegiance. No raised mugs.

Just a silence that felt... too careful.

Only one face didn't flinch.

Lilly's.

She sat across from him, her hands folded in her lap, blue eyes locked on his like the rest of the world had ceased to matter. If she blinked, he didn't see it.

"What happened?" she asked softly, her voice trembling with hope. "Did they get Vex back?"

Marko exhaled through his nose, the breath heavy with words unsaid.

"Not yet," he said, voice just above a whisper. "But people are angry. They want Devaultus to succeed. They want vengeance. They want Vex back."

He let the words hang there, like meat on a hook.

But the crowd didn't bite.

If anything, they pulled further away. A few heads dipped. One man rubbed the back of his neck and avoided Marko's gaze entirely. Another woman looked toward the back corridor, her fingers tightening around her mug like she was holding onto something more than ale.

And still, the glances. Quick flicks of the eyes, a language all their own. Silent conversation. Agreement... or warning?

The fire snapped behind him.

For the first time since entering the tavern, Marko felt cold.

A voice broke the uneasy quiet.

"I've met Lord Sakatorious," a man said, seated near the corner, arms crossed and brow furrowed. "Didn't seem all that bad to me."

Another voice chimed in before Marko could answer. A woman, older, with silver hair braided tight down her back. "He pays well, you know. Keeps the peace. I find it hard to believe he's the monster you make him out to be."

Marko blinked.

Something in the air shifted. Not just suspicion. Something deeper. More... *wrong*.

His eyes drifted toward one of the corridors branching off the main room. Narrow. Dimly lit. Doors lined both sides like ribs in a throat. One creaked open, and a man stepped out, smoothing his shirt and adjusting his pants with a satisfied little grunt. He didn't notice Marko watching.

Then another door opened. And another man followed. Same look. Same smug self-satisfaction.

How had he missed this?

His stomach turned.

Lilly caught the change in his expression. Her eyes followed his toward the hallway, her lips parting ever so slightly. She stood without a word, brushing her skirt down and moving toward a nearby table.

"Excuse me," she murmured as she passed.

She leaned in to speak to a patron. Then another. Her voice was low, but her movements were sharp. Deliberate. And she kept glancing back at Marko.

Cara, behind the bar, was watching him now, too. No warmth in her eyes. Just caution. Calculation.

Every gaze in the room felt like a blade on his neck.

Something was wrong.

Very wrong.

Marko stood slowly, his stool creaking beneath him.

"Perhaps... perhaps it's time I take my leave," he said, forcing a small smile, careful with every word. "I meant no offense to your Lord. It was simply a story. Nothing more."

Silence greeted him. Heavy, tight silence.

Then a voice, low and gravelly, spoke near the hearth.

"I dare say, lad... you've already done that."

Marko chuckled nervously, the sound dry and brittle. "Just a tale, my good sir. A bit of fireside nonsense. Nothing worth holding onto."

Another man grunted, unimpressed. Angry.

Marko slowly reached into his coat and pulled out a folded scrap of cloth, pressing it to his nose like it was just a casual wipe of sweat.

Then came the hiss.

Soft. Almost like a sigh.

Green mist began to snake along the floorboards.

Subtle. But growing.

The hearth's flames shimmered as the gas thickened.

And Marko? He didn't wait to see if they noticed.

Marko pulled his hand from his face, revealing a small device clipped discreetly to his nose. A purifier. Designed to filter out the very toxin now creeping through the room like a curse.

Around him, weapons were drawn, steel rang, but it was already too late.

The gas had seeped into every breath.

One by one, their eyes widened as their tongues began to swell. Panic spread like wildfire as airways constricted. Boots scraped. Chairs overturned. People clawed at their throats, gurgling, choking, dropping.

From around the corner, Lilly stepped into view, a similar device affixed to her nose.

She didn't run.

She didn't flinch.

She walked calmly toward the exit as she followed Marko.

Slipping through the tavern's front door, she took one last look over her shoulder.

Inside, the bodies were collapsing, twitching in silence. Eyes glazed. Lives snuffed out like guttering candles.

She would never get used to this. Being the hand that delivered death so directly.

Outside, under a sky littered with stars, the man she'd followed paused. He stood motionless in the moonlight, looking skyward as if listening to something ancient and cruel.

She caught up and slowed, watching him.

Then he began to ripple.

The illusion peeled away like smoke. Clothes shimmered, posture straightened. That tired, drunken storyteller faded... and in his place stood *Devaultus*.

He didn't glance her way.

Just kept his eyes on the stars.

Lilly let out a slow breath, tugged the pin from her bun. Her dark hair spilled down her back in a wave. From the warm nest at her cleavage, Jerry emerged, stretching like a shadow. His dark black fur was shimmering in the breeze. Four eyes blinking knowingly.

"That was close, Devaultus," she said.

Still, he didn't look at her. His gaze was distant, fire behind his irises.

Lilly fought with the weight in her chest, but she knew better than to mourn these people. She'd spent days among them. She'd seen the signs, the rooms, the behavior, their blind reverence for Sakatorious. There was rot in that tavern. Maybe the whole town.

They really had to work out a way for her to tell him. Before he got through that whole story.

She looked at him and smiled faintly.

"We'll get her back."

Devaultus gave the smallest nod. The kind that made the night lean in to listen.

"The world better hope so," he said, "I have no problem leaving it in flames."

Lilly believed him. Gods help her, she believed every word.

"You know," she said with a teasing grin, "next time, you should actually let me stab you. It'd sell the performance better."

Devaultus finally side-eyed her, brow twitching. "You've spent far too much time with Vex, Blight."

She grinned wider, teeth flashing.

And just like that, the two vanished into the night, silent shadows trailing after them, leaving behind a tavern steeped in death and decay, a mirror to the world outside.

# FROM THE AUTHOR

Thank you for reading *The Book of Devaultus*.

This wasn't just my first novel, it was a leap off a cliff with a dagger between my teeth and chaos strapped to my back. Every chapter carved from my own bones; every scene dipped in venom and ink. And yet, it's not about me.

It's about *him*.A man who isn't a man, a hero who isn't trying to be, and a war that began long before you opened this book. Devaultus, the knife in the night, the song you shouldn't hum too loud. He's chaos pushed too far. He's the whisper you ignore until it's far too late.

This tale is layered with lies, a storm dressed as a common man, and just enough twisted hope to make you wonder if redemption is worth the blood it takes to buy it. I wanted to explore what happens when someone chaotic and cruel *tries* to do the right thing... and keeps getting it terrifyingly wrong.

If you found yourself laughing at inappropriate moments, questioning your own moral compass, or rooting for someone you *really* shouldn't have, then it worked. Devaultus has that effect on people.

But this is only the beginning.

The story continues in the next book of *The Dark Deceiver Chronicles*, where shadows grow longer, masks fall, and the question isn't whether the villain will win...It's whether he *should*.

To every reader who gave this strange, sinister tale your time, thank you. Your feedback isn't just appreciated, it's ammunition. If something in this book stuck with you, hit you in the guts, or whispered in your ear long after you closed the final page, consider leaving a review or a comment. Every word helps this world grow sharper.

Until next time.Until the next chapter.And remember:

Monsters aren't born.They're created.

– J.A. Roggie

www.ingramcontent.com/pod-product-compliance
Lightning Source LLC
Chambersburg PA
CBHW021937110726
47901CB00003B/873